A fam...

Little Christ...
Miracles

Three sparkling, exciting romances from three
favourite Mills & Boon authors!

**In December 2009 Mills & Boon bring
you two classic collections, each
featuring three favourite romances
by our bestselling authors**

FOR CHRISTMAS, FOREVER

The Yuletide Engagement
by Carole Mortimer
The Doctor's Christmas Bride
by Sarah Morgan
Snowbound Reunion by Barbara McMahon

LITTLE CHRISTMAS MIRACLES

Her Christmas Wedding Wish
by Judy Christenberry
Christmas Gift: A Family
by Barbara Hannay
Christmas on the Children's Ward
by Carol Marinelli

Little Christmas Miracles

JUDY CHRISTENBERRY
BARBARA HANNAY
CAROL MARINELLI

MILLS & BOON

All the characters in this book have no existence outside the imagination of the author, and have no relation whatsoever to anyone bearing the same name or names. They are not even distantly inspired by any individual known or unknown to the author, and all the incidents are pure invention.

First published in Great Britain 2009
Harlequin Mills & Boon Limited,
Eton House, 18-24 Paradise Road, Richmond, Surrey TW9 1SR

LITTLE CHRISTMAS MIRACLES
© by Harlequin Enterprises II B.V./S.à.r.l 2009

Her Christmas Wedding Wish, Christmas Gift: A Family and *Christmas on the Children's Ward* were first published in Great Britain by Harlequin Mills & Boon Limited in separate, single volumes.

Her Christmas Wedding Wish © Judy Russell Christenberry 2006
Christmas Gift: A Family © Barbara Hannay 2005
Christmas on the Children's Ward © The SAL Marinelli Family Trust 2005

ISBN: 978 0 263 87145 6

05-1209

Printed and bound in Spain
by Litografia Rosés S.A., Barcelona

HER CHRISTMAS
WEDDING WISH

BY
JUDY CHRISTENBERRY

Judy Christenberry has been writing romance for fifteen years, because she loves happy endings as much as her readers do. A former French teacher, Judy now devotes herself to writing full-time. She hopes readers have as much fun reading her stories as she does writing them. She spends her spare time reading, watching her favourite sports team and keeping track of her two daughters. Judy's a native Texan but now lives in Arizona.

CHAPTER ONE

MOLLY SODERLING hurried back down the hall to the one patient who had been on her mind all through her break. Toby Astin. The eight-year-old had also found his way into her heart, ever since he'd come into the hospital three days ago, the victim of a car crash. The same crash that had killed his parents and two other adults, and had left the boy an orphan. Less than a month before Christmas.

Molly's heart ached for him. She knew exactly what he was feeling, as she, too, had lost her parents when she was a young child. She remembered how lonely she was the first Christmas without them, and every one since then.

In Toby's eyes she saw the loss he suffered; in his clinging arms she felt his pain. In the three days he'd been here, no one had come for him. Perhaps after the funerals someone would claim him. She didn't want Toby to be put into the foster care system as she had been.

As she turned down the pediatric wing, she saw two people clad in black enter his room. Perhaps they were mourners who'd attended the funeral for his parents today. According to his doctor, Toby's uncle and grandmother had phoned to ask for Toby to attend, but Dr. Bradford had refused.

He was concerned the boy might suffer depression.

Molly had disagreed with the doctor, but he wasn't going to listen to her. Having had to attend her parents' funeral when she was seven, she knew how comforting it had been to see others mourning their deaths also.

Molly sighed. Then, forcing a smile on her face, she turned into Toby's room.

"Molly!" he cried as if she were a lifesaver.

"Hi, Toby. Did you eat your dinner?"

"Yes, but—"

"Are you his nurse?" the man in the black suit asked abruptly, stepping toward her. He looked about thirty, with dark hair and striking blue eyes.

"I'm one of Toby's nurses."

"He seems extraordinarily attached to you."

Was it condemnation she heard in his voice? Her shoulders stiffened. "We've become friends," she said tersely.

Then she turned her attention to Toby. "Can I get you anything, honey?"

"I'd like some ice cream," he said hesitantly, shooting a look at the man as if he would object.

"Sure. I'll be right back with it."

She passed the older woman dressed in a black designer suit, leaning against the wall. She wasn't sure who the elegant-looking woman was. Maybe a family friend or maybe even the grandmother she'd heard mentioned. But no, she wasn't acting like a grandmother, at least none Molly had ever imagined.

"Excuse me, Ms. Soderling," the man called.

How did he know her name? Molly turned around. "Yes, sir?"

"We're taking Toby with us in the morning."

Before he could go on, Molly said, "I'm sorry to see him go. I'll miss him. Are you his guardian?"

"Yes, by default."

She stared at him, her eyebrows raised. Who would say such a thing, as if the boy was nothing more than a burden to be endured?

"The other couple, who also died in the car with Toby's parents, were named in their will as guardians. However, my mother and I are his only relatives. I'm an attorney and I filed the papers this morning to be named guardian. They've assured me it would be approved. I want to get Toby home so he can begin to heal."

"Good. He's been feeling lost since no one had come to claim him."

"The doctor in charge of Toby says he's very fond of you."

Molly frowned. "Yes, I told you we've become friends."

"He's eight years old. How could you be friends?"

Molly said nothing, turning to continue on her way.

"Wait!"

She didn't like the order, but she obeyed. No need to irritate the man if he was going away in the morning. "Yes?"

"Dr. Bradford said you didn't have any family here."

"Why would Dr. Bradford tell you that?" she asked carefully.

"Because I need someone to come with us to Dallas to take care of Toby and help him settle in."

"Sir, I'm a pediatric nurse, not a baby-sitter."

"I know. And I'm willing to pay your going rate, twenty-four hours a day, if you'll come with us in the morning."

"For how long?" she asked, startled at his offering.

"For a month. You'll make more than three times your salary, Ms. Soderling."

"I don't know if the hospital—"

"Dr. Bradford assured me he could spare you."

Molly didn't know what to think. "I'll have to talk to Dr. Bradford."

"He left a note for you at the nurses' station," the man said, as if that alone should persuade her.

He expected her to drop everything and go to Dallas for a month, as if it were nothing but a shift reassignment. Not that she had anything holding her here in Florida, especially at holiday time. Still, the man hadn't even introduced himself! "Excuse me, sir, but who are you exactly?"

"I'm Richard Anderson, Toby's uncle." As he spoke, he stood straighter, his shoulders back in a proud gesture. But he made no move to shake her hand.

Neither did Molly. "I'll go read the note," she said. And she walked away.

At the nurses' station, she got the Dixie cup of ice cream for Toby and asked the nurse on duty if Dr. Bradford had left a note for her.

"Oh, yeah. Sorry, Molly. I forgot to give it to you."

"Thanks, Ellen," Molly said, taking the note with her as she found a quiet corner of the floor to read it.

Indeed, Dr. Bradford had asked her to go with the Andersons to Dallas. Because of her rapport with little Toby, he thought her best for the job. He'd approved a month's leave for her if she decided to go. And, she guessed, to make her refusal harder, he added that Mr. Anderson had offered two hundred thousand dollars to the pediatric wing if the hospital could supply a nurse for the boy.

That much money could help the children, Molly knew. And she knew Dr. Bradford was counting on her love of the kids…

But a month in Dallas with the seemingly pompous Richard Anderson? Could she handle it? The assignment would span the holidays, and aside from some volunteer work, she had no Christmas plans. At the very least she wouldn't have to spend another Christmas alone. She could stand the thought of that. And she'd be with Toby.

Still unsure, she pocketed the note and brought the boy his ice cream. "Your wish is my command," she joked to Toby as she pulled the lid off the Dixie cup and held it out to him.

Though his arm and collarbone were in casts, he could hold the Dixie cup in his injured hand and eat with his right.

"Thank you, Molly. You're not going to leave, are you?"

The boy's sad blue eyes reached right down into her heart. "No, sweetie, I'll stay for a little while." She smiled as she pulled up a chair next to the bed. His frown transformed into a broad grin and he dug into his ice cream. How could she leave him? Not just now, but when he went with his uncle and grandmother?

"What's wrong, Molly?" Toby asked anxiously.

Molly knew her concerns were nothing compared to the tragedy Toby had experienced. She pasted a bright smile on her lips. "Nothing, sweetheart. Hey, would you like me to go with you to Dallas, where your uncle lives?"

"You could do that? And stay forever?" Toby asked, hope in his voice.

"No, but I could go and stay for a few weeks, during Christmas. Wouldn't that be fun?"

"Oh, yeah," Toby said, reaching up to hug her neck.

With his face buried in her hair, he whispered, "I don't want to go with them."

"I know, sweetie, but we'll be together and I'll help you."

"Okay," Toby agreed as he pulled back to look at her. "You'll really come with me?"

"Yes, your uncle has asked me to come." She settled the little boy back in his bed. "Now, eat your ice cream before it melts while I talk to your uncle."

And just like that, her mind was made up.

She stood and walked over to the man watching them with no sign of emotion. "I'll take the job, Mr. Anderson. When were you planning on leaving?"

"We have seats on an eleven o'clock flight tomorrow morning. We'll need to leave for the airport by nine, which means you should be here by eight to get Toby ready."

"Does Toby have clothes?" The shirt and pants the boy had been wearing had been bloodied and torn.

The man stared at her, as if he hadn't comprehended her question.

"Toby hasn't had any clothes since he arrived and we cut off his bloody ones. He'll need clothes for the trip."

With a weary sigh, the man said, "Of course. It'll take a little while because I've got to get my mother back to the hotel. But then I'll go to his house and pack his clothes."

Molly knew she was a sucker for the weary and down-trodden, but she couldn't help herself. "If you want, I could meet you there and help you pack up his things. It would save you a trip back to the hospital."

After a moment's hesitation, Richard Anderson nodded. "I'll take that offer. Thank you." He looked at his watch. "Can you meet me there at eight o'clock?"

"Yes, but I don't know the address."

He pulled a card and a pen out of his pocket and wrote an address on the back of the card. "Do you know where this is?"

Molly nodded. The address was actually close to her apartment. How strange. She'd lived just a few blocks from Toby. "Yes, I do."

"Then I'll see you there at eight o'clock."

Molly heard a warning in his voice not to be late. But she was always on time. With a nod, the man took his mother's arm and left Toby's room.

That was when Molly realized the older woman had remained in the back of the room the entire time. She hadn't taken a seat nor uttered a word to her grandson. Instantly Molly felt good about her decision. How could she have let this sweet boy go with these cold-hearted people?

Molly came back to Toby's side. "Was the ice cream good?"

"Yes. Are you really going to go with me tomorrow?" the little boy asked anxiously.

"Yes, I told you I would. And I'll be there all through Christmas. I've never been to Dallas. Have you?"

"No. I never met my uncle and my grandmother before."

How could that be? Molly wondered. They were family. But for Toby's sake, she tried to put a positive spin on it. "Well, you'll get a chance to know them now." She grinned. "I have to go if I'm going to be ready to leave in the morning. Ellen will come in and see you before you go to sleep. Okay?"

"Okay. You really are going with me?"

"Yes, Toby. I'll be here in the morning, I promise."

* * *

Richard Anderson pulled up to his sister's home in a nice neighborhood in Jacksonville, Florida. He dreaded going in the house. He'd missed Susan after her move to Florida. He'd talked to her on the phone some, but it hadn't been the same.

Nine years ago his father had been furious with his daughter. He'd blown up at her and had refused any consideration of reconciliation. Now it was too late for both of them. James Anderson had been a brilliant man, but when it came to his daughter he had been foolish. He'd lost her because of his anger, long before either of them had died.

When another car pulled up behind him, Richard automatically checked his watch. Good. The nurse was on time. It would be easier to enter the house with a stranger.

He got out of his car and waited until the nurse joined him. "I appreciate you coming, Ms. Soderling."

"Please call me Molly, and I'm glad I can be of assistance."

"My mother would've come, but the past few days have been hard on her."

"Of course. Shall we go in?"

Richard pulled the keys from his pocket. They had been handed to him by the funeral director, along with other items found in the clothing. He selected one that he hoped would open the door.

He'd guessed right. The door swung open and he followed the nurse into the house. He was hit almost at once with a wave of grief. The house showed so much of Susan. It was warm and cozy, a home where a family shared and loved.

He turned to the nurse, hoping to control his grief, and he saw the same reaction on her face. She hadn't even known Susan.

"Poor Toby," she muttered.

"Why would you say that?"

"Because I can see what he's lost," she said quietly, and he saw the sheen of moisture in her eyes.

Before he could think of anything to say, she said, "We'd better get started. Do you know where Toby's bedroom is?"

He shook his head. "I've never been here."

"Oh. Then I'll go look for it."

Richard decided he should remove any valuables his sister and her husband had before he hired someone to come pack up the house. What would he do with everything? What would Toby want to keep? Hard decisions to make on the spur of the moment.

He entered the master bedroom, neat and tidy, like Susan. And hard for him to enter. He looked in the closet and found his sister's jewelry box. Then he found a folder of their financial papers on her husband's side of the closet, and some cuff links and things in a small leather box. He assumed Toby would one day want them.

"Mr. Anderson?"

Molly appeared in the doorway of the bedroom. "Yes? And please, call me Richard."

"Am I packing everything Toby has or just enough for the trip?"

"Have you found any luggage?"

"Yes, it's stored in the third bedroom closet."

"Then please take everything you can, packing the immediate needs in the smallest bag. I'll be there to help you in a moment."

After she left the room, Richard realized how extraordinarily kind she had been to come with him and do the grisly task. It was like sorting through the bones. A very personal experience.

As soon as he'd gathered anything valuable, he carried it all to Toby's room. It was a perfect bedroom for a little boy.

Susan had loved her child. It showed in so many ways.

He stood there, not wanting to enter. Molly was folding clothes and putting them in the bags. He had to force himself to join her. "I need to put these things in one of the larger bags," he said, nodding down to the articles he held.

"Of course. If it's anything valuable, you should put them in a carry-on bag so you can keep them safe."

He frowned. "I guess you're right."

She pointed out a small bag he could use. When he got to the hotel, he could transfer it to his own carry-on bag or his mother's.

By the time he had those things stowed away, Molly had finished packing Toby's clothes. Then she packed some books from a nearby shelf.

"The packers will get those things," Richard said.

"I know, but I thought it would help Toby if he had some things of his own with him."

Richard agreed. Molly was very thoughtful.

"I can't thank you enough for coming with me to the house, Molly. It was difficult to—to come here."

"Yes, I know."

Molly reached for one more thing. A small framed picture of Toby with his parents. It sat on his bedside table.

He watched her but said nothing.

She was an attractive woman, he suddenly realized. Her

reddish-brown hair was shoulder length and simply styled. Her green eyes held so much sympathy, he didn't like to meet her glance. When she smiled, as she had at Toby, her face lit up a room. No wonder the boy was attached to her. She was like a warm fire on a cold night.

He backed away, recognizing a danger there. And he'd invited her to his home for a month. Was he crazy? No, just desperate. He had to protect his mother. Since his father's death eighteen months ago the not-yet-sixty-year-old had aged. She leaned on him, so needy in many ways. Now she had to deal with her daughter's death and the regrets she had.

How could she deal with an eight-year-old boy? And the child was frightened, since he didn't know them. Molly was the answer to both those problems. He'd made the right move hiring her.

"Uh, I really appreciate your help, Molly," he said again, preparing to set the tone for her visit.

"It's all right, Richard. I'm glad I could help."

"Yes. What I wanted to say is my mother is weak. She won't be able to deal with Toby. I'll need you to shield her from the boy's energy, as well as care for Toby. Will that be a problem?"

She seemed taken aback. But she raised her chin and said coolly, "No, that won't be a problem."

He'd upset her. Too bad. He had to protect his own. "Good. I work long hours, so I won't be there to make sure she's not disturbed, so I will appreciate your help. If there are problems, bring them to me, not my mother."

"Certainly," she said, her voice crisp.

"Are we finished?"

"Yes, of course."

He picked up the two big bags and she grabbed the overnight bag where she packed Toby's things for tomorrow. She also picked up the bag that held the valuables.

"I can get that," he hurriedly said.

The sympathy that had prompted her to come with Richard tonight was drying up. Molly glared at him and set the bag on the floor. Did he think she was going to steal something? "Fine."

She walked back into the living area of the house. The Christmas tree looked forlorn in the darkened room. Suddenly Molly stopped. "The presents. Should we—"

"We don't have room," was his clipped response.

Molly forced herself to keep moving to the front door. Every step she took was a betrayal to Toby. She could feel him protesting. The presents under the tree would be something he needed, not for what was in them, but for the memories associated with them.

"When will their belongings arrive in Dallas?" she asked.

"I don't know. I'll have to make arrangements tonight."

He sounded irritated.

Molly mentally shrugged. She'd done her best for Toby. She couldn't do any more because the man behind her didn't want her to.

She'd thought perhaps he was sad and exhausted at the hospital. Now he seemed surly and difficult. And she was going to live with him for a month? She must be crazy. At least he would be at work most of the time.

Poor Toby, in a house with a grandmother who needed to be protected from him, and an uncle who was never there. He'd gone from a loving home to what? A museum?

She would only be there a month, but she'd do everything she could to make a warm home for Toby.

She squared her shoulders as she marched out to her car. She wasn't going to worry about the man behind her, carrying most of the luggage. That was his choice.

After putting the small case in her car, she turned to look at Richard Anderson, who was loading the rest of the luggage in the trunk of his car.

"I'll see you at the hospital in the morning," she called.

"At nine o'clock. Please be on time. We don't want to run late getting to the airport."

With disdain, she replied, "I'm always on time, Richard."

Then she went back to her car, got in and drove away, leaving him standing there. So what if he didn't like her abrupt withdrawal. He shouldn't have been so snippy.

Immediately she felt remorse for her attitude. The evening had to have been difficult for him, even if he hadn't seen his sister in a while. And it must've been a long day, as she'd guessed at the hospital. She chastised herself for not showing more patience.

But Toby was a little boy. The man and his mother hadn't shown much compassion to him. Richard's concern had been for his mother.

The next few days would be difficult for Toby. But at least he would have her so he wouldn't feel alone. Richard might regret his invitation, but he wasn't going to get rid of her now, even if he wanted to.

She was going to be there for Toby.

For just a little while, and regardless of the heartache when she had to leave, she and Toby would be a family.

* * *

Molly was used to getting up early, but apparently her patient was not. She had to practically dress Toby without any assistance from him. "Toby, you're not helping me, you know."

"But I don't want to go," he said in a low voice. "Mommy and Daddy are—" He cut off on a sob.

Molly put her arms around him. "Sweetie, your mommy and daddy's bodies are buried here, but *they* will always be with you, in your heart. You just have to think about them and they'll come to you in your heart and in your memory."

"Really?"

"Yes, and one day, when you're older, you can come back to visit their graves. But they won't be there, because they'll be with you, in your heart."

Toby patted his heart. "Do you think they're here now?"

"Yes, I do. And they want the best for you."

"So you think they want me to go with my uncle?"

"Yes, because he'll take care of you. That's important."

"Okay," Toby agreed with a sigh.

"Good. Let's get your shirt on. I like it. It matches your eyes."

"That's what Mommy said, but I like it because it's easy to wear."

Molly smiled. "I see."

Once she got his shoes on him, she helped Toby get down from his bed. He had a cast on his left collarbone that ended on the upper part of his arm and the cast on his lower arm started just below his elbow. At least he was mobile.

She managed to get him discharged from the hospital and down at the front door five minutes early. She already knew Richard would be irritated if they were late.

Her bags were down by the door. She'd left them with

one of the greeters so she wouldn't have to drag them upstairs and down. She sat Toby down in one of the chairs for visitors and hurried over to get her bags.

"Molly!" Toby cried urgently.

Molly whirled around.

Toby was pointing to his uncle coming through the door.

"I'm coming, Toby," she called. Gathering her two bags, she rushed across the lobby to meet Richard at Toby's side. "We're ready," she announced.

"Good. Toby, can you walk?"

"Yes," the little boy said, his eyes big.

"Okay. I'll get your bag. May I take one of yours, Molly?"

"No, thank you. I can manage." She followed the two males out the door, keeping an eye on Toby. The boy kept looking over his shoulder at Molly, to be sure she was following.

Toby's grandmother was sitting in the front seat. Elizabeth Anderson smoothed back her graying hair and turned her blue eyes to Molly. The woman looked rested, Molly thought. She was glad someone was. She had just come off the night shift for the last six months and was still adjusting to working in the daylight.

She got in the back seat with Toby, wondering if his uncle was still irritated with her. Judging by his silence as he loaded the trunk, he probably was. Richard Anderson didn't appear to be the forgiving kind.

Toby sat very still as Molly put his seat belt on him. "Can she speak?" he whispered, nodding toward his grandmother.

"I don't know," Molly returned. After all, she hadn't heard the woman utter a sound, either.

"Is everything all right?" Richard asked, looking at them in the rearview mirror.

"Yes, Richard."

Before Molly could stop him, Toby leaned forward and said, "Are you my grandma?"

The woman seemed to freeze.

Richard answered for her. "Yes," he said in clipped tones.

Molly put a hand on Toby's good arm, warning him not to speak again. She didn't believe the woman was as frail as Richard believed, but she was certainly suffering grief at her daughter's death. That was enough for Molly to cut her some slack. For a while.

There was no conversation in the car. All the way to the airport, Molly held Toby's hand and squeezed it when he sent her a panicky look.

When they got out at the airport, Richard got a skycap to take care of their luggage. Then he turned to Molly. "Here are the tickets for the three of you. Please take care of my mother and Toby while I return the rental car. I'll meet you at the gate."

"All right." She nodded to the skycap who led them to the check-in line. She discovered they were flying first class, which made it possible to bypass the long line. In no time, she had checked them in.

"My son—" Mrs. Anderson said, looking as panicky as Toby.

"He'll be joining us at the gate, ma'am. He has to present his own ID, you know. Airport security."

"Oh, yes. Do you—do you know where our gate is?"

"Yes, ma'am. If you'll come with Toby and me, I have our tickets and I can find the gate. It's right over here."

Molly led the other two to the gate where their plane waited. She checked her watch. Richard had about thirty minutes to get there before their plane took off.

"Will my son get here in time?" Mrs. Anderson asked, her voice trembling.

"Yes, I'm sure he will. He seems to be very efficient."

"Oh, yes, he is."

Molly's words seemed to have settled down Toby's grandmother. She relaxed in her seat, but Molly suspected if Richard didn't get there quickly, she would start worrying all over again.

Toby leaned in against Molly. "Is he going to go with us?"

"Yes, Toby, he is."

Mrs. Anderson looked at Toby. "How old are you?"

Molly stared at her, her mouth agape. Toby seemed to be taken aback, too. His grandmother didn't know how old he was?

"I'm eight," Toby finally said.

"Oh, you were born a year after your mother married."

Toby looked at her curiously. "Did you know my mommy?"

The woman suddenly burst into tears.

For the first time since she met him, Molly discovered a desire for Richard's presence.

CHAPTER TWO

MOLLY discovered her desire for Richard's arrival wasn't a good thing.

"What have you done to my mother?" he demanded roughly as soon as he reached them.

"I didn't do anything to your mother. Toby asked an innocent question, that's all."

She regretted that comment, too, because the man immediately turned to glare at the boy.

When they announced the boarding of the first-class passengers, Molly immediately stood and returned Mrs. Anderson's ticket to her son. "Toby and I will go ahead and board."

After they were seated on the plane, Toby by the window, he leaned over and asked in a whisper, "Did I make her cry?"

"Not really, sweetie. I guess she's still emotional about your mommy. After all, your mommy was her little girl."

"Oh."

Toby tensed and Molly looked up to see Richard and his mother entering the plane. Their seats, it appeared, were across the aisle from her and Toby.

Richard nodded in her direction, but she said nothing.

Perhaps he would continue to blame her for his mother's tears. She didn't know, but she didn't see how she could be expected to have realized Toby's question would've brought that intense reaction.

There was no more conversation between them. Toby, much to Molly's relief, fell asleep after the first hour. Molly pulled out a novel she'd been reading and passed the time that way. When the pilot announced their approach to the airport, she woke Toby.

"The plane is landing. Don't you want to see where you're going to live?"

"Can you see it from the airplane?" Toby asked in surprise.

Molly chuckled. She'd already discovered Toby was very literal. "No, honey, I just meant you could see the area. You'll see your new home later."

"I miss my old home," Toby said sadly.

Molly hugged him to her, as much as the seat belts allowed. "I know you do. But you'll like this one, too, I'm sure." She hoped she wasn't lying.

"Okay," Toby whispered.

She held his hand while the plane landed and then taxied to the gate. Since he'd brought nothing on board with him, they were ready to exit the plane at once. When Richard indicated they should go ahead, Molly led Toby off the plane and to their baggage claim. She was sure the Andersons were right behind them, but she didn't turn to look for them, not wanting to give Richard that satisfaction.

Then that deep voice came over her shoulder. "If you'll point out your bags, Molly, I'll get them off the carousel."

"Thank you. They haven't come by yet."

When she saw her bags, along with Toby's, she pointed them out. A skycap loaded them on his pushcart.

"Molly, will you keep an eye on Toby and my mother while I go get my car?"

She heard the words not said. "And please don't make my mother cry."

"Yes, of course," she replied.

Molly led them to a bench where they could sit until Richard arrived with the car.

Much to her surprise, he pulled up in a medium-size SUV and got out, opening the back for the luggage. She had assumed he'd drive a Mercedes or a Lexus, since he was supposed to be rich. After she got Mrs. Anderson and Toby settled, she followed him into the back seat.

"Thank you for getting them loaded," Richard said as he slid behind the wheel.

"Thank you for loading the luggage." It seemed the only polite thing to say in response to his remark. Had he thought she'd remain standing on the sidewalk, unable to move without his guidance?

He flashed her a look in the rearview mirror. She smiled, determined to let him know she wasn't bothered by his attitude.

She turned her attention to the sights outside her window, pointing out interesting things to Toby.

"Where's the ocean?" Toby whispered.

"Um, I don't think there is an ocean nearby, Toby."

Toby appeared startled. "They don't have an ocean?"

"Actually, we do," Richard said over his shoulder, "but it's on the southern part of the state, which is about five or six hours away."

"Oh," Toby said softly.

"Did you go to the ocean a lot?" his uncle asked.

"Yes, with Mommy," Toby said.

"Susan always liked the ocean," Mrs. Anderson said, surprising everyone.

"Yes, Mom, she did."

No one spoke after that exchange.

When they got off the freeway, they turned into a neighborhood with large houses and big trees. The house whose driveway they pulled into was the biggest of them all. Both Molly and Toby stared at it in surprise.

Richard looked over his shoulder. "You can get out now. We're home."

Toby turned to look at Molly, panic on his face.

Molly squeezed his hand. "It's all right," she whispered, but she wasn't sure she believed it herself. The house was huge, but the stone façade made it look cold and unwelcoming. The air, too, was cold and windy, furthering the impression.

Molly was going to have to buy a coat. Good thing she was earning a lot of money on this job.

Pasting a smile on her face, she said, "Come on, Toby. It'll be fun. We can explore."

She helped the little boy out of the vehicle and shivered as a cold wind blew.

"Hurry inside so you'll be warm," Richard said.

Since they parked in the driveway beside the side entrance, Molly assumed he meant that door. She opened the door and led Toby inside. They were standing in a small entryway next to the kitchen.

Suddenly there was a flurry of movement as three

people rushed forward. Toby pressed against Molly, but the male and two female strangers passed them by and greeted the Andersons.

The younger woman took Mrs. Anderson by the arm and led her away. The man, tall and wiry, was sent to the vehicle to bring in the luggage. Richard consulted with the other woman.

Molly and Toby stood there, not sure what they were supposed to do.

Richard stepped toward them. "I'll show you your rooms if you'll follow me."

Molly nodded and followed him, Toby clinging tightly to her hand. No wonder. He had sounded as remote as a hotel employee. They went up a grand stairway to the second floor. He turned left and led them down the hall to two rooms side by side.

"These rooms are actually connected by a door inside. I thought you might want to leave the door open the first few nights Toby is here, Molly, if you don't mind."

"No, I don't. That's a good idea, right, Toby?"

Richard opened a door. "This will be your room, Toby."

Molly walked into the room with the little boy. "This is great, isn't it, Toby? You have a lot of windows and you can look at the garden behind the house. When it's warmer, you may be able to play there."

The man nodded. "Of course." Then he crossed to another door and opened it. "This will be your room, Molly."

It was beautiful, not what she expected. She laughed to herself as she realized nannies were housed in the attic only in gothic novels.

"Thank you, it's lovely, Richard."

He frowned, as if she'd said something wrong. What could it have been? She'd smiled at him, trying to be gracious.

"Yes, well, I need to see about my mother. If you need anything, please ask Delores or Louisa. They'll be glad to help you."

So they'd already been handed off to the staff. Molly nodded in response, but she didn't say anything. If she'd spoken, she might've said the wrong thing. The man had been kind to Toby when he'd shown him the room, but it was clear he was going about his business as usual.

One thing was certain: Richard Anderson did not have a kind heart.

One thing was certain: Richard was irritated with Molly. Condemnation fairly glowed in her green eyes. He had a lot of things on his plate. He'd brought her here to help Toby settle in okay. That was her job. And he wasn't going to be chastised for doing his job by someone he'd hired.

He shook his head as he went to the other end of the house where his mother's suite was located. Tapping lightly on the door, he stood waiting for it to open.

Louisa came to the door.

"I'd like to see my mother. Is she asleep?" he asked.

"No, sir." Louisa stepped aside and swung the door wide. Then she silently made her way out.

Richard took the chair opposite his mother, in a sitting room professionally done in southwestern decor. He noticed she looked tired, drawn, much the same as she'd looked for the past year and a half. The depression had taken its toll on her. And now, the funeral.

Before he could speak, she said, "You know, Richard,

ever since the incident between Susan and your father, I've regretted her leaving. But never like I regret it now." She looked up and there were tears in her eyes. "She ran away because of your father—but I had nine years to make it right and never did. I was too afraid to cross him." The tears spilled down her cheeks now as she said, "And after he died, I was too distraught and depressed to make the move. I thought I had more time…"

Richard reached out and took her hands in his, rubbing the tops of her hands with his thumb. Her skin was soft and firm, and he realized as he looked at her just how lovely a woman she was. Elizabeth Anderson had once been in the Dallas social scene, a benefactor, an organizer, a supporter of the arts. She had a closet full of designer gowns and suits for the variety of functions she'd attended and chaired. But in the last eighteen months she'd spent most of her time right here in this room. Had he done enough to help her through her hard time?

He could certainly help now.

"You know, Mom, the incident had nothing to do with you." Funny, he thought, how they referred to it—"the incident." As if giving it a generic name made it more ephemeral, less real. But the day Susan walked out couldn't have been more real. He remembered it as if it were yesterday, though it was almost a decade ago. It was the day everything changed.

Susan and their father, James, had always butted heads. He was an autocrat and Susan a free spirit—a doomed combination. When James laid down a law, he expected it enacted, but his sister had a hard time conforming; she was confident and eager and resented her father's strict hand. But that didn't deter James. He tried to control everything:

her clothes, her friends, her studies. But the day he'd tried to control her heart was the end. He'd found out she was seeing a young man behind his back, a young man from a working-class family who was studying to become a teacher. Kevin Astin was far from the rich, privileged, connected man James had wanted for Susan. He gave her an ultimatum: ditch him or get out.

Susan opted for the latter. In an hour she'd packed her bags and left Highland Park for good. In nine years she hadn't ever been back.

She moved to Florida with Kevin, whom she married almost immediately. And a year later they had Toby. The nephew Richard had never seen until yesterday.

In the intervening years he'd spoken to Susan twice, and his mother never, both fearful of James Anderson's wrath. Not that he'd ever been physical with them; but his disapproval took other forms, equally distasteful. Somehow it had just seemed easier to agree with him, or at least conform to him.

Richard realized he was equally to blame. Nothing, no one, should have kept him from his sister, kept Elizabeth from her daughter. But there was nothing either of them could do now, except pray for forgiveness. And care for Toby.

He told his mother all that, and she listened to him. After a while her tears stopped, her sobs turned into steady, even breathing. She held his hand and almost mystically he could feel her pain exiting. He knew nothing could ever erase the agony she'd suffered, but Elizabeth was on the way to recovery.

They talked about Susan, about what they remembered, about what they'd heard of her recent life at the funeral. Richard realized this felt more like a funeral than what they'd endured in Florida. This was a memorial to Susan Anderson Astin, who would live forever in their hearts, where she belonged.

Elizabeth smiled faintly. "I don't know what I'd do without you, Richard. But I do know what I intend to do." She stood up and looked around. "I intend to get out of the prison I've made of this room and start living again. The way Susan would want me to. And I intend to care for her son."

"That's the Elizabeth Anderson I know." Richard hugged her and she held him tight, conveying her gratitude in the maternal embrace.

"Now, Mom, I have to get to the office. I'll try my best to get home in time for dinner." For the first time in over a year, when he closed her bedroom door he knew his mother would be okay.

And so would he.

He walked back downstairs to the kitchen, where their cook, Delores, ruled. Now nearing fifty, the Mexican-American woman had worked for the Andersons for decades, as had her husband, Albert.

"Delores, I'm going to the office for a couple of hours. If the nurse or the child needs anything, please take care of them."

"Yes, sir, Richard."

Richard's law firm was located downtown, very close to their neighborhood, Highland Park, an exclusive area. It only took a few minutes to reach the parking garage connected to the building where the law firm had offices.

As expected, he found a pile of messages and mail on his desk that his secretary had sorted and opened for him. After dealing with those matters, he asked his secretary to gather the partners in his office for a quick briefing. Then there was a list of phone calls to be returned. By the time he'd finished half the calls, he put aside the rest of them for the morning and packed up to go home.

He'd probably already missed dinner. Normally he made it home for dinner at least three nights a week, or else his mother ate her meal upstairs in her suite.

Tonight, when he got home, he found the dinner table set for four. "No one's eaten yet?" he asked Delores as he came in.

"Your mother requested we wait for you."

"The boy didn't get too hungry?"

"No, sir. I gave Toby and Molly a snack about five."

"Thanks, Delores. Please call them down to dinner."

He carried his briefcase to his office, stepped into the connecting bath and washed his hands. Then he came back to the dining room.

Molly and Toby were standing there, seemingly unsure of where they should sit.

"Good evening. I hope your afternoon was relaxing?"

Molly nudged the boy. He said, "Yes, sir."

"Good, Toby. And you, Molly? Did you have a pleasant afternoon?" He was determined to show no prejudice to her.

"Yes, I did, Richard, thank you. We're all unpacked and we've familiarized ourselves with the house and your staff. They're all very nice."

"Yes, we're most fortunate," Richard said with a smile. "But it doesn't sound like your afternoon was very restful."

Molly raised her gaze to his. "Neither of us needed rest. Toby was curious about his new home. Albert even gave us a tour of the backyard after we unpacked."

"Weren't you cold? I noticed you didn't wear a coat on the trip."

"No, neither of us has a coat because it didn't get that cold in Florida. But Albert promised to drive us to a store to buy coats tomorrow."

"Good. I'll be glad to pay for them."

"If you insist, you can pay for Toby's. I'll pay for mine."

Richard frowned. He wasn't used to such resistance.

"Richard?" His mother stood at the door of the dining room.

He crossed over to take her hand and lead her to the table after kissing her cheek. "Hello, Mother. It was kind of you to wait for me to get home."

"I wanted our first meal to be a family one," Elizabeth Anderson said.

"Then let's all sit down," he suggested. He showed his mother to the seat at the head of the table. He indicated Toby and Molly should take the two seats to her left. As they did so, he sat in the chair to his mother's right.

Once they were seated, Elizabeth rang the small bell sitting beside her plate. Almost immediately, the kitchen door opened and Louisa entered with a tray. She carefully set a bowl of soup in front of each of them.

Toby leaned over to Molly and whispered, "What is this?"

Richard, hiding a grin, said, "It's broccoli cheese soup, Toby, one of my mother's favorites." He was feeling relieved that things were going so well. He'd gone to the office and his mother had rested, and the nurse had taken care of the boy, as he'd planned.

"Oh. Uh, it looks good."

"Very nice manners, Toby. Your mother would be proud

of you," Richard said softly. He didn't want to upset his mother, but Susan deserved her due.

Instead of bursting into tears as she normally would have done upon mention of Susan, his mother smiled faintly. Their talk had indeed helped her. "Yes, I believe she did a good job teaching Toby proper behavior."

"I agree, Mrs. Anderson," Molly chimed in. "I can't wait to try the soup. I haven't gotten used to this cold weather yet."

Richard laughed. "It doesn't get that cold here, Molly. Now in Colorado, this would be late spring weather."

"Where is Colorado?" Toby asked.

"It's a state north of here where a lot of Texans go to ski."

"Water-ski?" Toby asked.

"No, Toby, snow skiing."

"With real snow? I've never seen snow, except on TV," the boy confessed.

"Maybe after you get your casts off, we can fly to Colorado and try some snow skiing," Richard suggested.

"I'd like that!" Toby said in excitement. "Would you like that, Molly?"

"I'm sure it would be fun, Toby, but I'll probably be back at work by then."

Richard watched the enthusiasm fade from the little boy's face.

"But you could send me pictures of you skiing. That would be wonderful. You might even build a snowman for me."

"Could we do that?" Toby asked, looking at Richard.

"Sure, Toby, we could do that."

"Right now, though, you need to eat your soup before it gets cold," Molly said with a smile.

Richard watched her. While some people would have been overwhelmed by the quick transition, the gamut of emotions and personalities, Molly kept her composure. And she was wonderful with Toby. Now she not only offered a way for Toby to share his excitement with her, but she'd reminded him of his behavior.

The boy at once picked up his spoon and tried the soup. Then he looked at his grandmother. "The soup is very good."

"Yes, it is, isn't it? We'll have to tell Delores what a good job she's done," Elizabeth said, smiling at Toby.

"Am I supposed to call you Grandma?" Toby asked.

"Yes, I think that's what you should call me. Do you mind?" Elizabeth asked with more energy than she'd shown in months.

Richard stared at his mother. She looked better already, a gleam in her blue eyes he hadn't seen in a long time. He knew it would take time for her to regain her old self, but she was on her way. After all, she'd barely recovered from his father's death eighteen months ago, when she'd learned of Susan's death. Somehow, when he'd expected her to give up on life, she seemed to have found a new lease on it. Still, he'd have to keep a close watch on her to make sure she didn't overdo it.

When they finished their soup, Elizabeth rang her bell again and Louisa came in to remove their bowls. Albert followed with a large serving tray.

Richard drew in a deep breath of roast beef perfectly cooked with attending vegetables. He smiled at Louisa. It was his favorite meal. "Thank Delores for me, Louisa."

"Yes, sir," Louisa said with a grin.

They were all enjoying their meal when Toby asked a question that got their attention. "Don't you have a Christmas tree?"

Elizabeth assured him they did. It was in the living room.

"But I didn't see it today."

"You may have missed the living room, dear. It's the room by the front door. Some people call it a parlor."

"I don't think we went in that room, Toby," Molly said softly.

"You would remember it if you saw it, Toby," Elizabeth continued. "It's silver with gold balls on it. It's quite striking."

"No, Grandma, Christmas trees are green, not silver."

"Toby, some trees aren't real," Molly hurriedly explained. "They're made out of other things."

Toby looked puzzled. "Why?"

Molly looked at Richard, a clear plea for assistance.

"Real trees are messy, Toby. Plus, if you have an artificial tree, you can reuse it every year."

"Is that good, Molly?" Toby asked.

"For some people it is."

"I like green trees," Toby asserted. Then tears glistened in his eyes as he continued, "Me and Mommy and Daddy decorated our tree with all our favorite ornaments."

Molly leaned over and whispered something in Toby's ear and the little boy tried to wipe away the tears.

"Mrs. Anderson," Molly asked, "would there be a room where Toby could have a green tree this year? As a sort of memorial to his parents?"

Richard spoke up. "My mother can't—"

"Yes, I think we could do that," Elizabeth said at the same time.

"Mother, I don't think you can take on that task. It will be too much for you."

"It wouldn't be, Richard, if you'd help."

The other two were sitting quietly, watching the conversation between him and his mother. Richard almost groaned aloud. He had too much to do as it was. But he could tell his mother wanted to make the effort for her grandson.

"All right, Mother. In what room would you like to put the green tree?"

"I think my sitting room would do. Then we could enjoy it all day long."

"Of course you could, if you want an eight-year-old running in and out."

Molly spoke up. "Toby and I came across a garden room with a tiled floor and some pretty durable furniture in it. Wouldn't that be a good room for a real tree, so the pine needles won't stick in the carpet?" She looked at Richard.

"We don't use that room often in the winter. Do you think that would be a good idea, Richard?" Elizabeth asked her son.

"I'm sure it would be fine, Mom. Albert can take Molly and Toby out to find a tree tomorrow, if they want."

Toby frowned. "But the daddy always comes to carry the tree and tie it on the roof of the car."

Richard smiled. "We don't have a daddy here, Toby. I promise Albert can carry the tree for you. He's very strong."

"No, I think Toby is right," Elizabeth spoke with more authority than Richard had heard from her since he was a small boy himself.

"Right about what, Mom?" he asked.

"I think we should go as a family. That's what we did when you were a little boy. When you get home tomorrow evening, we'll go find a tree." She nodded, as if to punctuate her statement.

"I'm not sure when I'll be able to get home, Mom. I missed two days of work."

"Richard, I don't think you should miss buying the tree. This will be Toby's first Christmas with us. It's important."

Richard sighed, thinking of all the work he had piled up for him when he got to the office in the morning. And now he'd have to get home at a decent hour tomorrow night to go buy a blasted Christmas tree!

"And when will the presents get here?" Toby asked.

"Why, I suppose Santa will bring them Christmas Day," Elizabeth assured him with a smile.

"No, I mean the presents that were under our tree at home." Toby turned to Molly. "They will come, won't they?"

"I don't know, honey. I'm sure they'll get here sometime, but it might not be before Christmas."

"But they have to! I think Mommy wrapped up my puppy!"

CHAPTER THREE

ALL three adults stared at the little boy.

"What?" Molly asked, not sure she'd heard correctly.

"Oh, no!" Elizabeth said, covering her mouth with her hand.

Richard drew a deep breath. "Toby, I don't think that would've been possible. Puppies can't live in a closed-up box."

Once again tears formed in Toby's eyes. "But my mommy promised me a puppy for Christmas!"

Molly automatically put her arm around Toby. "Richard isn't saying your mommy wasn't getting you a puppy. He's just saying it wasn't wrapped up. She'd probably made arrangements for picking up the puppy on Christmas Eve."

"So I'll still get my puppy?"

Molly looked at Richard. She figured he should be the one to answer that question. She couldn't imagine a dog in their elegant home.

"Uh, no, I don't think so. We don't know where she'd purchased a dog."

Toby slumped back in his chair, devastation on his face.

Molly squeezed his shoulder and said softly, "Finish your dinner like a big boy, Toby."

He sat up straighter and looked at Molly for approval. She managed a smile for him, hoping he wouldn't realize how much she sympathized with him. It would only make him weaker.

"I'm sure Santa will bring you some wonderful presents, Toby," Elizabeth assured him.

Toby managed a smile for his grandmother.

Elizabeth immediately rang the bell. When Louisa entered, she said, "We're ready for dessert now, Louisa, please."

Richard looked at his mother in surprise. "We are?"

"Yes, I believe Toby has finished his meal and dessert will make him feel better." Again she smiled at Toby, ignoring Richard's half-filled plate.

With a sigh and a regretful look as Louisa collected his plate, Richard said, "Dessert must be good tonight, Toby. We don't always get any dessert."

"Me, neither. But I like dessert," Toby added, again managing a smile for his grandmother.

Molly hid her smile, afraid Richard would guess she was laughing inside about his consternation as his plate was taken from him. But he was being a good sport about it, which earned him marks in her book, in spite of his lack of warmth toward her.

Dessert was chocolate cake with chocolate ice cream—Toby's favorite. Molly ate some of it, but she didn't clean her plate like the two males did.

Elizabeth didn't touch hers, seeming more engrossed in Toby's enjoyment of the dessert.

After dinner was over, Molly suggested Toby tell his relatives good-night and she'd take him up to bed. Since saying good-night at home had included kisses and hugs for his parents, Toby hugged his grandmother, much to her delight, and kissed her cheek. Then he moved on to Richard and did the same.

To Molly's relief, both of them appeared grateful for Toby's nightly ritual. Molly took the boy's hand and led him up the stairs to his room.

"You did really well tonight, Toby," Molly told him as he was preparing for his bath. She'd already run the bath-water as soon as they'd reached his room.

He raised his head to stare at her. "What do you mean?"

"Well, you used good table manners, and you behaved very well when you realized you might not get a dog for Christmas."

"Yeah. I want a puppy so much. But I guess a dog wouldn't do so well in this big house. He might get lost."

"Yes, he might. After you have a bath, I'll read you a story," Molly said, trying to recall the books she'd packed. "I don't know which books I packed. Is there one you want me to read?"

"Any of the Berenstain Bear books. They're a lot of fun. And I can read them myself."

"Ah. Good. Then I'll let you read one to me tonight. And I might buy a copy of *Charlotte's Web*. Have you ever read that book?"

"No, but my mommy was going to read it to me if Santa brought me it."

"Okay. Well, tonight, we'll stick to the Berenstain Bears. Go hop in and take your bath. I'll go see if your uncle will loan you a T-shirt for the night. We should be able to get one of his over your casts."

"Do you think he'll mind?" Toby asked hesitantly.

"Why do you ask that?" She was afraid her attitude toward Richard might have been passed on to Toby without her realizing it.

"He—he scares me a little bit."

"I think that's just because you don't know him well yet. I'll be right back." Molly smiled at Toby and left his room. She didn't know how to avoid speaking to Richard. She wished she did. But she couldn't make a big deal about it. Otherwise, she might think about him like Toby did. As the enemy.

She ran downstairs, but she didn't find Richard in the dining room. She went into the kitchen and asked Louisa if she knew where Richard had gone.

"Yes, ma'am," said the Mexican woman about her own age. "He went upstairs to his room."

She got directions from Louisa and ran back up the stairs, turning to the right until she reached the bedroom opposite Elizabeth's. She tapped softly on the door and waited. But she couldn't shake the feeling that she was like Daniel about to enter the lion's den.

Richard settled in a comfortable chair in front of his fire-place, warmed by the fire. He had some legal reading to catch up on.

But his mind was filled with the evening he'd just spent downstairs. There was no question that Toby's arrival had changed the dynamics of the household. He was rethinking his plan of turning the little boy over to his nurse and continuing on with his life. After all, he had just about completed his reworking of his father's law firm. Instead of personal injury cases, he had changed the focus to corporate law.

He thought he'd finally be able to return to the pleasant life he'd always led. For the past eighteen months, he'd dealt with the law firm and with his mother. While he and his father had not agreed in many things, he had truly mourned his death. And feared he'd soon lose his mother. Tonight, as she'd focused all her attention on Toby, she appeared to have grown younger before Richard's very eyes.

He wondered if Molly had come to that same conclusion. He'd noticed how closely she'd watched his mother. It would be nice to be able to talk to her about his mother. After all, she was a nurse.

He shouldn't be thinking about Molly as a friend. He was paying her salary. That would be like asking Delores for advice. Of course, he'd done that. After all, Delores had been with them for more than twenty years. And Molly didn't look anything like the plump, dark-haired Delores, either. He immediately shut that thought away.

But thoughts of Molly persisted in spite of his efforts to concentrate on other things. Her hair had glinted in the light from the chandelier in the dining room, sparking more red tonight than he'd noticed before. Concern had filled her green eyes when Toby had made his statement about the puppy he was expecting. Richard had been tempted to laugh until he'd seen Molly's reaction.

With a sigh, he tried again to put away all thoughts of Molly. As beautiful as she was, she had no place in his life.

Unfortunately, for the last eighteen months no woman had had a place in his life, except his mother.

Prior to his father's death, he'd enjoyed a nice social life. However, with his father's death had come the opportunity to change the law firm's focus, which demanded most of his time. His mother had demanded the rest of it.

That was the problem, he realized. He was thinking of Molly because he missed…he missed having a woman in his life.

Just as he managed to focus on his reading, he heard a knock. With a frown, he rose and went to the door. Delores or Albert must have a problem. Normally they didn't disturb him after he'd gone upstairs.

Swinging open the door, he discovered his caller to be the woman he'd had on his mind. He could only think of one reason she would be there, and it wasn't one he was willing to cooperate with. At least not here.

"Molly?" he said, frowning at her.

"I'm sorry to disturb you, Richard, but I have a favor to ask."

"I don't think I'll be willing to grant that favor, Molly. It would be rather improper with my mother across the hall."

Her green eyes widened in shock as she took in his meaning, which made him realize he'd made a mistake.

"What do you want?" he asked, hoping she'd forget what he'd implied.

"I wanted to borrow a T-shirt from you for Toby. I'll buy him a couple tomorrow, but his shirts are too small to fit comfortably over his casts."

Her stiffened demeanor told him she hadn't forgiven him for the beginning of their conversation.

"Yes, of course, I'll get one for you," he said, leaving the door open. As he crossed the room to open a drawer, he tried to figure out how to apologize for his initial words without admitting what he'd actually thought. Or how his pulse had raced.

When he got back to the door, a white T-shirt in his hand, he said, "I'm sorry I, uh, reacted in the, uh, wrong way." He thought he sounded like a teenager speaking to a teacher.

"I can assure you I won't bother you in the evenings again, Richard."

Her words were cool, distant, and told him his apology hadn't gotten him very far.

"I'm glad to be of assistance, Molly."

She took the T-shirt from him and walked away with a muttered thanks. He watched her until she entered Toby's bedroom.

Damn, he'd messed up big time. He'd have to make it up to Molly tomorrow.

But how?

Molly and Toby came to breakfast after Richard had left for work. Elizabeth came down just a couple of minutes after them and they all enjoyed breakfast in a small room off the kitchen. It was a cozy room to eat in, and both Molly and Toby were more relaxed.

"Mrs. Anderson, can—"

"Please, dear, you must call me Elizabeth."

"Oh, thank you, Elizabeth. I wanted to ask if Albert could take me and Toby to a store to buy coats this morning, and maybe to a Christmas store to buy some ornaments for the tree?"

"Of course he can, and I'll go with you. Richard gave me strict instructions to pay for all your purchases today."

"Oh, surely not all of them. I'll pay for my own coat and anything else I buy for myself."

"He was quite clear in his instructions."

"Well, we'll see. Not having bought a coat before, I'm not sure what they cost."

"Are you thinking about a fur coat?" Elizabeth asked.

Molly stared at her. "Fur? Oh, no, not at all!"

"But a fur coat will last longer than a cloth coat. I've had a mink coat my husband bought me thirty years ago, and it still looks good even now."

Molly smiled. "But I'm going back to Florida. I wouldn't have any use for a fur coat. Nor could I afford it. I thought we'd go to Target and find reasonably priced coats."

"I usually go to Neiman's for clothes."

"I don't think Neiman's would have what we need, Elizabeth, but you don't have to accompany us. We'll be fine."

"Oh, but I want to go with you. It'll be fun. Richard left you a note to explain everything. I put it in the pocket of my robe so I wouldn't forget it. Here it is."

Molly unfolded the note. In it, Richard assured her, as his mother had done, that they would pay for whatever she wanted. He also cautioned her not to let his mother get too tired.

She could definitely follow that caution, but Molly didn't think she could let him pay for all her purchases if they were for her. She'd find a way around that order.

"Well, if you're going with us, plan on leaving at ten. Isn't that when the stores open?"

"I believe so," Elizabeth said. "That gives us almost an hour to get ready."

Molly smiled in agreement, though she didn't think an hour would be necessary for either Toby or herself.

When they met downstairs at the assigned time, Elizabeth was dressed in a chic wool suit that shouted designer. Molly was in slacks with a cotton sweater. They were the warmest clothes she owned. Toby was in jeans and a knit shirt that would fit over his casts.

"Albert promised to have the car warmed up so you two wouldn't freeze to death before we can get you coats."

"I'll have to thank him," Molly said, turning to the garage.

Elizabeth redirected her out the front door. "Albert has pulled the car around."

As Elizabeth had said, the car was warm and they barely felt the north wind that chilled the air. All three of them sat in the back seat while Albert drove the car.

When they reached Target, Albert let them out at the front door and promised to wait in the parking lot for them.

"This makes shopping easy, doesn't it?" Molly commented.

"Yes, it does. Albert is a dear." Elizabeth took Toby's hand. "You must hold my hand, Toby, so we won't get lost."

"Yes, Grandma. I won't let you get lost."

Molly wasn't sure who was protecting whom, but that was okay with her. They went to the children's department first and found a ski-jacket for Toby. They bought it a little large to fit over his casts. Elizabeth added some sweaters and long sleeve polo shirts to the pile, too. Then they went to the men's department to buy him some large T-shirts.

Molly explained to Elizabeth about them borrowing one of Richard's the night before.

"Then we should get at least four T-shirts," Elizabeth said. She put that many in their basket. When they reached the women's department, Elizabeth thought Molly should buy a good wool coat that would last for many years. Molly didn't remind her that she would be returning to Florida in a month.

Since the wool coat was navy and would go with almost anything, Molly was pleased with it. She added a couple of sweaters to the basket for her, too.

"Now, shall we look at the Christmas tree ornaments?" she asked.

"Oh, not here. There's a lovely Christmas store that I've been to before. They have all kinds of specialty ornaments. Let's go there," Elizabeth insisted.

Molly agreed. She managed to convince Elizabeth that she should pay for her purchases.

Albert sped them away to the store Elizabeth had chosen. Inside, everything shimmered and glowed as the ornaments were displayed beautifully. Toby was thrilled, especially when his grandmother told him he should pick all the ornaments. He raced around the store, not wanting to miss anything. But he made very thoughtful choices.

"He reminds me so much of Susan," Elizabeth said softly as she watched him make his selections.

"He is a terrific little boy, but you mustn't spoil him too much," Molly warned. "Susan taught him beautiful manners, and we wouldn't want her teaching to go to waste."

"You're quite right, dear, but as long as you're here with him, I'm sure you will keep him in line," Elizabeth said with a big smile.

Molly thought about reminding Elizabeth that she would be going back to her life in Florida after Christmas, but she didn't bother. Richard would make sure his mother knew that.

They returned home at noon, just in time for a wonderful lunch that Delores had prepared. Then Molly suggested everyone lie down for an hour or two so they'd be rested for the Christmas tree hunt that evening.

While Elizabeth and Toby took their naps, Molly removed the tags from their purchases, including the ornaments, which she carried down to the garden room. They'd bought a tree skirt and some colored lights, too. Toby had also chosen an angel to go on the top of the tree.

He had assured Elizabeth it looked just like the angel that had topped his tree in Florida. Though it was expensive, Elizabeth had declared it the perfect choice for the top of Toby's tree at their house, too.

Molly had enjoyed their shopping as much as the other two. Because she had no family, she usually only decorated a tiny tree that sat on her dining table. She was excited just looking at all the ornaments they'd bought. A big tree, with presents under it, filled her with an anticipation that she hadn't experienced since she was a small child with her parents.

Her parents had died in a car accident, much as Toby's had, but she'd had no relatives to take her in. She'd spent the rest of her childhood in foster homes. None of them had celebrated Christmas as she'd remembered it with her parents.

Now, though she was alone, she tried to make Christmas special for those around her. She'd already purchased Secret Santa presents for the patients in the hospital. Since she'd left early with Toby, she'd left the gifts with another nurse to pass out for Christmas.

She usually did a lot of baking, taking goodies to her friends at the hospital and neighbors in her apartment building. She would miss baking. Unless she could convince Toby to make Christmas cookies with her.

She smiled. She wasn't sure Delores would let them invade her kitchen.

When Toby woke up, Molly kept him busy by playing a game with him. She had a deck of cards with her and together they played more hands of Battle and Go Fish than she could count.

At five o'clock, Louisa knocked on Toby's door. Richard had called to tell them he would be there in half an hour to go find a Christmas tree. Could they please be ready?

"Yes, of course, Louisa. Have you told Mrs. Anderson?"

"Yes, ma'am. She said she would be ready, too."

Molly put the deck of cards away, reminding herself to buy some games the next time she had a chance. Toby was a smart little boy. She didn't want him getting bored. According to Elizabeth, he wouldn't be going to school until after the New Year, since most of the schools in town had ended their semester this week.

Toby could hardly contain his excitement. Molly took the child down early to wait in the garden room and discuss where they thought the tree should be placed.

When Toby finally decided on the corner of the room, she reminded him that Elizabeth and Richard might decide otherwise.

"Yeah, but I think Grandma will agree with me."

"You think so, do you?" Molly asked him with a grin.

"She's nice, isn't she?" he asked, smiling back.

"Yes, she is. You're a lucky little boy."

Toby's blue eyes clouded over. "I'm not lucky 'cause my mommy and daddy died."

Molly hugged him. "I know, sweetie, but the same thing happened to me, and I didn't have a grandma to take me in."

Her revelation caught Toby's attention. "Your mommy and daddy died, too?"

"Yes, when I was seven."

He immediately hugged Molly. "I'm sorry."

"Thank you, Toby, but it was a long time ago. I told you so you could appreciate your grandmother and uncle taking you in. That makes you a lucky boy."

"Did you have to live alone?"

Molly laughed. "No. I might've been better off if I had, but I was put in a foster home."

"What's that?"

With a sigh, Molly said, "It's a family who gets paid to take care of you. Usually they have too many people in the house and they don't have time to make you feel special. Like your grandma." Or even loved. In the two foster homes she'd lived in, they had assigned chores, but they hadn't shown appreciation or love for what she did. She'd almost felt faceless.

"That must've made you sad," Toby said solemnly.

"Yes, it did. But I—" She was interrupted by the sound of a car pulling into the driveway.

Toby rushed out of the room, calling over his shoulder, "I bet that's Richard!"

Molly sighed and followed him more slowly. The last

thing she wanted to show was enthusiasm for Richard's arrival.

Elizabeth was coming down the stairs as Molly reached the hallway.

"Is that Richard?" she asked.

"I believe so. Toby went to see. He's very excited about the tree."

"I am, too, for the first time in years." She reached the hall and took on a wistful look. "You know, we gave up decorating a real tree after the children went to college. It just didn't seem worth the effort without a child to enjoy it."

Molly smiled. "But you do have a Christmas tree in the living room. It's quite beautiful."

"Yes, but it's not the same. Now with Toby, I feel like I've been given a second chance at life. It's invigorating." She returned the smile and grabbed Molly's hand. "Let's go see if it was Richard."

The two ladies went to the side entrance and found Toby telling Richard about all their purchases that day.

"You must've shopped all day!"

"Not quite," Elizabeth said as she and Molly arrived in the doorway.

Richard stared at his mother. "You sound like you went with them. Are you too tired to go out now?"

"Absolutely not!"

Richard frowned as Toby and Elizabeth went out to get in his car. "I thought I warned you not to let Mom overdo it," he said harshly, blocking Molly as she started to go past him.

How dare he accuse her of not doing her job! She'd done as he'd requested—even if it hadn't been part of her employment arrangements. They stood mere inches apart, so close

Molly could feel the cold emanating from his overcoat. But she didn't back up. She raised her chin and looked him square in the eyes. "Did she sound exhausted to you?"

Richard held her gaze a few seconds, as if measuring her resolve. Then, finally, in one swift motion he turned and went out the door. "I'll hold you responsible if she has a breakdown."

CHAPTER FOUR

MOLLY pressed her lips together. She knew she had done all she could to protect Elizabeth. The lady was talking more and taking more interest in her grandson. If Richard thought that was going to damage his mother, well, he was dead wrong.

Molly knew then and there the only way she'd survive this assignment was to avoid the man altogether. That conviction lasted until she got to the car and saw Elizabeth had left the front seat for her—next to Richard.

Elizabeth must have seen her disgruntled expression, because she said, "I'm going to ride back here with Toby so we can discuss the tree he wants to buy."

Richard slanted at look at Molly. "Join me, won't you, Molly?" he said, sarcasm in his voice.

Okay, so he'd seen her reluctance. It didn't matter. She wasn't here for him. "Thanks," she muttered and circled the vehicle to climb in the front passenger seat.

Molly stared straight ahead. After last night, and again just now with Richard, she intended to keep her distance from this man.

"What kind of tree do you want us to buy?" Richard asked his mother.

"One that pleases Toby," she said.

"Do you have any preferences, Molly?" Richard asked.

"Not in regard to trees," she muttered, hoping that would be the end of any conversation.

"Do you always decorate a tree in Florida?" he persisted.

"A small one." She didn't want to talk to him about her life. It had nothing to do with him. He'd probably think her simple life was pitiful, but she'd created a happy life for herself. It hadn't been easy.

"Why?"

That got her attention. She turned to stare at the handsome man. What was wrong with him? "Because I enjoy Christmas, of course. Don't you?"

"Not particularly."

"Is your middle name Scrooge?"

His lips twitched at the corners. "No, not exactly."

"Well, I hope you'll make an effort for Toby."

"I won't need to. My mother seems to have the bit in her teeth. She'll probably hire someone to play Santa since she wants this Christmas to be special for him."

"Good for her."

"What do you want Santa to bring you for Christmas?"

The man was crazy. He didn't enjoy Christmas and yet he asked about Santa? Molly shrugged. "Nothing."

"Aha! So you're not a fan of Christmas, either!"

Molly scowled at him. "I love Christmas! But that doesn't mean I believe in Santa Claus," she added in a lower voice.

"Then why do you love Christmas if you don't expect to get something special?"

Molly shifted in her seat to look at him squarely. "Christmas isn't about getting something. It's about giving. That's the true meaning of Christmas!"

Or couldn't someone as handsome, rich and successful as Richard Anderson understand that?

Richard drove silently the rest of the way to the Christmas tree lot. The nurse had put him in his place.

Maybe he deserved it. He'd lost his enthusiasm for Christmas the last few years. Or maybe his enthusiasm for life. He wasn't certain.

But he sure didn't want to get into a spitting match with Molly. She seemed well-armed and he didn't like to lose.

He pulled to a stop beside the tree lot. "We're here. Mom, be sure you're wrapped up warmly. We're having a cold December this year. Toby, do you have your coat on?"

"Yeah," he called over his shoulder as he grabbed Elizabeth's hand and off they went toward the trees.

Left alone with Molly, he didn't know what to say. "I guess we should go find a tree," he ventured.

Molly nodded and set off after her charge.

"This one looks nice," he heard her say as he walked toward the trio weaving among the evergreens.

"Oh, no, it's much too short," Elizabeth said. "We need a bigger tree because our ceilings are high." She pointed to a tall one. "What about this one, Toby?"

"It's kind of skinny, isn't it, Grandma?"

"Absolutely right. Let's go look at that one over there." The two hurried eagerly in the direction Elizabeth had pointed. But Molly stayed behind, he noticed. He also noticed her shiver.

"Are you cold?" Richard asked, stepping closer to her.

She backed up. "No. I'm just adjusting to the change in the weather."

Richard nodded. He said nothing for another few minutes, just standing there amongst the trees. Finally he turned again to Molly. "Don't you want to go see the other trees?"

"Whatever they choose will be fine."

More silence. Then, after another few minutes, when Elizabeth and Toby were still darting around the lot, where each tree was staked to the ground like a mini forest, Richard was getting irritated.

"Mom, you and Toby need to choose one. It's too cold to remain out much longer."

He shot a look at Molly, expecting to find disapproval on her face, but she didn't look perturbed by his demand.

"Are you frozen, Molly?"

"N-no, I'm f-fine."

"Why didn't you tell me you were cold?" he asked in irritation. Grabbing her arm, he headed back to the SUV.

"What are you doing?" she demanded, resisting.

"I'm going to warm you up."

The look of horror on her face brought some interesting thoughts to Richard, but he hastily shut them out. "I'm going to start the engine and turn on the heater," he explained with a grin.

"O-Oh."

Once he got her in the front seat, he circled the vehicle and got in to start the engine. "Give me your hands," he said.

Molly stared at him again. "Why?"

"I'm going to hold them in mine. You should've bought some good gloves today when you bought your coat."

"I didn't think I'd be outside this long," she muttered. She finally extended her hands to him. He'd removed his gloves and the warmth of his skin began to penetrate hers.

He did nothing, just held her hands in his larger ones. Still, Molly could feel the heat all the way from her head to her toes. Under her coat she felt flushed. Being in this enclosed space, alone with Richard, was an amazingly intimate exchange with a man she didn't even like two days ago.

Too intimate.

She pulled her hands free. "I think they're warm enough now, thank you."

"Are you sure?" he asked, staring at her.

She felt her cheeks heat and she knew she had to have some distance. "Yes, thank you." She looked over her shoulder. "How—how is the tree search going?"

After telling her to stay inside so she'd be warm, he added, "I'll be back in a minute."

Then he located the two tree-hunters. "Molly is half-frozen. You've got to make a decision."

"We have, Richard. We just decided on this one," Elizabeth said, pointing to a nine-foot Douglas fir.

"Fine, go get in the car and I'll buy it."

"We need to stay here until you get the man's attention. You might buy the wrong tree."

Richard glared at his mother. What had happened to the gentle, indecisive lady he'd lived with for the past eighteen months? "Fine, Mom, I'll be right back."

He went back to the hut where the operators stood around a glowing fire in a half drum. Quickly indicating he was ready to buy his tree, he led one of the men to his mother's side. "This is the tree we want to buy."

"Well, now, you picked a fine one!" the man said with enthusiasm, which in Richard's experience meant that they'd picked an expensive one.

"Mom, take Toby back to the car so he won't catch cold," Richard urged. He handed his credit card to the man to move the process along.

Elizabeth and an excited Toby hurried to the car.

Ten minutes later, Richard had the tree strapped to the top of the SUV and they were on their way.

That was when Toby barraged him with questions, volleying one after the other.

"Did you see the tree?" the boy asked. "Isn't it great?"

"Yes," Richard replied. "You picked a nice one."

"Is it tied on good?"

"Trust me, it's not going anywhere."

"Will we be able to get it down?"

"Albert will help me." Richard couldn't stop smiling at his nephew's enthusiasm. He turned the tables and asked a question. "Do you think you bought enough ornaments for such a big tree?"

"We bought lots. Grandma told me we'd need that many."

"I wanted to be prepared," Elizabeth said.

"Yes, Mom, that was good thinking. I wouldn't want to have to shop for ornaments now. I'm hungry."

"Me, too!" Toby called. "I didn't get a snack today."

"I'm sorry. I'll have to speak to Delores about that," Richard said.

That remark brought Molly to life. "There's no need to speak to Delores. It's my fault we didn't have a snack."

"Why is it your fault?"

"I didn't ask for it. I forgot."

"I see."

He noted her anxious expression. Apparently he hadn't convinced her he wouldn't chew Delores out. The fact that he had never done such a thing hadn't occurred to her.

Elizabeth leaned forward. "Molly, don't worry. He's never said a harsh word to Delores. She might burn the next roast she cooks and that's his favorite meal."

Molly glared at him. "Oh, thank you, Elizabeth."

Richard grinned at her and she looked away.

Obviously Molly wasn't a forgiving woman. At least not to him. He figured Toby was easily forgiven. Even his mother seemed to be in Molly's good graces.

When they reached home, he sent the other three into the house and asked his mother to send Albert out. Together they'd unload the tree and put it right into the stand he'd purchased. They could take it right into the garden room.

A few minutes later, after the tree was standing tall in the garden room, water in its basin, he removed his overcoat and gloves and entered the dining room. It appeared the others were waiting for his arrival.

"I'm sorry to keep you waiting," he said as he entered.

"We had a cup of hot chocolate while we were waiting," his mother said. She rang the bell to let Delores know they were ready.

Dinner began with tortilla soup. Toby seemed even more skeptical this evening, but Molly encouraged him to give it a try.

"It's okay," Toby said with a shrug.

"It will warm you up faster than last night's soup," Richard said. "It's a little spicier."

"It's delicious, Toby," Molly said with a smile.

So the nurse had a stomach for Mexican food? "Have you had tortilla soup before, Molly?"

"Yes, of course. Florida has many Mexican restaurants."

"Oh, really? I would have expected Cuban restaurants, but not Mexican."

"They have both," she answered briefly and continued to eat her soup.

"How does the tree look?" Toby asked.

"Tall. It almost touches the ceiling."

"Do you have a ladder? We'll need one to put the angel on top."

"Yes, I have a ladder," Richard said, sighing, "but you may be too small to climb to the top."

"Richard!" Elizabeth protested.

"That's okay," Toby said calmly. "That's the daddy's job, anyway."

Richard smiled at the little boy. "You know, Toby, I may have to get a list of the daddy jobs. I'm not sure I know all of them."

"It's okay, Uncle Richard. I'll help you."

Uncle Richard?

He couldn't stop the smile that lit his face. This was the first time Toby had called him that. The first time anyone had ever called him that. He knew enough to not make a big deal about it and embarrass Toby, but he liked it. A lot.

Molly, however, leaned over to the boy and said, "You don't really have to make a list. He's just teasing you."

"No, I wasn't, Molly. Not having been a daddy, I don't know all the jobs a dad must do." He certainly hadn't learned the list from his father. The man hadn't spent a lot of time with his family, and when he did, he tended to control them, not be a role model for them. His mother had done the best she could for both him and Susan under the circumstances.

Molly gave him a quick, disbelieving look and turned her attention back to her soup.

"Richard, do you think we can decorate the tree this evening?" Elizabeth asked.

"No, Mom, it's already eight o'clock and Toby will need to go to bed after dinner. Besides, the limbs will look better in the morning. The man at the lot told me they had just put that tree up today."

"Right. Yes, we'll wait until tomorrow to decorate it. But you'll need to be here."

"Tomorrow's the last day before Christmas vacation, Mom. We close at noon."

"Oh, that's right. I'm so glad."

Molly stared at him. "You close tomorrow for Christmas?"

Elizabeth answered her. "It's a trend in Dallas. A lot of businesses close for the two weeks including Christmas and New Year's because so little work gets done. It's mostly parties."

"I see. But it's still a week and a half until Christmas."

"I decided to close tomorrow because it's Friday. Already work has slowed down, so there's not much point in holding everyone there when they want to go shopping and to parties."

"Ah. So you're not taking the vacation out of the goodness of your heart?" Molly asked.

Elizabeth rushed to his defense. "Yes, Molly, he is. His father never let his people have even one day off. They worked all the way through the holidays except for Christmas Day and New Year's Day."

Molly smiled at her hostess. "Of course, Elizabeth, it is generous of Richard."

Richard noticed he didn't get a share of her smile. Which meant, of course, that she didn't really believe he was being generous. Not that he could blame her after his remarks in the car earlier.

When dinner was done, Molly led a sleepy Toby up to his bed, after the good-night hugs and kisses he gave both Richard and his mother.

Elizabeth looked at her son once the other two were gone. "What did you say to Molly earlier about Christmas?"

"What do you mean?"

"I noticed you two talking in the front of the car when we were on our way to the tree lot. She got upset. Which, I think, led to that comment about your generosity."

"I told her I wasn't excited about Christmas."

"I was afraid of that. Don't you think it had something to do with your dad's death and then Susan's?"

Richard sighed. "I don't know, Mom. Christmas hasn't been very exciting since I was still a boy. There's a lot of rushing around and drinking and partying, but it seems kind of empty to me."

"I don't intend to go to many of the society parties this season, and I recommend you don't, either. I feel I have a second chance to make a life for Toby. I know I failed both you and Susan because I wasn't strong enough to stand up to your father. After his death, I was too despondent to make reparations. But Toby needs me now. And he needs you."

"I know, Mom. And I'll try to remember that I'm as close to a daddy as he's going to get now."

"I want to find things to do with Toby. Could you drive us around to see the Christmas lights one night?"

"Of course. Or if it's not too cold, we could take one of the horse and buggy rides around Highland Park."

"That's a wonderful idea, Richard."

"Do you think Toby would enjoy seeing *A Christmas Carol?* Or do you think he'd be afraid of Scrooge?" He could just imagine Molly's reaction to his suggestion.

"I think he'd love it. Are they doing that at the Theater Center?"

"Yes, I think so."

"Wait! I need to get a pen and paper so I can make a list. Then tomorrow I'll discover times and dates and can buy the tickets."

She rushed away from the table. Richard was surprised to find some enthusiasm growing in him for the holiday traditions. It helped that his mother was excited about them.

When she got back to the table, she wrote down his suggestions. He added a few more and decided Toby would be bored once Christmas passed.

"These are wonderful suggestions, Richard, and Toby will love them. He's such a wonderful little boy…and he reminds me so much of Susan."

"Yes, he does, doesn't he? She always demanded the

biggest Christmas tree, too." Richard couldn't hold back a smile, thinking of his little sister.

"Yes," Elizabeth said with a sigh.

"But, Mom, you're not used to all this running around. You have to be sure you don't overdo it."

"I will, dear. Molly is very good about that. Right now, Toby needs a nap every day because of the accident and his recovery. She's sending me to bed for a nap, too."

"Good. I like that."

"She's such a nice young woman. I know the doctor told us she didn't have any family in Florida, but does she have any family anywhere?"

"I don't know. I haven't asked her."

"I'll ask her. She shouldn't be completely alone in the world."

"A lot of people are, Mom. They survive."

"I know, but Molly deserves better."

Richard couldn't argue with that.

"Do you like our tree, Molly?" Toby asked her the next morning at breakfast.

"Very much, Toby. It's huge."

"Did you have big ones when you were little?" he asked.

"Not that big."

Elizabeth looked up. "Do you have brothers and sisters, Molly?"

"No, I was an only child, like Toby."

"Are your parents alive?"

"No," Molly said and smiled at Elizabeth. She appreciated that lady's interest, but she didn't want to tell her life story. There was no need for that.

"Molly's parents died when she was seven," Toby informed his grandmother.

"Oh, no! I'm so sorry!"

"It was a long time ago, Elizabeth. I'm fine."

"Did you go to live with family?"

"No, she lived in a—a what, Molly?"

"A foster home, Toby," Molly said with a sigh. Now she regretted telling Toby about her past.

"But I've heard being in a foster home is awful. Was it bad, Molly?"

"Not bad, Elizabeth. It—it was just not as nice as being with family."

"Well, this Christmas, we're going to be your family!" Elizabeth said with a big smile.

Molly silently groaned. She knew Richard would think she'd put his mother up to that idea. "Really, Elizabeth, that's not necessary. And please don't buy me gifts. I wouldn't be able to reciprocate in kind. I have a small budget."

"Money doesn't matter, Molly. But we've thought of all kinds of ways to celebrate Christmas. I'm supposed to check the times and dates of things Richard thought of last night. He was wonderful."

"How nice. What did he suggest?"

Elizabeth filled her in on all the plans. "And last but not least, we're taking you both to see Scrooge. Would you like that, Toby?"

"I don't know what that is, Grandma," Toby said.

"Oh, of course not, dear. But you'll like it. It's the story of a man who gets a second chance to be good at Christmas, like me."

"You're very good, Grandma," Toby said earnestly.

"Thank you, my angel," Elizabeth said with a big smile. "Oh, do you have a suit?"

"No. My daddy had suits, but Mommy said I shouldn't have one because I would outgrow it so soon."

"Well, I think we should get you a suit for Christmas. We can buy you another one when you outgrow it. Would you like that?"

"I guess so," Toby said doubtfully.

"That won't be your only present, Toby, I promise."

"You mean I might still get a puppy?" The boy couldn't hide his excitement.

"No, Toby, I don't think that's what your grandmother meant," Molly said hurriedly, trying to erase that image from his mind at once.

"Oh."

"Toby, your grandmother is being very nice to you," Molly said softly.

The boy responded by straightening his shoulders and smiling at his grandmother.

"Oh, Toby, you are such a dear boy," Elizabeth said.

"You're a good grandma, too."

Molly encouraged him to finish his breakfast. After he had done so, she sent him upstairs to wash his face and hands.

As soon as he left the room, Elizabeth said, "I know just what to get Toby for Christmas. A puppy!"

CHAPTER FIVE

"ELIZABETH, don't— I mean, don't you think you should discuss such a gift with your son before you say anything to Toby?"

"Why?"

"I appreciate your wanting to make Christmas special for Toby but Richard lives here, too. I don't think you should please Toby at the expense of your son. He loves you and tries to protect you."

"I guess you're right."

Molly was relieved Elizabeth seemed to change her mind. "I'm glad you realize how important your son is in your life."

"Yes, of course. I'll discuss the dog with Richard tonight."

"Elizabeth, have you thought how much a dog could disrupt your household?"

"Louisa?" Elizabeth called. The young woman immediately appeared from the kitchen.

"Yes, ma'am? Do you need something more?"

"Oh, not for breakfast. It was delightful as usual. No, I need to speak to Albert."

Louisa returned to the kitchen. Immediately, Albert appeared in the breakfast room. "Yes, ma'am?"

"Albert, do you know how to train a dog?"

"You mean to go outside and not in the house?"

Elizabeth nodded. "Yes."

"Sure, I can do that."

"So, if we got Toby a dog for Christmas, you could help us with that problem?"

"Yes, ma'am. Is he going to get a dog?"

"Maybe. Do you like dogs?"

"Yeah," Albert said, getting so excited he forgot his usual response. "I always had dogs until—I mean, when I started working for you and your husband."

"You and Delores have your own quarters here, Albert. Couldn't you have had a dog here?"

"No, ma'am. Your husband told me I couldn't."

"Oh, Albert, I'm sorry."

"It's all right, ma'am. He was probably right."

"Well, I'm sure Toby would share his dog with you."

Molly wasn't so sure about that.

"It's not definite, Albert. Elizabeth is going to discuss it with her son," Molly said. "Please don't mention it to Toby."

"No, ma'am, I wouldn't do that."

"Of course not, Albert," Elizabeth agreed. "That's all I needed. I wanted to be able to tell Richard you could help us."

"Yes, ma'am." He hurried back to the kitchen.

"I think this will work out well," Elizabeth said, smiling.

Molly wanted to warn her again, but she didn't think she should. Hopefully Richard wouldn't think this was her idea. If he thought that, he would probably ship her off to Florida before Christmas even got here.

* * *

Richard said goodbye to his happy employees. He'd passed out their bonuses at the party they had just before noon. It had been a good year and he believed in sharing the profits.

Wearily he returned to his office and loaded his briefcase so he could work on his cases at home. Clients being sued didn't care that it was Christmas.

When he got home, his mother and Toby were taking their afternoon naps. Albert had taken Molly to North Park, the shopping mall near their house.

"Do you have anything I could eat for lunch, Delores? All we served at the party were hors d'oeuvres and cakes and cookies. And most of it was gone before I had a chance to nibble."

"Of course, Richard. You want to eat in the breakfast room?"

"Yes, please. I'll go wash up and meet you there."

He often ate a late meal in the breakfast room. It seemed silly to have them serve him in the dining room.

Five minutes later, Delores presented him with a roast beef sandwich with chips and a Diet Coke. Perfect.

As he ate, the silence of the house seemed deafening. Perhaps it was the sharp contrast to the raucous party he'd just left, loud with holiday music and laughter. His employees knew how to kick off their shoes and have a good time, dancing to "All I Want for Christmas" and "Santa Baby" on his secretary's boom box. She'd even asked him to take a turn on the reception area-turned dance floor, but he'd declined. Somehow when he thought of dancing it wasn't his secretary but Molly he saw as his partner.

He'd had to literally shake his head to erase that image.

Then and now.

He ripped off a bite of his sandwich, determined to get control of his errant thoughts, when he heard musical laughter coming from the back door. Molly. She'd come into the kitchen with Albert, giggling at some private joke.

Once again the image of her in his arms was being painted by a master right before his mind's eye. She was dressed in red, a slinky, off-the-shoulder gown with high heels; her glowing hair kissed her shoulders, swaying with the rhythm of the music. As they danced, all the other holiday revelers faded away, till there was only them.

Richard lived the fantasy until the real thing appeared at the door of the breakfast room.

Molly came to an abrupt halt when she saw him sitting there.

He cleared his throat. "Good afternoon, Molly." Seeing her laden with packages, he asked, "Did you have a nice shopping trip? Why didn't Albert let you out at the door so you wouldn't catch cold?"

Still standing in the doorway, like a deer caught in the headlights, Molly replied, "I told him it wasn't necessary. After all, I'm not family. I work for you just as he does."

True, he thought, but Albert didn't appear in his day-dreams.

He kept that remark to himself. Instead he voiced, "He should at least carry your packages for you."

"I'm fine." Stepping back, she added, "Now, if you'll excuse me…"

"No." He couldn't let her go. For some reason he wanted her company right now.

What was wrong with him? It wasn't the spiked egg nog

he'd had at the office; there wasn't enough brandy in that to make him act so out of character. Whatever it was, he had to get himself under control. For Toby's sake.

Molly, he noticed, looked at him oddly. Covering for himself, he explained, "I prefer not to eat alone. Why don't you join me? Have a drink, at least." Not waiting for her assent, he called for Louisa and Albert, who appeared almost instantly. He directed Albert to take Molly's packages to her room, and Louisa to bring her a Diet Coke.

Molly tried to think of a way out of being in Richard's company, but she couldn't come up with anything. Toby was napping, as was Elizabeth. And he was her host… and her boss.

Dutifully she sat down—at the opposite end of the table. Apparently that wasn't good enough.

"Why so far away? Come sit next to me." Richard pointed to his left, and Molly reluctantly obliged.

"Your enthusiasm is overwhelming, Molly."

"I'm sorry, but I was capable of carrying my purchases upstairs."

"I'm sure you are, but why not relax and enjoy a drink?"

Louisa entered again and set down a plate of warm cookies.

"See? There's more to enjoy. Thank you, Louisa."

"Albert should be the one receiving the reward," Molly said stubbornly.

"He'll get warm cookies as soon as he gets to the kitchen again." He looked up as Albert entered the room. "You'd better hurry, Albert. Delores just baked cookies."

"I'm on my way." Albert grinned.

"Satisfied?" Richard asked after Albert left.

"Yes, thank you," Molly said, wishing she weren't. She knew Albert didn't have a tough job and that he was well paid. But that didn't mean he should wait on her.

"What did you buy?"

She stiffened. Richard wanted idle conversation? This was so unlike him. "Just some odds and ends," she replied.

"Did you enjoy North Park? I thought Toby might like to see it. Their holiday decorations are usually spectacular. Did they lift your spirits?"

"My spirits didn't need lifting, Richard."

"Oh, right, I forgot. You're filled with the Christmas spirit."

She shoved her chair from the table. "If you'll—"

He grabbed her hand and stopped her departure. "You haven't even touched your snack. You don't want to hurt Delores's feelings, do you?" Then, as if burned, he pulled his hand back. But her forearm still tingled from his touch.

What was going on here? her head screamed. Surely no nurse had that kind of reaction to her boss's touch. She almost chuckled when she thought of Dr. Bradford making her pulse race.

But the sixtyish Dr. Bradford didn't look like Richard Anderson.

Clearing her head, she sat back down. Then, in an effort to save herself, she picked up a cookie, ate it in two bites and drank half her drink. Anything to avoid Richard.

"One cookie won't satisfy Delores."

She looked up at him. Was he kidding?

At her skeptical look, he leaned in close and stage-whispered, "Should I call her in here and ask her?"

Molly leaned back, extending her arm fully to reach another cookie. "Will two satisfy her?" She took a quick bite.

"Maybe, if you take your time to eat it. But if you jump up and run away, not only will Delores be concerned, but my mother will be also as soon as Delores tells her."

Molly closed her eyes. When she opened them she said, "I can't believe you'd really let Delores tattle on me."

"I don't know why. Delores has been tattling on me for at least twenty years." Richard kept smiling.

"Twenty years? Delores has worked here that long?"

"Sure. She had Louisa's job for the first ten years. Then she took over the kitchen when our other cook left. She's been in cahoots with my mom all that time. She thinks she helped raise me."

Against her better judgment Molly smiled. "It probably did take two mothers to raise *you*."

"How many mothers did you have?" he asked.

"Just one," she said succinctly. Her history had already been discussed that day more than she liked.

"Where does your mother live?"

Molly stiffened. Then she said, "Seattle."

"And you didn't plan on going home for Christmas?"

"No, I didn't have the money for a plane ticket. Besides, it wouldn't be worth the trip for just one day." Molly hoped he wouldn't mention her lies to either Toby or Elizabeth. But she refused to pour out her history to this man. The truth made her sound pitiful, and she didn't want Richard's pity. She'd experienced that response many times in the past. Then she'd had to work hard to be treated normally.

"Oh, really? That doesn't sound like a woman filled with the Christmas spirit."

"I'm sorry to disappoint you."

"Feel free to call your mother, if you want. I won't charge you for the call."

"Thank you. That's very generous of you."

He studied her. "But you don't intend to take me up on the offer?"

"I'll call her on Christmas Day on my cell phone."

"I didn't realize you had a cell phone."

"I didn't know I had to tell you if I did," she said, her shoulders stiffening.

"No, it's not necessary. I'm glad to know you keep in touch with your family." Then he lifted the plate of cookies and offered her another one.

"Thank you," she said, taking her third cookie and eating it slowly, as if she were really enjoying it.

"You're welcome." Finally he sat back, giving Molly room to breathe. "What have you planned for Toby for Christmas?"

"I was hoping Delores would let us make Christmas cookies. We could decorate them and even hang some on the tree if Toby wants."

"He might prefer to eat all of them."

"I try to limit his sugar intake. Children tend to get hyper if they have too much sugar."

Richard grinned. "Then I approve of that idea. What else?"

"I had already thought of taking him to the mall."

"Good. Anything else?"

She wasn't going to mention her other idea. He wouldn't understand it. "No, that's all."

"Okay. Well, I'm sure Mom will appreciate your help. She's determined to make this a special Christmas for Toby."

"More than you'll ever know," Molly muttered, thinking about Elizabeth's idea of a dog.

"What did you say?" Richard asked, leaning forward, this time so close she could smell the subtle after-shave that clung to his neck.

"Nothing," Molly said quickly. She had to get out of here. "I've had three cookies, Richard, so I'll go upstairs now, if there's nothing else."

"Fine. I won't hold you. Feel free to leave."

She took him at his word.

After she left, Richard sat there for another few minutes, enjoying another cookie and thinking about her. He had to admit that was about the most enjoyable lunch he'd had in a long time. Then he picked up the two glasses and the plate of remaining cookies and carried them to the kitchen to kiss Delores's cheek and thank her for the quick lunch.

"Did the pretty nurse enjoy the cookies, too?" the dark-haired woman asked.

"She did, but she worries about her weight."

"For no reason."

Right, Richard thought. Her body was perfect, rounded where it should be, with a slim waist and high breasts.

Delores continued, "And she's very pretty."

"Yes, she is." In the right light her red highlights glowed, lighting up her creamy, flawless skin. And those green eyes…

"And kind to," Delores added.

She certainly was, not only to Toby but to his mother. With an easy— He pulled up short. Wait a minute. He knew what was going on here…

"Delores," he said in a warning tone. "Don't be putting

any ideas in my mother's head. I don't want her pressuring me to marry the nurse."

"You are prejudiced against nurses?"

"Of course not. But I've got about all on my plate that I can handle right now."

"Richard, you work too hard. You need to relax and enjoy life more."

He kissed her cheek again. "Right. As long as I make enough to pay your salary, I guess."

"Oh, you!" Delores exclaimed, slapping his arm and laughing.

Richard laughed too and then escaped the kitchen.

He knew his social life the past year and a half had left a lot to be desired. Now that things had settled down at the firm, he'd start rectifying that, right after the holidays. He'd find himself a nice woman, pretty and kind. A woman like Molly.

But the last thing he needed was his mother and Delores playing matchmaker.

Richard was in his home office working before dinner when the door opened and his mother came in.

"Do you have time for a little chat, Richard?"

"Of course, Mom. Are you having any problems?"

"No, of course not. Everything is lovely."

"Good, glad to hear it."

"But the subject of the dog did come up."

"How?"

"I told Toby that I thought we should get him a suit for Christmas. Needless to say, like most little boys, Toby was polite but not enthusiastic. I told him he would get other presents, too. He immediately guessed it was a puppy."

"Did Molly encourage him?"

"Not at all. In fact she deterred him. Even when I told her I wanted to get Toby a dog, she suggested I talk it over with you first."

"She wants to make me the bad guy, I guess."

"No. She just said you should have some say in the matter since you live here, too."

"I could move out if you want me to, Mom. I only moved back home so you wouldn't be alone after Dad died."

Elizabeth shook her head. "I love having you here, and with Toby living with us, I need you to be here. He needs a male presence in his life."

"Okay. So did you agree to talk to me about a dog?"

"Not at first. After all, it is my house."

"It is."

"But she said you loved me and tried to take care of me. She didn't think I should lose you just to please Toby."

"How kind of her."

"She was right, Richard. I was getting carried away," his mother said. "But I still want Toby to have his dog. So I wanted to talk it over with you."

"Okay. What do you want to say?"

"Albert loves dogs and he says he could help us train the dog so it wouldn't make a mess in the house."

"Good for Albert."

"He said your father wouldn't let him have a dog."

"I can believe that. He was a very controlling man as we both know."

"So if he can help us, why can't Toby have a dog?"

"I never said he couldn't, Mom."

"Oh, Richard, you are such a good son!"

"You might change your mind if the dog relieves himself on one of your pricey oriental rugs."

Elizabeth laughed. "A rug is replaceable. And it will make Toby so happy."

"What kind of dog do you want to get him?"

"I don't know. Do you have an idea?"

"One of the attorneys at the office has a dog that just had a litter of puppies about three weeks ago. I think they're chocolate Labs. They're good with children."

"Perfect. Can you call him and get him to sell us one?"

"Sell? I'm his boss!"

"I know, but—"

Richard laughed. "I'm just teasing you, Mom. I'll give him a call right away. Do you want him to keep the puppy until Christmas Eve?"

"Absolutely. I want it to be a surprise for Toby. Can you go get it after he goes to bed?"

"Of course, Mom. Did you ever consider getting me a puppy?" Richard thought of how much he'd wanted one when he was little.

"Yes. I pleaded with your father, but…he didn't like animals in the house. He didn't even want one in the yard. I'm sorry, son." She looked genuinely contrite.

"It's okay, Mom. I grew up just fine without a dog." He reached out for her hand. "I'm just glad we can give Toby one."

"I can't wait to tell Molly that you agree."

"I'm sure it will surprise her."

"Son, you're too hard on her."

"Not all that hard. By the way, I know the doctor told us she had no family in Florida, but did you know she has a mother in Seattle?"

"Oh, no, dear, you're wrong about that. Her parents died in a car crash when she was seven. She told Toby that. And she was raised in a foster home."

Richard frowned. "Maybe she told him that so he'd feel better."

"No, he told me this morning and I sympathized with her. She didn't say anything."

"She couldn't in front of Toby. That would've ruined her bonding with him."

"I'm sure you're wrong. Molly wouldn't lie about something like that."

Richard just shook his head. His mother had never believed bad things about him, either. Unfortunately sometimes he'd lied to her. And he'd always felt so guilt-ridden that he had to admit it afterwards. Maybe Molly would do the same.

"Molly, can I go outside for a little while?" Toby asked after he woke up.

"No, it's too cold outside. You don't want to be sick for Christmas, do you?"

"I guess not."

"Besides, I need you to do something." When Toby looked at her, a question in his eyes, she explained, "Think of something you can give to Richard and your grandmother for Christmas."

"But I don't have any money," Toby reminded her.

"I have some allocated for presents."

"What's allocated?"

"It means I have some money for you for presents."

He seemed to perk up then. "Really? That would be fun."

"Yes, we can go buy them and wrap them up. Then you can put them under the Christmas tree."

"I'd like that. But what can I buy them?"

"Nothing expensive, but maybe some monogrammed handkerchiefs for Richard and scented soap for your grandmother."

"Those aren't very exciting." After a few seconds of silence, during which he gave the subject some thought, his eyes suddenly lit up with excitement. "I bought Daddy a big flashlight. Mommy said he needed it and—" Reality hit him and suddenly those same eyes filled with tears. "I—I forgot he and Mommy aren't ever coming back. Are they?"

"No, honey, they're not," Molly said, reaching out and holding him in her arms. Comfort like this was all she could give Toby, though she ached to take away his pain. Still, she knew it helped to talk about the deceased; that was what everyone had told her. And they were right. Talking about them somehow kept them alive, at least in one's memory. "What did you get your mommy?" she asked him.

"Some perfume," Toby whispered. "I couldn't really afford it," he said, pausing to swallow the tears, "but Daddy said he'd help me 'cause Mommy really, really wanted it."

"I'm sure she would've loved it, baby."

"I—I know." He lay quietly in her arms, the excitement of Christmas lost in his memories of his life in Florida. "Molly, did they die because I wasn't a good enough boy?" he asked anxiously.

Molly hugged him more tightly against her. "Absolutely not. You're a very good boy. It was because someone in another car didn't drive safely. And God gave you your uncle and grandma to make up for losing your parents."

Toby sniffled but said nothing. Molly, her head resting on his soft hair, said, "Did you hear me, Toby? It's important that you know that. It wasn't your fault."

"Okay," he said with a sigh, turning his face into her sweater.

"You're not putting tears on my sweater, are you, Toby?" she asked, trying to put a teasing note in her voice.

"I'm sorry," he said, swiftly moving away from her.

"Oh, sweetheart, I was just teasing. I have other sweaters. I was hoping to make you laugh a little." She stroked his head and wiped away some tears with her fingers.

"I've been trying to be happy for Grandma. She likes it when I smile for her."

"I know she does, and that's very brave of you. But when it's just the two of us, you can cry if you want to. I'll understand."

"Thank you," he said softly and resumed his place against her. "I like the new ornaments we bought, but I wish I had the ornaments from our tree. Mommy helped me pick them out. There was one that had all three of us in a picture frame. And one of me when I was a baby. It was my first Christmas, but I can't remember it."

"I bet you were cute!" Molly said with a chuckle.

"Did you have an ornament like that?"

Molly squeezed him a little tighter. "Yes, I think I did, but—but it gets hard to remember."

"I don't ever want to forget Mommy and Daddy!"

"I don't think you ever will, sweetie. You're a little older than I was and you have that great picture of the three of you."

"Yeah. Daddy threatened to tickle me if I didn't smile at the camera. I wanted to go see Santa instead of having a picture taken. But now I'm glad I did."

"Me, too," Molly said and kissed him on top of his head. "Well, now I need to finish wrapping things so I can put everything away. And if you didn't like my ideas for presents, you can think of something else to get Uncle Richard and your grandma."

"Yeah, I need to think." He left her arms and wandered back into his room.

A few minutes later he ran back in. "We can get Richard a football!"

"Hmm, a football. He told you he likes to play football?"

"No, but I'm sure he would."

"And with whom would he play football?"

"I'll play with him!" Toby said in an excited voice.

"I see. You see, Toby, the art of gift giving is to get the person something he or she wants. Not something you want."

"Oh."

"Want to try again?"

"Yeah," he said, sounding discouraged.

Molly began wrapping the presents she bought that day for Elizabeth, Richard and Toby. They were inexpensive gifts, in hopes that they would enjoy them without feeling the necessity to reciprocate.

Toby wandered back in. "What are you doing?"

"I'm wrapping presents."

"Are any of them for me?"

"Maybe one or two," she told him with a big smile.

"Can I shake them?"

She handed him a box she'd already wrapped. He shook it diligently.

"It doesn't make any noise!" he complained.

"I never said it did," Molly said, grinning.

"Do I have any others?"

"Yes, but they aren't wrapped yet."

"Can I take them downstairs to put under the tree when you get finished?"

"No, sweetie. I'll take them down the night before Christmas. If I take them down early, Richard and Elizabeth might think I'm hoping they'll get me something. That's not why I bought the presents."

"Oh. Will they think that if I buy them something?"

"You're *supposed* to buy them presents. They're your family now."

Toby nodded as he digested the information. Then he looked her straight in the eye as he said, "You know what, Molly? I wish you were my family, too."

Molly had to look away, afraid he'd see the tears glisten in her eyes. When she looked up, Toby was gone.

She never got the chance to tell him she wished so, too.

CHAPTER SIX

RICHARD made arrangements with his friend to pick up a
Lab puppy for Toby on Christmas Eve. He hadn't asked
his mother if they wanted a male or a female, so he'd
chosen a male.

When Louisa knocked on his door to tell him dinner was
served, he followed her into the dining room to discover
the other three already at the table.

"You must all be hungry," he said with a smile as he
joined them.

"Yes, we are," Elizabeth said. "Toby and I napped
through our snack today. How about you, Molly?"

Richard raised his eyebrows and stared at Molly, eager
to hear her response. She didn't look up.

"I—I had a snack, Elizabeth. Richard was eating when
I, uh, came downstairs, and he insisted I join him."

"Well, that was nice of you, son."

"Yes," Richard said, "but Molly wasn't—"

"Very hungry!" Molly said a little louder than usual,
cutting Richard off before he could say anything else. This
time she glared at him.

So what did Molly not want his mother to know? That

she'd left the house, or that she'd used Albert? His mother wouldn't have complained about either of those things. He'd keep her secret…unless he needed something she didn't want to give him.

He immediately reminded himself he didn't mean it the way it sounded. But she seemed to be good at keeping secrets. Like her mother in Seattle.

Toby's question intruded on his thoughts. "Are we going to decorate the tree this evening, Uncle Richard?"

"Yes, of course. Are you excited about that?"

"I can't wait!"

"Good. Then all we'll need will be some presents to go under it."

"Yes, Molly—"

"Needs to take Toby shopping so he can buy some presents for the both of you," Molly inserted.

Richard could swear her hand was on Toby's leg, warning him not to speak. He checked with the boy. "Is that what you wanted to say, Toby?"

"Uh, yeah. Uncle Richard, do you like football?"

"As well as the next guy. I watch it on Sunday afternoons sometimes."

"No, I mean do you like to throw a football?"

"I haven't done that in a long time, Toby."

"But he played when he was in high school," Elizabeth added.

"Really? Could you teach me how to throw a football?" Toby asked with excitement. "My dad didn't know how."

"I could if we had a football."

Molly jumped.

Richard asked, "Are you all right, Molly?"

"Yes. Toby accidentally bumped into me," she said. "It's no big deal."

Richard looked at Toby's red cheeks. Were they sharing secrets between them? Was that why she'd interrupted Toby earlier? But why would they be arguing about football? That didn't make any sense.

"Would you like for Santa to bring you a football, dear?" his mother asked Toby.

"That would be great, Grandma," Toby replied. "You'll still teach me to throw it, won't you, Uncle Richard?"

"Sure, buddy, I'll do that. Unless it's still this cold outside. If it is, we'll have to wait for a thaw."

"Okay."

"Is there anything else you think you would like for a present?" his mother asked the boy.

Toby immediately looked at Molly and she shook her head.

"Uh, I'd like, uh, some books."

"That's all you can think of?" Richard asked.

"Um, yes. Don't you like books?"

"Sure, I like to read when I have some spare time. That hasn't happened for a year or two, but I keep hoping." He felt Molly staring at him.

"What's wrong, Molly? Does that make me a bad person?"

"No, not at all. I just feel sorry for people who don't read for pleasure."

"Me, too," he agreed with a wry laugh.

Molly looked away.

"Maybe Santa will bring you a book, Richard," Toby said with enthusiasm. Again Molly jerked.

"Is anything wrong, Molly?"

"No, no, nothing's wrong."

"I don't think Santa brings adults presents, Toby."

Toby stared at his uncle. "Really? I don't think so. Mommy and Daddy always got something from Santa."

Elizabeth responded when neither of the other adults had anything to say. "I'm sure you're right, Toby, if the mommy and daddy are true believers."

"Mommy and Daddy were. And I know Molly believes in Santa. And you do, Grandma, because you asked what Santa should bring me. So that only leaves you, Uncle Richard. If you believe in Santa, he's sure to come see us."

"I see. Then I'm sure I believe in Santa, Toby, because I'm sure he's going to come see you."

"And you, too, Uncle Richard. I want him to come see all of us, so we'll all be happy."

Richard exchanged a look with Molly. He could read the gratitude in her eyes. "That's very sweet of you, Toby. I'm sure we'll all receive presents."

"Good. Grandma, what will he bring you?"

"Oh, probably perfume."

"What kind do you wear, Grandma?"

"Chanel No 5. It's terribly expensive, so don't even think of getting me any," she said to Toby.

"Okay," he said with a sigh.

"Is something wrong, dear?"

"No, Grandma. Dinner is really good tonight."

"I'll tell Delores you said that, Toby. She'll be pleased."

"Grandma and I were talking about some fun things to do for Christmas," Richard began.

"You mean the horse and buggy ride? We can do that, can't we?"

"Yes," Richard replied. "And I thought we should go to the North Park Mall and see the decorations while we shop."

Molly shot him a look but he ignored it. "We can all go."

"But how do I buy presents for you guys if you're all with me?"

"I'll take you shopping for their presents, Toby," Molly told the boy, but her eyes never left Richard.

Refusing to back down, Richard said, "We can take turns going with you in the mall, while the others shop. I'd be glad for some all male time."

Toby's face lit up. "You mean just you and me?"

Richard smiled, continuing to watch Molly out of the corner of his eye. She seemed a little perturbed about that.

"Okay. We don't want to go tomorrow because the mall will be jammed on a Saturday. We can go Monday or Tuesday, if you want."

"That would be great!"

"You know, I think maybe the three of you should go. I might get too tired at the mall," Elizabeth said suddenly.

Richard frowned. "You're sure, Mom?"

"Yes, Richard, I'm sure." She smiled at Molly. "I'm sure the two of you can manage with one little boy."

"Of course we can, Mom, if you insist."

Richard looked at Molly. "So is Monday or Tuesday okay with you?"

"Yes, of course, but I can manage with Toby if you have other things to do."

She even smiled at him, which made Richard suspicious. Suddenly she wanted him to avoid doing anything for Christmas with Toby? Or was it him she was trying to avoid? Either way, she was going. "No, I'm looking forward to shopping with you and Toby."

"Certainly," she said, not meeting his glance.

Yep, something was definitely going on.

"Won't it be fun to go to the mall with Uncle Richard?" Toby asked as he was climbing into bed.

"I guess. But I'll give you some money beforehand. Don't spend more than I give you."

"I couldn't, could I?"

"Your uncle might offer you some money, but just tell him you have your own."

"Okay."

"Good. Now hop into bed so I can kiss you good night."

"Okay." After he got into bed, he held up his arms. Molly bent down and hugged him.

As he closed his eyes, Molly turned off the overhead light, leaving just the night-light burning, and hurried into her room. She wanted to finish wrapping the gifts she'd bought today.

She was almost finished when someone knocked on her door.

Immediately she began stowing the bags and packages under her bed. The knock came again. "Just a minute. I have to find my robe," she called. As soon as she had everything out of sight, she hurried to the door.

Richard was standing there. "Nice robe," he commented, raking his gaze over her.

Molly realized she'd forgotten to don her robe over her clothes. "Um, I forgot I was dressed."

Richard looked over her shoulder, but he couldn't see anything suspicious. "What were you doing?"

"I was reading."

"I don't see a book out."

"I—I just finished it."

He braced a hand against the doorjamb and leaned in. "You just seem awfully nervous about something."

"Did you come to my room for a purpose, Richard? Or did you just want to harass me?"

He immediately held up his hands, as if surrendering. "I just wanted to let you know that I told Mom your mother lived in Seattle. She was disappointed that you'd lied to her and Toby."

Molly closed her eyes. Then she opened them. "Fine. Thanks for letting me know."

"What was going on at dinner?"

"I don't know what you're talking about."

"Yes, you do. Toby kept kicking you. And you kept cutting me off."

"I didn't want you to tell your mother and Toby that I had gone to the mall today."

"Why?"

"Toby would be reluctant to take his nap if he thinks I'm going out without him. And your mother might think it was rude of me not to tell her I went out."

"That's a plausible answer, but I don't think it's the real one."

And he was right. But how could she tell him she didn't want anyone knowing about their quiet moments alone? Or, more appropriately, her reaction to those moments?

"Think what you like, Richard. I'm tired and I'd like to go to bed now."

Suddenly his roving eyes caught sight of a piece of red material in the floor. "What's that?" he asked.

She looked over shoulder and then began closing the door. "I need to go to bed now."

She forced him out of the doorway and closed it in front of him. He thought about pounding on the door until she opened it again, but his mother or Toby might hear him. Slipping his hands in his slacks pockets, he strolled down the hall, looking over his shoulder to see if she'd open the door, but it remained shut.

Finally he gave up and went into his room. He had a lot to think about. The nurse was being very secretive, and he couldn't figure out why.

Toby told her first thing the next morning that they'd forgotten to decorate the tree last night.

"You're right, Toby. We'll ask Elizabeth if we can do it this morning."

"Oh, good. Let's go down to breakfast at once."

"Wait a minute. Isn't that the shirt you wore yesterday?"

"Yeah, but I wanted to hurry. It was closest."

"I think you need to change shirts."

"But, Molly, it's hard work changing shirts."

"I'm here to help you."

The little boy turned back into his room. "Okay," he said slowly, indicating how little he liked what he had to do.

It actually didn't take that long, but they were the last ones down for breakfast. Molly hadn't thought about the fact that Richard would be there. He and Elizabeth were sitting at the breakfast table, enjoying pancakes.

"Good morning, dear," Elizabeth said at once. "You, too, Molly. How are you today?"

"I'm fine, Elizabeth. I'm sorry if we're late."

"Nonsense, there's no set time for breakfast, especially not on the weekends."

"Delores?" Richard called. "You've got two hungry customers."

"You want more, Richard?" Delores asked, coming to the door. "Oh, you mean Toby and Molly. I'll have your plates right out."

"Thank you, Delores," Molly called.

"That looks really good," Toby said, staring at his grandmother's plate.

When Elizabeth started to offer him a bite, Molly said, "No, Elizabeth, don't offer him any. He needs to learn to wait for his food. Or maybe he should learn to fix his own breakfast. It would teach him to be patient."

"Oh, don't go that far, Molly. If you do, I'll have to make mine, too. I'd feel spoiled if I didn't at least do as much as Toby." Richard smiled at the little boy.

Toby giggled. "That would be funny, wouldn't it, Uncle Richard?"

"Yes, it definitely would. And Delores would kill us for messing up her kitchen."

"What are you talking about?" Delores demanded as she came through the door. "Who's going to mess up my kitchen?"

"I was wondering if maybe we could make Christmas

cookies one afternoon, Delores," Molly hurriedly said. "But I promise we'd clean up after ourselves."

"Ah, you are a sweet lady, Molly. I guess Toby would like to do that, wouldn't you?"

"It would be fun. I—I used to do that with my mommy," Toby said.

Delores smiled at him. "Of course you can make cookies. I'll help and do the cleaning up myself."

"Thank you, Delores," Molly said softly.

Then Delores set two plates on the table, stacked high with pancakes. "Eat up so you can grow to be a big boy like Richard."

Molly laughed. "But I don't want to be a big boy, Delores. Why did I get so many?"

"So you can keep up with both of them." Delores went back to the kitchen, laughing.

"That'll teach you to challenge Delores," Richard said. "I learned that lesson long ago."

"I'm afraid he's right, dear," Elizabeth said, smiling. "She rules this house."

Having taken her first bite of delicious pancakes, Molly said, "I can see why."

"They're good, aren't they?" Richard asked.

"The best I've ever tasted. Do you know how she makes them, Elizabeth?"

"No, she won't tell me. She doesn't want me in her kitchen cooking breakfast."

After Molly turned to her pancakes, Toby said, "We forgot to decorate the tree last night." He looked at his grandmother, as if knowing he'd get support from her.

"I know, Toby. I realized it last night as I got into bed. But it was too late then. Is this morning all right?"

"Sure. Want to go now?"

"I think you should finish your breakfast first," Richard said, enjoying his second cup of coffee.

"Oh. I don't think I can finish all of them."

"Well, Molly has to finish hers." He shot her a twinkling look. "If she wants to keep up with us."

"Be careful, Richard," Elizabeth called as she stared at her son on the top of a stepladder. Toby and Molly were holding their breaths, too, as Richard put the angel on top of the nine-foot tree.

"I'm fine, Mom. Don't worry. Albert, is that straight?"

"Yes, sir, it sure is. Good job."

"Thanks. I'd rather you be up here instead of me, but Toby insisted."

"Yes, sir, I slipped him a fiver," Albert said with a laugh.

"What's a fiver, Molly?" Toby asked.

"He's teasing, sweetie. He's saying he gave you money to get Richard up on the top of the ladder instead of him."

"But I don't have any money—" Toby said.

Molly hushed him at once. "He's just teasing."

"But—"

Clearly the explanation wasn't working, so Molly tried a diversion. "Have you picked out the first ornament you want to hang, Toby?"

That distracted him, and Molly breathed a sigh of relief. The boy immediately turned to the table with all the decorations. She held her breath, wondering which he would choose. The last Christmas she shared with her parents was the only one she remembered. She'd hung the first ornament, a clear glass ball with the manger scene on it.

Toby had chosen one remarkably like it.

When he picked up that particular ornament, Molly sank her teeth in her lips to keep control of her emotion. Twenty years later and she still got emotional about the holidays.

"You might as well hand me some of the ornaments, Molly, before I get down off this ladder," Richard said.

"All right." She picked up several balls and handed them to Richard.

"One at a time, Molly," Richard said, handing back one of the ornaments.

Which meant she was stuck handing balls to him. Elizabeth and Toby were handling the rest of the tree. Molly said nothing, doing as Richard asked. But she'd hoped to do some decorating herself. She wanted ownership in this tree, too. It had been so long since she'd celebrated a Christmas so gloriously.

"Richard, that's enough balls up there. Come down off the ladder and let Molly hang some of the ornaments, too."

"Sorry, Molly, I didn't think. I would've been glad to trade places with you."

"No, thank you," she hurriedly said, adding in a low voice, "I'm afraid of heights."

"Really?" Richard asked in surprise.

"Yes, really."

"Here, I'll hand you ornaments, how about that?"

"It's not necessary, Richard. Toby's the one who needs to decorate the tree." She didn't want anyone to know how important decorating the tree was to her. Several years, she'd considered buying a big tree just because she'd enjoy decorating it, but she'd talked herself out of it. Money hadn't been plentiful, and in the past couple of years, she'd found other ways of celebrating Christmas. But this year—

"But we want you to have a good Christmas, too. After all, you're not going home for Christmas, either," Richard said casually.

Molly quickly looked at Toby, but he was busy putting an ornament on the other side of the tree. "Please don't say that in front of Toby."

"Oh, sorry, I forgot. That's the problem when you start telling stories."

"The story I told was to you!" she snapped. "I didn't want to tell you my situation. I knew you would make fun of me!"

Richard narrowed his eyes. "You're not serious, are you?"

"Yes, I am!"

"Okay. So hang some ornaments on the tree!"

"Thank you, I will." She blinked rapidly, trying to handle the sudden tears as she helped decorate the beautiful tree.

When they finished decorating, they all stood together, staring at the huge tree.

"It will look even better when we turn the lights on tonight," Elizabeth said. "It will look magical in the dark."

"I think it looks wonderful now," Toby said.

"Me, too," Molly agreed in an awed voice.

For the first time, Richard believed Molly's statement that she'd lied to him, not Toby. He thought the tree was nice, but he'd had big trees as a boy every year. His mother had seen to that. His father hadn't participated in decorating the tree, but his mother and whoever the chauffeur was at the time had helped him and Susan with the tree.

He fought the urge to put his arms around Molly. He'd be crazy if he did such a thing. She'd probably slap his face. His mother would order the wedding invitations.

"Now, Albert, you can put up the other decorations," Elizabeth said in a soft voice, as if she didn't want anyone to notice.

"What decorations, Mother?"

"I got Albert to get some lights to go around the room at the top of the wall. They'll blink like the Christmas tree."

"Oh, that will be lovely, Elizabeth," Molly said.

"Don't you want me to put up these, too?" Albert asked. He held up some greenery.

Richard recognized it at once as mistletoe.

"Mother!" he exclaimed.

CHAPTER SEVEN

IN SPITE of Richard's protest, the mistletoe went up all over the downstairs.

Molly made a mental note not to linger in any doorways. She didn't expect Richard to want to kiss her, but she didn't want to tempt fate. Not that she wasn't attracted to the man. That was part of the problem. She was. But she had no place in their world. Once Toby was settled in, she'd be back in Florida.

She released an unconscious sigh, thinking about the time she had to leave.

"Molly? Is anything wrong?" Richard asked.

They were all having lunch together, again in the breakfast room. Louisa was off for the day to be with her family, and it made things easier for Delores and Albert if they ate there.

"No, what made you think that?"

"You sighed," he said, watching her closely.

"Oh, I was thinking about a friend back home," she hurriedly said.

"A boyfriend?"

Molly shot him a puzzled look. "No."

"No boyfriend waiting for you in Florida? I find that hard to believe."

"A nurse doesn't have a lot of free time, or the energy to do much when she does," Molly said. She took a sip of tea, hoping that would end this ridiculous conversation.

"That sounds like my life. Since my dad died, I've been reworking our law firm, trying to bring it up-to-date and get back on top of the legal world in Dallas. I don't have much free time, and no energy when I do."

"Dear, I knew you were working long hours, but I didn't realize how hard it was for you," Elizabeth said. "I should've paid more attention."

"No, Mom, I'm fine. We're about to get to the point where I can take it a little easier."

"You should take a vacation as soon as you can," Elizabeth said. "I'll be here with Toby, so we'll manage just fine."

"I'm not sure, Mom. You might need me."

"Maybe we could get Molly to come back for a couple of weeks," Elizabeth suggested, looking at Molly expectantly.

"I doubt I'll get any more time off once I get back. My vacation is scheduled for July."

"Oh, dear, that's a long time away. You're not having any fun at all during Christmas," Elizabeth said.

"Yes, I am, Elizabeth. I'm enjoying myself immensely, I promise." Molly gave the woman her best smile. She couldn't let her think she was suffering. In truth, she wasn't. She was getting to do things she'd always wanted to do. Most of all, she was getting to spend time with Toby and know she was helping him adjust to his new family.

"All right, dear. Oh, I know what we should do, Richard. We should all go to lunch at Antares, in the ball."

"Mom is talking about the restaurant located in the ball on the Dallas skyline. You can see the entire area because the restaurant rotates while you're eating."

Molly swallowed. Her fear of heights made that prospect turn her stomach.

"Mom, I'm not sure—" Richard began.

Toby, however, was excited. "That sounds neat. Can we go, Grandma?"

"Yes, dear. I think we could do that Monday and then you three could do your shopping on Tuesday. Yes, that's what we'll do."

Molly said nothing, hoping either she would work up enough nerve to go, or she could plead a temporary illness that would keep her at home.

Richard caught her eye, silently asking if she wanted him to halt the plans. She shook her head. She'd deal with it on Monday.

"I think you need to take Toby to buy a suit today, Richard. Maybe they have something that would fit him, with his casts on. We can have it tailored after he gets his casts off."

Richard agreed. "What are you and Molly going to do?"

"Oh, we'll make some plans, organize our shopping, that kind of thing. We might even go to some stores, if you're not taking Albert."

"No, I'll drive my car. Is that okay with you, Toby?"

"Yeah. I like your car."

"Okay. Then, if you've finished your lunch, let's head out."

Molly and Elizabeth sat there in silence for several

minutes. Then Elizabeth said, "It's a lot quieter when they're both gone, isn't it?"

Molly laughed. "It is, but honestly I miss the noise. Richard is being very good to Toby."

"I think he loves him very much. He loved his sister and missed her when she…left the family. I know they talked once or twice, but he hated his father's behavior. In Florida, you didn't see him at his best. He was mourning Susan's death and trying to take care of me. I'm afraid I'd become quite a burden."

"But you seem to be doing very well now," Molly said, not sure what had brought on the change.

"Yes, I changed my attitude. I had something to live for. Toby needs me. Richard didn't need me, even though he would say differently, but I knew better."

"Then, in spite of the tragedy, I'm glad Toby has come to you and Richard. I know he's going to be happy here with you."

"I hope so. But you've made a big difference, easing him into a role in our home. I know Richard is paying you a lot, but what you've given Toby is priceless."

"Thank you, Elizabeth. Now, you need to rest for a while so I won't have to lie to Richard when he returns."

"I think I will, if you don't mind."

Molly stood as Elizabeth left the room. Then she gathered their dishes and took them to the kitchen so Delores wouldn't have to come get them. She made several trips, before Delores returned to the kitchen.

"What are you doing, child?" the cook demanded.

"I'm helping out. I'm going to load the dishwasher so you have time to do other things."

"Bless you, Molly. With Louisa not here, I'll admit it's a little difficult."

"Well, Elizabeth sent the two men to get Toby a suit and she's gone up to lie down, so I'm free. I'll do anything I can to help you."

"In exchange, I'll give you my recipe for pancakes."

"That's a deal, Delores. I'll be the belle of the ball in Florida if they taste your pancakes."

The rest of the afternoon, Molly worked in the kitchen alongside Delores, helping her prepare dinner for that evening. When Richard and Toby came in, they discovered Molly sharing a cup of coffee with Delores, laughing together at some of the cook's stories about Richard and Susan as children.

"What's going on here?" Richard asked.

Molly smiled at him. "I'm getting some good blackmail material from Delores."

"Delores, you wouldn't betray me, would you?"

"This little girl worked with me all afternoon. I'm giving her my pancake recipe!"

"You wouldn't give it to Mom, but you're giving it to Molly? And what do you mean, she worked in here all afternoon?"

"You know it's hard with Louisa gone. Molly helped me out."

"I thought you were going to make lists with Mom. What happened to that plan?"

"I sent her up to have a nap, and she hasn't come down. Maybe I should go check on her."

As if on cue, Elizabeth asked from the doorway, "What's everyone doing in the kitchen?"

"I was just coming to check on you," Molly said.

"No need. I'm here. But I didn't expect to find all of you in the kitchen."

"You're right, Elizabeth. I can't work with a crowd in here," Delores said.

"My fault. I was hoping I could learn some cooking tricks from Delores. Thanks for letting me visit with you, Delores," Molly said and slipped from the room. "Toby," she called over her shoulder, "come show me and your grandma what you bought."

That quickly cleared the kitchen, except for Richard. He looked at Delores. "She was helping you?"

"Yes. She said she had the afternoon free and knew Louisa was gone. She did the lunch dishes and then helped with the preparation for dinner."

"That was nice of her."

"Nice? That was really sweet of her. You can't find a sweeter person than Molly. Richard, you shouldn't let her get away!"

"Now, Delores, you know I'm kind of busy right now."

"Yes, but that's not important. Molly is what's important."

Richard just smiled and shook his head. Then he excused himself to find the ladies and get their compliments on his job of shopping with Toby. He'd gotten the boy a couple of pairs of slacks, a belt and several dress shirts to go with his suit. And he'd bought him his first tie, and a sweater to wear until his cast was off. It looked better than a jacket that was too big for him.

"Molly, can you tie a man's tie?" Richard asked.

"No, I can't. You'll have to teach Toby that particular skill," she told him.

Richard nodded. "I can do that. When he gets dressed in the morning, I'll tie his tie after breakfast."

"All right. Is he wearing his suit in the morning?"

"We're going to church in the morning. He'll wear his sweater, dress shirt and tie, with one of his new pairs of slacks. Will you join us?"

"Yes, I'd like that."

Richard smiled at her. "Good."

"Would anyone like to go to the movies tonight?" Elizabeth asked. "They're showing a film I'd like to see."

"What is it, Elizabeth?" Molly asked.

She named a current movie. "It's supposed to be quite funny and romantic."

Toby made a face that made Richard laugh. "Sometimes, buddy, we have to go to movies we aren't crazy about to keep the ladies happy. But we can always eat a lot of popcorn."

"I like popcorn!"

"Okay, we'll escort you ladies to the movies tonight. What time does it start?"

Elizabeth told him the time and he went back to the kitchen to make sure Delores could have dinner ready on time.

When he got back in the den, he heard Molly suggest that she and Toby stay home.

"No way. Toby shouldn't have to give up his popcorn, and you need some reward for helping Delores this afternoon."

"She helped Delores? You didn't have to do that, Molly," Elizabeth protested.

"It wasn't much. I enjoyed it."

"We're all going to the movies, Molly," Richard said firmly. "No arguments."

"You'd best go along with him when he uses that tone, dear. It means he's determined." Elizabeth smiled at Molly.

Richard held his breath. He thought she was tempted to challenge him, but he wanted her to go. When she nodded, he silently let out the breath he'd been holding.

When they reached the theater, it was already crowded. To get four seats together, they would have to sit down front. Elizabeth turned to Richard. "Toby and I will take one of the popcorns, and you and Molly take the other one. We're going to take these two seats."

Richard didn't know if his mother was trying to match-make or didn't really want to sit so close to the screen. Whichever the case, the result was the same. He was going to sit with Molly and share a bucket of popcorn. He couldn't admit to himself the reason his pulse was racing.

They settled into their seats just as the movie started. Richard put the popcorn between them, encouraging Molly to have some. Just then, a big man, weighing at least three hundred pounds, pushed past them to sit in the seat next to Richard.

Richard, uncomfortable, leaned toward Molly.

He whispered, "Sorry but I've got to move closer." Then he raised his arm and put it on the back of her chair.

When Molly saw the man on the other side of Richard, she scooted over as much as she could. Richard lifted the arm of the chair between them and moved even closer.

He told himself it was the only practical thing to do, but as the movie started, he found himself distracted by Molly's warmth and scent. When something funny happened on screen Molly laughed, and her low, sexy chuckle riveted through him.

Damn! He should've taken more time off the past year so he wouldn't leave himself vulnerable to the first woman who walked into his life in two years. This was ridiculous. He wanted to draw back, to remove his arm from around her, but there was no room.

A moment later, she leaned into him. "Don't you want some of the popcorn?"

"Oh, uh, yeah," he said and reached into the tub for a handful of popcorn. Molly got some after him and munched on the popcorn as if totally unaware of him. And he was practically a blithering idiot because he was pressed up against her.

After a while, he relaxed, out of necessity, and began watching the movie. It was funny and not too sappy. When it was over, he stood, along with Molly, and moved out of the auditorium.

The sensation of loss amazed him. He wanted to pull Molly against him and hold her there, but he couldn't do that. They moved out into the lobby and waited for Elizabeth and Toby.

"That was fun," Molly said.

"Yeah, it was." Richard took a deep breath, drawing in Molly's scent. It was a good thing they were getting out of this place.

Elizabeth came out with a sleepy Toby.

Richard moved forward and picked up the little boy. "I think this little guy is just about asleep on his feet."

"Yes, it's quite late for Toby," Molly said. "How did he do, Elizabeth?"

"He enjoyed it until we got about halfway through. I looked over and he was slumped down in his chair. I put his head on my shoulder and let him sleep."

"Next time we'll have to go to an earlier movie," Molly said.

So there'd be a next time? Richard thought. But he said nothing.

As soon as they got home, he carried Toby up to his room, closely followed by Molly and Elizabeth. Elizabeth parted with the others at the top of the stairs.

Molly opened the door to Toby's room and hurried ahead of Richard to turn down the covers. When he lay Toby down, she slipped off his shoes and then his pants. Richard slid down the zipper on his coat and managed to get it off. His shirt was knit and short-sleeved and Richard quickly got it off. Together, they'd managed to undress him in two minutes. The big T-shirt only took seconds.

"We did a pretty good job, didn't we?" Richard whispered with a grin.

Molly smiled back but she was busy covering the little boy up and kissing his forehead.

Richard was jealous. When that thought struck him, he took a step back. What was wrong with him?

"He was exhausted," Molly whispered. "Thank you for carrying him upstairs, Richard."

"No problem. Are—are you going to bed now?"

"Yes, I think I will. Good night," she said softly and stood there waiting for him to leave.

Damn it, where was the mistletoe when he needed it? "Good night. I'll see you in the morning."

He backed out of the room, finally breathing when he

closed the door. He took the long walk down the hall to his bedroom. He obviously needed some time to think. He'd been too close to Molly tonight and it had screwed up his defenses.

He just needed some time alone to resurrect his defenses. He didn't need a woman intruding into his life right now.

Molly had watched Richard's entry into his bedroom. Once he was out of sight, she slid out of Toby's room and tiptoed down the hall to the stairs. She wanted to see the Christmas tree in the darkened room, the lights shining like stars in the sky.

When she entered the garden room, she found the plug and turned on the lights. With a deep sigh, she sat down at the glass table, staring at the tree, perfect in her mind, and the lights glowing around the walls. The entire room seemed magical, as Elizabeth had predicted.

Molly sat there, soaking in that magic, the ephemeral lightness filling her soul. Maybe next year she would get a big tree, though not this big, so she could sit at night and enjoy the gleaming lights. Then she wouldn't have to sneak down to enjoy Christmas.

A slight noise awakened her from her dreams. She whirled around to discover Richard approaching. "What—what are you doing here? You went to bed!"

"You said you were going to bed, too."

"So you're spying on me? Do you want me to pay for the electricity I'm using?" She regretted her words as soon as she spoke. Richard and his mom had been more than generous to her. "I'm sorry. I shouldn't—"

"No, you shouldn't have. I came down to make some

coffee and saw the lights on. I thought maybe Albert had forgotten to turn them off."

"I'll turn them off now," she said, jumping up from her chair.

"I have a better idea," he said. "I'll go make some decaf coffee for both of us and we can enjoy it in here."

"Really, I should go to bed. There's no need—"

Instead of answering her, he bent down and brushed her lips with his. "Watch the lights," he said and walked out of the room.

Molly was completely flustered by that brief kiss. Why had he done that? Had he thought she'd flirted with him at the movies? She'd worked hard to make sure her voice sounded normal, even though he was pressed against her. She knew one thing. For all his complaints about lack of time, he'd found some time to work out somewhere. He was solid muscle.

She flushed from her head to her toes, glad he wasn't in the room. Even in the darkness, he might've noticed her blush.

Within minutes Richard appeared in the doorway, carrying two mugs of coffee. He set one in front of Molly and he took the seat next to her, pulling it even with hers. "We did a good job, didn't we?"

"Yes! The tree is beautiful," she said breathlessly.

"Are you okay?"

"Yes, of course. I just wanted— I enjoy seeing the tree at night. As your mother said, it's magical."

"I realized that when I saw you staring at it today. You were remembering trees in the past, weren't you?"

All she could do was nod.

"When did your parents die?"

She turned to stare at him. "You believe me now?"

"Yeah, I believe you. I'm not sure why you lied to me, but I believe you."

Abruptly she said, "I was seven."

"And you went to a foster home?"

"Several foster homes," she muttered.

Richard frowned. "Why did you change?"

"Well, let's see, in the first foster home, the dad was caught forcing himself on a couple of the older girls. So we were all moved to different homes. It's like starting all over again. The second foster home closed down because the mom won the lottery and didn't need the money she got from the state."

"She didn't mind letting you go?"

Molly gave a cynical laugh. "She dumped us so fast it made our heads spin."

"Then what happened?"

"My third foster home I stayed in until I was eighteen. By then I'd worked for three years and had saved as much as I could."

"What kind of work?"

"I was a telephone operator, part-time."

"How did you get into nursing?"

She shrugged a shoulder. "I got a scholarship. It didn't pay for everything, but most of it. I paid for the rest."

"And how—"

"No more questions about me. It's your turn. Was your dad as awful as he seems?"

"He was difficult. I try not to say too much, because I think Mom loved him, but he was controlling, self-centered. I managed to get along with him, but he considered females to be second-class citizens. Susan wouldn't buy that attitude. She fought him all the way."

"Good for her," Molly whispered.

"When my father tried to tell her who to love, that was the last straw. She moved to Florida with Kevin, Toby's father, and never came back. My father disowned her after that."

"I'm sorry, Richard." Sympathy was audible in her voice. "That must have been hard on you."

"Yeah. I called her a couple of times, but she obviously wouldn't come home for a visit, after Dad cut her out of his life. It was stupid on his part."

"Yes, it was." She sat there for a minute staring at the Christmas tree. Then she said, "Life's too short for such silliness."

"As we both know," he said softly. Then he stretched his arm on the back of her chair.

She thought about moving away, but the warmth of his arm felt good. They sat there in silence, looking at the tree. Molly had enjoyed the lights before he came down, but they were always better when shared.

After a few minutes, he pulled her a little closer and her head rested on his shoulder. They remained there for a long time. Somehow, in the darkness, she didn't feel like it mattered.

Molly enjoyed his closeness, but she knew when daylight came, the magic would end.

Molly enjoyed the visit to their church the next morning. They only went to the main service in the large auditorium, where the minister gave an intelligent and entertaining sermon.

The only thing that bothered Molly was that Elizabeth again took Toby's hand and led him into the pew first. Which left her between Toby and Richard. At least they didn't have to separate, leaving her with Richard. And they had plenty of room in their pew.

They went out to lunch after the church service since Delores had the day off.

"We should've gone to Antares today," Elizabeth said as they ate lunch at a local restaurant. "But I made the reservations for Monday."

"That's okay, Mom. I like the pies here."

"Richard, I don't know how you stay so lean, with all the desserts you eat. It's disgusting!"

Molly thought so, too, but she wasn't going to make any comments.

"I went to the gym every morning this past year, Mom. That's how I can eat all those desserts. And I enjoy every one of them."

"Maybe I should get up and go with you," Elizabeth muttered.

"You look lovely, Elizabeth. You have nothing to worry about," Molly assured her.

"Yes, but I pass up the desserts most of the time."

"It's probably better for you," Molly said, smiling in sympathy.

"So you're both going to pass up dessert?" Richard asked incredulously.

Molly looked at Elizabeth and at the same time they said, "No way!"

Richard grinned. "Looks like we're all having pie, right, Toby?"

"Can I have ice cream instead?"

"Sure, buddy, if that's what you want."

Toby nodded enthusiastically.

Molly again realized how close Richard and Toby were becoming. By the time she left, she thought Richard would be regarding Toby as his own son.

Toby would scarcely miss her.

She chastised herself for that thought. That was what she should hope for. And she should hope that she wouldn't miss Toby…or anyone else when she went back to Florida.

Maybe she should look for a job here in Dallas? No, no, that wouldn't be a good idea. She needed to cut her emotional ties to Toby at once. It would be easier that way.

"Hey, they have a Christmas tree here!" Toby called out.

"Yeah, they do, but it's not as pretty as ours, is it, Toby?" Richard asked.

"Ours is the best! Do they have one at the mall?"

"They always have at least one," Richard said, looking at Molly.

She knew he was thinking she should've answered the question since she'd been to the mall. "Didn't you go to the mall to get Toby's new clothes?"

"No, we went to a men's store at Highland Park Village, where we went to the movies last night."

"We're fortunate that we have a lot of specialty shops around here," Elizabeth said with a smile. "Whatever we're looking for, we can find nearby."

"How nice," Molly said. In her mind, she was thinking, "If you can afford it!"

Then, at Elizabeth's horrified glance and Richard's grin, she realized she'd spoken her thoughts aloud.

CHAPTER EIGHT

"OH, I'M SO sorry. I didn't mean to say that out loud!" Molly said, her voice filled with anguish. "You've both been so good to me, treating me like family, and I have no reason—"

Richard reached over and touched her hand. "It's okay, Molly. Mom didn't think about the fact that you might not be able to afford the shops around here."

"I don't have to be able to afford them. I'm not shopping for anything. I shouldn't have been so rude."

Elizabeth smiled at her. "Don't worry about that, Molly. I'm very fortunate and sometimes I forget that others don't live like I do. It's a good reminder to me."

"But I shouldn't have reminded you of that, Elizabeth."

"Let's call it quits on that subject, dear. Toby is ready for his ice cream and I'm going to choose my pie. What kind do you want?"

"I love apple, especially if it has a scoop of ice cream on it," Molly said, smiling.

"Hey, I didn't volunteer to pay for ice cream for you, young lady," Richard said, laughing at her.

"Richard!" Elizabeth exclaimed.

"Just teasing, Mom. I'll even pay for you to have ice

cream. It's all Toby's fault, of course. He's the one who mentioned ice cream first."

"But I didn't want pie!" Toby protested.

They all burst into laughter, which confused both Toby and their waiter.

"Come along, everyone. We don't want to be late for lunch at Antares," Elizabeth called.

Molly looked at Toby, dressed in some of his new clothes. "You look very nice, honey, but I think I'm going to stay home today."

"No, Molly, I don't want to go without you."

"You'll be fine. Richard will be there."

"No. I won't go if you don't."

Molly swallowed. She'd gotten ready for the lunch trip to downtown Dallas, but at the last minute, she didn't think she could go. "Toby—"

"Molly, Toby, come on. Richard is waiting."

"Come on, Molly," Toby said, pulling her hand as he headed toward the door of his bedroom. "We've got to hurry."

Molly gave up and followed him into the hallway. They reached the head of the stairs when Elizabeth came into view.

"Oh, there you are! Richard is waiting in the car. It's much warmer today than it was, but still, we don't want him to get impatient."

"No, of course not," Molly said, trying to forget their destination.

They hurried outside and got into Richard's SUV.

"I was beginning to think I was going by myself," Richard said as he backed out of the driveway.

Molly, sitting in the front seat, said nothing.

Elizabeth said, "Toby wasn't quite ready."

"I wasn't?" Toby asked.

"Actually, I was the slow one," Molly said in a hurry.

Richard looked at Molly. "No problem. It won't take us long to get there."

"Oh, good," she said faintly.

"You'll just love the restaurant, Molly. It's part of the Hyatt Regency Hotel. Very stylish," Elizabeth commented.

"I'm sure it's lovely, Elizabeth."

"Can we see our house from there, Uncle Richard?"

"With all the trees, probably not. But we can see the American Airlines Center where our pro basketball team plays. And we'll see the Trinity River, and the rest of downtown. We might even be able to see Six Flags Over Texas. I can't remember ever looking for it, but we'll try today."

"What is Six Flags Over Texas?"

"It's an amusement park, Toby," Elizabeth explained.

"Can we go there, too?" he asked.

"It's closed during the winter. You might get to go next summer."

"Molly, will you want to go, too?" Toby asked.

"No, probably not, Toby."

"Why not?"

Molly pasted on a smile as she looked over her shoulder. "Because I'll be back in Florida by then, Toby."

"Uncle Richard, does Molly have to go back?"

"Toby!" Molly exclaimed before Richard could answer. "I have to go back. There will be other children who are hurt and need me."

"But I need you."

"No, you have Richard and your grandmother, Toby. Remember?"

"Yeah, I guess so," he said sadly.

"Your grandma has planned a nice day for you, Toby. Don't ruin it for her," Molly said gently.

"No, I won't. Thank you, Grandma."

"Toby, look, there's where we're going," Richard said, pointing out a large ball up in the air, sitting on concrete pillars.

"Do we have to walk up there, Uncle Richard?"

"No, there's an elevator." He pulled the car into the driveway of the Hyatt Regency Hotel and stopped. "We're doing valet parking, so hop out, everyone."

Molly got out, but she didn't want to. She wanted to offer to drive around the block a couple hundred times until they came back down, but she knew Richard wouldn't allow that.

He led the way down a long escalator and Molly wondered why they were going down when the restaurant was up on top. But then they reached a bank of elevators. When the doors opened, Richard led them in.

Molly faced forward, prepared to close her eyes until they reached their destination. Behind her, Toby was chatting with Elizabeth.

Suddenly he said, "Look, Molly!"

Immediately Molly turned around only to see that what she'd thought would be the back of the elevator was actually a bank of windows that looked down on the quickly disappearing ground.

Just as her knees buckled, Richard's arms went around her and he pressed her face into his chest. "Don't look, Molly. Just stay here with me. We'll be there in a minute."

"I'm sorry to be such a coward," she whispered, on the verge of tears.

"It's not a problem. Toby doesn't understand. Neither does Mom."

"Why do you?"

"I've had an illogical fear or two. My dad insisted I get over them. As much as I tried, I couldn't."

"No, it's not something you can control."

"I was watching you, afraid you'd get upset, so I knew at once when you turned around, you weren't going to make it."

"Can I go back down?"

"Not now. We have to eat first. But don't worry, you won't have to sit by the window. I'll sit there, and I'll keep you safe."

"Thank you." Just as she said that, she heard the elevator door open. She raised her head and looked over her shoulder just as he eased her forward and out the elevator door.

Richard gave their name to the hostess who took them to their table. Richard held Molly back and let his mother and Toby go first.

When they stepped down on the lower level of the restaurant floor, Richard kept his arm around her and he steadied her with his other hand when she realized the floor was moving.

"Easy," he whispered. "We'll be at the table in a minute."

When they reached the table, Richard went in first so he had the window seat opposite Toby, and he pulled out the chair next to him for Molly.

"Richard, you should give Molly the window seat. She'll want to see everything," Elizabeth told him.

"Mom, Molly is afraid of heights. She'll be all right in

the chair she's in. If she wants to see anything closer, all she has to do is tell me."

"Oh, Molly, why didn't you say anything?"

"I—I didn't want to spoil everyone's fun," Molly said.

"Poor dear. Do you want us to leave now?"

"No, it's all right. Richard has promised to make it easier for me when we go down, so we might as well eat before we do that."

"You're being very brave. Isn't she, Toby?"

"Yes, but it's my fault," Toby said, tears forming in his eyes. "I told her I wouldn't come without her."

"Toby, it's okay," Molly said, reaching across the table to touch his hand.

Richard looked at the boy. "You need to be more thoughtful of others, Toby.

"Richard, don't. He's just a little boy!"

"Yes, but I don't think he realized how difficult it would be for you." He stretched his arm around her chair, as he had the night they'd watched the lights together.

"He's just come through a terrible ordeal. He'll be more thoughtful in the future."

"Okay, buddy," Richard said, reaching over and patting Toby's arm. "I know you're just a little boy. But part of growing up is learning to think about others."

"Okay," Toby whispered.

"Good, now we need to order," Elizabeth said. "Toby, what do you think you would like?"

"A cheeseburger," he replied without hesitation.

"You know what, Toby?" Molly asked. "I'm going to have the same." She smiled at the little boy.

The waiter came and they placed their orders. He

brought their drinks at once and Molly took a sip of her Diet Coke. It helped her feel a little better.

"Uncle Richard, did you look for the amusement park?"

"Not yet. Let's see, there's the Trinity River, so we're facing south right now. When we rotate west, we can look for it."

"How will we know?" Toby asked.

"There'll be a sign painted on the wall that says West."

"Okay, I'll watch for it."

Now that Toby's attention was off her, Molly slumped in her chair.

"You okay?" Richard whispered, leaning closer, his breath warm on her skin.

"Yes, but you shouldn't have blamed Toby," Molly returned.

"I won't have him spoiled by you and my mother. He has to learn to be responsible for his actions."

"I agree, but it seems a little harsh so soon after he lost his parents." She should know; she'd experienced that first-hand.

"I didn't beat him, honey. I just pointed out what he had done. I don't think that's too harsh."

"Well, I do, *honey*!"

"But you're not in charge of him. My mother and I are."

Molly's gaze fell to the table. She refused to look at him. She knew she wasn't in charge of Toby, but she cared for the boy. Surely Richard knew that. At the moment, she disliked Richard. And truthfully she didn't want to leave Toby with him.

"Was that truth too harsh, too?" Richard asked, watching her response.

She nodded, trying to hold back tears. She knew she was

too emotionally involved with Toby. Even with Elizabeth and Richard. Especially with Richard if she were honest. It seemed they shared a lot recently. So much for her vow to avoid him. She was used to being alone, and it was going to be difficult to forget her visit to Texas.

He pulled her a little closer to him, but she didn't rest her head on his shoulder like she wanted to. She didn't really have that right.

"Uncle Richard, look, it's here!" Toby exclaimed. "We're facing West!"

Richard responded to Toby, but Molly didn't look up. She could tell Toby was doing just fine. Could it be true, what Richard had said? Still, she wasn't going to admit to him that he was right.

The waiter brought their food. It was all beautifully served and looked great on the plate. Even though a hamburger was the normal American fare, it tasted better than any Molly had ever had. All in all, she had to admit, she enjoyed the lunch at one of Dallas's main tourist attractions.

Until they had to enter the elevator again.

She was still irritated with Richard, in spite of Toby's quick recovery. She was determined to manage without his help. But just entering the elevator, facing the windows for that brief walk, was hard.

When she hesitated, Richard took her hand and turned her around. "You can back in. I'll guide you."

"Thank you," she said stiffly.

Once they were in the elevator, she stood close to the door, her gaze fastened on it, waiting for it to open again.

"Need any help?" Richard whispered.

"No, thank you, I'm doing fine."

"Too bad. I enjoyed our ride to the top."

She said nothing. With her teeth gritted, she refused to bury her face in Richard's chest, as she'd done earlier. She wanted to. His warmth had felt good. But she mustn't take advantage of his goodness.

When the elevator door opened, Molly drew a deep breath of relief, knowing her ordeal was over.

Richard took her hand and led her to the escalator. She tried to pull her hand free, but she would've had to make it obvious to do that. With Elizabeth and Toby right behind them, she thought the best thing to do would be to wait until they reached the hotel lobby. He'd have to present their parking ticket to get the car pulled up.

When that happened, she turned back to Elizabeth and Toby. "Elizabeth, do you want me to sit in the back of the car with Toby on the way home?"

"Do you mind, dear? I'm feeling a little sleepy after our lunch. I believe I ate too much."

Toby took her hand. "Yeah, I'm tired, too."

"I guess you and Grandma both need your rest, don't you?" Molly said. "You were up way too late on Saturday night."

"Yeah, I don't remember the end of the movie."

"That's because you fell asleep. Richard carried you to bed."

"I didn't know that. He must be very strong," Toby said, a touch of awe in his voice.

"I suppose," Molly agreed, but she knew how strong he was. She'd felt his arms around her, too.

Not only did she remember the rock-hard wall of his chest, but she recalled his warmth, the security he provided her in the circle of his arms, the smell of his citrus aftershave. All things she should *not* be remembering now. Shaking off the thoughts, she got in the car and put her head back, willing them not to invade her mind again.

After a few minutes, her roving eyes betrayed her, landing on the rearview mirror where she studied Richard's reflection. His jaw was square, his dark hair perfectly groomed, his blue eyes focused on the road ahead. Say what you will, she thought, but he was one handsome man.

As if feeling her gaze on him, he looked up into the mirror and their eyes met in reflection. "You okay back there?" he asked.

"Y-yes," she stammered, feeling as if she were caught doing something illegal. "I'm fine. Toby's just a little tired."

"We'll be home in a few minutes."

When they got home, Molly roused a sleeping Toby and led him in, holding his hand all the way up to his room. Elizabeth accompanied them upstairs.

A few minutes later, Molly slipped back down. The door to Richard's study was closed. Even so, she tiptoed past the door. When she reached the kitchen, she found Albert sitting at the table having a cup of coffee.

"Albert, could you take me shopping for a few minutes?"

"Sure I can, Molly. You have more Christmas shopping to do?"

"Yes, just a little bit that I can't do at the mall tomorrow."

"No problem. Are you ready to go?"

"Yes. Can we go without asking Richard?"

Albert grinned. "Sure. He doesn't ever need me."

About an hour later, Molly hurried back up the stairs.

She heard a door open as she reached the top of the stairs, but she didn't turn around to see if Richard had come out of his office.

She didn't want to know.

Richard watched Molly's rapid ascent up the stairs, carrying a package. With a frown, he walked to the kitchen.

"Albert, did you take Molly out?"

Albert, sitting at the table with a fresh cup of coffee looked up in surprise. "Yes, sir, I did. Did you need me?"

"No, I was just curious. We're going shopping tomorrow."

"I know, but she had some shopping to do that she couldn't do in the mall."

Richard stood there staring into space.

"Want a cup of coffee, Richard?" Delores offered.

"Yeah, that would be great."

She poured him a cup of coffee, but instead of leaving, Richard sat down beside Albert. "Where did you take her?"

"To a camera store."

"She's buying a camera?"

"I don't know. I didn't go in the store with her. She told me she wouldn't be long, and she was right."

"It seems to me she has a lot of secrets."

Delores chuckled. "Of course she does. It's Christmas. Are you telling everyone what you're doing every moment of the day?"

Delores had a point.

"She's such a nice lady," the cook continued. "I wish she didn't have to leave."

"Toby feels the same way, Delores."

"So why don't you do something about it, Richard?"

"What do you want me to do? Hire a nurse as a nanny to Toby? He's not that small."

"I don't know. I just know I'll miss her when she's gone."

"When is she supposed to leave?" Albert asked.

"Mid-January," Richard muttered and took a sip of coffee. The longer she was here, the more he was dreading the date. But he couldn't admit that to Delores and Albert.

"She sure is pretty," Albert said.

"You got a crush on her?" Richard teased.

"Of course not. I'm old enough to be her father, but I like her. She's kind to everyone."

"Yeah, she is."

"And she's not a snob, like some people you know," Albert added.

"Okay, I get the picture. You both want Molly to stay. But I'm not able to take that on. I'm still working nonstop on office stuff, except for when I have to take Mom, Toby and Molly to do something for Christmas."

"It's about time you slow down. You don't want to be like your daddy," Delores said.

"No, I don't. But I have an obligation to the law firm. A lot of people depend on our success, not to mention the two of you. It would be hard if Mom had to start doing the cooking!"

"Well, you're right, but she could do more. It would probably be good for her. Toby is good for her," Delores pointed out.

"I know. I'm trying to keep him from being spoiled with two women fawning over him."

Delores grinned. "That's a hard job."

"I know. I upset Molly today. She hasn't forgiven me yet, but she will."

"How do you know that?" Delores wanted to know.

"Because Molly can't hold a grudge. It goes against her very nature. You know that."

"Yes, but I don't want you taking advantage of her!"

"So you want Toby spoiled?" Richard demanded.

"No. He's a fine little boy. Susan did a good job."

"Yes, she did. But it would be easy for him to get spoiled in this house."

Delores sighed. "I suppose you're right, but try not to offend Molly. I don't want her to leave."

"I know. Toby and Mom say the same thing. But none of you has come up with a way for Molly to stay."

"I have," Delores said. "You just marry her!"

"Don't be—" He stopped as he heard footsteps behind him. He spun around and saw Molly entering the kitchen. "Molly!" Had she heard Delores's comment? He searched her face and saw no reaction. Feigning innocence, he asked, "What are you up to?"

"I thought I might see if Delores needs any help again today."

The cook smiled. "No, I don't, but I appreciate the thought. Louisa should be here at two o'clock to help prepare dinner."

"She had a long weekend, didn't she?" Molly said with a smile.

"Yes. Her sister got married yesterday."

"How nice."

"Yes, it is. Do you like weddings?"

"Yes. I've only been to a couple, but they always fill me with optimism. You can see the hope on everyone's face."

"Half the marriages today end in divorce," Richard said.

"So people shouldn't get married?" Molly challenged.

"I don't think it's anything someone should rush into."

"I saw a report that couples who date for a long time are less likely to have a lasting marriage than those who marry more quickly." Molly crossed her arms over her chest, as if waiting for him to disagree with her.

"I read that study, too. I'm not sure I believe it, but they had some good points," he said calmly.

"It's time for you to get married, Richard," Delores chimed in. "After all, you're thirty." Then she looked at Molly. "How old are you, Molly?"

"I didn't think you were supposed to ask a woman her age," Richard pointed out.

Molly ignored him. "I'm twenty-seven, Delores."

"Perfect," Delores said with a smile.

Molly raised her eyebrows. "What's so perfect about being twenty-seven?"

Richard had understood Delores's comment, but he challenged her with his stare to explain what she meant to Molly.

Delores was unfazed. "I just think it's a good age. You're old enough to know your mind, but young enough to have some choices."

"I suppose." Molly got up. "I'm going to get some coffee."

"How about a piece of chocolate cake to go with it?"

"You holding back those sweets again?" Albert mock-complained. "What about for me too? And Richard?"

Richard nodded. He was in the mood for sweets, all right. One by the name of Molly Soderling.

CHAPTER NINE

THE afternoon coffee klatch was in full swing in the kitchen, Molly having taken a seat at the table with Richard, Albert and Delores, when Toby walked in.

"Molly? I tried to wake up Grandma, but she didn't want to get up."

Rising immediately to her feet, Molly said, "I'll go see if she's feeling all right."

Richard held his hand out to the boy. "I'm sure she's just tired," he explained. "Why did you want Grandma anyway?"

"'Cause she told me to come to her room when I got up and she'd read to me."

"Oh, that's right," Molly said. "She'd found a book you used to like her to read to you, Richard. She wanted to do the same for Toby." She ruffled the boy's dark hair and smiled down at him. "I'll just go check on her." With that, she left the kitchen.

"Is Grandma sick?" Toby asked Richard, concern in his voice.

"If she is, Molly will fix her up. After all, she's a nurse, isn't she?"

"I hope so," Toby said.

Richard could see the fear in his eyes. He hesitated to reassure him any more. After all, he didn't know if his mother was well. After his father's death, she was severely depressed, but she'd been so much better after they brought Toby home. He hoped she hadn't overdone.

Molly hung up the phone just as Louisa entered the room after a soft knock. "Is she all right?" the maid whispered.

"Oh, Louisa, you're here."

"Yes, I just arrived. How is she?" She nodded to the bed.

"I think she has the flu. I talked to her doctor and he's going to call in some medicine for her to take. Do you know her pharmacy?"

"Yes. Shall I tell Albert to go get it?"

"Yes, please. And do we have some Tylenol? She has a headache and is running a fever."

"Yes, ma'am. I'll get it." Louisa hurried into the bathroom and came back with a glass of water and the medicine.

"Thank you, Louisa."

When Louisa left, Molly put some pillows behind Elizabeth, then she managed to get her to take the Tylenol.

As she lay her back on the pillows, Elizabeth opened her eyes. "Where's Toby?" she whispered.

"He's downstairs. Don't worry about him. Why didn't you say you weren't feeling well?"

"I thought a nap would take care of it. What's wrong with me?"

"Your doctor said it sounds like the flu that's going around. He said to push the fluids and he would prescribe a pill that has helped some of his patients. But basically, you're going to be sick for four or five days."

"But it's Christmas!"

"Actually, it's not Christmas until a week from today. You should be feeling fine by then."

"But I have some shopping I need to do."

"I'll do it for you, or Richard can. Don't worry about things like that."

"I guess so. But I was going to read to Toby from a book Richard used to like."

"I know. I can read it to him in here, so you can see his reaction, if you want."

"Maybe later."

"Okay. Why don't you go back to sleep, and I'll check on you later."

Molly left her alone. As she pulled the door behind her, she almost ran smack into Richard's chest. She would have, if not for his strong arms that held her a foot away.

"How's Mom?" he asked.

"I gave her some Tylenol and she's gone back to sleep." When was he going to let her go? She wondered.

"I want to thank you for calling her doctor."

"No problem." She stepped back and he dropped his arms to his side. "She should be okay in a few days, but I'm going to have Albert pick up some masks. If you go in to see her, I want you to wear one."

"Is that really necessary?"

"It can't hurt."

"Okay."

"She was worried about doing some Christmas shopping. I'll be glad to pick up anything she knows she wants, but you might be better able to help her in that department."

"Okay. I'll talk to her the next time she's awake."

Molly nodded and walked past him.

"Where are you going?" he asked.

"I need to make a list of things I need for Elizabeth."

"If Albert is gone already, I'll go get whatever you need." He followed her back downstairs. "I've got paper and pen in my office," he said, opening the door to his office for her. "Come on in here."

She shrugged her shoulders and followed him in. It was a lovely room, with a lot of bookshelves and leather-bound volumes. A large desk dominated the room, but there was also a leather sofa with a coffee table in front of it. Molly sat down on the sofa and waited.

Richard pulled several pieces of blank paper out of a drawer and took a pen off his desk. He brought them to Molly and sat down beside her.

Though she was a bit unnerved by his closeness, she made her list. She made a note to ask Delores if she had any soup on hand.

"Delores can make some chicken soup," he said as he read her paper. "She'll be happy to."

"Good. Then this should do it." She handed Richard the list. "You know, I can come with you, if Albert has already left. Just let me check on Toby."

In the kitchen she spotted Toby munching a piece of chocolate cake. There was no sign of Albert, who'd apparently already gone.

Richard told Delores he was going to the store. "Want to go with me, Toby?" he asked the boy.

"Can I, Molly?" Toby asked, eagerness in his voice.

Molly looked at Richard. "Are you sure you want to take him along?"

"I thought it would give him something to do."

"Then maybe I should go with you."

"If you're coming, let's go," Richard said, holding Toby's hand in his. "We men are ready to go."

"You *men*?" Molly questioned with a grin.

Richard grabbed her hand with his free one. "Come on, young lady, or you'll be left behind."

In spite of the purpose of their shopping, the threesome had an enjoyable time. Richard wanted to get everything necessary to make his mother comfortable. In addition, because he knew Toby would need ways to pass the time, he found some puzzles and some videos for the boy. When he was about to add a game to his pile, Molly tugged on his sleeve. "Santa," she whispered.

He knew what she meant, and put the game back.

"Besides," Molly said, "I think you've bought enough. We don't want Toby to get spoiled, after all."

Richard looked at her smug expression. He knew she was paying him back for what he'd said earlier in the day.

The store clerk who had been helping them looked at Toby.

"Parents always worry about that kind of thing," he said, grinning at Toby.

"But they're not—"

"Arguing," Richard inserted. "We're not arguing. We're just trying to do the right thing. Right, honey?" He raised one eyebrow in Molly's direction.

"Yes, that's true, *honey*. Are you ready to go, Toby?"

"But we didn't buy that book you said you would read to me."

"*Charlotte's Web*?" Molly asked.

"Yeah, that one."

"Santa might bring it to you, so we'd better wait."

"Oh, okay."

As Toby walked a few steps ahead of them back to the car, Richard grabbed Molly's hand. "Santa has apparently been busy already. I didn't know my mother had done any shopping already."

"You never know." Molly didn't look at him, catching up with Toby to leave him behind.

He stared at her. He was learning to read Molly fairly well. There was something she wasn't telling him about the Santa items, but he wasn't sure what. Probably his mother had made her promise to say nothing.

When they got back to the house, Molly asked Richard to bring the humidifier upstairs to his mother's room. She took the glass of juice Delores held out.

"Do you think she'll want anything to eat?" Richard asked.

Delores spoke up. "I don't think so. She had some canned soup before, and I have chicken soup on the stove for later."

Richard nodded. "I'll tell her it's coming soon. It'll give her something to look forward to." As they turned to go, Molly reminded him, "Don't forget to put on a mask."

"What about you?" he asked as he pulled the masks out of one of the bags.

"I've already been in there. I'll be fine."

He swallowed his argument and followed her upstairs. It only took a couple of minutes to have the humidifier working. It wasn't long before he could tell a difference in his mother's breathing. Though she was still asleep, her breaths were less heavy, less labored. Molly roused her enough to get her to drink some juice, but after half a glass, she went back to sleep.

"Are you sure she's going to be all right?" he asked Molly.

"She'll be fine, Richard. I think the humidifier is already helping her."

"Yes, I agree. I would never have thought of that."

"I'm glad I could help. After all, I feel I owe you and Elizabeth so much for making me feel welcome."

Richard checked himself to keep from saying what came to mind. He'd wanted to say that Molly felt like family, like she belonged. It was an amazing feeling. He hadn't felt like anyone belonged to his family in a long time. Not even his own sister.

But he didn't give voice to those private thoughts.

When they got downstairs, Toby was waiting anxiously for news of his grandmother's condition.

"Toby, your grandmother is doing just fine. The flu makes her want to sleep all the time, but she's doing better, I promise," Molly said, hugging the little boy.

"I'm glad. I don't want Grandma to be sick."

"I know you don't. Why don't we go watch one of the movies Richard bought you?"

After Toby chose *Mary Poppins*, Molly took his hand and they started for the family room.

"I'll come watch it with you," Richard said, following them.

In the family room he settled down with Toby between him and Molly.

The door opened an hour into the video, Delores and Louisa bringing in several dinner trays to them.

"What are you doing, Delores?" Molly asked, stopping the video. "We can come to the table."

"Nonsense. Stay and watch the movie. We won't do this every night, but once in a while will be fun. Right, Toby?"

"Right, Delores," Toby agreed enthusiastically.

"But you have to promise to eat all your food."

"I will. I promise."

"Thanks, Delores," Molly added. "This is nice of you."

After Delores and Louisa had withdrawn, Molly started the movie again, and they ate their soup and warm turkey melt sandwiches.

By the time the movie ended, Toby was curled up between the two adults. "Wasn't that great?" he murmured drowsily.

"Yes, sweetie, it was."

"You want to take him up to bed?" Richard suggested. "I'll take the dishes to the kitchen before I come up."

"Yes, of course. Come along, Toby. It's your bedtime."

"What about Grandma? Won't she want me to hug her good night like I always do?"

"I'm sure she'd like that, but you can't because it might make you sick. When I go in to check on her, I'll tell her that you wanted to. Will that do?"

"I guess so."

Richard grinned at Toby. "It's the best way, Toby. You don't want to be too sick to come down on Christmas morning. That would be a horrible Christmas."

"Yeah, but—but I'm worried about Grandma."

Richard smiled at the little boy. "You're a good boy, Toby. I hope Santa brings you everything you want."

"Thank you, Uncle Richard. I hope the same for you."

Richard stood there, watching Molly lead Toby out of

the den to climb the stairs to bed. Toby was such a sweet boy. Richard realized how much Toby had changed his life. Before Toby and Molly's arrival, he'd worked fifteen-hour days for the past eighteen months. He'd had little interaction with his mother. He'd had no social life.

Now he was spending time with Toby and Molly and his mother. And his life was richer for it. Even after Christmas, he wouldn't work as much as he had been. He'd need to spend time with Toby.

It saddened him to realize how much he'd miss Molly.

He bent and picked up one of the trays and hurried to the kitchen. He didn't want to think about Molly leaving. Not tonight.

Delores protested his actions. She said she and Louisa could've gotten the trays.

"I'll let one of you get the others. I want to get upstairs before Toby goes to sleep. Is that all right?"

"Of course it is. Louisa fed your mom the soup. She didn't quite finish the bowl, but she did a good job."

He thanked Louisa, then made his way upstairs.

"If you and Molly want some coffee and bread pudding, you can come back to the den and I'll bring it in," Delores offered.

"Mmm, we might take you up on that."

Richard sped up the stairs to reach Toby's room just as he was crawling into bed in flannel pajamas.

"Hey, where did you get those pajamas, Toby? I've never seen them."

"Molly bought them for me. She said I'd catch cold wearing just a T-shirt."

"That was thoughtful of her, wasn't it?"

"Yeah. I like them."

Richard got his hug from Toby and watched as Molly received the same. Then they both tiptoed from the room as the boy snuggled under the covers and dozed off.

Molly started down the hallway and Richard caught up with her. But she bypassed the stairs.

"Where are you going?"

"I want to check on your mom."

He passed on what Delores had said, but she still insisted on checking on Elizabeth.

Waiting outside the door for Molly to emerge, he was grateful that Molly was here to monitor his mother's progress.

When she came out, she seemed surprised to find him waiting for her. "Is there something you need?"

"Yes, I need you to come downstairs to have dessert."

"Dessert? Oh, no, I couldn't— What is it?"

"It's Delores's bread pudding, and she makes the best I've ever tasted." He held his hand out to her. "Shall we?"

"I guess so, but it's not good for me to eat dessert every night. I'll have to start working out like you do."

"You can go with me whenever you want. I usually leave around seven." In his mind's eye, he pictured Molly in workout clothes and figured there'd be a riot at the gym with all the men rushing to be next to her.

"I don't think I can while your mother is sick. Toby would be lost if he woke up all alone."

"You're probably right. You're a very thoughtful person, Molly." It felt good to compliment her.

"Thank you. I try to be."

"Did you get money from my mother to pay for the pajamas, by the way?"

"No, I didn't."

Why was she so stubborn about this? He wondered. "Why not? You know, we're supposed to be responsible for Toby now."

"*I* decided to get him the pajamas. It wasn't something he had to have."

"I think it was. From now on, you need to get money from us if you buy Toby something."

Molly, he noticed, stiffened. "What I choose to spend my money on is my business."

Why was she getting upset? He was only looking out for her. "Toby *is* my business and you'll spoil him if you keep on buying him things."

That comment ignited her anger and her eyes sparked as she spat out, "I don't think flannel pajamas will spoil him!"

"Maybe not, but there's no reason for you to pay for them!"

"I think you—"

But Molly never got to finish her thought. Delores came to the hallway and yelled, "What's going on out here?"

CHAPTER TEN

MOLLY FELT like a kid caught with her hand in the proverbial cookie jar. She ducked her head. "Nothing, Delores."

Richard covered up, too. "We were just coming down for the bread pudding."

"Well, come on into the breakfast room. Albert and I thought we'd share it with you, if you don't mind."

"Of course not," Molly immediately said.

Richard kept silent and Molly thought he looked a little irritated, but that was probably because of their argument.

Albert brought in four bowls of bread pudding, while Delores carried a pot of decaf coffee and cups.

"May I get some milk for my coffee, Delores?" Molly asked as she stood.

"Of course. I didn't know you drank milk in your coffee."

"I especially like it late at night."

She felt Richard watching her as she added milk to her coffee. "I'd say she takes coffee in her milk," he commented dryly.

"I can always contribute to the groceries if you want, Richard," she returned coolly.

Delores stared at the two of them. "What is the matter with you two?"

"Sounds like an argument to me," Albert said, keeping his head down and eating his bread pudding.

Richard raked a hand through his hair. "I'm not arguing with Molly, really. But she's been spending her money on Toby's necessities and I think we should be paying the bill. She bought him pajamas."

"Why didn't you ask Richard for the money?" Delores asked her.

"Because I didn't think of it. I've had a lot to deal with."

Delores reached out and patted her hand. "That's true, dear." Then she turned to Richard. "Molly is in a strange city, living with strangers and yet she still manages to know that Toby will need pajamas."

Before Richard could respond, Molly explained, "It's my job to focus on Toby."

"And it's my job to pay for him," Richard retorted sharply. Then he drew a deep breath and let it out, speaking more calmly he said, "That's what I was trying to say earlier, Molly. You see, I've put all the money his parents left him into a trust fund for him. But I expect to pay for the day-to-day things. Not you."

Richard was right.

She hated to admit it, but seeing to the boy's financial needs was a guardian's job, not the nurse's. Why couldn't she see that earlier? Perhaps because she'd come to view Toby as more than a job. She'd come to love the boy.

She saw so much of herself in him, and as such, she wanted to tend to his every need, physical and emotional, the way she'd desperately hoped someone had done for her.

But that was up to Richard now. And Elizabeth.

"I understand, Richard. It won't happen again." She didn't even glance his way, lest he see the anguish in her eyes. Instead, she abruptly changed the subject. "This bread pudding is really good, Delores. What are the chances of prying this recipe out of you too?"

Delores smiled. "When you've got your bags packed and are walking out the door, I'll give you whatever recipes you want, young lady. And not a moment before!"

"You sound like you don't think I'm leaving," Molly said. "I'm due back at the hospital by the fifteenth of January."

"Are you anxious to go back?" Albert asked.

"Yes, and no. I've enjoyed myself here, Albert, getting to do things that I don't do at home. But I love my work."

"I'm just worried because Toby acts like you're his mom. And he's already lost one mom," Albert said with a sigh.

Molly felt like someone had ripped the chair from under her. Is that what Toby thought? Had she been so blinded by her own needs that she couldn't see it? Tears stung her eyes and she fought to keep them back.

Delores elbowed Albert in his side. "He'll be just fine. Don't you worry."

Richard added, "You've always told him that you were going back to Florida. It won't come as a surprise, Molly."

Their words offered her little comfort. Afraid she'd cry in front of everyone, she stood. "I didn't mean to make things worse for Toby. I should never have come here with him." She turned to bolt from the room.

Richard grabbed her arm and stopped her. "No, Molly." He stood up and took her by her shoulders, looking her in the eyes. "You've been wonderful for Toby. Don't you think otherwise." He pulled a handkerchief out of his pocket and wiped the tears from her eyes.

"Toby wouldn't have made it this far as well as he has without you. He still depends on you to help him. But once we get him enrolled in school and he starts making friends, he'll find it easier to tell you goodbye."

Molly looked up at him, her eyes stinging with tears. "Are you sure? I can leave right now if you prefer."

"Absolutely not! Toby would think I drove you away and he'd never forgive me."

"I could wait until morning and explain that I had to go back to the hospital. He'd understand that and he wouldn't blame you, Richard."

"You're staying until mid-January and I don't intend to discuss you leaving early ever again," Richard said emphatically.

He escorted Molly back to her chair. "Now finish your bread pudding before you hurt Delores's feelings."

Though she took a forkful, she couldn't help but search her mind for a way to fix the mistake she'd made.

After a few minutes of idle chitchat, Delores and Albert stood up to say good-night.

"I'm sorry for what I said, Molly," Albert told her. "I couldn't have been more wrong."

Molly smiled at him. "You didn't say anything I shouldn't have realized on my own. Don't worry about it. Good night, Albert."

When the couple left, Richard questioned her. "Do you really think Albert will believe you when your eyes look so sad?"

Molly snapped her head up. "I'm not— My eyes don't look sad!"

"Yes, they do. You can't hide your emotions very well, Molly. Everyone in the house knows how you feel. And they've all fallen in love with your bright smile and warm heart. You're going to have to make a big effort to convince Mom and Toby that you're happy here."

"I am happy here, but I don't want to do irreparable harm to Toby. He's suffered so much already."

"You won't. You've given him a new life and helped him adjust and that's what you need to do when he goes to school, too. He'll want to come home and tell you all about his day."

"Your mother will be here to talk to him."

"Yes, but she's not you. Now, come on up to bed and stop worrying about the future." He led her to the door and then paused.

"Yes? Did you think of something I should do?"

He looked up and then down at her. She automatically looked up and discovered what she'd forgotten.

Mistletoe over the door.

Before she could move away, Richard kissed her.

It wasn't the friendly peck she thought was supposed to happen if you stood under the mistletoe. No, his kiss was skillful and deep and…unlike any kiss she'd ever received.

When he finally raised his head, his gaze fastened on her, she tried to protest, but it didn't come out strong, as she'd intended. "Richard, you—you shouldn't have—"

He took her mouth again, cutting off her protest.

Which was just as well. Truthfully she wanted him to kiss her. Craved his kiss, actually, for a few days now. And she wasn't disappointed.

Richard made her body come alive, and she felt a tingling, a heat, from her head to her toes. No man had ever done that with just a kiss.

Now he looked at her, deeply, staring down into her eyes, his own blue ones smoldering with desire. She recognized the feeling; she felt it, too.

Dangerous, said an inner voice.

Richard was her employer, Toby's guardian, a benefactor to the hospital. She'd best control her desires and remember why she was here.

But his arms were like iron around her, his aftershave like a love potion, drawing her in…

Richard broke the spell he was weaving around her. "We'd better move out of the doorway before I get carried away," he said with a grin, as if his kiss had been a simple Christmas tradition.

As if released from a trance, Molly stammered, "G-good night, Richard." Then she turned and ran up the stairs as if a bogeyman was after her.

But no bogeyman kissed like Richard Anderson.

Molly drew back the curtains, inviting the glorious morning sunshine into the room. Then she woke up her patient. "Good morning, Elizabeth. How are you feeling this morning?"

"Better," Elizabeth said in a small voice.

"I brought up your breakfast. How about sitting on your chair to eat?" Molly put her tray on the coffee table in front of a stone fireplace. Then she built a fire, which seemed to warm the room as much with its orange flame as it did with its heat.

"Delores made you eggs and the apple-walnut muffins you like."

"I do like them," Elizabeth concurred. "Have you tasted them? I'll make you a deal. You try this one and I'll eat the other one." She gave Molly a sly look that made her laugh.

"Good try, Elizabeth." But she took the muffin anyway. Anything to get Elizabeth to eat and regain her strength.

Later when Molly got to the kitchen, she found Richard and Toby eating their breakfasts. Just seeing Richard again stopped her in her tracks. His hair was damp and dark from the shower, and his jaw had a sheen from a clean shave. Memories of their kisses last night assailed her, and she wanted to turn and run again.

As if he read her mind, Richard called out to her. "Come sit down, Molly. We need to get organized for our shopping trip."

Reluctantly Molly joined them at the table.

"I figured Toby and I would shop together first," she said, trying not to make eye contact with him. "After lunch you could take Toby for maybe half an hour. Then we'd be through."

"I don't think so," Richard returned emphatically.

Now she had to look at him. "Why not?"

"I'm going to need several hours with Toby, at least. We've got plans."

Molly's gaze narrowed as Toby and Richard smiled at each other. "I think maybe you've been plotting while I was upstairs."

"Of course. I figured we'd each get two hours with Toby. If we leave here at ten, we'll be at the mall by ten-fifteen. So I'll take him first, since I know the mall, and you can look around. Then we'll meet at twelve-fifteen or twelve-thirty, and have lunch. Then you get him from one to three."

"I'm not sure he'll last that long. He's used to taking a nap, you know," Molly said, smiling at Toby.

"I usually just read a book, Molly. I don't really sleep."

"Fine. But if you get tired, don't blame me!" Molly said.

"Are you mad at me?" Toby asked in concern.

She was mad—but not at Toby. She was mad that she'd have to spend the whole day with Richard. But she couldn't take it out on the boy. "Of course not, Toby. It'll be fun."

"Oh, I promised my mother Toby would visit her this morning, and I need a word with her, too. When should we do that?"

Molly looked at her watch. It was a little after eight now. "Not before nine-thirty, or nine forty-five. Louisa is going to check on her at ten."

"That will be great. Any questions?" Richard asked.

"No, but—your mother gave me this," Molly said, pulling out the envelope. "She said to use it to buy some things for her. I'm a little concerned about carrying around this much cash."

Richard took it from her and opened the envelope. "She asked you to buy some things for her?"

"Yes."

"I can offer to get them for her."

"No, you can't," Molly said, staring at him.

He looked at her until the reason dawned on him. Then he smiled and handed back the envelope. "I see. Well, that will be fine."

Molly shook her head, but she stuffed the envelope back in her jeans pocket.

"I'm going to do some work in my office until nine-thirty. Toby, do you have something you can do? Is there anything on television?"

"I'll go read one of my books. That's more fun."

"I think that's a wise decision. I'll come up and get you when we go to visit Grandma."

"Okay. May I be excused?" he asked.

Molly nodded to him. After all, he'd eaten his breakfast.

It didn't occur to her that she would be alone with Richard again until after Toby ran out the door. Impulsively she stood to take the dishes into the kitchen, hoping Richard would go to his office while she was gone.

When she came back into the breakfast room, he was still sitting there.

"Did you want something else, Richard?"

"No, I'm just moving slowly this morning."

She figured if she moved fast, she could get out of the breakfast room before he realized she was going.

"Well, I won't bother you, then," she said breezily as she rushed past him.

Suddenly, for someone who was moving slowly, he was beside her and caught her in his arms. Then he looked up. "Mistletoe, you know."

And he kissed her again.

CHAPTER ELEVEN

MOLLY couldn't get the kiss out of her mind.

She did the necessary shopping for Elizabeth, buying three gifts for Toby from Santa and the Blackberry for Richard. She had money left over, but she put it in her purse with the receipts from her purchases.

But every moment between purchases, she thought of the kisses Richard had been giving her. She supposed it could be the Christmas spirit filling him, but she didn't think so. She feared he thought she should entertain him at night by giving in to his advances.

Well, he had another thought coming. She certainly wasn't that kind of woman. She was there for Toby, and at the moment, Elizabeth. Not for him to toy with!

Not that she wouldn't want to. Truth be told, she found Richard very attractive. And since she'd been in Dallas, he'd mellowed a lot from the aloof, arrogant man she'd first met in Florida. He was seeming to adapt well to Toby's presence, making every effort to carve a place in his life for the boy. But for her to get involved with Richard would be a mistake. After all, any relationship with him had a definite end point. Mid-January, when she returned to the hospital.

No, she'd just have to control her urges when it came to Richard.

When she met the two males at the appointed place for lunch, she discovered they had made a lot of purchases. "Did you find something for Albert and Delores, and Louisa, too?" she asked.

"Yes, Uncle Richard helped me. And he said to give you back your money."

Richard rolled his eyes. "I told him to do that after we got home. He forgot that part."

"But, Toby, you needed money to buy all the gifts."

"I used Uncle Richard's money. He said it wasn't fair to use yours."

"I see," she said slowly, as Toby put five twenty-dollar bills in her hand. Richard probably couldn't have done anything to make her feel less a part of Toby's family than that. She fought back tears of loneliness. For a little while, she and Toby had been a family. It had been a great feeling.

But now it was gone.

"Molly, is anything wrong?" Richard asked, leaning closer to stare at her face.

"No, absolutely nothing. Let's eat."

Richard had suggested they eat in Neiman Marcus's tearoom. Molly stepped forward and a maître d' led them to a table for four. Once they were seated, Toby needed help with the menu. Molly started to help, but Richard beat her to it. She sat back, realizing Toby turning to Richard was a good thing, she guessed. It would make her departure easier on Toby.

And harder on her.

Richard was already pushing her away so Toby wouldn't be distraught when she left.

When the waitress came to take their orders, Molly asked for a separate check. Richard stared at her. Then he told the waitress to put all three of their lunches on one ticket and bring it to him.

The waitress agreed and Molly sat there in frustration until the woman had walked away. "You've made it clear that I'm not to pay for Toby, but I see no reason not to pay for myself."

"Because you're working for me. I pay for those who work for me."

"I see. So I'm like Delores and Albert? You pay when they go out to eat?"

"I do if they go with me. Don't be difficult, Molly. We want to enjoy our lunch, don't we Toby?"

Molly realized Toby was watching her with a worried frown. "Yes, of course, we do. What did you buy, Toby?"

"I can't tell you!" Toby said.

"Not even what you bought Delores and Albert?"

"Oh, those. Yeah, I got Delores a big bottle of cream of some kind that Uncle Richard said he thought she'd like."

"Oh, that's good. And what did you get Albert?"

"A box of cigars. Uncle Richard said smoking is bad, but Albert likes them and he only smokes them in his apartment."

"I see."

As if he were concerned about what she thought, Richard added, "Toby and I had a long talk about smoking, Molly. I'm sure he understands that he should never do it."

Their food arrived, and all three started to eat.

"What are you and Toby going to shop for after lunch?" Richard asked.

"Oh, odds and ends. I'm not sure since you've taken care of most of the gifts I intended to help him with."

Richard suddenly looked stunned. "I didn't mean to leave you out, Molly. I just wanted to be sure to pay for Toby's shopping. I can give you money if—"

"No, thank you. I have my own money."

That stopped all conversation. They ate in silence until they were finished.

"Did you like your lunch, Toby?"

"Yeah, but this is kind of a fancy place, isn't it?"

Molly smiled. "I doubt that your uncle would've chosen it if I hadn't come with you. This is a tearoom and usually just women come here to eat."

"Oh. I understand." He turned to Richard. "It's like when we went to the movie that Molly and Grandma liked."

Richard smiled. "That's right, Toby."

"Hey, Molly, did you see Santa Claus? I got my picture taken with him. Wanna see it?"

So Richard couldn't have waited for her to see Toby with Santa? Almost of their own will, her eyes sought his and she glared at him, at the same time she said sweetly to Toby, "Of course I do, Toby. Was it fun?"

"Yeah. I learned the truth about Santa last year in school, but I still like to pretend."

"I understand." She took the picture Toby handed her. "Oh, I like this picture. I'm so glad your uncle Richard had this taken. We'll need to get a frame for it."

"We got one already. I need to put it in there before it gets all bent."

"Yes. Maybe your uncle Richard will help you," Molly said pointedly and then felt ashamed of herself.

"No, I saved that job for you, Molly. I'm not very good at that." Richard smiled at her.

"I see. Of course I'll help you, Toby. Where's the frame?"

Toby bent over and pulled a nice frame out of his bag. Molly had the picture in place in a couple of minutes. Then she held it up for Toby and Richard to see. "How does it look?"

"Perfect," Richard said. "You want to go get your picture taken on Santa's knee?"

Molly was surprised by a wave of sadness. "No, it's only for children."

Her sadness must have shown on her face, because Richard asked, "Molly, are you all right?"

She nodded and lowered her gaze. "It's just…well, foster children didn't get to go to the mall and see Santa."

"Why not?" Toby asked.

"Because we knew he wasn't going to bring us what we asked for. We usually got a new pair of socks and a little doll for the girls and a truck or car for the boys."

"That's all?" Toby asked in horror.

"Toby, let's not talk about sad things," Richard said. "We want this Christmas to be a happy one for Molly, don't we?"

"Yes, we do. And we bought you some presents, Molly!" Then Toby clapped his hands over his mouth. "But I can't tell you."

Richard laughed. "Remind me not to tell you any more secrets, Toby, my boy!"

"Sorry, Uncle Richard. But I didn't tell her what they are."

"That's true. Okay, I'll forgive you."

"Phew, I'm glad."

"It's time for our shopping to begin, Toby," Molly said. "Are you ready to go?"

"I'm carrying some things to the car," Richard said before they could move. "Want me to take your bags, too, Molly? I'll promise not to peek in them."

"Are you sure?" Molly asked, trying to smile.

"I cross my heart, honey. No peeking."

"Okay," she agreed, wanting to leave him as soon as she could. He may not peek into the bags but he'd already pried into her heart. And she wanted to keep her feelings hidden.

After Richard took their packages, Molly and Toby went shopping. Toby wanted to get his uncle what Molly had chosen for Albert, a pocketknife. Molly steered him into a smaller version, more gentlemanly, that wouldn't be a bulge in Richard's expensive suits.

Molly had already bought Richard a mystery novel she hoped he'd make time to read now. She also bought him a DVD of a mystery movie she'd seen last year and liked.

By the time they met Richard, they had quite a few packages. She asked if they could stop at a store so she could buy wrapping paper and ribbon to make bows.

"You didn't have yours gift-wrapped?" Richard asked in surprise.

"I usually do the wrapping myself."

"I see. Of course. There's a store right over here that carries wrapping stuff."

"I won't be a moment if you and Toby want to wait in the car."

After Molly rushed into the store, Richard said, "You didn't tell her what we bought for her, did you?"

"No, I promise, Uncle Richard."

Molly came back to the car with a big package. "Do you have enough patience for me to get one more thing?"

"Sure," Richard said. "Where do you want to go?"

"It's right here. I'll hurry."

Richard saw that she was watching Toby. He turned to the little boy. "While Molly is doing more shopping, why don't you lie down in the back seat and rest. It's been a long day, hasn't it."

Toby seemed willing to rest a little. Molly nodded at Richard and hurried into another store. When she came out she had a large package in a plastic bag. She opened the back of the vehicle and stuck it in.

As she got in the truck, she saw Toby asleep on the back seat.

"Oh, good," she said with a sigh.

"You'd better hope he doesn't wake up. Once he smells that last purchase, it'll be hard to keep him away from it."

Molly nodded. "I know. I'm ready to eat it all now."

"We'll have plenty to eat on Christmas Day. Why did you buy that?"

"I always buy a small bag of caramel corn, but this year I'm sharing the holiday with all of you, so I thought I should get enough for all of us." She remembered caramel corn being a part of Christmas when she was a child; her parents always had some in her stocking on Christmas morning.

"I'm going to hide it until Christmas Eve after Toby has gone to bed."

"You'd better hope he can't smell it."

"I know."

When they got home, Richard carried Toby up to his room. The little boy didn't even wake up.

Then he came back down to help carry up the packages. Molly had sorted out her packages and left his alone.

"I didn't want to be accused of peeking," she said.

"Wouldn't matter because all mine are already wrapped."

"And you certainly have a lot."

"Yes, I'm a real Santa Claus," he said with a grin. It reminded Molly of how he looked just before he kissed her. She backed away.

"Well, I'll take my packages to my room so I can wrap them."

"Okay, I'll put mine under the tree."

Molly went up the stairs, forcing herself not to run to the garden room where the tree stood. She loved the idea of a big tree with lots of beautiful presents under it. But she'd sneak a peek later this evening. Alone.

The rest of the week sped by. One day they baked sugar cookies and decorated them with colored icing. To Molly's surprise, Richard joined them in the kitchen and then the breakfast room where they sat down to do the decorating.

They had a lot of fun. Richard teased Toby about his artistic efforts, but Molly teased Richard, telling him Toby was better at decorating than he was. They both agreed that Molly was better than either of them, and she assured them it was because she'd had lots of practice.

"You got to decorate cookies when you were a foster child?" Toby asked.

"No, but I usually bake cookies and decorate them to give to friends and people in the hospital."

"That's really nice, Molly," Richard said.

"Should we give some of our cookies to people in the hospital?" Toby asked.

"We could, Toby. But I'm not sure we'll have enough. Maybe we could just take cookies to the children's ward of a nearby hospital."

"That would be Presbyterian. I'll call and see how many kids they have in the hospital over Christmas. I bet it's not too many."

Richard checked and said they only had fourteen children who would be there a few days.

So the next morning, they took bags of cookies, some extra for the nurses on duty, and passed them out to the children in the hospital. Toby met and visited with another boy his age.

When they left the hospital, Toby hugged Richard and told him how lucky he was to have his uncle and grandmother.

Elizabeth was doing much better, getting a little stronger each day. But when they planned their horse and buggy ride to see the Christmas lights, she decided to pass.

It wasn't a terribly cold night, but the blanket the driver covered them with was welcome. Molly insisted Toby sit between her and Richard, so he wouldn't fall out. Both males looked at her like she was crazy, but she held her position. Mainly because she didn't want to sit next to Richard. She was afraid the evening would be too romantic, and she might succumb to the idea of snuggling up next to Richard.

Many of the residents of Highland Park had great light displays and the buggy moved slowly past them, giving Toby plenty of time to examine each one and pick his favorite. On the way home, he asked Richard about having a light display of their own next year.

Molly told herself she was pleased that Toby could think of the future without pain. He had made remarkable strides in the two weeks he'd been in Dallas. But she wouldn't be there next year to see their lights. And that made her sad.

"What do you think, Molly?"

"About what?" she asked in surprise.

"See, Toby, she wasn't listening. We were talking about the lights we should have next year. Do you have an opinion?"

"I can't decide whether I like the multicolored ones or the white lights. What do you think, Toby?"

"I like all the colored lights. But the white lights that had deer grazing on their lawns did look nice."

"Well, maybe we will try some lights next year. I'll have to contact one of the lighting companies that does the displays in March or April and let them bring some suggestions for us to choose from."

"You mean they don't do the lights themselves?" Toby asked, disappointment in his voice.

"I think it might take too long on a house as big as yours, Toby," Molly explained.

"Yeah, or the dad might fall and break his neck," Richard said. "I haven't forgotten who had to climb up so high just to put the angel on the Christmas tree!"

"But you did a great job," Toby said with a grin.

Once they got home, Toby rushed upstairs to tell Elizabeth all about what they'd seen. Which left Molly alone with Richard.

"Thank you, Richard. That was fun."

"Yes, it was, wasn't it? But I would've had more fun if you'd let Toby sit on the side and you sat next to me."

"I don't see that that would've made a difference."

"I could've cuddled with you under the blanket. Toby was so busy jumping up to see everything, he kept letting in the cold air."

"You survived."

"I did, but I would've had more fun the other way." He winked at her.

"Richard, you shouldn't—"

He pulled her against him and kissed her again. She'd told herself she'd hate it if he kissed her again, but she'd known she was lying. When his warm lips touched hers, she melted in his embrace and her arms reached up around his neck.

When he finally pulled away, she drew a deep breath. "I don't think we should do that anymore. There's no mistletoe here and your mother would be very upset if she saw us kissing."

"Do you think so?"

"Yes, of course. And Delores could've walked in on us at any time!"

"And you think she'd be upset, too?" He was smiling, with a glint in his eyes that worried her.

"I—I have to go upstairs," she said and hurried away.

Richard watched Molly's trim figure run up the stairs… away from him.

He thought she liked his kisses, because she didn't pull away. He hoped she liked them. As each day passed, he was realizing he needed Molly in his life. The past eighteen months had been horrible. At lot of the time he'd put in at the law firm had been necessary, but he was coming to realize that some of it had been because life had changed and he didn't know how to deal with it.

With Molly in his life, he didn't need to hide anymore.

She brought joy to his days. He loved having breakfast with her each morning, and all the Christmas activities were more fun with her along.

Of course, Toby was part of the fun, too.

He'd often thought he would one day marry and have children, but somehow that kept getting pushed back to some distant time in the future. Now he had Toby, a son, to raise. And, for a while, he had Molly.

He already had put some plans in place to try to convince Molly to stay. But he wasn't sure what her reaction would be. With a hopeful heart, he tried not to think she would turn him down.

When his mother started coming down for dinner again, they moved back to the dining room for that meal. Toby, no longer shy, talked a blue streak, telling Elizabeth about the things they'd done while she was ill. He talked a lot about their trip to the hospital.

"I think that was a wonderful thing you did, Molly, suggesting you take some cookies to the hospital."

"Thank you, Elizabeth, but it was Richard who checked with the hospital and got an okay for us doing that."

"Then, Richard, you deserve some praise, too. I think that it's time I go back to doing my charity work. And we should plan to make it a Christmas tradition to bring cookies to the hospital."

"I agree, Mom," Richard said. "By the way, have you eaten any of the cookies we made?"

"No, I haven't even seen them. Does Delores have them in the kitchen?"

"Yes, she's going to serve them for dessert tonight," Richard said. It was Saturday night before Christmas on

Monday. "She wanted you to have some now that you're not sick."

"Oh, that's a delightful idea. You must've made a lot of cookies," Elizabeth said.

"It took us two days to decorate all of them."

"Yeah, I pooped out, Grandma. I just watched them while I ate a couple of cookies," Toby said with a grin. "Uncle Richard said I was being lazy, but I told him I'd lost my artistic drive," Toby said in precise words, grinning at his uncle.

"What a con artist you are, Toby! You just decided you wanted to eat the cookies more than you wanted to decorate them," Richard retorted.

"I put the little silver balls on the stars you decorated!" Toby said. "That was decorating, too, wasn't it, Molly?

"Yes, sweetheart, it was. And there were a lot of cookies to decorate."

Delores, who entered the room in the middle of the discussion, carrying a plate of decorated cookies, said, "And maybe you would've been as inspired if you'd had a girl to kiss under the mistletoe like your uncle did."

Since Molly and Richard both turned red in the cheeks, no one had to ask who was doing the kissing.

CHAPTER TWELVE

"DOES that mean you're going to stay, Molly?" Toby asked, his eyes wide with contained excitement.

She shook her head. But before she could say anything, Richard spoke up. "I'll explain later, Toby." She wanted to hear his explanation. Exactly why was Richard kissing her under the mistletoe? Was it only because of tradition…or did he actually have feelings for her?

After dinner Richard took Toby aside for a man-to-man talk, none of which she could hear without being obvious. He must have explained himself well, though, because Toby didn't ask any more questions all night. Nor did Elizabeth, who was strangely quiet.

Even on Sunday, Christmas Eve, at services, Elizabeth didn't maneuver them together in the pew. They ended up together naturally.

"I love to go to church at Christmas time," Molly said as they were seated in a restaurant for lunch after services. "All the carols. Your church has a talented choir, Elizabeth."

"Yes, we do. And the decorations are beautiful. Especially the manger scene." Elizabeth referred to the living nativity, complete with real animals.

From the back seat Toby chimed in. "I liked the donkey. He kept eating all the hay."

"I'm sure they'll get more," Richard said. "I think you liked him because he looked like a big dog."

"Yeah," Toby admitted, grinning. "But my Sunday School teacher told us a story about a dog that was neat."

"I enjoyed Sunday School this morning, too," Richard said, his gaze on Molly. They had both gone to the Singles class together.

"What did you think, Molly?" Elizabeth asked.

Before she could answer, Richard said, "She thought she was surrounded by hungry dogs!"

"You had dogs in your class?" Toby asked with envy.

"No, sweetie," Molly hurriedly assured him. "Richard was referring to some gentlemen in the class who were…very welcoming."

"Yes," Richard said. "They all wanted to ask Molly out."

Toby looked shocked. Fortunately their meals, that they'd previously ordered, appeared at the table and gained the boy's attention.

Molly, however, noted Elizabeth's amused look.

In truth, Molly had been glad Richard had taken such proprietary interest in her. She was a little too shy for such determined interest as the men had shown. It would make her reluctant to attend that class again without Richard.

They met in the family room later on and watched the DVD of *It's a Wonderful Life*, having talked about the movie over lunch. They'd promised Toby they'd show him the holiday classic. He delighted when Clarence got his wings and declared his parents had become angels, too.

After dinner, they all went into the garden room and Richard turned on the Christmas lights. In the darkness they glowed softly, creating an atmosphere of magic.

Toby sighed. "Isn't it wonderful?"

"The lights, you mean, and the tree?" Molly asked. After he nodded his head, she said, "Yes, more beautiful than any I've ever seen, Toby."

"I think so, too," Toby agreed.

Richard and Elizabeth agreed, Elizabeth pointing out that Toby had chosen all the ornaments, so he should take pride in the tree.

Finally Molly told Toby it was time to go to bed, so Santa could come visit their house. He agreed and gave his normal hugs to Richard and Elizabeth.

Upstairs, he got in his flannel pajamas and knelt down by his bed to say his prayers, as he'd done every night in Dallas. Molly sat on the edge of his bed, waiting. But when he said nothing, Molly looked down at Toby. "Is something wrong, sweetheart?"

Toby lowered his head for a moment. Then he said, "Molly, do you think Mommy and Daddy will be upset that I'm happy?"

Molly's throat tightened for a moment and she fought the tears that filled her eyes. Then she reached down and lifted Toby into her lap. "No, baby, I think they'll be happy that you're happy. That's what they want. That's what every mommy and daddy want for their children."

"I've been worrying about that. I love living here with Uncle Richard and Grandma, and you, too. But I wish my mommy and daddy were here with us."

"Of course you do. They know you haven't forgotten

them, Toby. I told you they were in your heart. That means they know what you're thinking and feeling. It's okay to be happy."

Toby hugged her tightly. "Thank you. I knew you would know."

He kissed her on the cheek and then climbed into bed. "I love you, Molly."

"I love you, too, Toby."

She tucked him into bed and tiptoed out of his room. As she got to the stairway, on her way down to see if the coast was clear for her to take down her gifts, she ran into Elizabeth on her way up.

"Are you going to bed now?" Molly asked.

"Yes. We'll be getting up early in the morning. Richard said to tell you no one is to come downstairs until seven. I think he told Toby he should wake you up before he comes down.

"Yes, he did. I'll keep Toby up here until seven. Then we'll all go down together?"

"Yes, so we can all see Toby's reaction."

"Fine. Well, I hope you get a good night's sleep."

"I will. And you, too." Elizabeth smiled and then continued to her bedroom.

When Molly got downstairs, she didn't find Richard anywhere. She went to the kitchen to ask where he was.

"He said he had to run an errand," Delores said. "Albert and I were about to have a cup of decaf. Want to join us?"

"Yes, please, and thank you for asking. Are we having Christmas cookies, too?"

"I was afraid everyone would be tired of them."

"How could we be? It's like pure sugar," Molly said with a laugh.

They were enjoying their snack, chatting about their day, when they heard the side door open.

"Is that Richard?" Molly asked.

"I'll go check," Albert said, jumping up and running out of the room before anyone could call out.

Molly sat there for a minute before she asked Delores, "Did that seem odd to you?"

"Yes, it did. I wonder what those two are up to."

Only a minute later, Richard stuck his head in the door. "I'm going on up to bed. We've got to get up early in the morning. Good night."

Only after Richard had left the room did Albert reappear.

"Is everything okay?" Delores asked him.

"Uh, yeah, fine."

Shortly afterward, Molly went up to gather her gifts and take them downstairs in a big shopping bag. By the time she'd added them, the pile under the Christmas tree was ridiculously huge. But she stood there, staring at the big tree and all the presents, wanting to remember this very special Christmas. Would she ever have another one like it?

Richard was up long before seven o'clock. His roommate had insisted on getting out of bed at five-thirty. Of course, he should've been grateful, since the puppy promptly relieved himself on the throw rug by his bed.

"Thanks, you rotten little puppy. I'll be glad when you have a name, so I can chew you out properly."

Of course, he was already attached to the animal. He'd intended for it to sleep in a box in the corner of his room, but an hour of listening to the puppy's cries was enough to convince him to take the dog into his bed.

That warm little body curled up against his chest was unbelievably comforting. He had in mind a different bed partner in the future, but the puppy would do for now.

He talked the dog into another hour in bed before he got up and went downstairs, the puppy carried in his arms. He had a box prepared, wrapped in Christmas paper with holes poked through the cardboard and wrapping paper so the puppy could breathe, but he didn't want to put the dog in it until the last minute.

In the meantime, he wrote a letter from Santa to Toby and attached it to the bag of dog food sitting right in front of the tree, where it wouldn't be missed.

When he heard some stirring around upstairs, he hurriedly put the puppy in the box, placed the lid on it and moved to the foot of the staircase.

There was Molly, her reddish curls tumbling about her shoulders, dressed in jeans and a sweater, holding Toby's hand. He'd gotten dressed, too. Elizabeth was wearing a robe, looking comfortable and warm.

"I came down to turn on the Christmas lights," Richard called up the stairs. "Are you ready to see if Santa came to see us?"

Toby didn't wait until he finished. He was downstairs before the other two even started down.

"Steady, there, Toby. We have to wait for the ladies, you know."

"But you saw the tree. Did Santa come?"

"You know, I think he did, but I just glanced at the tree. I didn't want to spoil the surprise."

When the ladies reached them, Toby again took Molly's hand. Richard escorted his mother in first, followed by Molly and Toby. Elizabeth sat down in a chair, clearing Toby's sight to the tree. The first thing he saw was the letter from Santa to him.

"Santa left me a letter?" he asked. He pulled it from the sack it was attached to, not noticing what the sack was. Molly did notice, and Richard watched as her eyes widened.

Toby read the note. "I think Santa got me confused with another Toby. He thinks I have a dog."

Just then, they all heard squeaking.

Richard, to hurry the discovery along, because the suspense was killing him, said, "I think that box is making noises. Maybe you'd better open it quickly, Toby."

Toby looked at his uncle and then at Molly. Slowly he fell to his knees and reached out to take off the lid, his fingers shaking. The minute the lid came off, the excited puppy came up on his hind legs, trying to climb out of the box, his tail wagging frantically.

"Molly, look! It's a puppy! It's really a puppy!"

Richard saw the tears in Toby's eyes as he picked up the dog and hugged it to him. When Richard looked at Molly, he saw tears streaming down her face, too.

"Can I keep him, Uncle Richard? Is he really mine?"

"He really is, Toby. You get to name him and everything." While he talked, Richard moved to Molly's side and put his arms around her. He knew she was happy for Toby, but he hadn't expected it to make her cry.

She lay her head on his shoulder and he pulled a handkerchief out of his pocket to mop up her tears again.

"Molly, what can I name him?" Toby asked her.

"Whatever you like. I think he's a chocolate Lab."

"Chocolate? Oh, I know! I'll name him Cocoa, like the drink."

"That's a great name for him, Toby," Richard said. "And look, his leash is attached, so you can take him outside when you need to."

"How will I know?"

"You'll learn the signs, Toby, after you've cleaned up the messes he makes."

"Do you think he needs to go now?"

"No, I'm, uh, sure Santa took him before he left him behind."

"Oh. Uncle Richard, thank you for my puppy," Toby said, reaching up to hug Richard's neck. Richard had to bend down to his level but he straightened in a hurry, afraid Molly would move away from him.

Toby ran to his grandmother, too. "Thank you, Grandma! For a minute, I thought maybe Daddy and Mommy had told Santa. But then I remembered that Santa isn't real."

"He's real in our hearts, child," Elizabeth said.

"That's what Molly said about Mommy and Daddy, that they were in my heart."

"That's true," Elizabeth said softly, blinking rapidly.

"How about we open some presents?" Richard said. "Let me see if Albert and Delores are ready to come in." Before he left Molly, he dropped a kiss on her lips.

When Delores and Albert came in, Toby immediately showed them Cocoa. Then he asked Albert how he knew if Cocoa had to go outside. They had a brief discussion in lowered voices.

Richard picked up a package for Albert and asked Toby to carry it to him. Toby had to put his puppy in Molly's lap to do so. Then he carried a package to his grandmother. Molly played with the puppy, loving its silky warmth. In a minute, Richard bent down to her on the sofa and whispered, "Do I need to get you a puppy, too?"

"Oh, no! I mean, he's sweet, but I have to work and he'd be lonesome."

"A bike!" Toby suddenly shouted.

The tree had hidden the bike on the far side.

"Is it for me?" he asked hesitantly, as if afraid to hope.

"I don't know. It looks a little small for me, but it could be for Molly," Richard said.

Toby rolled the bike over to Molly, his face serious. "Do you think it's for you, Molly?"

"No, sweetheart. Your Uncle Richard is teasing you. The bike is for you."

"Wow! That's almost as good as Cocoa!"

"But you can only ride it in the backyard unless someone is with you, Toby. You must promise to obey that rule." Richard gave him a stern look.

"I will, I promise. In the backyard Cocoa can run along beside me!"

"True," Richard said with a smile. "I think I might as well pass out the other gifts. Toby seems too occupied with the two he's gotten so far."

Molly still held Cocoa while Toby fiddled with his bike, examining every inch of it. Elizabeth had a small gift she was opening, and Molly realized it was one she'd had made for her. She held her breath, hoping she'd made the right decision.

Suddenly Elizabeth burst into tears.

"I'm sorry, Elizabeth. I thought you'd— I can take it—"

Elizabeth clutched it to her breast. "No, I love it! I'm sorry I cried, but I wasn't prepared— It's wonderful!"

"What is it, Mom?" Richard asked, kneeling beside his mother.

Elizabeth held out a small jeweled frame with a picture of her daughter, Susan.

"That's Mommy!" Toby exclaimed.

"I know, sweetheart." She wiped the tears. "The pictures I have of her are as a little girl. Her father wouldn't let me keep any recent pictures of her."

Richard kissed his mother's cheek. Then he moved over and kissed Molly on the lips, taking her by surprise.

"That was very sweet of you, Molly."

"Thank you, but— Thank you. I, uh, borrowed Toby's small picture of him and his parents, and the photo shop was able to take her out and make a picture of just her."

"You cut up my picture?" Toby asked in horror.

"No, sweetheart, I would never do that. They can make a new picture without cutting up yours."

Richard unwrapped his book from her. "I've been wanting to read this. I've decided to slow down and enjoy life more. This will help me do that."

Albert was very proud of the pocketknife Molly had bought him. "I lost my last one and I've been planning to buy another, but I haven't. This is perfect."

Delores sighed when she opened her box of chocolates. "I can't wait to eat them," she said to Molly. "Thank you."

Toby had lots of presents, some from Molly, some marked from Santa. He received games and books, including *Charlotte's Web*. "Hey, look, Molly, now we can read a chapter every night!"

"Yes, sweetie, we can."

Then he unwrapped another gift from Molly. It was a frame with the picture of him and his parents enlarged to an 8 x 10. "Thank you, Molly!"

Molly had received some good-smelling perfume from Toby and a necklace and earrings from Elizabeth. They were beautiful cubic zirconia but glistened like real diamonds. Next Richard handed her a big box that intrigued her. She couldn't imagine anything that size.

When she opened the box, she stared at the contents, completely surprised. A bejeweled top in dark green with colored stones and gold ribbon all over it. Beneath that was a lush velvet floor-length skirt in the same dark green. She couldn't take her eyes off the outfit. It made her think of Cinderella, except that she, Molly, had no ball to attend.

She looked up to find Richard smiling at her.

"Is this from you?" she asked in surprise.

"Actually it's a second gift from Mom, but I picked it out."

"You did? It's beautiful…in fact, it's incredible. But I don't go anywhere I could wear it, Elizabeth, so maybe you should return it."

Elizabeth looked at her son. "That's your cue, Richard."

"I have to go to a New Year's Eve party, Molly. I was hoping you'd agree to go with me."

"Oh, no! I—I couldn't. I'm sure you have someone else to ask, Richard."

"No, I don't. I could find someone else, but she wouldn't be the woman of my heart, like you are."

Molly stared at him, speechless. What was he saying?

"I think you should take her to another room where you'll have some privacy, Richard," Elizabeth said, nudging her son.

Molly had no idea what was going on, and no time to figure it out. Richard tugged on her hands and she rose, handing Toby the puppy.

When they got to the family room, Richard didn't let her sit down. Instead he gathered her in his arms. "Is it a complete surprise, Molly?"

Was what a complete surprise? Molly still didn't follow. Or maybe, she realized, she was getting her Christmas wish. She looked up into Richard's blue eyes, alit by the morning sunlight streaming through the windows. Did she dare hope…?

He smiled at her then, and she knew. He loved her.

"But, Richard, I'm a nurse and I work long hours—in Florida!"

"I hope not. Not the nurse part, but definitely the Florida part. You can get a job here if you want, but not until you marry me. And then I think we should have children so Toby won't be spoiled rotten by you and Mom."

"You—you want to marry me?" Molly asked, wonder in her voice.

"I know we didn't start off too well, but once I got to know you, I haven't been able to resist you. I couldn't figure out a way to change our relationship except by kissing you. And you seemed resistant to that."

He should only know how much she'd wanted that kiss. "Not too resistant since you didn't stop."

"Oh, I haven't begun to kiss you yet, Molly Soderling soon-to-be Anderson. You will marry me, won't you?"

She yearned to say yes, but doubt still lingered in her pragmatic mind. "Are you sure we're compatible?"

He kissed her, one of those long, sweet kisses she loved. Then he whispered, "We are compatible, aren't we?"

"I—I think so. You're not just doing this because Toby wants me to stay?"

Richard chuckled. "I love Toby, but I don't think I'd ask a woman to marry me just to please him."

"Your mother likes me, too."

"That's handy, since she's going to be your mother-in-law."

"I hadn't thought of that! Oh, Richard, I'm so lucky."

"Now I'm jealous of my mother."

"Don't be. You're the one I want to spend my life with. But your mother and Toby make it even more special." Tears glistened in her eyes as she gazed at him. "I've always been alone. I was dreading leaving because I would miss everyone so much."

"And I couldn't stand the thought of you leaving, either."

"Now I'll never have to leave."

"And you'll always have wonderful Christmases."

"And most of all, I'll always have you," she said softly before she kissed him.

For the first time she surrendered to his kiss. It was the best kiss of all.

EPILOGUE

RICHARD was talking with Toby while he waited for Molly to come down. It was New Year's Eve and he was escorting Molly to the party he'd mentioned on Christmas Day.

A noise alerted him and he turned to stare up the stairs where Molly stood.

Now he knew how Cinderella's prince felt. Only he was the lucky one. His Cinderella was coming toward him, not running away.

The dress he'd picked out looked even better on her. It picked up the green in her eyes and made her hair look more auburn than brown. She looked gorgeous.

Her hair was done in a French pleat and she was wearing the necklace and earrings Elizabeth had given her for Christmas, too. She'd bought gold sandal heels and her nails had been painted a dark red. Every inch of her was perfect.

He met her at the bottom of the stairs. "You look wonderful," he whispered and kissed her.

"Don't mess up her lipstick, Richard!" Elizabeth scolded him. "I thought I had taught you better than that."

"Sorry, Mom. I'll let her apply more lipstick before we get out of the car."

"Doesn't she look splendid?"

"Absolutely," he returned and added another kiss.

"Does splendid mean pretty?" Toby asked. "'Cause I think Molly looks pretty."

"You're right, Toby," Richard said and kissed her again.

"No more compliments, Toby, or she won't have any lipstick on when they get to the party," Elizabeth warned. "Run along now, and have a good time."

Once they were in Richard's vehicle, Molly wrapped in his mother's black mink coat, she said, "I really do feel like Cinderella at the ball. Do I have to be home by midnight?"

"Probably, because that's the only way I'll be able to keep you to myself," Richard said. "By the way, I forgot to tell you on Christmas, but the jewelry my mom got you—"

"I know. I'm wearing them."

"I don't think you know this. They're real."

Molly stared at him, processing his words. "But that would mean…It's a diamond necklace! No, Richard, that can't be true!"

"It is. Mom wanted you to have your own necklace and earrings as a starter set. She's big on jewelry."

"But I can't wear real diamonds! I might lose them!"

"Don't say that or I can't give you your New Year's present."

Molly looked even more stunned. "A New Year's present? But I don't have one for you."

"Yes, you do. You just don't realize it yet."

He pulled over to the side of the road and parked.

Molly looked out the window. "Are we here already?"

"No. But I can't drive and give you your gift at the same time."

"But it's not New Year's yet."

"I want you to have this before we go into the party. Like a This Property Is Taken kind of sign."

She stared at him, having no idea what he was talking about.

Then he opened a small box he pulled from the breast pocket of his coat. "Are you sure you can't wear just one more diamond?"

She stared at the ring in the box, the size of the diamond stunning her. "It's huge! Richard—"

He kissed her several times before he allowed her to speak again. "Now, say yes."

"Yes," she said obediently. She knew what she was saying yes to and she had no hesitation.

He slid the ring on her finger. It was a perfect fit. "How did you know my size?"

"Mom guessed it when she was having you try on her rings."

"I hadn't thought of that."

"And will you wear the ring tonight?"

She smiled at him. "Of course. I don't want anyone thinking you're free."

He laughed. "Me, neither."

"Richard, when will we get married?"

"If I had a choice, it would be tomorrow."

"On New Year's Day? Aren't you supposed to be watching football all day?"

"I'd rather be marrying you, but I'm willing to wait until the first weekend in February. Mom says she thinks she can call in some favors and have it arranged by then. Will that be all right with you?"

"It sounds perfect."

"Give Mom the names of any of your friends from Florida and she'll send the invitations. Then call them and if they can come, I'll buy the plane tickets for them."

She threw her arms around his neck. "Richard, you never cease to amaze me. You are the most thoughtful man I've ever met."

"That's because I'm the luckiest man you've ever met. Getting to marry you is something I'll always be grateful for."

"I love you so much," she whispered as she got rid of the last of her lipstick in the best way possible.

At a late breakfast on New Year's Day, Molly showed her ring to Toby and Elizabeth.

"Oh, it's beautiful," Elizabeth said, a big smile on her face.

"Thank you, Elizabeth," Molly returned and kissed Elizabeth's cheek.

Toby watched them. Then Delores and Albert came in and congratulated Richard and Molly. After a couple of minutes of silence, Toby said, "Uncle Richard, how come Molly's the only one who got something for New Year's?"

"Well, it's not because it's New Year's, Toby. It's because we got engaged."

Toby sat silently for a few seconds and then his eyes grew large. "You mean you're going to marry Molly? And she'll stay with us forever and ever?"

Richard grinned. "That's exactly what I mean. Pretty cool, huh?"

"Oh, yeah!" He got up and hugged Molly's neck. "I'm so glad you're going to stay."

Molly hugged him tightly. "Me, too."

He sat back down in his chair and took a bite of his eggs and chewed them slowly. Then he looked at Richard again. "Does that mean you'll have some kids?"

"Hopefully, but we've already got one child to raise."

Toby sat there thinking about that. Suddenly he raised his head and looked at Richard. "Do you mean me?"

"Of course I do, Toby. I know you'll always love your mommy and daddy, but they can't be here, so Molly and I will be your new mommy and daddy."

"You will? And I can call you my mommy and daddy when I go to school, so I'll be like the other kids?"

"Yes, you can, Toby," Molly promised, a loving smile on her face. She hugged Toby and Richard did, too.

Toby looked at Elizabeth. "Isn't this neat, Grandma?"

"Yes, it is, Toby. We're so lucky to have a family like ours. We must never forget how lucky we are."

"No, I won't forget," Toby said soberly.

"Go get your coat, son," Richard said. "Albert and I are going to play football with you."

Joy broke across Toby's face and he ran from the room.

Richard kissed Molly goodbye and grabbed his coat, calling over his shoulder, "That was a good breakfast, Delores. Albert, are you ready?"

Toby came running to join them and the three males went to the backyard.

Molly leaned toward Elizabeth. "Life never stops, does it?"

"Thank goodness, no. It just keeps going. Just like our family."

* * * * *

CHRISTMAS GIFT: A FAMILY

BY
BARBARA HANNAY

Barbara Hannay was born in Sydney, educated in Brisbane and has spent most of her adult life living in tropical North Queensland, where she and her husband have raised four children. While she has enjoyed many happy times camping and canoeing in the bush, she also delights in an urban lifestyle – chamber music, contemporary dance, movies and dining out. An English teacher, she has always loved writing and now, by having her stories published, she is living her most cherished fantasy. Visit www.barbarahannay.com

Don't miss Barbara Hannay's exciting new novel, *Secret Outback Daughter...*, available April 2010 from Mills & Boon® Romance.

CHAPTER ONE

CHRISTMAS EVE. Oh, joy! For Jo Berry it meant sitting behind a shop counter in Bindi Creek, staring out through the dusty front window at the heat haze shimmering on the almost empty main street, and trying not to think about all the fabulous parties she was missing back in the city.

She was especially trying not to think about the office party tonight. Mind you, she had a feeling things might get out of hand. Her friend, Renee, was determined to nail a big career boost by impressing the boss but, apart from buying something clingy and skimpy to wear, her idea of pitching for a promotion usually involved clearing her desk of sharp objects.

Jo still clung to the belief that a girl could smash her way through the glass ceiling via non-stop slog and professionalism, without the aid of deep cleavage, or tying the boss up with tinsel.

Still, she would have liked to be in Brisbane tonight. She enjoyed her friends' company and it was great fun to be on the fringes of an occasional outrageous party.

It wasn't her friends' wild antics that had stopped her from partying in the city. Every Christmas she

5

took her annual leave and travelled home to help out in her family's shop.

And no, she wasn't a goody two-shoes, but honestly, what else could a girl do when she had a dad on an invalid pension and a mum who was run off her feet trying to play Santa Claus to half a dozen children while preparing Christmas dinner, *plus* running Bindi Creek's only general store during the pre-Christmas rush?

Not that anyone actually rushed in Bindi Creek.

At least…no one usually rushed.

Nothing exciting happened.

And yet…right now there was someone in a very great hurry.

From her perch on a stool behind the counter, Jo watched with interest as a black four-wheel drive scorched down the street, screeched to an abrupt and noisy halt in the middle of the road and then veered sharply to park on the wrong side of the road—directly outside the shop.

A lanky dark-haired stranger jumped out.

A very handsome, lanky dark-haired stranger.

Oh, wow!

He was quite possibly the most gorgeous man Jo had ever seen, not counting movie stars, Olympic athletes or European princes in her favourite celebrity magazines.

In spite of the layer of dust that covered his vehicle and the intense, sweltering December heat, he was dressed in city clothes—tailored camel-coloured trousers and a white business shirt, although as a concession to the heat his shirt was open at the neck and his long sleeves were rolled back to his elbows to reveal lightly tanned, muscular forearms.

Jo slid from her stool and tucked a wing of brown hair behind one ear as she stood waiting for the ping of the bell over the shop door. *Please, please come in, you gorgeous thing.*

But the newcomer lingered on the footpath, studying her mum's window display.

Jo couldn't help staring at him.

As he stood with his wide shoulders relaxed and his hands resting lightly on his lean hips, she decided there was a certain elegant charm in the way his soft dark hair had been ruffled and messed into spikes. And there was definite appeal in the very masculine way he rubbed his lightly stubbled jaw as he studied her mother's dreadful tinsel-draped arrangement of tinned plum puddings, boxes of shortbread and packets of chocolate-covered sultanas.

He lifted his gaze and peered inside the shop and, before Jo could duck, his eyes—light blue or green, she couldn't be sure—met hers. Darn, he'd caught her staring.

She felt her cheeks grow hot as he stared back. Then he smiled. But it was rather a stiff smile and she sensed instantly that he was searching for something. By the time he entered the shop her curiosity was fully aroused.

'Good afternoon,' she said warmly. He was close

enough now for her to see that his eyes were green rather than blue and fringed by the blackest of lashes. 'Can I help you?'

This time his smile was of the slightly crooked variety, the kind that should come with a health warning about dangers to women.

'I'll just look around for a moment,' he said, casting a doubtful glance at the bags of sugar and flour and the shelves of tinned food that filled the store.

As soon as he spoke Jo realised he was English. His voice was deep and rich—refined and mellow— reminding her of actors in Jane Austen movies and men who lived in stately homes surrounded by green acres of parkland and edged by forest.

'Look around as much as you like,' she said, trying to sound casual, as if divine Englishmen were a regular part of life in Bindi Creek. And then, because he wasn't a local, she added, 'Just sing out if I can be of any help.'

At times like this, when the shop wasn't busy, she usually amused herself by trying to guess what a customer might buy. What was this guy after? Engine oil? Shaving cream? *Condoms?*

From the far side of the shop he called, 'Do you have any dolls? Perhaps a baby doll?'

Good grief.

'I want the best possible gift for a little girl.' It was a command rather than a request. 'Little girls still play with dolls, don't they?'

'Some of them do. But I'm sorry, we don't have any dolls here.'

He frowned. 'You must have little tea sets? Or perhaps a music box?'

In a general store in the middle of the outback? Where did he think he was? A toy shop? 'Sorry, we don't have anything like that.'

'Nothing suitable at all?'

Think, Jo, think… She walked towards him along the aisles, checking the shelves as critically as he had. Food, household items and pet supplies, a few basic hardware products, a tiny collection of paperback novels… 'I assume you're looking for a Christmas present?'

'Yes, for a little girl. She's five years old.'

It was the same age as her little sister, Tilly. Jo shook her head. 'I'm afraid you're not going to have much luck here.'

She pointed to the old-fashioned glass jars on the counter. 'We have some fancy sweets and chocolates especially for Christmas.'

'I guess they might do.' He groaned and ran long fingers through his ruffled hair. Jo caught the glint of gold.

'I'd better get something as a fallback.' He began to pick up items at random—throw-away pens, Christmas decorations, a wooden ruler and a school notebook.

Thinking of the beautiful baby doll with a complete change of clothes that she'd bought in Brisbane for Tilly, Jo decided he definitely needed help. But given their limited stock it wasn't going to be easy.

How intriguing… What was this man doing out here in the middle of nowhere?

'How far are you travelling?' she asked.

'To Agate Downs.'

'Oh, I know that property. The Martens' place. It's not far. So you're looking for a present for the little girl they're caring for, are you?'

He looked startled. 'You know her?' He moved closer, his expression more intense.

'Ivy? This is a small town. Sure, I've met her. Do you know what she likes?'

His throat worked. 'No, I've never met her.'

'She's a lovely little thing.' Jo was being totally honest. She'd been quite smitten by the little girl. She had the most exquisite face Jo had ever seen on a child and her prettiness was all the more striking because it contrasted so strongly with the ugly scars on her arm. The poor little mite had been terribly burned in an accident a few years ago. 'Ivy's been in here to shop with Ellen Marten a couple of times this week.'

'Really?'

The eagerness in his voice and his eyes was perplexing. Jo looked at him sharply. Was she getting carried away or was there a resemblance between this man and the child? Ivy's hair was dark and her eyes were clear green like his.

What was going on? Could he be Ivy's father? Jo

didn't like to be too nosy, so she hadn't asked the
Martens about Ivy's parents, but she'd heard rumours
about a tragedy and there'd actually been talk about
an estranged father coming to claim her.

Her customer sighed and gave a little shake of his
head. 'I'd completely forgotten that a little girl at
Christmas needs a present.'

She felt a rush of sympathy. *Come on, Jo, do
something to help.*

'Would you like some of these?' she asked, lifting
the lid on a huge jar of chocolates wrapped in red,
silver and gold foil. 'Ivy's quite partial to them.' Just
yesterday she'd slipped the little girl a chocolate
when Ellen Marten wasn't looking and she'd been
rewarded by a beaming smile.

'I'll take the lot,' he said, looking exceptionally
pleased. 'And I'll have a couple of tins of the shortbread and a bag of those nuts.'

Jo lifted the metal scoop and said, 'Perhaps I could
gift wrap these things to make them look a little more
festive?'

She was rewarded by another of his dangerous
smiles. 'That would be wonderful.'

Leaning one hip against the counter, he folded his
arms across his chest and watched her as she began
to wrap his purchases in red sparkly paper. She felt
self-conscious as his green eyes watched her hands
at work, cutting and folding paper, reaching for
sticky tape and then measuring lengths of shiny silver
and gold ribbon.

If it had been any other customer she would have chattered away, but she was too absorbed by the mystery of his connection with Ivy.

He didn't seem in a hurry so she took her time making the gifts as pretty as she could, adding a sprinkle of glitter and a tiny white fluffy snowman on the chocolates.

'Thank you so much, that's terrific.' He reached into his back pocket for his wallet, extracted several notes and held them out.

She noticed the glint of gold again. He was wearing a signet ring, engraved with a crest and worn on his little finger.

'You will charge extra for all the trouble you've gone to, won't you?' he said.

'Not when it's Christmas.' She sent him a quick smile as she handed him his change.

She expected him to leave then, but he continued to stand there, looking at the bright parcels on the counter with a long distance look in his eyes, as if he were lost in thought.

'Was there something else?' she asked tentatively. She wouldn't mind at all if he wanted to stay longer. Nothing else like him was likely to happen to her this Christmas.

'If only I could take something more exciting, something Ivy would really love,' he said and he glanced behind him to the slightly dusty row of reading material and reached for a comic book. 'What about this?'

An Action Man comic? Jo did her best not to look shocked. 'I don't think Ivy's started school yet,' she suggested gently. 'I'd be surprised if she could read.'

He closed his eyes for a moment. 'It would have been so simple to pick up a toy in Sydney. There isn't time to ring a city toy shop and fly something out, is there?'

'Well…no. I shouldn't think so…' Goodness, if he was prepared to hire an aircraft, this must be important. He *must* be Ivy's father—and he must also be a man who made sure he got what he wanted. No wonder a box of chocolates seemed unsatisfactory, even with the pretty wrapping.

'There are no other shops around here?'

'No toy shops, I'm afraid. Not unless you want to backtrack about two hundred kilometres.'

With an air of resignation he began to gather up his parcels, but he moved without haste.

'You really want to make a big impression on Ivy, don't you?' Jo suggested.

He nodded. 'It's vitally important.'

There was an intensity in his voice and a sadness in his eyes that sent an unexpected tiny pain sweeping through her. How awful for him if he was Ivy's father, but had never met his daughter. And where was Ivy's mother? What tragedy had occurred? Jo's own family were very close and her soft heart ached for him.

'Well…thank you very much for all your help,' he said, turning to go.

Oh, crumbs. She felt rotten about sending him away with such inappropriate presents. 'Look,' she said to his back. 'If this present is really important, I might be able to help you.'

He turned and looked at her, his green eyes intense. Fuzzy heat flashed through her.

'I have a mountain of toys that I've bought for my brothers and sisters,' she said. 'Probably more than I'll need. If—if you'd like to take a look at them, you're welcome. We should be able to find some little toy to add to the chocolates.'

His green eyes studied her and she tried to look calm and unaffected, but then he did the crooked smile thing and her insides went crazy.

'That's incredibly kind of you.'

'I'll just call one of my brothers to come and mind the shop,' she said. 'Wait here.' And, before he could protest, she hurried away through a door at the back of the shop.

It led directly into their house.

Down the central hallway she rushed, heading straight for the backyard where she knew from the boys' shouts that they were playing cricket. And with every hasty step she fought off doubts.

She knew it was impulsive, but somehow this was something she had to do. Poor little Ivy deserved a proper Christmas present. And of course spending more time with Ivy's gorgeous father was simply a chore to be endured...

She managed to convince her brother Bill that he

was needed and then she almost ran back through the house. She was a touch breathless as she re-entered the shop.

The Englishman was still there, looking strangely out of place beside a mountain of dried dog food. He seemed to be making polite conversation with old Hilda Bligh, the town gossip.

'There you are, Jo,' said Hilda. 'I was just telling Mr Strickland that if the shop's empty we usually holler until someone comes.'

Goodness, Hilda already knew the man's name. No doubt the old girl had been treated to one of his dangerously attractive smiles.

'Sorry, Mrs Bligh, you know what Christmas Eve can be like. Here's Bill. He'll look after you.'

Jo glanced towards the Englishman, feeling rather foolish because she was about to invite him into her home and she didn't know the first thing about him. 'Can you come this way?' she asked him.

'It was very nice to meet you, Mr Strickland,' called Hilda Bligh, smiling after him coyly.

Jo led the man through the doorway and into the shabby central passage that ran the full length of their house.

'So you're Mr Strickland?' she said once they were clear of the shop.

'Yes, my name's Hugh—Hugh Strickland. And I believe you're Jo.'

Jo nodded.

'Short for Josephine?'

'Joanna.' She held out her hand. 'Joanna Berry.' Somehow it seemed important to shake hands—to make this exchange businesslike. But it wasn't exactly businesslike to have her hand clasped warmly by Hugh Strickland.

'I take it Hilda Bligh filled you in?' she asked.

'Indeed and with astonishing attention to detail.'

She groaned. 'I hate to think what she's told you.'

Hugh smiled. 'I don't think she told me what you scored on your spelling test in the second grade, but I believe I know just about everything else.'

'I'm sorry. Outback towns are so—'

'Exposing?'

Jo nodded her head and sighed. This really was the weirdest situation.

'Yes, well…' She took a deep breath. 'We'd better take a look at these toys. I'm afraid I'm going to have to take you into my bedroom.'

'Really?'

He didn't look shocked—he was too smooth for that—but Jo knew he was surprised. She made a joke of it. 'Of course I don't usually invite strange men into my room within minutes of meeting them.'

Amusement sparkled in his eyes. 'Mrs Bligh didn't mention it.'

Thank heavens he had a sense of humour.

'I've hidden the presents in there, you see, and I can't bring them out or one of the children might find them.' She turned and led him down the passage.

But, despite her matter-of-fact air, she was suddenly nervous. It didn't seem possible that she was actually doing this. She, ordinary, average Jo Berry, was taking a man who was a mixture of every gorgeous British actor she'd ever swooned over into her dreadful bedroom.

It was more than dreadful. She'd taken all her favourite bits and pieces to decorate her flat in Brisbane, so her room was as bare and as ugly as a prison cell.

It held nothing more than a simple iron bed with a worn and faded cover, bare timber floorboards, a scratched, unvarnished nightstand and an ancient wardrobe, once polished silky oak, but painted creamy-orange by her father during one of Mum's decorating drives. The old Holland blind that covered her window was faded with age and had a watermark stain where rain had got in during a storm several summers ago.

'Perhaps this isn't a good idea,' Hugh said. 'I can't take gifts from your family.'

'But isn't it vitally important to have a present for little Ivy?'

'Well…'

Without further hesitation, Jo dragged her suitcase out from under the bed. 'Luckily I haven't wrapped these yet,' she said, looking up at him over her shoulder.

And he was smiling again—that dangerous smile—with his eyes fixed directly on the expanding gap between her T-shirt and her jeans.

Heaving the suitcase on to her bed, she began hauling gifts out to pile on her bedspread.

What she was looking for were the stocking fillers she'd bought to help her mother out—small fluffy toys, plastic spiders, dress-up jewellery, fishing lures, puzzles…

But she more or less had to get everything out because these things were mixed in with the main presents—the action figures and video games for Bill and Eric; the books and CDs for the older boys; the 'magic' magnetic drawing board and hair accessories for Grace and the baby doll for Tilly.

She glanced up at Hugh and felt a pang of dismay when she saw the look in his eyes as he stared at the doll.

As baby dolls went, it was perfect. She'd been thrilled when she'd found it. It came in a little cane carry basket with a pink quilted lining and there was also a feeding bottle and a change of clothes.

'You have quite a treasure trove here,' he said.

'I need to negotiate a bank loan every year just to cope with Christmas,' she joked.

'Six brothers and sisters…'

'Mrs Bligh told you that too?'

He nodded and smiled, then looked back at the bed. 'I'd pay you anything for that doll.'

Jo thought of Ivy. She was such a sweet little thing and for a fleeting moment she almost weakened. But then she came to her senses. 'Sorry. Not possible. That's earmarked for Tilly.' She reached for a fluffy lavender-hued unicorn. 'What about this? Unicorns are all the rage with the pre-school set.'

One dark eyebrow lifted. 'I would never have guessed. I'm completely out of my depth when it comes to little girls.'

'Or there's this—' She reached for some multi-coloured plastic bangles, but stopped when she heard the sound of giggling on the other side of the door. Her stomach plunged.

Tiptoeing to the door, she listened. Yes, there was another burst of giggles.

Carefully, she opened the door a crack and found Tilly and Eric crouching there, their eyes dancing with merriment. 'Get lost, you two.'

'Bill says you've got a man in there,' said Tilly.

'That's none of your business. Now run away.'

Eric bumped against the door as if he wanted to push it open, but Jo blocked it with her hip.

'Is he your boyfriend?' asked Tilly.

'No, of course not. Now scram, both of you!'

Face aflame, Jo slipped back through the narrow opening, slammed the door shut and locked it again. Embarrassed, she rolled her eyes to the ceiling, hardly daring to look at Hugh, but when she did she saw that he was standing in the middle of the room with his hands thrust in his trouser pockets, wearing an expression that was a complicated mixture of amusement and impatience.

'I do appreciate your efforts.' He gallantly re-

mained silent about the antics of her siblings. 'But I
think I'd better be off.'

'Yes,' she said. 'Will you take the unicorn?'

'Are you sure you can spare it?'

'Absolutely. Right now, I'd be happy if you took
all the presents. I might yet disown my entire family.'

He flashed her a smile. 'Just the unicorn would be
terrific, thank you.'

Jo thrust the fluffy toy into a non-see-through pink
plastic bag and handed it to him. 'Done.'

As she hastily transferred everything back into the
suitcase and dropped the lid, Hugh reached for his
wallet again.

'No.' She shook her head. 'No money. It's for
Ivy.' Quickly she opened the door.

'I must say I'm terribly grateful to you,' Hugh
said. 'I would have hated to turn up at Agate Downs
on Christmas Eve without the right gift.'

His smile and his confession, delivered in his
beautifully modulated, polite English voice, had the
strangest effect on Jo. She had to fight off a weird
impulse to bar the door so he couldn't leave.

'Well,' she said, pushing such silliness out of her
head and turning briskly businesslike again. 'I
mustn't keep you any longer, Mr Strickland. I'm sure
you need to be on your way and I'd better relieve
Bill in the shop.'

He hurried off then. After delivering one last quick
but sincere thank you he made a hasty farewell, heading out the front door in record time.

Leaping into his vehicle, he pulled out from the kerb at the same reckless speed with which he'd arrived.

And Jo was left feeling strangely deflated.

Her thoughts returned to where she'd been before he'd arrived. Remembering her friends at the office Christmas party in the city, all having a ball.

While Hugh Strickland, possibly the dishiest man in the world and as close to Prince Charming as Jo was ever likely to meet, was riding off in his glittering coach—well, OK, his four-wheel drive. Roaring down a bush track.

Never to be seen again.

CHAPTER TWO

BINDI CREEK had its last-minute pre-Christmas rush shortly after Hugh left. It seemed to Jo that almost every household in the township, as well as some from outlying properties, suddenly remembered that the shop would be closed for the next two days and that they needed items vital for Christmas.

No doubt it was paranoia, but Jo couldn't help wondering if some of them had come to the shop just to spy on her. At least two of the local women hinted—with very unsubtle nudges and winks—that they'd heard from Hilda Bligh about Jo's *special* visitor. One of them actually said that she'd heard the Martens were expecting a visit from Ivy's father.

Jo pretended she had no idea what they were talking about.

Apart from these awkward moments, she was happy to be kept busy. The work kept her mind from straying Hugh-wards.

Brad and Nick, two of her brothers who worked further out west on cattle properties, arrived home around eight. They came into the shop and greeted her with hugs and back slaps and they hung about for ten minutes or so, catching up on her news. Then

22

they went back into the house for the warmed left-over dinner Mum had saved for them.

Jo ate a scratch meal at the counter and she was tired when it was time to close up the shop. She went to lock the front door and looked out into the street and took a few deep breaths. It was a hot, still summer's night and the air felt dry and dusty, but despite this she caught a hint of frangipani and night-scented jasmine drifting from nearby gardens.

Overhead, the Christmas Eve sky was cloudless and clear and splashed with an extravaganza of silver-bright stars. Grace and Tilly would be watching that sky from their bedroom window, hoping for a glimpse of Santa Claus and his reindeer. And Mum would be warning Eric and Bill not to spoil their little sisters' fantasies.

What would little Ivy be doing out at Agate Downs? Had she received her present? Had she liked the lavender unicorn? For a moment Jo let her mind play with the mystery of Hugh Strickland and this child. She could picture him very clearly as he climbed out of his vehicle with the toy unicorn clutched in one hand. Goodness, she should have put it in something more attractive than a plastic bag.

Thinking about him and his mysterious errand caused an unwelcome pang around her heart. She shivered and rubbed her arms to chase away goose-bumps. What was the point of thinking over and over about Hugh? Perhaps she was getting man-crazy. It was six months since she'd broken up with Damien.

She locked the doors, pulled down the blinds, locked the till and turned out the lights in the shop. It was time to slip into her bedroom to wrap her presents. Once the children were safely asleep, she would have fun setting the brightly wrapped gifts under the Christmas tree in the lounge room.

The Berrys enjoyed a no-frills Christmas Eve. She'd have a cup of tea with Mum and they'd both put their feet up. The older boys would sit out on the back veranda with Dad, yarning about cattle and drinking their first icy-cold Christmas beer, while she and Mum talked over their final plans for the festive meals tomorrow.

She hadn't quite completed the gift-wrapping saga when there was a knock on her bedroom door. 'Who is it?' she called softly, not wanting to wake her sisters in the next room.

'It's Mum.'

'Just a minute.' Jo had been wrapping her mother's presents—French perfume and a CD compilation of her mum's favourite music from the sixties and seventies—so she slipped these quickly under her pillow. 'I'm almost finished.'

When she opened the door her mother looked strangely excited. 'You have a visitor.'

'Really? Who is it?'

'An Englishman. He says his name's Hugh Strickland.'

An arrow-swift jolt shot through Jo. 'Are you sure?'

'Of course I'm sure.' Margie Berry's brow wrinkled into a worried frown. 'Who is he, love? He seems very nice and polite, but do you want me to send him away?'

'Oh, no,' Jo answered quickly. 'He's just a customer. He—he was in the shop this afternoon.'

'Yes, he told me that. He said you were very helpful.' Margie looked expectant, but Jo was reluctant to go into details.

Her mind raced. Why was Hugh here? He was supposed to be at Agate Downs. 'W-where is he?'

'I found him on the back veranda, talking to Dad and the boys, but it's you he wants. He asked for you ever so politely, so I told him to wait in the kitchen.'

'The kitchen?' Her bedroom had been bad enough and Jo winced when she tried to picture Hugh Strickland in their big old out-of-date kitchen, cluttered this evening with the aftermath of Mum's Christmas baking. Somehow the image wouldn't gel.

Jo was gripping the door handle so hard her hand ached as she let it go. This didn't make sense. 'Did you ask him why he wants to see me?'

Margie gave an irritated toss of her head. 'No, I didn't.'

Jo wished she had a chance to check her appearance in the mirror, but her mother was waiting with her hands on her hips and a knowing glint in her eyes. Besides, what was the point of titivating? Hugh Strickland had already seen her today and she would look much the same as she had earlier. Her smooth brown hair was cut into a jaw-length bob that never seemed to get very untidy and she wasn't wearing make-up, and there wasn't much she could do to improve her plain white T-shirt and blue jeans.

Just the same, she felt nervous as she set off down the passage for the kitchen, as if she were going to an audition for a part in a play but had no idea what role she was trying for.

Hugh was standing near the scrubbed pine table in the middle of the room and the moment she saw him she went all weak-kneed and breathless.

And that was *before* he smiled.

Oh, heavens, he *was* good-looking. She'd been beginning to wonder if perhaps her imagination had exaggerated how gorgeous he was.

No way. His dark hair was still spiky, but that was part of his appeal, as was the five o'clock shadow that darkened his strong jaw line. And beyond that there was a subtle air of superiority about him—a matter of breeding perhaps, something unmistakable like the born-to-win lines of a well-bred stallion.

But behind his charming smile she could sense banked-up emotion carefully held in check. What was it? Anger? Impatience? Dismay?

She wondered if she should ask him to sit down, but his tension suggested he'd rather stand. Why had he returned so soon?

He answered that question immediately when he held out the pink plastic bag she'd given him. 'I came to return this.'

Frowning, Jo accepted it. She could feel the shape of the fluffy unicorn still inside. Her mind raced, trying to work out what this could mean. 'Couldn't you find your way to Agate Downs?'

'I found the place,' he said. 'Your directions were spot on.'

'So what happened? Weren't the Martens home?'

'I turned back without seeing them.' A muscle worked in his jaw and he dropped his gaze. His face seemed to stiffen. 'I had second thoughts. It's the wrong time.'

'Oh.' What else could she say? This was none of her business. 'That's a—a pity.' A few hours ago it had been vitally important that Hugh made a good impression on the child. And it had seemed important that it happened *today*. Jo pressed her lips together, fighting the impulse to interrogate him.

He looked up briefly and she caught a stronger flash of emotion in his intense gaze before he looked away again. Was it anger? 'I didn't want to spoil Ivy's Christmas. I—I mean—her guardians knew that I was on my way, but I realised it would be intrusive.'

She wondered how Hugh Strickland would react if he knew that the locals were gossiping about him.

His eyes sought hers again. 'I suddenly thought how it would be for Ivy to have a strange man turn-

ing up on her doorstep on Christmas Eve, claiming—' He broke off in mid-sentence.

Claiming…what? Jo's tense hands tightened
around the package and the unicorn let out a sharp
squeak. She was so uptight that she jumped.

'So what will you do now?' she asked.

'I've found a room at the pub.'

'Oh…good.'

'I'll stay there till Christmas is over and I'll go
back to the Martens' place on Boxing Day.'

Jo thrust the unicorn back into his hands. 'If you're
still hoping to see Ivy, you must keep this. You'll
need it.'

Their hands were touching now, and as they both
held the package she was exquisitely aware of
Hugh's strong, warm fingers covering hers.

'No,' he said. 'I came here tonight because I
wanted to give this back to you in time for your
family's Christmas. There won't be the same pressing urgency for a gift for Ivy once Christmas is over.
And this was really meant for one of your sisters.'

He was looking directly into her eyes and making
her heart pound.

Their gazes remained linked for longer than was
necessary, and Jo knew she would always remember
the shimmering intimacy of his green eyes as he
looked at her then and the heated touch of his hands
on hers.

It was almost depressing to realise that memories of this handsome stranger were going to haunt her nights and linger in her daydreams…for ages into the future…

'Please keep the unicorn.' She felt so breathless her voice was hardly more than a whisper. 'Believe me, little girls always like presents.'

He sent her a quick smile. 'If you insist. I'll trust your deep understanding of what little girls like. The only one I know well is my goddaughter, but she's only six months old, so our communication has been somewhat limited.'

'Believe me, where presents are concerned, little girls are no different from big girls; they never get tired of receiving gifts.'

His eyes flashed confident amusement.

'But I'm sure you already know that.'

'Indeed.'

But then he seemed to remember something else and almost immediately his smile faded.

And the spell that had kept their hands linked was broken. Jo stepped back, leaving him with the unicorn, and Hugh looked away.

She drew a quick nervous breath. *Calm down, Jo. Stay cool. You're getting overheated about nothing. Nothing. He hasn't come back to see you and he'll be leaving again any moment now.*

'There's another thing I wanted to ask you, Jo,' he said softly.

Her head jerked up.

'I wonder if I can possibly impose on you one more time?'

Caught by surprise, she found herself blustering. 'How? W-what would you like me to do?'

'I want you to come with me when I go back to Agate Downs.'

Crumbs. 'Why me? I don't understand.'

'You already know Ivy—and you have so many brothers and sisters. I have no experience with young children. I can't even remember what it's like to be five.'

She tried to speak as casually as he had. 'So you think I can help you somehow?'

A muscle in his throat worked. 'Yes—if you could spare the time. I get the impression you've hit it off with Ivy already.'

'I'm afraid I'm not an expert at managing small children,' she warned him. 'You've seen how naughty Tilly can be.'

'But you're used to them. You're relaxed around them.'

'Well…' Jo's immediate impulse was to help him, but a nagging inner warning was hard to ignore. 'It might be helpful if I understood a little more about this situation,' she said carefully.

He nodded and then he looked directly into her eyes again. 'The situation's quite straightforward really. Ivy's my daughter.'

Right. Jo tried to swallow. So now she knew for sure. Did this mean Hugh was married? She glanced at his hands. The only ring he wore was the signet ring on the little finger of his left hand.

Sensing the direction of her gaze, he smiled wryly, lifted his hand and waggled his bare fourth finger. 'No, I'm not married. I only dated my daughter's mother for a while. And…her mother is dead.'

'Oh, how sad.' This changed everything. All at once Jo was adrift on a sea of sympathy. She said quickly, 'Why don't we sit down for a bit?'

He pulled out a wooden chair on the other side of the kitchen table. 'If I'm asking you to help with Ivy I should be perfectly honest with you,' he said. 'I only learned of her existence a short time ago.'

Jo watched the barely perceptible squaring of his shoulders and she sensed that he was working very hard to keep his emotions under control. 'That must have been a terrible shock.' Her kind-hearted urges were going into overdrive now. 'How come you only learned about Ivy recently?'

Hugh stiffened and she guessed she was delving deeper than he wanted to go. But he met her gaze. 'Her mother wrote a letter but it never reached me and she died shortly after Ivy's birth.'

Jo thought of the dear little bright-eyed Ivy who'd danced about their shop like a winsome fairy while her guardian had selected groceries. How sad that her mother never knew her.

How sad that Hugh still hadn't met her. Jo blinked away the threat of tears.

'It gets worse.' Hugh spoke very quietly. 'Apparently Linley suffered from severe postnatal depression and—and she committed suicide.'

'No!' A horrified exclamation burst from Jo. 'I'm so sorry,' she added quickly. Then she asked gently, 'And you never knew?'

'I thought she had died in a car accident,' he said. 'There was never any mention of a baby.'

Jo wondered if he was being so forthright to draw her into the task of helping him. Well, it was working. It would be hard to turn him down now, especially when his eyes held hers with such compelling intensity.

'Ivy's grandmother died recently and she left instructions in her will, demanding that I claim my daughter,' he said. 'Of course I wanted to do the right thing by the child, so I came dashing over here. But I've realised now that my timing is off. On Christmas Eve children are expecting Santa Claus, not strange men claiming to be their father.'

'Ivy might like you better than Santa Claus,' Jo suggested gently.

He sent her a sharp, searching look. 'So you think I've done the wrong thing?'

Jo gulped. This gorgeous, confident man was acting as if he really needed her advice. She sent him an encouraging grin. 'No, I'm sure you've made the right decision. I always believe it's best to follow your instincts.'

'So will you come with me when I collect Ivy?'

Her instincts screamed yes and Jo didn't hesitate to take her own advice.

'Of course I will. I've got a real soft spot for Ivy and, as you said, with six younger brothers and sisters I've got to be something of an expert with kids.'

'Absolutely.' Hugh glanced at the clock on the wall near the stove and jumped to his feet. 'It's getting late and I've taken up far too much of your time.'

Jo wondered if she should warn him about Ivy's scars, but perhaps that would only make him more anxious about meeting her. Or maybe he already knew. It might be best not to make a big deal about them.

Standing, she shoved her hands into the back pockets of her jeans and shrugged in an effort to look unconcerned. 'So we have a date for Boxing Day?'

He nodded stiffly. 'Thanks. I'd really appreciate your help.'

Then he turned and walked to the kitchen door. Jo followed.

'I hope you'll be comfortable at the pub,' she said as they stepped into the hallway. 'It's not very flash.'

'It looks perfectly adequate.'

'A bit lonely for Christmas.'

'I'll be fine.' Suddenly he looked very English, sort of stiff upper lipped and uncomfortable, as if he couldn't stand sentimental females who made fusses about Christmas.

Her mother appeared in the hall. 'Did I hear you say you're staying at the pub, Mr Strickland?'

Jo wanted to cringe at her mother's intrusion, but Hugh didn't seem to mind.

'Yes. It's basic but quite adequate.'

'You're not having Christmas dinner there, are you?'

'They've booked me in. Why? Is there a problem?'

'Oh, not the pub for Christmas.' Margie sounded shocked and she thumped her hands on her hips in a gesture of indignation. 'We can't let you do that.'

'I'm sure the food will be fine.' Hugh was beginning to sound defensive now. 'I'm told they do a fine roast turkey.'

'But you'll be all on your own. At Christmas.'

Jo could tell where this was heading, but it would look a bit weird if she suddenly leapt to Hugh's rescue by insisting that he would be fine at the pub.

'And you're so far from home,' her mother said. 'No, Mr Strickland, I won't hear of it. You must join us tomorrow. I know we're not flash, but at least there's a crowd of us. You won't feel lonely here and we're going to have plenty of food. I hate to think of anyone being alone at Christmas.'

Hugh's expression was circumspect—a polite mask—and Jo waited for him to excuse himself with his characteristic, well-mannered graciousness.

But to her amazement, he said, 'That's very kind of you, Mrs Berry. Thank you, I'd love to come.'

*   *   *

Hugh arrived punctually at noon the next day, bearing two beautifully chilled bottles of champagne.

Jo's dad, who drank beer, eyed them dubiously, but her mum was effusive.

'Nothing like a glass of bubbles to make the day special,' she said, beaming at him. 'But don't let me have any till I've got all the food on the table or I'll forget to serve something. Nick,' she called to her eldest son, 'can you find a bucket and fill it with ice? We don't want to let these bottles warm up and there's not a speck of room in the fridge.'

Jo had given herself several stern lectures while getting ready that morning. She'd chosen a cool summery dress of fine white cotton edged with dainty lace, and she'd applied her make-up with excruciating care. But, in spite of her efforts to look her best, she was determined to stay calm and unaffected by Hugh's visit.

She was so busy helping her mother to get all the food out of the kitchen and on to the table that she had to leave Hugh to the tender mercies of her father and brothers, but she heard snatches of their conversation as she went back and forth.

'Hugh Strickland,' said her dad. 'Your name rings a bell. Should I have heard of you?'

'I shouldn't think so.'

'What line of work are you in?'

'I'm in business—er—transport.'

'In the UK?'

'That's right.'

Her dad mumbled knowingly. 'I almost got a job in transport once—driving buses—but I wasn't fit for it. My chest was crushed, you see. Mining accident. Lungs punctured, so they pensioned me off.'

Hugh made sympathetic noises.

Jo chewed her lip and wondered if she should try to butt in and change the conversation. Her dad tended to carry on a bit.

But if Hugh was bored, he showed no sign. He was fitting in like a local. Clutching his beer in its inelegant Styrofoam cooler, he relaxed in a squatter's chair and looked surprisingly comfortable.

The family always gathered for Christmas lunch on a screened-in veranda shaded by an ancient mango tree. This was the cool side of the house, but Jo wondered if an Englishman would realise that. It was still very hot, even in the shade.

'Now, Hugh,' said Mum after everyone had found a place to sit and the family had been through the ritual of pulling crackers and donning unbecoming paper hats. 'You'll see we don't have a hot dinner.'

'That's perfectly understandable.' Hugh smiled bravely from beneath a pink and purple crêpe paper crown, which should have made him look foolish but somehow managed to look perfectly fine.

Her mum waved a full glass of champagne towards the table. 'There's four different kinds of salad and there's sliced leg ham, cold roast pork and our pièce de résistance is the platter of prawns and bugs.'

'Bugs?' Hugh looked a tad worried.

'Moreton Bay bugs,' Jo hastened to explain, pointing to the platter in the table's centre. 'They're a type of crayfish. If you like seafood, you'll love these.'

Hugh did like them. Very much. In fact he loved everything on the table and ate as much seafood and salad as her brothers, which was saying something. And then he found room to sample the mince pies.

And, not surprisingly, he was an expert dinner party guest, an interesting conversationalist, who also encouraged Nick and Brad to regale them all with hilarious accounts of the antics of the ringers on the cattle stations where they worked. And he enjoyed listening while the younger children chimed in with their stories too.

Knowing how tense Hugh had been yesterday, Jo was surprised by how relaxed he seemed now. No doubt he was charming her family to ensure her commitment to helping him.

She decided to relax. She'd been working hard all year in the city and had put in long hours in the shop during the past week and now she decided to let go a little and to enjoy the fine icy champagne. How in heaven's name had Hugh unearthed such lovely French champagne in the Bindi Creek pub?

Everyone raved about Jo's Christmas pudding of brandy-flavoured ice cream filled with dried fruit, nuts and cherries and afterwards her mum announced that she was going to have a little lie down. And everyone agreed that was exactly what she deserved.

'Jo, you take Hugh out on to the back veranda for

coffee,' she suggested, 'while this mob gets cracking in the kitchen.'

With coffee cups in hand, Jo and Hugh retired to the veranda. They leant against the railing, looking out over the tops of straggly plumbago bushes to the sunburnt back paddock and it was good to stand and stretch for a while; Jo felt she had eaten and drunk too much.

The air was warm and slightly sticky and it hung about them like a silent and invisible veil. Jo would have liked to run down to the creek, to shed her clothes and take a dip in the cool green water. She'd done it often before, in private, but she found herself wondering what it would be like to skinny-dip with Hugh. The very thought sent her heartbeats haywire.

They didn't speak at first and she felt a bit self-conscious to be alone with him again after sharing him with her noisy family. The slanting rays of the afternoon sun lit up the dark hair above his right ear, lending it a gilded sheen and highlighting his cheek-bone and one side of his rather aristocratic nose.

Eventually he said, 'Your family are fascinating, aren't they?'

'Do you really think so? It must be rather over-powering to meet them all in one fell swoop.'

He smiled as he shook his head. 'I think you're very lucky to have grown up with such a happy brood. They're so relaxed.'

She shrugged. 'They have their moments. Christmas is always fun.'

'I'm impressed that they'll take in a stranger, knowing next to nothing about him.'

Too true, she thought. Hugh had shared rather personal details about Ivy in his bid to enlist her help, but she knew next to nothing about the rest of his life.

'You don't come from a big family?' she asked.

'Not in terms of brothers and sisters. I'm an only child. I guess that's why I'm always fascinated by big families.'

'Sometimes I envy only children. It would be nice, now and then, to have that kind of privacy. Then again, I spend most of my time these days working in the city.'

His right eyebrow lifted, forming a question mark, but, unlike her, he didn't give voice to his curiosity, so there was an awkward moment where they were both aware that the rhythm of their conversation had tripped.

Hugh stood staring into the distance.

'Are you thinking about Ivy?' Jo asked.

At first he seemed a little startled by her question, but then he smiled. 'How did you guess?'

'Feminine intuition.' She drained her coffee cup. 'Seriously, it must have come as a shock to have a five-year-old dropped into your life.'

'It was a shock all right.' Taking a final sip of coffee, he set his empty cup and saucer on a nearby table and, with his usual gentlemanly manners, he took Jo's cup and set it there too.

'I feel so unprepared for meeting Ivy,' he said. 'I don't like being unprepared. How the hell does a bachelor suddenly come to terms with caring for a child?'

'He hires a nanny?'

'Well, yes,' he admitted with a wry grimace. 'A nanny will be essential. But I'll still have to do the whole fatherhood thing.'

'At least Ivy's not a baby. She can talk to you and express her needs. I'm sure you'll become great mates with her.'

'Mates?' He couldn't have looked more stunned if she'd suggested that Ivy would take over as CEO of his business.

'Good friends,' she amended.

'With a five-year-old little girl?'

Jo thought of the warm lifelong friendship she'd shared with her mum. 'Why not?'

Hugh shook his head. 'A boy might have been easier. At least I have inside knowledge of how little boys tick.'

'Don't be sexist. There are lots of little girls who like the same things as boys. Grace and Tilly love to play cricket and go fishing. So do I, for that matter.'

'Do you?' He regarded her with a look that was both amused and delighted, but then he frowned and with his elbows resting on the veranda railing he stared down into the plumbago bush. 'But what if Ivy turns on a horrendous scene? It would be horrible if she cried all the way home on the flight back to London.'

'Goodness,' cried Jo. 'You're a walking advertisement for the power of positive thinking, aren't you?'

For a moment he looked put out, and then he smiled. 'You're right. I'm normally on top of things, so I guess I should be able to handle this.' He sent Jo an extra devilish smile. 'With a little expert help.'

Gulp. 'Just remember Ivy is your flesh and blood,' she said. 'She's probably a chip off the old block.'

'Which would mean she's charming and well-mannered, even-tempered, good-looking and highly intelligent.'

'You missed conceited.'

Hugh chuckled softly and then he glanced up and seemed suddenly fascinated by something above her head. 'Is that mistletoe hanging above you?'

Jo tipped her head back. Sure enough there was a bunch of greenery dangling from a hook in the veranda roof. 'I can probably blame one of my brothers for that.' She rolled her eyes, trying to make light of it, but as she looked at Hugh again his smile lingered and something about it sent shivers skittering through her.

How silly. This reserved Englishman had no intention of kissing her. And, even if he did, why should she get all shivery at the thought of a quick Christmas peck?

But her jumping insides paid absolutely no attention to such common sense.

Hugh gave an easy shrug of his shoulders and his eyes held hers as he murmured ever so softly in his super-sexy English voice, 'Tradition is terribly important, Jo. And you're under the mistletoe and it *is* Christmas.'

Her stomach began a drum roll.

CHAPTER THREE

SOMETHING deep and dark in Hugh's gaze made Jo's pulses leap to frantic life.

Oh, for heaven's sake, calm down, girl.

Why was she getting so worked up about a friendly Christmas kiss?

Because Hugh is gorgeous!

She took a step closer to him and Hugh's hand cupped her elbow as if to support her. She hoped he didn't notice that she was trembling.

And then, without warning, he dipped his head. 'Happy Christmas, Jo.'

She pursed her lips for a quick peck and let her body tilt forward. But the anticipated peck didn't take place.

Instead Hugh's lips settled warmly on hers and suddenly he was kissing her. Properly. Or she was kissing him? It no longer mattered. All that mattered was that it was a full-on kiss.

She could blame the champagne. Or the heat. No, she would blame Hugh, because he was far too gorgeous and far too expert at kissing. There had to be some logical reason to explain how a simple mistletoe kiss became so thorough and lasted for such a long and lovely time.

Yes, she would blame Hugh because at some point his hands slipped around her waist, and then it was incredibly easy and seemed perfectly OK to nestle in against him. His arms bound her close against his strong, intensely masculine body and his mouth, tasting faintly of coffee, delved hers expertly and with daring intimacy.

Without warning, a flood of unexpected yearning washed over her. Her insides went into meltdown. Soft, hungry little sounds rumbled low in her throat as she pushed closer into Hugh.

Oh, man. Never had she experienced a kiss that was so instantly shattering.

The sound of footsteps brought her plummeting back to earth. With a little whimper of disappointment, she broke away.

Hugh let her go and he stood very still with his shoulders squared and his hands by his sides, watching her intently and not quite smiling. Only his accelerated breathing betrayed that he'd been as aroused by the kiss as she had.

Taking a deep breath, Jo shot a scowl back over her shoulder to see who'd interrupted them.

It was Bill and Eric and their mouths were hanging wide open.

'What's eating you two?' she demanded angrily. 'Haven't you ever seen someone get kissed under the mistletoe before?'

Eric's face was sheepish. 'Not like that.'

'Get lost,' she said, feeling flustered. 'Finish those dishes.'

They vanished. Which left her with Hugh, who'd gone quiet again. In fact he was looking so uncomfortable that she wondered suddenly if he regretted the kiss. Damn him. He'd probably only kissed her to get closer to her—to ensure that she would accompany him to Agate Downs.

But he'd been so passionate, so *involved*.

Good grief. She was trying to read too much into the kiss. Hugh had simply reacted to the Christmas tradition. And she'd been carried away. Look how calm he was now.

Nevertheless, their easy conversation was over. They carried their coffee cups back to the kitchen and soon afterwards Hugh said polite farewells and set off for the pub. He left without any special word for Jo.

She was left to be plagued by annoying doubts. And no matter how many times she told herself to be sensible, confusion about the passion in Hugh's kiss kept her churning for the rest of Christmas Day.

Hugh was nervous.

He hated feeling nervous. It was so alien to his nature. Normally he was always in control, but in all his adult life he couldn't remember feeling so helpless.

As he drove with Jo to Agate Downs, he had to keep taking deep, slow breaths to remain calm. Even so, emotion clogged his throat and he kept swallowing to be rid of it.

Jo seemed subdued too, and he wondered if she was remembering the kiss they'd shared yesterday. The chemistry of it had been rather sobering. It had caught him completely by surprise. He'd anticipated a harmless exchange beneath the mistletoe and had found himself launching a fully-fledged seduction.

He might have taken things beyond the point of sanity if her brothers hadn't arrived on the scene.

The rough outback track reached a rusty old iron gate where Hugh had turned back two days ago. Jo pushed open the passenger door. 'I'll get the gate.'

About ten minutes later, after they'd traversed a long paddock dotted with rather scrawny-looking cattle, the homestead emerged through the trees.

Jo frowned. 'I haven't been out here for years. This place is looking very run-down, isn't it?'

Hugh nodded. He tried to picture his daughter living here. The yard around the homestead was weedy and parched, with no sign of a garden, and as far as he could see there weren't any playthings to amuse a child—no tricycle and no swing hanging from the old jacaranda tree.

He felt a rush of adrenalin as he parked the car. Within a matter of minutes he would see Ivy, the unknown daughter he was to take home with him, the child he must adjust his whole life to accommodate.

He no longer doubted that he wanted her. Since

he'd learned of her existence he'd developed an astonishing deep-seated longing to see her and at some unfathomable soul-level he knew he already loved her.

But who was she? And how would she react to him?

Jo touched him on the shoulder and, when he turned, she handed him the unicorn, wrapped now in brightly coloured Christmas paper and topped by a crimson bow sprinkled with silver glitter.

'Don't worry about this, Hugh,' she said. 'Just be yourself. Believe me, Ivy is a very lucky little girl to have a father like you. She'll love you.'

A grim smile was the best he could offer.

At the front door they were greeted by a dark scowl beneath thick bushy eyebrows. Noel Marten stared glumly at Hugh. 'You must be Strickland.'

'Yes.' Hugh extended his hand. 'How do you do?'

'Hmm,' was all Noel Marten said and his hand-shake was noticeably reluctant.

'I telephoned to say I'd be here on Boxing Day,' Hugh added.

'Who is it?' called a voice from deep inside the house.

Noel called over his shoulder. 'It's him—Strickland.'

'Oh.' Ellen Marten came hurrying down the central passage, wiping her damp hands on an apron.

Behind her, at the far end of the passage, a small,

impish figure peered around a doorway. Hugh's throat constricted. There she was. Ivy. His little girl.

Jo reached for his hand and gave it an encouraging squeeze.

'Do come in, sir,' said Ellen Marten, but then she glanced at Jo and looked a little confused.

Jo beamed at her. 'Hi, Ellen. I don't suppose you were expecting me. Hugh's been telling me how excited he is about meeting his daughter at last.' She offered both the Martens her warmest smile.

'I invited Jo because she knows Ivy and she's had much more experience than I have with children,' Hugh explained rather stiffly.

'Right,' said Ellen, nodding slowly.

The far end of the hallway was quite shadowy, but when Hugh glanced that way again he saw the silhouette of a little girl jigging with excitement. His heart began to pound. The child's mother had been beautiful with a slim, pale fragility, luminous brown eyes and a halo of soft, golden hair.

Whose looks had Ivy inherited?

Ellen followed his glance back down the hallway. 'The little monkey; I told her to wait in the kitchen.'

'I don't want to wait,' shouted a very bossy little voice.

Ellen sighed. 'I'm afraid she's quite a little miss. There are times when I don't know what to do with her.'

'That's because you won't listen to me,' growled Noel. 'I know exactly what she needs.'

By now the little girl had sidled along the wall until she was halfway down the passage. She was wearing a pink gingham sundress and no shoes. A handful of pebbles lodged in Hugh's throat. He could see that her hair was a mop of curls as dark as his and she had a pale heart-shaped face with big, expressive eyes—green eyes that were dancing with mischief.

Her nose, mouth and chin were exceptionally dainty and feminine. Strong dark eyebrows and lashes gave her character, as did the intelligence shining in her eyes. He felt an astonishing surge of pride. She was his daughter. She was wonderful.

Ellen called to her, 'Come on then, Ivy. Come and meet your visitor.'

Your father, Hugh wanted to add, but he held his tongue. He stood very still, feeling terrified and trying very hard to smile, but not quite managing.

As if sensing his tension, the little girl came to a standstill. She pressed herself against the wall with her hands behind her back and she let her head droop to one side, suddenly shy.

'Come on now, Ivy,' Ellen Marten said sharply. 'Don't keep the man waiting.'

'No.' Ivy pouted. 'Won't come.'

Hugh's stomach sank. Ivy didn't want to meet him and he had no idea how to entice her. No doubt his friends in London would be amused by the fact that he, who could charm twenty-five-year-old females with effortless ease, had no idea how to win the heart of this five-year-old.

Ellen rolled her eyes and sighed again. Noel brandished a fist in the air and Hugh cast a desperate glance in Jo's direction.

And Jo, bless her, was the only person in the room who seemed quite free from anxiety. She flashed a cheery grin across the room to the child. 'Hi there, Ivy.'

'Hello,' came the almost sulky reply.

'I've brought you a special visitor.'

Ivy listened carefully, but she didn't budge.

'Don't you want to come and see the lovely Christmas present Hugh has brought for you?'

'What Christmas present?' Ivy inched forward a step.

'This one,' said Hugh nervously as he held out the bright package. Then, copying Jo's example, he squatted beside her.

'What is it?' asked Ivy, coming closer by cautious degrees.

Hugh hesitated and looked again to Jo. He had no idea about the proper protocol for divulging the contents of gifts to children.

But Jo didn't hesitate. 'It's a beautiful unicorn.'

Ivy came still closer. 'What's a unicorn?' she asked.

'It's like a pony,' said Jo. 'A magic pony.'

That did the trick. Ivy closed the gap.

Hugh was transfixed. Here she was—his flesh and

blood daughter, perfect in every way, with his hair colour and his green eyes. And ten neat little pink toes.

'Are you going to open this?' His husky voice betrayed his emotion and he was sure there were tears in his eyes.

Little Ivy stood staring at the package with her hands clasped behind her back. Her eyes shone with curiosity, but she shook her head. 'You open it.'

'OK.' Hugh began to rip at the paper and his daughter leaned close, her face a pretty picture of concentration. And, as the paper fell away, the unicorn was revealed in all its fluffy lilac glory.

Ivy's eyes widened. 'Is it really magic?'

'Ahh...' Hugh had no idea how to answer her.

Jo came to his rescue. 'See this?' she said, patting the pearly horn on the unicorn's head. 'This is what makes it magic.'

One little hand came out and Ivy touched the tip of the horn with a pink forefinger. 'How is it magic?'

'It brought your daddy to you,' said Jo.

If it was possible Ivy's eyes grew rounder and she looked at Hugh. 'You're my daddy, aren't you?'

He was bewitched, his eyes locked with hers. Ivy was a miracle.

Jo dug him in the ribs with her elbow and he remembered his daughter's question.

'Yes,' he said, swallowing hard. 'I'm your daddy.' Then, balancing on his knees, he leaned forward and kissed her very gently on her soft pink cheek.

Beside him Jo made a low snuffling sound that was suspiciously like a sob.

'Give your unicorn a hug,' she suggested in a very choked-up voice.

A dimple bloomed in the little girl's cheek as she smiled with excitement and then her arms came out to embrace the unicorn. And that was when Hugh saw...her left arm.

Oh, dear God. The little girl's arm had obviously been very badly burned and it was a mass of terrible scar tissue from her shoulder to her wrist. Some areas were bright pink and shiny and others were a heart-breaking criss-cross of thickened lesions.

A ragged cry burst from him. How in hell's name had this happened? Rioting emotions stormed him. Without a care for the surprised bystanders, he swept Ivy into his arms and hugged her and the unicorn to his chest. Then, cradling her close, he scrambled to his feet.

With his cheek pressed close to Ivy's, he squeezed his eyes tightly closed to stem the threat of tears and he kissed his daughter's cheek and then her hair.

'My little girl,' he whispered.

His heart almost burst when Ivy flung her little arms around his neck.

'My daddy,' she said softly and then she kissed his cheek.

Behind him, Hugh heard Jo's happy sigh of relief.

'I must say I've never seen her take to anyone so quick,' Ellen remarked.

Almost reluctantly, Hugh lowered Ivy back to the floor and then he turned to Jo. 'I need to speak with the Martens,' he said. 'Would you mind entertaining Ivy for a few minutes?'

'Not at all,' she said brightly. 'Come on, Ivy, let's take your unicorn for a flying lesson.'

As they left, Hugh took a deep breath and directed a searching look at the Martens. 'Right,' he said. 'I want straight answers. I want to know exactly what happened to Ivy. I need to know where and why, and I insist on knowing what's being done about it.'

For the first time in days he felt he was back in control.

When it was time to say goodbye to the Martens, Jo felt that they'd been genuinely very fond of the child, despite Noel's gruffness and Ellen's admission that caring for Ivy really was becoming too much for her. And, although they had prepared themselves and Ivy for the parting, they had shed tears at the farewell.

But the bonding between Hugh and his daughter was the real surprise. There was no problem about Ivy leaving. In fact she was excited about going away with her newfound father.

Now, as they bumped down the track back to Bindi Creek, Jo patted the unicorn. 'So, what are you going to call this fellow?' she asked in her brightest manner.

Ivy, who was sitting between Jo and Hugh, frowned and studied the fluffy animal carefully, turning it over and upside down. 'Is my unicorn a boy or a girl?'

Over Ivy's head, Jo and Hugh exchanged amused glances. 'What would you like it to be?'

Ivy giggled and rolled her expressive eyes as she gave this deep consideration. 'I think he's a boy. Like Daddy.'

'So do I,' said Jo. 'And now you can give him a nice boy's name.'

'Hugh?'

'Well…it might be confusing if Daddy and the unicorn both share the same name.'

'What about Howard?' suggested Hugh.

'Howard?' Jo gave a scoffing laugh. 'For a little girl's toy?'

'I like Howard,' insisted Ivy. 'I want to call my unicorn Howard.'

Hugh sent Jo a smug wink. 'You see? I know more about naming toys than you realised.'

'Howard he is then,' Jo replied with a wry smile.

Ivy grinned up at Hugh and her little face was a glowing picture of adoration.

Jo wanted to cry for them. It was just so sweet the way Hugh and Ivy were so delighted with each other.

By the time they reached Bindi Creek's main street Ivy had nodded off with her head resting against Jo's shoulder.

'Would you like to bring her back to my place?' Jo asked. 'It mightn't be very suitable for her at the pub.'

'I've imposed on your family too much.' He glanced at the sleeping Ivy, still clutching Howard. 'But I know what you mean about the pub. I'm sure a child would be much happier at your place.'

'She wouldn't be any trouble. We can put up a little stretcher bed in the girls' room. She'd love it.'

Hugh smiled just a little sadly. 'She might love it too much. I might never be able to drag her away in the morning.'

'Oh, I hadn't thought of that.' Jo thought about it now and was hit by an unexpected deluge of sadness. She'd been trying not to dwell on the fact that Hugh and Ivy would soon disappear from her life. 'I guess you'll want to try to book a flight home,' she said.

'That's already arranged.'

'Really?' He must have organised it during one of the dozen calls he'd made from Agate Downs on his cellphone. 'So when are you going back to England?' She tried to sound casual, as if she didn't actually care, but she wasn't successful.

'Tomorrow.'

'Heavens.' *For crying out loud, Jo, don't sound so disappointed.* 'You were lucky to get a flight so quickly.'

'I know people in the industry.'

'Oh, yes, of course. I forgot you're in the transport business. So do you get mates' rates?'

'A-ah, yes, something like that.'

'Well, don't worry about Ivy,' she said with a brave smile. 'She already adores you and she understands she's going to England with you. She'll be fine.'

Hugh reached his hand past Ivy and gave hers a squeeze. 'Thanks, Jo.'

She tried to smile.

Tilly and Grace had seen Ivy a few times when she'd been in the shop but they'd never spoken, so they were a little overawed when the beautiful little girl arrived with Jo and Hugh. But their surprise didn't stop them from asking awkward questions.

'What happened to your arm?' Tilly asked almost immediately and Jo wanted to gag her.

But Ivy was matter-of-fact. 'It got burned.'

'Does it hurt?'

'Not really. Not any more. It just looks different, that's all.'

'I asked Santa for a unicorn,' Tilly said next. 'But I got a baby doll instead. Do you want to see her?'

After that, the children got on with the fun of dressing up and playing with Howard and the doll and Ivy was in seventh heaven.

In the kitchen, Hugh said to Jo, 'How private are we here? Is this conversation likely to be overheard?'

'Very likely, I'm afraid.' She wondered what he wanted to discuss.

'Do you think you could come up to the pub with me, for a quick drink and a chat?'

She made the mistake of looking into his eyes and she felt a swift ache deep inside, which warned her that she shouldn't go anywhere near the pub—or anywhere else—with him.

For Hugh, taking her to the pub was a purely practical arrangement—probably to discuss something about Ivy. While she—fool that she was—would be madly wishing it could be a date. And that was crazy.

Then again, what good reason could she give for refusing to go?

'I'll ask Mum to keep an eye on Ivy for us,' she said.

They found a table in a corner of the tiny beer garden, tucked between the side of the pub and the butcher's shop, and covered by a green shade cloth that did little to relieve them from the sweltering heat.

'You'll be pleased to get back to England's winter,' Jo said, pressing her cool glass against her face and neck.

Hugh chuckled. 'Give me two days in gloomy London in late December and I'll wish I was back here.'

'So you live in London?'

'Yes. I have a house in Chelsea.'

'Chelsea? That's a very nice area, isn't it?'

'It's quite nice. Very central, handy for everything.'

Jo realised how very little she knew about this man, while he knew so much about her; he'd even been inside her bedroom.

'So,' she said, after she'd taken a deep sip of wine, 'what did you want to talk about?'

'Ivy,' he said simply.

Of course. Jo sent him her warmest smile. 'She's a darling.'

'She is, isn't she?'

'Absolutely. She's bright and spirited, with the potential to be naughty, I'm sure, but she's incredibly sweet and beautiful.'

Hugh smiled and then his face grew sombre. 'I thought my heart was going to break when I saw the scars from her burns.'

Ellen Marten had told Jo about Ivy's burns as the two women had packed the last of Ivy's belongings. At the age of two Ivy had been living at her grandmother's Point Piper mansion in Sydney where Ellen and Noel had been servants, and somehow she'd escaped from her nanny and toddled into the kitchen where she'd pulled a pot of boiling water from the stove.

She'd spent a lot of time in hospital and had had several skin grafts.

Jo reached across the table and laid her hand on his. 'Ivy will be OK, Hugh. She has you now. Don't feel too sorry for her. You're going to be a wonderful father. She's a very lucky little girl.'

'I'll make sure she has the very best medical attention. Luckily, I have an old school friend who's a top burns specialist.'

Hugh looked at her hand covering his and something in his expression made Jo suddenly nervous. She retracted her hand and picked up her wineglass.

Hugh stared hard at the white froth on the top of his beer. 'I want you to come back to London with us,' he said.

Her heart took off like a racing car.

'I know this is short notice and probably very inconvenient, but I would pay you well. The thing is, Ivy's obviously expecting you to be around. And you're so very good with her and once I'm back at work I won't be able to spend all my time with her.'

Crash. Jo's heart skidded straight off the track and into a barrier. He wanted her as a nanny.

Well, of course, what else did you expect, you dreamy nitwit?

She lifted her glass and took a gulp of wine. 'I'm sorry, Hugh,' she said, not quite looking into his face. 'I can't manage it. I've already got a good job in Brisbane.' Then, with a haughty tilt of her chin, she looked him squarely in the eyes. 'And I have a career plan. I've worked hard to get where I am. I'm afraid I can't just abandon everything here.'

He nodded thoughtfully, lifted his beer as if he was going to drink, and then set the glass down again. 'I'm sorry, I should have asked before this. What sort of work do you do?'

She hitched her chin a notch higher. 'I'm an accountant.'

He smiled. 'I'd never have picked you as an accountant. You seem too—'

'Too what?' she snapped.

His smile broadened to a grin. 'I was going to say relaxed.'

'So you're another one.'

'Another?'

'One of the millions who like to stereotype accountants.'

'Oh, touchy subject. My apologies.' Hugh lifted his beer again and this time he drank half of it quickly. As he set the glass down, he said, 'You're not accounting at the moment.'

'No,' she admitted. 'That's because I've taken my annual leave over the Christmas and New Year period, but I have to be back at work in a little over two weeks.'

Without hesitation, Hugh said, 'What about those two weeks? What are your plans for them?'

She was surprised by his persistence. 'I'm here to help Mum out with the shop—and to spend time with my family.'

Hugh nodded and his face grew serious.

Jo fiddled with the stem of her wineglass. She thought of what it would be like for Hugh on the long flight back to London with Ivy. How would he go about settling his little daughter into a big strange city like London?

Her natural inclination to be helpful kicked in.

'Do you have friends or family in London who can help you with Ivy?' she asked. 'What about a— a girlfriend?'

'My parents live in Devon. I have friends, of course, but—' He paused and sighed.

Jo waited…and an annoying anxiety twisted inside her.

'My girlfriend and I broke up recently,' he said at last.

Jo kept a very straight face.

'Actually, we broke up because of Ivy.'

'Really?' This time it was hard to hide her shock.

Hugh shrugged. 'No big deal. We were heading for the rocks anyway, but the crunch came when I found out that I had a daughter.'

'Perhaps if she met Ivy she might change her mind,' Jo suggested.

He shook his head. 'Not this woman. The point is that none of my friends would understand Ivy the way you do. It's not just that you have sisters her age. She's really taken to you and, besides, you understand what she's used to, and what she'll find strange about London.'

He was right, of course. She was sure Hugh could manage quite adequately without her, but she also knew she could be very useful. She could help to make the big transition smoother for Ivy.

'Do you have a boyfriend who'd object to your going away?' Hugh asked.

Jo gulped. ''Fraid not. I'm—um—between boyfriends at the moment.' There'd been no one else since Damien, but there was no need to mention that to Hugh.

Should she seriously consider his request? Should she do it for Ivy's sake? Could she go to London for just two weeks until Hugh found a really good nanny? 'How much would you pay me?' she asked.

She spluttered into her wineglass as he named a sum. 'For two weeks? That's out-and-out bribery.'

He smiled. 'I know.'

'What sort of transport business are you in?'

'Aeroplanes,' he said quickly, as if he wasn't eager to divulge details. 'There'll be no problem in getting you a seat on our flight.'

'I'll have to think about it.' Jo drained her wineglass and took a deep breath. She was determined not to be impulsive this time. She wasn't rushing anywhere simply because this charming Englishman had asked for her help.

Just the same, his offer was very tempting. If she tried to balance the pros and cons, there were so many pros... Two weeks in London...all that money...doing a good deed for Ivy's sake...

What about the cons? There had to be cons. She would be leaving her mother in the lurch, but Christmas was over. Besides, she deserved a bit of a holiday. What else? There had to be more reasons why she shouldn't go.

Hugh.

Hugh and his gorgeousness. Two weeks with him and she'd be head-over-heels in love with the man. Even though he would remain polite and simply treat her like a nice nanny, she would fall all the way in love and she'd come home an emotional wreck.

'Sorry, Hugh,' she said grimly. 'I'd like to help, but I can't. I really can't.'

He looked so disappointed she almost weakened.

So she jumped to her feet. 'What time will you call in the morning to pick up Ivy?'

'I'll collect her now,' he said crisply. 'There's no point in her spending any more time with you. She'd only get too attached.'

'What's the matter, love?' her mother asked as Jo returned to the house just before dusk. She'd taken a long walk by the creek after Hugh and Ivy had left and she'd shed a tear or three.

The silliest thing was that she'd been crying for Ivy as much as for Hugh. The thought of the two of them…

Enough. She had made her decision and it was time to forget about them. They were starting a new life together and she had to get on with *her* life.

'I'm just a little tired,' she said vaguely.

'Tired my foot,' scoffed Margie. Steam rose as she lifted the lid on a pot of vegetables boiling on the stove. 'You've done something silly, haven't you?'

'No, Mum.' Jo's voice developed an annoying squeak. 'I've been excessively sensible.'

'You've turned Hugh Strickland down.'

Jo gasped. 'How did you—?' She bit her lip hard. Turning away, she pulled out a chair and flopped into it and rested her elbows on the kitchen table. 'Yes,' she said. 'Hugh offered me money to help Ivy settle in London and I turned him down.'

Her mother replaced the lid on the saucepan and lowered the heat before taking a seat opposite Jo. 'You should have gone with him, Jo.'

'Of course I shouldn't. You need me here.'

'We'd manage without you.'

'Well, that's gratitude for you.'

'I'm grateful, love. You know that, but I'm sorry you didn't grab the chance to go with him. It would really make a difference for that little girl to have a friendly face among all those strangers in a foreign city.'

'I'm almost a stranger to her.'

'But already she's very fond of you.'

Jo sighed. 'Ivy will be fine, Mum. London's crawling with nice Aussie girls looking for work as nannies. Hugh will find one at the drop of a hat.'

Her mother's chest rose and fell as she released a long slow sigh. 'I thought you had more courage.'

'Courage? I'm not scared. What would I be scared of?'

'Hugh.'

A kind of strangled gasp broke from Jo. 'Don't be silly. He's a gentleman.'

'Of course he is. A very handsome and charming gentleman. That's why you're scared.'

'Mum!' Jo jumped to her feet. 'I don't want to talk about this. What would you know?'

'More than you could imagine,' Margie said quietly.

About to flounce out of the kitchen, Jo stopped. Her mother was looking…*different*…kind of wistful and sad…and Jo felt her heart begin a strange little wobble.

'There was a man, Jo—before your father.'

Jo was quite sure she didn't want to hear this.

'I've never forgotten him.'

Appalled, Jo wanted to leave, but was transfixed by the haunted regret in her mother's eyes.

'I was madly in love with him,' Margie said. 'And he wanted me to sail across the Pacific with him on a yacht.'

'Did you go?'

Her mother shook her head slowly. 'I wouldn't be telling you this story if I'd gone. I reckon I'd still be with him.'

A stab of pain pierced deep inside Jo. 'You don't know that. It mightn't have worked out.'

Her mother smiled sadly. 'Then again, it might have been wonderful. I'll never know.'

It was too awful to think of Margie Berry with another man. Jo thought of her mother's hard life—with an invalid husband and so many children.

'I don't regret my life,' her mother said. 'But I wish now that I'd gone. I might have been disappointed, but then…you never know.'

Margie had never given a hint that she wasn't happy, but the expression on her face now was like a window on another world. So many possibilities promised and lost...

Jo's throat was so tight she could hardly speak. 'But—but Hugh isn't asking me to go with *him*. He just wants a hand with Ivy.' She swallowed again. 'I'm not in love with him.'

'Pull the wool over someone else's eyes.' Margie stood and crossed the room and slipped her arm around her daughter's shoulders. 'I think you should go to London, Jo. You'll definitely be good for Ivy and, as for what else might happen, be brave, honey, and take the risk. At the very least it'll be a jolly sight more interesting than hanging around here for the rest of your holidays. And, believe me, you don't want to spend the rest of your life wondering what might have happened.'

The light was out in Hugh's hotel room when Jo gave a tentative knock at a little after eight. If he was already asleep she would slip away.

No chance.

The door opened quickly. And by the dim light of a fluorescent tube halfway down the veranda, she saw that he was shirtless, with a pair of unbuttoned jeans hanging loose around his hips, as if he'd just dragged them on.

'Hello, Jo.' His greeting was polite but lacking his usual warmth.

'Hi.' She swallowed and tried not to stare at his

rather splendid shoulders…or at the dark hair on his chest, trailing down… 'I'm sorry to disturb you.'

'I wasn't asleep.' He cocked his head back towards the darkened room. 'But Ivy is.' Stepping out on to the veranda, he closed the door gently. 'What did you want? Is anything the matter?'

'I—I wondered if it would be all right if I changed my mind—about coming to England.'

Hugh didn't answer straight away and he was standing close to the wall where his face was in shadow, so Jo was left hovering, filled with sudden doubts. Why on earth had she listened to her mother? This was crazy.

'I'd like to help you with Ivy,' she added.

'What made you change your mind?'

'I—I started thinking about her. She's had such a tough life, poor kid. I know everything's going to be fine for her now she has you, but if I can help you to smooth the way for her, right at the start—'

Again there was silence. Hugh's eagerness to have her help seemed to have vanished.

'Are you quite certain your family can spare you?'

'Yes, I've discussed it with Mum. She's actually keen for me to go.'

'Is she now?' For the first time, Hugh sounded faintly amused. 'Well, then.'

'Is—is your invitation still open?'

'It is,' he said at last.

Jo waited, feeling dreadful.

'So you're sure you'd like to come?'

'Yes.'

'You have a passport?'

'Yes, I do. I went to a conference in Singapore last year.'

'That's terrific,' he said and his smile was cautious as he extended his hand to shake hers.

That was all? A handshake?

Jo was horribly deflated as she walked home again—down the quiet main street, past the familiar, shabby little cluster of buildings that was her home town. The thought of swapping it for London had been so exciting. She'd been so worked up about reaching her decision and going to Hugh to tell him.

But somehow she'd kind of been expecting a little more enthusiasm from him. Another kiss perhaps…to continue what they'd started under the mistletoe.

Now she wondered if that had been the first and last kiss she'd ever share with Hugh. And an inner voice warned that trying to get close to Hugh Strickland would be dangerous.

In the middle of the street she stopped and she looked up at the vast star-speckled sky stretching overhead and she wished she'd stuck to her original decision.

Why on earth had she listened to her mother's fantasies about a might-have-been romance?

CHAPTER FOUR

HUGH was worried. Not about Ivy—his first fears had been for her, but she was travelling like a veteran. However, there was something not quite right with Jo.

It wasn't her initial hesitation over coming to England that bothered him; she'd been happy enough when they'd left Bindi Creek and she'd laughed at her father when he'd warned her not to expect too much of England.

'England's a good place for the English,' he'd joked and she'd dismissed his gloomy cautions with a good-natured grin and an expressive roll of her eyes.

'Say what you like, Dad, you won't put me off. I'm going with an open mind.'

The change began in earnest when they reached Mascot Airport in Sydney and Jo realised that they weren't flying in a regular commercial jet.

'You're worried my plane won't keep you in the air?' Hugh suggested when he saw her pale face.

'No, it's not that. It's just that I've never known anyone who owned his own jet, let alone his own airline company. I hadn't realised you were quite so—so seriously wealthy.'

He'd expected to be interrogated. A straightforward girl like Jo would demand that he laid all his cards on the table. But, to his surprise, she'd backed right off.

She was subdued on the flight—although she was wonderful with Ivy—reading to her, helping her with a colouring-in book, being excessively patient when Ivy insisted on colouring horses purple and chickens bright blue. And, when Ivy had had enough, Jo found a suitable movie from the video collection and she made sure the little girl was perfectly comfortable when it was time to sleep.

He'd thought that they might spend much of the flight chatting, getting to know each other better, even flirting a little, but Jo kept her distance. She seemed determined to stick to her role as nanny and nothing more—which was no doubt very sensible—but it left Hugh feeling strangely dissatisfied.

She seemed happier when they finally landed at Stanstead. They were met by Hugh's man, Humphries. And, as they drove across London to Chelsea, both Jo and Ivy peered from the car's windows with identical expressions of wide-eyed wonder. But when they turned into St Leonard's Terrace and pulled up in front of his house, Jo looked worried again.

'This is your new home,' she told Ivy. 'Isn't it grand?'

'It's very tall,' Ivy said, dropping her head back to look up. Then the little girl frowned as she viewed the other houses up and down the street. 'Why are all the houses joined on to each other?'

Jo laughed. 'So they can fit lots of people into London.'

Ivy turned to Hugh. 'How many people can you fit into your house, Daddy?'

'Quite a few if I'm having a party, but most of the time there'll just be the three of us. And Humphries. Oh, and Regina, my housekeeper.'

'Do you have lots of parties?' Ivy asked, excited.

'Not these days.'

At one time there had been an interminable stream of parties, but now Hugh realised with something of a shock that he was looking forward to a quieter life, getting to know Ivy.

And Jo.

He noticed that Jo was shivering in her inadequate jacket. 'First thing tomorrow, we buy you and Ivy decent winter coats,' he said.

'Don't worry about me,' Jo protested. 'I won't be here long enough to make it worthwhile.'

Her gaze met his and then skittered away. She was definitely tense. It was almost as if she was deliberately distancing herself from him.

Regina greeted them with offers of cups of tea or supper, but neither Jo nor Ivy was hungry.

'You're tired,' Hugh said to Jo, noting her drawn pallor. 'Let me show you and Ivy to your rooms.' Everything should be ready here. He'd telephoned detailed instructions to Humphries and Regina.

'Yes, I want to see my room,' cried Ivy excitedly. 'Is it pretty?'

'I hope you'll like it. Come on, it's this way. You'll have to climb some stairs. Here, let me help you off with your jacket.'

As they mounted the stairs Ivy slipped her trusting little hand inside Hugh's and he experienced an unexpected flood of well-being. This was his little girl and he was bringing her home.

'Here we are,' he said when they reached the third floor.

The door to Ivy's room was standing ajar and at the first glimpse the little girl let out a delighted 'Wow!' Her eyes danced as she let go of Hugh's hand and crept on tiptoe across the carpet. 'It *is* pretty!' she whispered.

Regina had done a good job, Hugh decided, noting the new bedspread and matching curtains in a pale yellow, blue and rose floral print. A little student's desk and chair had been set near the window, complete with a box of pencils, note pads, a little pot of glue, a child's scissors and, on the floor beside the desk, a little cradle and—

'A baby doll!' Ivy fell to her knees and her eyes were huge as she stared in wonder. 'She's just like Tilly's.' She scooped up the doll. 'Oh, thank you, Daddy.' Then she was on her feet and hugging his legs. 'Thank you, thank you.'

Hugh blinked back the tears.

Beside him, Jo bent down and picked up the unicorn that had been abandoned in the excitement. 'Look, Howard,' she said, holding the fluffy toy near the doll. 'You have a little sister.'

'Yes,' giggled Ivy, taking Howard and embracing both toys. 'I'm their mummy.'

'Now for your room,' Hugh told Jo. 'There's a connecting door here, but you and Ivy have your own private *en suite* bathrooms. Is that OK?'

'Is that OK, Hugh?' Jo cried, giving him a strange look. 'Are you joking? Of course it's OK. You've seen my family's home.'

Remembering how nine Berrys shared one bathroom, Hugh felt his neck redden. He hurried ahead of her. 'Well, anyway, here's your room.'

Jo followed him slowly, looking about her with a serious, grim little half-smile. She dipped her head to smell the violets and rosebuds in the crystal vase on the dressing table and then she stepped up to the big double bed and traced the pale gold silk of the quilt with her fingertips and then the pillowcases and the pretty trim on the sheets.

'Snow-white sheets with drawn-thread cutwork and embroidery,' she said. 'I'm going to feel more like a princess than a nanny.'

There was a knock on the door and Humphries appeared. 'I have Miss Berry's suitcase.'

'Good man,' said Hugh. 'Bring it in, please.'

After Humphries had left again, Jo stood staring at her luggage sitting on the carpet at the end of her bed. 'I'm afraid my battered old suitcase looks rather dingy in the middle of such a lovely room.'

'You can stow it in a cupboard if it bothers you.'

'Yes.' She took a deep breath and squared her shoulders before looking at him and her intelligent brown eyes regarded him with shrewd wariness.

'What's the matter, Jo? Is there something not right?'

'Now I see where you come from, I can't believe you fitted in so well at Bindi Creek.'

'The differences are superficial,' he said. 'You'll fit in here too.'

Her face pulled into a disbelieving smile. 'We'll see.'

He was tempted—*very* tempted—to slip a comforting arm around her shoulders, but the look in Jo's eyes prompted him to slip his hands into his trouser pockets instead.

Jo crossed her arms over her chest and fixed him with her steady gaze. 'A girl can handle just so many surprises, Hugh. I think you and I need to sit down and have a serious talk.'

'Now?'

'No, we're all too tired now.'

Hugh was feeling more wired than tired, but he said, 'OK, I'll leave you to make yourself comfortable. My room's further along the hall.'

Her face broke into an unexpected grin. 'I bet the master bedroom is really something.'

His body reacted in an instant. 'You're welcome to come and take a look, if you like.'

'Oh, no,' she said quickly. Too quickly.

'It'd be a fair exchange, Jo,' he responded flippantly. 'You've shown me yours, so I'll show you mine.'

It was meant as a joke. No matter how much he'd like to have Jo in his bed, now wasn't the right moment. But, to his surprise, instead of accepting the joke and smiling, or telling him to drop dead, she looked upset and blushed brightly.

He felt a surge of dismay. What had happened to the light-hearted, level-headed Jo Berry? The sight of her blush bothered him and, damn it, *stirred* him, arousing the very desire he wanted to quench.

While he struggled to think of a way to lighten the moment, a plaintive cry came from Ivy's room.

'Jo, where are you?'

'I'm here,' Jo called.

The sound of a sob reached them and she quickly hurried back through the connecting door. Hugh followed.

Ivy had abandoned her toys and was huddled on the floor in the middle of her bedroom with tears running down her face. When she saw Hugh and Jo, she began to sob loudly and Hugh felt a panicky rush of alarm.

'What's the matter?' Jo said, dropping to her knees beside the weeping child.

'I don't know,' Ivy wailed. 'I got scared.'

'It's OK, you're just tired,' Jo said, hugging her. 'And everything here's a bit strange for you. What you need is to get into your pyjamas and then into your lovely bed. You'll feel better in the morning.'

'Would a cup of warm cocoa help?' asked Hugh, desperate to help.

Jo sent him a grateful smile. 'That would be lovely, wouldn't it, Ivy?'

His daughter gave her eyes a brave scrub and then nodded and Hugh dashed downstairs to the basement kitchen—a man on an urgent mission. By the time he returned, Jo had changed Ivy into a frilly white nightgown and the little girl's face looked pink and white and clean as if Jo had washed her as well.

Hugh held out the mug of cocoa.

'It's not too hot, is it?' asked Jo.

'I don't think so,' he said, but he wasn't sure. 'See what you think.'

He watched with interest as Jo tested the mug against her inner arm, then frowned and took a tiny sip. There were so many things to remember about caring for a child, especially this child who'd already experienced one horrendous accident. He wondered how many mistakes he would make. He felt again completely out of his depth.

'This is fine,' Jo said. 'Yummy, in fact.'

Ivy accepted the mug, drank deeply and beamed at him. 'It's very yummy, Daddy.' But she only drank half before her eyelids began to droop.

Jo was sitting on the edge of Ivy's bed and she

gently took the mug from her loosening grip and set it on the bedside table. Scant seconds later Ivy's head reached her pillow and she looked as if she'd fallen asleep.

Hugh began to tiptoe away. 'I'll just be—'

Ivy's eyes flashed open and Jo frowned at him and set a silencing finger against her lips. Chastened, he stood very still.

'Don't go away, Daddy,' Ivy demanded.

'Don't worry, Ivy. Daddy will stay right here till you're sound asleep,' Jo reassured her and Ivy's eyes closed again.

Somewhat gingerly, Hugh sat at the end of the bed. 'I'm here, poppet.'

With her eyes still closed, Ivy smiled and she looked so sweet and angelic he felt a surge of pride. Emotion lodged in his throat as a rock-hard lump. Good God, he was turning as hopelessly sentimental as his elderly Aunt Daphne.

And yet…

There was nothing sentimental about the way he felt when he looked at Jo.

As they sat together in the lamplit silence, Hugh let his mind play with the fantasy of helping Jo out of her clothes and into bed. He wondered what the chances were that the light tan on her arms and legs extended to her thighs and stomach…

'She's such a beautiful little girl.'

Jo's soft voice intruded into his pleasant musings.

Hugh smiled. 'I'm dreadfully biased, but I'm inclined to agree with you.'

'I'd say she's sound asleep now.'

But Jo didn't move and neither did Hugh. They continued to sit very still, super-conscious of each other's proximity as they watched Ivy.

'I imagine her mother must have been beautiful.'

'Linley? Yes, she was.' He sighed. 'But I'm afraid she was rather like a beautiful soap bubble or a butterfly. I felt as if I never got to the essence of her.'

'Oh.' Jo seemed to consider this as she watched Ivy thoughtfully. 'I don't think Ivy's like that.'

'No,' Hugh agreed. Even at the tender age of five, his daughter possessed an inner strength he'd never sensed in Linley.

Jo turned to him. She looked calmer now and she smiled sleepily.

'You look tired,' he murmured.

'Mmm. I am rather.' A wing of her hair fell across her cheek and she tucked it behind her ear.

In the past few days Hugh had seen her do this many times. He knew that before long her silky brown hair would slip forward again and he couldn't resist reaching out now to touch the soft curve of her exposed cheek. Her skin was as soft as a rosy-gold peach. 'Thanks for coming here, Jo.'

'I suppose I should be thanking you. I've never basked in so much luxury.'

'Treat this place like it's yours. Take whatever you like.'

She looked a little startled and Hugh couldn't resist leaning forward to drop a kiss on her surprised pink mouth. He heard the sharp intake of her breath and it sounded so sexy and her open lips were so warm and sweet that he kissed her again.

She had the loveliest mouth.

'Welcome to Britain, Jo Berry,' he murmured as he tested the soft, lush fullness of her lips.

'I'm very happy to be here,' came her breathless, throaty reply.

Hugh couldn't resist deepening the kiss and her lips drifted apart in open invitation. He reached for her hands and as he rose from the bed she came with him, moving slowly, languidly, almost floating, as in a dream. Next to the bed he drew her close and kissed her again and then he slipped his arm around her shoulders and she drifted beside him and he guided her to the doorway.

No sooner were they were out of Ivy's room and in the hallway than they fell into each other's arms and in a heartbeat their lips and tongues were sharing secrets they hadn't dared to speak of.

Hugh knew he was sinking fast. Jo was so sexy. She sounded and looked sexy and she tasted and felt incredibly sexy…

His hands explored the gorgeous curves of her bottom, the soft slenderness of her waist and then they found her breasts—beautifully full and soft and round—their tight peaks straining against the flimsy lace of her bra. With a soft, voluptuous moan she arched, pressing her breasts into his hands.

Rampant need inflamed him. He was losing control…

But then he realised Jo was pulling away from him.

She gasped, pressing her hands to her cheeks. 'This can't be real. I must be more jet lagged than I realised.'

No.

He was about to haul her back into his arms, to hurry her away with him to his bedroom, but her dark eyes looked directly into his and her gaze was intensely eloquent, as if she were pleading with him, commanding him to agree that their kiss had been a mistake.

Had it been a mistake? *Had it?*

His tormented body cried no!

But as Jo backed further away from him he knew that yes…it probably had been ill-advised.

Things could get very complicated if he dragged her to his bed the very minute he got her inside his front door.

'I'm going to follow Ivy's good example and get to sleep,' she said.

Hugh took a deep, still ragged breath. 'I'll ask Regina to bring a light supper on a tray to your room.'

'Thank you. Some cocoa and a sandwich would

be lovely.' Without looking his way again, she walked quickly away from him and into her room.

Next morning Jo and Ivy appeared in the dining room just as Hugh was helping himself to bacon and eggs. He'd spent a restless night—the combined result of jet lag and Jo.

But he was relieved to see that both Jo and Ivy were looking more chipper. Jo was looking exceptionally pretty, dressed in cream corduroy trousers and a soft wool sweater in a very fetching shade of deep pink. It seemed the perfect complement for her nut-brown hair and eyes.

She made Hugh think of…wild roses…on a summer's afternoon…

In fact, he found that he was staring.

'So that's what a full English breakfast looks like, is it?' she asked, eyeing his loaded plate.

He grinned, relieved that she seemed to take last night's incident in her stride. 'If you want the works you get sausages and baked beans as well. Of course, you don't have to have anything cooked.'

'Can I have some orange juice?' asked Ivy.

'Say please,' Jo reminded her.

'Please, Daddy?'

'Of course.'

'I'll just start with a cup of tea,' Jo said, helping herself to a cup and saucer as Hugh poured orange juice from a glass jug. 'I love this pink and white striped china. You have so many lovely things, Hugh.'

His mother had given him the china. At the time he'd thought it was a strange choice for a bachelor's pad, but whenever he'd brought young women home they'd adored it, and so he'd decided it was a definite asset.

Jo smiled when she lifted the teapot from the sideboard. 'Silver. I should have guessed.'

'Are you sure you wouldn't like something to eat?' he asked. 'Scrambled eggs or poached, or—?'

Behind him a door banged.

And a sharply elegant blonde, wearing an ankle-length silver fox fur coat, swept into the dining room.

Oh, God, no. Priscilla.

Hugh had no chance to recover from the shock of seeing his former girlfriend before she flung herself at his neck.

'Darling, I heard you were back. I've missed you so-o-o-o much.'

Her arms latched around him and he was enveloped in fox fur as she pressed herself against him and kissed him on the mouth.

Stunned and angry, he struggled to extricate himself from her embrace. 'What are you doing here?' he gasped.

'What a silly question, Hugh, darling. I just had to be here to welcome you home.'

Hugh sent a quick glance in Jo's direction. She was looking as stunned as he felt. But Priscilla man-

aged, very deftly, to ignore Jo. Her gaze—perfect
blue, but crystal cold—flicked rapidly over her as if
she didn't exist, before settling rather nervously on
Ivy.

'And this is your little sweetheart,' she said, smiling a very forced, awkward smile.

Hugh glared at her. How could Priscilla do this?
She'd broken up with him the minute she'd learned
of Ivy's existence.

'You can't have us both,' she'd told him when she
learned he was going to Australia to claim his daughter. 'Who will it be, Hugh—the child or me?'

'She's my flesh and blood,' he'd reminded her.
'My responsibility.'

'But you can't drag her into our lives now.'
Priscilla had made his daughter sound like something
the cat might bring back from a night's hunting.
'What would everyone think, Hugh? I'd be a joke!'

It was the last in a string of disappointments he'd
experienced during their relationship. He'd had
enough of Priscilla Mosley-Hart's tantrums and was
more than glad to be rid of her.

He made no attempt to introduce Ivy, and so
Priscilla bent forward stiffly, from the waist, and
bared her teeth as she tried again, unsuccessfully, to
smile at the child.

'What's your name, sweetheart?'

Ivy didn't answer.

Priscilla's plastic smile slipped, but she tried another tack. 'We'll be seeing a lot more of each other from now on, sweetheart.'

But Ivy had the good sense to remain silent and she watched Priscilla through narrowed eyes, as if she sensed she was in enemy territory.

'Oh, well,' said Priscilla with the air of someone who'd done her very best and couldn't be expected to succeed when a child was so obviously uncooperative.

Not for the first time, Hugh regretted the manners that had been hammered into him from birth. Unfortunate rules about the way a gentleman treated a lady prevented him from grabbing Priscilla by the scruff of her extravagant coat and marching her back through the front door.

He pressed a bell for Regina and his round-faced middle-aged housekeeper appeared at the door. 'Regina, would you mind taking Ivy to the kitchen and fixing her some breakfast?'

'I'd love to.' Regina beamed at Ivy. 'Come with me, ducks. Come and see all the lovely things I have for you. You must be so hungry after flying all the way from Australia.'

To Hugh's relief, Ivy seemed happy to escape downstairs.

'I'll go, too,' said Jo.

'No,' commanded Hugh sharply. Then, more gently, 'Please stay, Jo.' He wanted her to hear first-hand that his relationship with Priscilla was over.

'*I* think the nanny should leave,' Priscilla said with a sniff.

Hugh ignored her. Under no circumstances was she going to win this round. He said, 'Let me introduce Joanna.'

'Joanna?' Priscilla seemed to freeze and she turned to Jo with some difficulty.

Hugh took Jo by the elbow. 'This is Joanna Berry. She has come over from Australia and has very kindly—'

Priscilla let out an uncertain titter. 'What a sensible idea to bring an Australian nanny with you. She can do everything for Ivy before you find a school to send her to.'

How had he ever thought he was attracted to this woman? She was getting more ghastly by the minute.

Jo was standing very still with her eyes downcast, studying an antique table napkin. In one hand she held her cup and saucer, but she seemed to be paying great attention to the monogram on the napkin, running her fingertip over and over the embroidered initial R.

Priscilla gave a toss of her head. 'Now can we have some privacy, Hugh?'

'Why on earth do we want privacy?' Hugh injected a thread of menace into his voice—one Priscilla couldn't miss.

'What's the matter with you? That's a strange thing to ask your fiancée.'

'My *what*?'

Priscilla's smile was very brittle. 'Hugh, dear.' She lifted her left hand and pushed at a wing of her expensive hair and an enormous sapphire and diamond ring glinted on her fourth finger.

'Bloody hell, Priscilla, what game are you playing?'

Holding out her left hand, she waggled her fingers at him, making the sapphire and diamonds sparkle. She pouted. 'Our engagement is hardly a game, Hugh.'

'Our engagement? Have you gone mad? What's this ring?'

'I bought it at a sale at Sotheby's. Do you like it? It's just like the one we planned.'

'Like *hell*. We never planned any such thing.'

Beside him, Jo set down her cup and saucer and stepped away. 'I'm out of here,' she muttered, but Hugh moved quickly and reached for her arm and, at his touch, she froze.

Clearly put out, Priscilla fiddled with the ring, twisting it back and forth on her finger.

'Just tell me whatever it is you have to say, Priscilla.'

Ignoring Jo as best she could, she said, 'I know you want to forget my silly little outburst about dear little Ivy. I don't know what got into me. I was shocked. I was shaken. I wasn't thinking straight and it was all a mistake. Of course I didn't mean it when I said I wanted to break up.'

'I'm sorry, Priscilla,' Hugh said quietly, while he

held Jo's arm in a tight grip. 'It's too late to change your mind. You gave me an ultimatum. I was to choose between my daughter and you, and I made my choice.'

'But darling, I wasn't thinking straight. Of course you have to have your daughter with you.'

'Our relationship is over.'

'Like hell it is!'

'That's my final word.'

Priscilla gaped at him and then she pouted coyly like a spoilt little girl. 'But I'm planning to marry you, Hugh. Surely you always knew I would. I've booked the church.'

'Cancel it.'

A breathless silence filled the room. Hugh could feel white-hot anger sluicing through his veins.

Priscilla's eyes narrowed then and she directed a venomous glare at Jo, before swinging a blistering glance back to Hugh. 'This is *her* fault. She's got to you, hasn't she?'

'Stop right now.' Hugh spoke through gritted teeth. He'd known Priscilla had her imperfections, but he'd never seen this side of her before. Had she hidden it, or had he been blinded to it? 'Of course this isn't Jo's fault.'

He was surprised by the force of the rising anger surging through him and by his overpowering desire to protect Jo.

A kind of light-headed wildness overcame him and he slipped a possessive arm around Jo's shoulders.

The simple gesture had the desired effect. Priscilla sagged in horror as if she'd been kicked in the chest by a kung fu expert.

But she quickly rallied. Hatred flashed in her eyes. 'I can see she's got her nasty little claws into you already.'

'I'd advise you to shut up, Priscilla.'

She ignored him and directed her glare straight at Jo. 'You might be sleeping with him, but don't fool yourself that he would ever consider marrying you.'

Hugh felt a violent shudder pass through Jo and something inside him snapped. He had to defend her from this assault, even if it meant fighting dirty.

'That's exactly where you're wrong, Priscilla.' Hugh paused for dramatic effect.

Jo gasped.

And Priscilla screamed. 'You're not planning to marry *her?* You're mad. This is crazy. Your father will disinherit you.'

'Rubbish. He's delighted.'

'Now just hang on a minute,' interrupted Jo. Obviously embarrassed, she wrenched her arm out of Hugh's grasp. 'This is getting totally out of hand.' Outrage flashed in her eyes. 'I've had enough of listening to you two fight. I've more important things to do. I'm going to check on Ivy.'

With that she stormed out of the room—determined not to be involved in their little game.

Priscilla's lips curled into a sneer as she watched Jo leave. 'She might be a fast worker, but she's timid and flighty. She'll be the same as Linley Quartermaine. One thing's for sure, she won't last—not as your nanny—or as your fiancée.'

'It's time you left,' Hugh told her coldly. He should have chucked her out twenty minutes ago.

In desperation, Priscilla tried again to smile. 'You don't mean that, Hugh. I came here to tell you—'

'Leave right now, Priscilla. You've said more than is wise.'

She rolled her eyes. 'Don't you believe it; I've hardly begun.' And then, with a chilling, calculating smirk, she turned and sailed out of the opposite door from the one Jo had used.

Moments later Hugh heard the sharp click of her high heels in the marbled entry hall and shortly after that the front door slammed. And Jo came back upstairs.

She marched into the dining room, her face tense and tight and her hands planted on her hips, ready for battle.

'How's Ivy?' Hugh asked her quickly.

'She's fine—eating you out of house and home. I'll join her just as soon as we've had our little *chat*.'

'Jo, I'm sorry about that. Priscilla was abominable.'

'Yes, she was. But what are you up to, Hugh?'

He flinched.

Momentarily, her face crumpled. 'Why on earth did you let her think we're getting married?'

She looked so wretched a stab of pain pierced him in the chest.

To defend you and help me, he thought. 'To get through to her. To finish it,' he said.

'Surely you can wriggle out of a sticky situation with an old girlfriend without dragging me into it?'

'I know it was reckless of me, but at the time I was so furious with her.'

Jo glared at him. 'You didn't even deny that we're having sex.' She gave an accompanying stamp of her foot to show how very mad she was. 'You more or less said yeah, it's a red-hot relationship and we're going to get married.'

'That's not what I said at all.'

'It's what you implied.'

Hugh felt a surge of annoyance. He'd just had one woman take centre stage when he should have dropped the curtain on her. Now here was another!

He sighed. 'I was trying to defend you. I'm sorry.'

'It's a bit late for apologies. Priscilla's walked out of here convinced that we're having sex—which is dead wrong! And she thinks we're going to be married. Wrong again! What have you achieved? I can't see that you've done me any favours.'

Feeling cornered, he scratched the back of his neck. 'You have to admit, it was almost worth it to see the look on her face when she thought we were going to be married.'

Jo rolled her eyes to the ceiling, but a moment later a little smile tweaked the corner of her mouth.

'She did look like she'd been slapped in the face with a kipper.'

But then she gave an annoyed toss of her head. 'Don't try to sidetrack me, Hugh.' Eyeing him warily, she added, 'Just make sure you tell Priscilla the truth and tell her soon.'

The phone rang in the next room and he ignored it.

But Jo dived for the door. 'That might be Mum. I couldn't ring her last night because of the time difference, but she's expecting to hear if I've arrived here in one piece.'

She dashed to answer it, but she was back in less than a minute. 'It's your father,' she said, looking and sounding shaken.

Bloody hell.

'He's just congratulated me on my engagement to his only son. He was very polite and charming, but somehow I don't think he sounded too happy about it.'

Hugh groaned. The minute Priscilla had been out of the door she must have rung his father on her cellphone.

'You'd better sort it out, Hugh. I'm not prepared to continue this charade just so you can keep your Priscilla at arm's length.'

'Yes, you're right. I'll explain.'

The strange thing was, he thought as he headed to the phone, that for one reckless moment marrying Jo had seemed to make perfect sense.

CHAPTER FIVE

WHAT a mess! What a dreadful, dreadful mistake she'd made by coming to England—to Chelsea—to this house, Hugh's house. She should never have listened to her mother.

As Hugh went to answer the phone, Jo was awash with tears. The door closed behind her with a gentle click and she stumbled across the room to put as much distance as possible between herself and Hugh's conversation with his father.

She felt terrible. She'd already been tired after the long flight and a long, restless night of tossing and turning as her mind wove fantasies about her and Hugh and now—*this*.

Priscilla was ghastly.

Of course she was rather beautiful in a plastic, ultra-expensive, super-model kind of way. And men fell for that sort of thing—but how could Hugh have ever liked her?

But then she knew nothing about him really. *Nothing*. Well, one thing. She knew that he had to be seriously wealthy—or seriously in debt. He apparently owned his own aviation company and this house was five storeys tall and in one of the swankiest parts of London.

But that was all she knew and there were so many questions screaming around inside her.

And the biggest question was how he could so casually claim to be marrying her. It made a complete mockery of her deepening feelings for him.

With an angry little huff, she looked out through the dining room window—actually, it was a pair of full-length French windows—and they opened on to a little balcony edged with a dainty wrought iron railing. Elegantly decorated porcelain pots on the balcony had been planted with carefully pruned topiary trees, each tree consisting of three neatly clipped balls.

Around each trunk a large red bow had been tied, presumably to provide a touch of Christmas. She wondered if they'd been Priscilla's idea.

Outside the house, the sky was winter white. Across the street there was a row of tall trees so bare that she could see right through the branches to a large playing field and a big, rather grand old building.

'That's the Royal Hospital.'

Hugh's voice sounded close behind her.

Jo's heart leapt as she swung around. 'I didn't hear you come in. That was a quick conversation.'

'Charles the Second had the hospital built for returned soldiers,' Hugh said. 'It was designed by Christopher Wren.'

Why was he suddenly talking about hospitals and history? 'What's the matter, Hugh?' He looked rather pale. 'Did you explain to your father that the engagement was all a mistake?'

He looked a little ashamed and awkward but, to her relief, he nodded.

'Thank heavens for that.'

'But I wasn't able to talk him out of coming up to London. He and Mother are coming up from Devon soon.'

'Well… I suppose they want to meet Ivy.'

Hugh sighed. 'Yes.' Turning back to the table, where his bacon and eggs still lay cold and untouched, he said, 'I've rather lost my appetite. Why don't I ask Regina to do something quick and easy— some fresh tea and hot buttered toast? Would that suit you?'

'Yes, of course, thank you.'

He disappeared and was back in a matter of minutes. 'Breakfast is on its way.'

'Hugh, before Regina and Ivy get here, *I'd* like to get a few things straight.'

Hugh flexed his shoulders, squared his jaw and then grinned at her.

Jo wasn't in a grinning mood, but his smile wrought its usual havoc on her heart. She tried to hide her distress behind a small smile. 'I think it's only fair that I know exactly who I'm dealing with while I'm working here,' she said.

'You're not working here, Jo. You're my guest.'

'If I'm not working, why did you offer me a great deal of money?'

Hugh didn't seem to have an answer.

'So,' Jo resumed, 'I'd appreciate it if you'd answer a few questions.'

'What would you like to know?'

'What school did you go to?'

He looked taken aback. 'Why do you need to know that?'

'*Please*… I'd just like to know.'

'OK, I went to Eton.'

'Right.' She'd been afraid that would be his answer. 'And that signet ring on your little finger. It has a crest that matches the one on the teapot and the teaspoons.'

'You're very observant.'

'Is it a family crest?'

He glanced idly at his little finger. 'Yes.'

Jo picked up a starched linen table napkin. 'What about this initial R? Is it significant?'

'Jo, you've missed your calling. You should drop accountancy and take up law. I feel like I'm being cross-examined.'

'And I feel like a mushroom.'

'A what?'

'Someone who's deliberately kept in the dark.'

With a helpless shrug, he said, 'The R stands for Rychester. My father, Felix Strickland, is the Earl of Rychester.'

Oh, my God.

Jo's face flamed as she thought of how well Hugh had seemed to fit in at Bindi Creek, eating a

Christmas dinner of cold salads on the veranda with her family, listening politely to her dad's corny jokes and her brothers' risqué campfire stories.

She gulped. 'Does that mean—it doesn't mean—you're not related to the Queen, are you?'

'Good heavens, no.'

'So, what are you called? Does an earl's son have a title?'

'In formal circles they stick a Lord in front of my name, but you don't have to worry about that.'

Oh, heavens. What had Lord Hugh Strickland really thought of her family?

She remembered the wistful, dreamy look on her mum's face when she'd urged her to go to London with Hugh. Poor Mum. If she'd been hoping for a romantic outcome from this venture, she was in for a major disappointment.

What a joke. What a disaster! How had Jo Berry from Bindi Creek entertained even the tiniest romantic fantasy about an involvement with an heir to a British earldom?

Far out! Her fledgling dream seemed so foolish now. She was such a child. 'I wish you'd told me, Hugh.'

'But I wasn't keeping it a secret. I just didn't see the need to make a big deal about my family. It's only a title.'

Taking a deep breath, she folded her arms across her chest. 'What about your parents? I bet they're not as low-key about all this as you are. I'm sure your father was very relieved to hear that you haven't rushed into an engagement with the hired help.'

Hugh gave an exasperated shake of his head. 'If it's any consolation, my father has never liked any girl I've introduced to him. Priscilla was at the top of his list of pet hates.'

Jo awarded Hugh's father a mental tick for his good taste. 'And, speaking of Priscilla, what about her? Does she have blue blood too?'

'Her father has a minor baronetcy.'

Damn! Somehow, Jo hadn't expected that. Silly of her, but she'd hoped to hear that Priscilla was *nouveau riche*—with a father who'd made all his money doing something that was generally frowned upon— like robbing banks or making pornographic movies.

But Priscilla was an aristocrat. All Hugh's circle were probably aristocrats—a club of exclusive peers of the realm. Jo's sense of alienation, her hurt and simmering anger, erupted. Tears threatened, stinging her eyes. 'I can't believe I let myself get into this mess.'

'Jo, don't be upset.'

'Why not? I have every right to be upset. Maybe it doesn't bother you that your old girlfriend is running all over London spreading the word that you're sleeping with your daughter's nanny—or worse, that you've got yourself engaged to a money-grubbing nobody from Australia.'

'I doubt Priscilla has the energy to stir up trouble.'

Jo didn't believe him. After four years working in

a city office, she'd witnessed enough broken affairs to know that a woman scorned had masses of energy and could cause all kinds of damage.

What a mess. If she wasn't very careful she would start crying, but she was too proud to break down in front of Hugh, so she squeezed her eyes tightly shut and took so many deep breaths she was in danger of hyperventilating.

'Jo, I really am very sorry to have caused you this distress.' Hugh's voice sounded worried. His hand touched her cheek.

Her eyes flew open.

His face was very close to hers and he was looking at her so tenderly she almost broke into very noisy sobbing. And then he gave her his endearing, crooked-sad smile. 'I can't bear to see you upset,' he said ever so gently. 'You're such a sunshiny girl. I want you to be happy here.'

She blinked—twice—and forced a watery smile. Hugh's gentle concern was breaking her heart. 'Don't worry about me,' she said, holding bravely on to her smile. 'I'm fine.'

'No, you're not.'

'Then I'll *be* fine, very soon.'

Hugh leant just a little closer and dropped a quick, warm kiss on her forehead. It was just a brotherly kiss, but it was very nice. Jo drew a deep breath. And then suddenly Hugh's hand was at her waist and he dropped another kiss on to her cheek.

A second kiss was *not* brotherly. A flash of awareness zigzagged through her—and an unbearable longing for him to kiss her again.

But she knew she shouldn't let that happen. Not again. She should step away from him. Right now. Even if he wanted to, she mustn't let him kiss her the way he had last night. She mustn't submit. Hugh must realise how susceptible she was to his—

Oh, man. She'd hesitated too long.

His lips were already on hers. His hands were bracketing her face and he was taking a delicious sip at her top lip, and now, oh, *yes*, he was tasting her lower lip, drawing it gently between his teeth. And there was no way she could ask him to stop—especially when his hands shifted to her hips and, with a soft sound that was half a sigh, half a groan, he covered her mouth with his.

Her legs turned to liquid as he drew her against him. She could feel the hardness of his arousal and he began to kiss her with a thoroughness that stole her breath. His lips and tongue were hot and demanding—delving the soft, warm recesses of her mouth.

His hands slipped under her sweater to touch her bare waist and, just as it had last night, a wild longing broke loose inside her and he went on kissing her, as if he needed her desperately, as desperately as she needed him.

'Look what I found.'

A voice sounded in the doorway.

Breathless, stunned, they sprang apart. Jo's heart was going haywire.

Ivy came into the room with a huge fluffy marmalade cat in her arms. 'I found this pussy cat,' she said with a beaming smile.

Jo's head and heart were still spinning and she couldn't think of a thing to say. And then she felt a rush of shame. What must Ivy be thinking?

Hugh recovered first. 'Well, hello there.' His greeting sounded just a little breathless and he sent a quick sideways glance to Jo before he addressed his daughter. 'So you found Marmaduke?'

'Yes, I've been exploring and I found him under the stairs.'

'He's Humphries's cat, so be gentle with him.'

'And guess what else I found?'

Hugh glanced Jo's way again and he sent her a quick, worried smile. 'What else did you find?'

'Your Christmas tree, Daddy. Come and see, Jo, it's beautiful.'

'Hang on,' said Hugh. 'Here's Regina now with Jo's breakfast.'

As Hugh hurried to help his housekeeper with the heavily laden tray, Jo took a deep, steadying breath. The after-shock of Hugh's kiss seemed to reverberate all the way through her.

But thank heavens Ivy hadn't been upset by the sight of them pashing each other to oblivion.

Hugh looked particularly light-hearted as he joined her at the table. His eyes held Jo's for a shade longer than was necessary. Why? Was he flirting? She couldn't bear it if he was playing games with her.

She thought again of her mum and suddenly remembered her promise to phone her. 'Excuse me,' she said, jumping to her feet. 'I need to telephone home. Mum will be frantic.'

'By all means.'

'I'll be back in a minute.'

She supposed it must have been jet lag that hit her as she dialled her home phone number. She felt vague and disoriented and teary. But at least she managed to convince her mother that everything was absolutely fine and that she was very, very happy. However, she found the white lie exhausting and it was a relief to hang up.

Just as she did so, the phone rang again.

Jo started. Heavens, she was jittery. And then she stared at the phone, wondering if she should answer it. What if it was Priscilla, or Hugh's father?

She took a step back and looked through the doorway to the dining room. Hugh was busy showing Ivy how he liked to cut his toast and he paid no attention to the phone.

Her hand shook a little as she lifted the receiver. 'Hugh Strickland's residence,' she said and her voice came out squeaky and thin.

'Oh,' said a male voice. 'You must be Jo.'

'Yes, that's right.' She wondered nervously how this person knew about her. She thought of Priscilla and her stomach clenched.

'It's Rupert Eliot here,' the voice said. 'I'm a friend of Hugh's.'

He had a very nice voice, cultured and beautiful like Hugh's, and just as warm and friendly.

'Would you like to speak to Hugh?'

'No, that's not necessary. Hugh's coming to our party on New Year's Eve and Anne and I were hoping you could come too.'

He must have made a mistake. Surely he mustn't know she was the hired help. 'I'll—er—tell Hugh straight away,' she said.

'We're looking forward to meeting you, Jo,' Rupert added. 'Hugh rang me from Australia and said you were helping him with little Ivy. Make sure Hugh brings Ivy too. There'll be other children here and they'll be good playmates for her, so the sooner she gets to meet them the better.'

'That sounds lovely,' Jo said, feeling dazed. 'Thank you. Thank you very much.'

'We'll hope to see you on Friday then.'

Back in the dining room, as Hugh poured Jo a lovely hot cup of tea and plied her with toast, she told him of the phone call and he wasn't the least surprised.

'Rupert's my oldest and best friend,' he told her. 'His six-month-old daughter, Phoebe, is my god-daughter.'

She must have looked worried because Hugh rushed to reassure her. 'You'll really like Rupert.'

'He isn't a Lord or a Duke or anything, is he?'

Hugh grinned. 'He's an Honourable, but honestly you'd never know. He doesn't have a snobbish bone in his body.'

'He did sound rather nice on the phone.'

'Anne, his wife, is really wonderful. She's a mad keen gardener and just dotes on Phoebe.' Almost wistfully, he added, 'Rupert and Anne fell in love when they were both eighteen and they're as happy as pigs in mud.'

Jo decided she very much liked the sound of Rupert and Anne. But what on earth would she wear to their party?

Hugh, however, was one step ahead of her. He'd already made plans for a shopping expedition.

And later Jo decided she must have fallen under some kind of spell because, for the rest of the day, she had let Hugh lead her and Ivy to shops and exquisite boutiques all over Chelsea and Knightsbridge.

There had been a great deal of dashing about, jumping in and out of tall, sturdy, square-looking black taxi cabs, which Hugh had said was easier than taking his car and trying to find parking spaces.

The prices of the clothes were high enough to send Jo into credit cardiac arrest, but Hugh had taken complete charge of the purchasing and wouldn't listen to any of her protests.

By the time they'd arrived home, she and Ivy had an astonishing number of purchases, including beautiful winter coats for them both and a gorgeous, utterly *divine* red evening gown for Jo from a shop in Sloane Street.

'You'll need something glamorous to wear to the Eliots' party,' Hugh had insisted.

And, as she hadn't packed anything remotely formal, she'd had to agree.

Hugh had taken charge of the whole thing. He'd pointed the gown out to the assistant. 'I want Miss Berry to try that one. Take her away and if it fits and she likes it, we'll have it.'

'Would you like to see the young lady in the gown?' the assistant had asked.

'No,' he'd replied, sending Jo an unexpected wink and one of his bothersome smiles. 'Keep it as a surprise.'

There had been just one sticky moment when Ivy had spotted the toy department in Harrods and Hugh had been eager to rush in there and buy her the lot.

But just as he'd been about to dive inside, Jo had stopped him. 'I wonder if that's a good idea,' she'd said.

'Don't be a spoilsport, Jo.' She suspected that his look of stubborn resistance was one his own nanny must have endured on many occasions when he was a boy. 'It's not as if Ivy has a houseful of toys.'

'But already this week you've given her Howard and the baby doll and her beautiful new bedroom with all those school things and now an entire wardrobe of lovely clothes…'

'You think my money will spoil her?'

'If she gets too much too quickly.'

His eyes had twinkled as he smiled another charming smile. 'I've turned out OK, haven't I?'

Jo gave a roll of her eyes. No way would she comment on that. 'Ivy's not used to luxury.' As she said this, Jo had wondered if it was her own reaction she was talking about. It was hard not to feel uncomfortable about being surrounded by such wealth. It was such a far cry from home.

But then Hugh had let out an exaggerated, moody sigh and grinned. 'You're probably right. Women always know best.'

By then Ivy had already wandered right inside the toy department and she was entranced by a wind-up pig chugging across the floor.

'Can I have him, Daddy?' she'd asked as Hugh approached.

'Maybe not today, poppet.'

'But I want a pig!'

Hugh shot a here-we-go glance back to Jo. 'If you're very good I promise I'll buy you a pig another day,' he'd said as he reached down and scooped her up.

She'd begun to protest.

'It's time to go home to Howard and baby doll,' he'd said.

'And Marmaduke?' she'd asked, her eyes brightening quickly.

'And Marmaduke,' Hugh had agreed.

'Yes, let's go home. I love your home, Daddy.'

Hugh's eyes had gleamed with a suspicious sheen. 'It's your home too, poppet.'

As Jo slipped into her sumptuous bed that night, she was exhausted but almost too excited to sleep. A whole day with Hugh had been intoxicating. He'd been so much fun, so generous, so solicitous, and so full of compliments, both for her and for Ivy.

She knew that the inevitable was happening; she couldn't help herself. Even though she'd started out by trying to resist Hugh, she was falling way past head over heels and into the deepest depths of being hopelessly in love with the man.

And all the time they'd been shopping—when she'd been under his spell—and remembering his kisses—a romantic future beyond the brief two weeks had almost—*almost*—seemed possible.

The problem was that now, as she lay alone in the dark, listening to the muffled sound of distant traffic on the King's Road, the happiness of her day with Hugh seemed unreal.

Of course she would be going back to Australia at the end of the two weeks. Hugh had his little daughter. He and Ivy were wrapped up in each other.

They didn't really need Jo at all.

CHAPTER SIX

'DADDY?'

Ivy's voice came through the darkness just as Hugh passed her room.

Her door was halfway open and he gently pushed it further. 'Did you want something, poppet?'

'Can you tuck me in?'

'Yes, if you like.'

A newly purchased night-light in the shape of a toadstool stood on Ivy's bedside table, casting a warm pink glow across her bed, making her look rosy and prettier than ever, and Hugh felt a swift clutch of emotion.

'You look rather nicely tucked in to me,' he said, eyeing her neat bedclothes. 'What would you like me to do?'

'Daddy,' Ivy scolded. 'Tucking me in doesn't just mean tucking me in.'

'It doesn't? What does it mean then?' He felt lost again for a moment.

Ivy's bottom lip stuck out and her dark brows drew down into a stubborn frown. 'You should know.'

'Should I?' He swallowed a constriction in his throat. For the life of him he couldn't ever remember his own father tucking him into bed when he was a youngster. His mother had…but mothers and nannies were different, weren't they…and he'd been sent away to school when he was quite young. 'I'm sorry, Ivy. I've never had a little girl before.'

She turned her head to the side and looked towards the door that led to Jo's room. 'Jo knows what to do.'

'Well, yes.' Hugh sighed. 'That's because—because she has little sisters.' As Ivy continued to look sulky, he said, 'I'd love to tuck you in properly, sweetheart.'

'Don't call me that word.'

'Sweetheart? Why not?'

'That's what *she* calls me.'

'Who? Jo?'

'No. Gorilla.'

Gorilla? She meant Priscilla, of course. Hugh had difficulty suppressing his smile.

'I promise never to call you the S word again,' he said solemnly. 'Now, tell me what Jo does when she tucks you in.'

Ivy patted the bed. 'She sits here.'

'Oh, yes, of course,' said Hugh, lowering himself on to the edge of the bed.

'And she tells me a story, but you don't have to tell me a story.'

That was a relief. Hugh knew he wasn't much of a story-teller.

He watched Ivy looking up at him with trusting

expectation and he realised with a rush of happiness that there was no need to ask her what Jo did next. 'I've just worked out what a daddy should do now,' he said.

'What?' she asked, her green eyes sparkling suddenly.

Hugh picked up her hand. 'I should eat you up, starting at the fingertips.' He growled playfully as he began to nibble.

'No,' Ivy squealed, delighted.

'No? Then I should tickle you,' he suggested, tickling her ribs.

'No, no,' she protested amidst a flood of giggles.

'Have I still got it wrong?' He gave a deep, exaggerated sigh. 'Then, there's nothing for it, I'll just have to cuddle you and kiss you goodnight.'

'Yes!' With an excited cry she held out her arms.

And Hugh gathered her up.

His heart swelled. She was his little girl. His very own. She felt so tiny and warm and she smelled of clean nightgown and the delicately scented special soap Jo used to bathe her sensitive skin. And she clung to him, her little heart beating against his. He kissed her cheek.

'I love you, Daddy.'

'I love you too, poppet.'

He hugged her again and then released her and she sank happily back on to her pillow.

'I like that name.'

'Poppet?'

'Yes.'

'Good. I like it too. It's my special name for you.' He kissed her forehead.

'I'm so glad you came and founded me. Ellen told me you would come and I've been waiting for you for so-o-o long.'

Hugh's heart ached for her. 'I'm glad I found you too. Now, goodnight, sleep tight.'

'I will.'

Ivy reached for Howard and closed her eyes and Hugh's throat tightened with a welling of emotion, stronger than anything he'd thought possible. He was astonished and deeply moved by how quickly and completely his little girl had opened her heart to him.

As he watched her, she hugged the unicorn closer and the sleeve of her nightgown bunched, revealing the terrible burn scars on her arm, and he felt a sharp, savage twist to his heart, so intense that he thought he might actually cry. Fearful that Ivy might open her eyes and see his distress, he turned and walked quickly to his own room. What fierce, sweet agony it was to be a father. He wondered if he was adequate for the task.

He slumped on to the side of his bed and began to unbutton his shirt, lost in thought. So much tragedy had clouded his daughter's early life.

And yet in spite of that she was such a lively, spirited, loving little thing. But she had big battles ahead of her.

No matter how carefully he chose her school there

would be inevitable taunts about her burned skin from some of the children. And in the future, as she grew, she would have to face more trips to hospital and more painful skin grafts.

If Ivy was going to remain lively and spirited and grow into a happy, well-adjusted adult, she needed strong, positive, loving forces in her life.

Was he man enough for the task?

Until very recently he'd been a rather selfish man, but now he had little choice; he had to change. As his father had been telling him for years, he had to take life more seriously. The thing was, he found running a business and making money relatively easy. Personal relationships were more problematical.

His friendship with Rupert and Anne Eliot had been one of his sounder personal choices. His selection of women, on the other hand, had been lots of fun but less prudent. His girlfriends usually proved to be more decorative than reliable.

Priscilla was a prime example.

Damn.

The shoe he'd just removed fell to the floor with a thud as he remembered. He'd promised Jo he would phone Priscilla and set the record straight. But he'd had so much fun taking Jo and Ivy shopping today he'd forgotten.

He would have to plan his speech very carefully before he rang. It was important to hit exactly the right note and it wasn't going to be easy. First he had to squash Priscilla's assumption that he'd been sleeping with Jo; and then he had to confess that he'd lied about asking Jo to marry him; and finally he needed to block any opportunity for Priscilla to belittle Jo in any way.

Rather a tall order—especially when he also had to ensure that Priscilla was left in no doubt that he wanted her out of his life—and he most definitely didn't want her anywhere near his daughter.

It was mid-afternoon the next day before he made the call. He was at his office in the city, where he'd been attending to urgent business that couldn't be left until after the New Year weekend. But his guilty conscience was nagging him and at last he punched Priscilla's speed dial number into his cellphone.

She recognised his number even before he spoke. 'Hello, Hugh,' she purred. 'What a delightful surprise. What can I do for you, darling?'

He thought he'd prepared for this call, but suddenly his concentration—super-focused when dealing with business matters—was distracted by a kind of sixth sense, a vague feeling of unease, a suspicion aroused by the fact that Priscilla sounded far too relaxed and happy.

Was she plotting something?

'Darling?' Priscilla's voice repeated.

She'd never called him darling when they'd been a couple, and the hollow meaninglessness of the endearment set his teeth on edge now. 'Good afternoon, Gorilla, I hope you're feeling calmer today.'

'I beg your pardon?'

'I said I hope you're feeling—'

'Not that. What did you call me?'

'I don't know. I called you Priscilla, didn't I?'

'It sounded like Gorilla.'

Had he really made that slip? 'Good God, no,' he protested. 'Impossible. So, how are you?'

'Calm as a millpond. We're having an absolutely fab time—afternoon tea at The Ritz.'

'How nice.' It had been raining heavily since lunch time and taking tea in one of the city's grand hotels while the rain fell on others less fortunate outside was a predictable, Priscilla-style activity.

He could picture her adopting her Marie Antoinette pose as she lifted a crystal champagne flute or a teacup—azure blue with a thick gold rim—or took a leisurely nibble at a dainty cucumber and smoked salmon sandwich. Yes, she *would* be at The Ritz; he could even hear a string trio playing Mozart in the background.

Somewhat reassured that she was out of harm's way, Hugh refocused his attention on his line of attack.

'You'll never guess who's here with me,' she said.

Distracted, it took a moment or two for her question to register. 'Oh?'

'Jo and Ivy.'

'What?' Fine hairs rose on the back of Hugh's

neck. His gut clenched as he leapt from his swivel chair. Jo and Ivy had gone sightseeing today.

Priscilla chuckled. 'Isn't it a lucky coincidence?'

Like hell it was.

'I ran into the poor things just as they were leaving Hyde Park.'

It was more likely that she'd been stalking them.

'Hugh, you should tell your international visitors never to go out in London without an umbrella. The poor darlings were absolutely drenched and it was freezing cold. Poor little Ivy could have caught pneumonia. Of course I insisted on giving them a lift to The Ritz to dry off.'

By now Hugh had grabbed his coat and was shrugging his shoulders into it as he clutched his cellphone to his ear. 'How are they?' he barked as he rushed out of the office.

'They're absolutely peachy *now*, darling. Jo's enjoying a cup of Earl Grey and Ivy's stuffing herself with scones and strawberry jam and cream.'

Hugh knew this pretence at cosiness was nonsense. There was no way Priscilla would make such an about-turn without a reason. A rotten, sneaky reason.

He was absolutely certain she hadn't extended such a conciliatory gesture to Jo out of the goodness of her heart. As the lift shot him to the car park in the basement, he tried to think of a way to keep the conversation going. He needed to distract Priscilla from whatever she had planned.

But, just as he reached his car, Priscilla said, 'Oh,

sorry, Hugh. We have an emergency. Ivy needs to go to the ladies' room.' And she hung up.

He considered calling straight back again, but chances were she wouldn't answer and he decided instead to concentrate on his driving. He needed to make his way through the rain and the traffic as quickly as possible.

He felt ill with dread as he steered his car through driving sheets of rain, but as he turned down Piccadilly, he tried to convince himself his fears were illogical.

Priscilla might have turned nasty, but she wasn't evil. And what could happen to Jo or Ivy at The Ritz? The place was swarming with staff trained to watch over their patrons and to attend to their every whim.

Swerving into Arlington Street, his tyres sent up a spray of rainwater and another shower as he came to a halt quite close to The Ritz's commissionaire. But the good fellow, dressed in his greatcoat and top hat and armed with a huge black umbrella, greeted him with his customary courteous smile.

'Would you like us to park your car, Lord Strickland?'

'Thanks,' Hugh muttered, tossing the keys to him. He had no time for their usual exchange of pleasantries as he dashed through the rain to the huge revolving doors.

Where were Jo and Ivy?

His gaze darted everywhere as he strode through the spacious lobby. He had no idea if Priscilla was here or in The Ritz's famous Palm Court restaurant. Most people needed to make a reservation for afternoon tea in the Palm Court and Priscilla might have done so but, then again, she was a notorious queue jumper.

One thing was certain; when Hugh found her, he was going to make sure that the first message she got was to get the hell out of his life. He wasn't prepared to have her anywhere near his daughter—or Jo!

And then suddenly he saw Priscilla, walking through the lobby, looking about her in much the same manner as he was. Alone.

Surprised to see him, she blinked. 'Hugh, what are you doing here?'

'I came to have a word with you.'

Something in his tone must have alerted her. She looked suddenly wary. 'Hold it, Hugh. Don't say a thing you might regret. The most important thing right now is to find your daughter.'

'What?' Hugh felt as if he'd been slugged. 'What the hell do you mean?'

'The poor little sweetheart. I'm trying not to think the worst, but dear little Ivy has disappeared.'

'How could she?' Hugh roared so loudly that several heads turned their way. 'What have you done?' He couldn't bear this. He grabbed Priscilla's arm. 'Where's Jo?'

'Who knows where Jo is? She panicked and took off. She's no good in a crisis.'

That was rubbish but he didn't have time to argue. 'Where was Ivy when you last saw her?'

Priscilla shrugged. 'She went to the ladies' room and didn't come back.'

'Where? Which ladies' room? Have you searched every cubicle?'

She slipped her arm through his and snuggled against him. 'Come with me, darling. I'll do my best to show you where she was last seen.'

Hugh shook her off. 'Just lead the way and be quick about it.'

As they rounded a corner Jo came towards them. And, in spite of Hugh's terror, he felt an immediate lift in his heart. But, to his surprise, she was walking at a sedate pace and she didn't seem particularly distressed.

'Have you found Ivy?' he demanded. But it was a foolish question. Surely if she'd found the child she wouldn't be alone.

'Not yet,' she said calmly. 'But I'm sure she'll turn up soon.'

Her composure annoyed him. 'How can you be so sure? Have you alerted the staff?'

'Yes, and I'm sure they'll find her. She must have gone exploring.'

'What about the police?'

'The police, Hugh?' Her brown eyes rounded with surprise. 'No. I didn't want to overreact.'

Hugh ploughed frantic hands through his hair. 'I can't believe this.' He reached for his cellphone.

'What are you doing?'

'Calling the police, of course.'

Jo laid a restraining hand on his arm. 'Just a minute, Hugh. Calm down. Ivy has been missing for ten minutes. Isn't it a bit early to call the police? We don't want to make a fuss about nothing. I'm sure she'll turn up any minute now.'

What had happened to warm, caring Jo? 'How can you be so damn casual?'

'This is a big hotel and a little girl has wandered off,' she said. 'But, for goodness' sake, the place is full of very nice, charming people, who will be only too happy to help her to find us.'

Her forehead creased as she peered at him more intently. 'Do you really think London is a mass of kidnappers just waiting to jump on her?'

Yes, he wanted to shout. A part of him knew he was overreacting but he just didn't know what a father should do in a situation like this.

But, at that very moment, Jo glanced past his shoulder and smiled. 'Look, just as I thought. Here she is.'

Hugh spun around and a desperate, choking little laugh broke from him. There was Ivy walking along the corridor, holding hands and chatting happily with an elegantly dressed, sweetly smiling elderly lady.

The moment she saw him, Ivy let go of the woman's hand and rushed forward excitedly.

'Daddy!' She hurled herself at his waist. 'What are you doing here?'

Hugh was so overcome, so suddenly confused, he couldn't speak. He simply patted Ivy's head while she clung to him and, although his heart was galloping like a steeplechaser, he noted that her hair was only a little damp and her clothes weren't wet at all. Obviously Priscilla's claim that she'd been drenched was an exaggeration.

He heard Jo thanking the elderly woman profusely and he took a deep breath and blinked several times to try to clear his eyes.

Jo knelt in front of Ivy. 'Where were you? We've been searching everywhere. You gave Daddy a terrible fright.'

Ivy gave a puzzled shrug. 'Gorilla took me to see the big Christmas tree and told me to hide there. She said it was a game and I had to wait there for you to find me, Jo. But you didn't come.'

'That scheming—' Hugh spun around, looking for Priscilla, and realised that Jo was doing the same.

'Where is she?' they both asked simultaneously.

But it was rather obvious that she'd taken off.

Jo's lip curled into a very un-Jo-like malicious sneer. 'She plotted this.' She shook her head in disbelief. 'She was trying to make me look bad—trying to prove that I don't know how to look after Ivy.'

'I can't believe you got in the car with her.'

Jo sighed. 'She made me feel terribly guilty about having Ivy out in the rain. But Ivy's coat has a hood. She was fine, really.' She darted Hugh a shrewd glance. 'How did you get here so fast? Did Priscilla phone you?'

'No,' he said. 'As a matter of fact *I* was ringing *her* to—' He broke off, not keen to admit that he still hadn't carried out his promise to set Priscilla straight.

With one arm around Ivy, holding her close, he watched the play of emotions on Jo's expressive face as she stood regarding him with her arms wrapped over her middle.

'You haven't spoken to her yet, have you?'

'I was about to.' He knew that was the lamest excuse under the sun.

'No wonder she tried to quiz me. She still doesn't know, does she? It's your job to set her straight, Hugh, not mine.'

'I'm sorry.' He chanced a smile. Jo was looking very fetching in an ivory-cream sweater, tweed skirt and knee-high brown leather boots that he'd bought her in Knightsbridge yesterday. 'What did you tell her?'

'Oh, what does it matter?' she cried angrily. 'I should never have spoken to her. I shouldn't have let her persuade me to come here with her.'

He stepped towards her and reached out to pat her shoulder, but she jerked away quickly and sent him a sharp hands-off look.

He had to hand it to Priscilla. She'd managed to upset everyone.

'I'll take you home,' he said.

'Goody.' Ivy beamed.

Jo merely nodded. And then, 'I'll fetch our coats.'

As they approached the heavy revolving doors, Jo took Ivy's hand and Hugh let them go ahead. Through the glass, he could see a policeman on the footpath, talking to someone. And then, as the door rotated and he stepped into the next available space, Jo and Ivy reached outside.

Hugh shoved at the door and pushed his way forward.

The policeman turned. 'Lord Strickland?'

'Yes?' Hugh snapped. 'What do you want?'

'We've received a report that your little daughter is missing.'

Damn.

CHAPTER SEVEN

JO WOKE to the shrill ringing of a telephone.

She lay in the semi-paralysed state of the still-half-asleep and it seemed to take ages for her mind to kick into gear. When it did, she remembered that she'd been dreaming about phone calls…lots of phone calls… *weird* calls…from home, from Priscilla, from her boss in Brisbane, even one bizarre call from Queen Elizabeth the Second.

As she pushed her bedclothes aside and swung her feet over the edge of the bed, the phone downstairs rang again, and she wondered if it had been ringing a lot this morning. Perhaps it was the sound of many phone calls that had penetrated her sleep and prompted her strange dreams.

Had something happened? Some kind of emergency?

Her mind flashed back to last night. Hugh had been moody and distracted, but he hadn't wanted to talk about it with her. In fact he'd gone out.

Ivy had been dog-tired and had fallen asleep quite early, but Jo hadn't been able to sleep till after midnight. She hadn't heard Hugh come home.

Again the phone rang. What was going on? Her

122

feet sank into the deep pile carpet as she hurried to check on Ivy. She was gone.

Her first reaction was to panic, but then she told herself that was silly. Nevertheless, she washed her face quickly and dressed in haste, paying no more attention to her hair than to drag a quick brush through it before she rushed downstairs.

And, of course, there had been no need to panic.

Ivy was at the dining table, still in her pyjamas and with her hair a mass of sleep-tousled curls, and Hugh was helping her to take the top off a boiled egg that sat in a bright red hen-shaped eggcup.

He offered Jo a rather grim smile as she hurried into the room. 'Good morning.'

Ivy waved a gleeful spoon at her. 'We started breakfast without you.'

'Sorry, I slept in.'

'That's no mean feat, considering all the phone calls,' said Hugh.

So she'd been right. There had been a lot of calls even before she had woken. 'Why so many? What's happened?'

Hugh shrugged as if to make light of her query, but then his face twisted into an angry scowl. 'Have a cup of tea before you try to face the day.'

'What does that mean?' she asked as she lifted the silver teapot.

He didn't answer, but his scowl remained stiffly in place as he watched Ivy dip a finger of toast into her softly boiled egg.

'Come on, Hugh, tell me what's happened.' The worried tension in his eyes frightened Jo. 'Does it involve me?'

'I'm afraid so.' His glance shifted to a folded newspaper lying on the dining table.

Jo's teacup rattled against its saucer and she set it down quickly. She felt ill. 'Don't tell me there's a story in the paper. Priscilla hasn't run to the press?'

'Don't worry, it's a load of nonsense. And this is a discredited rag. No one takes any notice of it.'

'If no one takes any notice, why have there been so many phone calls?'

Even as she spoke, the phone rang again in the next room. She glanced expectantly at Hugh. 'Are you letting the answering machine deal with them?'

'Humphries is handling all the calls,' he said. 'He's doing a sterling job, diverting press enquiries to my PR fellow and vetting the private messages. I'll deal with those later.'

Jo's gaze flashed back to the newspaper—a potential time bomb just sitting there on the table—looking innocuous in the middle of all the breakfast things.

Hugh leaned closer to Ivy. 'Poppet, how would you like to have breakfast down in the kitchen with Regina again?'

She grinned. 'And Marmaduke?'

'Yes, Marmaduke will be there too.'

'Can I take my egg?'

'Of course.'

'Is Jo coming?'

'No, Jo and I need to talk about something.'

Hugh's ominous tone caused a lead weight to settle in the pit of Jo's stomach. She reached for the paper as soon as he and Ivy left the room, but she didn't want to read whatever was printed there.

And yet, if it involved her…and if the entire London populace already knew what it said…she had to face the worst.

The paper shook in her hands as she unfolded it and scanned the headlines. At first she couldn't see anything except general news stories. But then she saw a column—*Nelson's Column*—down the left-hand side and Hugh's name jumped out at her.

Sinking into a chair, she began to read.

The Lord's Love-Child

Publicity-shy and supposedly squeaky-clean Lord Hugh Strickland, only son of the Earl of Rychester, has finally blotted the family's impeccable copybook.

Not one to do things by halves, the charming Lord Hugh is now at the centre of a growing scandal featuring the suicide of an abandoned lover and the sudden appearance of an illegitimate child, flown from Australia earlier this week.

Obviously the powerful and influential family went to great lengths to keep this a dark secret, particularly the fact that Strickland's love-child, a sick and delicate little girl, has a severe deformity.

No! Oh, God, no! Dropping the paper, Jo covered her face with her hands. How could they say something so terrible about Ivy? This was much worse than she'd feared. She wasn't sure she could bear it.

Could it get any worse?

Sick with dread, she forced herself to read on…

And it could have remained a family secret but for the bungling of an unqualified Aussie nanny who lost the child on her first outing in London yesterday.

A lost child sparks a call to the police, which in turn alerts the media (to keep you fully informed of the scandalous facts, dear reader)…and, as usual, this column is delighted to provide a vital link in the info chain.

How does a nanny lose a child on a visit to one of London's grandest hotels?

Perhaps it's not surprising when the attractive but totally disoriented nanny only has eyes for Lord Hugh…

The nanny, one Jo Berry, has no training or qualifications for the task (her previous experience has been with cattle, sheep and wombats) but apparently she's the hottest thing that the dashing Lord set eyes on when he made a mysterious visit to the wilds of the Australian outback recently.

It is obvious that the relationship is much more than nanny to Strickland's love-child and a source close to the family reports that an engagement has been announced to shocked family and friends.

But perhaps we shouldn't be too harsh on poor Miss Bindi Creek (Yes, dear readers, there is such a place, I assure you).

It's no wonder she forgot she was guarding a defenceless little girl whose medical condition requires constant attention.

Jo Berry probably had stars in her eyes, visions of diamond rings, a society wedding and a honeymoon spent rolling naked in the Rychester estate money.

But here's some free advice for little Miss Bindi Creek:

'You can lose the diamonds, darling, or even the engraved family silver…but not the daughter of the heir to the estate of the Earl of Rychester.'

The fiery old Earl himself is about to intervene and even this intrepid reporter wouldn't want to be around when that happens!

So, readers, stand by for official denials about any impending marriage and watch for the imminent return of Miss Bindi Creek to her distant native soil.

Jo thought she might throw up.

Each sentence was like a knife thrust. She couldn't bear it. She'd heard of gutter press but she'd never imagined such awful journalism was possible. There were so many lies. Every word was a lie.

Unable to bear the sight of that ghastly print, she

closed her eyes, but from beneath her lids tears spilled down her cheeks. Hurt and indignation welled in her throat.

'Jo, it's a beat-up column by a broken-down hack.'

Hugh's voice startled her. She hadn't heard him return.

Looking up, she slapped at the newspaper in her lap. 'This is Priscilla's work, isn't it? This is all because of that stupid smokescreen engagement.'

'Yes,' he admitted. 'I didn't expect her to be so quick off the mark—or so vicious.'

Tears blinded her. She was trembling with anger and outrage.

'Jo, I promise you, I've dealt with Priscilla now. Last night. She won't cause you any more problems.'

'*She doesn't need to!* She's already done her worst.' With an angry yelp, Jo tossed the paper on to the floor and stomped on it. 'How can any journalist write such filth? Everything in it's a lie. They're all vicious lies. It's totally, totally despicable. One hundred per cent wrong. It's vile.'

Pressing her fingers against her lips, she tried to stop her mouth from twisting out of shape.

But she couldn't stop herself from crying. She felt violated. Betrayed.

Hugh reached for her and she tried to bat him away, but he drew her close and she was too overcome, too helpless to hold back. Her head fell on to his strong, bulky shoulder and she clung to him as she sobbed her heart out.

'I'm sorry, Jo,' he said in a husky whisper. 'I'm really sorry that this has happened.'

She wanted to be mad at him. She *was* mad at him. But he sounded so genuinely sorry that she found herself forgiving him.

And, as her sobbing slowed, she realised that it was rather comforting to nestle into his reassuring strength, to feel his protective hand stroking her head. He was actually being rather patient with her. He wasn't annoyed by her tears as many men might be. He held her as if he had all the time in the world.

He held her as if he cared. Really cared. And that made such a difference.

When at last she felt calmer, she lifted her head. 'This must be awful for you too, Hugh.'

But all he said was, 'I'm furious and incensed for you and for Ivy.'

She stepped away from him and her eyes searched his face, trying to read his true feelings beneath the calm, handsome façade. 'I guess this is what people with high profiles have to put up with.'

'Yes, it goes with the territory. But don't worry, this will backfire on Priscilla. She'll be *persona non grata* among our friends.'

There was a careful knock on the door behind them.

Hugh turned. 'Yes, what is it?'

Humphries took two steps into the room. 'I have a message from the QC you asked me to contact.'

'Good man, what did she say?'

'She's afraid that a successful action is unlikely, sir—and going to trial would be very messy and distressing.'

'I see.' Hugh's green eyes were thoughtful as he stood with his hands on his hips. 'I can't say I'm really surprised.'

'Why not?' Jo couldn't help asking. 'There isn't a grain of truth in that column. Surely you can sue them? The whole thing's a stack of garbage.'

'Yes, it's a stack of garbage, but unfortunately it's garbage piled on top of some basic facts.'

'Facts?' she cried. 'There's nothing factual.'

'Thank you, Humphries,' Hugh said and, with a courteous bow of his head, Humphries left them.

Hugh turned back to Jo. 'I'm afraid we're just going to have to ride this out. There's no point in getting tangled up in a long and drawn out court case and having the media stirred into a frenzy.'

Jo frowned. 'What did you mean before—about facts? Where were the facts?'

Letting out his breath slowly, he leant a hip against the table and folded his arms over his chest. 'Well, there's Linley's suicide...'

'OK,' she said slowly. 'That might be true, but I didn't lose Ivy yesterday. And to say that Ivy is deformed! That's a terrible thing to say about such a beautiful little girl.'

'I agree totally.' Hugh ran a hand down his face and released a long sigh. 'But can you imagine the pain of arguing in court about whether Ivy was lost

or hiding—or—or whether she's beautiful or deformed?'

'No,' Jo admitted, shuddering. Hugh was right. It
would be horrendous. 'And I guess I'll just have to
live with all that rubbish about Bindi Creek and the
claim that I wouldn't know how to care for anything
except wombats. But it—it's—'

She clamped her mouth shut to stop herself from
swearing. If she wasn't careful she would be in tears
again.

'I doubt anyone will believe that about you, Jo.'

'But then there's the problem of the engagement
announcement,' she said. 'I assume you set Priscilla
straight last night, but what about everyone else?
What are you going to tell them?'

'About our plans to marry?'

The question seemed to resonate in the room as if
a gong had been struck. Hugh continued to lean
against the table, not moving at all.

But a tiny smile sparked in his eyes.

And a sudden shiver rippled down Jo's spine.

'I don't know,' he said at last, letting the words
roll out slowly. 'Maybe we shouldn't get too uptight
about denying our wedding plans. After all, it's New
Year's Eve.'

Jo gulped to try to rid herself of the sensation that
she'd swallowed a marble. 'What's New Year's Eve
got to do with it?'

His eyes shimmered with an intensely intimate glow.

And for some inexplicable reason Jo couldn't breathe.

This was ridiculous. Anyone would think she and Hugh had something going—an *understanding*—that they were actually contemplating marriage.

And, just to make things worse, her skin flashed hot and cold as she remembered the way he'd kissed her, the way she'd kissed him back.

His mouth tilted into his familiar heartbreaking smile. 'Today marks an important milestone. We've known each other for an entire week, Jo.'

A week. Had it only been such a short time? She felt as if she'd known Hugh for ever.

He was still smiling. 'So it wouldn't be rushing things if we made our engagement official, would it?'

Of course he was teasing her. He had to be. *The cad.* She wasn't in the mood for playing games.

It wasn't very sporting of him. Even if he was the future Earl of Rychester and the best-looking man in Greater London, and even if his ancestors had been bedding their serving wenches for centuries, Lord Hugh Strickland should know better than to play around with his daughter's twenty-first century nanny.

Her emotions were already fragile this morning and now she could feel her anger shooting high— volcano style. It would serve Hugh right if she called his bluff.

Come to think of it, why shouldn't she? It would

do him the world of good if he got some of his own back.

With a coolness that reflected nothing of the havoc inside her, she threw back her shoulders and looked straight into his cheeky smiling eyes. 'What a terrific idea, Hugh. We can make a formal engagement announcement at your friend Rupert's party tonight. Actually, why stop there? I'll alert the Country Women's Association in Bindi Creek to be ready to cater for our wedding reception. That would be fine with you, wouldn't it?'

She allowed herself a small, self-satisfied smirk as she waited for his reaction.

But, when it came, it wasn't quite what she expected.

Hugh didn't laugh. He didn't chuckle. He didn't even grin.

He suddenly looked impossibly serious. Colour stained his high cheekbones and he stared at her with a breath-robbing intensity.

For lo-o-ong seconds they stood watching each other, while Jo's heart pounded and her preposterous counter to his joke echoed back at her from every corner of the room.

What was the matter with Hugh? He must know she wasn't serious. He knew she was going home at the end of next week.

Suddenly overcome by the tension that seemed to have seized them both, she dropped her gaze and stared at her hands instead. For heaven's sake, someone had to break the silence. She took a deep breath. 'And if tonight's going to be the big night, you've only got the rest of the day to come up with a spectacular proposal.' And then she chanced an anxious glance his way.

And at last he reacted.

For one brief moment he frowned. Then his right eyebrow arched as he flicked back the ribbed cuff of his black cashmere sweater and looked at his wristwatch. 'So we have till midnight?' Without warning, he sent her a roguish smile. 'That means we still have fourteen and a half hours. Plenty of time for me to propose.'

Jo gulped. Was she seriously overreacting, or was this nonsense getting completely out of hand? But as she struggled to think of a response, the front door bell rang.

And Hugh's merriment vanished. 'Humphries will get that,' he said, suddenly businesslike. 'If either of us answers the front door we might find our photo in the paper tomorrow.'

'Really?' It hadn't occurred to Jo that there might be paparazzi lurking outside Hugh's house. She was standing near a window where the curtains had been drawn open, and she couldn't resist taking a quick peek.

'Jo, stay away.'

Too late! There was a bright flash from the foot path.

She jumped back. 'I'm sorry, Hugh. I didn't think they would notice me up here.'

From the hall came the sound of the front door slamming, and then a man's voice. 'Damned press. Every last one of them should be hanged, drawn and quartered.'

'But not by you, Felix,' a woman's voice said. 'There was no need to swing at that young man with your umbrella.'

'Ah,' said Hugh with a strange look that expressed a mixture of pain and virtuous duty, as if he'd swallowed unpalatable medicine that he'd been told was good for him. 'Now you'll have the pleasure of meeting my parents.'

'Already? I thought they were coming up from Devon?'

Hugh managed a tight smile. 'By helicopter.'

Oh, good grief. Jo pressed damp palms against her thighs and found herself standing to attention. She didn't feel ready to meet the earl and his wife. Not before breakfast.

To add to her surprise, Hugh crossed to her side and slipped a friendly arm around her shoulders. 'Don't look so worried, Jo. They'll love you. You're the daughter-in-law they've always wanted.'

'Stop it, Hugh. How can you keep joking about that?' She was furious that he could be so playful about such a serious subject. How insensitive of him to tease her now, when he must know she was stressed to the max!

Even if Hugh's parents hadn't read the column in the paper they were sure to have heard about it. They would know by now that she was the incompetent, careless nanny who'd managed to lose their grandchild between bouts of leaping into bed with their son.

If only she could scurry downstairs to join Ivy and Regina in the kitchen.

'Oh, God, Hugh,' she whispered in sudden panic. 'How do I address your parents?'

'Call them Felix and Rowena,' he whispered back.

'Hugh!'

He grinned. 'Or Lord and Lady Rychester—whichever takes your fancy.'

She half-expected Humphries to come to the door and announce the earl and his wife, the way butlers did in movies, but when the door opened a somewhat matronly woman hurried into the dining room and Jo had no chance of getting her knocking knees under control.

'Hugh, darling.'

'Mother.'

Holding out her arms, the woman gave Hugh a kiss and an enthusiastic motherly hug.

Jo bit back an involuntary gasp of surprise. She wasn't sure what she'd expected Lady Rychester to look like—probably someone with a regal air and a haughty, cold beauty like Priscilla's. She certainly hadn't anticipated a woman who was shorter than herself, almost plump, with soft salt and pepper curls and warm, smiling brown eyes.

Hugh's mother even had an outdoorsy glow about her. She was not unlike how Jo's own mother might look if Margie Berry ever had the funds to dress in classic black trousers, a cream silk blouse teamed with a Hermes scarf, and pearl studs in her ears and a single strand of perfectly matched pearls at her throat.

Jo had barely got over that shock before Hugh's father, who'd been having a word with Humphries, strode into the room.

The earl was a different story—a taller, thinner, more stiff-upper-lipped version of Hugh. His eyes were very dark, almost piercing jade-black, and they made him look more than a little frightening.

Lord Rychester greeted Hugh with a grunt and a handshake. 'Had to fight through a pack of vultures to get to your front door,' he grumbled.

And then he fixed his sharp-eyed attention squarely on Jo.

CHAPTER EIGHT

HUGH intervened quickly. 'Mother, Father, I'd like you to meet Joanna Berry. As you know, she's kindly come with me from Australia to help Ivy settle in. I couldn't have managed without her.'

Hugh's mother clasped Jo's hand between hers. 'I'm delighted to meet you, Joanna. It's so kind of you to help Hugh.'

'How do you do, Lady Rychester?' Jo said and she wondered if a curtsey was in order.

'Pleased to meet you, Joanna,' the earl said more formally.

Jo offered her hand. 'How do you do, Lord Rychester?'

Oh, heavens, this felt seriously scary.

How had a chance meeting with Hugh in her family's humble shop in Bindi Creek lead her to this?

'My dear, I can't imagine what you must think of our outrageous British press,' said Hugh's mother. 'I'm so sorry.'

Jo could have kissed her. 'Thank you. It's very kind of you to say so.'

'We've had a dreadful morning,' admitted Hugh.

'Damn tabloids,' muttered the earl and his piercing gaze speared Jo. 'Don't give them a victory, lass.

You're not going to charge off home to Australia because of this, are you?'

'Not yet, sir.'

'Jo hasn't even managed so much as a cup of tea this morning,' said Hugh.

'Can't have that,' said his father. 'Let's get a fresh pot. I could do with a cup.'

Hugh smiled. 'I'll organise fresh provisions.'

Lady Rychester was casting a curious glance towards the door leading upstairs. 'I'm dying to meet Ivy,' she said. 'Is she awake?'

'She's in the kitchen,' Hugh told her, 'eating a soft boiled egg with toast soldiers.'

His mother's eyes shone. 'Oh, the little darling.' She turned to Jo. 'Is she very shy?'

'No, not really.' The eager light in the other woman's eyes touched Jo's heart. She'd been so caught up with feeling nervous that she'd temporarily forgotten how important this meeting must be for Ivy's grandmother. Now she felt a rush of empathy for her.

'I'll fetch Ivy, shall I?' asked Hugh with a proud smile that advertised how very much he was enjoying his new role as a father.

'Darling, please do.'

It was only after Hugh had left that Jo remembered Ivy was still in her pyjamas. Worse, her hair wasn't brushed and her face was probably covered in egg.

Cringe. Hugh's parents might be prepared to overlook the preposterous claims in the newspaper, but they would be less charitable when they saw evidence of the nanny's incompetence with their own eyes.

Nervously, she asked them if they would like to sit down. But they had only just taken their seats when a piping voice could be heard coming up the stairs.

'Have I really got an English grandmother, Daddy?'

'Yes, don't you remember? Jo and I told you about her yesterday. She's upstairs.'

'Is she a fairy grandmother?'

'No, just a regular grandmother.'

'A hairy grandmother?' Ivy was giggling at her own joke.

Jo held her breath. When Ivy got overexcited she could be quite silly.

'A scary grandmother?' Ivy giggled again as she and Hugh walked into the room, hand in hand.

Despite the pyjamas and the tumbled curls, Jo thought the little girl looked very appealing. Her face was scrubbed clean. *Thank you, Regina.* Her lively eyes were dancing with merriment and no amount of stray curls could mar her exquisite features.

But when Ivy saw Hugh's parents she came to a halt and Jo was reminded of the morning when she and Hugh had arrived at Agate Downs and the child had been overawed to see strangers.

'Ivy,' she said, holding out an encouraging hand.

'Your grandmother and grandfather have come all the way to London especially to meet you.'

But Ivy seemed to have frozen to the spot. She clung to Hugh's hand and eyed her grandparents from a safe distance, assessing them with solemn, frowning wariness.

Hugh looked a little out of his depth. 'Come on, Ivy, say hello.'

'Hello,' she said and then she lowered her gaze and dropped her bottom lip.

Sensing an awkward moment that could escalate into an uncomfortable scene, Jo jumped to her feet. 'I have a good idea. Why don't we take Grandmother upstairs to show her your new bedroom? You can introduce her to Howard and Baby and you can show her some of your nice new clothes.' *And I can tidy you up and get you dressed.*

Ivy seemed to think this over.

The little minx, thought Jo. She's playing with us.

But suddenly the little girl took a delighted skip forward. 'Yes,' she said, eyes twinkling once more. 'That's a very good idea.' She held out an imperious hand to a rather bemused Lady Rychester. 'Come on, Grandmother. Come with Jo and me and we'll show you my lovely new bedroom.'

'Well done, Jo. I couldn't have managed without you. I categorically *could not* have survived this day without your help.'

It was mid-afternoon and Hugh was sprawled on

a sitting room sofa, where he'd collapsed the minute his parents had left to visit friends in Mayfair.

Jo, curled in an armchair opposite him, was rather stunned by the enormous relief Hugh had expressed.

'I can't believe they took Ivy with them,' he said.

'They want to show off their granddaughter,' she responded. 'They're absolutely smitten with her. It's wonderful, isn't it?'

'The amazing thing is the adoration seems to be mutual. Ivy really took to them, didn't she?'

'That's not so surprising, Hugh. I thought your parents were rather sweet. I was afraid of your father at first, but he's a softie underneath that upper class crust.'

'He's a softie around you,' Hugh amended. 'You have no idea how differently my father behaved today compared to the way he usually treats my women.'

'Perhaps that's because I am *not* one of your girlfriends.' Jo hurled a cushion at him.

Hugh caught it and hugged it to his chest and then he grinned at her. 'You might not be mine yet.' He glanced at the clock on the mantelpiece. 'But it's half past three. Only nine hours left till midnight. Time's running out, Jo.'

She let out a wail of impatience. 'I'm getting tired of this ridiculous game.'

'Then perhaps I should propose to you now.'

Yeah, right.

'For heaven's sake, Hugh, give that subject a

miss!' She hurled another cushion his way but, to her horror, it went sailing over his head and knocked a beautiful porcelain vase from the sofa table behind him.

She leapt to her feet, appalled by the mess she'd made. The vase had broken into three pieces and rose petals, flower heads and stems were scattered in a sodden heap. And, of course, there was a pool of water soaking into the white wool carpet.

'I'm so sorry. I'll get something to mop up the mess. Was that vase expensive? It's not Ming or anything is it?'

Hugh jumped from the sofa and caught her hand as she hurried past. 'It's Meissen, but don't worry.' Holding her hand tightly, he drew her close. Within a heartbeat her face was only inches from his.

'Hugh, I—I've got to get a bucket or—'

'Or nothing.'

Jo gulped for air. Up this close, Hugh was breathtaking. Literally. 'But the carpet. That stain should be treated quickly.'

'There's another matter that requires more urgent attention.'

'What—what's that?'

His hand slid down, pressing into her lower back, bringing her pelvis suddenly against his. 'I desperately need you, Jo.'

Oh, God. His words plunged straight between her legs and she felt a shocking, violent eruption of desire.

With one hand holding her close, Hugh used the other to trace a line with his fingertip along her jaw, down her throat to the V neckline of her sweater, and his green eyes burned with such wicked, devilish heat she felt her breasts swell and her nipples grow tight with unbearable longing.

So quickly. Just like that. She'd become an incendiary bomb about to explode. If Hugh kissed her, if he lifted her sweater, if he touched her anywhere *intimate* she would disintegrate. She'd be lost.

'No,' she managed to whisper. 'Don't.'

'Come upstairs,' he urged and his voice was low— a hot chocolate, super-seductive rumble. 'You want me, Jo. Don't you?'

Of course she did, but that wasn't the point. 'Please, no. Let me go.' Shoving her hands into his chest, she pushed him away from her.

And to her relief as well as her dismay, he did exactly what she asked. He let her go.

Breathless, panting, she staggered backwards, almost overbalancing.

Hugh looked as if he might follow her and she held up a shaking hand. 'Hold it.'

His eyes narrowed.

'I think you're getting a little confused, Lord Strickland. I'm here to look after your daughter, not to be your girlfriend.'

'Jo, don't be angry. Just be honest with yourself. And with me.'

'I'm sorry, Hugh, but why shouldn't I be angry?

Sex was not part of our agreement. Maybe you're used to having the pick of whichever English girl you fancy, but despite what's reported in newspapers here, Aussies aren't all that impressed by titles.'

He stood very still with his shoulders squared. His chest expanded and compressed, as if he was breathing hard. His eyes smouldered with dark, banked heat. 'What if I were to tell you that I think I love you?'

Oh, no, don't do that to me. Jo gaped at him, too stunned to come up with an answer.

In his eyes she saw naked emotion that made her want to cry.

How had this happened? Something was wrong. She was the vulnerable one. She didn't have the power to hurt Hugh Strickland. But he could break her heart.

On the verge of tears, she pressed her lips tightly together as she tried to get her emotions in check. 'Why? Why do you have to be who you are?'

'What the hell does that mean?'

She released a desperate strangled sigh. 'If you were an everyday average Englishman, it would be different.'

'You mean you might be upstairs naked and in bed with me right now?'

Jo gulped. 'Yes…perhaps.'

His frown was accompanied by a troubled smile. He scratched the back of his neck. 'Excuse me, Miss Berry, but aren't you contradicting yourself?'

It was Jo's turn to frown. 'No, I don't think so.'

'But one minute you're telling me you're not impressed by titles and the next you're saying that my title is so damned impressive it's scaring you off.'

Finding herself suddenly at sea, she flapped her hands helplessly. 'There's no point in discussing this. I'm going upstairs. To *my* room. I—I need to paint my nails for tonight.'

'By all means.' A weary smile flitted across Hugh's face. 'You'll want to look your very best for tonight.'

Confusion stormed inside her as she hurried upstairs. What was the matter with her? In her secret heart she'd been hoping for a romance with Hugh, and now that she had the chance she was running scared like a terrified child.

Running scared because Hugh thought he might love her—which was exactly what she'd hoped, but had never dreamed was possible.

It wasn't possible. Hugh was confusing lust with love. Very soon he would come to his senses and realise his mistake and she would be grateful for her lucky escape.

In her room, she took out the small bottle of dark berry-red nail polish to match the beautiful dress Hugh had bought her. One thing Hugh had said was right. Tonight she needed to look as glamorous as possible if she was to have any hope of measuring up to his friends. But her hands were still shaking so badly she had no chance of applying the polish.

Ivy and Hugh's parents would be home soon and then she would be busy getting Ivy ready for the party and she'd have no time for herself.

Acting on a sudden desperate whim, she snatched up the bottle and tore back downstairs, not glancing to the sitting room where she'd left Hugh but continuing all the way to the kitchen, where Regina was ironing and listening to the radio.

'I'm sorry to bother you, Regina.' Jo held up the little red pot of polish. 'I was wondering if you could lend me a steady hand.'

'Heavens, love, it's a while since I painted a fingernail, but I'll give it a try. It makes a change from ironing.'

After switching off the iron and lowering the volume on the radio, Regina pulled out a chair at the kitchen table. 'Let's see if I still have the knack.'

'It's so good of you. I'm too nervous and shaky,' Jo admitted.

'Don't be nervous about going to Rupert's house,' Regina said as she shook the bottle. 'He's the loveliest, kindest man.' Regina sent Jo a sudden shrewd glance. 'That Priscilla Mostly-Tart won't be there, will she?'

'Priscilla *who?*'

'Mosley-Hart. Sorry, Jo. I know I have a hide to call her names.'

But Jo couldn't resist a small smile. 'I don't think she'll be there. She's out of favour. If she turns up,

Hugh will have her clapped in irons and taken to the Tower.'

'About time Hugh came to his senses.' Regina painted a steady stripe of crimson on to Jo's thumbnail. 'You have lovely hands.'

'Thank you.'

As she finished the first nail, the housekeeper let out a laughing shout of triumph. 'Look at that. Perfect. I haven't lost my knack.' She dipped the little brush back into the polish. 'Just relax and enjoy yourself tonight, ducks. I have a very good feeling in my bones. I think you'll come home on cloud nine and won't that be a wonderful way to start the New Year?'

CHAPTER NINE

HUGH had never felt more uptight than he did that evening as Humphries drove him with Jo and Ivy to the Eliots' house. His feelings for Jo had thrown him into a complete tailspin. He'd never been so undone.

He'd fallen in love—*really* in love—and it was no fun at all. He couldn't imagine a condition that rendered a man more helpless. More joyous. More tormented.

He was racked by gut-wrenching pre-party nerves and he hadn't felt this tense about taking a girl to a party since his teenage years.

During the past week there'd been times when he'd convinced himself that his feelings were returned. He'd caught Jo looking at him with a special soft light in her eyes. He'd seen the way his sudden appearance in a room could make flushes of colour come and go in her cheeks. And when he'd kissed her, her lips and limbs had responded with a trembling, sweet desperation that couldn't be faked.

She was such a contrast to Priscilla who'd been so in love with his title and money that she'd been willing to gamble everything in a bid to win him as a husband.

What bitter-sweet irony it was that Jo had thrown

his riches and privileges at him as her reasons for keeping him at bay.

'Oh, look.' Jo was craning her neck to look out through the car window. 'I think I can see snow.' She turned back to him, her eyes shining. 'Is it, Hugh? Is it snow?'

He blinked and saw fluffy white flakes spinning and gleaming in the glare of street lights and head-lights. 'That's snow all right. Haven't you ever seen it?'

'No,' Jo and Ivy answered together and they gave little squeals of delight as they leaned forward, watching with mouths and eyes wide open.

'It's just beautiful,' said Jo.

But her happiness depressed Hugh. He glared at the pretty flakes. In his current mood the snow seemed to emphasise the vast differences between Jo's world and his.

'I'm afraid most of the snow we get in London usually melts or turns to slush almost as soon as it reaches the road,' he felt compelled to warn her.

But she wasn't going to be put off.

'It doesn't matter.' Her face was flushed with the enchantment of it all. 'Look Ivy, it's real snow. Now I'll be able to tell everyone at home that I've seen it.'

Hugh swallowed a sigh.

When they arrived at the Eliots' the white flakes were still drifting softly about them and as they stepped out of the car the scene before them was picture perfect—the Eliots' lovely house with lights glowing from every window, the falling snow outside and the promise of warmth and gaiety within.

And then the door opened and a blast of music from a dance band greeted them and Rupert, who'd beaten his butler to the door, was grinning broadly and urging them to hurry in out of the cold.

Inside, they were immediately surrounded by a grand and welcoming spectacle—warmly tapestried walls, dazzling chandeliers, glittering mirrors and pieces of silver, beautiful flower arrangements and polished parquet floors designed especially for dancing feet.

Introductions were made amidst a great deal of laughter and happy chatter accompanied by hugs and kisses. The Eliots' butler hurried to help Ivy and Jo with their coats. Jo smiled as she thanked him and then she turned slowly, looking a little overwhelmed as she took in her surroundings. And Hugh felt as if he'd turned to stone.

He stood stock still, rooted to the spot by the sight of Jo in her lovely red dress.

She was beyond beautiful.

The deep crimson gown was perfect for her. Its colour offset her dark brown hair and eyes and highlighted the rosy tints in her complexion and the delicious deep red of her mouth. The dress's fabric was soft, skimming close to her figure without clinging. The cut was daring, with a deep plunging back and a tantalising low neckline, which somehow, mercifully, kept Jo's modesty intact.

The combination of boldness and decorum sent fire shooting to his loins.

'Is something the matter, Hugh?' High colour sprang into her cheeks. 'Don't you like the dress?'

He tried to answer, but his heart seemed to fill his throat.

'What about my dress, Daddy?' demanded Ivy, not to be outdone. 'Do you like it?'

He dragged his gaze from Jo to his daughter in her new winter dress of emerald-green velvet that matched her sparkling green eyes. 'It's beautiful, poppet. You both look—' He had to take a breath. 'You both look like princesses.' He turned to his best friend. 'Don't they, Rupert?'

'Absolutely gorgeous.' Rupert shot a knowing look Hugh's way. 'So gorgeous I'm going to have to ask you both for a dance.'

Ivy was suddenly shy and turned to whisper to Jo, who gave her a reassuring pat.

'Ivy's worried because she doesn't know how to dance,' she told Rupert.

'Then I shall teach you,' he said to Ivy with a charming grin as he held out his hand to her. 'Come on, let's go.'

Which left Hugh and Jo alone.

A waiter offered them a tray of drinks and they made their selections—champagne for Jo and Scotch for Hugh—and for a short while they stood together without talking, while they watched Rupert take Ivy's hand and spin her around. Within seconds the child was beaming with delight.

'Oh, there you are,' called a voice. It was Anne Eliot, so there were more introductions and happy chatter. 'I thought we'd let the children party with us for an hour or so and then our nanny will take them upstairs,' Anne explained. 'Don't worry about Ivy. There are plenty of children here to keep her happy and plenty of beds for when she gets tired.'

She dragged them off then, so that Jo could be introduced to other guests and, as Hugh might have expected of guests at the Eliots', no one raised the question of the newspaper column and it was all very pleasant—until Jack Soames asked Jo to dance.

She responded after only the slightest hesitation and as she and Jack headed out on to the dance floor Hugh toyed with the idea of asking one of the other women to be his dancing partner, but he was hopelessly mesmerised by Jo. Leaning against a marble pillar, he clutched his glass of whisky and watched her dancing and smiling—and suffered.

Once or twice, Jo sent a brief, anxious look his way, but on the whole she paid a great deal of attention to Jack and she looked as if she was enjoying herself. Very much. Almost as much as her partner.

'That Jo of yours is charming.'

Hugh started as Rupert's voice sounded close beside him.

Rupert raised a sandy eyebrow. 'You're not yourself tonight, old chap.'

Hugh grunted and muttered a deliberately incomprehensible reply.

'You're not letting that idiot from *Nelson's Column* bother you, are you?'

'No, not at all, but it's been hard for Jo. I blame bloody Priscilla for the whole thing.'

'I hear old Mosley-Hart's lost all his money,' Rupert said. 'Some crazy get rich quick investment that went belly up.'

So that explained why Priscilla had been so dead keen to get herself engaged when he'd returned from Australia, thought Hugh. It was all about money.

'I must say your little Ivy is absolutely delightful,' Rupert added in an obvious attempt to soothe his friend.

This time Hugh smiled. 'She's fantastic, isn't she? I'm so lucky. I still can't quite believe I'm a father, though. But we've gotten to know each other very quickly. I adore her.'

His friend didn't reply at first. 'I take it you're referring to your daughter?'

'Naturally.' Hugh felt his face flush and shot Rupert a warning look.

'But if I'd been talking about Joanna Berry, your answer would have been the same, wouldn't it?' Rupert said with clear disregard for Hugh's warning.

Hugh opened his mouth to deny it. But what was

the point? Rupert was his oldest friend and could read him like a book. 'Yes,' he said softly and then he downed his Scotch in a swift gulp.

Rupert signalled for a waiter to bring them fresh drinks and, once they'd made their selections, he said, 'Unless I've lost my ability to sum up a person at a first meeting, I'd say you've hit the jackpot this time, old fellow.'

Hugh frowned.

'Don't pretend you don't know who I'm talking about.'

'So you like Jo?' Hugh couldn't resist asking; the question mattered a great deal.

'Yes, and I don't just mean that I like the look of her.' Rupert took a sip of wine. 'Although it's hard to ignore that lovely figure.'

Hugh glared at him. 'When will you ever give up? You've been a stirrer since our school days.'

Rupert smiled. 'Actually, she's very different from the women you usually mistreat. No offence, Hugh, but I consider that a plus.'

Hugh knew what Rupert meant. They were both familiar with his tendency to be blind-sided by women of rare physical beauty and his habit of moving on as soon as he got to know them.

But then he'd met Jo and he hadn't been swept away by stunning looks. He'd been pleasantly charmed by a pretty girl with a sweet, warm smile. And now, after a week in her company, he was completely spellbound by her rare and beautiful spirit.

For him, Jo's ordinary prettiness had blossomed and deepened into a more stirring, more compelling beauty than any he'd encountered.

'I'll tell you something else I like about your nanny,' said Rupert.

'Mention her body again and you put our lifetime friendship in jeopardy.'

Rupert chuckled. 'Seriously, I like what she's done to you.'

'Done to me? I'm a wreck.'

'Exactly. And I'm very pleased to see it. It's about time.' From behind rimless spectacles Rupert's clever blue eyes shone with a beguiling mixture of sympathy and delight. 'You've never felt this miserable over a girl before, have you?'

'No.' After a bit, Hugh said, 'I love her.'

'Does she know how you feel?'

'Yes. No. Sort of.' He stared at the drink in his hand. 'I've made a complete hash of trying to tell her.'

'Well, there's no need to rush these things.'

'There is, actually. She's going back to Australia at the end of next week.'

Rupert lifted both eyebrows. 'I'll admit a deadline injects a certain degree of urgency.'

'Yes. I've got to pull a rabbit out of a hat.'

Hugh sighed. Rupert and Anne had it all—a relationship that was as secure and constant as it was passionate. And deep down he was certain that he could have that with Jo. If only he could find the right words...

Rupert's hand clasped his shoulder. 'Be careful, my friend. A proposal of marriage isn't the same as securing one of your business deals. Women don't respond well to pressure.'

Hugh wasn't so sure about that as he watched the couples out on the dance floor. Hal Ramsay was cutting in to replace Jo's partner and, as soon as she began to dance with Hal, the music slowed to something soft and bluesy.

Next minute Hal was drawing her in—and his hand, damn it, was dangerously close to her lovely bare back. For crying out loud, the man had a wife of his own and Jo was smiling at him as if he'd offered her the sun and the stars.

What a pity Hugh was spoiling everything.

Jo didn't know what to make of his behaviour tonight. Why wasn't he dancing and having fun? She'd been sure that the dashing and charming Lord Strickland would be the life of the party.

She was having a great time. It was so exciting to be in such a lovely house, wearing such a beautiful, beautiful gown. She felt totally welcome. The Eliots were charming and friendly and so were their guests. No one so far had been snobbish or condescending. No one had mentioned *Nelson's Column*. No one had asked awkward questions about her relationship with Hugh.

But, instead of enjoying himself, Hugh was standing aloof, watching her with the frowning stare of an old maidish chaperon.

Well, maybe not old maidish. Not Hugh. He looked far too manly and gorgeous in his superb black tails. Brooding and moody might be a better description.

What was the matter with him? Surely he wasn't upset with her? She couldn't believe that his teasing about proposals and engagements was serious. As for his comment about loving her—she would be naïve and foolish to think that had been any more than smooth words rolling off the tongue of a skilful seducer. They were worlds apart and she had to remember that.

She was determined to have fun this evening in spite of Hugh's sulky mood. Tonight was a one-off chance for an Aussie chick in London to check out the way the upper-crust partied. She owed it to the girls back in the office to soak up every glamorous detail so she could give them a blow by blow report when she—

'Excuse me.'

Hugh's voice stopped her thoughts and her dancing mid-track.

Her head jerked up and her eyes met his. Green. Gorgeous. Black-fringed. Oh, man. Her heart began a strange little dance, completely out of time with the music.

Hugh tapped her partner's shoulder. 'I'm sorry,

Hal, but your time's up,' he said, flashing a tight-lipped version of his charming smile. 'My turn.'

Hot and cold shivers darted over Jo's skin and she felt an urgent need to protest, or to find an excuse to avoid close contact with Hugh. The dance was about to end, wasn't it? Shouldn't she check on Ivy?

But her partner was politely stepping away and within a heartbeat Hugh had usurped his place, taking her hand in his and placing his other at her waist and then drawing her close.

Too close. She couldn't breathe.

The dance was no more than a simple slow shuffle in time to the music. Nevertheless she stumbled.

'I'm sorry,' said Hugh. 'Did I trip you?'

She shook her head, suddenly too breathless, too anxious to speak. Oh, dear heaven, why did she have to react to Hugh this way? Why couldn't she be calm and sensible, the way she'd been when she'd danced with the other men? She was quite an uninhibited dancer normally. Now, for the life of her, she couldn't untangle her feet.

She bumped into Hugh again and the impact of their bodies was only slight, but that was all it took— a brief brush of his chest and thigh—to set off flashpoints of reaction all over her.

Hugh leaned back a little and studied her face. 'You look a little pale, Jo. Perhaps you need a drink?'

'Thank you.' It would be a blessed relief to stop dancing.

His hand settled at her waist as he steered her from the dance floor and she could feel the burning imprint of his thumb on the bare skin at her lower back.

'Why don't you try a brandy?' He looked about for a waiter. 'It's supposed to have medicinal benefits.'

But now that he wasn't touching her Jo felt more composed. 'I don't need brandy, thank you. I'd just like some water, please.'

He came back from the bar with a tall crystal tumbler filled with ice and water and, as he watched her drink it, a worried frown creased his forehead.

'That's better,' she said, forcing a smile as she finished half of it. 'This is a lovely party, Hugh.'

He nodded. 'Anne and Rupert always put on a good show for New Year's Eve.'

Jo looked towards the foot of the staircase where a young fresh-faced woman had gathered several of the children. 'I think that might be the Eliots' nanny getting the children ready to go upstairs now. I'll go and find Ivy and make sure she understands what's happening.'

'Good idea. I'll come with you.'

That wasn't quite what she'd had in mind.

Ivy and another little girl were playing peek-a-boo around a pillar at the side of the dance floor.

'But I'm not ready to go to sleep yet,' she protested when she saw Hugh and Jo approaching.

'All the other children are going upstairs now,' Hugh told her.

'No, I don't want to!' Ivy's bottom lip projected in a familiar pout.

Time for some gentle coercion, Jo decided. 'Wouldn't you like to sleep upstairs with your new little friends?'

'In the same room?' Ivy asked, suddenly interested. 'Like Tilly and Grace?'

'Yes,' said Jo, although she was quite sure that the Eliots' nursery would be nothing like the humble bedroom her little sisters shared.

Remarkably, that was all it took for Ivy to agree.

'After everything else that's happened this week I'm surprised Ivy remembers Tilly and Grace,' Jo said as they watched the chattering children climb the stairs.

Hugh smiled. 'You'll have to admit that your family's rather memorable.'

Something in the way he said that lifted fine hairs on Jo's skin. She looked up at him and he smiled again, but it wasn't a particularly convincing smile. She was sure she could sense a shadow of sadness behind it.

She was afraid to ask, but then the words spilled out anyhow. 'Is something the matter, Hugh?'

His eyes pierced her. 'I need to talk to you, Jo.'

'OK.' She felt suddenly breathless. 'I'm listening.'

'Not here.'

Her heart hammered as she looked about her. The Eliots' nanny and her little flock of children were almost at the top of the stairs. To her right, Anne

Eliot was helping an elderly white-haired woman into a chair and offering her a glass of sherry. A couple nearby were sharing an apparently uproariously funny joke. No one was paying any attention to Hugh or Jo. 'You can talk here, can't you?'

'No,' he said, reaching for her hand. 'Come upstairs with me.'

'Upstairs?' she squeaked.

'There's a little conservatory on the next floor, and there's something I want to show you.'

Rolling her eyes at him, she made a nervous attempt at a joke. 'That's not very original, Lord Strickland. What have you got up there? Etchings?'

His mouth quirked as he gave her hand a tug. 'I promise this is all above board. It will only take five minutes.'

'Oh, very well.'

At the first landing, he pushed open a door to the right and they entered a small informal dining room. Hugh didn't turn the light on, but on the far side of the room pale moonlight spilled through a snow-covered glass-roofed conservatory on to potted palms and flowers.

'Wow!' Jo forgot to be nervous as she walked towards the glass-walled room. 'This is so pretty.' She stepped into the conservatory and was met by the scent of roses. She looked up and saw enchanting little banks of snow lying against the ribs that joined the glass panels—and, higher, the moon shining through a break in the clouds.

But then she turned back to Hugh and in the moon-washed shadows she saw the look of deep intent in his eyes. Her heart leapt. 'Oh, God, Hugh, why have you brought me here? You're not going to try to seduce me again?'

He held up his hands. 'I'm on my very best behaviour, Jo. I want to ask you to marry me.'

She felt a slam of panic. 'But you can't. You mustn't keep this silly joke going.'

'I love you.'

'Don't say that.'

'Why shouldn't I love you?' Hugh stepped towards her and his voice was husky with emotion. 'You're a miracle, Jo Berry.'

She mustn't let herself listen to such temptation. 'I'm going home in a week, I'm only here to help you with Ivy.'

He took her by the shoulders. 'This has nothing to do with my daughter. I want you for myself.'

She wanted to cry. Her dream had come true. But now that it had, it felt terribly wrong. She felt a rush of tears. This was so surreal.

'Why can't you believe me?' Hugh whispered.

Wriggling her shoulders out of his grasp, she took two steps back. 'It—it's too much like a fantasy—a fairy tale. I'm Jo Berry from Bindi Creek and you're—you're Prince Charming. I shouldn't even be here at this party, dressed in this gorgeous gown and dancing with your blue blood friends. I—I should be with the Eliots' nanny, taking the children to the toilet or settling them down to sleep.'

Hugh ploughed a frantic hand through his hair. 'You're letting that damned *Nelson's Column* get to you. Either that or you're deliberately underselling yourself.'

'I'm being realistic.'

'How's this for realism?'

Hugh took something from his breast pocket. It was difficult at first to see what he held in his hand, but then he moved slightly and she caught the unmistakable sparkle of gemstones.

Her heart jumped as if a shot had been fired.

'This was my grandmother's engagement ring,' he said. 'I've never offered it to another woman, but I very much want you to have it, Jo.'

This couldn't be happening. She was dreaming. She had to be.

'There are five stones,' Hugh continued in his low, deeply beautiful voice. 'Three diamonds and two rubies and, according to the story my grandmother liked to tell, the five stones represent five words. *Will you be my wife?*'

The conservatory seemed to swim before her.

'Jo,' Hugh whispered, 'please say something.'

She blurted the first words that came into her head. 'I think you've taken this too far.'

'What?' The little jewellery box in his hand shook. 'You can't really believe this is still a joke.'

She pressed a hand against her clamouring heart.

'What else can it be? Think about it, Hugh. You've already hinted at our engagement once when you didn't mean it. That's pretty fast work for a couple who've only known each other a week. Maybe it's getting to be a bad habit—a quick fix solution. How can I be confident that you really mean it this time?'

He gave an impatient shake of his head.

'A marriage proposal! That's for life, Hugh. It would make more sense if you propositioned me again. Can't you see that?'

Surely she'd made perfect sense. Why was he being so stubborn? 'Can't you see how rushed this is?' She felt compelled to fling him her trump card. 'After all, you still have Priscilla's things in your bedroom.'

He frowned. 'When were you in my room?'

'This afternoon.'

She'd gone there after Regina had painted her nails. She'd felt a sudden need to apologise to Hugh for the immature way she'd rebuffed him. And she'd decided to tell him the truth…that she fancied the pants off him. She could be persuaded to change her mind…

But when she couldn't find him in the lounge she'd gone upstairs and she'd stepped into his bedroom…

'You still have a box of Priscilla's things on the floor just inside your bedroom door,' she told him now. 'Her name is marked very clearly on the side.'

Hugh groaned softly. 'Humphries was going to deliver that box to her but with all the phone calls and nonsense in the press he's been distracted. I'm sorry.'

'I'm not sorry. It was a timely wake up call for me.'

He gave another impatient shake of his head. 'I was never in love with Priscilla, Jo. Even before I learned about Ivy, I had realised that Priscilla and I were headed for misery. And that was before she walked out on me at the very time I needed her support.'

'Well, I can't help wondering if you'd change your mind about me too,' said Jo. 'What guarantee do I have that in a month or two there won't be a box of my things waiting for Humphries to deliver to me?'

She swallowed and bothersome tears sprang to her eyes. 'I'm sorry, Hugh. I'm not prepared to take a gamble on that.'

In the moonlight she saw the way his face stiffened. 'Is that your final word?' he asked.

Every part of her wanted to say no.

He remained standing very still. Very British and stiff—and he looked more dashing and gorgeous than ever in his dark formal evening clothes.

'Is it your final word?' he asked again.

She opened her mouth to say yes, and then she shut it. She thought of her mum and the wistful dream that had sent her flying here to London with Hugh. And then she thought of the box of frilly negligées in Hugh's room and she imagined the words Joanna Berry written in black felt pen on the side.

'Yes,' she said. 'It's my final word.'

Hugh looked down at the ring in his hand and then quickly closed his fist over it. 'Forgive me for taking up your time.' With a grim, tight face he slipped the ring into his pocket.

He made a movement as if he planned to take her elbow, but then he thought better of it and, without another word, he turned and walked away from her.

In the moonlit silence Jo watched him disappear and she wondered how on earth she could face the New Year without him.

Jo's mum telephoned several nights later. 'So how's it all going, love?'

'Terrific.' Jo gulped back the homesick tears that threatened the instant she heard her mum's voice. 'I've been having a really good time.'

'You don't sound too happy.'

'Must be a bad line. I'm fine, Mum. And Ivy's fine. How are you and everyone at home?'

'Oh, we're all chugging along the same as always. Not much news. Eric broke his arm. Silly kid jumped out of a tree, trying to frighten Grace.'

'Heavens. Poor Eric. I hope he's not in too much pain.'

'He'll live.'

'Give him my love. Give everyone my love.'

'I will. So…what have you been up to, Jo?'

'Well… I think everything's just about organised for Ivy.'

'Organised? How do you mean?'

Being organised and efficient was the way Jo had survived the past week. Luckily, it was how Hugh had chosen to conduct himself as well. They'd both been super-organised, mega-efficient and they'd deflected any superfluous emotion to Ivy.

'Hugh's had Ivy checked out by Simon Hallows, a fantastic burns specialist, who went to school with Hugh. You should have seen how gentle and kind he was with Ivy, Mum. And he's been able to set Hugh's mind at rest about what can be done for her in terms of future surgery as she grows.'

'The poor little lamb. She shouldn't have to go through all that.'

On the other end of the line there was the sound of a chair scraping and Jo could picture her mother sitting down, settling in for a comfortable chat. 'So you went along to the doctor's with them, did you?' Margie asked.

'Yes, Hugh wanted me there.'

'That's nice, love.'

The sentimental warmth in her mum's voice made Jo nervous. She'd done her best to squash Margie's wistful yearning for a romance between her daughter and the handsome English gentleman. She'd told her about Hugh's money and his aristocratic family and about Priscilla and the havoc she'd caused.

What else did it take to get the message across?

'We've found Ivy a school,' she said, hoping to steer the conversation away from uncomfortable topics. 'We've spent three days going to inspections at all the schools Hugh's friends have recommended, and he's found a lovely one only a few streets away from his house.'

'Sounds perfect. Does Ivy like it?'

'Loves it. Can't wait to start. You should have seen her face when she saw the little English schoolkids in their uniforms. The girls wear little green blazers and pleated skirts and knee-high socks. And the boys wear the cutest little green peaked caps. I think Ivy wanted to bring one of the boys home to keep him as a pet.'

Deep chuckles sounded on the other end of the line.

'And this afternoon we finished the interviews for a new nanny,' Jo added quickly.

'Oh?' There was no doubting the sudden tension in Margie's voice.

'It was such a hard choice. There were lots of very suitable girls, but I think Ivy will get on really well with the one we've settled on.'

'So you really are coming home?' Margie made no attempt to hide her disappointment.

'Of course I am. My holiday's almost over and I have to get back to work. I've already told you I'm flying out on Saturday.'

'I thought Hugh might have persuaded you to stay.'

'Well, he hasn't,' Jo said sharply, too sharply, but

it couldn't be helped. This wasn't her favourite talking point.

'Has he tried?' Margie asked.

'No.'

'I don't believe you.'

Oh, heck. There was nothing for it but to bite the bullet. 'Well, yes, he tried to talk me into staying—and not just as Ivy's nanny. But it wouldn't work, Mum.'

'Jo!'

'It wouldn't! Hugh came to his senses and realised his mistake.'

Jo was aware of a movement behind her and she turned to see Hugh in the doorway. She felt a rush of panic—her chest squeezed tight and her face felt as if she'd been sunburned. How long had he been there?

He'd taken up a casual pose, with his hands thrust deeply in his trouser pockets, his shoulder propped against the doorjamb and one foot crossed over the other.

The expression on his face was anything but casual.

Oh, God.

'Are you sure he wants you to go home, love?'

She could hardly hear her mum's voice above the pounding in her ears. Snatching her gaze from Hugh's, she twisted the phone cord with frantic fingers. 'Y-yes,' she said.

It was true. Hugh hadn't once this week tried to

convince her to stay. He'd never mentioned the engagement ring or his feelings. He'd been the perfect courteous, polite English gentleman.

Until now. It wasn't very gentlemanly to listen in on someone else's telephone conversation. The way he watched her was downright intimidating.

There was a deep, loud sigh on the other end of the line.

'We mustn't talk for too long now, Mum,' Jo said, glancing again briefly in Hugh's direction. 'This call must be costing you a fortune.'

'Before I forget, can you thank Hugh for the lovely letter he sent?'

Again Jo's eyes flew to Hugh and he regarded her with a dark, brooding vigilance that sent her heart-strings twanging. She turned her back on him. 'What did you say? Something about a letter?'

'Yes. Hugh sent us the loveliest long letter. He must have written it last week, but it's only just arrived.'

'That—that's nice. OK, I'll thank him.'

Her mother gushed on. 'It was beautifully hand-written and he thanked us for sharing Christmas dinner with him. Said he'd never enjoyed a Christmas more. And he invited us all to England.'

'You're joking.'

'No, seriously. He thought we'd love his family's farm in Devon. And he went to the trouble of telling each one of us specific things we'd enjoy.'

'What—what kind of specific things?'

'Well…let me see…' There was a crackle of paper. 'He said Brad and Nick should try polo because they're such good horsemen…and Bill and Eric could go exploring on the moors…and Tilly and Grace would love the little Dartmoor ponies. And if we go in the spring there'd be wild flowers and market villages that I'd love and he has a good trout fishing stream for your dad.'

Jo sent a quick, frantic glance back over her shoulder to the doorway. Hugh had gone again, leaving as silently as he'd appeared. She ought to feel relieved, but she felt strangely bereft. She forced her mind back to the conversation. 'Hugh didn't actually name everyone in the family individually, did he?'

'Yes, he did, love. He remembered the names of everyone. I thought he must have checked them with you.'

No, no he didn't.

'Wasn't that nice of him?' her mum added.

'Very.'

Jo couldn't believe it. None of her friends in Brisbane had ever been able to remember the names of all her brothers and sisters—not even her flatmates—and she'd been living with them for four years and they'd even visited Bindi Creek with her.

She'd known Hugh for two weeks. He'd spent one day with her family. One day and he could remember them all—Nick, Brad, Bill, Eric, Grace and Tilly.

OK, so he had an excellent memory for names. There was no need to get all choked up about a man's memory. 'Well, I'm sorry you won't be coming over here now,' she said.

'Yeah,' Margie sighed.

'Mum, I'm looking forward to seeing you all very soon.'

There was silence from the other end of the line.

'Mum, are you there? I should say goodbye now.'

'All right. Goodbye, love.'

'I'll see you really soon.'

'Yes, have a safe trip.' Her mum sounded so dejected as she rang off that Jo burst into tears.

CHAPTER TEN

'NO AIRPORT farewells,' Jo insisted. 'It would be too traumatic for Ivy.'

Somewhat reluctantly, Hugh agreed.

And so the goodbyes took place at St Leonard's Terrace.

He watched the shining dampness in Jo's eyes as she hugged Ivy for the last time. He watched her tight white face as she held out her hand to shake his. He watched her back—ramrod straight—as she walked to the car behind Humphries.

And he saw that she didn't look back and she didn't wave once, not even as the car turned the corner.

The plan was that Humphries would drive her to Heathrow while Hugh stayed behind to keep Ivy entertained with the wind-up pink pig he'd ordered from the toy department in Harrods.

But how in hell's name was a man supposed to entertain a child when his heart was breaking? Especially when the child persisted in asking awkward questions about when Jo was coming back, or why there had to be a new nanny.

'I don't want a new nanny. I want Jo,' she repeated over and over as they sat on the floor in her bedroom and made a poor attempt to play with the toy that had so delighted her a week ago.

'You'll like Sally, your new nanny,' Hugh said, wishing he could dredge up an enthusiasm he couldn't feel.

Ivy's lower lip pouted ominously. 'But I love Jo.'

'Jo explained it to you, poppet. She has to go home to Australia. Now, look at this lovely fat pig. Isn't he funny? He's walking right under your bed. I think we need to get Howard to—'

'I don't want Jo to go to Australia,' Ivy said, pushing the treasured toy away. 'I want her here.'

'Well, aren't you a Miss Bossy Boots?' Hugh wondered how he would cope if his daughter threw a tantrum.

'Why did you let her go, Daddy?'

He wasn't ready for that question. 'I don't know,' he whispered hoarsely.

Ivy stared up at him with curious green eyes. 'Daddy, are you crying?'

'No.'

'You are.'

'No, no.' He blinked hard. 'It's just something in my eye.'

Scrambling to her feet, Ivy looked worried. She pushed her little face close up to his till their noses were almost touching and she stared anxiously into his eyes. 'You *are* sad,' she said. 'You're very sad.'

'Just a little.'

'Is it because Jo had to go away? Doesn't she love us?'

'I'm sure she loves us, poppet, but she loves her family too.'

'Does she love Tilly and Grace better'n us?'

Hugh forced a smile and he hugged Ivy close. 'She couldn't possibly love anyone more than she loves us.'

'Don't worry, Daddy. She'll come back.'

'No, poppet, you've got to understand Jo's not coming back.'

Ivy's eyes were huge. 'She's gone for good?'

'Yes.' Hugh sighed.

From her lonely seat in the back of the car, Jo watched the streets of London flash past. This was her last glimpse of the famous city. There would be no more chances to visit London's wonderful museums or art galleries, or to go to lovely concerts like the one Anne Eliot had taken her to in St Martin-in-the-Fields.

Never again would she take Ivy for walks along the Thames Embankment, or go to the King's Road to buy sweets from the little shop around the corner.

Worst of all—very, *very* worst of all—there were no more chances to see Hugh and Ivy.

She'd come to the end. The final page. And she'd discovered what she'd suspected all along; her story was a gritty reality drama, not a fairy tale.

She'd accused Hugh of creating a fairy tale but, if

that were so, he would have found a way to stop her from leaving. He would have done the Hollywood thing—chased after her and swept her into his arms and vowed his undying love for her. Or he would have found a magical fairy tale way to *prove* beyond doubt that he loved her.

Instead he'd shaken her by the hand.

And he'd said goodbye with a strange little stiff nod of his head. How jolly British!

How bloody awful! Her face crumpled and her tears overflowed and streamed down her cheeks. And her chest hurt with the awful pain of wanting Hugh. It was her fault that she'd lost him. She'd walked away from him. But she loved him! Oh, dear heaven, she loved him so much.

She loved looking at him, she loved talking to him, she loved being with him and she loved making plans for Ivy with him. She loved his friends, his parents, living in his house, his city...

There wasn't a thing about Hugh Strickland that she didn't love.

Another torrent of tears poured down her face and she reached into her pocket for a tissue to stem the flow. Along with the tissue, a stiff piece of paper came out of her pocket and, as she mopped her face, she stared at it lying in her lap.

Actually...it wasn't a sheet of paper; it was an envelope—with a single word written in spiky black handwriting.

Jo.

It was Hugh's handwriting.

Her heartbeats seemed to stop and then they began a querulous thumping. She turned the envelope over and slipped her little finger beneath the flap. *What on earth could it be?*

Inside, there was a single sheet of notepaper and something else. Something small. Her eyes caught a glint of gold and her hand trembled as she reached inside.

A ring! Oh, dear Lord. Hugh's grandmother's engagement ring. Her heart picked up pace until it thundered. Her hands shook so badly she almost dropped the ring, so she slipped it on to her finger for safe-keeping and opened the piece of paper to read a handwritten message.

Dearest Jo,

I am desperately in love with you. I know it's hard for you to believe; it's all happened so quickly—how can I convince you?

I feel as if my past has happened in another lifetime, and all I know now is that with you by my side I could live my life as it's meant to be. If you were my wife I would be the happiest man in all history and I would devote my days to making you happy too.

If ever or whenever you decide that you want me, all you need to do is slip this ring on your finger and come back to me and I'll be yours for ever.

If you return the ring I'll know that I've been wrong in thinking you love me too.

I love you.

Hugh

'Pigs don't usually go in the same pen as unicorns,' Hugh patiently explained to Ivy.

His daughter frowned at him. 'Why not?' She didn't like being corrected.

'They eat different things.'

'Unicorns eat grass. What do pigs eat?'

'Oh, grain and scraps—almost anything really.'

An impish grin suffused Ivy's face. 'Like you.'

'Are you calling me a pig?'

She giggled. 'Yes, you're a pig, Daddy. You eat almost anything.'

'I beg your pardon. I don't think I can let you get away with that. Little girls who call their fathers pigs must be tickled.'

'No.'

'I'm going to have to tickle you to death.'

'No!' Ivy shouted again, but she was giggling too and her fate was sealed.

Toys scattered as the two of them tumbled sideways on the carpet. Next minute Hugh was on his back holding Ivy up in the air at arm's length and the little girl was laughing and squealing.

'Is this a private party or can anyone join in?'

Hugh paused in mid-tickle. His heart jolted hard. Had he heard what he thought he'd heard?

He turned.

And there was Jo standing at the top of the stairs, just outside the doorway to Ivy's room.

Her face, framed by her neat brown hair, looked pale and yet bright spots of colour stood out in her cheeks. She sent them a rather wobbly smile.

'Jo!' Ivy screamed. 'It's Jo, Daddy! I told you she'd come back!'

As soon as Hugh lowered her to the floor Ivy dashed across the room to fling herself at Jo, and Hugh's heart pounded so fiercely he felt it might burst through the wall of his chest.

Jo was back.

Jo, smiling across at him as she hugged Ivy. Jo, with raindrops in her hair and with sparkling, lovely eyes—looking as if she might cry.

Hugh swallowed the painful lump in his throat.

Silver tears glistened on her lashes as she looked at him. 'You remembered all their names,' she said.

'I did?' He had no idea what she was talking about, but he pushed himself to his feet.

'My family. My brothers and sisters—you remembered their names.'

'That's why you came back?'

'It was so sweet of you to remember, Hugh.'

She wasn't making sense. Hugh felt his elation falter.

But then Jo held out her hand—her left hand—and he saw the twinkle of rubies and diamonds.

He wasn't sure who moved first, or how they came together. All he knew was that he was holding Jo at last. He was clasping her tight, breathing in the special fragrance of her, feeling her arms around him and her sweet body pressing close, and she was welcoming him with open lips, kissing him, wanting him.

'I love you, Hugh,' she whispered against his lips. 'I love you. I love you. I love you.' She kissed him on his mouth and on his chin, on the underside of his jaw, his throat and then his lips again.

Laughing, he caught her eager face between his hands and held her still so that he could return her kisses, so that he could kiss her soft, warm mouth and her salty tears. And then he hugged her to him, almost afraid that she might disappear.

'Daddy! Stop it, you're squeezing Jo too hard!' Impatient little hands tugged at their clothing.

Breathless, they broke apart and looked down at Ivy as if she'd just arrived from outer space.

'Ah, poppet,' said Hugh. 'Why don't you run down to the kitchen and see if Regina has afternoon tea ready for you?'

'Has she made chocolate cake?'

'Perhaps. Why don't you go and ask her?'

'OK. See you.' At the top of the stairs, Ivy turned back and she eyed them warily. 'Make sure Jo doesn't go away again.'

'Don't worry, Ivy, I promise I'm here to stay,' Jo assured her.

His daughter set off happily downstairs and Hugh took Jo's hands in his and looked again at the ring. It suited her hand beautifully. 'I've been so worried,' he said. 'I didn't know if you would find this, or when you'd find it, or how you'd react, or what you'd do, or whether—'

Jo stopped him by placing two fingers against his lips. 'It's OK, Hugh. I'm here.'

And then they were lost in another kiss—an unrestrained, lush and lingering kiss—a kiss that released at last all the loving and longing that had lain in their hearts.

It was much, much later that Jo told him her story. 'We were on the approach into Heathrow. You know where all those big hotels are. Poor Humphries didn't know what to make of me when I started blubbering that we had to turn around. He was so worried I'd miss my plane. It took me ages to convince him that I *wanted* to miss it. Once he realised I was serious he broke the speed limit to get me back here.' She blushed sweetly. 'To you.'

Just for that Hugh kissed her again. 'You do understand that I truly love you, don't you?'

'Yes, Hugh.' She lifted a hand to gently caress his cheek. 'Yes.'

'I'm the luckiest man alive.'

She dropped her head on to his shoulder and Hugh pressed kisses to the back of her neck. 'I know I've been far too rushed about this, but when can we be married? Is six months too soon?'

'Oh, goodness, six months?' Her eyes danced with silent laughter. 'I couldn't possibly wait that long.'

EPILOGUE

FROM *Nelson's Column:*

One of the best kept secrets on the London social calendar last week was the sudden and very private wedding of Lord Strickland, long-time Chelsea bachelor and owner of Rychester Aviation.

Always first with the spiciest news, this column blew the lid off Hugh Strickland's clandestine romance with Australian nanny, Jo Berry.

We made startling revelations and saucy suggestions about what would happen to the unfortunate miss from Down Under.

Humble pie is not usually on the menu in this column. However, dear readers, I will eat a large slice since my predictions about this couple fell so wide of the mark.

Who would have guessed that True Love would play an unexpected hand, and that Miss Bindi Creek would become Lady Joanna Strickland, wife of the future Earl of Rychester?

This columnist was somehow overlooked by the minions who prepared the guest list for the Strickland-Berry wedding, as were most others apart from family and a few close friends, who gathered at the chapel on the Rychester estate in Devon.

However, I can report that the bride looked radiant, the bridesmaid very sweet, and that the post-wedding celebrations continued for several days.

I am reliably informed that Jo Berry's extended family from Australia were flown over on one of Strickland's private jets. No small order considering there are enough Berrys to field a cricket team.

My spies tell me that the honeymooners—with a little companion—have been seen in the French Alps, in New York and in Tahiti...and I have no reason to doubt any of them.

CHRISTMAS ON THE CHILDREN'S WARD

BY
CAROL MARINELLI

Carol Marinelli finds writing a bio rather like writing her New Year's resolutions. Oh, she'd love to say that since she wrote the last one, she now goes to the gym regularly and doesn't stop for coffee and cake and a gossip afterwards; that she's incredibly organised and writes for a few productive hours a day after tidying her immaculate house and a brisk walk with the dog.

The reality is, Carol spends an inordinate amount of time daydreaming about dark, brooding men and exotic places (research) which doesn't leave too much time for the gym, housework or anything that comes in between and her most productive writing hours happen to be in the middle of the night, which leaves her in a constant state of bewildered exhaustion.

Originally from England, Carol now lives in Melbourne, Australia. She adores going back to the UK for a visit – actually, she adores going anywhere for a visit – and constantly (expensively) strives to overcome her fear of flying. She has three gorgeous children who are growing up so fast (too fast – they've just worked out that she lies about her age!) and keep her busy with a never-ending round of homework, sport and friends coming over.

A nurse and a writer, Carol writes for Mills & Boon® Modern™ and Medical™ lines and is passionate about both. She loves the fast-paced, busy setting of a modern hospital, but every now and then admits it's bliss to escape to the glamorous, alluring world of her Modern™ heroes and heroines. A bit like her real life, actually!

Don't miss Carol Marinelli's exciting new novel,
Innocent Secretary…Accidentally Pregnant,
available January 2010 from Mills & Boon® Modern™.

CHAPTER ONE

'HEY!'

Coming out of his office, chatting away to a rather pretty, rather blonde physiotherapist, Consultant Paediatrician Nick Watson was flattened against the wall as Eden Hadley rushed past, visibly upset.

Visibly, because Eden was incapable of hiding her emotions. Along with wearing her heart on her sleeve, her expressive face told anyone who cared to look exactly what she was thinking, and right now it didn't take a degree in psychology to work out that she was far from happy. Her pretty full mouth was set in a grim line and her dark brown eyes flashed angrily as Nick caught her arm to halt her progress. Her long, dark, chocolate curls fell out of her loose ponytail as she swung around to confront him.

'Just leave it, Nick,' Eden said through gritted teeth.

'Leave what?' Nick frowned, gesturing for her to wait as he said goodbye to the physiotherapist. 'Thanks for that, Amber, it's been very helpful.'

'Any time, Nick. Call me if you need to discuss Rory's ambulation programme further.' Amber smiled and Eden felt her already gritted teeth starting to grind as the tall slender physio continued talking, completely unfazed by Eden's presence. 'In fact, call me anyway— I'll look forward to it.'

'Well, she certainly knows how to get her message across!' Eden bristled as Amber waltzed off, her back impossibly straight, flicking her blonde hair as she did so.

'She was just being friendly.' Nick laughed. 'Just what is it that you have against physios?'

'Their glowing health,' Eden moaned. 'Their toned bodies and white smiles. I could go on for ever. I haven't yet met one with a single vice. You just know that they'll be tucking into a cottage cheese salad for lunch, know for a fact that they don't smoke.'

'Neither do you,' Nick pointed out, and then shook his head. 'Let's not change the subject. This is my ward, Eden, and if there's a problem I need to know about it.'

'There isn't a problem,' Eden insisted. 'At least, not any more.'

'Eden, you've lost me.'

Taking a deep breath, she finally faced him. 'Donna just called an impromptu meeting to discuss the revised Christmas roster.'

'Oh.'

Instantly his eyes glazed over. The nursing roster was way down on Nick Watson's list of priorities. So long as his precious patients were happy then so was he. But, Eden reminded herself, Nick was the one who'd stopped her, who had demanded that she tell him what was wrong, and Nick who had insisted that she voice her problem. And voice it she would.

Loudly!

'This will be my second Christmas on this ward,'

Eden choked. 'And now it seems I'll have to work night shifts for both! Donna's been hounding me to use up my annual leave as I've got five weeks owing. I was supposed to be having a full week off, given that last year….' The spitfire that was raging was doused a touch as Eden realised the inappropriateness of this conversation, but Nick, with a very noticeable edge to his voice, quickly filled her in.

'You had to work over the Christmas and New Year period because of what happened to Teaghan…'

Damn! She didn't say it, but the word spat like a hot chip between them. Eden slammed her forehead with her hand, wishing she could take it all back, wishing that Nick hadn't chosen that particular moment to come out of his office and demand to know what the problem was.

Eden had been so angry she'd chosen to take her fifteen-minute coffee-break away from the ward in an attempt to cool down before she said something she'd surely regret, but unfortunately she had done just that. The tragic events that had taken place the previous December hadn't just affected Eden's off-duty roster—the whole ward had gone into numb shock when Teaghan Camm, Associate Charge Nurse and fiancée to Nick Watson, had driven home after a night shift and apparently fallen asleep at the wheel. She'd suffered injuries so severe that she hadn't even made it into the emergency resuscitation room.

Eden could still recall that morning as if it had happened only yesterday.

As the nurse in charge that morning, it had been she, Eden, who had taken the call from Emergency. She had heard how the vibrant young woman, who had left the

ward only an hour or so before now lay dead a few
floors below. It had been Eden who had located Teaghan's personal file and relayed her parents' telephone
number to Sharon, the nurse supervisor who had been
with Teaghan in Emergency. She could still hear
Sharon's devastated voice as she'd asked Eden whether
she wanted her to come up and tell the staff.

'I'll do it,' Eden had said, not wanting to but knowing Sharon should be there to wait for Teaghan's parents to arrive.

'What about…?' Sharon had hesitated and Eden had
been too stunned, too shocked to fill in the gap, just
screwed her eyes closed as Sharon had stumbled on.
'Nick has to hear this privately, Eden.'

'I'll tell him first, away from everyone else.'

'Perhaps I should send up Brad, the emergency consultant,' Sharon suggested. 'Maybe another doctor should
be the one to tell him—although whoever it is who breaks
the news, it's not going to change the outcome.'

Looking out of her office, Eden had seen one of the
porters stopping to talk to the ward domestic, her
shocked expression telling Eden that the unpalatable
news had already started filtering its way through. She
had seen Nick at a patient's bedside, sharing a joke with
the child's mother, utterly oblivious to the fact that in
the same building at that very moment, his young fiancée had lain dead.

'I think I'd better tell him now.' Eden swallowed
hard. 'The news just hit the ward. I don't want him to
hear this on the floor. Send Brad up, though. I'm sure
Nick will have a lot of questions.'

It was among the hardest things she had ever done in

her life. As a senior nurse on a busy paediatric ward, Eden had seen more than her fair share of tragedy, had sat more times than she wanted to remember with devastated parents as terrible news had been broken, had even delivered it herself when the occasion had merited it, but to survive she managed to retain some degree of professional detachment. Though tears were sometimes shed, they were always controlled. She constantly reminded herself that, as much as she was hurting, it was worse, far, far worse for the parents, and the last thing they needed was an overly emotional nurse.

But this was personal.

Very personal.

She hadn't particularly liked Teaghan, had never taken to the rather loud, over-confident woman, but she'd never in a million years have wished this on her, and Eden was realistic enough to realise that her own judgement of the woman was probably tainted. Tainted by the fact that she, along with every other woman at the Royal, was just a tiny bit in love with Nick Watson.

'Nick.' He looked up as she came out of the office, gave a tiny questioning frown as she'd asked him if she could have a word.

'What's the problem?' Blond, happy, smiling and utterly oblivious, he strode in, took a seat when she asked him to do so. 'What have I done wrong this time?' He grinned.

'Nothing,' Eden croaked, then cleared her throat, willing herself to get on with it.

They were friends.

Sure, she'd only been there three months, but since the first shift they'd worked together they'd clicked, gently teasing each other, pre-empting each other's jokes, moaning together as friends did.

And now she had to break his heart.

'Nick, there was an accident in the city this morning…'

'Yeah,' Nick moaned, 'that's why I was late. Why?' His voice was suddenly serious. 'Are there kids involved? Should I go down to Emergency?'

'Nick.' She halted him almost harshly, and as his green eyes met hers they widened just a fraction, perhaps realising that this had nothing to do with work and everything to do with him. She felt as if she were wielding an axe, watching him wince as each blow was delivered. 'It was Teaghan's car.'

'No.' He shook his head, absolutely denying it, but a muscle was pounding in his cheek, his jaw muscles tensing as he refuted her words. 'She wasn't going anywhere near the city. She'd just done a night shift. Teaghan's at home, asleep…'

'Nick, it *was* Teaghan in the car,' Eden said firmly. 'She was wearing her ID badge, and Sharon Kennedy, the nurse supervisor, has confirmed that it's her. She was brought here a short while ago…' She knew, because of her training, that there must be no room for doubt as you delivered the news, that words like 'she didn't suffer' or 'everything possible was done' had no place yet in this horrible conversation. They had to come later. There could be no room for false hope. Raising her mental axe, trembling inside as she did so, Eden delivered the final, appalling blow. 'Nick, Teaghan was pronounced dead on arrival.'

And she watched—watched as her words felled him. Watched that carefree face crumple before her eyes, watched as he seemed to age a decade in a matter of seconds. Every sound was somehow magnified—a scream from a child on the ward, a baby crying in the background, IV pumps singing loudly for attention, the linen trolley clattering past her office, the world moving on as it stopped in its tracks for Nick. She didn't know what to do, knew there was nothing she could say that could make it even a tiny bit better. She crossed the short distance between them and put her arms around his tense shoulders, felt the squeeze of his hand as he gripped her arm, the shudder of his breath as he leant his head on her chest, one low sob the only noise he made. His pain was palpable and she held him, held him for a time so small it was barely there, caught him as he went into freefall, tears spilling out of her eyes as she witnessed his agony.

'I have to go to her…'

The tiny moment to process was over, replaced now with a blinding need to see Teaghan, to maybe put right a million wrongs, to do something, anything. He stood up, dragging a hand over his mouth, swallowing back the scream he was surely suppressing. His eyes again met hers, tortured eyes that begged for answers, begged her to take it all back, to somehow erase what she'd said. But all she could do was stare back helplessly, tears spilling down her cheeks as she felt his devastation. Then he was gone. His arm knocked a pile of papers off her desk in his haste to get to his fiancée, the chair toppled over as he dashed past it, he collided with the porter who was wheeling the linen trolley. His feet pounded as he ran down the corridor and Eden just stood there, white-faced and shaking, not moving until Brad Jenkins, the emergency consultant, appeared grim-faced at the door, taking in the chaos Nick had left in his wake.

'You just missed him,' Eden said, the words shivering out of her chattering lips. She braced herself to call the staff in, to tell the rest of her colleagues the terrible news. 'He's gone to be with Teaghan.'

'I'm sorry.' Eden hadn't said it on that fateful day, but she said it now, turning troubled eyes to him. Here she was moaning about the roster, and the fact that she'd had to work last year as well. It suddenly seemed beyond petty, given all Nick had been through, given what had happened to Teaghan. 'That was absolutely thoughtless of me,' Eden apologised again, and Nick gave a small forgiving smile.

'So why do you have to work this year?'

'It doesn't matter.' Horribly embarrassed, cringing inside, Eden made to go, but again Nick halted her.

'Let's talk in here,' he suggested, gesturing for her to go into his office, but Eden shook her head.

'The nursing roster isn't your problem, Nick. I was just letting off a bit of steam.'

'Then let it off over a decent cup of coffee.'

He walked back into his office, clearly expecting Eden to follow, and for a moment she stood there, not quite sure she was up to an impromptu chat with Nick right now. Since Donna had dropped her bomb about the Christmas roster, Eden's emotions had been bubbling dangerously close to the surface, and fifteen minutes alone with Nick was the *last* thing that was going to calm her down.

Nick was the main reason she had wanted Christmas off in the first place!

A week at home with her family, a week away from the city, a week of horse riding and clearing her mind, far away from the pressure cooker she found herself in whenever Nick was near.

'Eden!' Nick's impatient voice snapped her attention back. She took a deep breath and headed into his office, determined not to let him glimpse the effect he had on her.

Nick Watson's ego was already big enough, without another boost.

'Still take sugar?' Nick asked, not looking up.

'Please.' Perching herself on a chair, Eden forced a smile as Nick handed her a coffee, pleased that her hands were steady as she took the cup. 'I really am sorry about what I said...'

'Don't worry.' Nick waved a hand as he sat down. 'I'm OK.'

'You're sure?' Eden checked, but she wasn't just talking about her little *faux pas* earlier. 'This time of year must be awful for you.'

'Actually, no.' Nick shook his head. 'I'm too busy to even start feeling sorry for myself. There's too many parties and dinners and, of course—'

'Women,' Eden finished for him with a slight edge to her voice, which she quickly fought to check.

'I was about to say work.' Nick grinned. 'But now you mention it...! Anyway, enough about my social life. How come they're making you work over Christmas again? I thought the ward policy was one year on, one year off.'

'It was,' Eden sighed, 'until Ruth went off on early maternity leave. *Apparently* her blood pressure's high.'

'Apparently?' Nick raised an eyebrow, picking up the tiny note of cynicism and Eden winced.

'That sounded so bitchy, didn't it? But I've guessed for months that she wasn't going to make it to Christmas, especially given the fact that she was down to work night shifts on Christmas Eve and Boxing Day. Donna called us all into the office earlier and asked for volunteers to take Ruth's shifts.'

'I'm assuming you didn't put your hand up.'

'No!' Eden took a sip of her coffee before she continued, 'No one did. And then it started.'

'What started?'

'"Timmy's only two" or "It's Jamie's first Christmas". Even Becky, who's supposed to be my friend, chimed in that it's "Conner's last Christmas while he still believes in Santa".' Nick grinned as she mimicked her various colleagues' voices and a tiny smile wobbled on Eden's lips. 'I don't have a defence, given that I'm a paediatric nurse on a paediatric ward, I, of all people, should understand that children want their mums to be there on Christmas morning so Donna asked if I'd mind working it.'

'You could have said no,' Nick pointed out, and then laughed. 'Hell, Eden, why didn't you just say that you weren't prepared to do it? Why can't you just say no to Donna?'

'I tried!' Eden wailed.

'How?'

'I pointed out that if I work a night shift on Christmas Eve I can hardly be expected to drive to Coffs Harbour on Christmas morning unless they want me to doze off at the…' Her voice trailed off again as the conversation tipped where it shouldn't. 'Last year my dad drove all the way down to Sydney and stayed at my flat overnight just so that I could be with my family on Christmas Day, but it was just too much for him. It's a six-hour drive after all—it was actually too much for me as well. We both ended up sound asleep for the best part of the day—just about missed Christmas altogether. I can't ask him to do it again this year.'

'What about your flatmate, Jim?' he asked. 'What's he doing for Christmas?'

'He's going to Queensland for the Christmas break. Actually, he's been trying to persuade me to come with him and his friend. Maybe I should tell Donna that I'm going to be away and take him up on it. '

'Maybe you should.'

Eden pulled a face. 'I don't think so. There's only so much damage one's liver can take. As much beer and barbequed prawns as you can stomach isn't really my idea of Christmas.'

'You can't be on your own.' Nick shook his head, but Eden just gave a wry smile.

'Believe me, Nick, I'd rather be. I've already had about three invites for Christmas dinner from my guilty colleagues…'

'And?'

'Timmy may only be two…' Eden rolled her eyes '…but he's an absolute monster. And as much as I adore Conner, I see enough kids' tantrums in a day's work…' She gave a small shrug. 'You get the picture!'

'I do.' Nick grinned back. And it was funny, Eden mused, that even after a year of relative silence they could slip back so easily into their own shorthand, pick up on the tiny vibes without explanation. 'And I suppose the fact that Becky's also a strict vegan had nothing to do with it.'

'Caught.' Eden managed a weak smile. 'I guess if I want my turkey and ham, I'll have to cook it myself.'

'There's always the canteen.'

The look Eden shot him wasn't particularly friendly but Nick merely roared with laughter. 'It will probably be in the high thirties,' Nick pointed out. 'The last thing you'll want is a huge roast.'

'Wrong.' Eden pouted. 'I love Christmas dinner, pudding, mince pies…' She closed her eyes for an indulgent second, imagining her parents' dining room at home, the air-conditioning on full blast as the table groaned under the weight of ham and turkey, roast pork, little sausages wrapped in bacon and mountains of Christmas crackers with their cheesy presents and even cheesier jokes. But Nick threw a bucket of water over her fantasy.

'Well, if it makes you feel any better, I'd love to have your problem. I've practically begged to work this Christmas but the powers that be have decided, given my *circumstances,* that they know best, and that what I really need is a nice little break over the festive season with my family.' Nick's low groan told Eden that it was the last place he wanted to be, and she blinked at him in bewilderment.

'But it's Christmas!' she said, and it should have been explanation enough, but as Nick just grimaced, Eden let out a wail of indignation. 'It's Christmas,' she said again. 'How could you not want to spend it with them? I thought you adored your family?'

'I do.' Nick rolled his eyes. 'And they adore me, so much so that they want to see me happy, which I am, of course, but they beg to differ. Happy to them means…'

'You *can* say it, Nick.' Eden smiled.

'OK.' He took a deep theatrical breath. 'They want to see me in a relationship!'

'I thought you were.' Eden blinked innocently. 'With Shelly from Emergency—oh, no, sorry, I meant Phoebe from ICU.' Another blink, a tiny frown as she tried to place a name, and she heard Nick's intake of breath as he realised she was teasing him. 'What about that intern—oh, what is her name…?' She clicked her fingers a couple of times as Nick actually managed a small blush. 'Tanya, that's the one. Whatever happened to her?'

She already knew the answer! Nick's initial devastation at Teaghan's death had slowly been replaced by a curious arrogance as he'd headed off the rails, his undeniable charm working its way around the hospital and leaving devastation in its wake. But even though it was considered almost an insult not to have been dated by Nick during the last twelve months, not once had Nick attempted to cross the line with Eden. And even though she valued what was left of his friendship, even though the last thing she wanted was to be another of his conquests, Nick's indifference to her on the romantic front was breaking Eden's heart.

'Tanya and I are just friends,' Nick said. 'You're reading far too much into it."

'*We're* just friends, Nick.' Draining her coffee-cup, trying not to show just how much that admission hurt, Eden stood up. 'Or we used to be.'

'What's that supposed to mean?' Nick asked, but Eden just shrugged.

'Nothing.'

'It didn't sound like nothing. What did you mean?'

'Just that things have changed lately,' Eden admitted. 'Sometimes I feel as if I hardly know you any more.'

'You're being daft.' Nick grinned.

'Perhaps I am, but take it from me, what Tanya feels isn't merely friendly, so tread carefully. Anyway, enough already about your love life, Nick. I'd better get back out there. I can hear the meal trolley coming and I've a feeling someone's about to kick up a fuss when they find out I swapped her order.'

'Priscilla?' Nick checked almost needlessly, referring to a nine-year-old with a penchant for chicken nuggets. 'I'm going to have to speak to her mother again.'

'Well, tread carefully,' Eden warned. 'Remember that she's a high-profile lawyer.'

'So maybe she'll appreciate some straight talking,' Nick countered. 'Hell, we're so bogged down in politically correct jargon these days, so terrified of being sued, it's a wonder anything useful gets done in this place; Priscilla's a great kid, but unless someone spells it out to Rose, unless someone actually sits that woman down and tells her to stop feeding her kid rubbish, we may as well send her daughter home with a packet of cholesterol-lowering pills and a post-dated referral to a psychologist to deal with the *issues* of bullying.'

Eden shot him a worried look but, as politically incorrect as Nick could be at times, more often than not his straight talking hit the nail on the head.

'The other kids are starting to tease her.'

'If I were nine, I'd tease her,' Nick moaned, and thankfully he wasn't looking so he didn't see a tiny smile flash on her lips as she pictured Nick Watson as a cheeky blond nine-year-old. 'What the hell is Rose doing, calling her Princess in front of the other kids?'

'It's her pet name.'

'Then she should save it for home. Are you going to do it?' Nick added as she headed for the door. 'Work Christmas, I mean?'

'It looks that way,' Eden sighed.

'You need a baby of your own,' Nick said with another grin, and Eden gave a wry smile back.

'It's probably the only way I can guarantee getting next Christmas off—I'd better step on it.'

'You'd better,' Nick responded dryly. 'Given that they take nine months…'

'I was referring to work, Nick,' Eden said.

CHAPTER TWO

PRISCILLA, or Princess as her mother called her, was in for investigation into her recurrent constipation and abdominal pain, which had culminated in many trips to her local GP and a lot of absences from school. As a private patient, initially her mother had demanded a single room for her daughter, but thankfully Nick had been able to persuade Rose that her daughter would benefit from being among her peers, and after a rather prolonged negotiation Rose had finally agreed.

Even though she was in a public ward, Priscilla still demanded private patient attention, pressing the call bell incessantly, complaining loudly about the food and the lack of her own television—to the amusement of her fellow patients, who were starting to tease the little girl and calling her by her nickname of Princess, though not in the affectionate way her mother delivered it.

As annoying as Priscilla could be, as demanding as she was, despite the other nurses' grumbles when allocated to look after her, Eden actually enjoyed looking after the spoilt little girl. Fiercely intelligent, she had a wry sense of humour. Very pretty, she was also very overweight and had her exhausted working single mother wrapped around her rather podgy little fingers. She was completely used to getting her own way—and quickly, please! Since she'd discovered that the call bell by her bed summoned attention quickly, Priscilla was abusing it to the max, despite the fact she wasn't on bed rest. However, before Eden again explained that fact, first she had to be sure that there was nothing wrong with the little girl.

'What's the problem, Priscilla?' Eden asked, smiling as she made her way over to the bed.

'This isn't the dinner I ordered.' Frowning down at her plate, Priscilla stabbed at a defenceless piece of roast chicken and vegetables. 'Mummy ticked the chicken nuggets for me—look.' She held out the menu card for Eden, but Eden didn't need to read it to know what was on it.

'You had nuggets for dinner last night,' Eden explained patiently, 'and the previous night as well.'

'Because I like nuggets.'

'Do you remember that Dr Nick said you were to have more variety in your diet? Well, instead of having chicken nuggets, why not try having some roast chicken and some of the lovely vegetables?'

'I don't like vegetables.' Priscilla pouted, her bottom lip wobbling, tears filling her big blue eyes, and Eden was grateful that Priscilla's mother wasn't there because it was at about this point that Priscilla was used to adults giving in. But Eden stood her ground, undoing the little pack of fruit juice and pouring some out for Priscilla.

'When Mummy comes I'll tell her to go and get me some nuggets from the take-away.'

'You're going to turn into a nugget one of these days.' Nick was there, ruffling Priscilla's hair, grinning broadly and completely ignoring her tears. 'I told Eden that you were going to eat some veggies for me tonight, Priscilla. Now, you're not going to make me look silly, are you?'

'I hate veggies,' Priscilla snarled, slamming down her knife and fork with a clatter that alerted her fellow patients to the start of yet another of Priscilla's rather too frequent dramas.

'Come on Princess, eat your veggies,' Rory, a cheeky ten-year-old with his leg in traction, called out.

'Yeah, come on, Princess,' Declan, a five-year-old post-tonsillectomy patient chimed in.

'Cut it out, guys,' Eden warned, pulling the curtains and shutting out the delighted audience while Nick stood firm with his patient.

'Roast chicken and vegetables are what's for dinner tonight—' He didn't finish. Priscilla's meal tray crashing loudly to the floor, courtesy of a flash of temper, interrupted the conversation. Her angry face stared defiantly at both Eden and Nick, awaiting their reaction as a few cheers erupted from the other side of the curtains.

'Whoops,' Nick said calmly, which clearly wasn't the reaction Priscilla had been expecting. Her angry face puckered into a frown, her expression changing from fury to utter indignation as Nick calmly continued talking. 'Not to worry. Accidents happen. Eden can ring down to the canteen and order you another dinner.'

The tears started again, angry furious tears, her pretty face purple with rage.

'Do you need a hand?' Becky asked, arriving with the

mop and bucket as Eden picked the remains of the meal off the floor. 'Her mother has just arrived,' she added in a low tone to Nick as she bent down to help Eden.

'What's going on?' Rose Tarrington clipped into the ward on smart high heels, her petite frame in an expensive chocolate brown suit, well made-up eyes frowning as she pulled open the curtains and surveyed the mess.

'Priscilla knocked over her dinner,' Nick responded calmly. 'Sister's just going to order her another one.'

'But she won't eat that.' Rose pointed a manicured finger at the messy remains. 'I know you want her to have some variety, but you can hardly expect her to suddenly start eating roast meat and vegetables overnight!'

'The other children are,' Nick broke in, staring around the ward at the other three children, all eating their dinners.

'Look, Princess.' Rose made her way over to her daughter's bedside and cuddled the distraught child. 'Why don't you do as the doctor and nurses say? Eat your dinner and then, if you do, I'll go over the road and get you some ice cream.'

'Could I have a word at the nurses' station, please, Ms Tarrington?' Nick broke in, and Eden watched as the woman stiffened.

'I'm just talking to my daughter.'

'It won't take long.' Nick's voice was even but it had a certain ring to it that told everyone present he wasn't about to take no for an answer.

'Becky can stay with Priscilla,' Nick instructed. 'Eden, would you mind joining us, please?'

Eden rather wished he'd allocated her to clean up the mess and sort out Priscilla. A nine-year-old throwing a tantrum she could deal with blindfolded, but a brutal dose of honesty, as only Nick could deliver it, wasn't going to be particularly pleasant, though it was called for.

The endless talks with the nursing staff, doctors and dieticians clearly hadn't made the slightest bit of difference to Rose or Priscilla's behaviour and now, Eden guessed as she followed Nick to the nurses' station, the kid gloves were off. Nick's only priority was his patients.

'Have a seat.' Nick gestured to the tense woman, barely waiting till she was seated before diving in.

'I've asked Sister Hadley to sit in so that we can all be on the same page,' Nick explained. 'For Priscilla's sake, we all need to be taking the same approach.

'We don't seem to be getting very far, do we, Rose?' Nick started softly, but Rose Tarrington clearly wasn't in any mood for a gentle lead-in. Brittle and defensive, she stared angrily back at Nick.

'Perhaps if you stopped focussing on my daughter's diet and found out just what the hell the problem is with her stomach, we'd start to make some progress. Priscilla's been in here a week now and apart from a few blood tests and an X-ray, she's had nothing done for her.' Rose's hands clenched in frustration, her legs tightly crossed. She was the complete opposite to Nick, who sat relaxed and open in the chair opposite. 'Oh, and an ultrasound,' Rose spat, more as an afterthought. 'We could have done all that as outpatients. I'm not asking for favours, but given the fact my daughter's a private patient...'

'That has no bearing.' Nick shook his head. 'I have a mixture of private and public patients on my list, Rose, and I can assure you they all receive the same treatment from both me and the staff on the ward. Yes, as a private patient Priscilla could, no doubt, have had all these investigations done speedily as an outpatient, but, as I explained to you in Emergency when I admitted your daughter, given that Priscilla has already missed out on a third of her schooling this year, it really is imperative that we find out what's causing her abdominal pain and causing her to miss so much school. Which…' As Rose opened her mouth to argue, Nick shook his head, speaking over the angry woman. 'Which we have,' he said firmly. 'The abdominal X-ray showed that Priscilla was chronically constipated, the ultrasound told me that there was nothing acutely wrong and her blood work confirmed my clinical diagnosis. Priscilla is anaemic, her cholesterol is high…' He paused for a second, only this time Rose didn't jump in to argue, this time Rose closed her eyes as Nick gently but firmly continued. 'Now, I could put on her on some iron tablets. However, that would only cause further constipation. To counter that, I could prescribe a fibre supplement, but I don't think Priscilla would drink it. I could, of course, give her laxatives, but the thing is I'm not prepared to do that when all she needs is a varied, healthy diet and an increase in her physical activity.'

'That's all she needs, is it?' Rose's tired, angry eyes were bulging as she spoke. 'You've seen what she's like when she doesn't get her own way. I work ten-hour days and, yes, it's easier to pick up a take-away than to start cooking, but what am I supposed to do when it's the only thing she'll eat. I can hardly let her go to bed without eating…'

'You could,' Nick replied, but Rose just scoffed.

'You obviously don't have children, Doctor. Don't you think I already feel guilty enough about the hours I work, without spending every evening fighting with my daughter over what she wants for dinner and sending her to bed hungry? No doubt you'll be telling me soon to cut down my hours and start spending more *quality* time…' Tears came then, choking, angry tears, her tiny, exhausted frame heaving, her hand pressing on her mouth as she tried to hold it all in. Nick still calmly sat there, not remotely embarrassed, pulling a couple of tissues from the box on the desk and handing them to her before pressing on.

'I wouldn't dream of telling you to cut down your hours, Rose. I'm aware that you're a single parent. You're doing an amazing job—'

'Don't patronise me,' Rose snarled as she blew her nose. 'Don't try and tell me I'm doing well when you clearly think I'm an unfit mother.'

'No one thinks that.' Eden said, her voice a gentle interlude from the painful conversation. 'We're not ganging up on you, Rose, we all just want to do the best we can for Priscilla. Nick isn't suggesting that you're an unfit parent. If that were the case, we'd be having this conversation in an office with a case worker present so, please, let's try and not go there.'

Standing, Eden fetched a drink of water for Rose from the cooler, a tiny nod the only response from Rose as she handed it to her. Nick waited as Rose had a drink and then continued.

'Eden's right. I don't think that for a moment.' Nick shook his head. 'And you're right as well. I don't have kids, but my sister is a busy GP with three little ones and is in the process of getting a divorce. I've heard from Lily all about the guilt, the endless juggling and the pressures of trying to do the right thing.'

'It's just so hard,' Rose choked.

'If it carries on like this, Rose, it's going to get harder,' Nick said as Rose frowned. 'Priscilla is so constipated that if the situation continues, very soon she could end up with some overflow.' When Rose frowned, Nick clarified his words and Rose closed her eyes as he did so. 'She could have episodes of faecal incontinence. Priscilla has already told some of the nursing staff that she gets teased at school about her weight. Can you imagine how much harder it will be for her if she starts to soil her pants as well?'

Eden half expected an argument, but all the fight seemed to go out of Rose. The hotshot lawyer was gone, leaving just a terrified mum sitting on the chair. 'She already has,' Rose whispered through pale, trembling lips. 'Only once, but…it's all my fault, isn't it?'

'We're not going there, remember? We're here to deal with the things we can change, and the past isn't one of them.' Nick gave a very nice smile, peeling another wad of tissues out of the box. 'Come on, Rose, blow your nose and stop the tears and let's work out what we're going to do.' He glanced over at Eden and she took her cue.

'At the moment Priscilla's used to getting food as a reward and she's using it to her advantage,' Eden explained. 'For example, you said to her tonight that if she ate her dinner then you'd get her an ice cream.'

'It's all I could think of to get her to eat her dinner,' Rose admitted.

'How about, leaving out the "if",' Eden suggested. 'Try "Eat your dinner, Priscilla, and then I'll read to you" or "then we'll watch a movie together" or "then I'll help you with your homework".'

'Spend some *quality* time with her?' Rose asked, only this time it was said without contempt.

'For want of a word, only in this case it's time you would usually spend arguing,' Eden responded. 'In the morning, you can do the same: "Eat your breakfast and then you can watch some television."'

'Make it non-negotiable,' Nick said, 'but at the same time make out it's no big deal. Be matter-of-fact about it—she *has* to eat her meals, and by that I mean the meals you provide for her, not the ones she demands.

'And I choose my words carefully, Rose,' Nick winked, and to Eden's amazement Rose actually managed a pale smile as he continued. 'I'm not telling you to grow a vegetable patch and start steaming broccoli every night. Just a normal balanced diet is all Priscilla needs—you, too, no doubt. I'm assuming here that you're not tucking into the fries and nuggets yourself?'

Rose shook her head.

'Cheese on toast around midnight?' Nick asked.

'Something like that,' Rose admitted.

'Me, too,' Nick sighed. 'How about you, Eden?'

'I'm more a bowl-of-cereal girl.'

'Stop boasting.' Nick grinned. 'We're all guilty of it, Rose. We've all got jobs that demand too much of us so we grab something to eat when we can or when we absolutely have to. But as you pointed out, Eden and I don't have kids, so we *can* mess up our own health. Look, if you can afford it, why not get your meals delivered for a few weeks? You could choose your menus together, there are a few companies that provide that type of service.'

'And that would be OK?'

'Absolutely.' Nick nodded.

'And,' Eden added, 'if it makes things easier for you, for the next couple of days why not let us deal with Priscilla at mealtimes?'

'Shouldn't *I* be telling her?' Rose asked wisely. 'Given that I'm the one that's going to be dealing with her at home.'

'You should,' Eden said, 'but it's going to be difficult the first few times. Priscilla isn't going to take very kindly to the rules suddenly changing and we can take some of the strain for you, so long as you support us. As Nick said, if we're all working as a team there's a better chance of getting results. Why don't you come in at mealtimes and if Priscilla starts to kick up, tell her that you're going to the canteen for a coffee and that the nurses will ring down once she's finished her dinner?'

'You'd do that?'

'Definitely.' Eden nodded, peering over Rose's shoulder as an orderly arrived with a fresh meal. 'How about we start now?'

'She's not going to like it,' Rose warned.

'Good,' Nick said, standing up and shaking Rose's hand warmly. 'Because I'm sure you could use a coffee and a bit of time alone to think about what we've just said. And for the record, Rose, I wasn't being patronising before. You are doing an amazing job—Priscilla's funny, intelligent and incredibly perceptive.'

'Thank you.' Rose blushed. 'She really is my little

princess.' Nick opened his mouth, then clearly thought better of it. Now, perhaps, was not the time to tell Rose to curb her pet name, at least around Priscilla's peers. 'I'll just go to the washroom and freshen up. I don't want her to see that I've been crying.'

As Rose scurried off, Eden expected Nick to do the same, but instead he remained. 'Thanks for your help. Hopefully some of it got through to Rose.'

'I think a lot of it got through,' Eden replied generously. 'You were really good with her.'

'Probably because I've had a lot of practice around tearful women lately,' Nick said, but as Eden's lips pursed his face broke into a slightly incredulous smile. 'You're really quick to think the worst of me, aren't you, Eden? When I said I'd been around tearful women lately, I was actually referring to my sister, Lily.'

'Oh.' Blushing, Eden scuffed the floor with her foot. 'Well, you can hardly blame me for assuming…' Her voice trailed off, and Nick did absolutely nothing to fill the uncomfortable silence. Eden willed Rose to hurry back, terrified that if she looked up, Nick might catch a glimpse of the jealous feelings that seemed to choke her whenever she pictured him with another woman. However, her mouth was moving ahead of her mind and wretched emotions were taking over. Wincing inside, yet completely unable to stop herself, a tiny slice of truth came out. 'I just don't like seeing people used, that's all.'

'Used?' She could hear the frown in his voice without looking up, and Eden knew she'd gone too far, knew that she had to pull back now before irretrievable damage was done, before Nick realised how much she was hurting. Forcing a very cheeky smile, she dragged her eyes back to his.

'Yes, used, Nick. Just because you're blond and gorgeous, it doesn't mean that you don't have feelings, too!' And even though he smiled at her joke, it didn't quite reach his eyes and Eden knew her attempt at recovery hadn't quite succeeded. 'I'm allowed to worry about you—that's what friends do.'

The smile was back in his eyes now, and Eden gave an inward sigh of relief as Rose appeared.

'Good luck,' Nick called as Eden and Rose headed back towards Priscilla's bedside, just in time to see Becky setting up the replacement meal tray.

'Oh, look.' Rose smiled. 'Roast chicken—yum!' Her tone was a touch forced, but Eden was pleased to see how hard she was trying. 'Now, come on, eat up your dinner and then you can read to me.'

'I'm not eating that filth!' Priscilla snarled. Her hand moved towards the tray, but Eden was too quick for her.

'Oh, no.' Eden held onto the tray, holding the young girl's angry glare. 'There are plenty more trays down in the canteen, Priscilla. I can ring down for more all evening if I have to, but we're not wasting good food like that.'

'Well, I'm not eating it.' Priscilla's bottom lip was working overtime and she squeezed out a tear for effect. 'Mummy, I don't like roast chicken!'

'That's what's for dinner tonight, Priscilla.' Rose took a deep breath and Eden felt sorry for her, knowing how hard it must be for her to be firm when her daughter lay in a hospital bed. 'Now, it looks so nice that I'm going down to the canteen to have some dinner myself. When you're finished, Eden here will ring me and I'll come back up.'

'Mummy!' Priscilla wasn't squeezing tears out now—they were coming thick and fast of their own accord. 'Mummy, don't leave me!'

'As soon as your dinner's finished, darling, I'll come back up.' Hiding tears of her own, Rose turned quickly, hurrying out of the ward. Eden ran after her as Becky stayed with a shrieking Priscilla.

'She'll be fine,' Eden soothed. 'You did so well.'

'I can't do this every night,' Rose sobbed.

'You won't have to,' Eden said. 'As soon as Priscilla realises that you're serious, she'll start eating properly. Rose, just remember that all you are asking is for her to eat her dinner, not walk on hot coals. There's nothing unreasonable or unfair about what you're doing.'

'I know,' Rose gulped.

'Now, go and have a coffee or dinner. I promise that we'll look after her and as soon as she's made a reasonable effort with her dinner, I'll ring you.'

'And if she doesn't?'

'I'll ring down for you anyway.' Eden smiled. 'But let's stay positive.'

In fact, by the time Eden returned to the bedside, the tears had stopped and Priscilla was sitting upright with her arms folded pointedly, not looking up as Eden made her way over.

'Thanks, Becky.'

'No worries.' Becky grinned, scooting off to check on her own patients.

'Your mum has just gone to have some dinner,' Eden said, picking up a rather impressive book on Priscilla's bedside. 'Is this yours?'

When Priscilla didn't answer, Eden pressed on, un-perturbed. 'It's a huge book for a nine-year-old.'

'It's easy.' Priscilla bristled.

'Well, I don't think so—all those funny names and spells and trying to work out who the baddy is….'

'You've read it?' Priscilla blinked, curiosity overriding her anger for a moment.

'Not this one,' Eden admitted, 'but I've read four in the series and I'm hoping someone will get me this one for Christmas.'

'But it's a kid's book.'

'So?' Sitting down at the bedside, Eden peeled off the cover on Priscilla's dinner. 'Come on, Priscilla, eat your dinner and then I'll call downstairs for Mum to come up. She said you were going to read to her tonight, and she's really looking forward to it.' Pretending to ignore her, Eden concentrated on the blurb at the back of the book as Eden slowly picked up her knife and fork.

'I don't like broccoli.'

Eden flicked the pages, deliberately not looking up.

'Eden, I *really* don't like broccoli.'

'Neither do I.' Eden smiled. 'OK. How about you eat everything else? If you do that, you can leave the broccoli.'

'I don't like carrots.'

'Priscilla.' Eden's voice held a warning. 'If you eat all your carrots, potato and chicken, *then* you can leave the broccoli.' Turning back to the book, she flicked the pages. 'Where are you up to?'

To an onlooker, Eden knew she probably looked as if she was doing nothing but sitting on the bed as Priscilla slowly worked her way through her meal, but, Eden knew exactly what she was doing; knew she had

the best job in the world. Rose had trusted her enough
to go down to the canteen and Priscilla was actually eating her dinner. They might not be cutting-edge science,
but tonight she and Nick had hopefully made a difference, a huge difference, in a little girl's life.

And Priscilla did very well!

Eden's heart swelled with pride as finally the plate
was if not clean then almost so. Priscilla had even had
a small piece of the broccoli.

'Well done, honey.' Eden grinned and picked up the
tray, careful not too make too much of a fuss but also
wanting to acknowledge Priscilla's effort. 'How about
I go and ring down to the canteen for your mum?'

'Are you on in the morning?' Priscilla asked, and
Eden shook her head.

'I'm on another late shift. I'll come and check on you
a bit later. You enjoy reading to your mum.'

'How did Priscilla get on with her dinner?' Nick asked
a while later, when Becky was on her supper break and
Eden was giving a grumpy six-month-old named Justin the last of his bottle.

Eden loved this time of night on the children's ward.
At seven the main lights were switched off and the curtains drawn and, despite the light Sydney evening outside, the whole ward was plunged into darkness, filled
with the sounds of babies' and toddlers' final protests
as their parents or nurses soothed them off to sleep, the
background drone of the television in the older children's rooms. Usually with Donna, the unit manager,
gone and most doctors long since headed for home there
was a chance for Eden to take her time feeding a baby

or sit on a bed and have a chat with a lonely patient or just catch up with the mountain of paperwork involved in nursing these days. It was one of the main reasons she often volunteered for the late shift.

'Good.' Eden said. 'Rose is going to go through tomorrow's menu with her a bit later on and I'll pass it all on to the night staff. Hopefully, if we all keep it up, she'll be a different girl in a few days. Becky and I are both on another late shift tomorrow, which will make things easier when Rose comes in. How come you're still here?' she added.

'I'm not.' Picking up his briefcase, he gave a tired smile. 'Unless my pager goes off between now and the car park. I'll see you tomorrow.'

'See, you, Nick.' Eden smiled back. 'Have a good night.'

'I will if you don't call!'

No doubt a thousand doctors were jokingly saying those exact words to a thousand nurses even as Nick spoke them, but for Eden they hurt like hell.

The hardest part of the entire day was about to ensue.

She kept a professional smile in place as he picked up his briefcase and walked out of the ward, wondering who he was on his way to see, wondering who was filling the long hours till she saw him again.

Wondering where the loyal man who had been engaged to Teaghan had disappeared to…

Maybe he felt her eyes on him, but for some reason as he reached the door he turned around, then walked back the length of the ward in long purposeful strides. Eden figured he must have forgotten to sign for something or was going to remind her about a patient.

'I've been thinking about our mutual problem.'

'Mutual problem?' Eden frowned, shifting Justin on her knee into an upright position, his little face held between her thumb and finger as her other hand rubbed his back.

'Christmas.' Nick said with a note of exasperation, as if the conversation they had had a few hours ago should still be at the front of her mind.

'I'll sort something out,' Eden said airily. 'Though I have to admit I'm not particularly looking forward to ringing my parents tonight and telling them I'm not coming home.'

'Will they be upset?'

'Not upset.' Eden shook her head. 'Just sorry, I guess, and worried that I'll be on my own.'

'But you don't have to be on your own,' Nick said, and Eden just shrugged and turned her attention back to the babe in her arms, continuing to rub his back in an attempt to bring up the wind she was sure was there. 'Why don't you spend it with me and my family?'

Despite a very loud burp from a very little baby, Eden carried on rubbing his back, determinedly not looking at up as her cheeks started to colour, waiting for Nick to roar with laughter or make some wisecrack to show that he was joking, but when finally she did jerk her eyes up to look at him, she was shocked to see that his face was deadly serious.

'It makes perfect sense,' Nick insisted. 'My sister's kids are spending the day with their dad and they won't be there till the evening so there won't be any tantrums, and my mum's an amazing cook so you can have the massive roast dinner you're dreaming of. At least you can tell your parents when you ring them that you're not going to be on your own.'

'And what's in it for you?' Eden asked directly, her eyes narrowing as Nick blushed slightly.

'I just don't like the thought of you being on your own,' Nick attempted, but Eden just slowly shook her head.

'What's in it for you, Nick?' she asked again.

'Well, if I hinted to Mum that we were seeing each other, I guess that would buy me a few months of grace.'

'You mean get them off your back?'

'Something like that. Think about it, Eden. It would be good for both of us and you'd have a great day, I can guarantee it.'

'So why not ask one of your many admirers? I'm sure Tanya's hoping for an invitation to meet your family.'

'Exactly.' Nick rolled his eyes. 'I spoke to her last night and unfortunately you're right—she was hoping…' He gave an embarrassed shrug. 'Suffice to say an invitation to Tanya to spend Christmas with me and my family could only confuse things, whereas with you and I…' He gave another shrug. 'Well, we'd both know that there was…'

'Nothing in it,' Eden finished for him as his voice trailed off. 'Thanks but, no, thanks.'

'Why not?'

Somehow she managed a smile as she placed a nappy over her shoulder and rested Justin against it as she stood up.

'Playing your girlfriend for a day, just isn't my idea of a fun Christmas,' Eden said. Heading down the ward and coming to Justin's room, she pushed the door open. 'You'll have to come up with someone else, Nick.'

'Think about it,' Nick said, but Eden shook her head.

''Night, Nick.'

As the door closed behind her, she placed Justin in his cot, soothing him gently as he struggled to open his heavy eyes. She listened to the sound of Nick's footsteps going down the ward and felt the sting of a great salty tear as it rolled down her cheek.

Stupidly, she'd dreamed of that very moment.

Secretly dreamed of Nick asking her to be with him and his family, the thought of sharing Christmas with him a fantasy she'd harboured—only not like this.

Never like this.

CHAPTER THREE

'SHE'LL never agree.' Becky shook her head as Eden wrestled with six feet four of hulking pine tree, dragging the beast the length of the nurses' station then levering it up to its full height. 'Donna *always* has it on the far side of the nurses' station.'

'Where no one can see it,' Eden retorted.

'Where it doesn't get in the way,' Becky countered with a grin. 'She'll have a fit when she sees that you've moved it.'

'Then she shouldn't have asked me to sort out the Christmas decorations, "given that the ward's so quiet".' Eden's rather purse-lipped impression of her senior rapidly faded as Becky gave a quick cough and started shuffling a pile of papers in front of her. Eden sucked in her breath as Donna Adams arrived at the nurses' station with a mountain of empty boxes. She was clearly not in the least impressed with what she was seeing.

'*What*, may I ask, is the tree doing there, Sister?'

'I thought it was more visible,' Eden attempted. 'That more of the children would be able to see it from their beds.'

'It's in the way,' Donna clipped. 'This is a hospital,

Eden, not the local shopping centre. If, or rather when, there's an emergency the staff have enough to deal with, without manoeuvring crash carts around a blessed tree.'

'But there's plenty of room.' Eden stood firm, determined not to back down, determined for once in her life to stand up to Donna. 'I've measured it. And, yes, this is a hospital, but it's also a children's ward—'

'Nice tree!' Nick announced, depositing a mug of coffee and smothering a yawn, clearly oblivious to the argument that was taking place. 'When are the decorations going up?'

'Once Sister Hadley moves it back to the other side of the nurses' station,' Donna said tartly, and as Nick's eyes darted between the two women, Eden saw a twist of a smile on his lips as he picked up on the tension. 'I was just explaining that the reason we keep it at the far side of the table is that in the event of an emergency we need to be able to manoeuvre the trolleys—'

'There's plenty of room,' Nick broke in. 'They're not supermarket trolleys, Donna, we do have some control over them.'

'But the patient files are kept there.'

'Then move them,' Nick responded. 'It's much better here—more of the kids can see it.'

Given that Nick was the consultant, the argument was effectively over, but Donna wasn't particularly gracious in defeat, thrusting a pile of empty boxes in Eden's direction. 'You can wrap these for under the tree, and I do not want to come in tomorrow morning to mountains of tinsel and fake snow over all my windows and plastic Santas stuck to the wall. Could we try and aim for tasteful?'

'Children and tasteful don't exactly mix,' Eden muttered, but only when Donna was safely halfway down the corridor and heading for home! 'What is her problem?'

'She just likes to remind everyone she's the boss,' Nick answered, scribbling furiously on some notes and not looking up as he spoke. 'She's a honey really.'

'Only because *you're* the real boss.' Becky grinned, leaning over and peering down the corridor to make sure Donna really had left before rummaging in her wicker basket under the desk. She pulled out a container and shovelled a delectable-looking slice of cake on a paper towel and placed it beside Nick's mug. 'Here you go, Nick, have some chocolate cake with your coffee. 'Eden?' she offered, but Eden shook her head.

'Not for me, thanks. I'd better get on with this tree, given that I'm going to be seeing so much of it.'

'Oh, Eden, I am sorry about that, but it wasn't just for me that I said no.'

'I know,' Eden admitted. 'It's hardly fair on Conner as you worked last year.'

'It's not just Conner who'd be upset.' Becky let out a low sigh. 'I don't think Hamish would have taken it too well if I'd had to tell him that I was going to be working. Believe me, his tantrums lately are worse than anything Conner can pull off.'

Eden carried on listening to Becky's woes as she climbed onto a footstool, unraveling a bundle of fairy lights as she did so. She felt horribly self-conscious all of a sudden, acutely aware of Nick just a few metres away. Not that he was paying any attention, Eden consoled herself, tugging down her dress with one hand as she reached

up to the top of the tree with the other and started draping the lights—he was too wrapped up in his notes.

'You should check them first.' Nick's voice caught
her unawares and she swung around too quickly, embarrassed but grateful that, almost like a reflex action, he
reached out his arm to steady her. 'Careful, Eden,' he
warned, and Eden was grateful for the semi-darkness,
which meant that Nick couldn't see her blushing, which
she was—furiously. His fingers tightened around her
wrist. 'Do you want me to do it?'

'Do what?' Eden blinked, her mind having wandered
well away from the subject.

'To check the lights for you,' Nick explained patiently. 'Before you go to all the trouble of decorating
the tree, first you ought to plug them in to make sure
they're working.'

'Oh, Nick!' Eden simpered. 'What on earth would we
do without you?'

'That's why he's a doctor,' Becky said in a proud, vil-
lage-idiot type of voice, and Nick started to realize he
was being teased. 'Because he's so clever.'

'I was only trying to help.' Nick moaned, finally getting around to his coffee and cake. 'I'll keep my mouth
shut next time.'

'Please.' Eden grinned, resuming the difficult task as
Nick picked up his cake and eyed it greedily.

'I've just realised that I'm starving.'

'Well, enjoy.' Becky smiled. 'Eden didn't want any
so there's another piece here if you fancy it.'

Quite simply, Eden couldn't resist it. Still on the
footstool, the fairy lights poised in her hand, she turned
her head to watch Nick's face as he took a bite of the

moist chocolate sponge and Becky pushed the container holding Eden's slice towards him. 'Help yourself, Nick.'

It was sheer poetry in motion. Nick closed his eyes, just as one did when one was about to sink teeth into something divine. Eden watched as he took a very generous bite of the chocolate cake and then witnessed his eyes snapping open. The public school system had certainly done its job when they'd taught young Nicholas his manners because his moan of horror turned in an instant to a groan of approval.

'What ingredients do you use, Becky,' Eden asked innocently, turning her attention to the tree and smothering a smile, 'to get it so moist?'

'Tofu,' Becky smiled. 'Though I swear a good soy milk helps—none of that genetically engineered rubbish. And Hamish has found a store that does the most delectable vegan chocolate chips. I'm going to make one of those for Christmas—this was just a practice run. You will come,' Becky checked, jumping up as a buzzer went off. 'I'll get it.'

'What the hell is it?' Nick choked, using the paper towel Becky had thoughtfully provided but for a reason she had never intended!

'It's awful, isn't it?' Eden giggled. 'All her food's the same. It looks fantastic, but when you taste it. Don't!' Eden yelped as Nick went to toss the rest of his cake in the waste-paper basket. 'She'll see. Use the sharps bin.'

'I gather that you've done this before,' Nick said in a loud whisper, shoving the remains into the sharps bin, which had a closed lid that hid the contents from sight.

'Many times,' Eden admitted.

'You absolutely cannot go there for Christmas. It's

no wonder Conner and Hamish are throwing tantrums if that's what Becky's trying to feed them!'

'What can I say to her?' Eden giggled again. 'She knows that I can't get home and, given she was there when I found out, it's not as if I can pretend I've got other plans.'

'You could have,' Nick reminded her, but thankfully her pager bleeped, giving Eden an excuse not to get into the uncomfortable topic. Glancing down at her neon yellow pager, the numbers displayed were instantly recognisable as Accident and Emergency. As Eden was the admitting nurse for the paediatric unit that evening and all admissions had to come through her in order to be allocated, it could only mean one thing—a new admission was on the way.

'Eden Hadley, admitting nurse for Paeds,' Eden said as she was connected, listening to an unfamiliar nursing sister and scribbling down an initial diagnosis as Nick looked on. 'Chest infection or difficulty feeding.' She shared a wry grin with Nick as Emergency attempted to shuffle their patient to the top of the list. 'And he's three years old. Have we had him before?'

An incredibly long wait ensued as the nurse attempted to locate the patient's history, reeling off a long list of complaints until finally Eden halted her.

'Ben!'

'No,' came a hesitant voice down the line. 'The name I've got is Maxwell Benjamin Reece, he's a three-year-old with Down's syndrome. He's also…' The nurse lowered her voice and Eden rolled her eyes, finishing the sentence for her.

'HIV positive. He's familiar to the ward, but he goes

by the name of Ben. Could you let the staff who are dealing with him know that, please? Who's with him?'

The frantic scribbling on her notepad had stopped— Ben was familiar to anyone who worked on the paediatric unit and Eden didn't need to write down his past history. She gave a frown as the emergency nurse cheerfully declared that he had come in accompanied by Lorna, a social worker. It became clear that, yet again, little Ben was a ward of the state, that he'd had a chest X-ray and that they wanted to send him up soon as they were getting pretty full. Maybe it would be better if he was in familiar surroundings.

'Send him straight up,' Eden said, replacing the phone in its cradle.

'Ben?' Nick checked.

'Minus his new foster-parents.' Eden ran a hand through her hair, pulling out her tie and collecting all the loose curls that had fallen out and replacing them, an automatic gesture she did ten, maybe twenty times a day,

'What's the diagnosis?'

'They're fumbling to get one.' Eden gave a tight smile. 'Why don't they just admit that little Ben's too much like hard work?' Closing her eyes for a moment, she instantly regretted her words. It wasn't for her to judge. Ben wasn't just her favourite patient. Everyone, from cleaner to consultant, adored Ben, but, as cute as he was, he had been dealt more than his fair share in life. Genetic, social and hereditary problems seemed to have aligned when he had been conceived. 'I'm just sick of seeing him passed around, Nick. It just doesn't seem fair that one little boy should have to put up with so much.'

'He's happy,' Nick said soothingly.

'Is he?' Eden wasn't so sure. 'He just doesn't know any better, Nick. He's never been given a chance.'

And though no one could have expected a drug-addicted teenage mum to deal with a Down's syndrome baby, if Ben's mum had only revealed her pregnancy earlier than in the labour ward, had received antenatal care and been diagnosed as HIV positive, then she could have taken some measures that could have lowered the chances of her transmitting the disease to her son. Sophisticated antiretroviral drugs could have been given during pregnancy and labour, even in the period following birth, but Ben had received none of these. Only when his mother's results had come back ten days post-birth had her HIV status been revealed, and despite the best preventative treatment her HIV status had been passed on to her son. As the weeks had dragged by into months, as endless foster-parents had tried and failed, little Ben was constantly returned to the hospital. It would seem that hospital was the only home this little boy knew. But Nick seemed to understand how Eden was feeling.

'Someone will come along soon for him.'

'When?' Eden asked, not even attempting to hide the bitterness in her voice. 'He's not going to live long, Nick—you and I both know that. I just really hoped…' She didn't finish, couldn't, tears stinging her eyes.

'Really hoped what?'

'That he'd get one Christmas with a family, that this foster-placement would work out…' Eden choked, 'One Christmas of being of spoilt and cuddled, one Christmas being loved…'

'Ben doesn't go short of cuddles,' Nick pointed out, 'All the staff love Ben. He'll get all that here.'

Eden shook her head. 'Twenty-eight kids will get that here, Nick—the nurses will make sure of it—but most kids that are here over Christmas are here because they're very sick. We're stretched to the limit normally, but especially over Christmas. Most of the children will have parents and siblings, aunties and uncles to dote on them, and Santa will come and visit. We'll do our very best for Ben, but no matter how hard we try it's not the same as…' she took a deep breath '…a family Christmas. As much as you mock it, Nick, as much as we all grimace sometimes at the thought of it, we wouldn't have it any other way. And that little guy has never had it, not even once.' Eden shook her head, more to clear it. She couldn't allow herself to get so involved, it wasn't healthy for anyone. 'I'd better go and get a cot ready— he's already on his way up.'

One look at those big brown eyes and Eden was instantly reminded why Ben was everyone's favourite— it wasn't just sympathy for his ailments that evoked such a response, it was all to do with a little guy who could melt the hardest heart at fifty paces. His dark hair was a wild mop around his little face, his almond-shaped eyes were always expressive, and his cute mouth broke into a wide grin despite the bottle he was half-heartedly sucking on as Eden greeted him.

'Hey Ben, we've missed you!'

'*Den!*' Ben answered, and Eden was thrilled that he remembered her name. He'd only just started to talk a few weeks ago when he'd last been admitted as a patient, and *Den* had been one of his early words, *more* being near the top of the list.

More milk.

More chocolate.

More cuddles.

But his first word had been the one that had torn at Eden. Whereas most children started their vocabulary with a gummy *mum* or *dada,* Ben's first word had been *no.*

No to the endless drips and IVs, *no* to the mountain of medicine he had to take and, saddest of all, *no,* when his favourite nurses' shifts ended and they popped in to say goodnight.

Lifting him up off the trolley, Eden expertly negotiated the oxygen tubing and carried him to his freshly made-up cot. She propped Ben up on a couple of pillows she had prepared so that he remained semiupright to allow for greater chest expansion and strapped an oxygen saturation probe to his fat foot. There was no murmur of protest. Ben was way too used to the procedure to fuss, as most toddlers would have.

'I'm just going to speak to the nurse and then I'll be back, Ben.'

The nurse giving handover didn't have much more information to give than she'd had over the telephone. 'He's reluctant to take fluids and mildly dehydrated and his ears are clear. But he wasn't about to let us look down his throat…'

'Typical Ben.' Eden smiled, knowing how much Ben hated having his throat examined. 'Why hasn't he got an IV?'

'The doctor thought we should rehydrate him via a nasogastric tube first.'

'But he hasn't got one in,' Eden pointed out.

'We tried to put it down but he got very distressed.

We're trying him with his bottle.' The nurse didn't quite meet Eden's eyes as she answered and even before her next question came, Eden already knew the answer.

'Has he been given any antibiotics?'

'Oral,' the nurse said, pointing to the prescription chart. 'He's only got a mild infection—this admission seems more social.'

Lorna, the social worker, gave a murmur of agreement. 'The family just couldn't cope. We're going to have to look for some alternative type of placement. Ben's just proving too hard to place with a family. His medical needs are so time-consuming and behaviourally he's very demanding as well…'

'Because he's confused,' Eden argued futilely. 'Once he settles into a routine he's fine. Look how good he is here.'

'I know,' Lorna sighed. 'But it's looking more and more likely that Ben's going to end up in a residential unit—there aren't many foster-families out there capable of looking after a child with Ben's needs. I'll speak to Donna first thing tomorrow and pencil in a team meeting for the end of this week. We really do need to look at some other options for Ben.'

'Donna?' The emergency nurse asked.

'She's the paediatric unit manager,' Eden explained as she took the admission notes and X-ray films, her heart sinking at the thought of Ben living out his short life in a long-stay residential facility. 'As you can probably tell, we all know Ben pretty well. What bloods have been done?'

'None.' The emergency nurse gave a rather too casual shrug. 'It was a locum and he's not used to taking blood from a child. He thought it might be better for Maxwell, I mean Ben, if the paediatrician did it on the ward.'

It would have been easier to say nothing, to just take the notes and say goodbye, but Eden simply couldn't just walk away.

'Did you remind the doctor about universal precautions?'

'I'm sorry?' Confused, the nurse frowned back at her.

'Did you remind the doctor that every patient, regardless of their symptoms or status, should be treated as if they have a communicable blood disease?'

'I don't know what you mean,' the nurse said, but from the colouring in her cheeks she clearly did.

'We *know* Ben's HIV positive,' Eden said tersely. 'Remind the doctor for me that it's the patients we don't know about that should cause us the most concern.'

'Eden.' As the emergency nurse stormed off, Lorna touched her arm. 'Don't go getting upset.'

'Why don't they just admit that they didn't want to put an IV in, rather than coming up with all that nonsense about pushing fluids and the doctor wasn't used to taking blood from children? What the hell's he doing a shift in Emergency for? It's a cop-out and everyone knows it!'

'Just who are you really cross with here, Eden?'

'Don't try your psychobabble on me, Lorna,' Eden said, running a worried hand over her forehead. 'Do you really think he's going to end up in residential care?'

'He might,' Lorna said warily. 'Look, Eden, there's nothing you can do. We've been over and over the options and there's just no way that you can manage—'

'Manage what?' Nick's voice had both women jumping, and Eden shot an urgent look at Lorna as Nick frowned at the two of them, clearly expecting to be brought swiftly up to date.

'We were just discussing Ben's long-term care,' Lorna said warily. 'Discussing his options.'

'And what exactly is it that Eden can't manage?' Nick asked, his question direct, his eyes swinging between the two women who were both taking great interest in the floor all of a sudden.

'Nothing,' Eden mumbled. 'I was just moaning about the staff in Emergency, how they didn't take any blood or put in an IV. Lorna just pointed out there was nothing I could really do to change things, that technically they'd done nothing wrong.' A lousy liar at the best of times, Eden scuffed the floor with her foot, only letting out a relieved breath when Nick, clearly not impressed, stalked off.

Eden looked anxiously at Lorna. 'You won't say anything?'

'Why would I?' Lorna shrugged. 'You've done nothing wrong.'

'Thanks.' Eden gave a tense nod. 'It's just if anyone found out, they'd think…'

'That you were too involved?' Lorna finished for her. 'Which you are, Eden.'

'I can handle it,' Eden said stiffly, but Lorna didn't look particularly convinced.

'You know my pager number—if you need to talk any time, call me.'

Nick was already midway through his examination by the time Eden arrived at the cot-side. She smiled down at Ben as Nick gently probed his abdomen.

'Could you hold him for me while I check his ears and throat?' Nick asked.

Eden happily obliged. She picked Ben up and took a seat, holding his head against her chest as Nick carefully checked one ear and then deftly turning Ben around so that the check could be repeated on the other side.

'Now for the fun bit,' Nick said in a dry tone.

Eden held Ben tightly, one hand clamped on his forehead, as Nick attempted to check his throat. But this was the part Ben hated. Instantly he clamped his jaws tight, shaking his little head furiously as Nick waited with his lolly stick and torch poised for when he finally gave in and opened his mouth.

'Come on, buster,' Nick coaxed. 'It's only going to take a second.'

And as Ben finally gave in, his mouth opening in a sob of fury, Nick pushed down his tongue and peered down his throat. Ben squealed his protests and Eden waited, waited for the cursory examination to be over, for the torch to flick off and for Nick to throw the lolly stick into the plastic bag, but instead Nick was pushing the stick harder. Ben gagged and Eden's knuckles were white as she struggled to hold his head still. Nick peered around the child's mouth. For an appalling second Eden thought she might let go, that she might just rip that blessed lolly stick out of Nick's hand, might tell him to stop looking for things that she didn't want him to see.

But she didn't.

Instead, she held Ben firmly, fear—pure, naked fear—growing in the pit of her stomach. Cold fingers of terror touched her heart as Nick finally pulled out the lolly stick, but instead of taking Ben from her as he always did, instead of comforting the sobbing child, he pulled off his gloves and gently probed the little boy's neck, his fingers working their way slowly down to his axilla.

'Lay him on the cot for me.'

Nick's voice was flat, his eyes not meeting Eden's as she did as she was told. She watched as he pulled off Ben's nappy and carefully examined his groin.

'He's a bit dehydrated. We should put in a drip and do some bloods.'

'I can try and give him a bottle. Maybe once he's settled...' She stopped talking as Nick almost angrily shook his head.

'He isn't drinking because his mouth is sore,' he explained. 'He's got oral candida.' Children the world over got thrush—there were two babies on the ward at this very minute with the same condition—but the huge difference was that Ben was three years old and was HIV positive, and thrush was one of the warning signs in a child like Ben that his condition could be tipping over into full-blown AIDS. 'He's got enlarged lymph nodes, Eden.' Nick's voice bordered on the apologetic, as if the news he was delivering was somehow his fault. 'And from his notes he's lost weight since his last admission. We need to do a full lab screen and see exactly where we are.'

The treatment room was the place of choice for performing procedures. Any child upset on the ward made the other children anxious and where possible patients were moved to the treatment room well out of earshot of the other children. Even though Ben's skin would be numbed, the insertion of an IV and taking of blood was distressing for a small child, especially one like Ben who, even if he couldn't feel it, knew exactly what was happening and his tears and distress would upset the other children on the ward. But Ben had passed through the doors many times and Eden felt him stiffen in her arms as she carried him along the corridor. 'It's OK, sweetheart,' Eden said softly. 'Dr Nick's just going to fix you up with a drip so we can make you feel better very soon. He'll be very gentle.'

They worked well together. Eden held the reluctant toddler firmly as he bucked and struggled to get off the treatment bed, one hand gripping his arm tightly as Nick attempted to bring up a vein. She talked to Ben all the while, smiling down at him as Nick cut up tape, knowing full well that IV access in a child had to be secured very firmly if a repeat procedure was to be avoided.

'I'm in,' Nick said, but Eden didn't move, just held on tightly to Ben while Nick secured the bung then put an arm splint in place, immobilising Ben's little arm and then applying a huge bandage.

'Leave a gap,' Eden reminded Nick, because the IV site needed to be checked regularly to ensure that the line was patent and there were no signs of infection.

'Done.'

Only when Nick had said that word did Eden relax. At that point a child would normally be handed to his parents for a well-earned cuddle and Eden was more than happy to fill in, but Nick did the honours, scooping up his patient and holding him firmly.

'I'm sorry, Ben, but that nasty old drip is going to make you feel much better soon.'

His clipped public school voice was supremely gentle and his firm grip still tender. Eden watched as Ben relaxed under Nick's touch, the exhausting day catching up with him. His sobs became less urgent, fading into a hum, each blink of Ben's eyes lengthening in time as Nick cuddled him to sleep.

'He's going to sleep,' Nick said. He didn't lower his voice but kept it steady. Most babies were soothed by background noise, comforted by an adult presence, but Ben in particular was more than used to the constant hum of a busy hospital ward.

'Keep on doing what you're doing, Nick. Ben's almost impossible to get to sleep. I'll go and prepare his cot and set up the IVAC. You've got time?' she checked, knowing a lot of doctors didn't list rocking babies in their job description.

'I'll make time,' Nick said, not looking up, just holding the little guy tight. Eden had anticipated his answer—Nick's patients came first always.

Of course, as soon as they laid him down, Ben awoke and, despite his sore throat, screamed loudly, his face purple as he simultaneously coughed and wept. All Eden could do was hold his hand and rub his forehead. She willed sleep to arrive for him so that his tortuous day would be over, but again and again Ben fought sleep. Every time Eden thought he was, and attempted to slip out of the room and check on the rest of her patients, Ben would break into distraught sobs, his oxygen saturation dropping markedly as he vomited.

'Should you give him something to settle him?' Eden asked, watching anxiously as Becky and Rochelle ran the length of the ward. She knew that she really ought to be out there, helping.

'I'd rather not when all he wants is a cuddle.' Nick let out a weary sigh, but suddenly his voice brightened. 'I've got an idea. Wait here!'

As if she had a choice!

Turning her attention back to Ben, Eden offered him his soother again, gently pushed him back down on the pillow, feeling resistance in every muscle. But suddenly he relaxed, the soother in his mouth slipping as his red, chafed face broke into a smile that could only be described as wondrous.

'Hey!' Eden grinned back. 'What do you see, little guy?' Turning around, following Ben's gaze, a smile broke out on her own face as she stared at the still crudely decorated Christmas tree, naked of tinsel and with the star at the top missing. But the lights she'd draped were turned on now, twinkling and flashing, and, Eden decided as Ben's sobs gave way to tiny whimpers, never had a tree looked more beautiful.

'See the lights,' Eden whispered. 'They're all little fairies, little fairies looking out for Ben…' She couldn't go on, the words that normally came so easily as she soothed a distressed child off to sleep just too hard to say tonight. The words stuck in her throat as she wrestled with her tears, sniffing loudly and trying to smile down at the little boy.

But Nick was there now, tucking in the sheet around a now sleepy, docile Ben. Taking Eden's arm, he led her out of the room and into the first private available space, which happened to be the store cupboard.

'He's got full-blown AIDS, hasn't he?' Eden gulped, waiting, hoping for Nick to deny it.

Instead, he gave a tired shrug. 'We won't know that

until the blood results comes back but, I have to admit, it doesn't look great.'

'It could just be a simple case of thrush, though,' Eden said hopefully. 'And just because—'

'Eden?' Nick broke in, his voice questioning, his eyes narrowing as he stared down at her, taking in the swollen reddened eyes, the trembling hands, her top teeth biting her bottom lip as she made an effort to keep from breaking down. 'Why don't I feel like I'm talking to Ben's nurse here? Why do I feel like I'm comforting a parent?'

'I'm allowed to be upset,' Eden retorted, pulling a tissue out of her pocket and blowing her nose. She pulled herself together and forced a smile. 'Look, I'm fine. It was just a bit of a shock, that's all. I really was expecting this to be a social admission. When you looked down his throat, I wasn't expecting you to find what you did. It just threw me.'

He continued to stare down at her, those green eyes taking in every flicker. She could smell the citrus tang of his aftershave, see the power in his arms, and for a second all Eden wanted to do was lean on him, to weep into his chest, to feel those strong arms comfort her, to have him tell her that it was all going to be OK, that little Ben was going to be fine.

But, quite simply, she couldn't, and, Eden realised, the horrible truth starting to sink in, neither could Nick say that Ben was going to be OK. So instead they stood there, for what seemed the longest time, Eden forcing a smile, pretending she could deal with this as Nick weighed up whatever was on his mind.

'We'll go for a drink when your shift's over.'

'A drink?' Bewildered, she stared back at him. As friendly as they had once been, their relationship, if you could call it that, had never extended outside the hospital walls. A stupid flame of hope started to fizz in her stomach but instantly Nick doused it.

'Or we can talk tomorrow at work, in front of Donna, but I really think the conversation we're about to have should take place well away from the ward.'

'I'm in my uniform,' Eden protested.

'So?' Nick shrugged. 'We'll go to Kelly's over the road, you'll match everyone there!'

CHAPTER FOUR

Nick had been only half joking.

Kelly's was a favourite haunt for hospital staff and one Eden stayed away from. Sure, she'd been there for a couple of birthday celebrations and leaving dos, but generally she avoided it. Too many nurses waiting for too few doctors, there was a certain needy air to it that Eden didn't ever want to buy into. And her feelings about the place were only confirmed as she walked in with Nick. The crowded bar was filled with hospital personnel popping in after a late shift, but despite the fact it was crowded, despite the fact if Eden had walked in alone, no one would have turned a hair, as Nick walked in behind her, the atmosphere shifted suddenly. There was a buzz of expectation in the air and Eden could have sworn half the women in the place suddenly seemed to suck in their stomachs and flick their hair. Curious glances were being shot in her direction as Nick guided her to a table at the back before going to get them both a drink.

Eden watched as he attempted to make his way to the bar. His name was called from several directions, groups dispersing as everyone suddenly decided that they too *needed* to go to the bar. Eden wondered for a moment what it would be like to be that beautiful, to have that effect on a crowded room. Could Nick really be blamed for taking his pick?

'Here.' Pushing a glass towards her, he smiled as she took a sip, watching her face screw up. 'Gin and lemon,' Nick said without apology. 'I thought you might need it.'

'If I'd wanted a gin, Nick, I'd have asked for it. I happen to be on an early tomorrow,' Eden snapped, feeling defensive.

'I'm not planning on getting you drunk and having my wicked way with you, Eden.'

Unfortunately! Eden gave a weak smile as the thought popped into her head.

'I'm worried about you.' As she opened her mouth to argue, Nick overrode her. 'I was actually worried about you during Ben's last admission. I spoke to Donna about it.'

'You spoke to Donna?' Appalled, she stared back at him. 'But why?'

'Because every shift you were looking after Ben.'

'It's called continuity of care,' Eden retorted. 'It's far better for Ben if he sees a familiar face.'

'But is it doing you any good?' Nick didn't back down an inch, confronting her angry stare with a firm one of his own. 'You're too involved, Eden.'

'I'm not.'

'So what were you talking to Lorna about this evening?' She could feel his eyes on her as she fiddled with her straw, took another sip of her beastly drink and tried to come up with an answer. 'If you won't tell me, Eden, I'll go and speak to her myself tomorrow.'

'Please, don't involve Lorna.' Instantly Eden shook her head.

'Then tell me.' Nick said simply, and as her hands shot up to her hair he reached for her wrist. 'Stop fiddling with that blessed hair-tie, Eden, and tell me what's going on.'

'Nothing's going on,' Eden said. 'I haven't done anything wrong.'

'I know that,' Nick said softly. 'Come on, Eden, tell me.'

His hand was still on her wrist. Her other hand fiddled with her straw and suddenly Eden was glad Nick had bought her a gin. She took a sip, feeling the sharp taste on her tongue, the warmth as she swallowed it causing enough of a mental diversion to stop the fresh batch of tears that she simply couldn't cry here of all places.

'Last time Ben was here, when we were having trouble placing him again,' Eden started, screwing her eyes closed, not sure how Nick was going to react, 'I asked Lorna about the possibility of arranging temporary guardianship for me. I wanted to be able to take Ben out now and then.' She couldn't look up, could feel Nick's hand tighten around her wrist. She could maybe have got away with leaving it there, but she knew Nick was too shrewd to accept half a story, that, no doubt, he'd follow it up and find out the whole truth anyway. Despite her reluctance to tell him, as she tentatively continued, there was also a feeling of relief, an unburdening as she finally told Nick the truth. 'Lorna wasn't keen, she gave the same warnings about getting too involved, but when I spoke to her properly, told her that it wasn't just about Ben, it was something I'd always wanted to do, she was really helpful.'

'Is it something you've always wanted to do?' Nick checked, and Eden nodded.

'My mum and dad are respite carers,' Eden explained. 'For as long as I can remember, once a fortnight or once a month we'd have some kid staying over, coming to the movies with us, perhaps to give their parents a break or, like Ben, to give them a break from the hospital. So I knew it was possible. Lorna gave me a lot of literature to read and part of it was about becoming a foster-parent. I thought you had to be married or a couple, certainly not a single working mum, but when I looked further into it, I realised that I actually fitted the criteria.'

'Oh, Eden.'

'Please, don't.' She put up a shaking hand, could hear the worried note in his voice. 'It isn't going to happen. If Ben were a normal healthy three-year-old, perhaps I could have managed it, but working shifts and everything, and with Ben's age and medical conditions, there was no way I could arrange child care while I worked. It was a complete non-starter. Still, I did go through the channels to become a respite carer, but by the time I'd been approved Ben had been allocated foster-parents.'

Her glass was empty now, and she didn't argue when Nick signalled to the bar staff for another round. She just managed a wry smile that Nick could manage waiter service in a packed bar and was grateful for the relative silence that followed as their drinks were brought over.

It was Eden that broke it.

'I suppose you're going to tell me I'm too involved,'

'I don't have to, Eden. I'm sure you already know that.'

Eden nodded.

'We have to maintain a professional distance.'

'I do,' she choked. 'Or I have. I know that we're not supposed to get too close and in ten years of nursing I never have. Sure, I get upset when a child's very sick or dies, everyone does, but till now it's been part of the job, a horrible part perhaps, but I could still see the bigger picture. It's just with Ben, I don't feel there's anyone really pulling for him, there's no one in his corner, fighting for him.'

'We all are,' Nick pointed out, but Eden shook her head.

'All he wanted tonight was a cuddle and, yes, he got one, but only for as long as the ward would allow it. I know that's just how it is, that as a nurse there's nothing I can do to change it. It's just…'

'Just what?'

'I adore him,' Anguished eyes met Nick's and she watched as he flinched. 'I'm supposed to feel guilty for even saying it.'

'You're crossing the line, Eden.'

'If I handed my notice in tomorrow and went off to some developing country to work with HIV-infected orphans, everyone would wish me well and tell me I was doing a great thing…' Nick frowned, clearly having no idea where she was heading. 'If I handed my notice in tomorrow to become a foster-parent for handicapped children, a few people might scratch their heads but again everyone would wish me well. But if, heaven forbid, I do it back to front, if I actually get attached to a patient who doesn't have anyone to call his own in the world, suddenly I'm crossing a line, suddenly I'm getting in too deep. We're supposed to care, but not too much, we're supposed to get involved in people's lives and still hold back.'

'We have to if we're going to stay sane.'

'But it's not a light switch, it's not something we can just flick on and off at will. We don't choose the people in our lives who are going to touch us. Sometimes, like it or not, it just happens…'

And something in her voice must have reached him because she felt the fight go out of him. A pensive look came over his face, his eyes softening slightly as he looked over at her.

'If you look after him, you're going to get hurt, Eden.'

'I know.' A brave smile wobbled on her lips. 'And if I don't look after him, if you stop me from being allowed to nurse him, then I'm going to get hurt even more.'

'Donna needs to know.'

'No!' Eden shook her head firmly, but Nick just stared right back.

'I can guarantee Donna's felt the same at some time in her career.'

'I doubt it.'

'I can guarantee it,' Nick said. 'And so have I.'

Her eyes jerked up to him.

'Lucy Wright, two years old with a cerebral tumour. I was a doing my paed internship and everyone, including my parents, told me it was just because I was young and relatively inexperienced, that it was because it was my first real experience with a terminally ill child, but even though I agreed with them to keep them quiet, the fact is, Lucy was just a great kid. I can still see her smile when I walked on the ward. She was blind,' Nick added, 'but she knew, just from my footsteps, that it was me. And, yes, I was young and relatively green and, yes, it was my first real experience with a terminally ill child, but I cried more than I ever have since over losing a patient when she died. Since then, to this day, I haven't cried that way again. And it wasn't just because she was two and that she didn't deserve it and that life wasn't fair. I cried, quite simply, because it was Lucy.'

'We've all been there, Eden. That's why you need to tell Donna, so she can help you through it.'

'But Donna!'

'Yes, Donna,' Nick said firmly. 'That's why she's the unit manager, Eden. You've told me, so surely you can tell her.'

'Ah but I had two gins and a jukebox playing in the background when I told you.' Eden smiled, but her heart wasn't really in it. With Nick it had been easy to open up, but with Donna it would be completely different. Eden just couldn't imagine telling the austere, immovable woman what was on her mind, let alone her actually understanding.

'I could talk to her for you,' Nick offered.

'You!' Eden said a touch ungraciously, but Nick just smiled.

'Yes, me, Eden. I am quite good at that sort of thing in case you haven't noticed.'

'Of course I have,' Eden said, chewing nervously on her bottom lip. 'If you do talk to her—I mean, if I do agree—you will tell her that I am capable of looking after Ben?'

'With support,' Nick said, and finally Eden agreed.

'With support.'

'Nick!' The falsely cheerful tones of Tanya, the orthopaedic intern, caught them both unawares. 'I haven't seen you in here for a while.'

'I've been busy,' Nick responded, barely even bothering to look up, but his distinct lack of enthusiasm did nothing to deter Tanya.

'I was just going to the bar. Can I get you anything?'

'Not for me.' Nick shook his head and drained his glass. 'We were just leaving.'

'Really!' The smile was still in place but Tanya's eyes were distinctly frosty as she shot a look at Eden. 'Well, maybe next time, then.'

'Maybe not,' Nick said frostily. 'Come on, Eden.'

'Nick!' After the icy blast of the air conditioner the thick warm air was uncomfortable as they stepped outside. Eden could still feel the sting of her own blush as she swung to face him outside, their uncomfortable, rapid, exit from the pub hadn't been quite quick enough for Eden to miss the glitter of tears in Tanya's eyes and she was appalled at the way Nick had treated her. 'That was a bit harsh.'

'She'll get over it,' Nick said casually, and Eden shook her head, scarcely recognising the man who was standing in front of her. But Nick stood his ground. 'Eden, sometimes you have to be firm.'

'You don't have to be rude, though!'

'Maybe I do,' Nick said through gritted teeth. 'Just leave it, Eden.'

So she did, walking in uncomfortable silence along the street towards her home, still reeling from seeing a side to Nick she'd never thought she'd witness.

'What a difference a day makes,' Nick said, breaking the silence. 'This time yesterday you were furious that you had to work at Christmas, and now I bet you're just a little bit pleased.'

'A bit,' Eden admitted, but her mind was still whirl-ing. The pain in Tanya's eyes had been real.

'You could have told me earlier you know, Eden,' Nick said as they arrived at the entrance to the town house she rented with Jim, who was clearly home and taking advantage of Eden's absence because the windows were practically vibrating to rock music. 'I mean, not just as a doctor but as a friend.'

'We haven't been friends for a long time,' In the dark-ness she was somehow able to admit the truth. 'Not re-ally. Sure, we talk about work and have a joke and that, but since Teaghan died…'

'It's been hard, Eden.'

'I know,' Eden answered. 'Well, I don't know exactly, but I can imagine. But you have to admit, Nick, things have changed. We haven't really been friends since Tea-ghan's death.'

'We were, though.' She couldn't see his expression in the darkness, but she could make out his profile, the hollows of his cheekbones as he stared down at her, the flash of his teeth as his mouth moved. 'We didn't know each other for very long before Teaghan died, but with some people I guess you just click.

'I've missed you Eden.'

His admission caught her completely unawares. There was a tiny raw note of urgency in his voice that she was too terrified to interpret, too scared of misread-ing the signs and making the biggest, most embarrass-ing mistake of her life.

'I've missed you too, Nick,' Eden answered care-fully. 'And I'm glad that we're talking again, glad that we're back to being friends.'

'Hey, Eden.' The front door swung open. Jim was standing in a pair of shorts and not much else, apart from a can of beer in hand, the thud-thud of his stereo spilling out onto the street. 'I was just putting the bins out.'

'And waking half the street,' Eden scolded. 'Since when did you put the bins out? Jim, this is Nick, he works at the hospital, Nick, this is Jim, my resident idle backpacker.'

'Who always pays his rent on time, though,' Jim answered cheerfully. 'Good to meet you, Nick. Fancy a cold one?'

'Not for me,' Nick answered, equally cheerfully. ''Night, then, Eden.'

''Night, Nick.'

There was a beat of a pause, a tiny moment of hesitation, and Eden wondered how to fill it. Suggest a coffee perhaps, say that she'd see him tomorrow…kiss him on the cheek even, just as a friend would, but Jim clattering past with the garbage bin completely broke the moment.

'I'd better get in,' Eden said, 'and turn down the music. I don't know why, but Jim has the uncanny knack of making me feel like a parent!'

'Really!' Despite the darkness she saw Nick's eyes widen. 'It seemed like the other way around to me.'

And, walking off, he left her frowning.

CHAPTER FIVE

IT WAS an incredibly shy Eden that walked onto the ward the following morning. She'd only had two drinks the previous night yet she felt as if she'd been at some wild party, the events pinging in and spinning her further into confusion—revealing the truth about Ben, Nick's behaviour towards Tanya and, strangest of all, that tiny moment at the end where she'd wondered if he might kiss her, or had it been, if she might kiss him?

'Good morning, Sister.' Donna was there, neat and trim, sitting on her office chair in the crowded handover room, queening it over everyone. Eden felt her heart sink at the prospect of what was undoubtedly to come later. 'Have a seat.' Pointedly Donna looked at her watch. 'We're just about to start. But before we do, we're expecting a new admission from Emergency—a two-year-old with rash and fever for investigation. She's also markedly dehydrated. I don't have her name just yet. Bruce, the registrar, has seen her in Emergency and she should be up soon—I've allocated Isolation room 2 for her. Right!' Donna nodded graciously to the night sister. 'Let's begin.'

The ward was pretty much as Eden had left it on her

late shift, apart from a couple of admissions overnight
from Emergency and ICU. A few of the patients were
about to be discharged, which heralded a busy day for
all. Discharges caused a lot of paperwork and no sooner
had the discharge meds been given and the patient
wheeled out of the ward then Emergency would be on
the telephone, hoping to fill the freshly empty bed.

'Now.' Donna peered at her list. 'Does anyone have
any preferences?' Turning in her chair, her sharp eyes
swivelled around the room. On any other day, at this
point Eden would have jumped right in, would have
asked to take care of the isolation rooms, but, given that
Nick would be talking to Donna later, Eden decided
against it.

'I wouldn't mind having Bay 1,' Eden responded. 'I'd
like to see how Priscilla goes with breakfast and lunch
today.'

'Fine,' Donna agreed. 'You've got young Rory going
to theatre for debriding of his wound—he's third on the
orthopaedics list,' Donna reminded them. 'And Declan's
being discharged now that his nausea and vomiting has
finally stopped, so no doubt you'll have a new admission. And then you've got the new boy, Peter, going
down for circumcision—he's second on the general sur-
geon's list.'

'And very hungry,' the night sister added. 'Hopefully
they won't take too long with the first patient.'

'Now, I've got a management meeting at twelve,
Eden,' Donna carried on. 'So if your bay's OK, can you
take over from me then?' She didn't wait for Eden's response, turning instead to the rest of her team. 'OK, Rochelle, you can help Becky with the isolation...' As

Donna continued allocating duties, Eden stayed, initialling each patient on her list with the nurse that was looking after them, so that if there were any enquiries or drugs to be checked, Eden would know who to go to.

'She's in fine form this morning,' Becky whispered as they made their way out of the office. 'Must have had her Prozac!'

'I hope she took two,' Eden responded.

'Meaning?'

'I'll tell you later.'

'How come you didn't take the isolation rooms?' Becky asked, pulling a stethoscope off the rack on the wall and grabbing a tympanic thermometer.

'I'll tell you that later, too.'

She hadn't expected to see Nick so soon. Even as Eden entered the bay and saw the curtains drawn around Priscilla's bed, she figured seven-thirty a.m. was a bit too early for Nick. But then again…

Seeing his highly polished shoes beneath the curtain, Eden allowed herself the indulgence of a quick cringe, burying her burning face in the mountain of linen she'd piled onto her trolley in preparation to make the beds. But she'd forgotten her audience and instantly regretted her actions as a thoroughly bored Rory decided to ask what exactly her problem was!

'Are you feeling sick, Eden?'

'Cool,' Declan responded. 'She's going to faint.'

'I'm fine,' Eden said quickly. 'I'm just checking that I've got enough linen.'

'In case you've wet the bed,' Declan teased Rory.

'In case you've been sick…' Rory answered back.

'Enough,' Eden snapped, heading for the television, but Rory called her back.

'We're not allowed to watch it until *Princess* has had her breakfast.'

'Her name's Priscilla,' Eden said as her finger recoiled from the 'on' button. Heading for her trolley, she peeled off a gown and some towels. 'OK, Rory, I'll get you a bowl and you can have a wash and then I'll come and help you into a gown for Theatre, but first I'm just going to check on Priscilla…'

'Morning.' Nick appeared from behind the curtain. Unlike Eden, he was utterly together, his newly washed blond hair, still damp from the shower, flopping over his forehead as he stared down at Priscilla's chart, his aftershave, his suit, his presence just a sheer, delectable notch above the rest. 'Can I borrow you, Eden?' He gestured and Eden duly headed out of the bay.

'How is she?'

'Fine.' Nick gave a half-laugh. 'Or at least she will be soon.'

'I'm not with you.'

'I've listened to her stomach and there are a few rumblings. I'm expecting the train in at any moment!'

Even Eden managed a laugh. 'So the veggies are working?'

'Priscilla isn't going to know what's hit her. I'll come and check on her later this afternoon. If she's still in pain I'll have to order another abdo X-ray, but I'm pretty sure we can avoid it. I think she'll be feeling a lot better soon.

'How are you?' he added, shifting the conversation to the personal.

'Fine,' Eden gulped.

'Good.'

The conversation would have continued, but at that point a rather frantic-looking Priscilla appeared at the curtains and Eden knew from the rather pained expression on the little girl's face that this conversation would have to take place later.

'This way, Priscilla.' Eden smiled as the little girl bustled past. 'I'll be with you in a moment. And, remember, don't flush till I've been in.' She turned to Nick. 'I think the train's just pulling in.'

'About time,' Nick answered, stepping out of the way as Eden ducked past.

'How are you doing Priscilla?' Eden asked, knocking on the bathroom door a good fifteen minutes later. As the lock slid open and a pale-faced Priscilla peered out, Eden decided that if anyone thought nursing was glamorous, they clearly hadn't read this part of the job description.

'Not very well.'

Priscilla looked as if she were about to faint as Eden let herself in.

'On the contrary.' Eden somehow grinned, pushing the flush button. 'In fact, Priscilla, I'd say life's just about to get a whole lot better for you!'

Eden walked Priscilla back to her bay and as the little girl went to climb back into bed, Eden instead suggested she sit in the chair to have breakfast. Not leaving any room for argument, Eden started to strip the bed.

'I'll give you some nice fresh sheets. Oh, here comes breakfast now.'

Priscilla didn't look particularly impressed with her cereal and fruit but at least she didn't throw it on the floor this time. Instead, she ate it with a pained expression at each mouthful, which Eden pointedly ignored as she guided Declan towards the showers.

'Your mum should be here soon for the doctors' round.'

'And then I'll be going home?' Declan said. 'I was only supposed to be in for the day.'

'It happens that way sometimes,' Eden said, turning on the taps for him and checking that he had soap, before putting out his toothbrush and paste. 'Now, give your teeth a good brush after your shower.'

'I know.' Declan, unlike some five-year-olds who expected you to do everything for them, was clearly waiting for her to leave before getting undressed.

'Have you got everything you need?'

'Yep.'

'Press the buzzer if you don't feel well…'

'I'll be fine.' Mr Independent shooed her out and Eden smothered a grin then headed off to the nurses' station to check all Rory's notes were ready for his trip to Theatre.

Rory had been knocked off his bike by a motorist three weeks previously. Thankfully he had been wearing a helmet which had, according to his notes, saved him from a serious head injury as he'd bounced, head first, off the car's windscreen. But his leg and pelvis hadn't fared quite so well. Rory had sustained a fractured right femur and shattered pelvis, along with a nasty degloving injury to his left thigh, which was requiring regular trips to Theatre for cleaning and debridement. This morning the orthopods were going to take a skin graft from his right thigh to cover the nasty wound and hopefully hasten healing.

Even though the night staff had assured her every-thing was ready, Eden double-checked. She was glad that she did—Theatre handover was not the best place to find out that something had been missed!

'Problem?' Donna asked briskly as Eden let out a moan.

'Professor Baines has written in the notes that he wants Rory to commence IV gentamycin *prior* to going to Theatre.'

'Then you'd better get on and give it,' Donna re-sponded, then tutted loudly as Eden shook her head.

'It hasn't been prescribed.' Eden doubled-checked Rory's prescription chart then flicked through the notes in case a new one had been started. 'No, it's not writ-ten up anywhere.' Reaching for the phone, she paged the intern for Professor Baines's ortho team. 'The team is not going to be too thrilled,' Eden muttered. 'No doubt they're starting to scrub.'

Tanya certainly wasn't!

Tanya let it be known in no uncertain terms that this should have been picked up sooner, that the team was already scrubbed and about to start the list, but Eden wasn't in the mood for unnecessary dramas—it wasn't as if Tanya was going to be operating!

Holding the phone away from her ear, Eden gave an exaggerated eye roll as Tanya continued to moan.

'Look,' Eden said finally, 'I'm sorry it wasn't picked up earlier, but if you'd written up the prescription when Professor Baines gave his order, we wouldn't be hav-ing this conversation. Now, are you going to come and write it up?'

'Presumably that's a yes,' Eden said dryly as the phone clicked off. Suddenly remembering Donna was present, Eden coloured up a touch, wondering if she'd sounded rude. 'She wasn't exactly helpful,' Eden said. 'She was blaming the ward…'

'When the mistake was hers,' Donna said through pursed lips. 'Good for you for standing up to her. And don't take any cheek when she comes up or *I'll* be having a word.'

If Tanya had been irritated before, when she flounced onto the ward a few moments later and put a name to the face that had been on the phone, she was seriously put out! Her usually pretty, elfin face scowled as she leant over the desk and scribbled on the prescription chart.

'This should have been picked up sooner,' she muttered, but Eden refused to rise to the bait, concentrating on paperwork of her own. 'Perhaps if the nurses on this ward weren't out till all hours…'

Eden shot her an appalled look, scarcely able to believe that Tanya could be so personal, so petty, but before she could think of a suitable retort Donna came up with one for her.

'I think that's quite enough, don't you, Doctor?' Donna's voice was pure ice. 'As Sister Hadley has pointed out, this was your mistake and just because the professor is giving you a hard time about having to leave Theatre, I'd suggest you learn from your mistake and move on.' She took a deep breath, positively withering Tanya with her eyes as the young intern flushed. 'And if you're referring to the fact that the consultant of this ward and one of my senior nurses were over at Kelly's last night, discussing a patient on this ward then, frankly, Doctor, my advice remains the same. Get over it and move on.'

'Ouch,' Eden winced as Tanya strode out of the ward. She turned shyly to Donna. 'Nick's obviously spoken to you.'

'He has.' Donna nodded. 'Let's get this gentamycin started and then we'll go into my office.'

Unlike Nick's office, Donna's was incredibly neat. Taking a seat behind her desk, she gestured for Eden to sit down, which Eden did, her heart hammering in her chest, her hands fidgeting in her lap. She wondered what on earth Donna was going to say—but it was actually Eden who spoke first.

'Thank you—for what you said to Tanya, I mean.'

'You're a member of my team, Sister,' Donna said, and Eden took a deep breath, knowing they were moving on now to the real reason they were there. 'I was actually already intending to have a talk with you about Ben before Nick spoke to me about it. I'd noticed how fond you were getting of him, how you always ask to look after him and that you often stay behind after your shift has ended.'

'I've never compromised his care.'

'Of course you haven't. Sister. You don't think that you're in trouble, do you?'

'I don't know,' Eden admitted. 'I feel as if I've done something wrong.'

'Eden.' Donna dropped her title. 'Behind that uniform you're a human being. That's why nurses will never be replaced by robots or machinery—it takes real people to do our job, and real people have real emotions. If Ben had a loving parent or even one relative who cared for him or came in and visited him, I know that you wouldn't be feeling this way—Ben would be one of your favourites, a patient you had a soft spot for, one that moved you more than most perhaps. But Ben doesn't have anyone. There's a huge gaping hole in this little boy's life and I can see how you might want to fill it.'

Of all the people she'd expected to understand, Donna had been the last, and Eden felt a sting of tears in her eyes as her senior spoke with more insight and compassion than Eden could have ever predicted.

'You know that my husband's paraplegic?' Donna asked, and Eden nodded. 'Do you know where I met him? I was nursing on a spinal unit,' Donna said, not waiting for Eden to answer. 'I was twenty-six years old and had worked on the unit for five years, since I'd qualified, and I loved every minute of it. We had the patients from the first day of their injury when they were transferred to us right through to when they moved to a small apartment while we prepared them for going home. I looked after David the whole way through and somewhere along the way we fell in love.

'But that was twenty-five years ago. Not only did we have to deal with the scorn of my nursing colleagues, but my parents were appalled too—they said that David was using me, that if he hadn't had his accident he'd never have even looked at me…' She smiled at Eden's appalled face. 'The reason I'm telling you this is that in those days there was no support—no one to talk to. I had to leave a job I loved as if I'd committed some sort of crime. Thankfully nursing's moved on a lot since then.

'Now!' Rather more crisply, Donna continued. 'I've discussed this with Nick and we're both more than happy for you to look after Ben, with a couple of provisos.'

'Which are?'

'Firstly, and most importantly, if Ben collapses or his condition rapidly deteriorates, you're to summon help, make your patient safe and, so long as numbers allow, you're to step aside. I don't think it would be in either of your best interests to be involved in decision-making in an emergency situation.'

Eden nodded thoughtfully, actually relieved that that decision had been made for her.

'I'd like you to talk to me, weekly at least, so we can be sure how you're dealing with everything. If you don't feel you can discuss things with me, I can arrange—'

'That won't be necessary,' Eden interrupted. 'You've been really helpful.'

Donna gave a small nod. 'And finally, given that the paperwork has already been done with Social Services, I'm more than happy, so long as Ben's health permits, for you to take him out for short intervals—with the necessary precautions, of course—though not while you're on duty. If you take Ben off the ward it has to be as his carer, and therefore you'll need the doctor who's on call that day to come and assess Ben and approve him leaving.'

A sharp, familiar rap on the door ended the conversation. As the door opened, Eden didn't need to look up to know that it was Nick.

'Donna, sorry to interrupt. I've just been speaking to a GP who wants to send a direct admission to the ward—a four-year-old who's just come back from overseas with query malaria. Can I use the last ISO room?'

'It's already taken.' Donna stood up. 'We're getting an admission from Emergency but ISO five is only in there because the parents demanded a single room.'

'I really do need it.'

'Then I'll tell the parents their child will have to move onto the main ward,' Donna said crisply. 'I warned them at the time this might happen.'

'How was it?' Nick asked as Donna bustled off. Instead of rolling her eyes, as was usually the case when Donna left the room, Eden found herself smiling.

'Good.' Eden blinked. 'Better than good. She was great. I can even take Ben out for short periods—if he's well enough, of course.'

And even though Nick smiled, somehow it didn't quite reach his eyes. His green eyes held hers for just a fraction too long, and she registered the tiny swallow in his throat.

'What is it, Nick?'

When he didn't answer straight away, Eden answered for him.

'His bloodwork's back, isn't it?'

Nick gave a hesitant nod, 'This isn't easy, Eden.'

'I know,' Eden whispered, because she did. In this very office, just a year ago, it had been Eden breaking bad news to Nick. Even though the circumstances were entirely different she knew how hard it was for him to be standing here now and hurting a friend because, just a year ago, she'd done it to him. Clearing her throat, Eden willed her voice to hold. 'What do his results show?'

'They're not all back yet and we'll need to do a lot more tests, but things aren't looking good for him. I've just been discussing his case with the infectious diseases consultant. As you know, Eden, it doesn't suddenly happen. AIDS is just what its name says: a syndrome. But unfortunately Ben is starting to display some of the more obvious signs.' He paused for a moment, allowed her to process the news before he gently continued. 'There are stages to this disease, Eden, and it looks as if Ben's HIV status has shifted.'

'He's going to die?'

'One day.' Nick nodded. 'And sooner than he deserves to, that's for sure. But with aggressive medication, with the right environment...'

'He's behind the eight ball already, then,' Eden rasped, choking back angry tears as Donna breezed back into the office.

'All sorted!' she said crisply. 'Eden, the orderly's here to take young Rory to Theatre.' Donna's sharp, knowing eyes swivelled between Eden and Nick. 'Is everything all right?'

'I was just discussing Ben's results with Eden,' Nick answered.

'I see.' Donna paused for a second before addressing Eden. 'Will you be OK to work, Eden?'

Eden nodded because, quite simply, she had to be. She couldn't afford the luxury of crying. Donna had offered her support through all this, but if Eden was going to break down whenever the news was bad for Ben, clearly things would have to be revised.

There would be time for that later.

'I'll be fine,' Eden said firmly, making her way out of the office and staring down the corridor she saw Ben through the massive glass windows of his ISO room. He raised a podgy little hand as he recognised her, his round face breaking into the widest of smiles as his beloved *Den* came into his view. Dragging in a deep breath, swallowing the tears that seemed to be choking her, somehow Eden managed to wave back, somehow she managed to give him a huge bright smile before heading back to her patients.

CHAPTER SIX

'WHERE'S Dad?'

Pulling open her front door, Eden blinked into the darkness, shocked to see Nick standing there, appalled that he should see her looking like this and confused at his question.

'Dad?'

'Jim,' Nick said, as if that should explain things, but when Eden just stared back at him, he explained further. 'Does he usually put the bins out?'

'Never.'

'Or stand on the street till you've waved off your friends?'

'Actually, yes…'Eden's mouth dropped open as a rather unwelcome penny dropped. 'Nick, you've got it all wrong. Jim and I are just housemates. He was just being…' Her voice trailed off, tiny seeds of doubt that had been sown over the past few weeks starting to sprout. 'Oh, that's all I need,' Eden murmured. 'Do you really think he likes me?'

'Take it from me.' Nick smiled. 'Where is he, then?'

'Gone to get some pizza.' Eden gave a tiny shrug. 'Trying to cheer me up.'

'Am I going to be asked in?'

'Sorry.' Pulling the door open wider, Eden stepped back. 'Of course.' She said it as if she meant it but really she'd have loved to slam the door in his face and dart upstairs for five minutes. Swollen red eyes weren't her only problem tonight. A scruffy pair of denim shorts and a halter top without the necessary accessory of a strapless bra wasn't exactly the look she was aiming for, at least not where Nick was concerned.

Stop it, Eden mentally scolded herself, padding along the floorboards in bare feet and showing Nick through to her unfortunately untidy lounge, reminding herself that Nick couldn't give a damn what she looked like on that level, he'd made that perfectly clear. She knew exactly why he was there.

'I assume you've come to check on me.' Sitting down on the sofa, Eden tucked her legs under her. 'To make sure that I'm *coping* with the news!'

'And are you?' Nick asked, ignoring her sarcasm. Bypassing the chair she'd assumed he's sit in, he sat himself down on the sofa beside her and Eden could feel him taking in her swollen eyes and reddened nose.

'Better now,' Eden admitted. 'I've had a good cry, thumped a few pillows. Jim's been great. It was my turn to cook but, as I said, he's insisted on going out and getting pizza. Do you want me to ring him,' she offered, 'and tell him to get some more? You're very welcome to stay.'

Nick shook his head. 'I'm actually on my way over to my parents'. I just wanted to see how you were doing.'

'Well, I'm fine,' Eden said in a rather falsely bright voice. 'It was nice of you to think of me.'

'I had an ulterior motive.' Nick gave her the benefit of a rather devastating smile. 'I was rather hoping you'd had a rethink about Christmas. You've no idea how much easier my life would be if I could tell them I was bringing a date.'

'Nick!' Eden wailed, wishing he'd just drop it. She had enough to weep about tonight without this as well!

'Oh, well.' Nick shrugged. 'Nut roast for you, then!'

'Looks that way,' Eden sighed.

Nick stood up, and Eden did the same. Now he hadn't got what he'd obviously wanted, the conversation was clearly over.

As he reached the front door Nick turned around. "Would it change your mind if—?"

'Nothing will change my mind Nick.'

'Hear me out, Eden. How would you feel if Ben came with us?'

'Ben?' Her mood shifted from irritated to angry. It had been an emotional enough day without Nick using Ben as some kind of pawn. 'You'd use a three-year-old kid to get your way…'

'Hey!' Nick's single word halted her. 'I know you're upset, Eden, I know this has cut pretty deep for you, but for your information, I've been looking after Ben since the moment he was delivered. I resuscitated that little boy when he was born. It was me who diagnosed his Down's syndrome and it was me who opened an envelope one Monday morning and found out he was HIV positive. For three years I've been trying to save his life and today I've found out that it isn't going to happen— and as hard as it might be for you to deal with this, you're not the only one this news has affected.'

His outburst had her reeling, her own self-absorption shaming her now. He'd had to shout it for her to see it.

In his own way, Nick loved Ben—they all did.

'I'm so sorry.' Tears were close but she held them back, the sympathy card not one she wanted to play here.

'What you said the other day, when he was first admitted, about how you wished he could have just one Christmas, one day of being the centre of everyone's world…' Nick's eyes met Eden's, holding her gaze with possibility. 'We could give him that, Eden. Not a whole day perhaps, but for a couple of hours at least we could give Ben the Christmas he deserves. My parents were saying when I went over how much they're going to miss having the kids there at lunchtime, given Lily's divorce and everything. It would be so nice to have Ben with us, so nice to spoil him.'

'You'd really do that?'

'Of course,' Nick said, as if he was surprised she'd even had to ask. 'You can go home after your shift and grab a few hours' sleep, and once I've finished dishing out the presents at the hospital, I'll pick up Ben and come and get you.'

'Are you Santa this year?'

'I am.' Nick grinned. 'And I make a very fine one, too, even if I do say so myself. So what do you say?'

'And your parents will be OK, with his HIV status and everything?'

'They won't turn a hair.'

'There won't be any other kids there?' Eden checked. 'He shouldn't come into contact with any—'

'Hey.' Nick halted her again, only more gently this time. 'I'm a paediatric consultant, Eden.' He smiled at her embarrassed blush. 'So, can I tell my parents you're coming?'

'Yes.' Eden nodded, her first genuine smile of the day breaking out on her full mouth. 'Yes, please.'

Despite decorating the tree at work, despite the mountain of empty boxes she'd wrapped and placed around it, Christmas hadn't really seemed to be happening for Eden, but waking up the next morning, hearing a Christmas jingle on her alarm radio, the date caught up with her all of a sudden—seven days to Christmas and she hadn't done a thing.

Not a single thing!

'Oh, hell!'

Peeling back her sheet, Eden jumped out of bed and hit the floor running. She greeted a bleary-eyed Jim in the kitchen and gratefully accepted the coffee he poured.

'Who are you ringing?'

'The bank,' Eden groaned. She pulled her credit card out of her purse and keyed in the digits, hitting the hash key and keeping her fingers crossed as she listened for her available balance. 'If I post my prezzies today, do you think they stand a chance of getting there?'

Of course, first she had to buy them!

Her parents were easy to buy for, or at least predictable—for her father a CD of marching pipers which, Eden realised as she handed over her card for the first of many times that morning, at least she wouldn't have to hear this year, and for Mum a twelve-month supply of some impossibly expensive facial treatment that promised everything but coffee in bed in the morning!

On, ever on, until every last present for her family

was wrapped and stuffed into a postpak and Eden queued up at the post office with the bulging box and a half-used roll of sticky tape that she still had to pay for, trying to fathom what on earth she should get for Ben and for Nick's family, given that they were having her for Christmas dinner. And, of course, for Nick himself! Over and over Eden had to quell her mounting excitement, over and over she had to replay Nick's rather harsh words to her. He'd told her there was nothing between them, had told her to her face that this was merely an exercise to get his parents off his back, but as she watched the shop assistant wrapping his present, she went the whole hog and added an extra two dollars to the bill to add a bow. Eden allowed herself the tiny indulgence of a daydream, imagined for a moment that this was how Christmas would always be.

'Who's the lucky bunny, going home?' Eden asked, walking into her allocated bay on the Ward, incredibly pleased to see Priscilla sitting on Rory's bed and playing a board game with him.

'Me.' Priscilla grinned, looking up from the game. 'Dr Nick said I could go home this afternoon. Mum's finishing work early to come and get me.'

'Well, good for you,' Eden said as Priscilla turned her attention back to the game.

Picking up Priscilla's chart, Eden turned to the food chart that was being kept on the girl, checking off the contents of the tray and filling in what Priscilla had eaten. 'How did you go with lunch today?'

'OK.' Eden shrugged, not bothering to look up, and her nonchalance was the best reward of all. The fact she'd eaten a plate of steamed fish and vegetables and a bowl of jelly was just as it should be—no big deal.

'How are you doing, Rory?' Eden asked as Priscilla skipped off to the loo. She popped the tympanic thermometer in his ear and watched as he shrugged his shoulders.

'OK.'

It was a very different *OK* to Priscilla's, and not for the first time Eden realised Rory had been having a hard time of it lately.

'A bit fed up, huh?' Eden asked.

'I guess so.' Rory gave another apathetic shrug and let out a long sigh. When Eden didn't rush to fill the long silence, Rory finally elaborated. 'Priscilla's turned out OK now she's stopped all her whingeing.'

'And now she's going home?' Eden asked, sitting on the bed. 'Like Declan did. You miss him, don't you?'

'Even if he was just a kid, Declan was cool.'

'Declan,' Eden whispered, 'was way too cool to be five! You know,' she continued, 'that once Priscilla's gone home her bed will be filled within a few hours. Before you know it, there will be another kid in there…'

'Waking me up in the middle of the night because he doesn't know where the call bell is, or because his mum's gone home.' He gave a very weak smile. 'As soon as I've broken them in they're ready to go home.'

'You're really very good with the other patients,' Eden said. 'I know they can be a pain sometimes, but the night nurses tell me you're a real help at night if one of the other children are upset. Dianne, the night sister, told me that one night you had one of the little ones sitting on your bed at three in the morning playing a game with him when he was missing his mum and the nurses were all busy.'

A hint of a blush darkened his cheeks.

'That's really kind of you Rory.'

'I guess.' Rory was pleating the sheet and Eden noticed that his nails needed cutting, but she made a mental note rather than saying anything. She wanted to wait until Rory elaborated, finally he voiced what was really on his mind. 'School breaks up today. For Christmas,' Rory added, and Eden nodded.

'You'll be back at school by the time the summer break's over.'

'Yeah, but who will I be sitting with?' Rory growled. 'You get to meet your new teacher on the last day of term and choose who you'll be sitting beside next year. I bet I'll be sitting on my own.'

'I'll bet you're not.' Eden gave him a little nudge with her elbow. 'It might seem an age to you since I was eleven, but I can remember it very well. I can remember there was this girl in my class called Alison Davies…'

'Did you like her?' Rory asked, and Eden screwed up her nose.

'She broke her arm, just her arm, mind—nothing near as bad as you—and she was only away one week. Well, the day she came back, everyone crowded around her, wanting to sign her cast. All the teachers said that we had to be nice to *Alison*.' Eden pulled a face and managed to make Rory smile with an alarmingly good impersonation of a jealous, petulant eleven-year-old. Even her voice adopted a preadolescent surly ring. 'Everyone wanted to be *Alison Davies's* best friend.'

'Yeah?'

'Yes.' Eden grinned and corrected at the same time. 'You're going to have metal rod sticking out your legs, which is way more cool than a cast. You, Rory, are going to be fighting them off with a stick.'

'Really?'

'Really,' Eden said. 'I'm working over Christmas— well, I'm on nights for Christmas Eve and Boxing night and then back for four nights over New Year—and I for one can't wait.'

Rory gave a very dubious frown. 'Who'd actually want to be here?'

'Me.' Eden smiled. 'Christmas is great on the children's ward.'

'For the little kids,' Rory said, but Eden shook her head.

'For everyone. I know this is probably the last place you want to be right now but, believe me, Rory, you'll remember this Christmas for ever.'

Rory gave her another dubious look. 'I doubt it. Anyway, it's not as if there's a Santa or anything.'

'Isn't there?' Eden said, treading very carefully as she spoke. Rory was at that horribly awkward age, caught between childhood and adolescence, hearing from his mates that it wasn't really true yet wanting to believe all the same. Eden thought about it for a moment and then shook her head. 'I don't care what anyone says, there's definitely magic in the air at Christmas. You're going to have a great day, you just wait and see.'

They weren't empty words either—Christmas in hospital really was a special time and Eden felt a pang of guilt at her own selfishness, knowing the huge effort everyone went to to ensure that those who had to be there really did have a Christmas to remember. As the countdown started, the atmosphere, not just in the children's ward but around the whole hospital, heightened. A job lot of Christmas earrings must have been purchased because everywhere Eden looked the floor was being mopped or the meals were being delivered by women of all ages with twinkling Santas or snowmen dangling from their ears. The admin staff joined the party, too, with tinsel wrapped around their badges. Every ward in the hospital was decorated in its own unique way, there were massive hampers at every nurses' station, and whether you were going to borrow an ampoule of penicillin or beg for a few hospital gowns till the linen was delivered the following morning, undoubtedly a book of raffle tickets would be waved in your face—the proceeds going to raise funds for that particular ward.

Even Donna, who had insisted on good taste, stunned everyone by arriving on the ward with a stack of tabards she'd made herself for the nursing staff to wear. And when Eden arrived on Christmas Eve she was delighted to find her navy culottes and white shirt, transformed by the red tabard, covered in reindeers and jolly fat Santas that Becky handed her as she followed her into the changing room, grabbing the opportunity, while the ward was quiet, for a quick five-minute gossip before handover.

'Donna made these?' Eden checked, tying the tabard at the sides and putting in her various pens and a small torch.

'She did.' Becky grinned, sitting down on the bench and idly flicking through an ancient magazine as Eden got ready to start her shift. 'Though I'll bet she'll want them returned washed and folded by Boxing Day!'

'I am sorry,' Becky said again, for probably the hundredth time since the roster had been rearranged, looking up from her magazine and catching Eden's eyes in the mirror. 'I really feel awful that you're stuck here tonight instead of zipping up the freeway with a back seat full of presents.'

'Well, don't be.' Eden shook her head, wrapping a bit of tinsel around her ponytail. 'It's not as if I'm replacing you, Becky. You were never supposed to be working.'

'I know,' Becky sighed, 'but my house is ten minutes away. You're missing out on being with your family.'

'Becky.' Eden turned from the mirror and smiled at her friend. 'I admit I was a bit put out at first, but I soon got over it, and, as it turns out, I'm actually glad I'm working tonight. It means I'm going to spend Christmas day with—'

'Nick Watson.' Becky gave a dreamy sigh. 'You know, if I'd have known that was part of the deal when Donna asked for volunteers, I'd have put my hand straight up.'

'Becky!' Eden grinned, ignoring, for a moment the fact Becky had deliberately missed the point. Despite her smile, Eden was more than a touch concerned about the constant jaundiced air that seemed to surround Becky whenever she spoke about her marriage. 'What about Hamish?'

'What about him?' Becky rolled her eyes but her expression changed, not just her face but her entire body drooping. Her shoulders slouched, her face dropped into her hands and Eden watched as a tear slid out between Becky's fingers. Crossing the room, Eden sat down on the bench and put her arm around her friend.

'What's going on, Becky?'

'You tell me.' Becky gulped. 'He's out every night, meeting Vince or George or whatever name he can come up with.'

'People are busy around Christmas,' Eden soothed. 'Loads of parties and drinks after work.'

'Hamish doesn't have a job,' Becky pointed out, and Eden felt her heart sink. 'And even if I stretched the boundaries and gave him some grace, how come he's out every night until three in the morning?' Becky's tear-streaked face turned to Eden. 'We normally get up at six and meditate for half an hour before the kids get up, but Hamish is so worn out from the night before, I can barely raise a good morning, let alone…'

'What?' Becky frowned as Eden's hand tightened on her shoulder. Eden had nowhere to go except the honest truth.

'I love you dearly, Becky,' Eden said, her lips trying so hard not to twitch. 'And I know that none of this is funny. I just can't get past the bit about you meditating…'

'Philistine!' Becky managed a very wobbly smile. 'You should try it someday.' The tiny diversion was over and Becky took a deep breath. 'I love you too, Eden, but I hate the fact I'm sitting here on Christmas Eve pouring my heart out to you, telling you that my marriage is as good as over. He's all grumpy when I ask him where he's been, says that we've been married for ten years and that surely by now I should be able to trust him.'

'And do you?' Eden asked, but Becky just shrugged. 'He could just be…' Eden struggled to come up with a scenario, but Becky was only too happy to fill her in.

'Playing around?'

'I didn't say that.'

'You didn't have to.' Becky blew her fringe skywards. 'I know I'm not the world's tidiest wife or the best cook…' Very deliberately Eden didn't comment. 'And I know that Conner's not exactly the world's most disciplined kid, but I truly thought those sort of things didn't matter to Hamish, I really thought we were a team.'

'Talk to him,' Eden urged, and Becky nodded.

'I'm going to…'

'Just not tonight, huh?' Eden said perceptively, and Becky crumpled.

'I just want Conner to have a great Christmas. Once that's out of the way, I'm going to ask him just what the hell's going on. He's either in or out of this relationship as far as I'm concerned, not somewhere in between.'

'It will be OK,' Eden soothed, but with more conviction than she really felt. She hated the fact her friend was in so much pain, but felt powerless to help. She wished she had a little bit of the Christmas magic she'd promised Rory in her tabard to sprinkle over Becky. 'You're going to be fine, Becks.'

'I know,' Becky gulped, wiping her cheeks with her hands and standing up. 'Knowing my luck, I'll end up paying *him* spousal maintenance or, worse, he'll sell one of his stupid paintings the day I sign the divorce papers.'

'It isn't going to come to that,' Eden said, standing up as well, glancing at her watch and seeing it was just after nine. 'We'd better go into handover.'

'Thanks, Eden.' Becky sniffed. 'I feel better now.'

'I haven't done anything,' Eden pointed out.

'I was thanking you in advance.' Becky grinned. 'If I leave Hamish, Conner and I will be on your doorstep!

'Joke,' she added, linking her arm through Eden's and heading out onto the ward.

Even though the conversation had been gloomy, the mood on the ward wasn't. Every television was tuned to *Carols by Candlelight,* and the tree looking prettier somehow. The whole ward hummed with expectancy. 'Bet you can't wait for tomorrow.'

'I can't,' Eden admitted. 'I feel like a kid myself I'm so excited.' And despite what you think, it has nothing to do with Nick Watson.'

'I know,' Becky sighed. 'I was just teasing.' The conversation stopped as they reached ISO one. A tuxedo was out of place on the children's ward, especially one worn with a surgical face mask, but the tall, blond man wearing it, checking the charts outside the cubicle, carried it extremely well!

'I thought you were supposed to be at the doctors' ball,' Becky chided him.

'I'm just checking his meds,' Nick answered, ripping off the mask. 'And making sure that his day leave order is signed for tomorrow.'

'You could have rung for that,' Becky pointed out. 'And since when did you have to wear a mask to check a chart?'

'He was crying.' Nick held his hands up in a helpless gesture. 'What was I supposed to do?'

'Out, Cinderella,' Becky shooed. 'Go and have some fun. It's Christmas Eve!'

'Well, if you insist.' Nick grinned. ''Night, ladies.'

''Night, Nick,' they both answered.

'I'll pick you up around eleven?' Nick checked as he headed off, turning around, for a brief moment his eyes meeting Eden's.

'Fine.'

'Gorgeous, isn't he?' Becky sighed, but just as Eden was about to agree she realised the conversation had turned back to Ben and both women stared through the glass for an indulgent moment at the little boy sleeping on his back, his thumb half in, half out of his mouth, dark eyelashes fanning his permanently red cheeks.

'I really admire you, you know. Sometimes I feel myself getting a bit too close, getting too attached to a poor little mite that's got no one. Do you remember Dwain?'

Eden shook her head.

'He was before your time, a little guy from the Solomon Islands with leukaemia. He was just gorgeous.'

'What happened?'

'Nothing.' Becky shrugged. 'I knew I was getting in too deep so I told Donna I was getting too attached and asked not to have him allocated to me any more. And that was that.'

'But was it?'

'No.' Becky shook her head. 'Believe me, you're doing the right thing, Eden, sometimes it hurts more to walk away.'

From every room the television had the same picture, and obs were taken and meds given to the background noises of *Carols by Candlelight,* various celebrities from around Australia delivering the Christmas message through song, and on more than a few occasions Eden found herself darting into the pan room to take a steadying breath or blow her nose, only to be met by Dana or Rochelle doing exactly the same thing. The ward round on Christmas Eve on a children's ward was both the saddest and happiest place to be. Happy because who couldn't be moved by the excited chatter, the expectant faces, the palpable air of excitement as the children were tucked in for the night? But it was tempered with sadness too, sharing a pensive, brave smile with a parent who knew they had to make the most of this night, who knew, more than any parent ever should, that this Christmas was special, and that the best they could do was make the very most of this precious child that had touched their lives.

Turning off the television and quietly tying a stocking to Ben's cot, Eden gazed down.

CHAPTER SEVEN

'I'LL just take this,' Eden said, retrieving the bedpan from Rory in virtual darkness, knowing how embarrassed he was by the whole procedure, 'and then I'll come and check your temperature. Merry Christmas, Rory.'

'Yeah.'

Returning two minutes later, Eden pulled out her pen torch and flashed it so she could locate his ear, pushing in the probe and listening for the almost simultaneous bleep as his temperature was recorded.

'You've got a new roommate,' Eden whispered.

'How old?'

'Twelve.' In the darkness Eden grinned as she felt Rory's interest go up a notch. 'He's feeling pretty sorry for himself. He fell off his skateboard yesterday evening and had to go to Theatre to have his arm set.'

'Was he wearing pads?' Rory whispered back, by now an expert on accident prevention.

'No.' Eden shook her head. 'I think he'll need a bit of cheering up, given it's Christmas and everything. Can I leave that to you?' She just made out Rory's nod in the darkness and even though it was six a.m., even though Rory was no doubt about to drift back to sleep,

Eden was just too excited to resist. 'Why don't you have a drink?'

'I'm not thirsty,' Rory said.

'You should drink lots,' Eden insisted. 'The doctor told you that. I'll just turn on your bedside light and pour you some water.' Flicking on the light, she fumbled with the jug and poured the reluctant Rory a drink. Seeing that he'd gone back to sleep, she pulled out her thermometer again, 'Sorry, Rory, I have to take your temperature again.' As Rory's eyes flicked open, Eden picked his chart off the end of his bed and started to fill it in, smothering a smile as Rory, despite the bulky traction, pulled himself to a sitting position.

'What's this?'

'What?' Eden frowned.

'This,' Rory said, gesturing to the massive bedspread covering him, with just his foot, hanging from the traction, sticking out the end of the bed. 'What's all the writing?'

'I don't know.' Eden stared at the hundred or so squares that made up the bedspread. 'What is all the writing?'

'It's from school,' Rory yelped, forgetting to whisper, his face lighting up as he read all the signatures. 'From my year. There's Davey and Glen and there's Shalya…' His fingers pointed to each individual square, three weeks of lethargy disappearing as he stared at the vast expanse of messages and pictures, each one just for him. 'And that's my teacher, Mrs Park. She says it was good I was wearing my helmet…' A tiny frown puckered his brow as he momentarily looked up at Eden. 'How did this get here? Did you put it on?'

A loud squawk from the isolation rooms gave Eden the perfect excuse to give him a very queer look. 'Me? Since when did the night staff have time to make your bed? This is from your school?'

'Yeah!' Rory stared from her to the blanket. 'If you didn't put it here, then who did?'

'I have no idea,' Eden said, but her audience was lost. Rory's attention turned back to the friends he was sure by now would have forgotten him, his Christmas already made—and it wasn't even five past six.

'Happy Christmas, Rory.' Eden smiled. Yes, he was ten years old, but he wasn't too big for a cuddle and despite her earlier protests Eden was happy she'd worked Christmas Eve as two bony arms wrapped around her neck.

'Happy Christmas, Eden, you're the coolest one here. '

'Flatterer!' Eden grinned, cuddling him back. 'But guess what? So are you!'

Six a.m. onwards was always chaotic at the best of times. Every child had their observations taken and recorded, waking babies needed to be fed, drugs and IV antibiotics had to be given—all hopefully before the arrival of the day staff at seven. But Christmas morning was, of course, even more chaotic than usual. A stocking had been placed at the end of each child's bed and each child demanded and merited more than a quick greeting on this very special day. The ward had fewer patients, due to the fact that elective surgery was cancelled over Christmas, but that also meant that the patients that were unfortunate enough to be in hospital over

Christmas really needed to be there and were therefore quite poorly. That was the reason the morning round had been started fifteen minutes earlier. Blowing her fringe skywards as she glanced down at her watch, Eden wondered if she was ever going to be finished in time.

'Morning, Sister, and Merry Christmas!'

'Good morning.' Eden smiled as Donna waltzed in, immaculate as always, but instead of heading straight to her office, as was her usual practice, Donna pulled one of her hand-made tabards out of her bag and proceeded to put it on.

'Where do you want me?'

'Sorry?' Eden gave her a slightly bemused look. 'It's only six-thirty.'

'It's also Christmas morning.' Donna gave a rueful smile. 'Why don't you give me that thermometer and the medicine charts and you can get on with the feeds? Young Justin is wide awake and singing for his bottle!'

'She's a good egg really,' Dana, the night nurse Eden had been on duty with, said as they met in the milk room, where Dana was making up a jug of formula and Eden was warming a bottle. 'She does this every year.'

'I don't remember her coming in last year.' Eden frowned, shaking a few drops of milk onto the back of her wrist to check it was the right temperature.

'Because she was on a late shift,' Dana explained. 'She stayed till nearly eleven on Christmas night, doing the obs and meds and letting us get on with settling a ward of thoroughly over-excited, over-fed children. Who are you feeding?' she asked.

'Justin,' Eden answered with a smile, 'which will take about two minutes flat. He's such a little guts!'

'Well, Ben's starting to wake up. Do you want me to pop his dummy in and hopefully drag it out so that you can feed him his morning milk?'

'Please,' Eden answered, and not for the first time she was so pleased the truth was out. Far from her colleagues criticising her, they had bent over backwards to support her—this morning was a prime example. Despite his age, Ben usually drank from a training cup, but in the morning and to settle at night he still loved to have his bottle and no one was in any rush to deny Ben this small pleasure. It wasn't so much the method of feeding he loved but the contact that came with it, being taken out of his cot and cuddled in for five or ten minutes. Dana, like the rest of the team, had been only too willing to leave that pleasurable duty to Eden.

'Oh.' Eden smiled as she pushed open Justin's door and saw his mum standing there, going through Justin's stocking, smiling as she pulled out the soft teddy, rattle and little box of chocolates that Eden had placed there when she'd take Justin's two a.m. obs. 'I was just bringing him in his bottle.

'Merry Christmas,' she added, handing over the bottle. 'The chocolates are for the mums, by the way!'

'That's really kind. Merry Christmas, Eden.' A tired-looking Jenny took the bottle and picked up her angry bundle. 'And Merry Christmas to you too, little man.' Kissing her baby on the top of his head, she sat in the large chair and started to feed her son. 'The others aren't awake yet, so I thought I'd come in and give him a cuddle and then dash back to the madhouse. Justin probably won't even know the difference, but I couldn't bear to go the whole of Christmas morning without seeing him. We're all going to come up after dinner—I know it's only supposed to be two visitors—'

'That's fine,' Eden broke in. 'And I can guarantee Justin would rather it was you than me giving him his bottle. Do you want me to take a picture?'

'A picture?'

'We've got a Polaroid camera on the ward—why don't I take a photo of you both and you can take it back home?'

Finding the camera and taking the photo actually took longer than it took for Justin to drain his bottle, but Jenny was so thrilled with the result it was more than worth it.

'Here you go!' As Eden came out of Justin's room, Dana handed her Ben's bottle. 'And don't rush. Donna's like greased lightning this morning. All the meds are done and a lot of parents are here too, giving the feeds, so take your time.'

'*Den!*' Even before the door had opened, just a glimpse of his warm milk and his precious Den through the glass and Ben's tears turned off like a tap.

'Happy Christmas, Ben.' Eden smiled, and though she wanted to scoop him up for a cuddle, first she changed his nappy and then, after washing her hands, pulled open the curtains. 'Look at the sun!' Eden pointed to the bright sky, just a few tiny wisps of cloud visible that would no doubt be burnt off by the time Ben had finished his bottle. 'And what's this?' Pulling the stocking off his cot, she handed it to him, but Ben didn't know what to do with it so Eden helped him, pulling out two shiny packages that Donna had bought with wards funds and carefully wrapped.

'You soon worked that one out.' Eden laughed as Ben

pulled at the shiny paper, clapping his hands in excitement at the mirror Santa had bought him. 'It ties onto your cot,' Eden explained, doing just that, marvelling at the thought Donna had put into each present because Ben was over the moon, grinning at his reflection and banging the looking-glass with his chubby hand. If Ben wasn't quite so thrilled with his next gift, Eden was—the ten dollars allocated to each child had clearly been ignored in Ben's case, because the smart navy shorts and trendy T-shirt Eden helped him to unwrap were just divine.

'You,' Eden said, finally picking him up and giving him a cuddle with his bottle, 'are going to look so handsome!'

It was actually a reluctant Eden that left the ward!

She hadn't been lying when she'd tried to cheer up Rory the previous night because, whether or not there was a Santa, there certainly was magic in the air! But it wasn't just Ben or the other children that had Eden wanting to linger just a little while longer, more the thought of seeing Nick, dressed up as Santa, but she knew that she'd regret it later—a few hours' sleep very much the order of the day if she was to have any hope of making it through lunch.

Fat chance.

She was more excited, almost, than any of the children had been last night. By the time Eden had showered and rung her family, opening the presents they had sent her and squealing over the phone in delight as she pulled out clothes, make-up and some hair straighteners, it was impossible to get to sleep. The beautiful sunny blue sky that had greeted her when she'd gone in to Ben was burning through her flimsy curtains now and, though she'd never in a million years admit it to Jim, the house was horribly quiet without the drone of his blessed music. By nine-thirty Eden had given in, choosing instead to inspect her presents rather more carefully.

Ceramic hair straighteners. Pulling them out of the box, Eden read the accompanying leaflet and looked at the before and after photos with tongue firmly in cheek. But for the hell of it she plugged them in anyway and, sure enough, it was only ten seconds or so before the red light started flickering to indicate they were ready and only another ten seconds before Eden was utterly and completely hooked! She gaped in admiration as her chocolate curls literally melted away, staring open-mouthed in wonder a mere fifteen minutes later at the sleek, dark curtain that hung around her shoulders. And now that she'd got the straight hair she'd always dreamed of, it seemed a shame to stop there. Her minimal make-up routine was transformed as she opened jar after jar of the latest mineral make-up, *buffing* the make-up into her face, *sculpting* her cheeks and *accentuating* her eyes until, Eden was positive, she could have walked down any street in New York with her very groomed head held high.

'They're divine,' Eden breathed down the phone, a second phone call most definitely merited. 'I love them.' Her voice trembled slightly. 'I love you all, too.'

'And we love you,' Lena Hadley replied. 'You're going to be OK today?'

Eden could hear the worried note in her mother's voice. 'Mum, I'm going to be fine. Look, I know it isn't the Christmas we planned but, as much as I miss being with you all, I'm going to really enjoy spending it with Ben.'

'I know,' Lena answered, and even if she didn't say it Eden could hear the inevitable 'but'.

'I'm OK, Mum. You, better than anyone, should understand that just because I'm close to Ben—'

'It's not you being with Ben that worries me,' Lena broke in, and Eden bit hard on her lip as her mother perceptively continued. 'I've given a few tots a Christmas to remember over the years and I know that the pleasure outweighs the pain, it's you spending the day with Nick that worries me.'

'We're just friends, Mum.' Eden shook her head into the phone. 'That's all we've ever been.'

'Eden?'

'OK!' Her mother's single word had Eden raking a hand through her newly straightened hair. 'Maybe I did have a crush on him when he was engaged to Teaghan, but that's been over for ages. Mum, he's dated more women in the past year than I can count and, no matter what way I look at it, I can't justify it. And I'm certainly not going to be another of his conquests—whatever game Nick's playing to get over Teaghan, I'm not about to be a part of it!'

'Good,' Lena replied. 'But I'm just asking you to be careful today, Eden.'

'I will be,' Eden said, blushing to her roots as she peeled back the curtain, wondering how, at twenty-eight years of age and with a few hundred kilometres between them, her mother could still make her feel guilty when she hadn't even done anything! 'They're here— I'd better go. Merry Christmas!'

'Merry Christmas, darling, and be careful!'

She had to be!

One look at Nick as he climbed out of his car and Eden felt her heart stick somewhere in her throat, her mother's warning merited now because, even if it was only through her window, the Nick she was witnessing away from the ward, out of the smart suit or theatre gear, was a dangerous combination indeed. Effortlessly smart, he was dressed in smart beige shorts and a black T-shirt and somehow he managed to look as smart and as groomed as he had last night in his tuxedo. The T-shirt accentuated his muscular frame and the impossible blondness of his hair. It was the first glimpse of his legs Eden had ever been privileged to see—and what a privilege. Muscular, tanned calves striding up her drive, casual leather thongs on his feet. Eden replayed her mother's warning in her head as she pulled open her door, utterly determined to feign a casual greeting, to hide the butterflies dancing in her stomach, willing herself not to fall for his undoubted charms.

Nick Watson was danger personified.

'Where's Ben?' Eden asked, peering somewhere over Nick's shoulder to the smart silver car on the nature strip.

'Merry Christmas to you, too…' Nick started, but his voice faded in mid-sentence. He was used, too used, to seeing her in uniform or casually dressed. He'd never glimpsed this side of Eden—and what a side! Those dark chocolate curls replaced with a sleek glossy curtain. Always beautiful, today she was stunning, from head to toe. Suddenly the straightforward was terribly complicated; suddenly Nick was stalling, reaching into his pocket for his sunglasses and putting them on before answering her. 'He's asleep in the car, I've left the air-conditioning on. Still, I don't want to—'

'I'm ready.' Eden practically snapped the words, utterly perturbed all of a sudden.

Even with his eyes hidden behind dark glasses she could feel the weight of his stare, every sense in her body screaming an alert, the delicious scent of him reaching her nostrils. His hair flopped forward as he bent to pick up the mountain of bags Eden had in the doorway and she had to ball her fists, dig her nails into her palms just to stop from reaching out and running her fingers through it. As Nick headed off to the car, Eden took a moment longer than was necessary to lock the front door, dragging the warm midmorning air into her lungs. Nerves caught up with her all of a sudden as she walked down the garden path, acutely aware that the powder blue linen dress her sister had sent her was maybe just a touch too short, her beaded sandals clipping on the pavers, her hand trembling slightly as she pulled open the passenger-side door.

'He's worn out.' Eden smiled, craning her neck to see Ben.

'Don't be fooled,' Nick answered. 'He's just having a power-nap—you should have seen his face when Santa came into his room. He just about pulled off my beard, he was so excited.'

'He looks great.' Eden smiled fondly, because Ben did. Out of the hospital pyjamas and dressed in *real* clothes, he looked just like any other toddler clutching a soft toy and dozing in his car-seat.

'So do you!' And there was nothing light or flip about Nick's voice, his statement delivered in a low, husky voice. Eden jerked her head to face him and even with the barrier of his shades she could feel the admiration in his gaze. 'You look stunning, Eden.'

'It won't last.' Somehow it was Eden who managed light and flip. 'My mum bought me some hair straighteners but, despite the promises, I doubt they're quite up to a warm, humid Sydney Christmas.' She was babbling—too much—wishing Nick would just tear his eyes away, wishing he would start the engine so that she could remember how to breathe again. 'Nick…' Nibbling on her thumbnail, she decided to broach one of the many things about today that had been bothering her.

'Eden?' A tiny smile twisted on his lips as he heard the nervousness in her voice.

'We haven't spoken about—I mean, we haven't worked out what we're going to say.'

'About?'

'Us!' Eden answered with a note of exasperation. 'Your parents think we're dating, so if they ask…'

'They won't.' Nick shook his head firmly. 'Just stick with the truth—we've been working together for fifteen months. We can leave the rest up to their imaginations. I'm not expecting you to start pashing me over the mince pies. Of course, if you get a sudden urge, I won't object.'

'I won't,' Eden said quickly, too quickly perhaps.

'Won't object or won't get the urge?' Nick teased. 'Look, Eden, all you have to do today is enjoy yourself. Do you think you can manage that?'

'Yes.'

'And relax, too!' Nick added, but Eden let out a rather drawn-out sigh.

'You might be pushing it there.' But now the conversation was back to the familiar friendly they did so well, now that the horrible thick tension that had suffocated her finally disappeared, Eden managed what only a few seconds ago had seemed near impossible—finally she relaxed. Her face broke into a smile, she pulled her seat belt around her and sank back into the seat.

'Here,' Nick offered, as Eden gave the strap a few futile tugs. 'It can be a bit tricky.'

'Is there something you haven't told me, Nick?' Eden teased as he leant over and slid the belt across.

'What?' A tiny frown appeared over his glasses.

'Since when did you take to wearing blusher?' Eden laughed as he pulled off his sunglasses and checked himself in the rear-view mirror, the remnants of Santa's rosy cheeks still in place. 'Here.' She rummaged in her bag and pulled out a moisture wipe. As her hand met his cheek Eden rued the stupid mistake she'd made in an unguarded moment, the wipe dragged over his cheek, a tiny turn of his head brought him right into her personal space and even as her hand pulled away, even as she managed some idle comment about the make-up being gone now, she knew he was going to kiss her. She had anticipated the moment so acutely that when his lips met hers there was no element of surprise, no awkward jumping, just the delicious, utterly decadent feel of his mouth on hers, a kiss that had hung between them since the day they had met. Feeling his flesh beneath hers, the weight of his lips moving a delicious fraction, the scent that was so much Nick way more intimate now as she breathed him in, she relished the moment, a heady taste of his flesh, and even if it only lasted a couple of seconds, if it was practically over before it had started, it couldn't remotely have been described as friendly,

'Happy Christmas, Eden.' His eyes pierced hers,

black pupils almost masking the vivid jade, his full lips darker than she remembered, hair blonder, more beautiful than she had yet acknowledged. It was like finally seeing some long revered work of art close up for the first time.

'Happy Christmas, Nick.' It was all she could manage and yet, at that moment, all she wanted for him, for herself and for Ben, too. Pulling away, she swallowed hard. 'Happy Christmas.'

The purr of the engine starting was a blessed relief, a chance to press her flaming cheeks against the cool, cool glass, her lips stinging from the brief encounter, trying and failing not to read too much into it, trying to convince herself that he didn't move her.

If Eden's tiny rented home was a mere stone's throw from the hospital, then Nick's parents' was a brief walk to choose the stone before you threw it—only the Watsons' stone definitely landed on the *right* side of the hospital! The narrow, hilly Sydney streets were easily negotiated until they came to the beach road, where the car glided through the light traffic. Eden stared out of the window at the gathered parties on the beach, some hunched around gas barbecues, some spreading blankets and emptying picnic baskets, others for the moment ignoring the food and running into the tempting Pacific Ocean. Even though she couldn't hear them, she smiled as she envisaged their excited screams as the bracing, invigorating surf met their hot bodies.

'The water looks heavenly.' Eden commented, only it wasn't idle chit-chat, just something that had to be said as you drove along the Beach Road and stared at the endlessly divine, constantly moving backdrop.

'Did you bring your bathers?' Nick asked, and Eden shook her head.

'If you want to swim I'm sure—'

'I'm not borrowing your mum's, OK?' Eden half snapped. As much as she loved the beach, as tempting as the water looked and as determined as she was to keep Nick at a very friendly arm's length, there was no way, *no way* she was heading down to the beach in some matronly bathing apparatus on loan from Nick Watson's mother.

A girl had some pride!

Flicking on the indicator and slowing down as he approached a gap in the tea-trees, a tiny sealed road Eden hadn't known existed came into view. Nick turned the car left towards the beach, when most mere mortals would have turned right, and if the view had been gorgeous before it was spectacular now. The water was so close as Eden pulled open the passenger door and stepped out, she half expected to feel it around her ankles, Nick's family home, completely stunning, was set low in the sandy rocks, the white rendered walls accentuating the blues and greens of the ocean behind. A real estate agent Eden certainly wasn't, but even a novice like her could pick out the luxurious extras—an outside shower to rinse off as you walked back along your own private beach path, the lap pool running along the side of the house. The cosy Christmas lunch Eden had envisaged for Ben seemed to be rapidly fading. The sun beat hot on her neck as she walked round to the back of the car and woke the sleepy Ben.

'Hey, Ben.' Eden smiled, picking up the docile bundle as Nick gathered not just Eden's many bags but Ben's, too.

'You two don't exactly travel light,' he grumbled, leading the way along the sandy path as Eden, clutching Ben, completely unsure of their reception, walked shyly behind.

Her doubts vanished even before they reached the veranda—the door flung open and Christmas greetings rang out, not just to Nick but to Eden, too, and most importantly to Ben!

'Hello, Eden!' A very slender woman who looked about eighteen introduced herself as Lily, Nick's sister. 'We're all dying to meet you.' She smiled, 'Nick's told us so much about you. And you, too, Ben,' she added to Ben, whose head was tucked into Eden's shoulder, weighing up the stranger with his almond eyes. Clearly Lily passed the test because Ben suddenly lifted his head and grinned, his smile widening as they all stepped into the house.

'Eden!'

If Lily and Nick were stunning, here was the reason.

Vivian Watson was as tall and elegant as Nick yet as delicate and slender as Lily, her Nordic hair tumbling over her tanned shoulders, her smile revealing perfectly capped teeth. Any visions Eden might have had of matronly bathers were instantly dismissed—designer clothes clearly the go for Mrs Watson. Never had Eden been more grateful for her usual blast of insomnia that morning, the two hours or so she had spent getting ready worth every sleep-deprived moment! Hugh Watson was tall, but rather less groomed, with wild grey hair and rosy cheeks. He welcomed the trio into his home.

But as ravishing and sophisticated as Vivian Watson first appeared, her smile was genuine, her affectionate greeting welcoming, and as she ushered them through to the family room Eden's nerves abated—not only because of the glass of Buck's Fizz that was thrust into her hand but by the whimper of delight Ben gave at the massive Christmas tree. It was a tree that would certainly have passed Donna's request for good taste—the heavy pine branches dressed only in silver, from the star at the top to the pile of boxes at the bottom.

Wriggling to be let down, Ben stood on the polished floorboards, dancing on the spot in excitement, enchanting everyone with his eager smile. Clearly Ben was a fast learner, because he was pointing at the mountain of presents and making his way over.

'Ben.' Gently Eden pulled him back, but Vivian just laughed and took the little boy's hand, and Ben smiled up as if he'd known her for ever.

'Are you going to help me give out the presents, Ben?' Vivian asked, dropping to the floor and pulling out a very large silver box which she handed to him.

'Careful, Ben,' Eden said nervously, knowing that Ben's only reaction would be to peel away the beautifully wrapped paper. 'Give it to….' Eden waited for Vivian to step in but, clearly used to children, she just laughed, watching delightedly as a thoroughly over-excited Ben tore at the paper with gusto, drooling with delight as a shiny red fire engine was revealed. In a matter of moments the floor was littered with paper, hours of careful choosing relegated to a few moments of excited frenzy. Eden blinked at the fabulous sarong that fell out of her package, the sheerest fabric decorated in myriad colours and tiny circular mirrors around the hemline. She hoped the rather less impressive photo frame she had purchased for Nick's mother would suffice, but she beamed with delight and promptly produced a digital camera, snapping Ben, Nick and Eden gathered around a purple plastic guitar, capturing their smiling faces.

'Here.' Nick passed a slim parcel to Eden and she turned it over in her hands, trying to guess the contents, before handing Nick the present she had bought for him. She chewed her lip as he peeled off the wrapper and blushed as he gave a crow of delight.

'I've been wanting to read this!'

'It's just a book,' Eden mumbled, not sure if he was merely being polite or was actually pleased with her choice. Knowing how much Nick loved his sport, she'd bought a tennis-star-tells-all biography, and if the reviews were anything to go by, there were a few hours of reading pleasure ahead of him. Peeling open her own present, she gave a reluctant laugh as a bikini fell into her hand—thankfully not the four-triangles type but some trendy hipster shorts and a halter-neck top, exactly what she'd have chosen for herself if she'd had her credit card handy!

'You've all bought way too much.' Eden shook her head in bewilderment at the pile of presents surrounding Ben, but Vivian shooed away her protests.

'Nonsense. We're just so thrilled to have a child here for lunch. We'd have been moping around otherwise. Christmas is all about children. We all need someone to spoil on a day like this, and who is more deserving than little Ben?'

Who indeed?

Always a happy boy, today he was positively glowing. Gone for ever were the hospital pyjamas and standard-issue soap, thanks to a thoughtful gift from Nick of slippers and a dressing-gown. There was even a little electric toothbrush in a bulging toiletry bag filled with soaps, powders, creams and brushes, just like any other loved child would have had in hospital. But it wasn't the guitar or the fire engine or the clothes that had him smiling, it was being the centre of attention, being enveloped into a warm, loving family. And Eden realised that, however much Ben might or might not know, he certainly knew that this was special.

'Right.' Vivian stood up and smoothed her dress. 'I'm going to throw you all out for an hour or so, so that I can get the place ready for Christmas dinner—unless you'd like another Buck's Fizz, Eden?'

'Not for me.' Eden shook her head. 'Alcohol and night shifts aren't exactly an ideal mix.'

'Nick?' Vivian offered, waving the jug in her son's direction. 'Surely you can have one.'

'Surely not, if I'm driving,' Nick said rather tightly, and for a moment a flicker of tension crackled in the air, no doubt memories of last year bubbling to the surface. 'Once I've dropped Ben off,' he relented, giving his mum an apologetic, brief embrace.

'Here.' Without prompting, Lily appeared with a tube of sunscreen and a pair of bathers for Ben. 'We have an inexhaustible supply of kids' bathers in this house.'

'He isn't toilet-trained.' Eden hesitated, but Lily just gave a casual shrug.

'I think I've got some training bathers somewhere, I'll go and have a look. I'll get him ready for you if you like while Nick takes you over to the cottage and shows you where you're both sleeping so you can get changed.'

'Sleeping?' Eden's startled voice had Nick looking up.

'Eden's only here for lunch.' Nick grinned. 'I can only inflict you lot on her in small doses. There's a cottage in the grounds.' Nick explained to Eden. 'I generally use it when I'm sleeping over, as my mobile phone goes off at all hours. Come on, I'll show you the bathroom.'

How casually she'd said it, Eden mused as the door closed behind her. No wonder the Watsons had accepted her so easily. No doubt they were used to Nick drifting in with his latest girlfriend in tow. Peeling off her clothes, Eden thanked her lucky stars that she'd thought to shave her legs in the shower that morning. Wearing bathers didn't particularly bother her. Most of her spare time was spent at the beach so she was nicely tanned and the stomach that peeped out between her hipsters and halter top was, if not flat, at least toned. Only her breasts caused her a moment of angst as she tied the flimsy threads at the back of her neck, hoping there would be enough support for her rather ample bosom. She stared down at the rather impressive cleavage jiggling beneath her and wished it wasn't quite so noticeable.

'Ready?' Lily looked up from rubbing cream into Ben's shoulders as Eden walked into the lounge. Despite the sarong Vivian had bought her, which was tied loosely around her waist, despite the fact she was probably more covered than the last time she'd been in this room, despite her earlier bravado about wearing bathers, as Nick looked up, she registered the bob of his Adam's apple as his eyes flicked over the length of her body. Suddenly Eden felt woefully underdressed. She could feel a blush scorching her cheeks and her nipples protruding into the Lycra fabric just at the sight of him.

Chocolate brown board shorts slung low on his hips, his stomach flat and taut as he stood up, a smattering of blond hair on his chest. There was nothing she'd have changed about Nick. Like a digital image unfolding on a computer screen, her mind processed it slowly, the golden hair darkening slightly as it met his navel, snaking down his lower stomach, a decadent sensual arrow. Eden jerked her eyes away, trying to busy herself organising Ben, but Lily had beaten her to it, finishing off applying the sunscreen and popping on his sun hat.

'An hour,' Vivian called as the foursome headed off to the beach. 'Don't be late.'

They easily could have been!

Strolling along the damp sand, feeling the waves licking their feet, Ben squealed with delight as the waves chased his little legs, the one truly endless game that the ocean always won. But Ben gave it his best shot, running away over and over again from the waves that chased him, until Nick hoisted him up on his shoulders and ploughed into the surf, waist deep in water as Lily clicked away.

'It's great to see him looking so happy.' Lily smiled, one hand shielding her eyes from the fierce midday sun, squinting as she focussed on the happy duo.

'I wasn't sure whether or not to bring him,' Eden admitted. 'I didn't know how he'd cope in a strange house, but he's having an absolute ball.'

'He is,' Lily agreed, 'but I was actually talking about Nick. It's nice to see him looking so relaxed.'

'Last Christmas can't have been good,' Eden sighed,

picking up the pace as Lily started walking. 'It must have been awful for you all.'

'It was.' Lily nodded. 'But then again the Christmas before that wasn't particularly great either.' She gave a tight shrug. 'This is the first time in a long time I've seen Nick actually looking really happy, and I'm not just talking about since Teaghan died.' Picking up her long legs, she raced out into the surf to join Nick and Ben, leaving Eden standing there, staring at the trio in the water, the jigsaw that was Nick, the jigsaw she'd spent the last year reluctantly piecing together and finally achieving a rather unsavoury fit, suddenly tossed up into the air, the pieces lying in a confused scramble now, just the same four corners that she'd started with.

Good-looking, funny, clever and—Eden realised as if for the first time, bidding a mental farewell to her newly straightened hair and racing into the surf to join them…

Terribly, terribly kind.

CHAPTER EIGHT

HUGH and Vivian hadn't wasted a single moment of that hour, because when they arrived back, dripping wet and laughing, as they opened the bi-fold doors, for a moment the causal chatter stilled. Everyone took in the magnificent table that had been laid. It groaned under the weight of its fare, the silver cloth barely visible beneath the berries and candles, the red plates and crackers. And pride of place in the middle went to a magnificent turkey, with *all* the trimmings!

'Eden loves her food.' Nick laughed as Eden let out a low groan of pleasure.

'It's not just the food,' Eden chided, 'it's everything. Oh, Vivian, it all looks wonderful.'

She wasn't just being polite. The air-conditioning had been set to arctic to battle the hot summer sun and an oven that must have been on since six a.m.—a full roast was no mean feat when the mercury was nudging forty degrees. Everyone sped off to various rooms, changing in record time, and arrived back at the dining table with hair still dripping.

'It's amazing, isn't it, Ben?' Eden smiled and placed him in the high chair, taking in the wide eyes as he surveyed the scene he was for once the centre of. She had to swallow hard for a moment and there was a dangerous sting in her eyes as she pulled a cracker with Ben. Nick helped him and held onto the stick so that Ben won,

'Happy Christmas, buddy.' Nick kissed his podgy cheek, and if ever there was a moment Eden wanted to capture it was that one.

Gone for a moment was Maxwell Benjamin Reece, a three-year-old with Down's syndrome and HIV positive, replaced instead with Ben Reece just as happy and as excited as a three-year-old should be on this special day. He discovered a passion for roasted parsnips, turned his nose up at Brussels sprouts and clapped his hands when Vivian pulled the curtains on the delectable view and Hugh brought in the flaming Christmas pudding.

'Cream or brandy butter?' Vivian waved a plate at her and Eden struggled to make a decision. 'Or bed?' Vivian grinned. 'I think you've earned it.'

'Sounds wonderful,' Eden sighed, smothering a yawn, 'but Ben's due back at the hospital at around three. I'm scared if I lie down now I won't wake up till tomorrow.'

'You're not the only one.' Nick smiled, nodding to Ben who had dozed off in his high chair, his face covered in ice cream, spoon still clutched in his hand. 'Why don't you both lie down? I'll wake you at three.'

And even though she opened her mouth to argue, not a single word of protest came out. Why shouldn't she lie down? Why should she rush Ben back to the hospital when he still had a precious hour?

'You won't think I'm horribly rude?' Eden checked,

but the entire Watson clan just rolled their eyes and shooed her away.

'I'll take you over to the cottage,' Nick said, but when Eden frowned he softened it with a smile. 'You won't get any sleep in the house. Mum's on her third sherry *and* she's just discovered the karaoke machine!'

They walked through the garden in amicable silence, Nick carrying a sleeping Ben. Eden struggled just to keep her eyes open and barely took in her surroundings as Nick gave her a very brief tour of the essentials, pointing out the phone, kitchen and bathroom before pushing open a bedroom door. Never had a bed looked more tempting!

'You'll come and wake me?' Eden said.

'Yes. Have a good sleep.' Nick closed the door.

Eden didn't need to be told twice. Not even bothering to pull back the sheets, she just laid Ben down on the pillow before gratefully stretching her exhausted, utterly full body out on the bed, smiling as Ben cuddled in to her.

'You're not that hard to get to sleep really, are you?' Eden whispered. 'You just want someone with you.'

A deep voice summoned her. Nick's face swam briefly into focus as she struggled to open her eyes.

'It's three o'clock. We ought to be getting Ben back.'

'Mmm.' Sleepily she agreed and struggled to sit up, but as Nick pushed her back down onto the pillow she didn't resist.

'I'll take him back. You have a sleep, you're exhausted.'

'I'll be OK.' Eden shook her head. 'Just give me five minutes.'

'Go to sleep,' Nick whispered, and it sounded so easy, so completely straightforward she was tempted to comply.

'Give Eden a kiss, Ben, and she'll see you tomorrow.'

'Den!'

His perpetually wet lips splashed onto her cheek and she held him close for a fierce second.

'Den and Ben.' Even though her eyes were closed she could hear Nick's smile as he said the words and lifted Ben up off the bed. 'Come on, buddy, let's get you back.'

Opening her eyes in the darkened room, Eden took a moment or two to orientate herself. Fumbling for her watch, she was bemused to see that it was after six, stunned to realise it was Christmas Day and absolutely horrified to find that Ben wasn't lying beside her.

'He's fine.' The door was pushed open and Nick smiled as he made his way over. 'You were completely out for the count so I took him back to the hospital myself.'

'How was he?' Eden asked, sitting up and trying to give the impression she was, if not entirely together, at least awake!

'Great,' Nick said, his smile widening as he sat on the bed beside her. 'He was just great, Eden, he had the best day. I've never seen a kid so happy and so tired at the same time. Mum printed off a couple of the pictures on the camera and he's lying in his cot back on the ward in his new pyjamas surrounded by his new toys, with his new CD playing and a photo of us all in his hand.'

'I didn't say goodbye,' Eden started, but Nick shook his head.

'You did. You just can't remember it. He gave you a kiss.

'How about some supper?' Nick asked, changing the subject and standing up. 'My sisters' kids are here now and mum's put out a cold buffet.'

'I should get back,' Eden said, but Nick wouldn't hear of it.

'For what, Eden? You can't be on your own on Christmas night.'

'Why not?' Eden shrugged. 'Anyway, once you've given me a lift, you can relax and have a drink, enjoy Christmas night with your family.'

'Stay,' Nick said. 'Stay here the night.'

'With you?' Eden said startled. 'I think that's pushing the deal a bit, don't you?'

'I can sleep on the sofa, or if you'd rather I didn't stay here, I could ask Mum to make up the bed in the spare room over at the house,' Nick offered.

'And ruin your little charade. Oh, come on, Nick, I'm sure you can manage to behave yourself for one night.' She gave a tiny tight smile, a slight edge to her voice, which she quickly modified. 'After all, we both know we're just good friends. It's no big deal.'

But it was.

Even as Eden agreed, even as she casually shrugged and nodded, she could sense the folly of her decision, hear her mother's warning words ringing in her ears. Sure, at the moment the talk was flowing easily and they were the friends that they supposedly always had been, but as she wandered up to the main house and through to the lounge, saying hi to Lily's kids and helping herself to the gourmet buffet, she could feel Nick's eyes on her, feel the strong current of emotion beneath the apparent calm surface, knew deep down inside that things weren't all they seemed—however brief the kiss, something had happened in the car. A point of no return had been passed and tonight things would come to a head.

Tonight, she would find out where she stood.

Lily's children had clearly inherited more than a few Watson genes! Fair and good looking, they were all thoroughly spoiled and had a rather haughty arrogance that Eden assumed was hereditary when you were born with wealth, brains and beauty.

'Are you Uncle Nick's new girlfriend?' Aqua green eyes, identical to her uncle's, narrowed as they eyed Eden. Nick's precocious niece, Harriet, stared rudely at Eden as she shuffled her food around her plate.

'I am,' Eden replied carefully, consoling herself that it was more a lie by omission. After all, she was a girl and, as Nick had pointed out on rather too many occasions, she was also a friend.

'Are you two going to get married?'

'Harriet!' Lily chided as Eden took refuge in her turkey sandwich. 'Don't be so personal!'"

'Well,' Harriet sniffed, 'I heard Nanny say Eden was staying the night in Uncle Nick's room, so I certainly *hope* that they're getting married.'

Fortunately Eden had a mouthful of turkey at the time and was saved from comment, but she was sorely tempted to poke her tongue out at the impossibly bold child and privately wished Lily would put them all to bed. But, as the evening progressed, when it became clear the little treasures were going to be up longer than the adults, Eden finally gave in and relaxed. The plates were cleared away and the corny party games that were so much a part of Christmas unfolded, and Eden found herself joining in. Finally, when she was exhausted, she flopped on the sofa and the yawn she was smothering was interrupted as she laughed out loud as Harriet took to the karaoke machine, belting out a song. Her brothers joined in and, turning, Eden was slightly startled to see a sparkle of tears in Lily's green eyes.

'They're having such a good time,' Lily sniffed. 'I've been so worried about Christmas, wondering how they'd cope, what with their dad and I breaking up and everything—we parted in April,' Lilly added.

'I'm sorry,' Eden responded, feeling horribly out of her depth, wondering just how much, as Nick's *girlfriend,* she should know. 'It must have been a difficult time for you all.'

'It was.' Lily nodded. 'I was running around trying to help Nick. Well, you'd know yourself the state he was in, riddled with guilt, barely sleeping, a complete mess really…'

Lily was too deep in her own thoughts to register Eden's frown. By April Nick had appeared well over Teaghan, in fact, if she remembered correctly, by April Nick had been well on his way to his second girlfriend and coping remarkably well, nothing like the shattered man Lily was portraying.

'I was so busy trying to be there for Nick I didn't realise until it was too late that my own life was falling apart.' This time she did notice Eden's frown. 'Another woman,' Lily explained, with more than a dash of bitterness. 'There I was, feeling sorry for him working so hard, and all the time…' She let out a low mirthless laugh. 'I'm sorry, you don't need to hear all this. I'm just finding it hard to keep the smile painted on at the moment. This time last year I thought I knew where I was going, had this vision of the future, and it didn't include being a single mother.'

'Don't be sorry,' Eden said. 'My friend's going through the same thing at the moment, or at least she thinks she is. She's just hoping to make it through today without upsetting the kids so that they can have a good Christmas, and then she's going to confront him.'

'The things we do for our kids,' Lily said softly, looking over to her brood dancing and laughing as if they didn't have a care in the world. They waved back to their mum who grinned and waved back. Eden could only admire her, just as she had admired Priscilla's mum, women who somehow held it together, somehow kept things going, somehow managed to keep on keeping on, despite being on their own.

The rather sombre mood on the sofa was lifted when Nick finally wrestled the microphone from Harriet, and both women laughed as he showed that he really was the biggest kid in the room, singing loudly, his face one of pure concentration as he tried to follow the little ball over the lyrics on the TV screen as the kids all fell about laughing.

'He can sing, too,' Eden said dryly.

'Yep.' Lily laughed. 'There's nothing my brother can't do if he sets his mind to it. You know, I'm really glad that you two finally got it together.'

Oh, how Eden would have loved to have probed further, how she wanted to ask just what Lily meant. Instead, she had to make do with sipping her drink, grateful for the diversion when Vivian stood up and clapped her hands. 'How about a game of charades?'

'How about we call it a night?' Nick said, coming over and smiling down at Eden who was clearly having trouble keeping her eyes open. A few hours' sleep in the afternoon not quite enough to keep her partying into the small hours.

'You stay,' Eden offered, but Nick shook his head.

'I'm tired, too. I've been up since six.'

The goodnights took for ever and for Eden they were surprisingly hard. The family she had shared Christmas Day with had already wormed their way into her heart and she was achingly aware that it wasn't just goodnight she was saying but probably goodbye, too, that the game of charades had started long, long ago and that her allotted time slot in Nick's vibrant life was nearly over.

'They're great.' Eden smiled when finally they were at the cottage. She felt impossibly shy now, the exhaustion that had sedated her moments ago disappearing, nerves catching up as she faced Nick alone for the first time that day. 'They've all been so nice. I feel absolutely wretched that we've deceived them.'

'What they don't know can't hurt them.' Nick shrugged, pulling a pillow off the bed. 'I'll crash on the sofa.'

'Nick.' Eden gave a dry laugh. 'It's only about two feet long and there aren't exactly a load of spare sheets. Just sleep in the bed.'

'You're sure?'

'So long as you don't snore.' Eden grinned. 'Not that it would matter—I'm so tired I'll be out like a light in a couple of minutes anyway.'

In record time Eden peeled down to her knickers and bra, jumped into the bed and pulled the sheet around her, pretending not to watch as Nick pulled off his shorts and T-shirt, stripping down to his boxers. She was as rigid as a board as Nick slowly climbed into his side of the bed, and as she felt the indentation of the mattress beside her she desperately tried to keep her breathing even as Nick flicked off the light. Not that it made much difference. The full moon over the bay cast a silver glow around the room. 'I've had a fabulous day.'

'So have I,' Nick agreed. 'In fact, it's been the best Christmas I can remember in a long time, and it's thanks to you, Eden.'

'To me?'

She felt him roll over to face her, but still she lay staring at the ceiling, terrified to face him, terrified he might somehow read the blatant desire in her eyes. 'You've made this Christmas really special.'

She didn't know what he meant—whether he was referring to Ben or that he had been saved a few awkward questions from his parents. But his face was right beside her now and she was powerless not to look at him. Her head turned on the pillow and she swallowed hard as she finally faced him, the eyes that had held hers in the car staring down at her. All she could do was gaze back, gaze back at the man she had always, since the moment she'd set eyes on him, loved. Knew there and then that, however much she fought it, however much she didn't understand it, she loved him and probably always would.

'I hate going to bed on Christmas night.' Her voice trembled slightly. 'Hate knowing that Christmas is over.'

'It doesn't have to be,' Nick whispered, and Eden knew exactly what he meant.

For a moment the voice of reason sounded loudly in her mind, her eyes taking in the effortlessly beautiful man that lay before her, a man who had broken more hearts in this last year than she cared to remember, a man who would undoubtedly do the same to her. But need was taking over, tossing aside reason, soothing her with impossible truths—that surely she could deal with this, that one night with Nick was enough to see her through, that because she knew what she was getting into, maybe it wouldn't hurt too much…

'I've always wanted you, Eden.' Nick's voice was thick with emotion, his finger tracing the contour of her cheek, and she screwed her eyes tightly closed, trying to summon up the mental strength to push away what she wanted so dearly. 'I've always wanted you.'

His repetition was enough to convince her, enough to drown out the warning bells, and Eden knew, as she had known since she'd agreed to stay the night, that this moment had been sure to arrive, the thrum of sexual tension that had hung in the air between them demanded this natural conclusion. And more selfishly perhaps, as wonderful a day as she'd had, as much pleasure as there was in giving as well as receiving, Eden wanted her own Christmas magic now, wanted to peel away the wrappers on the one present she'd secretly wished for for so long now, wanted to feel him, to touch him, to be held by him, to know him as only a lover could.

Her eyes stared into the endless depths of his. No need for barriers now, the desire, the passion she felt was there for him to see. He read her so well, his beautiful face swimming out of focus as he softly lowered his lips to hers, the sweet, sweet release of his mouth on hers, the cool of his tongue languorously exploring her mouth a delicious backdrop as their bodies met.

He turned her to face him and she felt his naked skin against hers, the brush of his thigh, the quiet strength of his arm around hers. And all she could do was kiss him back. She relished the feel of his skilful hand on her, expertly undoing her bra. His hand cupped the swollen weight of her full breast, his mouth leaving hers now and exploring the hollows of her throat. Eden revelled in it—his expert touch, the sheer intimacy of sharing a bed, sharing each other.

What she lacked in skill she made up for in willingness. There wasn't a more decadent scent in the world than that of a man in full arousal and she dragged it in, drew on its aphrodisiac power, Nick's sheer naked delight in her body imbuing her with boldness. She ran a tentative finger along the snaking trail of his abdomen that had teased her earlier, fumbling with the elastic of his boxers and sliding them down over his snake-like hips. As Nick wriggled out of their confines she laid eyes on his naked body for the first time.

Eden stumbled into her own paradise, capturing the full delicious length of him in her hand, marvelling at the silky texture, the ominous strength, running a curious, needy, teasing finger in ever-decreasing circles.

'Careful.' Nick's gasp was deep, his breathing rapid, and if ever Eden had felt empowered it was then. For a moment in time at least she held Nick Watson in the palm of her hand, and it was she, Eden, calling the shots.

'Why?'

The innocence of her question belied the wanton smile on her lips, her fingers working intimate magic, feeling the delicious swell of him beneath her touch as Nick's breathing came harder. In the moonlight she could see the planes of his stomach, the golden dust of hair, the generous length of him rising, the pleasure to be had in giving clearer now because Eden's breath was coming faster. His fingers dug into her breasts as his other hand cupped one buttock and it was Nick taking control now, Nick guiding her down onto him, Nick parting the petals of her most intimate place, Nick gazing up at her, holding her steady as she slid down his glorious length.

Capturing the peach of her buttocks, he guided her towards oblivion, that distant beat nearing now, Nick so deep inside her body, inside her head that for a second she resisted the deliciousness, not wanting to give in, not wanting it to be that easy, not wanting it all to be over, feeling the final, thrusting swell of him, the tension in his body beneath her, until Eden gave into her own blessed release, reeling at the force of her orgasm, almost violent in its intensity, robbing her of any semblance of control. Her neck arched back as she dragged him in deeper, a rush of heat fanning her throat, scalding up her spine, making her giddy with sated lust, heady from spent emotions, the last embers of her fire dying down, until spent, utterly exhausted, she lowered her head to his chest, listened to his heart pounding in her ear, the sheen of his damp chest on her cheek mingling with an involuntary tear that slipped out of one eye.

'Hey.' Nick rolled her on her side, wiping the salty tear away with the nub of his thumb.

'I'm fine,' Eden whispered. 'I'm just...' But she didn't finish, couldn't even attempt to find the words to describe how she felt at that moment, lying in bed with Nick's strong arms around her, her body weak, exhausted but supremely satisfied, the breeze of the ceiling fan cooling her warm flesh, a glimpse of a perfection she had always known existed, a feeling of coming home.

'Happy Christmas, Eden,' Nick whispered, kissing the top of her head, dragging her just a fraction closer towards him.

She nodded into the darkness even though his words didn't require a response because, quite simply it was the happiest Christmas she'd known.

CHAPTER NINE

THE shrill ringing of Nick's mobile phone had Eden sitting up before her eyes had even opened. She wrapped the sheet around her and blinked as Nick jumped out of bed and pulled on his boxers, clearly, due to his profession, used to being abruptly woken. Raking his blond hair into almost perfect shape, he headed out into the hall with a very brief 'I won't be long'.

Without even looking at her watch, Eden knew they had both overslept. Bright sunlight streamed through the windows, emphasising the chaos of the discarded clothes and rumpled bed, her naked body beneath the sheet swift confirmation, if Eden had needed it, of what had taken place last night. But instead of reeling in horror, instead of burning with shame and burying her head beneath the sheet, Eden gave a contented sigh and lay back on the pillow, staring at the ceiling and fondly recalling their love-making, remembering the bliss of being held by him, the tenderness in his eyes and, best of all, the depth of his words.

He'd always wanted her.

As he walked back into the bedroom, utterly confident, completely without regret, Eden turned to face him, smiling as he placed a brimming cup of coffee on the bedside table. She took a grateful sip.

'I thought you could use a coffee.' Nick gave a very tight smile and Eden frowned at the stilted voice. 'And then I'm going to have to take you home, I just had a phone call…' He didn't elaborate further, just gave a shrug of his shoulders. 'If you need a couple of paracetamol or anything, I can get them for you.'

'Sorry?' Bewildered, she frowned at him, trying to catch his eye and realising he was avoiding her gaze, the implication behind his offer starting to sink in. 'Nick, I barely had anything to drink last night. I certainly don't have a hangover.'

'I was just offering.' Nick gave another tight shrug and Eden stared at him, perplexed. All she knew was that she had to tell him her truth, couldn't let him think for even a moment that last night was something she regretted, that she could be so easy as to tumble into bed and make love with a man on nothing more than a whim.

'Nick.' Her hand reached out to touch him, capturing his forearm in her fingers, holding it as she spoke, trying somehow to recapture the closeness that had so recently been there. 'I don't regret last night for a moment. Last night wasn't something that happened just because I was feeling tired or emotional or because I'd had a few too many to drink. Last night was because of how I feel about you, how I've *always* felt about you.'

'No!' Shaking his head, he shrugged off her hand, his voice when it came harsh and unfamiliar an utter contrast to the man that had softly held her only a matter of hours ago. 'Eden, we're friends, that's all we've ever been. Last night was just….'

'Just what, Nick?' Eden croaked, eyes wide in her pale face, reeling from the mental slap to her cheek he had just delivered.

'One of those things,' Nick answered, his voice ominously flip. 'Two friends getting a bit emotional, perhaps.'

'Nick.' Eden was struggling to keep her voice down, struggling to fathom the change in him, refusing to believe that things could change so quickly, that he could use her so readily, could toss her aside so easily. 'Last night you said that you'd always wanted me, last night—'

'I didn't.'

His denial floored her, his absolute refusal to admit the truth so incredible that all she could do was stare at him, her mouth open but no words coming out, shame burning onto shame, a dark blush of humiliation spreading over her cheeks.

'I didn't say that, Eden,' Nick insisted, as he looked her straight in the eye and swore that black was white. 'You're getting things mixed up.'

'Oh, I'm mixed up all right!' Eden retorted. 'I'd have to be, to be stupid enough to get into bed with you.'

'Eden.' His voice was incredibly calm, as if it were she, Eden, who was the one with the problem, his barefaced lies, his outright denial, his complete about-turn clearly par for the course for Nick. 'I'm sorry you're feeling this way—'

'No, you're not,' Eden interrupted, her face incredulous as she stared back at this stranger. 'And don't presume to know how I'm feeling, Nick, don't presume a single thing about me ever again.' Draping the sheet around her, Eden stood, and if awkwardness about her breasts had taught her one thing, it was how to pull on a bra and knickers while still covered, those awkward adolescent days at the swimming pool finally coming in useful for something! 'Is that the line you use to get women into bed, then? Make out it actually means something to you, tell whoever it is that you're shagging that night that you've always felt something for them?'

Her words hit their mark. Nick winced at her unfamiliar crudeness, but he didn't back down and for Eden it was the final straw. She hated herself for it, hated the shame that had assailed her, last night sullied now for ever. But if she hated how she felt, at that moment she hated Nick more, and it gave her the strength to continue, to tell him in harsh, whispered tones exactly what she thought of him. Eden was grateful for that moment, glad of a chance to vent her anger, to say what was on her mind before remorse took over, knowing that the next time she faced him it would be she, Eden, looking away.

'You're a user, Nick Watson. I don't know what your problem is, whether you're trying to sleep your way out of your own grief or, worse, you've just forgotten how to care any more.

'Well, don't worry, Nick, I won't be hanging around and making a nuisance of myself. I won't be coming up to you in pubs and trying to buy you a drink, like Tanya was, in some pathetic hope that we can take a trip down memory lane…'

A muscle was leaping in his cheek, but apart from that he was completely motionless.

Emotionless

'You used her, Nick, the same way you used me,'

Eden said, confused, bewildered but completely in control. Not bothering to ask permission, she picked up a comb from his dresser and ran it through her hair before slipping on her sandals. 'Now, can you, please, take me home?'

Because they were nice, decent people who didn't deserve their Christmas to be spoilt, Eden managed a friendly smile and a few polite exchanges as she said farewell to Nick's family, but tears were dangerously close as she walked out to Nick's car. Despite her casual wave as Nick pulled out of the driveway, her whole body was trembling inside, scarcely able to fathom that things could have gone so horribly wrong, that she could have misread him so badly, that the man she loved could treat her like this.

Had loved.

A tiny spark of hope flared inside her as Eden mentally corrected herself—a woman's survival instinct kicking in, the knowledge that she would get through this, that she would come out the other side. And that knowledge gave her the strength to turn to him as he pulled up outside her house, to look him in the eye and keep her voice even as she spoke.

'I'd appreciate it if you didn't tell anyone what happened last night.'

'What do you take me for?' Nick responded, clearly irritated by her request. 'You know I wouldn't say anything.'

'But I don't know you,' Eden pointed out, as his eyes refused to meet hers and he turned his face away. 'I'm looking at you, Nick, and I don't even know you, but I'm telling you this much—I'll smile and I'll be friendly and I'll be completely professional, but don't be fooled, don't for one minute think that I've forgotten what a sleaze you really are. Don't ever, even for a second, think that I've forgiven you.'

Opening the car door, she swung her legs to the pavement outside and stood up, frowning as Nick called her back.

'What?'

'You forgot these.' He still wasn't even looking at her, just staring fixedly at the street ahead as one hand held up the bag with the presents she had acquired yesterday. But in a small defiant gesture Eden declined, instead slamming the car door closed and heading up the drive. She pulled out her keys and, despite her shaking hands, slid the key easily into the lock, opening the door and stepping inside. With the door safely closed behind her she stared at the blinking light on the answering machine, knowing it would be her mother checking that everything was OK, that Eden had heeded the warnings and kept her head.

And only when she heard the purr of his engine, only when she knew that he was really gone, that Nick wasn't coming back, did she let out a strangled sob and finally give in to the tears that had been there since he'd walked back into the bedroom that morning, since he'd offered her a coffee as he'd cruelly ripped out her heart.

CHAPTER TEN

'CAN you believe that all that time he was working at the post office?'

A delighted Becky tucked in the end of the sheet at the bottom of Rory's bed as Eden did the same on the other side, sliding it up under Rory, as he held onto his monkey bar, and tucking it in at the top.

'There was me thinking…well, you know, and all the time he was saving up to buy me these!' Fondly she touched the diamond studs in her ears and Eden gave her patient a small eye roll, smiling as Rory gave one back.

For the most part, this type of conversation took place away from the bedside, but Rory, beyond bored with the hospital routine, delighted in being included in the nurses' more private conversations and loved being made to feel special.

'Aren't they lovely?' Becky said for the hundredth time. 'You should have seen my face when I opened the parcel.'

'They're gorgeous,' Eden agreed. 'Aren't they, Rory?'

'Yep.' Rory nodded, winking at Eden as he spoke. 'You look great in them, Becky!'

The bed changed, Eden and Becky carefully tucked

in Rory's beloved blanket. Since Christmas morning, when he'd received his gift, Rory had been a different boy indeed, the despondent gloom that had shrouded him gone now. He felt safe in the knowledge that he hadn't been forgotten by his peers.

'Are you two both on night shift, then?' Rory checked, and Eden nodded.

'You've got us for the next four nights, so you'd better behave.'

'How come you have to do so many nights, Eden?' Rory asked innocently, completely unaware of the battles that went on behind making up the nursing roster.

'It's just the way my shifts fall,' Eden said casually, smiling as Donna came over to say she was leaving. Her jacket was on and her bag firmly on her shoulder, ready to call it a night after a long late shift.

'But that will mean you have to work Christmas Eve and New Year's Eve,' Rory said loudly, completely un-abashed by Donna's presence, blissfully unaware of the politics of hierarchy. 'It doesn't seem fair that you have to work both.'

'It's no big deal,' Eden said, smothering a smile as Becky gave a delighted grin behind Donna's stern face, both women scarcely able to believe their luck that Donna had heard what Rory had just pointed out!

'Could I have a quick word, you two?'

They headed off to the nurses' station, no doubt, Eden thought, to be told that if they got a quiet few moment there were several hundred cupboards that needed cleaning or a mountain of stores to be put away. But Donna had other things on her mind. 'I've just had a call from Emergency and we're getting a new admission—a five-year-old presenting with her first seizure. She's mildly febrile but, given her age, the emergency staff don't think it was a febrile convulsion. I've allocated ISO 2 for her until we know what's going on.'

Eden jotted the information down on her pad, slightly surprised at the seriousness of Donna's voice and the fact she had pulled both staff members away to tell them about the new admission. PUO, or pyrexia of unknown origin, and a first seizure were both fairly routine, but as Donna continued talking Eden's pen stilled over the paper and, unlike Becky, realised in an instant why they had been called aside.

'Her name's Harriet Mason.'

'Martin?' Becky asked.

'No, Mason,' Donna reiterated. 'You both need to know that this patient is Nick Watson's niece—he's down in Emergency with her now, but even though it's Dr Watson on take tonight, young Harriet has been admitted under the care of Dr Timms so if there are any problems in the night, instead of consulting one of Nick's team, you'll need to ask switch to page one of Dr Timms's team, though naturally, if it's an emergency or she starts seizing, it will just have to be the doctor nearest who treats her. Hopefully it won't be Nick.'

'Hopefully,' Eden agreed. 'How long till Emergency sends her up?'

'I told them to bring her when they're ready. I shouldn't think they'll be very long.'

With that in mind Eden and Becky headed off to set up the room, turning back the bed and putting out a gown and kidney dish in case Harriet felt sick, checking that the oxygen and suction were all connected and in proper working order.

'Do you want to take her?' Eden offered rather too lightly, colouring up a touch as Becky gave her a rather quizzical frown, no doubt puzzled. On night shift it was generally a case of whoever saw the patient first was the one who admitted them, but the last thing Eden needed right now was a close encounter with Nick. It had been hard enough maintaining an air of professionalism the few times their paths had crossed over the last few nights, but the fact his niece was a patient and that Eden knew Lily could only make things difficult.

'Sure,' Becky replied. 'Eden, is everything OK?'

'Everything's fine.' Eden replied stiffly, needlessly rechecking the wall-mounted suction again.

'You never really said how your Christmas went,' Becky pushed. 'What it was like at Nick's.'

'I had a great day,' Eden answered, forcing a smile and turning around. 'Ben did, too. Nick's family made us both very welcome.'

The sound of the ward doors opening thankfully ended the difficult conversation, and Eden peered out of the window. 'Your patient's here, Becky. I'll go and do the meds and then I'll give Rochelle a hand with the obs and settling.'

'Save some work for me,' Becky called, waving to the shadowy figure of the porter pushing the gurney along the darkened ward as Eden dashed off and set about her work. But as much as she feigned indifference, it wasn't only Nick's presence that was upsetting her. The fact Harriet had been taken sick so suddenly had a knot of anxiety tightening in Eden's stomach, coupled with a surge of sympathy for Lily, who had already been through so much this past year, and a genuine hope that Harriet would be OK.

'How's Harriet?' Eden asked a short while later when Becky came to help with the night round, catching up at the nurses' station and checking the IV antibiotics.

'Good,' Becky replied. 'She's on two-hourly neuro obs, her temp's 37.8 and she seems comfortable with it. Her mum's staying the night.' Becky shot her a sideways look. 'She was asking after you. She said you had a great time on Christmas *night!*' Swallowing hard, Eden deliberately ignored Becky's not too subtle push for information but, not remotely fazed, Becky carried on fishing. 'I thought you were only there for a few hours at lunchtime.'

'I stayed for supper,' Eden said lightly, tapping a bubble out of a syringe.

'And breakfast, too?' Becky giggled but it faded midway, seeing the anguished look on Eden's face. 'Oh, Eden, I didn't mean to…' Helplessly she flailed, 'Eden, I had no idea—'

'Leave it, Becky,' Eden's voice came out more sharply than she'd intended, but a ride on the rumour mill was the very last thing she needed right now. 'I mean it, if you breathe a single word to anyone…'

'As if I would,' Becky soothed, concern growing in her kind eyes as Eden rapidly blinked back a threatening tear. 'Eden, what on earth happened?'

'I can't talk about it.' Eden shook her head, taking a tissue from a box and blowing her nose, but Becky was insistent.

'But it might help,' Becky said. 'Look at all my troubles with Hamish. You were there for me, Eden, and you know I'd never breathe a word. And who knows? It might even help.'

'It won't,' Eden said firmly.

'It might.' Instinctively Becky's hand reached for her earlobe, fingering one of the precious jewels Hamish had bought for her, and Eden managed a weak smile.

'Believe me, Becky, there's going to be no little box with a bow for me. I know you'd never breathe a word, I trust you implicitly. It's just that I insisted that Nick not say anything to anyone. It's only fair that I do the same.'

'Fair enough.' Becky nodded 'But if you change your mind, you know that I'm here for you.'

'Thanks,' Eden sniffed. 'Now, let's get on with checking these drugs or we're never going to finish. Poor Rochelle's done practically all the obs herself.'

'She's good, though,' Becky observed. 'Considering she's just a grad nurse, she's incredibly efficient.'

'How's Harriet?'

The sound of Nick's voice behind them had both women jumping, and never had Eden been more grateful that the conversation had shifted to Rochelle. The last thing she needed was for Nick to see how upset she was. Thankfully, Becky had it all under control, turning her smiling face to Nick and somehow managing to greet him in the same easygoing way that she always did.

'She's doing great, Nick,' Becky answered, as Eden busied herself with the IV drugs, laying out the open prescription charts and placing the kidney dishes with the checked medication on top, then attaching a little sticky note to each kidney dish with the schedule time clearly visible. Impeccably organised, especially where medication was concerned, Eden was glad of the distraction, glad to be able to busy herself as Nick and Beck chatted on. 'Her obs are still stable, just a little bit febrile—37.8 I've given her a drink of milk and she's settling to sleep.'

'And Lily?' Nick checked. 'My sister?'

'Like any other mum, worried out of her mind and trying not to show it. Harriet's in ISO 2.'

'Thanks.' Nick nodded, but didn't head off. Instead, he tapped Harriet's details into the computer and checked to see whether or not any labs were back on her. 'You know that she's due for an EEG in the morning?'

'All booked.' Becky smiled. 'Any blood results back yet?'

'Just her U and Es,' Nick replied, 'which are all normal. Emergency's really busy, so I think Harriet's bloods will take a while to come back. Can you let me know when they do?'

'Sure,' Becky answered, looking up as Eden came over.

'Ready to give the IVs?' Eden asked, then, smiling casually, she greeted Nick. 'Hi, Nick, I'm sorry to hear about your niece.'

'Thanks.' Nick forced a smile of his own. 'I'd better go and say goodnight to her and then I'll be in my office tonight. Call me if there's any change.'

'We will,' Eden assured him.

As he marched off Becky let out a tiny gasp of admiration. 'Wow, you're good. Talk about laid-back. How on earth did you manage it?'

Eden gave a mirthless laugh. 'A full year of practice, Becky.'

* * *

The round took for ever and by the time the charts were all filled in and ruled off for the next day, it was already half past two.

'Do you want to go for your supper break?' Becky offered Eden as a tired-looking Rochelle returned from hers.

'You go,' Eden answered. 'Cot three's due to wake any moment. I'm just warming a bottle for him in anticipation.'

Becky stood up gratefully, smothering a yawn as she did so. 'I won't say no. I'm exhausted. I'll just stretch out in the staffroom. If I'm not back on time, come and call me.'

'Will do,' Eden answered, after all her years in nursing still baffled how anyone could manage to sleep on their break and come back to work afterwards saying that they felt better for it. Eden had tried it once and had sworn never to do it again, preferring to use her break to flick through a few magazines or read a book. 'Is there anything that needs doing while you're gone?'

Becky shook her head. 'I'm up to date. Just some oxygen sats to be done on cot one at three a.m.' Her face suddenly dropped. 'Oh, and Harriet will need another set of neuro obs at three. I can stay if you like and go after—'

'I'll be fine,' Eden assured her, consoling herself that Lily would no doubt be asleep. She was determined not to let her personal life interfere with her work. 'You go. Enjoy your break.'

As Eden had predicted, Justin awoke a couple of minutes later and because she was the most senior RN on the ward Eden put on a gown and bought him to the desk, cuddling him as she gave him his bottle.

'He's been here for ages,' Rochelle said, peering at

her notes. 'Why has he been kept in so long? There doesn't seem to be anything wrong with him.'

'It's complicated,' Eden replied warily, smiling down at the baby as he guzzled his bottle. 'Justin was bought in a few weeks ago with failure to thrive. He was losing weight and not taking his feeds well.'

'Well, that's certainly improved.'

'That's exactly the problem,' Eden responded. 'He put on weight and was discharged, only to present to his GP a couple of weeks later with further weight loss. He's been in all this time having tests to see what the problem could be.'

'But they've all come back as normal,' Rochelle said, staring down at her notes. 'Clearly he's taking his feeds well now, so why don't they just send him home?'

'Here's perhaps not the best place to talk about it,' Eden said tactfully, 'but when Becky gets back from her break, if we get a chance we can go into the office.'

'Oh.' Rochelle's eyes widened, staring from Eden to Justin and shaking her head. 'But his mum adores him,' Rochelle said.

'We'll talk later,' Eden said again, because the nurses' station, even if it was in the middle of the night, wasn't the place to discuss such things.

Jenny did love Justin, there wasn't any doubt on that score, but for so far inexplicable reasons whenever the child had been left in her care, he had not only failed to thrive but had actually lost weight and was suffering from malnutrition to the point where he had rickets from a vitamin D deficiency. After exhaustive investigations the medical and social workers were coming to the unpalatable conclusion that young Justin might be a victim of a rare and controversial syndrome by the name of Munchausen's by proxy—that his mother was somehow using Justin as a tool to satisfy her own attention-seeking needs, causing harm to her child to fill whatever it was that was missing in her own life.

The nurses' station certainly wasn't the place to talk about it.

'Do you want me to do the oxygen saturations on the baby?' Rochelle offered as Eden rose to take Justin back to his cot. 'And then I can do the neuro obs.'

'I'll do the neuro obs,' Eden said, tactfully not adding that Nick would rather one of the more experienced staff members looked after his niece. Given the fact that he was the consultant on the ward, Eden could understand the unspoken request.

Never had she been more grateful for that split-second decision as she crept into the room to perform Harriet's neurological observations. A gnawing sense of foreboding niggled at her as she flicked on the overhead light and saw the awkward angle of her head on the pillow, but Eden didn't let it show. Instead, she smiled as an exhausted Lily stretched in the reclining chair by the bed and yawned a greeting.

'Hi, Lily,' Eden said. 'I'm just going to do Harriet's neuro obs and then I'll let you get back to sleep.' Gently she shook Harriet on the shoulder, calling her name a couple of times until Lily herself intervened, rousing her daughter from her deep sleep. 'Come on, honey,' Lily called. 'You remember Eden. She's just going to do your obs again. Remember how they shine that light in your eyes and you have to answer some questions?'

'Hi, Harriet,' Eden said softly as those familiar green eyes stared back at her. 'Do you remember me?'

A confused look flickered across the child's face and she shook her head slightly.

'It's the uniform,' Lily said firmly. 'Harriet, it's Eden. Remember she was with us for Christmas?'

'Do you know where you are, Harriet?' Eden asked, that niggling feeling increasing as the same confused eyes stared back at her.

'What's your name?' Eden asked, desperate to hear the little girl speak, her breath stuck in her throat until finally Harriet softly mouthed the word.

'She's tired,' Lily said quickly. 'She was at her father's all day. I think he took them to the beach. She'll be much brighter by the morning.'

'Harriet, can you squeeze my hands for me?' Eden said, placing her hands in the little girl's and feeling the pressure that she applied. 'Good,' she said, pulling back the sheet. 'Can you wiggle your toes for me? That's a good girl,' Eden encouraged her. 'Now, I want you to lift your legs up for me.' Putting her hand on Harriet's calf, she encouraged her further, noticing with growing disquiet that Harriet had already fallen back to sleep. 'Come on, Harriet, push my hand away.'

'She's exhausted,' Lily insisted. 'Look, I really think that she needs to sleep, Eden. I know you have to do these obs but surely, given that it's three a.m....'

'I'm nearly finished,' Eden replied. 'I'm just going to shine a light in your eyes, Harriet, and then I'll let you rest.'

Shining the torch into Harriet's eyes, Eden didn't comment as Lily replaced the sheet around her daughter.

'Can I turn off the light?' Lily asked, and Eden nodded, slightly taken back by Lily's lack of concern.

'Sure,' Eden answered, frowning as she left the room and heading straight for the telephone. But even before she'd put out the page for Dr Timms's registrar, Nick was at the desk, obviously having set his watch alarm. He asked her how Harriet's obs had been.

'I'm just paging Dr Timms's registrar to discuss them,' Eden answered carefully, unsure how she should proceed, acutely aware that in this instance Nick was far from objective but wanting a doctor's opinion all the same.

'What's wrong Eden?' Nick's voice was not to be argued with. 'I'm not going to jump in with all guns blazing, I just need to know what's going on. Why are you paging the registrar? What's the problem with Harriet?'

'I'm not sure,' Eden admitted. 'I didn't actually see her on admission because she's Becky's patient, but she's at supper break now. I've just gone to do Harriet's two-hourly obs and…' Her voice trailed off, and she chewed her bottom lip as she attempted to voice her concern. 'On paper she seems fine, and admittedly it's the first time I've really seen her since she arrived from Emergency, but to me she seems altered.'

Nick gave her a worried look. 'Altered' was exactly that—an altered state of consciousness, a slight inappropriateness that wasn't always definable. 'She's answering questions, and she's obeying commands, but she just doesn't seem right. There's also a slight nystagmus.'

Nick's concerned frown deepened a fraction—nystagmus was a flickering of the eyes that was often a normal presentation in people but it could also indicate a neurological problem. 'I've had a quick look at the admission notes and it hasn't been recorded.'

'Because there wasn't one,' Nick said, dragging in a deep breath. 'What does Lily say?'

'I didn't mention the nystagmus to her but she didn't seem concerned at all. Lily seems to think that she's just tired. Perhaps she was the same on admission,' Eden offered, but privately she doubted it. Becky had given no indication of concern. 'Maybe I'm just overreacting.'

'I hope so,' Nick said. 'I'm going to check on her.'

'I'll come with you,' Eden said, calling Rochelle away from the saturations she was checking. 'Rochelle, I've just paged Dr Timms's registrar. When he calls back, can you ask him to come and review Harriet Mason?'

'What shall I say is wrong?'

'Just say that Dr Watson is in with Harriet now and that he'd like a doctor to come and assess her.' Eden called over her shoulder, and headed off to Harriet's room. But midway she halted, a gut feeling that couldn't be explained stopping her in her tracks. Heading back to the desk, she summoned Rochelle again.

'Go and knock on the staffroom door and ask Becky to come back from her break.'

'She's just gone back to sleep, Nick,' Lily was saying as Eden slipped into the room. 'Can't we just let her rest?'

'We need to check her,' Nick said firmly, running a careful eye over Harriet who was seemingly dozing on the bed.

But Eden just knew Nick was seeing the same as her, the awkward position that she was lying in, her head rotated awkwardly on the pillow. Lily was clearly less than impressed with the further intrusion and sucked in her breath, in irritation as Nick pulled back the sheet, gently rousing the little girl and noting her reaction to verbal stimulation.

'Hi, Harriet.' His voice was far less formal and he repeated the greeting a couple of times before gently shaking Harriet's shoulder.

'She's exhausted, Nick,' Lily argued, and Eden turned to the irritated woman, confused as to why, when Lily was a doctor herself, she would argue the point over something so that was obviously necessary. Then Eden realised that it was fear talking, that Lily quite simply didn't want to admit to the possibility that Harriet was really unwell. 'That's why she's not waking up—the poor kid is worn out.'

'Perhaps,' Eden conceded, 'and Nick will take into consideration the fact that Harriet is very tired, but it is imperative that he does a full examination on your daughter before we leave her to rest.'

A tiny nod from Lily indicated her consent and, knowing it was better for the young patient if her mother was included, Eden guided her closer to the bedside as Nick commenced his examination. Even though not by even a flicker did Nick betray his anxiety, as he moved the little girl's head to her chest Eden could tell that he was concerned. She'd worked alongside Nick for a long time now and could read from the tiny subtle shifts in his expressions, the way the lines that fanned around his eyes deepened, that Nick wasn't at all happy with what he was seeing.

'How are you feeling, Harriet?' He smiled down at his niece, who just stared back at him.

'Harriet, I need for you to talk to me. Are you sore anywhere?'

Again Harriet didn't answer, just stared back at her uncle with confused, anxious eyes.

'She answered you before?' Nick checked, and Eden gave a worried nod. 'Yes, well, when I say she answered, she just mouthed her name.'

'Harriet.' Lily's voice wobbled slightly. 'Answer Nick for me, honey.'

'Nick.' Something in Eden's voice dragged his attention away from the child. He watched where Eden's finger was pointing—a tiny red patch of skin no bigger than a pinhead with a small clear blister above it.

'That wasn't there before?' Nick asked, and there was definitely an urgent note to his voice now.

'No.' Eden shook her head. 'When I did her obs I checked for any rash. Let's sit you forward, Harriet,' she said immediately, not waiting for Nick, knowing he would want to examine Harriet's torso. 'There's another one,' she said, pointing to a small blister on her back as Nick looked behind Harriet's ears. 'And a few coming out here.'

'What going on?' Lily asked, staring at the faint rash on Harriet's body. 'What have you found…?' Her voice trailed off as she saw the emerging rash on her daughter, a hand smothering a sob as Nick flashed a torch in Harriet's eyes and repeated the reflex response check with a tendon hammer, gently reassuring the little girl when she let out a moan of protest.

'It's OK, Harriet, you can rest now. I'm just going to have a word with your mum and then I'll be back. Eden, can you get some acyclovir IV started?'

'She's got chickenpox, hasn't she?' Lily gulped. 'And if she's having this type of reaction it means that—'

'We'll talk outside,' Nick broke in quickly. Lily's tension could only upset Harriet further and Eden bit hard on her lip as he guided the frantic woman outside, pressing the buzzer on the wall three times in a code that told the ward that a member of staff required some rapid assistance. The emergency bell was only used when the situation was extremely serious.

'What's happening?' 'Rochelle asked.

'Have you called Becky?' Eden asked, barely able to disguise her irritation when Rochelle shook her head.

'I was on the phone with Dr Timms's reg. He's at home but he's going to come in soon.'

'What do you need?' Becky was back, summoned by the emergency bell and awake in a second.

'Her neuro obs are decreasing. Nick just examined her and it looks as if she's got chickenpox. Could you get me some acyclovir and a flask of saline? Nick will write it up when he gets back. And could you get the lab on the phone for Nick? He's going to want to speak to them.'

'Chickenpox?' Rochelle questioned, clearly bemused at her colleague's behaviour, but Eden didn't have the time to enlighten her. 'I'll explain later. Tell the switchboard to urgently page Dr Timms's registrar and let him know he needs to be here now!'

Even though it had only been fifteen minutes since Eden had done a set of observations she repeated the process, checking Harriet's vital signs. Though her pulse and blood pressure were relatively stable, Eden noted a marked decrease in her respiratory rate.

'Harriet!' Eden's voice was sharp, attempting to rouse the girl verbally. When the child responded to neither her voice nor a shoulder shake, she tweaked Harriet on her earlobe, calling her name in an urgent voice.

'Harriet!' Rubbing her sternum, Eden watched as Harriet's arms made only a small attempt to push her away, and Eden knew that her condition had deteriorated rapidly in just a few moments and that a rapid response was needed. Pushing the bell three times, she applied oxygen to the girl as Rochelle again dashed to the door.

'Get Nick—now!' Eden ordered. 'Actually…' She went over Harriet's symptoms in her head. Even though there was a consultant on the ward, Eden made a rapid decision. 'Get Nick in here and when you've done that call the medical emergency team and bring the crash trolley to the bedside,' she ordered, realising that the team needed to be summoned as in a matter of seconds Harriet could further deteriorate and require intubation.

'Shouldn't you run it by Nick?' Rochelle asked, but Eden flashed her a firm look. 'Just do it now, and get someone to stay with the mother.'

Attaching the oxygen saturation probe to Harriet she saw that despite the oxygen her saturation was only on ninety per cent, which was rather low. Flashing a torch into her eyes, Eden noted that her pupil responses were present but the little girl who had been talking only fifteen minutes ago, who had been celebrating Christmas and singing her heart out just a few days ago, was now slipping into unconsciousness. Eden felt her throat tighten as Harriet's body stiffened beneath her. The seizure she had anticipated had begun. Rolling Harriet swiftly onto her side, Eden willed the overhead chimes to go off, for help to arrive, relief flooding her when she heard Nick's footsteps and the door burst open as he rushed in.

'She just started seizing,' Eden explained. 'I've called a MET.' She held her breath for a second after she said it.

Rochelle hadn't been far off the mark when she'd queried whether Eden should run it by Nick first, given that he was on the ward. But Nick just gave a nod. He closed his eyes for a fraction of a second, as if willing his mind to clear, as if summoning the strength to push emotion aside and deal with this dire situation objectively. And even if she hated him for all he had done to her, Eden felt sorry for him now. To witness his own niece so desperately ill and to be the only doctor nearby would be a horrendous burden.

As the chimes went off overhead Becky arrived with the large red crash trolley, pulling up diazepam for Nick to give intravenously. But despite the drug, Harriet's seizure continued, and even though Eden knew the chimes that were ringing overhead were being played throughout the entire hospital, that at this very second the medical emergency team would be running towards the children's ward right now, the alarm on Harriet's oxygen saturation machine was going off too now. Her saturations were dangerously low and despite the diazepam, she continued to seize.

Rochelle was swinging into action now, moving chairs and tables out of the way to make room for the large trolley that was being wheeled in. And even though the emergency personnel were beginning to arrive, the situation was becoming more dire as Harriet's saturations dropped even lower. Nick started to pull off the bedhead and remove the pillows from under Harriet's head as Eden pulled open the intubation tray. She was grateful when the anaesthetist arrived. Nick at least would be spared from having to intubate his own niece.

'What's the story?' the anaesthetist asked, making straight to the head of the bed, assessing the situation with calm, knowing eyes and listening intently as Nick bought him up to speed.

'Five-year-old, admitted with first seizure. Neuro obs have rapidly deteriorated and we noted a classic chickenpox rash. She started seizing again.' Nick hesitated for a second. 'She's also my niece.'

'Should you be in here, then, Nick?' the anaesthetist asked, but didn't wait for an answer, his mind solely on the patient.

'How long has she been seizing now?' the anaesthetist asked, his finger probing the pulse in Harriet's neck then listening to her chest for air entry as Harriet's tiny body continued to convulse.

'Six minutes,' Eden responded, glancing down at her watch. 'She's had three lots of diazepam.'

'She can't keep on like this,' The anaesthetist was rummaging through the crash trolley, expertly pulling up the drugs of his choice. 'Let's paralyse and intubate. Sister, can I have some carotid pressure, please? Nick can you—?'

'I'll stay, thanks, Vince.' Nick's voice was calm and measured and completely in control but, glancing up briefly, Eden could see the sheer terror in his eyes and she was grateful when he stepped to the back of the room. He had realized that heroics weren't needed now, that the best he could do for his niece was stand back quietly and trust her life to his colleagues.

Eden's heart was in her mouth as Vince gently extended the little girl's neck. Eden applied the necessary pressure to allow the endotracheal tube to pass more easily and with her other hand passed him a laryngoscope, which allowed him to visualise the throat as he passed in the ET tube. His fingers snapped impatiently for Eden to pass the connections to the oxygen supply, waiting for the bag to inflate. It probably only took a couple of seconds but it felt like for ever.

'Has she had any acyclovir?' Vince asked, and Eden shook her head.

'We only just noticed the rash—'

'It's ready,' Becky broke in. 'It's all been checked.'

'Then let's get it started,' the anaesthetist said grimly. 'Can you ring ICU and let them know I'm bringing her straight up?' His foot was already kicking off the brake and Eden moved quickly, disconnecting the oxygen from the wall and attaching it to the portable cylinder, moving the monitors and dripstand onto the bed to prepare it for transfer as Becky dashed off to alert ICU.

'What's happening?' Dr Timms's registrar stood breathlessly at the door after a mad dash from the car park, his car keys jangling in his hand.

'I'll tell you on the way.'

'ICU wants ten minutes,' Becky called as she ran along the ward. Everywhere lights were flicking on, mothers alerted by the overhead chimes and commotion, babies abruptly woken from sleep crying for attention, but for now the sole concern was Harriet.

'ICU can keep on wanting,' Vince responded, continuing to move along the corridor and bagging Harriet as the rest of the MET staff pushed the bed, one running ahead to hold the lift doors open. 'This child doesn't have a spare ten minutes.' He glanced over at Nick, whose face was seemingly impassive, but Eden knew he was lacerated with pain. 'I'm sorry, Nick, I forgot you were here.'

'Just do what you can, Vince.' Nick's lips were white. 'Don't worry about me.'

Becky was grabbing Harriet's notes, running to catch up with the entourage, and Rochelle was wheeling the crash trolley back to the nurses' station. For a small slice of time, Eden and Nick were left alone, and for the first time in her life Eden truly didn't know what to say, didn't know how on earth to comfort him. Dragging her hair tie out, she ran a helpless hand through her hair and a tiny ghost of a smile dusted his taut lips at the familiar gesture.

'You don't have to say anything, Eden. This isn't anyone's fault.'

'I know that,' Eden choked. 'I just…' Helplessly she stood there, wanting so much to reach out and comfort him, to somehow convey that she felt his pain, but those days were long gone now. Her fists bunched at her sides as she struggled to keep her emotions in check. 'I'd better tell Lily what's going on.'

'I already know.' A tiny figure emerged from the darkness, fear, pain and grief etched on every feature. Nick was on the ball because just as Lily's knees buckled he caught her. Strong arms wrapping around his sister, he guided her down the long lonely walk to ICU and all Eden could do was stand there and watch them leave.

CHAPTER ELEVEN

'BUT how?' For what seemed the hundredth time Rochelle voiced the question that no one could really answer as Eden struggled to feed a restless Ben.

The ward had long since been cleaned up, the crash trolley restocked. In theory Eden could probably have gone for her break, but sitting down and flicking through a magazine held no particular charm right now so instead she was attempting to settle Ben, who no doubt was picking up on Eden's heart still thumping in her chest and refusing to take his bottle. Rochelle stood at Ben's doorway, clearly stunned at the rapid turn of events and desperately needing to talk.

'I mean, the poor kid's only got chickenpox!'

'It's very common.' Eden nodded. 'Unfortunately, in some cases the side effects can be severe.'

'But it all happened so quickly,' Rochelle said.

'That's the way it is with children,' Eden explained. 'They can hold their vital signs for a long time, appear relatively well, but when their condition deteriorates it can be extremely rapid. That's why we do such frequent observations on the children's ward—they can't always tell you themselves that they're not feeling well.'

'If I'd done Harriet's obs, would I have picked it up? I mean, his mum's a doctor and she didn't seem concerned. What chance would I have had?'

'I don't know,' Eden admitted, 'but I can guarantee that next time you do a set of neuro obs and every time for the rest of your nursing career, you'll remember what just happened and be on the lookout for anything that doesn't seem quite right.'

'He's nearly asleep,' Rochelle observed, smiling from the doorway at Ben. 'He likes it when you're talking.'

'He does,' Eden said fondly gazing down at a now relaxed Ben. His eyes were closed and he was sucking hard on his bottle. She took the opportunity to explain in a bit more detail what had just happened to Harriet.

'As I said, chickenpox can have some quite nasty side effects, one of them being viral encephalitis, which means an inflammation of the brain. Now, in Harriet's case, the inflammation caused the seizure that brought her to Emergency. Often, first seizures are sent home and followed up with outpatient appointments, but because Harriet was febrile it was decided to keep her in hospital for observation.'

'But she didn't even have a rash.'

'She didn't have to,' Eden patiently explained. 'The fact she was febrile and had had a seizure indicated there was some type of infection going on. It could have been nothing more than a mild ear infection, but until a diagnosis was made no one could be sure. At the back of the doctor's mind would have been the possibility if not of viral encephalitis then certainly meningitis—that's why she was kept in isolation until we knew exactly what was going on.'

'But will she be OK?'

And that was the one question, as much as she wanted to, Eden couldn't really answer.

'I don't know, Rochelle,' Eden admitted. 'They've started her on some strong antiviral medication and they'll probably give her some steroids to reduce the inflammation to her brain, but it really is going to be a case of wait and see.'

'Could she have brain damage?' Rochelle asked, and even though her question was merited, Eden closed her eyes in horror, scarcely able to comprehend herself that the vibrant beautiful girl she had shared Christmas with now lay in Intensive Care in a critical condition.

'She might,' Eden said softly. 'But there's one good thing about working with children. As quickly as they decline, they also pick up very rapidly. Let's just hope that's the case with Harriet.'

But despite her confident words, despite the hope she tried to imbue, as the night progressed, as notes were written and the morning round commenced, the horror of what had taken place never left her mind. Her heart ached for Lily and what she must be going through, and even though she was loathe to admit it, even to herself, she felt desperate for Nick, for all he had been through and for all he was suffering now.

When handover had been given and the day staff had been bought up to date with the night's events, Eden pulled on her jacket and slipped into Ben's room for a quick goodbye. She knew she had to go up and check on Harriet's progress before she left the hospital.

She knew that, despite her own pain, she couldn't walk away without letting Nick know she was thinking of him.

Bracing herself, Eden entered Intensive Care. Introducing herself to the nurse in charge and checking it was OK, she made her way over to Harriet's cubicle, standing quietly outside the glass window and staring in.

'How is she?' Eden asked as Lavinia, one of the charge nurses she vaguely knew, came up beside her.

'About as sick as a five-year-old can be. The mother's just gone to ring the father. Apparently they're separated. Imagine the poor guy when he picks up the phone and hears this news.'

'How's Nick?' Eden asked, already knowing the answer.

'Beside himself, of course. He thinks that he should somehow have worked out what was wrong sooner. He's berating himself that the acyclovir wasn't started down in Emergency. As if, I told him, we're going to start acyclovir on every febrile child that comes into the hospital.'

'He's just scared, I guess,' Eden said, staring through the glass at Nick. Draped in a white gown and even with a mask covering his face, the raw anguish was visible in his eyes and all she could do was repeat Rochelle's words.

'The poor kid's only got chickenpox.'

The worst thing about night shift was Eden's total inability to sleep during the day, and that morning was no exception. Lying on her back, she stared wide-eyed at the ceiling, going over and over in her head the previous night's events, wondering over and over if something—anything—could have been done that might somehow have changed the outcome.

'Oh, Nick.' The words shivered on her lips, the face that had haunted her for days swimming into focus every time she closed her eyes. Even though she was still reeling from his callous rejection, she was completely unable to hate him. Her mind was a horrible jumbled mess. She was furious with herself for crying over someone she didn't mean a thing to yet unable to stop.

Giving in, Eden padded into the kitchen. The house was impossibly quiet without Jim. She dropped two pieces of bread into the toaster and pulled some margarine and Vegemite out of the fridge, comfort food definitely the order of the day! There was something infinitely comforting about tea and toast in bed. She stared unseeing at a midmorning chat show on her faithful portable TV, watching as a relationship guru shared his wisdom, listening to the appalling mess people made of their lives and realising she'd done exactly the same.

Becky was wrong, Eden decided, her mind finally made up. Placing her plate on the bedside table and flicking off the television, she shut down other people's problems and for once really concentrated on her own.

The hardest thing wasn't walking away, it was staying to watch love die.

Her mind made up, Eden closed her eyes.

The first real sleep she'd had since Boxing Day finally washed over her.

CHAPTER TWELVE

'Is this about Ben?' Donna stared at the sheet of paper in front of her, rereading the neat handwriting once again before looking over to where Eden sat at the other side of the desk.

'In part,' Eden admitted. 'But there are other factors involved.'

'Are you going to enlighten me?' Donna asked, frowning as Eden shook her head. 'You're not giving the ward much notice, Eden.'

'I've got a week off after tonight,' Eden pointed out. 'And after that I've still got four weeks' annual leave owing. I know it might be difficult to fill the roster, but—'

'I'm not worried about the roster,' Donna broke in. 'I'm worried about you, Eden. I can fill a few shifts, but I can't replace a dedicated, knowledgeable paediatric nurse so easily. I thought you were happy here.'

'I am,' Eden answered, desperately trying to keep her voice even, to keep her emotions in check and just make it through this awkward interview. 'Or, rather, I have been. I just think I need a change.'

'And you have to leave tonight?' Donna frowned. 'On New Year's Eve?'

'I know it's a lot to ask—but I just want a fresh start.' Eden swallowed. 'I saw a position advertised in the intensive care unit at the children's hospital. I want a fresh challenge.'

'You're sure?' Donna checked. 'There's nothing I can say to make you change your mind?'

'Nothing,' Eden gulped, and she braced for the protest, for Donna to dig deeper, to try to get to the bottom of things. Instead, she was standing up and offering her hand, which almost reluctantly Eden took.

'Then I wish you well, Sister. I'll be happy to provide a reference for you.'

'I'm sorry if I'm leaving you short,' Eden attempted, slightly taken back by the ease in which Donna had accepted the news.

'We'll manage.' Donna smiled. 'I need nurses who want to be here, Eden.'

'I know.' Eden nodded.

'You haven't exactly given us time to arrange a leaving do or a collection—'

'I don't want anything,' Eden broke in. 'I just want to slip away.'

'Run away perhaps?' Donna said, raising an eyebrow, but when Eden didn't react instead she offered her hand. 'Good luck, Eden.'

And that, Eden realised, as she shakily made her way into her last handover, was that. No fanfares, no tearful goodbyes. She could walk away with her head held high.

So why didn't it feel good?

* * *

'I don't believe her,' Becky huffed as Donna marched off the ward without even stopping to say goodbye. 'It's New Year's Eve, for goodness' sake, and she expects us to take the Christmas decorations down.'

'Well, we're not,' Eden said. Becky had, no doubt, been expecting a small murmur of protest, but there was a definite note of defiance in Eden's voice that had Nick, who was on the phone, looking up. 'It's still Christmas. Decorations aren't supposed to be taken down until Twelfth Night, which isn't until the sixth of January.'

'Try telling that to Donna,' Becky said, rolling her eyes.

'I will,' Eden responded. 'There's no way I'm taking them down. It's bad luck.'

'Actually,' Nick corrected her, covering the mouthpiece with his hand 'it's bad luck to leave them up after the sixth.'

'Same thing,' Eden retorted.

'Hey, I'm on your side,' Nick sighed, putting down the phone. 'Frankly, I could use all the luck I can get tonight. They're going to extubate Harriet.'

'I heard,' Eden said. 'She seems to be responding well to treatment.'

Nick gave a very tentative nod. 'We'll know more once they take the tube out. There's still a long way to go, but at least she's fighting. I'll be in Intensive Care if you need me.'

'We won't,' Becky responded. 'For once the ward's just about empty and I, for one, intend to make the most of it. We deserve a quiet night after the last few we've had.'

'Well, I'm off,' Nick answered, clicking off his pen and placing it in his top suit pocket. For an indulgent moment Eden stared, capturing this moment, tracing his features with her eyes, trying to somehow etch them on her mind, knowing that it might be the last time she saw him. 'And don't you dare take down those decorations. Happy New Year, ladies.'

'Happy New Year, Nick,' Becky said. 'We'll ring Intensive Care later and see how Harriet is. Good luck!'

Maybe he felt the weight of her stare, maybe he sensed there was something going on, but Nick stared at Eden for a long moment, frowning slightly at her pensive face.

'Good luck with Harriet,' Eden croaked.

'Thanks, Eden…' Still he stood there and Eden was sure there was something he was about to say, but whatever it was he chose otherwise, giving her the briefest of nods and heading off to Intensive Care.

Ben seemed to know something was up and refused to go to sleep, giggling and waving every time Eden walked past the room. When he didn't know she was watching he played peek-a-boo with the mirror that was attached to his cot, the absolute cutest he had ever been, as if making some last-ditch effort to win her heart.

'Den,' he squealed when she finally came into the room and pulled on her gown, going through the familiar routine of changing his nappy before feeding him, catching legs that were kicking their protest and dressing him in his new pyjamas, brushing his teeth for him. Finally, when all the chores were done, she cuddled him close and gave him his bottle.

'You're going to be fine,' Eden said firmly, as if to

convince herself. 'Donna was telling me this evening that Lorna's found a wonderful new home for you. There will be lots of other children there, lots of friends to play with.' Tears that couldn't fall tonight threatened to choke her, a residential unit the very last thing she had wanted for Ben. If Eden hadn't been sure, she knew then she was making the right decision. She couldn't bear the thought of seeing Ben when, as was inevitable with his condition, he was readmitted, knowing that the one thing the little guy really deserved, really needed, was going to be denied.

That he'd never have a family.

'Fifteen minutes till midnight,' Becky said as Eden came and sat down, taking a grateful drink of the coffee Becky had made her. 'And the Christmas tree lights are still on. We're going to be in trouble in the morning.'

'We'd better take them down before the morning,' Eden sighed.

'What happened to your sudden streak of assertiveness?' Becky grinned.

'It scared the life out of me. You know how useless I am at saying no. Do you mind if I take first break?' Eden asked. 'I might head up to the roof and watch the fireworks over the harbour.'

'Go for it,' Becky said, then screwed up her nose. 'Bloody fireworks. I refuse to watch them on principle. Imagine burning thousands of dollars that could be spent providing meals for some poverty-stricken country.'

The diamond rocks in Becky's ears would provide a whole new irrigation system, Eden felt like pointing out, but realised her bad mood wasn't Becky's fault. Eden didn't say anything, just pulled on her cardigan and headed out of the ward, taking a moment to stop and stare at Ben, who was finally asleep, the sheet she had tucked around him discarded on the floor, his little bottom sticking up in the air, thumb firmly in mouth. Eden thought her heart would break.

The roof of the hospital was a fairly open secret and Eden half expected to find a crowd gathered there to watch the New Year firework display, but clearly the other wards weren't as quiet as the paediatric unit tonight and Eden stood alone, staring out to Sydney Harbour, seeing the elegant shape of the Opera House and the impressive sight of the Sydney Harbour Bridge. Hundreds of boats were out on the water in prime vantage points. Despite the warm night air, Eden shivered, pulling her cardigan tighter around her, jumping when she heard footsteps coming up behind her. Even before she turned Eden knew it was Nick.

'How is she?' Eden asked, and for a moment she thought the news must be bad when she saw the sparkle of tears in his eyes, the sheer tension in his face. But he gave a small hesitant nod, even managed a smile.

'So far so good.' His voice was thick with emotion. 'There's still a hell of a long way to go, but her eyes are open, she's moving her arms and legs and she recognises us all.'

'Thank God,' Eden whispered, and Nick nodded.

'I really thought we were going to lose her, Eden. When you think how bad it could have been, this really is a Christmas miracle.'

Eden didn't answer, just stared out into the night sky, waiting for the firework display to start, praying for this year to be over so she could get on with her life, yet terrified all the same, wondering how her life would be this time next year.

'You're leaving, aren't you?' His question was direct and Eden stiffened beside him.

Her first reaction was to deny it but, a useless liar at the best of times, finally she gave a short nod. 'I asked Donna not to say anything.'

'She didn't,' Nick answered. 'I just guessed.'

'How?'

'I was watching you work earlier. I don't know, something told me you were preparing to leave.' He hesitated for the longest time. 'Is it because of what happened between us?'

'It's because of a lot of things,'

'Ben?' Nick asked, and Eden nodded.

'I know now why we're not supposed to get involved. It isn't just for the patient's protection, it's for us as well.'

'You can still see him, Eden,' Nick pointed out. 'You can provide respite care, take him out for a day, even if he is in a children's home.'

'It isn't enough,' Eden choked. 'I thought it would be, thought if I could just have a little piece of him, make him happy some of the time, then that would make things better. But it hasn't and I just can't do it any more. I think it would be easier for me if I didn't see him at all.'

And for a second there Eden truly didn't know if she was talking about Ben or Nick, her agony blurring things into one painful mass.

'When do you leave?' Nick asked, his voice tentative,

and Eden saw a flicker of regret in his eyes when she answered.

'This is my last night Nick.'

'No.' Fiercely he shook his head. 'Eden, don't go, not like this…'

A massive crash in the distance ended his protest as the whole night sky lit up in a glorious display of colour. They stood watching the new year come in, the spectacular fireworks in the distance lighting up Sydney Harbour, the joyous sounds of revellers in the streets below. And even though there was plenty to focus on, she was achingly aware of Nick beside her, and the fact that she didn't know what to say or what to do. As hard as leaving was, staying would be torture—seeing him every day and knowing she couldn't have him, living on the pathetic hope of an occasional drink or—who knew?—perhaps the odd night together when Nick was feeling lonely and she didn't have the power to say no. A final fanfare of green and gold sparkled to the heavens, the bridge emblazoned with the numbers of the new year that would be forever etched on her heart. A year of new beginnings, but right now she had to get through the painful ending. She turned to him and offered a tremulous smile for her own inadequate words as she wished Nick well.

'I hope…'

'Hope what, Eden?'

'That this year's kinder for you.'

And a New Year's kiss was appropriate, a kiss good-bye, letting go all that could have been. But even as his lips dusted hers, Eden felt the shameful response of her body. Her own hands reached for him and she lost herself in that kiss, offering comfort. He drank it from her, the pent-up misery, the utter wretchedness of the past few weeks were momentarily suspended.

'Don't go, Eden.'

'I have to,' Eden said finally. 'Because this isn't fair on me, Nick. And I'm sorry if I can't be what you want, sorry that I can't just be a casual date or even a friend or colleague, because I just wasn't made that way. All I want to do, all I've ever wanted to do, is love you. And I'm not proud of that, especially as for some of the time you were engaged to Teaghan. I know you'll never feel for me a tenth of what you felt for her, but what you did to me the other night was cruel in the extreme. Nick, you used me and then you pushed me away, made something that was so right suddenly dirty and cheap, made me feel guilty for even caring about you. And I just can't get past that, Nick. I can't pretend that I'm OK with it for even a moment longer. I'm not going to let you use me the same way you used Tanya and countless others. I'm not going to be one of your diversions just so that you can deaden the pain of losing Teaghan.'

Pushing him away, she headed for the stairwell, appalled at what she had just admitted, that again she'd revealed the depths of her feelings to a man who simply didn't know how to love. But she was relieved, too, relieved that finally she'd admitted the truth.

'Eden.' She could hear him calling, but she chose to ignore him, pressing furiously on the lift button and jumping inside when it opened. She let out a sigh of relief as the doors closed and the lift descended. She rapidly made her way back to the safety of the children's ward, knowing Nick couldn't confront her there. Ben was still asleep and Becky exactly where she'd left her, except for the addition of a radio playing softly at the desk, a pile of notes waiting to be written—the whole world just moving right along.

CHAPTER THIRTEEN

'CAN I have a word, Eden?' Nick's voice was sharp, but Eden didn't look up. She'd already said more than she'd intended, already boosted his already over-inflated ego a touch further but, more importantly, Eden knew she couldn't carry on the conversation without breaking down and was determined to leave with what was left of her dignity intact. 'Eden,' Nick snapped, but still she ignored him, picking up a pen and grabbing a pile of obs charts.

'Where are you up to, Becky?'

'Room four,' Becky answered nervously, her eyes swinging from Nick to Eden. 'But I can do the charts if Nick needs to talk to you.'

'He doesn't,' Eden said through gritted teeth, grabbing a ruler and drawing an angry red line through the chart on the desk in front of her, wishing he would just go away and leave her to die in peace!

'Oh, but he does,' Nick responded, and from his tone Eden knew there was no arguing with him, that if she didn't go into his office the whole ward was about to become privy to her private pain. 'We can either go into my office, Eden, or I'll say what I have to say here. What's it to be?'

Becky and Rochelle sat up straighter, visibly perking up at the prospect of front-row seats. Even a tired-looking mum walking past the nurses' station with her baby's bottle in her hand paused at the desk, pretending to need a tissue.

'I won't be long, Becky,' Eden bristled, standing up. 'Two minutes at the most.'

In a final stab at assertion Eden refused to follow him, marching angrily ahead and flinging open *his* office door, turning angrily to face him as Nick closed it behind him.

'How dare you embarrass me like that in front of my colleagues?'

'How dare you say what you did and then walk away?' Nick's face was taut, his lips set in a grim line, but Eden refused to back down.

'I'm only speaking the truth, Nick. It's not my fault if you don't like it.'

'You don't know the truth,' Nick barked, an angry muscle leaping on his cheek. Every muscle in his body seemed coiled like a spring and Eden jumped back. In all the time she'd known him, not once had she seen him angry, not once had she seen him anything other than relaxed and in control. 'And you don't know the first thing about guilt either!' Anguished eyes held hers, pain she had never before witnessed, even when she'd broken the tragic news of what had happened to Teaghan, was there now for her to see.

'What have you got to feel guilty about, Nick?' Eden asked, but her voice was softer now. 'It was an accident…'

'We were breaking up when it happened,' Nick rasped. 'Or, rather, I'd just broken things off.'

'I'm sorry.' Eden closed her eyes in regret for him. 'But it doesn't mean that it was your fault.'

'Do you know what her last words were to me?' Nick asked, and Eden shook her head. '"Your *girlfriend* is on duty this morning, Nick, you don't have to deny it any more!" That was the last thing she said to me, Eden. She stormed out of here, full of rage and bitterness. It's no wonder she wasn't concentrating on the road.'

'Nick.' Again Eden shook her head, struggling to say the right thing. 'It still doesn't mean it was your fault. Couples break up—'

'It was over you, Eden!' Her mouth snapped closed as Nick overrode her. 'As soon as you started working here, Teaghan got it into her head that I liked you. We'd been having problems for ages, we'd nearly broken up the Christmas before, but this thing between you and I brought it to a head.'

'But there wasn't anything going on between us,' Eden whispered, her own face pale now, finally understanding Nick's guilt because her own was starting to trickle in. When Nick slowly shook his head, looked into her eyes and willed her to admit the truth, the dam burst, the trickle turning into a torrent as the truth was finally out.

'Yes, Eden, there was,' Nick said slowly. 'As much as I denied it to Teaghan, as much as I refused to admit it to myself, I did have feelings for you.

'I always have.' Nick's own eyes were swimming with tears now. 'And I always will, Eden. That night when you were upset about Ben, I was out of my mind with jealousy. I didn't want it to be Jim cheering you up, Jim going for pizza and trying to comfort you—I wanted it to be me.'

'I wanted it to be you, too,' Eden admitted. 'I just didn't want to risk getting hurt, didn't want to be another woman hanging onto your every word.'

'You're wrong about what you said about Tanya. I haven't slept with anyone except you since Teaghan died.' He registered her slightly incredulous look. 'I haven't,' he insisted. 'Sure, I've tried dating a few times, but I've always made it clear from the start I didn't want a relationship. But no matter how much I tried to deny it, no matter how much I wanted to somehow prove Teaghan wrong, I *did* want a relationship. And the only person I wanted to be with was you.'

'You told me that on Christmas night, Nick,' Eden pointed out, 'but it didn't stop you from tossing me aside the next day.'

'Her parents rang.' His voice was so low she had to strain to catch it. 'They wanted to know if I was coming to the cemetery with them, and all I could think was that you were lying in my bed, that Teaghan had been right about it all along. That I betrayed her because I'd always wanted you.'

She saw it from his side then, glimpsed the great abyss of his grief—meaningless attempts at relationships in an effort to run from the truth, trying to deny feelings that had always been there.

Always been there.

'You didn't kill her, Nick.' Her voice was amazingly calm. 'And neither did I. We've done nothing wrong.'

'Then why doesn't it feel that way?' Nick asked. 'Why do I feel so guilty for loving you?'

Which was a big difference from wanting. Eden's breath caught in her throat as the true depth of his feelings were revealed.

'I love you, Eden.' Crossing the room, he wrapped his arms tightly around her and buried his face in her hair, dragging in her scent, holding onto her as if he couldn't bear to ever let her go. 'I love you,' he said again, but more forcefully this time, as if shutting out the demons that had haunted him. Pulling away slightly, he stared down at her, captured her face in her hands and said it all over again, without shame or regret now, a burden lifted for ever as the simple truth was revealed.

'I love you, too,' Eden whispered. 'Always have and always will.' A terrible thought suddenly occurred to her, her forehead creasing as Nick smiled down at her. 'I've just handed in my notice!'

'Good.' Nick said, raining butterfly kisses on her face as she nervously chewed her bottom lip.

'It isn't good,' she protested.

'Oh, but it is,' Nick said. 'You can apply for your job all over again tomorrow. Donna will take you back, but you can tell her that you'll only accept under certain conditions.'

'Which are?'

'Absolutely no night duty,' Nick said, 'and next year you have all of Christmas off.'

'Fat chance,' Eden mumbled, but, given it was only the first of January, she didn't really care, and there was a whole delicious twelve months to fill in between now and then.

'You won't be working, Eden,' Nick said firmly. 'This time next year you'll be taking care of a family of your own.'

EPILOGUE

'YOU'RE DOING TOO much.'

Seeing Eden standing in her uniform, pulling a hastily prepared casserole out of the oven, Nick dropped his briefcase on the floor. Crossing the kitchen, he kissed her full on the lips before resuming his protest.

'Eden, I thought we'd agreed no night shifts. You're looking really tired.'

'I know,' Eden admitted. 'But it isn't the odd night shift that's making me tired…'

'The whole point of you working for the hospital bank,' Nick broke in, 'is so that you can pick and choose your shifts!'

'The ward is really short,' Eden said, buttering jacket potatoes and scooping the casserole over them. 'It's only for one night.'

'That's what you said last week,' Nick reminded her, grabbing a spoon from the drawer and scraping the dish. 'And the week before. When are you going to start saying no?'

'You didn't mind my inability to say no last night.' Eden cheekily grinned. 'Anyway, one night a week isn't going to kill me.'

But Nick just rolled his eyes. 'Well it's sure as hell going to finish me off. Have you any idea how much this one plays up once you've gone to work?'

'Then don't wake him,' Eden answered. 'There's no need to check on him five minutes after I leave the house.'

As if on cue, the sound of footsteps running along the hallway had them both turning and watching as an elated Ben scampered towards them, clearly delighted at the sound of Nick's voice.

'Home!' he squealed as Nick scooped him up and showered him with kisses.

'Yep, buddy, I'm home!'

Home was Ben's favourite new word! In the six months since they'd become permanent foster-parents, Ben said it a thousand times a day. *Home* as the car rounded the corner and their weatherboard house came into view, *home* whenever Nick came in at night or Eden arrived back in the morning, the single word making him smile each and every time it spilled from his smiling chubby face.

'Donna was saying that the Christmas roster is already done. She wanted to know if I wanted any shifts.'

'I hope you told her no!' Nick said with a note of alarm. 'This will be our first Christmas as a family so no way are you working a single shift in December—or January either, come to that.'

'I'm not,' Eden said, placing the plates on the table and helping Ben into his seat as Nick cut up the little boy's dinner. 'And I won't be working next Christmas either,' Eden added, holding her breath, waiting for Nick to look up. But he was tucking into the rather burnt casserole and trying to feed Ben at the same time.

'Good,' Nick said, totally missing the point.

'You know I went to see the doctor today,' Eden started, finally catching his attention.

'I meant to ring you about that. I asked the GP to fax Ben's bloods over to me when they came back. Well, I spoke to the ID consultant about them and he's thrilled. He says that Ben couldn't be doing any better—'

'The GP told me,' Eden broke in, wondering why on the films it always looked so easy, how with one tiny shift of the head the penny would suddenly drop. A sledgehammer would be the only thing that would get Nick's full attention tonight! 'I won't be working next Christmas because—'

When Nick's pager chose that moment to go off, Eden thought she might burst with frustration as he headed off to the phone to ring the hospital.

'Nick, I'm trying to talk to you.'

'I'll just be a moment.' Picking up the phone, he flashed an apologetic smile, punched in the hospital's number and introduced himself to the switchboard operator. All Eden knew was that she had to say it now or he'd be on the phone for hours!

'I'm pregnant, Nick!'

He stopped dead. His whole body went stock still. Only his eyes moved taking in her nervous, excited face, a slow, incredulous smile breaking out on his face as he digested the news. Suddenly remembering he was on the phone, he apologised to the switchboard operator, saying that he'd call back.

'Thanks very much!' he said, replacing the receiver and crossing the room. 'Switchboard sends congratulations! How long have you known?' he went on.

Eden glanced at the oven clock. 'Three hours and five minutes.'

'And you didn't tell me.' Nick grinned, but there were tears sparkling in his expressive eyes.

'I've been trying to,' Eden said. 'Since the second you got home. *That's* why I'm looking so tired, *that's* why I went to the doctor and *that's* why I won't be working next Christmas—because it will be our baby's first one!'

'You're not working tonight either,' Nick said, refusing to budge as Eden begged to differ. 'No way,' Nick said. 'You, Eden Watson, are going to learn how to say no! I want you here at home tonight—both of you,' he added, his hand brushing her stomach. She captured it, holding it there and revelling in its warmth.

'*Home!*' Ben repeated loudly, making them both jump—his little face filthy from five minutes' neglect, smothered in chicken casserole, his hair matted with jacket potato.

'Home,' Nick agreed, kissing her deeply before continuing. 'With your family.'

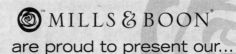

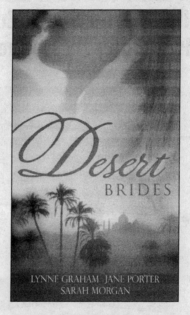

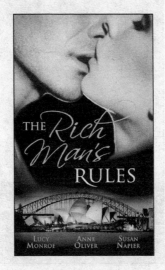

HOT ENOUGH TO MELT
THE WINTER SNOW!

Four brand-new stories where you'll be:

Stranded with the sexy healer

Trapped in his arms

Snowbound with her ex

Captive with the bad boy

Available 18th December 2009

www.millsandboon.co.uk

millsandboon.co.uk Community

Join Us!

The Community is the perfect place to meet and chat to kindred spirits who love books and reading as much as you do, but it's also the place to:

- **Get the inside scoop from authors about their latest books**
- **Learn how to write a romance book with advice from our editors**
- **Help us to continue publishing the best in women's fiction**
- **Share your thoughts on the books we publish**
- **Befriend other users**

Forums: Interact with each other as well as authors, editors and a whole host of other users worldwide.

Blogs: Every registered community member has their own blog to tell the world what they're up to and what's on their mind.

Book Challenge: We're aiming to read 5,000 books and have joined forces with The Reading Agency in our inaugural Book Challenge.

Profile Page: Showcase yourself and keep a record of your recent community activity.

Social Networking: We've added buttons at the end of every post to share via digg, Facebook, Google, Yahoo, technorati and de.licio.us.

www.millsandboon.co.uk

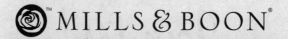

Kay Stephens was bo...
She spent the first sev... ...her working life as a librarian, and since then has written several short stories and a number of novels, including *West Riding* and *North Riding*, both set in the Yorkshire she knows so well.

Also by Kay Stephens

West Riding
North Riding
Pennine Vintage
The Soaring Fells

Stones of
Calder Dale

Kay Stephens

HEADLINE

Copyright © 1993 Kay Stephens

The right of Kay Stephens to be identified as the Author of
the Work has been asserted by her in accordance with the
Copyright, Designs and Patents Act 1988

First published in Great Britain in 1993
by HEADLINE BOOK PUBLISHING PLC

First published in paperback in 1994
by HEADLINE BOOK PUBLISHING

10 9 8 7 6 5 4 3 2 1

ISBN   0 7472 4273 9

Typeset by Avon Dataset Ltd, Bidford-on-Avon

Printed and bound in Great Britain by
HarperCollins Manufacturing, Glasgow

HEADLINE BOOK PUBLISHING
A division of Hodder Headline PLC
Headline House
79 Great Titchfield Street
London W1P 7FN

ACKNOWLEDGEMENT

For advice and information while researching the background of this book I am very grateful to Mrs Irma Bull of the Royal Institute of British Architects. I am also greatly indebted to Mr A. E. Bartholomew who supplied further details from his involvement with the education and examination of architectural students during the period covered by *Stones of Calder Dale*.

Chapter 1

Helen Clegg smiled, all the excitement of the drive down from Yorkshire surpassed by a new elation. Nobody would stop her now. Everything was possible if you wanted it enough to work as hard as you could. Wasn't she standing here, gazing across the Avon at the proof? The Shakespeare Memorial Theatre, opened just a month ago on 23 April. *And it was designed by a woman.*

Beside her Marian sighed, sounding exasperated. 'How much longer? We've stood here for hours, while you've done nowt but gawp.'

Helen grinned. 'Sorry. I was getting carried away. But it's been nothing like an hour, not much more than twenty minutes.'

Her sister laughed. 'Happen you're right, only my legs are growing numb with hanging around. And what's it all for? You haven't a snowball in hell's chance of ever becoming an architect.'

'She did,' Helen persisted, nodding towards the theatre, 'Elizabeth Scott.'

'I daresay, but you're still not being realistic. You've got a decent job, Helen, you want to hang on to it. Especially living up north like we do. I haven't forgotten being out of work a couple of years back in nineteen-thirty. There were two million of us unemployed.'

'I know.' She felt guilty about wanting more than other folk. 'But that doesn't stop me longing to do the job I've always fancied.'

'You've allus been full of fancies! They're not for folk like us, lass, can't you see? We should be content if we've brass to enjoy life with, and maybe enough to set up eventually in a nice little home.'

But seeing how she'd made her sister's grey eyes turn misty, Marian smiled and gave her an affectionate squeeze. 'Don't take on so, love. Tell you what − if you promise never to let on at home, I'll leave you on your own for a bit to study the place.'

'Would you? I'd love to do a few sketches.'

'Aye, go on then. See you back at the hotel.' Marian looked at her watch. She was meeting Denis in ten minutes. He was an Assistant Stage Manager at the theatre, could only spare her half an hour or so before she and Helen were due to go in for their evening meal. 'Just don't speak to anybody, think on,' she warned over her shoulder as she turned away.

Briefly, Helen gazed wryly after her nineteen-year-old sister, who was trying to look all grown up while barely restraining the urge to run. From the way Marian talked, nobody would think she was the one dashing off for a covert meeting. Not that any of this made much sense; Helen herself was only fifteen, yet she'd been brought along on this visit to Stratford upon Avon because their parents didn't believe Marian should come here alone.

Maybe they had a bit of an idea that their Marian might be up to something. They hadn't said owt, but they must be aware by now that her blonde hair and blue eyes, to say nothing of her long shapely legs, got all the young chaps interested.

Determined to make the most of this opportunity to concentrate, Helen felt in her pocket for the pencil and pad she always carried, leaned against one of the trees that guarded the riverbank, and began to draw. She wished she was totally enthusiastic about the design of this place, it looked too ordinary to her. But that feeling didn't stop her being thrilled that a woman had completed the design, any more than it could possibly curtail her own deep-seated ambition.

Commencing her sketch with its riverside terrace, Helen sensed that the theatre might be growing on her. With a matinee in progress, and actors glimpsed by the long windows of what evidently were dressing rooms, it was coming to life. And, as she had read since its opening, it was after all a functional structure, designed for presenting Shakespeare's plays to best effect. Until tonight when she was to judge the interior for herself, she would try and curb her desire for a more attractive building, truly in keeping with Stratford itself.

She had fallen in love with the town already: its picturesque timbered houses and inns, the streets better suited to horse-drawn vehicles than cars like the Austin Seven which Marian handled with startling dexterity. And the small hotel in Warwick Road where she herself was treated like an adult, and her sister aired all the graces which seemed to flow so readily from her slight figure. Maybe this instant affection for Stratford had encouraged her wish for a more classical setting for Shakespeare. There was her preference for good Yorkshire sandstone as well — almost every place built in brick like this began with a disadvantage in Helen's eyes!

After half an hour she had roughed in the outline of the theatre, and quite a lot of detail around the terrace overhanging the river. She'd need more time for getting all the windows in proportion. That could wait till tomorrow. She looked forward to coming back here. She'd be surprised if Marian hadn't arranged to see Denis again.

Smiling to herself, she stuffed her sketch pad into her pocket and paused for a second to watch a pair of swans take flight and land again on the Avon. How lovely the river here was with its meadows and gardens and Holy Trinity Church; so different from the Calder back home, pressing between the mills it had drawn to its banks.

Heading for Clopton Bridge and the walk towards Warwick Road, Helen began marvelling again at their Marian's audacity — the cool way she'd brazenly announced she felt she needed a break, and that she was thinking of Stratford. 'You know how I've always liked a good play.'

If either Mum or Dad had suspected there was more to it than that, they hadn't said. And it wasn't like either of them to keep silent if they were bothered about what was going on. But then they'd never been told how Marian had met Denis when she was trying to get hold of a fancy dress costume and had come up with the brilliant idea of approaching the company at the Grand Theatre in Halifax. Naturally, they'd heard nothing either of Denis's insistence on attending the party with her. Helen knew the whole story off by heart, and how keen on him Marian had become, how upset she'd been when he got this better job backstage here. Stratford had seemed so far away.

Still, she herself wasn't sorry their parents had stipulated that she should accompany her sister. As they had pointed out, if the girls shared a room, it wouldn't cost so much more. Relieved that her plan hadn't been quashed, Marian had volunteered to pay her sister's rail fare — but hadn't explained they weren't actually travelling by train. Denis had left his car behind in Halifax for repairs. Marian had

4

promised to drive it down to Stratford.

'Isn't it grand that you can afford to pay for her, love?' their mother had exclaimed while they were making plans. They'd had to scrimp to finance their elder daughter's training in shorthand and typing, but that period out of work had been short and she was earning good money now in a solicitor's office.

All Marian wanted was a job that brought in enough to give her a bit of independence. She liked a good time and, now that she'd met Denis, needed to be able to see him as often as she could.

Helen sympathised with that, even if her sister's earlier obsession with partying had seemed proper daft.

It was Marian, though, who frequently expressed doubts about *Helen*'s sanity. 'All that studying, when you could be out enjoying yourself! You must be wrong in your head.'

But Helen had always meant to do well at school. Dad had been determined that both girls would better themselves. He himself had never risen above chief maintenance man at the toffee works, and wasn't going to have his daughters in factory jobs.

Helen had a good head for figures and had been taken on in the accounts office of a local carpet mill. Delighted simply to have her in a job where she didn't get her hands mucky, Dad had been unable to grasp the fact that she wasn't contented. When she'd attempted yet again to explain her ambition he'd tried to laugh her out of it.

'Nay, love, it's time you put such ideas out of your head. Architecture's no sort of a job for a lass — you'd be getting wed and having bairns long afore you'd got anywhere near qualifying.'

Her father hadn't been the only one to ridicule her hopes. Mum was always too kind to do more than

5

smile to herself whenever architecture was mentioned, but that smile revealed every ounce of her doubts.

Going up the steps into the hotel, Helen was wondering if this meeting with Denis would accelerate Marian's hopes of getting married. That *would* be a surprise for everybody at home. Not that Marian had ever seemed unlikely to marry early; with her slender figure and eyes that challenged you to laugh life in the face, she entranced folk.

And I certainly don't! Helen thought ruefully, running up to their room. She was tall and big-boned like Dad, and if she even glanced longingly at a cream bun the inches piled on in all the wrong places. Tonight, she was going to need time to work on her mid-brown hair and on her face which always seemed merely serviceable. She wanted to look different. Denis had got her and Marian tickets for the stalls.

The play was *The Merchant of Venice* and Helen had resisted the temptation to read it through before coming away. She wanted each scene to be new to her, just like everything here.

Any reservations she might have had about the exterior of the Memorial Theatre were forgotten as she and Marian went in through one of its tall glass doors. The foyer seemed full already. People with all kinds of accents were exclaiming and enthusing and greeting each other. Folk were pressing together, some edging through the crowd or waving to friends. Women were wearing gorgeous dresses, daringly low-backed and cut to flare out as they neared the ground, but many so tight around the hips that Helen wondered however they'd manage to sit. A lot of the men wore evening dress which transformed even those with the most ordinary of features.

After thanking the young man who'd checked their

tickets and indicated the direction of their seats, Marian began gabbling on again about Denis and how important his backstage job was. Helen could no longer concentrate on what she was saying. In any case, she'd heard it already all through their meal.

Suddenly, she was standing quite still in the aisle, oblivious to amused looks from people obliged to detour around her. When Marian turned and hurried back to give her sleeve a tug, she came to with a lurch. She'd been stunned by it all — how well designed everything was, and how tasteful. She stared slowly all about her, up towards the balconies and the boxes then finally at the stage.

'Eh, isn't that grand!' she gasped. 'Why did I have any reservations about the outside? This couldn't be better.'

As soon as they were seated, Marian opened the programme, found Denis's name in tiny print, nudged Helen's arm.

She tried to enthuse with her sister, listened again to how marvellous he was, reminded herself that but for Denis's move to Stratford she wouldn't be here. She owed him and Marian a bit of attention.

But her other senses were diverted. Her ears alone occupied, she drew in a deep breath, savouring the atmosphere of anticipation in the buzz of conversation as people took their seats, and savouring as well the smell of new carpeting and upholstery. Running a hand along the seat back in front of her, she turned to her sister.

'What do you reckon, was this woven in t'West Riding?'

Marian groaned. 'I haven't the faintest idea. You're not here to dissect every little detail. And if you don't look at the programme you'll not know the first thing about what is going on.'

Helen read through the cast list. 'I've heard of Fabia Drake, the one that's Portia. Don't know any of the others.'

'Not Randle Ayrton? Denis says he's very much the big star.'

She shook her head. But once the play began it barely mattered to Helen that she was unfamiliar with the actors – she was enraptured.

'Gosh,' she said during the interval, 'I never knew Shakespeare could be so exciting. And isn't Randle Ayrton good? He makes you understand how Shylock feels, even when you're meant to hate him.'

It was Portia, though, especially in the trial scene, who ultimately won her admiration.

'She would, of course,' said Marian, suddenly serious when Helen confided in her after all the final curtain calls. 'She's a strong, determined woman. Just your sort.'

Helen gave a little, nervous laugh. But they were lingering while other people filed towards the doors. On her insistence, they were going right to the back of the auditorium to view it all from there.

'I'd give anything to build somewhere as good as this.'

'Oh – build it yourself as well, would you?' Marian mocked.

'You know what I mean. *Design* somewhere.' But Elizabeth Scott had begun with a big advantage. Both Gilbert and Giles Scott were relatives. Helen herself had only determination. Could that be enough?

She remained motionless, breathing in the scent of new wood, and a trace of recently dried paint which mingled with the still strong odour of new upholstery and carpeting. It was quite different from where they'd been sitting; there, she'd also been conscious of the smell of the painted set which wafted to them on

8

the draught each time those magnificent heavy curtains opened.

How must it feel if you were the person behind all this — if your plans had been the foundation of such a tremendous scheme? More than ever, Helen knew that architecture was the only thing that inspired her. As soon as she got back to Halifax, she'd tackle Dad again.

Daniel Clegg was strict — some of Helen's friends thought him dictatorial — but he wasn't unkind. She had intended using the car journey back to Yorkshire for working out what to say to him. But it hadn't turned out like that at all. Denis had agreed to drive them home like this on Sunday, then set off back to Stratford straight away. But Marian argued that *she* would drive to Halifax. He'd taught her, hadn't he, so that she could take over?

Unfortunately, Marian behind the wheel when Denis was there was quite different from the girl who'd so impressed her younger sister while they travelled down to Warwickshire. Her driving today consisted of screeching around corners and generally compelling the little car to struggle for maximum speed on roads that seemed to have acquired far more bends since the outward journey.

'Steady on, darling,' Denis protested regularly. He was an easy-going man, as a rule, whose hazel eyes and straight dark hair combined with a rugby forward's build to make him appear powerful.

But Marian was at her dizziest, giggling at his alarm. When they finally drew up a street away from their grey stone terraced house, Helen felt as though she'd been through her grandmother's mangle.

She was no less sure, though, that the time had come to try one last time for the career she wanted. Once

9

they had finished tea, and their parents had listened to Marian's edited account of the holiday, Helen asked their father if she could have a word with him. Her sister and mother were staring with curiosity they didn't bother to disguise. Because of having only the one living room and a small kitchen, there wasn't much scope for talking in private.

'It's about being an architect, I'm afraid,' Helen began. 'Yes — again. Seeing the Shakespeare Memorial Theatre has made me sure I'll always regret it if I can't even give studying a chance.'

'Nay, love — I thought you'd decided to be sensible, that you were putting them ideas behind you.' Her father hardly knew how to continue. He'd been flabbergasted when he first learned of Helen's notion. Where had she got it from? It must have been somebody at school; it had never been thought of here.

His own parents were simple folk: his father had been a blanket weaver, his mother in service. Wanting both his girls to do well, he had visualised nothing more ambitious than office work for them. He hadn't been brought up to believe ordinary people should want to get that far above themselves.

'Eh, lass,' he said at last. 'I'm proud of how well you've done at school, you know that. Let that be enough. That, and being set on to do figure work. Don't be allus moithering for more.' He'd been reared as a non-conformist. Perhaps believing simplicity was a virtue made it hard for him to appreciate the value of ambition. He became uneasy, suspecting he might be to blame for first instilling ideas of Helen's bettering herself — which suddenly were getting right out of hand.

'If I find out about all the studying I'd have to do, and if there's scholarships that I could go in for, would you consider it? Would you, Dad — please?'

But her father was only shaking his head, troubled by this abnormal ambition which threatened to disrupt all their lives.

'I don't want to talk about it any more, do you hear? We're ordinary folk, love. We've nowt behind us to finance studies that'd go on for donkey's years.'

For a time after the visit to Stratford Helen tried to will herself to accept life in the office at the carpet works. She hated her parents thinking her ungrateful for the start they had given her. And she didn't like the feeling that she made Dad uncomfortable because he was unable to provide the education she desired.

Marian hadn't helped when she announced her intention of marrying in the near future. Helen wouldn't forget the Sunday tea when her sister had brought that out into the open.

'I'm thinking of going to Stratford again before so long,' she'd said carefully as she cut the fat away from her slice of boiled ham.

Their mother had frowned. Kathleen Clegg hadn't had a holiday for over six years, since the General Strike in 1926 made surviving harder than ever, especially here up north.

'Nay, lass, you've nobbut just got back from your last trip.'

'How can you afford it?' their father asked. 'And what makes you so keen on the place?'

'It's a young chap, I'll bet,' his wife observed, before her elder daughter could speak.

'Whatever makes you think that?' Marian began.

Kathleen interrupted smartly. 'You were that elated afore you went, *and* when you got back. But that soon wore off. And for long enough now you haven't been going out as much as you used to. What happened to that friend of yours, somebody here in Halifax that were teaching you to drive a motor car?'

Smiling, Marian gave a little shrug. 'I ought to have known you'd put two and two together, shouldn't I? I didn't tell you at first because — well, I didn't like you getting concerned when it mightn't come to anything.'

'And will it — come to owt, I mean?' their father demanded, thinking already that he should have had some warning if he was going to be landed with providing a do for his daughter's wedding.

Marian's smile widened, her blue eyes glowed. 'Aye, Dad — so long as you're not bound to object. Denis rang me up on Friday . . .'

'Rang you up?' Kathleen asked. Who did their Marian know who had a telephone?

'Aye, at work. It's him that's got a job in Stratford these days, you see. And he's missing me a lot. He wants us to get married.'

'Now just a minute, lass,' Daniel interrupted, aware now that this daughter of his hadn't been quite straightforward about her motives for the original visit to Stratford.

He didn't like the sound of their Marian plotting to go off to meet this chap, and liked even less the holes he detected in her tale when questioned about how much time she'd spent alone with him. Helen was dragged into it because of their parents' initial supposition that she and Marian had spent all their time together. And because the sisters had always automatically supported each other, Helen was the one reprimanded for conniving with Marian.

'I'd never have let you go,' Kathleen had declared then, 'I'd not have had an easy minute if I'd thought the pair of you weren't together the whole time.'

It had taken days for Daniel Clegg to come round to agreeing to see Denis when he came up to the West Riding. 'If you do get wed, though — and I only say *if*

– you'll have to make a few sacrifices yourself, Marian. I'll give you a reception somehow, that's only right. But I can't run to providing your frock an' all. You'll have to wait till you've saved enough for that.'

Being told to bear that in mind hadn't dampened Marian's eagerness; she was that keen to marry Denis, she'd go to the altar in one of the theatrical costumes he could borrow, if that was the only way. But that was a feeling she couldn't mention at home; she had hedged when questioned about Denis's work. She had written to him emphasising that he must stress how secure his job was when he came to speak to her father.

Helen didn't know how her sister had the nerve to keep so much from their parents, and privately admitted that she thought Marian had been daft not to put them in the picture completely once the matter was aired. Neither Mum nor Dad would like learning the whole truth later on. There'd only be more trouble while Denis was here. Meanwhile, her own problems worsened. With a wedding on their hands, and one less wage coming in after, there'd certainly be no hope of Helen's throwing up her job to start studying. She hadn't a cat in hell's chance of going in for architecture.

On Monday morning Helen was sitting at her desk, reading while she waited to begin work. She always got into the office early; today more than ever. She'd had to get away. Marian was as daft as a brush, giggling and singing up and down the house because she'd got her own way. From what Helen could gather, Denis had been given a hard time of it but he had got Father to agree to their marrying. Ever since she'd been told, Marian had gone potty. She'd even danced their father around the room – something Helen had never seen before, Daniel Clegg wasn't accustomed to letting himself go like that.

'I'm glad you're suited, Marian,' Mum had remarked, her expression dour. 'I hope you'll look back on this happily in a year or two. It's not a rest-cure, you know, marriage. You'll soon find that keeping good meals on the table and a decent roof over your heads isn't quite the fun you expect it to be. And don't forget you're giving up a good job to move down yonder. Is there much short-time round Stratford?'

The weekend's events were forgotten now, though, while Helen examined photographs of Broadcasting House which had recently been opened in London. It did look grand, especially with Eric Gill's figures of Prospero and Ariel. She'd read about the building ages ago when the plans were first approved and construction was beginning.

That was what had started her off longing to design buildings. Miss March, who taught art and had always encouraged Helen's natural flair, had been studying copies of drawings of Broadcasting House. Seeing her pupil's interest, she'd told her to come along after school and they'd examine them together. Miss March's father had been an architect so she was more interested than most in such designs. The journal in which they had appeared had carried other articles about new buildings. Helen had been so fascinated that Miss March had let her keep it. Dog-eared now from much re-reading, it still emerged regularly from her drawer in the dressing-table she shared with Marian. Or had done until the new situation at home made her hopes even more improbable.

These photographs of Broadcasting House which had appeared in the Sunday papers were renewing her longing to create something equally important, making her aware of the years stretching ahead and how she would grow to resent her tasks in the carpet works' office.

'Why so glum, Miss Clegg? You've hardly had time for the place to get aired, I trust you're not fed up here already?'

The voice was their Senior Accounts Clerk's, and he wasn't normally so sharp with her. But then Helen wasn't frowning as a rule, and nor did she often look so despondent.

He wasn't an unkind man, and he'd already recognised Helen's talent for putting her back into hard work. 'What's up then?' he inquired.

'Nothing,' she said hastily, concealing what she was studying. It would never do to let on here that she wasn't wholehearted about her job. There'd be plenty of lasses thankful to take over from her.

But he had glimpsed one of the photographs. 'Broadcasting House, isn't it?' he said, wondering what seemed so fascinating about that to a girl of her age.

'Yes, it is actually,' Helen admitted, her face flushing.

'Interested in architecture, are you?'

'Well — yes. Not that there's much chance of it ever coming to owt.'

He looked pensive. 'You never know. You've a smart head for figures — that's something which would stand you in good stead.'

Helen hadn't really considered before that her ability with arithmetic would be useful if she were able to follow her chosen career. She'd found geometry easy to understand as well. Somehow, awareness of this made the whole prospect seem less impossible again. And that article in the paper had reminded her about Miss March. She'd be a fool if she didn't at least go and ask her advice.

Fenny March lived in a massive house on Albert Promenade which on that Saturday afternoon seemed to glow golden in the June sunlight.

'We can sit outdoors if you like?' Fenny suggested.

Helen happily agreed. Screened by laburnum and lilacs from the road, the terrace was raised above the rest of the front garden. The view across and over the Promenade was magnificent: distant mauve-tinged hills, their slopes densely wooded, and a sky far more blue than you usually saw above Yorkshire. This distance from the edge of the escarpment, the industrial valleys didn't show.

'I've always liked the Rocks,' Helen confided, and sensed her former teacher smiling at her. 'That's what we allus called it when we were little. Of course, I suppose it was more the rocks themselves that attracted us in those days, rather than the view from the top here.'

'There's a cave as well, isn't there, not very far down?'

'You knew it an' all! Just above the top path that meanders through the woods.'

'I used to play there a lot, while this house was being built.'

'Did — did your father design it then?'

'He did indeed. Must be forty years since now. I'll have to ask him the date when I see him tomorrow.'

'You mean he's still alive?'

Fenella March laughed. 'Why do school mistresses always seem too old to have parents?'

'I never said, I mean — I wouldn't . . .'

'I know that, Helen. Come on, don't go all embarrassed on me. You're here to talk, aren't you? Seriously, I suspect. And that's what we shall do, just

16

as soon as I've poured this tea. It must have brewed by now.'

Glancing sideways towards the house, Helen was studying its large windows, the arched doorway, the pleasing slant of the slate roof. And the glorious stone itself. She examined the matching slabs of the terrace where they were sitting, the myriad shades from palest cream to burnt orange with minute crystals that sparkled beneath the sun. There were darker layers also, black even and dark blue, incredible contrasts to the overall gold.

'You love sandstone, don't you?'

She laughed. 'It always looks far nicer than brick! I was going to tell you. I've been to Stratford, saw the new theatre.'

'Designed by a woman.'

Helen met Fenny March's eyes, grey like her own, though paler. Eyes that always seemed understanding.

'I was coming to that. But about Stratford — I was a bit disappointed that the theatre looked so . . . well, plain on the outside. I might have liked it better if it hadn't been brick. But I loved the interior — it thrilled me. Our Marian thought I were proper daft.'

'You went there with Marian? How is she?'

'Very well, thank you. Can't talk about owt but getting married.'

'So that's on the cards, eh? Somebody local?'

'No. It's caused a bit of a rumpus at home. Denis works in the theatre, backstage. That's how the trip to Stratford came about. Marian met him when he was working here in Halifax, at the Grand.'

Miss March's eyebrows, threaded with grey like her hair, were steadily soaring.

Helen grinned. 'That's right — the idea isn't too popular at home. Dad gave his consent, but I think he

17

knew that if he didn't Marian was quite likely to run off to Denis any road.'

'She always did tend to be somewhat unconventional.'

'Unruly — wasn't that what most of the staff at school called her?'

Again they laughed, but affectionately.

'And you, Helen — always just the opposite. That is why you're here today, to talk about your future?'

'I feel awful about it. I wish Mum and Dad could understand. It isn't that I'm ungrateful for my job. I do know how lucky I were to be taken on as soon as I left school.'

'But the carpet factory office isn't what you want?'

'I never told you, did I? Everybody but you — the Head, our form mistress that last year — said how well I'd done. They knew, of course, the circumstances at home. That the most Dad could ever manage would be to give me the sort of course our Marian had taken. And I'd turned that down. I'd no wish to end up a secretary.'

'So tell me now — when it's too late to offend those who were so delighted about the position you secured — what is it your heart's so set on?'

'I think you've guessed, haven't you? Architecture. Can't seem to put it out of my head.'

Fenny March grew very thoughtful. Helen imagined the teacher's anxiety on her behalf: the length of training, the years while she would be earning little or nothing.

'The studying'd take too long, wouldn't it? Mum and Dad only just make ends meet as it is. And now with our Marian's wedding to pay for — then there'll be one wage less after she's gone.'

'All a bit daunting, eh, love? Don't think I can't appreciate all the difficulties. Do you know what I believe, though?'

18

Dispiritedly, Helen shook her head. 'Go on.'

'There's generally good cause why a longing – an ambition – remains rooted in the soul against reason, or so it seems. Certainly against practicalities and opposition. Maybe you're not meant to foresake all that you want to do. Happen that's what hope exists for.'

'But it's five or six years, isn't it, the training?'

'All of that. Could be more if you only study part time.'

'And I couldn't live on fresh air meanwhile, could I?'

Miss March shook her head. The pale eyes seemed to look beyond Helen, way into the past. 'I had an ailing mother. Father was often away from home, visiting sites.'

'So you'd have become an architect if you could have?'

'I haven't regretted teaching.'

'*But . . .*'

'Quite.' She paused. 'I don't believe you should resign yourself, surrender all hope. Not quite yet. There might be something we can do.'

Chapter 2

Helen had never seen so many biscuits. Thousands of them passing on the conveyor belt, still soft, hot from the oven, and smelling — always smelling. This sweet, cloying smell had met her as she walked up the road from the tram on that first evening four years ago, and had clung with her ever since. Some days she hardly noticed it; other folk did, of course, on her clothes and in her hair. Alex was always complaining. Despite how meticulous she was about having a strip wash as soon as she got home, and keeping her hair short so that it dried quickly. Thank goodness some people still wore their hair bobbed.

It was worth it, though, was enabling her to survive. She had completed over four years of studying at Leeds College of Art. There was nothing now to stop her becoming an architect. Eventually.

And but for that talk with Miss March, none of this would have happened. Helen would never forget how good Fenny March had been, going the very next day to the nursing home where her father was, telling him all about her former pupil's ambitions. There had been meetings after that, sitting in the over-warm room in that lovely house in Harrogate, listening to the old man's grumbles about the staff there and the other residents. Listening, and waiting — until he came to the point and began discussing architecture. Then once he'd begun he had been transformed, with vigour in the lined face, colour in faded blue eyes, strength in shoulders wearied by too many years of living. And, on the very first day that Helen had met him, there'd been his satisfied smile as he put the proposal to her.

'Tell you what I'm going to do, lass — and it's as much for Fenny here as it is for you, so you mustn't ever get cocky about it. I'm going to create a scholarship so's you can study. No, hang on a minute, don't go thanking me till you hear all the conditions.' He had paused there, enjoying the tension almost as much as he was enjoying the ability to give again, at his age. 'I'm naming it the Fenella March Bursary. Yes, Fenny, my mind's made up — you didn't think, did you, that I'd forget what you sacrificed?

'And now, young lass, we come to what's expected of you. You'll have enough to see you through college, that's all arranged. But once you begin earning, you'll put some of it back. All of it, if you can without stinting yourself. It'll be there again then — ready for the next one that deserves a bit of a hand.'

Helen had immediately invested one shilling and sixpence in obtaining a form to apply for architectural probationership, affirming to herself that there could be no turning back.

The scholarship didn't cover all her living expenses, of course, and nor had it been intended to. Mr March was a firm believer in the fact that folk most appreciated something for which they'd had to work. That was certainly the word for the biscuit factory job, especially these days while they were producing presentation tins to mark George VI's Coronation. With the abdication at the end of 1936, they'd had to abandon all the tins bearing King Edward VIII's picture. But this occupation didn't make heavy demands on her already over-taxed brain, and it

22

definitely didn't require the kind of concentration which had been necessary in the carpet mill office.

Strangely, Helen had been rather sad to leave her first job, the place where she'd come to appreciate putting in a full day's graft and being paid for it.

And she had hated explaining at home that though Mr March's generosity was enabling her to begin at college, despite this evening work, she couldn't contribute so much to the family budget.

Dad had surprised her with his equable acceptance of what was happening. They were sitting at the chenille-covered table in the living room which was dominated by a Victorian sideboard which Kathleen Clegg regretted inheriting because, being mahogany, it showed every mote of dust. Helen had always loved the piece, especially its mirrors and intricate carving, and she enjoyed polishing its twisted columns.

'We'll manage somehow, love, remember that,' her father had said. 'Your mum and me both want what's best for you. And if we couldn't give it to you, we're glad somebody else has the means. We mightn't be enthusing as much as you'd like about what you're doing, but that's only because we're older, can foresee more of the problems. It's such a long time, Helen, such a large slice of your life to be taken up wi' learning.'

'We're just afraid, you see,' Kathleen had added, grasping her husband's arm in a gesture that showed their unity. 'Afraid as how you might be sorry later on that you've had to study for so long, and so hard. And happen afraid an' all that you might miss out on having a life of your own because you'll be that intent on putting all you've got into your work.'

She had hugged them both, loving them all the more after learning that their reservations about her career were based only on concern for her.

Shifting all her weight on to one foot, she raised the other, trying to flex her toes. The shoes she wore to the factory were old because no matter how regularly the floor was cleaned there was always some residue of biscuit waste. Standing so long in one place, just watching that all the freshly baked biscuits were flawless, really took it out of your feet and ankles; especially when it also seemed to make your feet spread until you could do with a size larger shoe. And because the task was so monotonous there wasn't much to take your mind off your complaints.

Helen had liked her first job in the factory rather better. That had been on the packing line where there had been other women and girls to talk with, the chance to have a laugh. And it hadn't been nearly so hot. The trouble was all the supervisors and charge-hands knew that she was only staying here while her training in architecture continued, and so weren't above giving her the worst jobs. The only good thing about this one was the opportunity to think over all that she'd been learning in recent weeks. She could also look forward to anything special which was coming up.

Next year a few of the more advanced students in her grade were going across to the Continent. Travelling to see some of the famous buildings from past eras, they would actually go as far as Italy. Helen hadn't believed she'd be able to afford the trip, but old Mr March had insisted that it was something she must not miss. He had described magnificent ancient buildings in Rome and elsewhere, and some that weren't quite so old. There was an abbey church at Einsiedeln which he still recalled very clearly. She had known then that she would have to go somehow, and had begun making the necessary economies.

Instead of getting the tram all the way to the factory each evening, she was walking a good mile of the distance. That saved only a few pence each week, but it would mount up. And she'd started taking bread and dripping from home to eat at lunch time at college. By only spending on cups of tea there, she was already accumulating a tidy sum. The exercise might counteract the fatty diet, and it would take more than this stringent economy to spoil her life at college.

Helen had loved it there wholeheartedly since the first day which she still recalled so clearly. Some of the students had seemed rather nervous as they went up the steps and through the heavy doors. She was just so thankful for the opportunity to study there that she strode eagerly towards the board displaying class lists.

Seeing 'Helen Clegg' just three names down gave her such a thrill that she was all but running as she found her way along the corridors. Four or five students had arrived ahead of her and were grouped around their tutor's desk. She had met Mr Wilkinson at her interview, and although his blue eyes could appear cold and daunting, they also took on an occasional crinkle of amusement.

Mr Wilkinson was smiling when she entered, and called to her: 'Ah – Miss Clegg. Over here, if you please. Do you know any of the others?'

She hadn't done, and the only name she recalled immediately afterwards was Alexander Stone's. As Tod Wilkinson explained, Alex was the son of Joseph Stone, one of the most respected architects in the Halifax area. Helen had discovered that day that she was the only female architectural student in their year; within a week she was suspecting that this was the cause of Alex's special interest in her.

From the start he had ensured that they sat close together in class. By the end of the month he'd offered to run her back and forth to college. That was when Helen had been obliged to explain about her evening job. To her surprise, Alex had applauded her determination.

'Gosh, but you make me think I've had it too easy!'

For years his father had been introducing Alexander into the family practice, taking him to new sites and then returning with him at various stages of construction. And, of course, there was the prestige of the name. Nobody in Halifax remained unaware of Joseph Stone — an alderman of the borough, from a family which had produced several councillors. During this Coronation Year, he was Mayor of Halifax.

'Pity I'm nowhere near qualified yet,' Alex had confided to Helen yesterday lunch time. 'Father's employing a chap to cover for him this year, otherwise the business would suffer from his absences for attending functions.'

She had expected that Alex would be eager to be in on the reception at the Town Hall for King George and Queen Elizabeth's visit. But the other day he had laughed at the suggestion.

'You don't know me at all if you can say that! Father's in his element when he's climbing socially — 'fraid I'm not, old thing.'

'But the King and Queen . . .'

He shook his head with its rich golden waves of hair all the more emphatically. 'I'd not cross the street to look at them. The monarchy ought to be abolished. Why hang on to them? They're no better than us. You saw how Edward went to pieces over that woman . . .'

Helen grinned. 'Mrs Simpson's attractive enough. Thought you'd be all for her.'

'Hardly. Not when she had him sacrificing his job. And it is just a job, Head of State. To my way of thinking, they'd do better to have a politician in ultimate charge, somebody who's had a grounding in ruling the country.'

'Surely the royal family has?' Helen ventured.

His grey-green eyes narrowed. 'Some, maybe.'

'Well, I think we shall soon find that the new King and Queen are champion leaders.'

Alex wouldn't have that, and when they turned to analysing which of the current politicians he would support it soon was clear that Alex was a bit of a Bolshevist. Helen was quite fascinated. She'd never come across anybody who wasn't very much a Royalist. This discovery led to further arguments between them which only ended in yet another agreement to disagree.

Their opinions seemed to differ on most things, as they had ever since the beginning of that first term when, as soon as Helen felt at home, she'd started saying what she thought. Their first clash had concerned Alexander's personal life — which wasn't really anything to do with her, but she'd been that incensed she'd had to comment.

Walking into class early one morning, Helen had caught him laughing with Harold Tilsley, another student, evidently about his previous night's outing.

'So, Harold, I said to her: "If you don't like it, love, you can walk home. It's only another couple of miles." Naturally, she suddenly grew more amenable.'

Harold laughed. 'You'd have thought she'd have given her eye teeth to ride around in your father's Rolls-Royce, anyway.'

'Ah, but it wasn't eye teeth I was intent on extracting from her, was it?'

'And did she — you know — cooperate entirely?'

'Not quite, worse luck. Still, half the fun's in the pursuit, isn't it, old chap? And even in my own little Morris I don't have much trouble finding . . .'

'. . . a willing victim?' Helen interrupted, her face flaring with anger. She felt degraded on behalf of all females who seemingly were expected to consider Alex Stone's attentions a privilege. 'Do you know what? The way you behave is as common as muck! And I thought you were supposed to be better off nor most of us. Has it never occurred to you that the lasses you hope will cheapen themselves for you mightn't have had all your advantages? That they'll be flattered just to go out with you, though Lord knows why. And all you can think of is ruining 'em for settling down with a decent fellow.'

The only thing that placated her was that it wasn't Alex but Harold who laughed. 'Is that right, Alex? Are you so expert you ruin their hopes of finding another fellow who's as good at it as you are?'

More than a little shocked, for her non-conformist father never permitted even a vague allusion to anything connected with sex, Helen had refused to say another word to either of them.

By the following day when she still answered in monosyllables whenever Alex addressed her, he was growing more perturbed than she would ever have imagined. That evening he was waiting outside on the college steps.

'I'll give you a lift home from Leeds,' he offered. 'And you have my word I don't class you in the same category as my girlfriends.'

'That's as may be,' She retorted. 'And thanks, but it makes no difference any road. I have a job to go to.'

'A job?'

'Aye — some of us have to earn a living.' That was when she'd explained about the biscuit factory and had been thankful that she didn't have to bring him into line for ridiculing that as well.

In fact, when he proved to be so understanding

28

about what she was doing, she'd felt quite sorry she didn't hold with the way he carried on with other members of her sex. He was a bit of a funny mixture. Maybe all men were — she'd not had the experience to be sure. And certainly, from what she'd seen of their Marian's Denis, *he* wasn't the one who'd put himself out in their household. Still, Marian was happy enough now they were married and starting a family.

'Aren't you ever going to settle down?' she asked Alexander in the car on the way to the factory. As she'd understood it, shortage of money was all that normally kept people apart. 'Or do you plan on continuing to use every lass that falls for you?'

He didn't like that. 'It's only girls who're out for a good time, you know. Ones who are of a like mind to myself, believing there's time enough in the future for being serious.'

She wondered where love came into it, but that wasn't something she'd ever ask Alexander Stone. He seemed so full of himself that it'd be just like him to think she was getting keen on him. Later, though, outside the biscuit works, he'd nearly made her late, he was so intent on explaining how he felt about *her*.

'Don't write me off entirely, Helen, please? I want to make it clear that you've already earned far more respect from me than any of that lot I go out with. You're going be a brilliant architect, I can sense that by now, and I've got to hand it to you for tackling evening work to help pay your way. Whatever happens, you'll always have my admiration.'

Soft talk, she'd thought, running across the setts to clock in. But, strangely, in all these intervening years, Alex's attitude towards her had actually reinforced what he'd said that evening.

They got a lot of enjoyment out of their classes, and

29

this was greatly enhanced for Helen by their common-room arguments about architectural styles. Over the years, it had become accepted in their crowd that Alex was in favour of ultra-modern, while Helen always spoke up for traditional, even Gothic lines.

Their first disagreement had concerned Bull Green House which had been opened during 1932. Whilst Helen accepted that it was a great improvement on the rough ground surrounded by hoardings which once had occupied the site between Bull Close Lane and King Cross Street in Halifax, she would have preferred a more elaborate building.

'Nay, but it's meant to be functional,' Harold Tilsley had argued. 'You don't want something like Manor Heath.'

'Oh, I don't know,' Helen had begun. She'd always loved Manor Heath, an elaborate mansion built for John Crossley, the son of the famous carpet manufacturer.

Before she could say any more, Alexander was asserting his view. 'Bull Green House isn't nearly modern enough. Halifax ought to be looking at what's being constructed elsewhere.'

'Such as?' Helen inquired, waiting for him to cite the Shakespeare Memorial Theatre as an example. She wouldn't mind telling him that she'd seen it, and what her impressions were of the exterior.

But Alex was thinking of places even further afield. 'There's the *Daily Express* building, for one. And the Hoover factory in west London — that was designed by a New York firm.'

None of the others had first-hand knowledge of either so his argument had fallen rather flat, but Helen had noticed ever since that Alex relished any discussion which made him appear more up to date than the rest.

Strangely, though, their very different ideas on architecture hadn't prevented friendship developing between them, any more than their totally dissimilar backgrounds had created a barrier. This had been proved on the day that the entire class was invited to The Stone House, the home which Alexander's father had designed for himself on the hillside overlooking Brearley, along the Calder Valley.

Reared in a back-to-back house just off Queen's Road, Helen had struggled for years against her initial envy of school friends who lived in through houses. Even though Kathleen Clegg's addiction to housework was no less than any Yorkshire housewife's, and the living-room furniture always gleamed from her daily dusting, Helen had felt uncomfortable in the past about bringing new friends home. They couldn't help but notice the carpet worn threadbare under the table which had been moved to conceal the thinnest places, and the old-fashioned fireplace that Helen was obliged to black-lead every Saturday because Kathleen wouldn't have a daughter of hers growing up unskilled in housewifery.

Worst of all, though, was having to explain to folk that the lavatory was out in the yard. Time and again, both she and Marian had begged their father to have a way through constructed so that going right outside was unnecessary. Daniel Clegg had been just as persistent in his assertion that he'd do nothing of the kind.

'*If* I had the brass for that,' he'd told them the last time the matter was raised, 'I'd be spending it on summat we could appreciate all the time, not on a necessity out of sight. I'd see your mother had an electric oven, and have this range taken out of the house.' Helen had started noticing recently how the living room was always referred to as 'the house', a fact which she supposed had roots in the past, though it seemed illogical to her. Maybe it went back to a time when people and their stock shared the one building, and the family quarters could then rightly be termed 'the house'?

Visiting Miss March's home along Albert Promenade had, at first, been an awesome experience. Helen had felt quite inhibited and constantly watched what she said, but that was only until Fenny March's ability to comprehend a girl's mind had put her at ease. Knowing something of the background of her past and present pupils, Fenny had skilfully bridged the gulf between them by concentrating on things that were familiar. Her father had scorned over-stuffed furniture, for instance, and his old Windsor armchair proved to be similar to one in Helen's home. The kitchen range had been a larger version of the one in the Cleggs' living room and, best of all, the set of balloon-backed dining chairs was similar to those inherited from Helen's grandmother. Having established that they had several items in common, Fenny had then succeeded in drawing Helen out on the subject of her pastimes.

Overshadowed as they were by her love of architecture, her other pursuits were few, but both Daniel and Kathleen Clegg were avid users of the public library and had passed on to Helen a great love of reading.

'You'll never lack an interest so long as you read,' Fenny had assured her, beaming, and they had settled to chatting about their favourite authors.

I wish I believed this visit would be half as easy, Helen had been thinking on the day she set out with her fellow students for The Stone House. From their homes between here and Leeds, they had converged on the centre of Halifax where they were catching the tram to Brearley. That must have been over a year ago now, she reflected. The trams had been replaced by buses along the Calder Valley during 1936.

She could hardly credit now that it was so long since she'd got to know Alex's father. He had so impressed her that the day was still fresh in her mind.

It had been hot, and she and her fellow students had clattered upstairs on the tram, scarcely aware of its juddering and swaying, so interested were they in Mr Wilkinson's account of The Stone House. Evidently, Joseph had drawn up the plans while he was only a student himself. Adjusting details, amending elevations, but always keeping the building substantially the same, he had preserved the drawings until he was successful enough to afford to have the house constructed by the best builders in the West Riding.

'If anything demonstrates the power of hanging on to a dream, that house does,' Tod Wilkinson enthused, his eyes gleaming.

Somehow, even the more rebellious among them remained a little awed, and it was in this mood of quiet anticipation that they descended from the tram at Brearley. Alex was waiting for them, and they surged across the road and began the climb up a narrow lane. Pausing occasionally for stragglers who stopped to admire the view across to the other steep hillside, Alex chatted with their tutor and those of his fellows who had breath remaining from the uphill climb.

Suddenly, his home was in sight from a bend in the lane where a drive took off at an angle between tall wrought-iron gates.

'Come on, Helen, let's have your arm,' Alex said then, drawing her with him to the head of the group. 'I've been telling Father about you, he's mightily impressed.'

She was still wondering whatever she might have done to impress someone of the stature of Joseph

Stone when they arrived at the steps leading up to the studded oak door.

A manservant admitted them, and sent a pair of darkly dressed maids to usher them into the reception room where their host awaited them.

Joseph Stone was taller than his son, though his shoulders stooped from all the years at a drawing board. His hair was as luxuriant as Alexander's and equally wavy, but greying to a pleasant shade midway between gold and silver.

'Welcome, all,' he exclaimed, his smile encompassing the entire group as they flowed about the room. But his eyes swiftly focused on Helen. She noticed his slight nod which appeared to be of approval.

'So you're the lass who's staggered this son of mine by proving to have an uncommon grasp of architecture?'

She felt the flush surging upwards from her neck, and the other students gawping, for all the world as though they'd never before noticed she was of a different sex.

Mr Stone deserved an answer, though, and she exerted considerable will-power to make her voice light and conversational.

'You're very kind,' she said. 'I hope you won't be disappointed. I'm rather afraid Alex may have over-exaggerated in the build-up he's given me!'

'Miss Clegg is always too modest,' Mr Wilkinson remarked, coming to shake Joseph Stone by the hand.

It seemed that the two were already acquainted and had arranged between them this tour of the house. Helen was glad to have attention diverted from herself as they were invited to examine the room in which they were standing.

'You'll see the windows are large,' Joseph Stone began, 'that was one of the first things I decided on.

Plenty of light in the place, and full benefit from the view.'

They followed him to look out towards the far side of the valley, three or four of them clustering at each of the five tall windows.

Helen felt Alex gazing at her, awaiting her reaction. Beyond the road and the River Calder soared grassland and wood — so many different greens she'd never finish counting them. 'By, but that beats rows of grimy terraces!'

He wasn't grinning back at her. Emotions seemed to war on his face. Surprise was surrendering to something closely resembling tenderness.

His father had heard too. She could sense him looking at her over the heads of her fellow students. His expression wasn't so easy to read, yet she sensed the warmth of understanding.

Helen turned from the view and blinked her eyes to try and refocus her concentration. Joseph Stone was indicating the large marble fireplace and the alcoves to either side.

'A shameless copy of Adam styling,' he confessed, smiling. 'I knew I'd not afford the genuine article, even if I could locate one and have it transported here. So I made sketches — visiting well-known houses in much the same way as you do yourselves. Providing that it's not at the expense of expressing your own individuality, I see no harm in acknowledging that there are certain masters worth emulating.'

'So you see, Father's a bit of a fraud,' Alex murmured into Helen's ear.

His remark was noticed. His father shrugged, but then as an afterthought turned on Alex. 'Right, boy, let's see how much better you are! Take over the description — you've heard it oft' enough.'

Beside her, Alex had flinched at 'boy' but Helen

soon realised that there was nothing immature about his response to the challenge.

'Thanks, Father,' he said smoothly, leaving the group to stand in the centre of the room.

'The alcoves, which you see accommodate some of the family glassware and china, were constructed to draw the eye down from the height of the room, and create a more intimate atmosphere around the fireplace.'

Helen could picture a log fire in the massive grate, and folk sitting on the two brocade sofas facing each other across a long low table.

'As I said, the ceiling's high. Its vaulting is of wood though modelled on a cathedral's stonework. Some might call it ostentatious.'

Joseph chuckled. 'And old fashioned, eh, Alex?'

'Some might.'

The rest of the class were grinning, relaxing already, a few of them wishing, like Helen, for a father whose architecture might aid their own. But Alex was continuing, directing them to inspect the columns ranged in a line parallel with the windows.

'Though these appear to support the vaulting, their main purpose is to provide a dividing point in the room. Father's gatherings aren't always of large numbers; by setting sofas, side tables, and other furniture between the pillars, guests are confined to the smaller area. Works quite well, too — feels much cosier than when we use the entire space.'

Watching their host's face, Helen detected a smile which seemed to reveal that he'd been unaware of his son's approval of the concept.

'Anything more in this room, Father?' Alex inquired.

'Not unless you wish to elaborate on the doors or the surrounding embellishments?'

'What can I say? Doors of mahogany, as you can see. And they are set in stone which has been carved to echo the decoration around each window.'

The entrance hall was next to be inspected and Joseph resumed the description. 'I'll admit to ostentation here – and again to being influenced by other men's ideas.' He paused, letting them gaze at the staircase curving to left and right from the centre rear, with balusters which had to be less fragile than they appeared.

'The Royal Hotel in Scarborough, wasn't that where you gleaned the notion?' said Alex.

'To your disgust!' Smiling unconcernedly, Joseph Stone addressed them all. 'I hope you've learned by now that an understanding of architecture doesn't necessarily involve appreciation of all its facets. Indeed, healthy disagreement breeds new attitudes, fresh concepts. Eh, Helen?'

'Somebody's been talking,' she exclaimed, feeling suddenly as though only she and Alex were here with his father.

'Those two will never agree,' somebody observed.

'I hope not either,' Harold Tilsley put in. 'We'd have a dull old time if it weren't for those two arguing for their different tastes.'

'Good, good,' Alex's father approved.

'You don't say that while I'm disagreeing with you,' Alex remarked.

That was met with laughter. 'I should think not, indeed. You'll mind your place here, son. Keeping you down has done you no harm so far.'

Helen was thinking that Joseph Stone's idea of keeping folk down seemed extreme lenience in comparison with her own father's. She'd never considered either she or Marian were particularly repressed, but they wouldn't have felt they could speak up like this to

Dad in front of a lot of visitors. And discussions at home, even in private, didn't allow for serious questioning of parental opinion or taste.

The rest of the tour of The Stone House had proved equally enjoyable, and just as much of an eye-opener. It was no wonder that all the way back in the tram the rest of the class were envying Alex his father as much as his home.

Even now, all this time afterwards, Helen had a clear picture of Joseph Stone, could readily recall his voice. And while she stared at the conveyor belt with its interminable rows of biscuits, she thought back again to that lovely house on the hill, its elegant gables, the portico at the front entrance, and all those windows enhanced by intricate stonework.

If she wasn't so much of a realist she'd dream of one day building a similar home for herself. I wonder why Alex is so keen on severe modern stuff? she reflected, as she had so often after seeing The Stone House. Was it purely reaction to his father's affection for something different?

Somehow, the certainty that Joseph Stone had approved of her meant a lot. Helen awakened in the night sometimes and felt warmer for suspecting he also might be glad they appreciated similar traditions. And much good will it do me, she told herself, when the cold draught from the empty iron fireplace in her room brought her back to reality.

I mustn't ever become discontented because I don't live among folk like that, she reminded herself quite regularly. When I've done training somebody somewhere will employ me in their practice. Until then, I'll be gathering experience and I'll enjoy it all, especially when there's things coming up like that trip to Europe.

Since seeing Alex in his home environment Helen had grown to realise how likeable he could be. She couldn't help admiring the authority with which he spoke. But there was more to it than that. He was so attractive that she couldn't feel anything but pleased when he took her arm, or even when his arguments about architecture were directed at her. She could hardly wait for the day when they would all set out together for the Continent.

Chapter 3

'I'm beginning to suspect you're not really interested in architecture at all,' Helen had said first thing that morning. They were in Lucerne now, where they had arrived late the previous night. The rest of them had been up early to begin the tour arranged for their interest. Alex had come down to breakfast just as they were gathering in the foyer around their English-speaking guide.

'Make my apologies, there's a love,' he whispered to Helen. 'Say I'm ill or something. I can't bear another day of inspecting fusty old buildings that look as dead as the folk who created them.'

Alexander was disappointing Helen a great deal. Being unbearable, in fact. She wasn't the only one who'd sharpened their tongue on him. Even Harold Tilsley had ceased to laugh at his behaviour. No one had expected Alex to enthuse about the historic buildings of Rome or Florence, but he had made such a show of being bored while they were exclaiming over the magnificence all around. And in Pisa he had outright distressed their guide by leaving the rest of the party who were fascinated, wandering around the Baptistry, the Cathedral which was begun way back in 1063, and of course the leaning tower. Alex had claimed the early March weather, even in Italy, was too cold for him.

Although she had passed on his excuses today, Helen was livid. But at least he wasn't ruining the day for the other nine students in their group. She forgot him entirely while they viewed the courtyard of the Ritter House, marvelling that its triple-storeyed arcading was constructed in the sixteenth century. And now they'd moved on to cross by the covered wooden bridge, Helen felt she could remain here all day, inspecting all the paintings which illustrated the history of Lucerne.

'The tower here once was a belfry,' their guide explained, then grimaced. 'It also contained a torture chamber.'

Looking out from the fourteenth-century bridge, first to one side and then the other, Helen sighed with sheer pleasure. Who'd have imagined she'd ever see a place that was so beautiful? It couldn't be more different from the industrial West Riding. She'd have such a lot to describe to Mum and Dad when she got home. Across the water were red-roofed buildings, every one of them clean and bright because there wasn't all that dreadful mill smoke. Nearer at hand the antics of the waterfowl made her smile, briefly reminding her of Stratford swans.

Some of the others paused beside her, asking where Alexander was, and surprising her because it seemed that over the years they'd grown to accept that a special relationship bonded the pair of them.

And did it? she wondered, after recounting his casual dismissal of the outing. Today she'd no wish to be associated with his arrogant offhandedness, but normally . . . ? She supposed she'd always been glad to have one person in their class who could be relied on to be friendly to her. At the beginning there had been a few occasions when some of the other young men had appeared dubious about having a girl among them.

These days, they took her for granted. But was there more than a certain closeness between herself and Alex following that visit to his home?

'Alex is a real old grouch, all of a sudden,' Harold Tilsley remarked. 'You're better without him.'

'Aren't we all?' she laughed. 'Come on — let's walk to the end of the bridge, then we'd best be off to wherever our guide wants our next stop to be.' It was their last day in Lucerne and she wanted to see as much as she could.

They arrived back at their hotel as some of the other guests were coming downstairs for dinner. Alex was standing in the reception area, clearly watching for their party.

He strode straight towards Helen. 'Sorry, old love, I've been a bit of a boor. But you know me and all these old ornate places. They're too rooted in the past for me.'

'They're not all ornate. You should have seen the old bridge.'

'I did, on my own, this afternoon.'

'Good. Everything's all right then.'

'It isn't though, is it? Not between us.'

'It's no worse than it's been sometimes in the past. You have your opinions, I stick to mine. We'll neither of us change in that.'

'I'd like to make it up to you, though. We could stay on here, let the others go back home without us.'

Helen's eyebrows arched. 'Nay, Alex just a minute. I know too much about you, remember? I'll not fall for that one.'

'Have you never believed me? Not ever, right from the start? You're the one girl I respect, Helen. There'd be no funny business. We'd still have single rooms, and keep to them.'

When her hesitation continued he took her arm.

43

'We could hire a car, see something of the scenery round about. That *is* something we could enjoy together.'

Hiring a car, however, generated further disagreements. After waving off their fellow students amid a chorus of the remarks they'd anticipated about why they were remaining in Lucerne, they got into the Volkswagen and looked at each other.

'Where to then?' Alexander inquired. He genuinely wanted to patch things up with Helen. Even he himself wasn't entirely sure why he'd felt so miserable throughout this trip. It certainly hadn't been at all as he'd imagined. Maybe he hadn't anticipated how obtrusive the others would seem. And the low temperatures hadn't helped – he'd pictured them strolling beneath the warm Italian sun, there was nothing romantic about battling to stand up against icy winds. Here in the mountains it was worse still, with occasional scatterings of snow. At this minute ice was frosting the car windows.

'Just drive,' Helen suggested. 'It's all new to us, isn't it?' She was, in fact, feeling uncomfortable now about her swift decision to stay on here with Alex. But she had wanted to find out what it was that had troubled him so much that he'd behaved badly. He wasn't really lacking in basic courtesy; if he was trying to sort out some problem she could only help by getting him on his own. Seeing the others depart, though, had left her with a strange foreboding.

Alex took the road hugging the shore of the lake and they stopped eventually to have lunch in a restaurant overlooking the water. As they ate a traditional fondue he began to realise how relieved he was that the two of them were alone. Helen might not be the prettiest young woman he'd known – she was taller and rather heavier than the girls he usually took out – but she had an intelligent face which glowed with enthusiasm. Her grey eyes were extraordinarily appealing. One straightforward glance was enough to stir him.

Alexander enjoyed being stirred. He'd always relished having a female in their class; had been glad he'd ensured they sat near to each other. These days, especially during this trip, he'd discovered that he resented her attention being diverted away from him. And what was wrong with that? He had promised he meant her no harm. All he wished was to spend a bit of time concentrating on something more personal than architecture.

'How about going back to the hotel this afternoon?' he suggested. 'We could sit for ages talking over tea — they do serve tea — then have a really relaxing evening.'

'What about the car? I thought you'd hired it so we could get around here . . .'

'There's tomorrow, and the next day. Where do you want to go, anyway? You don't know anywhere.'

'There's the abbey at Einsiedeln.' She'd seen on the map that it wasn't all that far away, and had been wondering ever since they crossed the Channel how she might manage to get there.

'You're off again about old buildings, aren't you? Drat it!'

'It *is* why I came to Europe. I thought it was the same for you.'

'If you must know, I pictured the two of us exploring places together. Thought it'd be fun.'

'And so it has been. I've loved every minute.'

Alex saw how true that was, watched her beautiful eyes glinting with joy. Again he felt dejected, aware that he'd contributed nothing to her enjoyment. And that was his own fault. By withdrawing because he'd resented having the others around, he'd missed the opportunity to share her pleasure. Worst of all, though, was learning that she had been content without him.

'We'll go somewhere tomorrow — where shall it be?' he asked, trying again to recover the easy relationship with her on which he'd hoped at last to establish something more intimate.

'I've made my suggestion,' Helen reminded him quietly.

'But Einsiedeln's so baroque. Its interior is far too ornate. You know that's not my style. Anywhere but there, love, anywhere at all.'

'You choose then. It's the only place I can think of.'

It had begun snowing by the time their meal was over, and Alex hadn't come up with any alternative for the afternoon and evening, or for the next day. Wearily, Helen agreed to return to their hotel.

The evening wasn't a success. She was so full of all the amazing buildings she'd seen in Florence and in Rome, she couldn't keep them out of the conversation. And Alex's expression repeatedly revealed his displeasure.

'Do you really dislike architecture?' she inquired gently, ready to sympathise if Joseph Stone had insisted Alex should follow this career.

'Not in the least, but I don't believe in living in the past. The things I build will show future generations something of now — of this age, Helen, not just echoes of the past.'

'But the past has lasted, and can teach us so much.'

'Which we adapt and improve on.'

'Granted.'

'The things I design are totally modern, built around my ideas. *Mine*.'

'You say that as if you're designing already. We've none of us started yet.'

'That's where you're wrong,' he said, surprising her into staring at him across the table. 'You knew I'd spent some time in Father's practice, surely?'

'Yes, but . . .'

Alexander was smiling at last. 'I made him give me a chance. A year or two since now. It was during the summer when we'd no classes. I persuaded Father to allow me just one design of my own. I really worked at it, love, put all I'd got into it.'

'And?'

'I pulled it off! Even he could find no more than one or two minor flaws. I couldn't believe it myself. He only altered a few lines on one elevation.'

'What sort of building is it for?'

'Nothing very grand — a farmhouse. But a very good farmhouse — Yeoman's Grange. I'll take you there when we get home. It's only a little way farther up the Calder Valley from us, on the hillside just beyond Mytholmroyd.'

'It's been completed already?'

'Last year. July.'

'But you never said. Not to Mr Wilkinson, nor to any of us.'

'Wilkinson wouldn't have approved, you know he thinks we've got to progress at his rate. He wouldn't like me getting ahead of the class.'

'But the rest of us?'

'And have it coming out in front of him? Somebody in a class the size of ours would have let it slip.'

'I don't think it would have mattered. Still, I'm pleased for you. A bit envious an' all. Must be marvellous to see your plans come to life.'

'It is pretty special.'

Even though she was delighted that Alex had confided in her, Helen didn't believe that he should close his mind to so much that had been devised by past masters of their profession. And nor had he the right to dismiss her opinions — was that just because she was a woman? She was too keen to remain silent about her feelings, too young to know not to persist.

'Just be fair — see for yourself,' she finished, as they walked slowly towards the stairs. 'Come with me to Einsiedeln, and come with an open mind. I'm so certain there'll be something you can like.'

Alex was no less sure that she was wrong. By daylight next morning when they met over an early breakfast he was, if anything, more adamant.

'You go if you wish, Helen. Take the car and go there. It won't do a thing for you.'

She hesitated, drawn by the possibility of seeing the abbey, and knowing that she'd be unlikely to come this way again. What was it their Marian had always said? 'This isn't just a practice for life, you know. If there's summat you want, it mightn't be offered again.'

'Well, when my brother-in-law taught me to drive, he said it'd open up opportunities. I suppose this is one I'm not going to miss.'

Helen had been scared more than once during the journey. She'd soon found there was a vast difference between driving on familiar roads in Yorkshire and here in the Alps, especially when sudden flurries of snow increased the danger of her not noticing all the icy patches. But the instant that she saw Einsiedeln in the distance every scrap of unease drained from her.

Standing out from the monastery buildings as well as from the little town itself, the twin towers seemed to urge her towards them. Farther along the narrow road, Helen glanced between conifers and noticed how white the abbey gleamed, contrasting with the green pastures beyond, the blue of Lake Sihl and of the sky. Only the snow-covered mountains had a similar brilliance.

Einsiedeln was even better close to. After parking opposite the front of the abbey, Helen gazed towards the elegant façade. But she was too exited to remain where she was, and moments later was approaching the heavy door.

Her first sight of the interior was so staggering that she stood for several seconds just inside the entrance. The sun, low in the sky, beamed in through the windows, silhouetting the Chapel of Grace which stood isolated in its black marble, but glowing from within when she approached the chapel's open gates. The glow, far brighter than any sun, was golden, seeming to hang in clouds and numerous light rays, and surround a black-faced Madonna and Child. Both were robed in red silk embroidered with gold. Below their feet an altar frontal echoed the colours.

When Helen finally began to move away from the chapel her eyes were so dazzled that the panels in gold relief decorating its dark exterior looked dull, and she felt drawn to continue staring towards that source of light above the altar.

Gradually, though, she was becoming aware of the rest of the area where this chapel within a church was housed — of splendid arches and columns of white embellished with gold and touches of red. In a daze, she backed away from the chapel to begin examining the building which soared above and about it. She had never seen such magnificence. Very slowly, she walked around, pausing by every arch, glancing upwards towards each window.

The sun seemed to have disappeared yet still the abbey shone, its carvings and its statues growing out of intricate gilded ornamentation. And then, just when she had progressed in a half-circle so that glancing back she saw the rear of the Chapel of Grace, Helen looked straight ahead of her. The amazing beauty which she'd seen already was only a portion of the whole.

Beyond this splendour were further sections, even more gloriously decorated, with painted cupolas. The mural she could see from here was of the Last Supper. In the far distance beyond the magnificent nave and delicately wrought gates was the choir.

It was inside the choir, whilst admiring the ornate abbot's throne, that Helen began to feel overcome. She'd expected masses of decoration, no baroque building would be lacking in that, but nothing had prepared her for so much within the one edifice.

Suddenly aware that she needed to get away from it all, if only for a short while, she began hurrying back through the different areas of the abbey towards the door.

Fumbling in her confusion, she struggled to turn the handle and all but stumbled as she went through to the open air.

She steadied herself against the wall, was compelled to lean for a moment against the icy chill of its stone. A bitter wind keened across this broad plateau amid the Alps, knocking out of her what little breath still remained, making recovery even more difficult.

A few snowflakes fluttered over her face, landed on closed eyelids, making her conscious that she'd shut her eyes as she attempted to come to terms with all that she had seen. How ever could Alexander belittle so much loveliness, and the craftsmanship which, over the years, had contributed to its creation?

'Excuse me, are you all right?'

She opened her eyes to find a young man studying her with concern. Snow gathered on his dark hair while he waited to see that she was all right.

'Yes, I – yes, thanks.' She managed a smile, and saw his rather thin lips curving in relief.

'You were . . . overwhelmed?' Sherry brown eyes smiled understandingly. His face was surprisingly gentle though his clothes — black trousers and sweater — hinted at a certain austerity of character.

Helen's laugh was rueful. 'Thank goodness you didn't want me to explain. I'd never have found the words!'

The man glanced about as though looking for somebody. 'You came here alone?'

Again she laughed, this time more freely. 'It's 1938, remember. Women have learnt to drive cars. We're even allowed out unescorted!' But then she realised that her joking response might have been misconstrued.

'Sorry, I didn't mean to be rude, but you looked so astonished that I'd come on my own today.'

'You're not on holiday out here alone then?'

Helen shook her head. 'Not really on holiday either. I'm studying architecture. A group of us have been to Italy. We're staying in Lucerne now.'

'Are you driving back there straight away?'

'I suppose so.'

'You're up to driving, are you?'

If it had been Alex implying otherwise, she'd have soon put him right, but this fellow was genuinely worried that she might not have recovered sufficiently from the impact of the abbey.

'You're too observant. I'll be all right in a few minutes.'

'And even better after a coffee or something.' He glanced away from where they were standing. 'There's a cafe.'

When Helen nodded, thanking him, he smiled once more. Before striding off, he grinned and fastened the top button of her tweed coat for her, turned up its fur collar. Neither Alex nor any of the other students ever paid her such small attentions.

'You're being very kind,' she said, and repeated the words minutes later when a steaming cup of chocolate was placed before her. 'And I still feel a bit of a fool. I was . . . well, the only word's gobsmacked! It was such a shock, you see. Alex had refused to come with me. As a matter of fact, he spends most of his time condemning ornate buildings like this. Driving over to see the abbey, I was beginning to wonder if I was wrong — if I shouldn't like it.' She paused. 'Oh, isn't "like" an inadequate word? I was so overcome, in awe of it all.'

'I know the feeling.'

And *she* knew at once that these weren't empty words. They smiled again at each other.

'It's funny, you know,' Helen continued, 'Alexander and I have been pals since the day we started art college, yet we never agree on architectural styles. And he is rather forceful.'

'Then you should be too, surely? Your opinions are just as valid as his, or anyone else's.'

'I'm not so certain about that. Alex should know what he is talking about, his father's Joseph Stone, the architect. I'm afraid I'm the old-fashioned one in the class. And that's not good, not when I should be thinking by now about the sort of job I'll have eventually.'

'How much more training's ahead of you?'

'A lot, though the worst's behind me. But even if I pass my finals at the first attempt there's still the practical side, with a firm of architects.'

'And what will you tell this Alex about today? The abbey?'

'That it moved me.' Suddenly, she was forced to confront the full significance of the experience. 'That I wanted to be a part of it, longed to have a share in

52

creating something so lovely.' Her voice lowered. 'And that I wished, for the first time in many a year, that I was sure I believed in what it stands for.'

'And you're certain that you don't?'

'I've had plenty of time to weigh it up. Church, an' all that. My father's a strict non-conformist. He tried for ages to get me to go with him.'

The sherry-coloured eyes sought her own again, briefly, before he glanced away to the spoon with which he was tracing intricate designs on the table cloth. 'We are talking of belief, you know, not proof. Faith, not the certain knowledge of an established fact.'

'But . . .' Helen began, then sighed. She'd never yearned before to belong amid so much that witnessed to reverence.

'Have you never considered that willingness to keep an open mind might be enough? For a start, at least.'

'No, I haven't. You either believe or you don't. And no amount of wishing for the comfort of belief . . .'

'Comfort?' he interrupted, and snorted. His eyes glinted with some private wry amusement, and were very searching.

He made Helen feel awkward. She glanced at her watch.

'I'd better be on my way. Thank you very much for the hot chocolate — sorry, I don't remember your name.'

'Chris. Christopher Maitland. You ought to return to the abbey, you know, give it another chance. The first impact is pretty startling. You're too disadvantaged to take in all that's there. Even the material side.'

'I know. I might do that, if there's time. Depends what else Alex wishes to see before we leave for home. That's the thing about architecture — wherever you go, there's so much that's interesting.'

Christopher smiled, rising with her, finding money for the bill without taking his gaze from her face. 'I'm sure. You're fortunate that your occupation is something so . . . tangible. It must prove very rewarding.'

Helen grinned. 'You'll have gathered by now that I'm rather obsessed. Like now. So carried away that I haven't even asked about your work.'

'I'm a student,' he said hastily.

While they were saying goodbye, Helen was struggling not to show her surprise. She was twenty-one now, he looked two or three years older . . . and still studying?

As she carefully followed the road over the mountains to Lucerne she felt as if the breathless awe she had experienced in the abbey had returned, and sensed it had somehow become intensified by her meeting with Christopher Maitland.

Alex wasn't in the hotel when she arrived back that evening, but while she was changing for dinner she glanced out of the window and saw him crossing the road towards the entrance. He was arm-in-arm with a flaxen-haired girl who was laughing up at him.

Berenice was at their table when Helen went down to the dining room. Smiling, Alex introduced them. 'Berry is here for a couple of days,' he explained, 'before going on to Zurich where her parents live.'

She was a pleasant enough girl, half-English, and talked excitedly throughout their meal. Afterwards, Helen couldn't recall what had been said, certainly little of any consequence, although she soon grasped the fact that Berry and Alex had spent most of the day together, and intended doing so tomorrow.

Nodding her approval, Helen smiled. 'If it's not terribly inconvenient, I wonder if you'd drop me off somewhere near Einsiedeln? There was so much to see

I only absorbed half of it today.'

'Use the car again, I don't need it,' Alex said airily.

It seemed Berry had a car of her own. Helen wasn't surprised that Alex had taken up with someone so evidently well heeled. Very much his sort, she supposed. But she was neither perturbed nor curious about the kind of relationship which might be developing between the pair. All she wanted at present was the freedom to follow old Mr March's advice and take a really thorough look at the abbey.

This time, entering the church, Helen felt a difference. Still awe-inspiring, still overwhelming, it now seemed more significantly a place of worship. She was conscious immediately of her nostrils prickling with the aroma of incense, of the rays of the pale sun focused on the dark marble of the chapel housing the Black Madonna, and of the urge to go and kneel near the chapel gates.

Unaccustomed to kneeling, she simply stood there, gazing at all the gold surrounding the image. All at once, she felt very alone, shut out maybe by her years of disbelief yet aching to be at one with something which she knew might be found here.

Silently, a darkly clad figure came to kneel beside her. Helen did not need to look to identify him, but smiled affectionately when she eventually gazed down at his bowed dark head.

Christopher grinned as he got to his feet. 'I saw the car, guessed where you would be,' he whispered.

Helen smiled back, pleased to see him again, wondering now if it was as much in the hope of this encounter as to see the abbey that she'd returned.

His hand rested lightly on her shoulder as they began walking around.

'Some of this was designed by Caspar Mosbrugger,

55

wasn't it?' Helen remarked.

Christopher nodded. 'And the Asam brothers were responsible for many of the frescoes. But this is only one of the many consecrated buildings to appear on this site. Way back in nine hundred and thirty-four, a monk came from Strasbourg, and that was the beginning of the monastic community here.'

'Does anything remain of the original buildings?' Helen asked, following him into the nave.

He shrugged. 'Haven't yet found that out,' he admitted. 'But I do know that a succession of fires destroyed parts of the earlier monasteries and the abbey.'

Because he was able to enlighten her about life within the order here as well as some of the history of the buildings, Helen remained fascinated. It wasn't for some while that she even considered anything beyond their glorious surroundings.

When they finally went out into the cold mountain air, Christopher smiled down at her again. Without asking he led the way across to the familiar cafe.

She felt quite easy with Christopher now. He might have been an older brother who was taking trouble to ensure that she enjoyed her visit. And she was itching to know more about him.

'Yesterday, we talked about me,' she began, smiling over the rim of her cup. 'Today I insist you have your turn. You say you're a student. What are you reading?'

He didn't reply immediately. He was looking into her eyes, thinking what an exquisite pearl colour they were. Yet it wasn't her loveliness that enchanted him so much as her manner. She could be direct, yet there was more sensitivity there than in many who made straightforwardness their virtue. She appealed to him far more strongly than any other woman he had met.

Not that he was an expert. Quite the opposite.

'For a degree at present,' he eventually answered carefully. 'Master of Arts, nothing special.'

'Which university?'

'Leeds.'

'That's where I'm studying — the College of Art.' She wanted to add that they could meet up, but knew she'd never suggest that. Women might have steadily taken more of a hand in determining their own lives since the day they'd ensured their right to vote, but there were still many areas where the man should lead. Her years among a class of male students had encouraged a feeling of equality, but she'd been indoctrinated in certain beliefs — and they most certainly didn't allow for any forwardness in young women.

Talking as they had on the previous day, they scarcely noticed how time was passing except when hunger compelled them to order soup and rolls, followed by Apfel Kuchen.

It was Chris who at last glanced at his watch. 'When do you have to be back at your hotel?'

'That can't be the time!' Helen exclaimed, but a glance towards the darkening sky confirmed how late it was. Then her smile returned. 'But I can't regret one moment of today. Thank you, Christopher.'

By the time they had settled the bill and emerged it was completely dark. There had been a light snowfall, beneath which the ground was icy. Beyond the abbey and its environs there was no sign of even one light shining from the town.

'Fog, filling all the valleys,' Christopher observed, frowning. 'Helen, I don't want you driving in this.'

'I'll be all right. I've got to get back.'

'Then I'll drive you there.'

'You can't. Aren't you staying in Einsiedeln?' She

had felt certain that he was located somewhere in the town here.

'Doesn't matter. I could always stop overnight in Lucerne.' Anything was better than thinking of her tackling that drive alone in this treacherous weather.

Helen agreed — with considerable relief. She hated fog and, not having her own car, was unused to driving in conditions as bad as these.

They had travelled barely a couple of miles — very slowly, for the icy road surface made them even more vulnerable to running off the road — when Christopher drew up on to the grass verge.

'I'm sorry,' he said, switching off the engine. 'Can't see a thing. I can't risk both our lives by continuing.'

'It's all my fault,' said Helen swiftly. 'I was irresponsible, not even thinking about the time. I was too interested in our conversation.'

His smile was momentary, and disappeared all too quickly.

'What'll we do?' she asked.

'Wait. Hope it'll clear.'

It was Christopher who eventually found the path to one of the mountain huts constructed as a refuge for skiers. Rather than lifting, the fog had intensified. Helen had shivered twice and he'd insisted on leaving the car. When they located the hut, though, she was puzzled by the grim air lurking behind his relief.

'It'll be infinitely warmer than the car,' he told her, yet still she noticed how tense he seemed.

He was right about the interior of the hut. She smiled appreciatively when he closed the door behind them. There was a torch beside the doorframe and he beamed it around their tiny quarters, revealing not only an oil lamp but a primitive heating stove. He lit them both while she took folded blankets from a well-insulated chest.

'Come and warm your hands,' he suggested, kneeling beside the stove.

Helen joined him at once.

Close beside him her perfume was drawn out by the heat, a fragrance that alerted all his senses. Chris knew he ought to move away, creating space between them. But Helen leaned her head against him in a gesture as innocent and as affectionate as a kitten's.

'If I had to be marooned here, I'm glad it's with you,' she admitted. She so enjoyed his company, relished the absence of the contention that always came with Alex's presence. And then there was the way Alex was with women. Look how readily he'd picked up with Berry! Despite his assurances, she'd not have felt easy alone with him here.

'Helen, don't . . .'

'But it's the truth. I thought you liked me being direct?'

Christopher didn't respond. How ironic to find himself isolated here with the one girl who could make him forget everything he was committed to.

'Chris — forgive me for asking, but are you married?'

He shook his head, and swallowed. 'No.'

She stirred slightly. Her hair brushed his cheek. Sighing, he rose and crossed briskly towards the blankets. He felt her watching him and could only guess her thoughts. Before he'd controlled the emotions making him move from the stove, she was beside him again. Unfolding the blanket, he discovered that was precisely what it was — huge, but only one.

'I suppose the idea is that you keep each other warm,' Helen said lightly. 'Come on.'

'You take the blanket. I'm all right.'

'Rubbish! You'll be frozen.' She paused, looking

into his eyes in the thin light from the lamp. 'What's wrong?'

He shook his head.

'We're fully clothed, for Heaven's sake!' Helen exclaimed. 'And not just a couple of fools.'

Still Christopher did not speak. Even last night, after seeing her only the once, he'd been too disturbed to sleep for wanting her. The longing had flared again today with renewed urgency. It might be endured from the other side of a cafe table. Here, it threatened to overwhelm him.

Helen was smiling. 'I'm going to take a risk,' she said forthrightly, 'and admit that I was hoping we might see each other again, once we get back to Yorkshire. I know we've only just met, but we seem to share so much.'

'Helen, please . . .'

She looked straight into his eyes. Christopher could not doubt the affection in her gaze, nor that it bordered on the emotion he was feeling for her. He tried to move away again, and felt his will weakening. Just this once, he thought. Just once . . .

Her kiss was impulsive, so unexpected that it took him by surprise.

'You see,' she said huskily, 'I'm drawn to you as well, Chris. It's not something to regret, my dear.'

'You don't know what you're saying.'

Again she kissed him, stopping his words with lips that prevented his from remaining aloof. Inwardly he groaned, yet could not let her go. He was kissing her feverishly, urging her lips to part for him. Her arms slid around him, anchoring him against her. He felt her fingers press his back.

Desire leapt within him in a million pinpoints of light and warmth.

Helen sighed against his lips, surrendering all

memories of the years when studies and work had left no time for love. For so long now she had struggled to learn, turning herself into the self-sufficient individual she was never meant to be. Here with Chris she had already discovered so much that could colour her life. She longed to discover more.

Abruptly, he broke away from her. His hands went to hers, wrenched them away.

'No, my dear.'

But his voice was soft and tremulous. And it confirmed to Helen all that she'd suspected. Now she knew he felt as she did, she couldn't accept that he meant this should not continue.

'It isn't just sex, is it?' she said. 'I'll agree it's very swift, but does that have to mean it's wrong? I'd not let anything happen – *you know*. I wasn't brought up to do owt like that without getting married, but . . .'

'Helen, my dear, I'm sorry. We shouldn't even continue seeing each other. I told you I'm studying – it's for the priesthood.'

'A priest?' she gasped. Eventually, after considering, she smiled. 'Happen I should have guessed. You'll be pretty good.'

They talked after that, about their very different careers and about Einsiedeln, no longer acknowledging anything that had passed between them. After a time they slept fitfully, backs to one another and drawing some comfort from the solitary blanket.

Although the fog had vanished, Chris insisted on driving her into Lucerne next morning. When he drew up outside the hotel he offered his hand.

'Goodbye then,' he said, and released her fingers. Briefly, he caressed her cheek. 'Take care of yourself, Helen.' His voice was ragged. Hurriedly he got out of the car, slammed the door and strode away without glancing back. She watched him hail a taxi, and then it drove away too quickly.

Inside the taxi Chris sat rigid, his hands thrust into his pockets. He was shivering violently in shock, biting on his lips as he tried to will control into a body which seemed drained.

He closed his eyes. 'God help us,' he prayed urgently.

Chapter 4

'Where the hell have you been?' Alexander jerked open the car door. 'I've never been more worried in all my life.'

Still shattered by the finality of the goodbye she'd said to Christopher, Helen stared at him, bewildered.

'I don't see why. You were with Berenice. Why bother about me?'

'You stopped out all night. And Berry's parents rang yesterday, insisted she went home. Why the blazes didn't you let me know where you were?'

'I couldn't, Alex. The fog came down, I spent the night stranded in a sort of refuge for skiers.'

'We'd better cut the explanations, get on our way. I've packed for you, paid the bills. We can sort out finances later.'

Watching him dash back into the hotel, Helen realised that the luggage placed just inside the glass doors was theirs. That Alex had been waiting there for her.

'Just a minute,' she began indignantly when he'd flung their cases into the car. 'I didn't hear you asking if I was ready for going home yet. If you think you're taking me back as some sort of punishment . . .'

'I don't, and I'm not,' he snapped, getting into the driving seat. 'We're quitting Europe as fast as we can because we've got to. Hitler marched into Vienna yesterday evening. We're not staying this close to the Austrian border, nor to Germany.'

'Hitler did what?' she asked incredulously.

'Marched his armies into Vienna. And was well received, by the sound of it. Not surprising, considering he was born in Austria.'

'Oh, Lord! Right then – I agree, we've got to get home. Thanks for packing my stuff, Alex. Sure you found everything?'

He started up the engine. 'I double-checked. Had time and to spare – I couldn't sleep so was up around four.'

'I am sorry you were so alarmed. But there really was no need.'

'Good. Then we'll forget the whole business.'

I'll never do that, thought Helen as Alex eased out into the traffic. There's no possibility that I shall ever forget Einsiedeln, and certainly not the man I met there. For the first time in years the prospect of learning more about architecture, even of qualifying, seemed less than exciting. She believed she would recover the urge to work, but nothing would be the same.

'It won't be the same, you know,' Alexander began, startling her by appearing to tune in to her thoughts. But then he continued: 'If we end up with a major conflict on our hands, building will cease. Or the sort that interests us will. There'll be government constructions but precious little else.'

'It mightn't come to war,' she said, wishing with all her heart that there was some means of influencing the future. If only she'd known all this yesterday in the abbey, she could have . . .

'We can only pray that the powers concerned have more sense.'

Pray? thought Helen, wondering how much he

really meant of what he'd said — and how she'd known him so long yet it was still so shallowly.

'There's nothing folk like us can actually *do*,' Alex added, 'not to affect their decisions.'

Grimly, Helen recognised how true she felt that was. Yesterday — ah, well, *yesterday* she'd been close to accepting there might be a means of harnessing some higher intervention.

'The future's being taken out of our hands. That's how I feel, any road,' said Alex dourly.

Helen was no more willing than he to accept the threat of war, yet she could not visualise any way of ensuring that they hang on to peace. Moments ago the prospect of returning to further her career had seemed less appealing; now she supposed that being allowed to do just that was the best she could hope for.

It wasn't yet an hour since she and Christopher had parted, but reality had come between them, as insurmountable as concrete walls. Away from him, she had her emotions sufficiently under control to recognise how many-faceted their brief relationship had become. Maybe if it had remained purely a matter of being attracted to each other, it would have troubled them less.

A priest. This man she'd grown too fond of was a priest. How could she have let that happen? Ordinarily, she wouldn't have been drawn to anyone connected with religion. But then — ordinarily she'd have found an abbey to be no more than an interesting structure.

'No time to look at any of the towns we pass through, I'm afraid,' Alex told her, and she was glad. Her senses were too raw for that. Pleasure would feel as bad as pain while this great gap yawned in her life.

'You're not saying much,' Alex remarked at last. 'Not scared are you, by Hitler's tactics? Britain won't enter the conflict yet awhile.'

'I'm not scared of that, no. I'm just tired out. I didn't sleep much either.'

She stayed quiet throughout their journey across France. Only when they were aboard the ship heading towards Dover did she begin to realise she must exert herself and take up her life again.

The interlude in Einsiedeln must become no more than that — an interval as beautiful as the abbey itself. And even if it was love that had brought Christopher and herself together, it was love of a special kind — blissful, thrilling to the senses and imbued with tenderness. But the truth of their situation was much harsher. There could be no future for them together in the real world.

The first few weeks back in Yorkshire were grim. Knowing that Chris would have returned to studying in Leeds didn't help Helen to settle to her own work. Some days, feeling that he was so near made dismissing the thought of him impossible. She went about the city, across the Headrow, along Briggate or Bond Street, in and out of Lewis's and Schofield's, often seeing in the distance a darkly dressed man with black wavy hair. And always being obliged to quieten her disappointed, racing heart because the man proved to be a stranger.

Even in class, mention of some religious building or other would resurrect mind pictures of the abbey, and of his face, his smile.

Helen hadn't reckoned with this inner yearning which reawakened so readily and remained to torment. And she certainly hadn't expected to discover she possessed a curious strain of morality which appeared to protest repeatedly, if silently, because of his calling. I didn't know, she often reminded herself. Until it was too late, I'd never once suspected there'd be a reason like that for not seeing him ever again.

But after a time, even the hours spent in the biscuit factory ceased to be surrendered quite so frequently to thoughts of Christopher. The threat of war had faded a little at home; in thanks for that, she willed herself to concentrate more intensely on her studies.

Alex reverted to his normal self, holding forth on the latest new buildings, deriding her affection for older styles. Their class went over to Halifax to study its eighteenth-century Piece Hall, and Alex started by asserting they were all barmy to bother looking at that. But during the course of their visit he began to reverse his opinion. The rooms, constructed in three tiers, were well planned for giving previous centuries of cloth merchants space and a bit of privacy for negotiating deals. And although the entire construction was colonnaded, it wasn't over-ornate.

'Maybe it was quite functional, for the time,' he conceded. And had them all grinning. 'What's wrong now?' he demanded, and several of their fellow students laughed. 'You lot look at me as if I'm the only one that's at all progressive.'

'Happen you are, Alex,' Helen suggested, though she was well aware that Harold Tilsley, for one, had been showing around photographs of the De La Warr Pavilion in Bexhill-on-Sea, and extolling it as the epitome of modernity.

They had all been obliged to hear Harold out on how it was the first new Continental public building in the modern style, concrete-clad but built of light-weight steel. That day, he had very evidently risen in Alexander Stone's estimation. Today, Helen noticed Harold was giving Alex a funny look, as if wondering if he could be believed.

She decided to have a bit of fun. Ever since visiting

Europe she'd felt more confident in her own judgement. Leaving the Piece Hall and beginning to walk uphill into the shopping streets, she paused and pointed over to their right.

'I daresay you'll have come round to realising that's very good an' all, Alex, won't you?' she exclaimed, pointing towards the Town Hall.

He all but spluttered with indignation. 'Never! Never, in this world. Talk about Victorian . . .'

'But it was designed by Barry — that's prestigious enough for owt — and I'll bet your dad would emphasise how *functional* it is!'

Glancing through the group towards her, Alex spotted the amusement in her grey eyes and groaned. 'All right, you've had me on. But you'll be laughing the other side of your face soon enough, when you begin looking for work and get turned down for being so out-moded.'

The other students were enjoying the exchange which was, after all, one of the many to brighten their hard slog. Helen, however, although continuing to smile, was privately uneasy. Hadn't she herself wondered from time to time if there would be a place for an architect who leaned so much towards styles out of the past?

'Do you think I'm old fashioned?' she asked her sister that evening.

Still holding the spoonful of egg which she'd been trying to persuade her small son to eat, Marian turned to her. 'Well, if you aren't, I don't know who is!'

'Thank you very much.'

Her sister smiled over her shoulder then returned to tidying the rim of egg yolk from around Mark's face. 'You shouldn't ask such daft questions. You leave yourself wide open. I hope you have more sense while you're at college.'

'But that's what it's all about really. There's always been Alex and me at opposite ends. He's allus been in favour of Art Deco and all that, and I suppose I'm just stuffy.'

Their father interrupted at that. 'Well, I don't pretend to know much about it, but there's some grand buildings gone up during the past ten years, and not all of them modern-looking. I'm thinking of the Viceroy's House in New Delhi – proper grand that was. I still have the picture that I cut out of t'paper.'

'Aye, but that was Edwin Lutyens, you see. I'm not reckoning I'll ever be as good as him.' She was pleased as well as surprised, nevertheless, that her father had been so interested in any building.

'Does it matter then?' Marian asked, as she moved Mark's high-chair and sat down at the table. 'Being old-fashioned, I mean?'

Helen's grin was rueful. 'Eh, I don't know. I'm afraid it might, if I don't fit in with other architects in the practice.'

'I can imagine that might lead to difficulties,' Marian said, nodding as she straightened her chair so her sister could take the next one to it.

'I'll just have to wait and see, I suppose. Any road, I'm already having to adapt some of my ideas in order to fit in with our student projects.'

'You'll find just the place, I'm sure,' Kathleen asserted, coming through from the kitchen with a tureen of tripe and onions. 'And it's only what you deserve.' She was that proud of the way their Helen had stuck to this course. Nobody on either side of the family had ever tackled anything that involved half as much studying.

Seeing the tripe, Marian wrinkled her nose, glanced sideways at Helen, and then remembered. Mum and Dad were being very good, keeping them and the two children for nothing until Denis started his new job. She'd made up her mind it was only fair not to let one word of complaint disturb things.

Marian had learned a lot during nearly six years of marriage. And if her love of fun had had to be suppressed sometimes, there wasn't much else that had gone by the board. She and Denis still got on well together, and even her mother could find nowt wrong with young Mark and Linda. They had had to be good for much of their short lives; Marian and Denis had often been in rented accommodation, sometimes with actors from the company as neighbours who had needed quiet at home while they were learning lines.

It seemed a long time now since they'd set up house so optimistically in Stratford. Although his job there had lasted until just the other week, their circumstances had changed. First Linda had come along, and then Mark, and there'd been no chance of Marian herself going out to work while she had them to look after. They'd been obliged to give up their first home, and that was when they'd started living in flats, most of them in houses owned by the theatre. The car had been sold. Denis now travelled around by motorbike which Marian hated.

They had moved back to Halifax so she could be near her mother who would help with Linda and Mark, freeing her to look for a job. Once Denis started as Assistant Stage Manager at the Grand Theatre in Leeds they would begin saving again for a place of their own.

Marian smiled to herself, watching the way her father was encouraging Linda to come to the table. Now she'd started school, she always wanted a pencil in her hand, or a slate pencil. Helen had bought her a wooden-framed slate, and it certainly made sense being able to clean the drawings off so that Linda could start all over again.

'I reckon she's taking after you, you know, Helen. It's allus houses she's doing.'

'Isn't it the same with all children? They're easy to draw.'

'It'd be nice, though, wouldn't it? You'd be able to teach her all she needs to know.'

Helen laughed. 'I doubt that. By the time I get to the end of my training, I'll have forgotten what I learnt at the beginning.'

'But I thought you'd have to remember it all, love?' Kathleen protested seriously. She tried to grasp everything it involved, but subjects like 'theory of construction', 'specifications' and 'professional practice' were beyond her.

'That is the general idea, Mum,' Helen replied patiently. 'It's only me going on about it taking forever.'

'We did warn . . .' Kathleen began.

Her husband cut in, smiling. 'You're taking our Helen too serious again,' he exclaimed. 'You only have to look at her to know she loves the work.'

'Our Helen's a serious young woman,' Marian announced, over the top of their father's voice.

All the adults plus young Mark laughed.

'What did you say that's funny, Mummy?' Linda inquired. She hated not understanding what was going on.

Marian gave her a hug. 'Eh, love, it was summat and nowt. I was only being daft.'

'You tell me off for that.'

'I do, an' all. And I'm afraid that's something that's going to happen for a long while yet. Not fair, is it?'

The child shook her blonde curly head, and her grandfather stroked the silky-textured hair. 'Never mind, Linda love — we have our bit of fun, any road, don't we?'

Greatly attached to each other, Daniel Clegg and his granddaughter spent hours playing dominoes or snakes and ladders. And the toffees he brought home from work contributed enormously to his popularity.

'What time will Denis be in?' Kathleen asked. She had finished serving out portions of tripe and onions and returned the lid to the tureen ready to put it back in the oven.

'Can't be sure, Mum, sorry.' Marian felt embarrassed already. Denis knew his in-laws liked to eat as soon as her father had washed after work. Her husband had been out all day in Leeds. One of his pals was the Stage Manager at the theatre and that was how Denis had heard about the job. And not having started there yet wasn't keeping him away. She knew how it would be, an' all — a few pints in the local every time they weren't needed backstage.

If they weren't so short of brass she wouldn't mind his drinking. He always knew when to stop, and it did put him in a good mood and usually made him quite amorous. That was one thing that hadn't changed — he was a lovely man, especially in bed. Marian had been worried for a long time after Mark's birth because they would never get on their feet if they risked having another. But then she'd been to one of the clinics opened by Dr Marie Stopes. She wouldn't dare mention that visit in her mother's hearing but it had put her own mind at rest.

Their Helen *was* old fashioned an' all, Marian reflected, remembering the day she'd told her sister how you didn't have to have children if you didn't want any more. Helen had been appalled. Even when Marian had explained that she'd only wanted her to benefit from what she'd discovered, Helen had still looked at her as though she was doing something really wicked.

'How can you see a couple of lovely children like your two, and wish to prevent any more being born!' she'd exclaimed.

'Just you wait,' Marian had retorted. 'Your turn'll come. And happen sooner than you think, after you've had all these years scrimping and saving. You'll have nowt behind you if you get married. You'll be too scun up to have a load of children round you.'

It was a pity their Helen was taking so long to qualify, Marian thought. She'd be a grand little mother, more practical in lots of ways than she herself was.

Helen's career called for a great deal of practicality these days. The students were often expected to visit sites – assessing their suitability, measuring up, and planning drainage and all the other essential services which must be incorporated in every building project.

She relished these outings which made the future seem nearer, and loved surprising her fellow students. The first time had been one murky November day while they were down by the River Aire in Leeds where an old warehouse had burned down. Developers were planning a mill there, but when Helen and the others arrived to inspect the site the original place wasn't quite demolished. Half a dozen rats shot out and some of her companions went ashen with shock. They seemed quite put out because she hadn't flinched. And she often proved herself their equal in physical tasks. She was glad now that she had a strong frame, had nearly forgotten the days when she'd envied her sister's fragility.

And Alex didn't seem to think there was much wrong with her. Ever since the trip to Europe he'd appeared less eager to go out with every attractive girl he could find. He made such a point of hanging around Helen when they were visiting construction sites that the other students were forever ribbing them. What the others didn't know was that she was often invited to Alexander's home now.

The first time she returned there, she had been wondering why it was that Joseph Stone had pressed his son to ask her to join them that Saturday. Rather anxiously, she had got out of Alex's car in which she'd been driven to Brearley. They had stopped on the way at her own home, so that she could clean up and change after spending the morning under instruction at a site where foundations were being dug.

At home, her parents were just starting their midday dinner, but they had welcomed Alex warmly enough when he was introduced to them.

'I'll just pop mine back in t'oven while I pour you a cup of tea, lad,' Kathleen Clegg had exclaimed, seeming far less perturbed than Helen had expected. 'I'm glad we're getting to know one of Helen's friends at last.'

'Aye,' Daniel had added, as Helen went into the kitchen to wash. 'And since you're a Stone, I suppose you'll be one of the family that's architects already?'

'That's right, sir. My father's Joseph Stone.'

It was after Helen had changed and reappeared at the foot of the stairs, though, that she really learned how well they were getting on together. Having reached their second course, Kathleen and her husband were inviting Alex to try a portion of sponge pudding.

'Go on, lad,' said Daniel. 'Helen's mum makes the lightest pudding in t'West Riding. It won't spoil your dinner at home.'

Handing him a plate, Kathleen was beaming. 'You

needn't let on to your own mother that you've already had a bit of summat to eat.'

'Actually, Mrs Clegg, we only have a housekeeper. I'm afraid my mother's been dead for many a year.'

'Eh, you poor love! Well, just you think on − if you ever want a bit of extra comfort, you know where to come.'

'You have lovely people,' Alex had told Helen warmly as they sped along Burnley Road.

But she had been less than happy about the impression she was likely to make on Alex's father when there were no other students to fill the conversational gaps.

She had reckoned without Joseph Stone's determination to learn more about her. During the period since her initial visit he had gradually probed until discovering from his son that Helen's course at the college had been facilitated by the bursary from old Mr March.

'I'm glad to learn you know Seth March,' he began as soon as he had given her a glass of sherry.

'You know him as well, do you, Mr Stone?' she exclaimed, her grey eyes shining delightedly.

'March taught me a lot, I'll have you know. When I was articled he was one of the bosses. Couldn't have had a better chap in charge, either. Firm, he was, but rightly so. Made us work damned hard but was generous with his knowledge. And with his brass as well − he footed the bill for a trip abroad for me and another lad. Took us to see some fine buildings. Berne was one place we visited, and the Abbey at Einsiedeln . . .'

Alex groaned.

His father gave him a look. 'Did you get to see Einsiedeln? You never said.'

While Alex shook his head, Helen smiled. 'I went there, though.'

'I didn't think it'd be his cup of tea. You liked it, I'll bet?'

'I said at the time that "liked" doesn't really express it.'

'I agree, my dear, heartily.'

After that kind of a beginning, Helen couldn't spend the afternoon feeling awkward with Joseph Stone. During the meal he continued drawing her out concerning the places she had visited in Europe. 'Waste of time asking him,' he declared, inclining his head towards Alex, 'he won't elaborate on anything he saw out there.'

'You know the reason, Father.'

Joseph gestured dismissively with a large, neatly manicured hand. 'You'll learn, given time, all this modern stuff you fancy isn't necessarily always best.'

During subsequent visits to The Stone House Helen had discovered that she wasn't the only one who grew tired of Alexander's perpetual support of contemporary styling. One evening Joseph reminded him he was becoming a bore, and pointedly began questioning Helen about her other interests. He thoroughly approved of her love of reading, and surprised her by having a taste for recent fiction. They found a common affection for J.B. Priestley, and discussion of his books soon led to comparing notes on the plays he'd written.

This brought Alex back into the conversation, and both men were interested to learn of her brother-in-law's job at Leeds Grand Theatre.

'You never told me he worked backstage,' said Alex.

'Mustn't have cropped up,' Helen replied, although she thought she had mentioned the fact some time during the past few years. It occurred to her then that, much as she liked Alexander, he didn't always take a lot of interest in other folk.

One Sunday during that summer of 1938 she was invited to his home for dinner. She'd had to check on the time she'd be expected to arrive — knowing how very much more grand the Stones' lifestyle was than her own family's, she had thought they would dine in the evening.

The meal, however, was at one o'clock and, although accompanied by a good claret — sheer luxury to her — it was essentially the kind of meal her mother would have prepared. After chatting with Alex and his father while they finished coffee, Helen was asked if she had any plans for the afternoon.

'Well, no, not really.'

Joseph beamed. 'Then I'd like to take you both over to Todmorden. There's a site I want you to see.'

Because none of them was dressed for trudging over rough earth from which chunks of sandstone still protruded, they remained in the car when they arrived there. But Joseph ensured that neither Helen nor his son missed anything.

'They're just starting to level the site, as you can see. It's a factory we've planned here — you, Alex, will be glad to know it's on modern lines. There's enough many-storeyed eyesores in these parts, with their uninspiringly featureless walls. This one's going to be different. Lighter, constructed in steel, then concrete-faced. And the windows will have a bit of character as well as serving their purpose. It's time we got away from rows of them, all looking alike.

'We're going to use the features of the land itself, as well,' he continued, pointing out the curve of the hillside as it embraced the area being cleared. 'The wall facing that way won't be straight but will follow the line of the hill. That's where the offices will be, with plenty of glass to prevent their being overshadowed. I'd wondered at first about putting offices at the front of the building, it's where they're usually placed, and there's a view over yonder towards the stream that's just out of sight from where we are.'

Joseph grinned. 'It was the boss who put a stop to that, claiming there'd be no work done if I made the outlook too pleasant. As it is, I'll give them some space between the offices and the hillside. And that'll no doubt come in useful for parking. It won't be long before everybody in business will get around by car.'

On their way back to Brearley, Helen noticed Alex smiling to himself. He nudged her arm. 'Look up there — quick. That's Yeoman's Grange, the house I designed, the one I told you about.'

Helen heard his father's laugh, but she was more interested in trying to lean near enough to the car window to see the house properly. They were too close to the hill for her to gain more than a brief impression of a large, well-proportioned building whose clean new stone was gleaming in the sunlight.

'Go on,' said Joseph genially. 'You've indulged me by letting me show you my latest scheme. I reckon we can indulge Alexander this once.'

He turned off to the left up a lane so narrow that Helen feared for the Rolls-Royce's gleaming bodywork while they swung around bends between the drystone walls. 'Oh, do mind your lovely car!'

Joseph Stone laughed. 'You like it then? Bought this in 1929.'

'It's gorgeous. I love the blue sides. They contrast so well with all that black. Does this model have a name?'

'It's a Phantom, my dear — Cabriolet de Ville.'

But now they were there, looking down on the farmhouse, able to appreciate its economical lines and flat roof, unusual for the West Riding.

'I said he was daft letting them go ahead with their ideas for a roof like that,' Joseph told her. 'But the folk who live there insisted, and they have a point. Whilst they have one bit of a garden, the rest is given over to the farm animals. They'd never manage to keep a larger area to themselves.'

'There's a grandmother lives with them, and she's not so fond of cows coming that close they almost get into the house,' Alex explained, 'And they've got several youngsters in their teens. I gather they use the roof a lot, for sitting out with the old girl in summer. It isn't so noticeable from here, but that's an edging wall for safety.'

Helen was nodding. 'I like it, Alex, I really like it.'

He pretended to be overcome. 'God, I never thought I'd live to see the day!'

She grinned. 'And the view is terrific — they certainly had to ensure that didn't go to waste.'

It was that evening when Joseph Stone first put the suggestion to her. They had pressed her to stay for tea and were sitting afterwards in a small drawing room, watching the sun dropping towards the far hill, darkening the full-leafed trees until their fresh greens turned the shade of cypresses.

'Have you thought yet where you'll work once you're qualified, Helen? I'd like you to consider the possibility of coming to Stone's.'

She was staggered, so astonished that she could hardly frame a coherent sentence.

'Oh. Mr Stone, I never in all my wildest imaginings . . . I mean — well, you'll be taking Alex full time naturally, and . . .'

'Think about it,' Joseph interrupted with a smile. 'A decision like that needs a lot of consideration.'

'Oh, but — I mean I'm not in the least reluctant,

you mustn't think that for one moment.'

'She's simply "gobsmacked" — that's one of your favourite words, isn't it, Helen?' Alex put in.

She laughed awkwardly. 'It's just about the only word for what I'm feeling, aye!'

And so no decisions were made, but Helen was delighted and immensely heartened to learn that Joseph Stone wanted her to work with him. She was less certain how his son viewed that prospect. And she was beginning to realise that she'd sacrifice quite a lot rather than disturb Alex.

As autumn came to the West Riding, however, in strong winds that tore the leaves from trees and buffeted folk walking its steep streets, Helen noticed that Alexander appeared undismayed by his father's offering her a position with the family firm. In fact, he seemed friendlier than ever, frequently taking her out to some eating house that was beyond her own pocket, or to the newly constructed cinema in Broad Street.

They had argued the first time, just as usual, over merits and demerits in the cinema's styling. But then they had laughed at themselves, and hugged each other in the sudden recognition that their friendship had weathered worse conflicts.

Helen and Alex returned to Todmorden on a Saturday afternoon in October. The site to which Joseph Stone had taken them was unrecognisable now, the offices all but completed and the adjoining factory level with the first-storey windows.

Joseph himself was growing over-familiar with the place, and had no desire to spend leisure hours there, but both Helen and his son enjoyed going along to inspect progress. They were sufficiently near the end of their training to be able to realise how they would feel when visiting the site of one of their own buildings.

'Do you want to stop for tea in Hebden Bridge?' Alex asked, reluctant to have Helen leave him. Although admitting it to no one, he was growing dissatisfied with generally seeing her only in company. And yet with her he needed more encouragement than he ever received before he would suggest they spend more time together. She was so different from the girls he'd known that even after all this time he wasn't really sure why she wasn't more responsive. She wasn't seeing any other chap, yet still she seemed to be holding back.

Helen was glad to have tea out with him. She'd never liked autumn — it always made her aware that the end of another year was approaching, making her think of all the things she hadn't yet achieved. This year, she still couldn't get Christopher Maitland out of her head, and seemed unable to return to the way she'd once been, content with her own company.

Before heading towards the cafe, they turned up their collars against the cold and strolled over bridges and through the narrow streets, trying to picture Hebden Bridge as it had been in the days when the weaving of cloth first moved from cottages into some of these forbidding mills and became an industry. Many of the factories and rows of terraced houses had changed hardly at all during the intervening years, but the local people had.

Watching some of the women in their shorter skirts and permed hair, Helen smiled to herself. How their grandmothers would have stared.

While they were having tea Alex asked how much she knew about this part of the Calder Valley. 'There's a lot gone on here. Have you ever heard of Nutclough Fustian Manufacturing Company, for instance?'

When she said she hadn't, he was happy to enlighten her. He admired workers with initiative. 'They got together round about 1870 — a band of fustian cutters. You know what fustian is, of course?'

'Some kind of cloth, isn't it?'

He nodded. 'Cord — corduroy. There's a great deal made round here. Anyway, they formed a highly successful producer-cooperative, one of the best in Britain. Not only that, they believed in education for adults. One of the weavers of fustian became involved in founding the Workers' Education Association.'

They talked so long that when they finally emerged from the cafe it had grown dark and all the gas-lamps were lit. Alex grinned.

'I suppose we'd better be getting back. Are you going to spend the evening with us?'

'Eh, I'd love to, thanks, but I ought to be on my way home. They'll be wondering wherever I've got to.'

'You can phone them, can't you?'

Helen gave him a look. 'Do you really think we run to having a telephone!'

'Sorry, I . . .'

Helen giggled. 'Don't go all uncomfortable about it. I'm not.'

Alex had driven half a mile or so, however, when they had to draw in to the kerb to make way for a clanging fire engine. A further mile along the road, they saw two more appliances tearing along from the direction of Halifax. Watching them turn off up the hillside, Helen noticed Alex had slowed the car again, and was staring, appalled.

'Oh, God — oh, no!' he exclaimed, before following the fire engines up the steep lane.

'Oh, Alex, it isn't . . .'

The farm which they had stopped to admire during their previous journey out here was ablaze. With only one eye on the walls lining the lane, Alex drove on, most of his attention riveted on the glow from the flames.

They were halted by a police officer before they could take off down to Yeoman's Grange itself. Four fire engines were filling the yard, a fifth was stationed in the nearest field. Alex wound down the car window.

'What about the family — have they got out?'

The policeman nodded. 'Aye, sir, thank goodness. The blaze was spotted by one of the farmer's lads coming home for his tea. He dashed in and made them all leave afore it got a proper hold, like.'

'Where had this lot started then?'

'Don't ask me. It'll be the fire brigade as has to fathom that. Though, to me, it looked like it had begun in the barn. That were well alight when I got here.'

'But that's yards away from the house.'

'I know, and I'm only surmising. It's not for me to hazard even a guess as to how it spread.'

'Where've the family gone then? To a neighbour's?'

'First of all, to leave the animals there. Then they'll go on to a brother of the old lady's, I think. Do you know them then, sir?'

Alexander nodded, swallowing. He choked on the smoke as the officer moved away to speak to one of the firemen.

'Dear, dear, what a tragedy,' said Helen, unable to think of anything to say that could make Alex feel any better. 'Let's get home.' She could see how distressed he was. 'There's nothing you can do, love.'

'How can I just drive off?' he demanded. 'How the heck can I?'

He got out of the car, leaving the door ajar as he ran towards the fire officer. He'd never have an easy minute if he didn't find out how the blaze had started.

The policeman was asking if all the farm animals had been rescued.

'Most of 'em, aye,' the brigade chief replied. 'They lost one of their cows and they're not sure they've got all the hens safe, but the rest's accounted for.'

'Where are they then?' Alex inquired, coughing as he tried to peer through the smoke and the flames silhouetting what remained of the buildings.

'I gather that the poultry were outside when it began, and they fluttered and scrabbled their way over into yon field. The cattle were rounded up. They were being led to t'farm next door when we got here. The milking parlour were t'other side of the barn. It'll not be fit for use, even if it's still standing tomorrow.'

'Did it begin in the barn?' asked Alex.

Both men gave him a dubious look. 'You don't belong to this place, do you?' the policeman said.

'No, but I designed the farmhouse.'

'I see.' The fire officer sighed. 'And it's not been finished more than a few months either. Well, sir, can't do no harm to tell you we believe it began in the barn, though what caused it to flare up is less certain.'

'But how on earth did it spread across to the house?'

'That we do know — the young chap who was on his way home saw it happening. He were right up yonder, on his way down through the fields, when he spotted the barn was ablaze and heard all the pandemonium the cattle and poultry were making. And then he saw that one cow, the poor bugger that set light to the house. Like a torch the beast was. Came tearing across the yard from the barn, its hide on fire. It panicked, made for the open house door. It was floundering, struggling to get in over t'step, when this lad caught up.'

'And the entrance hall had wooden panels,' said

Alex, aghast. 'They were that pleased with their panelling.'

The fire officer shook his head regretfully. 'Aye, it caught straight away by all accounts, from a bit of a curtain that the missus here allus kept across the door.'

'I remember that curtain. I thought it spoiled the whole effect, but she would have it. Said it kept flies out while she had the door open and prevented draughts in winter.' Alex was coughing repeatedly now and was compelled to turn his head away from the worst of the whirling smoke. He became aware of the heat, searing his face and hands even from this distance.

'We'll just have to be thankful there was no loss of life — human life, I mean,' said the policeman.

'But I don't understand — how could the family fail to hear all the commotion?' Alex asked.

'According to the son that got them out, they were all at the far side of the house, having a meal after they'd finished milking, and they had the wireless on.'

Watching him walk dispiritedly back towards the car, Helen yearned to put her arms around Alex. When he eventually sank on to the seat beside her, she saw in the light from the dashboard that his face was blackened with soot. The grime was streaked in channels below his eyes, and she sensed that it wasn't only the stinging smoke which was causing his tears.

'Do you want me to drive?' she asked, glad when he nodded and there was something she could do for him.

Except for coughing and blowing his nose, he remained silent until she had driven along as far as Brearley and taken the lane leading up to The Stone House.

'Stop here, will you?' he said in a voice that rasped when they approached the entrance to the drive.

'What is it, love?' Helen asked gently as she parked

the car and set the handbrake.

The car reeked of burning and Alex kept coughing. She'd have thought that all he'd want by now would be to go indoors.

'Just give me a minute, Helen.'

She saw that he was weeping still, making no attempt to check his distress.

'Eh, Alex love, come here.'

She drew him to her, held him while he cried out all the despair that had enveloped him while he stood there watching the first place he'd ever designed destroying itself.

Chapter 5

The night that fire ruined Yeoman's Grange was etched on to Helen's memory. Long after she and Alex eventually went into his home and began describing the horror of it all to Joseph Stone, they were still profoundly shaken.

She was disturbed most of all by how changed Alex was after witnessing the blaze — but maybe it was truer to say that he'd never before permitted anyone to see him moved. Certainly his father seemed staggered that Alex had taken it so to heart. It was the first time Helen had seen Joseph being gentle with his son.

After giving him a glass of Scotch, he stood behind his chair with a hand on each of Alexander's shoulders. 'You've had to endure something which I'm thankful to say I've never had to suffer. You'll not dismiss in a hurry such violent destruction of a building you designed, your first one and all.'

'I'll be all right once I get over the shock.'

But Alex had been quite unlike his usual self, and when Helen was leaving for home he drew her to him as if he couldn't bear her to go away. He kissed her on the lips, something else that was new, then looked her straight in the eyes. 'You've been marvellous to me today,' he said. 'I shan't forget.'

For weeks afterwards he remained subdued. It hadn't helped when the cause of the fire was officially given as spontaneous combustion of damp straw.

If the barn hadn't been in use for segregating the sick cow which panicked and spread the blaze, the farmhouse might have survived.

Even becoming involved in discussions with the builder who was to reconstruct Yeoman's Grange did little to brighten Alexander's spirits. And since he seemed to wish to spend any free time with Helen, she too began to suffer from an irrational dread of other things proving impermanent.

She thought afterwards that it was perhaps this that made him so understanding on the day he was confronted with another person's loss. It was a Saturday, Helen and her fellow students were meeting that afternoon to study Shibden Hall. She decided to spend the morning telling old Mr March how thrilled she had been by the abbey at Einsiedeln. For ages after returning to Yorkshire her emotions had been too sore for her to wish to relive memories of Christopher and her visit there. More recently, believing that she'd been neglecting the old man, she'd felt awkward about seeing him.

Today, however, she resolved to put that right and telephoned Fenny's home to make arrangements. There was no answer and she was astounded when the operator said the phone had been disconnected. Wondering what on earth was going on, Helen set out, walking briskly as far as the Marches' house on Albert Promenade.

But the place was locked up, no one came when she rang the doorbell repeatedly, and somehow it all looked totally deserted.

Helen was glancing back towards the house after closing the gate behind her when a woman called to her from the next-door garden.

'Are you looking for Miss March, love?'

'Yes. Do you know where she's gone, please? It's not like her to set out on a Saturday except to see her father. And it's early yet for that, I was going to go with her.'

'Eh, dear – you haven't heard then?'

'Heard what?' asked Helen, alarmed. Surely she wasn't about to learn that the old man was ill, or worse still had died?

'You'd better come in for a minute.'

Inside the elegant sitting room Fenny March's neighbour waited until Helen was seated. 'It's going to be a nasty shock, I'm afraid. Did you know Miss March had a sister lived in Austria?'

'No I'm afraid not, but . . .'

'Fenella was worried about her, naturally. She was married to somebody in the university there, I believe. And with them being Jewish . . .'

'I didn't know Miss March was.'

'No? Well, I don't think she was a practising Jew, not for a long time. Anyway, that's why she went out there – to bring her sister back with her.' She paused, swallowed, looked at Helen as though weighing whether she could take the truth.

'Go on – please.'

'If she'd got there sooner, it might have done some good. From what she'd been telling me, lots of folk have managed to get friends and relatives over to England or even to America.'

'But what happened to Miss March?'

'Eh, love – I'm right sorry to have to tell you this. I know you've visited her for years. I've seen you in the garden and so on. I'm afraid she was killed.'

'Oh, God! Oh, no . . .'

'I'll never forget that date, just over a fortnight since. On t'tenth of November there were firebomb attacks on all the synagogues in Vienna.'

'And her sister — was she killed as well?'

'We don't believe she was, though any news you get is unreliable. So far as I know, Fenny March had gone with this sister to her synagogue. I expect they wanted a bit of strength from somewhere to prepare them for the journey. I think word of Fenella's death only reached her father because of her having a British passport.'

'Poor old Mr March. He must be devastated.'

'Aye, he is very cut up about it. Me and my husband went to see him as soon as we heard.'

'He's still in the nursing home, I suppose?'

'Oh, yes.'

'I must get over there straight away.'

Crossley and Porter School clock was striking eleven as Helen thanked the woman and left. She realised that if she was relying on buses to get her to Harrogate and back she wouldn't be in time to join the other students that afternoon. Nor would she be up to going on anywhere. Feeling in her handbag for change, she headed for the nearest telephone kiosk.

'Can I speak to Alex, please, Mr Stone?' she said urgently. 'It's Helen.'

'What's up?' he inquired anxiously as soon as he came on the line. 'Dad said you sounded upset.'

'I am, very. Oh God, Alex, something dreadful's happened. You know the Marches — Fenny who taught me art, and her father who created the scholarship for me?'

'I remember, yes.'

'Well, it's Fenny. She's — she's dead.'

'That's sudden.'

'She's been killed, in Austria — Vienna, I think. I didn't know but they're Jews apparently, and . . . there was a lot of destruction. All the synagogues.'

'I heard about it on the wireless earlier this month. But how?'

Helen told him the rest. Before she'd finished speaking he was offering to drive her over to Harrogate. 'Doesn't matter about Shibden Hall, we can go there any old time.' He told her to go home and wait for him there. He'd be with her in less than half an hour.

Mr March looked rather better than Helen had expected, and his eyes lit up when he saw who was visiting him.

'By, but I'm glad to see you, young Helen. I wondered if I'd ever set eyes on you again.'

'I know I've been neglecting you, and I'm sorry. I'm sorrier still, more upset than I can ever say, to hear about your Fenny.'

'Aye, aye, thank you.' He swallowed, shook his head wearily. 'It's a bad do. When you get to my time of life you don't expect to outlive your offspring.'

'Is there — is there any word of your other daughter?'

'No, love, no. I don't suppose there will be, not while there's so much trouble out there. I'm afraid the best I can hope is that she's been interned — that way, she might survive.' He sighed and cleared his throat. 'All we can do is carry on somehow. I'm glad you've come. It's you young folk we must concentrate on now.'

Looking up, Mr March became aware for the first time of Alexander. But before Helen could introduce them, he was smiling.

'By, but I can guess who you are — specially with Helen thinking of nothing but architecture. You'll be Joseph Stone's lad. There's no mistaking your features.'

Talking of their common interest and filling in

Mr March on how Joseph Stone's practice had progressed seemed to ease some of the sadness. Only when they rose to leave did the old man's expression become grave again. He turned towards Helen.

'Just think on, that's all I ask of you, *think on*. Like I said at the beginning — it's the Fenella March Bursary. As we told you, she had to give up hopes of becoming an architect. Through you and them that benefit after, she won't be forgotten.'

Helen wept most of the way back to Halifax in the car, venting all the emotion held in check whilst visiting Mr March.

The November drizzle drove between the hills. As they crossed North Bridge, she felt a gentle hand on her arm. 'Where to, love? Shall I take you to your family or back to our place?'

She didn't know what she wanted to do, only that she didn't really wish to be with anybody. She shrank from talking about the cause of her distress even to her parents. No one had been in while she was waiting for Alex. Her mother had been busy with Saturday shopping and Dad at his customary football match.

Making the decision for her, Alex headed for his own home. He'd already told his father what had happened. There'd be no need for explanations.

Neither of them had eaten since breakfast. After the briefest of conversations, Joseph Stone left the two of them together in the big panelled dining room. Helen had no appetite, but when Alex attacked the cold beef and salad provided by Mrs Hartley their housekeeper, she made an effort to eat something.

'It's really knocked the stuffing out of me,' she confided afterwards as they sat over a pot of tea.

'That's only to be expected, love, it was such a shock,' said Alex. 'I'm just glad you let me know. You certainly shouldn't have gone over to Harrogate on your own to see Mr March.'

'Thanks for being there. That was all that made it bearable.'

Alexander's company became the thing that most helped Helen to accept the loss of Fenny March, which had made her feel she'd had to grow up very suddenly. Her attachment to her former teacher had been neither fiercely dependent nor nurtured by frequent meetings, but Miss March had been there and Helen still needed at least one person to understand how she felt about her work.

The stress of their final year was upon them, making patience thin at times, but she and Alex were old enough friends now for there to be less chance of any serious friction. If they argued, they bore no grudges, and even when exhausted by revision and exams they still could laugh, mostly at themselves.

Helen was delighted when Joseph Stone repeated his suggestion that she should consider joining his practice. 'You and Alex couldn't be more different in your approach to architecture, but that's all to the good. You'd temper his wilder excesses and he might urge you forward into this twentieth century!'

She smiled and told him that there was nowhere else she'd rather work. And then privately, during her first week there, Joseph Stone said the one thing which set the seal on her sense of achievement.

'I'll never let on to Alexander, Helen, so this'll only be said the once, but you've more natural flair than he'll ever possess. I'm fortunate you've consented to come to us.'

She gladly gave up the evening job at the biscuit factory, and was surprised when the other young women clubbed together for a leaving party and a present. Because she was so absorbed in her architectural studies she had never made any real friendships there; these tokens reassured her that they hadn't thought her entirely stand-offish. And the gift, a set of pens and pencils, delighted her.

When she showed them to Alex in the office, he appeared perturbed.

'What's up?' she asked. 'I thought it was a lovely present. They'll come in ever so useful.'

'I know,' he said. 'I know.' He squeezed her shoulders, and sighed. 'I suppose I've come to forget that you've had to budget for every thing you've ever needed. This has made me realise that I'd have loved to have provided these for you.'

'That's nice, but does it matter? I've got 'em now.'

Alex remained serious. 'You don't see, do you? I've always had so much, it's time I was making up to you for what you've sacrificed.'

She felt touched by this unfamiliar side of him, and began wondering if she'd been blind to what Alex might be feeling for her.

They were too busy, however, for her to dwell on such thoughts.

Joseph Stone was a typical Yorkshireman who believed in obtaining value for money. He had never employed more staff than he required, and almost before they had settled in behind their draftsman's desks, both she and Alex were expected to take their full share of the work.

They were sent out from the office, initially with Frank Barclay, Joseph's right-hand man. They worked long hours: surveying new sites, checking each other's measurements because neither of them would risk errors, and then incurring Frank's displeasure for being slow. They also accompanied him to Council offices while local bye-laws regarding construction were checked, and spent hours discovering where essential services such as drainage were situated.

They inspected partially built factories and houses, chatting with all sorts of building workers until they both felt they had a thorough understanding of far more than the theory of construction which they had studied. Joseph Stone occasionally tossed them a casual word of praise; more often, he merely told them what they next ought to master.

Alexander frequently grumbled about the pace his father expected from them. Helen was simply thrilled to be actually working at last, and thankful to be able to give her mother a decent amount of board money and begin putting something back into the bursary.

At home life was congenial. Both parents were proud as well as relieved that she had only this final practical year to complete. The threat of a world war seemed to have abated, and they were also less worried by now about Marian's situation. The last few years when Kathleen's willingness to care for her grandchildren enabled Marian to work had paid off. Denis had been promoted from Assistant to Stage Manager at Leeds Grand Theatre, and this together with Marian's earnings had ensured them the deposit on a house near Roundhay Park.

Although she spent a lot of time in Alexander's home, he was still an infrequent visitor in Helen's. Inwardly, she knew that this was largely due to her reluctance to invite him there. No matter how well her talent for design developed, she remained rather inhibited by her background and how different it was from his. She wasn't going to let herself become any keener on him unless she had more assurance about Alex's feelings towards her, but he wasn't a man to reveal what they were and gave the impression that he was in no hurry to change a lifestyle that relied on material comfort. Another difference in attitudes.

Helen had never thought that when he did finally surrender his freedom it would be to settle with somebody as ordinary as herself. It was more likely to be for a girl similar to that Berenice, the one he'd clicked with in Lucerne.

She would be sorry if it came to that; she hadn't doubted since the night of the fire that she was fond of Alex. And while she was still so upset by Fenny March's death his concern often warmed her. Even if their affectionate relationship never developed beyond the occasional hug, or perhaps an arm coming about her when something disturbed her, he was always around and she couldn't help being glad that was so. She often noticed how attractive he was, with those lovely grey-green eyes.

It was a wonder that he hadn't prevented her thinking so much about Christopher Maitland since that short encounter in Switzerland. She still frequently needed to remind herself that Chris was only one out of lots of men whom she might meet — that she ought to relegate him to the back part of her mind.

Helen was remembering him on the day in March 1939 when she and Alex set out on the first job they were tackling unsupervised. Driving through an area of Leeds which wasn't familiar from attending the College of Art, she noticed a Hall of Residence connected with the University. It made her ache to see Christopher again.

But Alex was talking, in an ebullient mood now that they were being allowed to exercise a little initiative. He wouldn't let her lapse into reverie. Life was too interesting. They were making for Knaresborough where land acquired by a Halifax businessman was to be used for building a house which seemed to Helen almost a mansion.

Under Joseph Stone's briefing, she and Alex had drawn rough plans and elevations which, after a few alterations, had proved acceptable to their client. Before preparing more detailed plans, they were now going to survey the land, measuring and checking levels. They also had appointments with council officials to formalise arrangements.

Drawing up plans with Alex had been an uneasy process. They still argued over so many aspects of design. Helen had visualised a house something like Shelf Hall, a distinguished mansion of considerable elegance for their part of the West Riding. As she'd anticipated, Alex favoured a far less complex structure with none of the adornments which enhanced the Hall's exterior, and certainly with nothing resembling its portico.

Helen had been delighted, though, when their initial drawings were submitted. The prospective owner had suggested having rather more ornamentation, and the final designs were developing some of the characteristics which she'd originally intended.

Today, however, they were happy together, embarking on their task and looking forward to being entrusted with the groundwork, and to making contact with the builders who had been appointed.

'We'll take some time off as well,' Alex promised suddenly. 'I've squared it with Father.'

'Are you sure about that?' Helen asked, not quite able to forget the time abroad when Alex had been anything but conscientious about his purpose in going there.

'Of course. We're working now, aren't we? That's different altogether from when we were just students. I shan't let him down — and I'll make sure you don't.'

'Steady on,' she reminded him. 'We're supposed to be equals. You're not here to keep an eye on me.'

He laughed. 'Thought that might make you sit up! But you do ask for it, you know. There's many a time when you behave as if you're the only one endowed with a sense of responsibility.'

'Am I that bad?'

Alex smiled sideways at her. 'Actually, you're much better than I give you credit for — in lots of ways. You've been a good pal to me, more than once. And you're the only woman I can say that about!'

Helen studied his face as he concentrated on the traffic and on avoiding the tramlines that bisected the setts of the roadway. She *did* like him. His hair appeared darker here in the car and had a tiny hint of copper in among the golden waves. His eyelashes were long enough to make her or any woman envious, and his mouth had firmed up these past few years, adding a pleasing air of determination to the smile which so often could be winning.

'What is it?' he asked lightly. 'Are you making up for the months when we haven't had time to look at each other?'

She chuckled. 'Happen so. Must admit it's not often I do.'

'I'm well aware of that.' And now the seriousness in his voice surprised her. 'Whereas I could describe you in so many different ways, Helen. Your absorption, and all the emotions you show when you're beside me at the pictures. The way your hair slides over your cheek when you're at your drawing board. The way your eyes glow when you're happy. No one I know has more expressive eyes.'

Helen was so surprised she couldn't think how to reply before Alexander continued.

'Then there's your strength. So often when we're on site I'm astonished by the way you baulk at nothing. And since that awful fire at Yeoman's Grange, well —

you've become special to me.'

By speaking of that night, showing how close he considered they had grown, Alex was sweeping away a lot of her misgivings. Helen felt quite moved. She'd never been so sure that she mattered to him.

Helen had been to Knaresborough before, of course, but never this early in the year. With few visitors in the town, and many of its residents evidently keeping out of the keen north wind, their view of the river seemed very different. The houses clustered about and beneath its bridge looked cosier and more compact as though the chill enforced their close proximity.

'I do love Knaresborough,' she exclaimed, and began hoping there would be an opportunity to wander around the castle. 'It's not a bit like any other town I know.'

'There's certainly no other in these parts with a cave resembling Mother Shipton's.'

'When I was quite little Mum and Dad brought us here, and our Marian got me ever so scared. She really convinced me that Mother Shipton still lived there. "She'll turn you into stone," she said, and nobody could get out of me why I wouldn't stop blubbing.'

'Something tells me I wouldn't take to your Marian.'

'Oh, but you would. All the chaps always have done. Still do, in fact, even though she's been married for years. Marian has a way with her. She's got the most gorgeous blue eyes and blonde hair. That and being so slim make her look fragile. Isn't that what you all go for?'

'For a passing fling maybe, not necessarily for anything lasting.'

Alex was parking the car outside their hotel. As the engine died he turned to her. He was smiling, and not

99

at all in the manner that so often was calculated to ensure he got his own way. Helen realised yet again how happy she was to be with him.

They spent the afternoon on site, checking dimensions and aspects, and confirming the precise area which the house itself would occupy. The owner had chosen wisely. There would be a view of hills to the rear and, beyond its own garden, the house would overlook the steep slope down towards the River Nidd.

'Wouldn't mind living here myself,' said Alex. 'What about you?'

'It's certainly very lovely, though we'd be a bit of a way from work!' She wondered if he fancied a house as grand as this would be.

'Could always open up another branch of Stone's, here or in Harrogate . . .'

Although they weren't very serious, these remarks made Helen think. Did Alexander wish perhaps that their relationship could develop into something deeper?

How much she herself would want that she wasn't entirely sure. He'd been just a pal for such a very long time. She hadn't had romantic ideas about him. Yes, things were changing, but was she ready for settling down? For admitting that hanging on in the hope that she'd someday meet another man who would affect her in the way that Chris had done was unrealistic?

Their work finished for the day, they returned to the hotel to wash and change, then got back into the little Morris. Alex wanted them to spend the evening in Harrogate, and had booked a table in an elegant hotel overlooking the Stray where they lingered over dinner.

Helen was thankful she'd brought her best frock, and that it had long sleeves. This early in spring the evenings anywhere in Yorkshire were cold. Of deep blue artificial silk, it was nicely draped, and she'd always felt it made her look slimmer.

Alex was very smart in a dark suit and tie, worn with an extremely white shirt. His hair was freshly washed, gleaming under the lights of the hotel dining room. He seemed much happier than he had for ages, entertaining her with recollections of things that had happened in their long period of training. Although most of what he said was light-hearted, much of it was illuminating. He was far more observant than she had credited. And a great deal of his interest had focused on herself.

'I didn't know,' and 'You never said at the time,' she remarked repeatedly, until Alex began laughing.

'You needn't have labelled me a total boor,' he teased.

Helen smiled back at him. 'I never have.'

'Your selective memory has discarded the early days then,' he contradicted. 'When you reprimanded me for my attitude to women.'

'Oh, that! No more than you deserved.'

'I agree.' His eyes looked more green than grey tonight, and were glinting. 'I only hope you consider I might have improved with age.' Surprising her, he reached across the table to cover her hand with his.

'Helen,' he continued, totally serious now, 'I couldn't admire you more – and that's quite some admission from someone like me who doesn't go in for pretty speeches.'

Silently, she agreed. And she wasn't at all sure how to respond. This unfamiliar Alex made her feel quite differently towards him, but along with this new excitement he seemed to be generating a touch of alarm in her, inner suspicions that she might not be entirely safe.

They strolled after their meal – beneath the street lamps and glancing about them to the elegant spa

101

buildings and the now darkened gardens for which Harrogate was famed. The night air was cool and when Alex placed an arm around her Helen began feeling reassured as well as warmer, and as if any sense of threat she had detected had been imaginary.

Driving the short distance back to Knaresborough he was preoccupied, speaking only once or twice and then just to make sure that she was warm enough now. After he had drawn up near the hotel entrance, he turned to her and smiled.

'I've loved this evening, Helen. The whole of today, in fact. Can't help wishing it needn't end just yet. We're not the same, are we, away from home? It's as if we've rid ourselves of everything routine and mundane.'

She smiled. 'I know. And I've enjoyed every minute, thank you. The meal tonight was so nice, and the way we talked.'

He kissed her then, more fiercely than ever he had before, his mouth possessing hers insistently as though he couldn't bear to be parted from her. 'Let's go indoors.' His voice was husky.

Hand-in-hand they crossed the foyer and sauntered up the wide staircase. When Alex paused beside the door of his room, he pulled her hand towards him, held it against his chest. The cloth of his coat was cold from the night air outdoors.

'Let's talk for a while longer, eh?'

She smiled again as she nodded. What an idiot she'd been ever to wonder if he could be interested in her. They shared so much − such a lot that Helen wanted to use every minute finding out other ways in which they complemented each other.

His room seemed slightly cramped, smaller than the one she'd been given. Helen noticed that its furnishing was completed with a large armchair and a glass-topped occasional table.

Alex took her coat and hung it on the door before removing his own and unfastening his jacket. He was smiling when he turned back to her. 'Soon have you feeling warmer, love.'

He paused beside the gas fire, finding a match to ignite it and then adjusting the flame. The only other light in the room was from a single Art Deco lamp at the bedside.

Watching Alex as he walked towards her, Helen grew aware that she felt slightly dizzy, and strangely conscious of a longing to have her hand in his again. Had she stopped needing to prove her self-sufficiency?

'Come here,' Alex said gently, taking her hand as she had hoped and drawing her with him towards the chair.

Sitting, he pulled her down on to his lap. She heard him sigh and his head came towards hers. His lips traced the line of her jaw, lingered below one ear, and travelled to her throat.

'I've waited so long for this,' he admitted, kissing her mouth.

Briefly, she wondered why he *had* waited. Patience was hardly a quality she'd have associated with Alex Stone. But then this couldn't have happened earlier. As well as being distracted by overwork, she had been too inhibited to respond. Maybe for both of them there had been a need to surrender old ideas?

Whatever their reasons for delaying, there could be no doubting the excitement they felt now. With each kiss it mounted, sending tremors coursing through Helen. Only once before in her life had she experienced such delicious attraction. This time there was nothing to keep them apart. She didn't have to stop and think. Alex was as free from ties as she herself was.

'I do so love you, Helen.' He sounded astonished — as astonished as she was that such feelings were overtaking them. 'You're such a vital part of my life. I hope you know that?'

She kissed him eagerly, willing her whole being to convey the love they were discovering. Alex began stirring against her, thrilling her with the strength of his passion. Through the silky textured dress, he was caressing her breast, making her wonder if she was at last turning into a beautiful woman.

That was what had been so special about today. Every moment seemed to emphasise this new phase in their relationship. By his admission this morning about noticing her over the years, Alex had introduced her to the joy of being admired.

Maybe Marian was right, thought Helen, and I *had* neglected to make time for this aspect of growing up. I've never had anything to be vain about, but it is lovely to be made to believe that I can thrill and be thrilled, just like every other girl. That I don't necessarily have to continue sacrificing everything else in order to succeed in my career.

Suddenly, her entire future looked brilliant. They could work well together when they tried, and Alex knew her so thoroughly that he would always understand the strength of her feelings about her job. And now there was this growing attraction, the headiness of discovering that he needed her. She felt as if glowing coals were burning deep inside her, as reassuring as they were exciting, because she was loved.

His tongue parted her lips and tested the sharpness of her teeth. Their kisses grew feverish, demanding, exhilarating.

'I need you so much, love,' said Alex urgently, the hand circling her breast creating tumult inside her. His

104

touch on her lips grew gentle now. He seemed pensive. 'You've been the other half of myself for so long, making me forget every other girl.'

Helen was not far from tears when she recalled how she had feared he might think her too ordinary. Everything seemed blissfully simple. They had grown so close without realising, so close that they needed only each other. She slid a hand beneath his shirt.

The touch of her fingers on his back awakened in Alex a fiercer yearning, willed him to trace the line of her ribcage, her hipbone, and then down over her firm stomach. Feeling her response was heightening all his feelings, urging him to unite them. But she had promised nothing — in words had given no encouragement. And Helen was the last person he would take if there remained one ounce of doubt about her agreement. 'Don't you believe we belong together after all this time?' he pressed her.

Helen thought of couples belonging together — of Marian and Denis weathering hardship to form a family. And she thought of herself and Alexander, and of their future which now appeared solid, assured. Hadn't they earned some happiness after concentrating on all that studying? Didn't they deserve some enjoyment? Of each other — perhaps of having a family?

'Happen so, Alex love, happen we do.'

His mouth instantly returned to hers. Helen thought how pleased her parents would be that Alex wanted her. But thinking was growing impossible. His lips and these caressing hands lured from her a longing that raged as every nerve ending came alive beneath his touch.

His kisses traversed her throat, and then lower to her breast's curve beneath the edge of her dress.

'Take this off, eh?' he suggested, smiling. 'It's getting creased.'

Helen hesitated, but Alex was working on the row of tiny buttons at the back. He urged her to stand, slid off her frock so swiftly that her only embarrassment was for the cheap petticoat she wore. He pulled her back to him at once, love in his eyes now, in his words and in his touch.

'You're so lovely, Helen,' he exclaimed, his mouth yet again covering hers while his hands drew her hips towards him.

She had never expected to feel eager like this. Hadn't dreamed that his delight in her would make her wish this nearness might last until the morning.

A small sound startled them both. The sigh of the gas fire going out. Some time afterwards Alex noticed that Helen's bare arms had grown cold.

'You're getting quite chilled, my love. Time we shifted from here.'

The thought of going to her own room while she felt so overwhelmed by longing was unbearable. She shook her head. 'I'm all right, Alex.'

'Don't be silly. I'm going to take care of you.'

He pushed her gently from his knee, rose and gathered her to him.

Stilling a sigh, Helen held him away, turned to pick up her frock.

'Not yet.' Smiling, Alex was removing his jacket, shaking his head. He slid his fingers down her arm to grasp her wrist.

'This is right for us,' he asserted as they moved towards the bed. 'We know and love each other, don't we? We've both waited that long, we're hardly rushing headlong with somebody we don't know.'

Helen couldn't argue about that. She was ready for love, more ready than she had known. And there was

106

no one else for her, no one who wasn't forbidden. Alex needed her. Accepted her as she was. She couldn't live the rest of life on regrets.

'I want you so much it hurts,' he said, his eyes darkening as they entreated her. 'And you'd be being cruel to yourself to refuse — you know that, love, don't you?'

Wordlessly, Helen acknowledged how true that was, that this craving was a kind of pain. She couldn't endure it for ever. 'I know,' she murmured at last.

His lips returned swiftly to her mouth. The hand about her wrist tightened. She stirred in answer to his urgency.

Conscious of nothing but this amazing need, she scarcely noticed she was slipping beneath the covers. Briefly, Alex paused to discard his clothing. He drew her towards him swiftly, across the chilly sheet to his warmth. With his arms about her she felt the last traces of her old anxiety evaporate like frost on the moors encountering morning sun.

'You see,' Alex whispered into her neck, 'how good you make me feel.'

Helen had wondered once why Marian wanted to make love if it wasn't so she'd have babies. Now she marvelled at her own failure to understand. But tonight was as much to make Alex happy as for herself.

He was taking charge, easing away her under-clothes. And then his fingers were bliss, focusing all her yearning until she gasped out his name. Slowly at first, he entered her, and his loving began to accelerate. The seconds of pain were brief, she gave herself freely to savouring with him the life pulsing between them. Holding each other completely, they gave and took and gave yet again.

Afterwards, when they had dozed, she awakened to see Alex smiling.

'You're wonderful, Helen,' he said. 'Thank goodness you're mine.'

Chapter 6

Helen felt as if her emotions were the yo-yo that she had watched her niece trying to master the week before. Alex had again made love to her on their second night in Knaresborough, and she had revelled in the exhilaration. Sharing herself with him induced such feelings of belonging and being accepted exactly as she was. It had seemed as if Alexander's importance in her life had developed over the years precisely for this purpose. Now, though, they were driving back into Halifax and the familiar buildings and no less familiar mist of mill smoke had jolted her back to a realisation of all the facts.

She sensed already that as soon as Alex left her and drove out towards The Stone House she would acknowledge that deep down, beyond this excitement, she was perturbed. And sure enough, when he drew up at the end of her street and spoke, her heart began plummeting.

'We must do that again sometime,' he said with a grin. But the kiss he gave her felt almost off-hand.

Walking along the street and through the yard to the front door, she started wondering if he ever intended their relationship to progress in the way she had supposed. Had all he'd said about loving her been merely the result of passion?

'How did it go?' her father inquired eagerly. 'Did

you manage to get that site surveyed?' He had taken enough interest in Helen's training to learn a few of the terms, and was glad that she seemed to appreciate being able to talk over the work involved.

'Yes, thanks,' she answered quickly, then turned to greet her mother who was coming out of the kitchen.

'You look tired, love,' Kathleen exclaimed. 'I expect you didn't sleep so well in a strange bed, eh?' When her daughter didn't respond she persisted. 'Everything's all right, isn't it?'

'Yes, of course. I'll just take my things upstairs.'

Helen closed the door of her own room thankfully, put down her suitcase and sank on to the bed. She flinched, she was very sore from the ferocity of their lovemaking; but worse than the pain by far was this sudden uncertainty. She had pictured Alex insisting that he must come in with her and speak with her parents. She had imagined him so eager to announce their decision to marry that he'd be unable to delay for even a few hours. Instead of that, what was it he'd said? No more than that they ought to repeat going away together *sometime*.

Her mother called from the bottom of the stairs that they had waited tea for her, and was she ready?

Helen felt anything but ready for sitting at the table and behaving with any sort of calm while they taxed her with the inevitable questions about the trip to Knaresborough. All at once anxiety about her future was overshadowed by more immediate worries. How was she to behave in anything resembling her normal manner?

The meal was such an ordeal that she fully expected one or other of her parents to ask what had happened to change her so completely, but they appeared to have reached their own conclusions. When the evening was finally over and she rose to go up to bed, her mother smiled.

'You seem altogether different for being away for a bit. I think it's done you good — you seem much more self-contained.'

Thank goodness you can't know, Helen thought as she kissed them both goodnight. Thank goodness you don't suspect the truth that I'm containing!

Only the following morning, however, she was shaken into realising that the whole story could emerge. Preoccupied with wondering how on earth Alex would behave when she saw him in the office, she was getting washed at the kitchen sink when Kathleen turned aside from the toast she'd been making.

'Whatever's that mark on your neck?' she asked, and came closer. 'Is it that Alex Stone who's been giving you love-bites?'

'Where?' Helen looked in the mirror.

'You'll not see it, it's round the side here. It was him, I take it?'

'Yes. Actually, Mum — we're in love,' she announced rashly, praying that Alexander's declarations were genuine. 'I daresay he'll be wanting to talk to you both before long, about us getting married.'

'I see. Well, we'll have to find out what your dad thinks about that. Not that we could put a stop to it, not with you being over twenty-one.'

Helen's anxiety found a fresh dimension. 'Would you, Mum — try to prevent us marrying?'

'I can't say it's an idea I'm in favour of, not by any stretch of imagination. He's nice enough, just — not our sort. I don't want you stuck with somebody who'd always make you feel at a disadvantage . . .'

'Nay, don't say that! Alex isn't like that at all — we've both had the same training, haven't we? We're equals, him and me.'

111

'Oh, aye? And I suppose I just *imagine* that he lives in that big house out yonder, that his father's been an alderman for years, and has been the mayor. That they own the firm which only employs you.'

'And which won't be employing me much longer, if I don't get a move on. I'm afraid we'll have to discuss this another time,' said Helen, relieved to have a reason for getting away.

'Happen it's as well. Let me think about it all. There's only one good thing about this, as far as I can see — you were brought up proper so we've no cause for worrying that you'll let the situation get out of hand. You know what I mean. You want to be more careful, though, love. If you've got him that worked up that he's leaving marks like that on your neck, you're not being fair expecting him to hold back every time.'

Helen's journey on the bus to work was miserable. Concern as to how Alex might react on seeing her again in their everyday environment had been submerged by an enormous weight of guilt. She couldn't be relieved because her mother assumed so automatically that she had kept Alex's desire in check. On the contrary, she felt as if she'd have been glad to have the truth in the open. That would, at least, have reduced the complexity of her own emotions. And it might even have made her parents more ready to accept that she and Alex would marry.

Whatever am I thinking? she asked herself silently. She couldn't really be even considering such a disgrace preferable to this confusion?

Alex and his father, together with Frank Barclay, were at their drawing boards. The offices of Joseph Stone and Associates, situated near the church high on the hillside at Luddenden Foot, were full of light flowing in through large windows designed to facilitate close work. All three men responded to Helen's good morning, and Alex winked in her direction.

'You had a good trip, I gather?' Joseph Stone observed, beaming. 'I'm delighted with you both. From what I hear, most of the essential services to the site are in hand. And as to the actual survey — well, the quick glance I've already taken at your notes seems to confirm that all's in order.'

Later that day he also indicated that he would send them out together again. 'Just one more time. After that, I'm going to have you work independently of each other for a while. It's the only way I'll assess with any accuracy what your capabilities are.'

After they had finished in the office that evening, Alexander waited for Helen and walked down the hill with her to the bus stop.

'Marvellous, isn't it, that the old man will send us off again on a job? Something to look forward to. And in the meantime we must see more of each other, of course. There'll be evenings out, and weekends. You could stay with us, couldn't you? The house is plenty big enough for us to lose ourselves away from everybody.'

'That depends . . .'

'Depends? On what, for heaven's sake?'

Helen glanced along the road towards Mytholmroyd. She didn't want to say this and then just leave it because the bus was coming.

'Well, love — you know . . . what we intend in the future. I thought — well, while we were away I believed you meant that you were thinking about us getting married.'

The dulling of his grey-green eyes was only momentary, there was hardly any hesitation before he gave her shoulders a squeeze. 'Well, naturally, that's what I want. But these things take time, don't they?

You're not so unreasonable, I'm sure, that you'd say we have to wait now until that's all sorted out?'

What made matters worse was Helen's own suspicion that she would be unable to compel Alex to wait. She was too much of a realist to deny to herself that she had enjoyed making love. If her body hadn't been reminding her throughout the long day that he was near, her silly heart would have been prompting her to notice him. I've fallen for him and no mistake, she acknowledged during the bus ride home. She just wished that she could feel one hundred per cent certain that her falling had not been into a trap.

The discussion she'd been anticipating began as soon as she and her mother had cleared away after their evening meal. Instead of sitting in his favourite armchair, Daniel Clegg was at the table, shifting around a Woolworth's notebook and pencil on the brown chenille cover.

'From what your mother says, it's time we had a talk. I gather that wedding bells might be in the air, if we can agree to it.'

'Now, Daniel,' his wife interrupted, finishing drying her hands on her apron before drawing out a chair. 'Remember what we said — we're not going to cause any ructions . . .'

'That's as may be. But our Helen's got to hear what I have to say.'

'Go on, Father,' Helen prompted. She was willing herself not to flinch, nor to give any sign of her growing misgivings about what had happened in Knaresborough.

'We're not daft,' he continued. 'And, much as you might think that unlikely, we were young ourselves once. We understand as how you and this Stone chap have been thrown together for years while you've been studying . . .'

'Yes, but along with a lot of other students, Dad. You've got to remember that, and that now we've — chosen each other.'

'Chosen?' He snorted dubiously. 'Or is it that it's turned out very convenient for him that you're allus around now you're working for them? Isn't it only to be expected that he'd try summat on?'

'You make that sound as if I'd no will of my own about this — it isn't all one-sided, not by a long chalk.'

'Fancy him, do you?' He regarded her curiously, making Helen suspect that it was only today that her father had realised she possessed the feelings of a normal woman. 'Aye, well, he's a fine-looking young man, I'll grant you that.'

'But handsome is as handsome does,' her mother put in.

'No need for that, Kathleen. We're not trying to make out the chap has behaved badly towards our Helen. Not as yet.' He paused, seeking words. 'You see, love, it's for your own good . . .'

Helen swallowed down a groan.

Daniel cleared his throat. 'Your mother and me think you'd be best deciding to wait. It's not asking a lot — we're not saying you mustn't end up with him. Only that you must bide your time. And we think you'd be well advised to stop at home on the next occasion when he's planning one of his trips.'

Helen felt her colour rising. 'It wasn't Alexander's idea this time. And actually his father's already arranging for us to go off to . . .'

'Then he can unarrange it,' Daniel snapped, rage suddenly gripping him. 'I'm not having a daughter of mine gallivanting off like that on her own with a single young fellow.'

'But this is business, Father, a job of work.'

'Nay, there were more to it than that afore, from

115

what your mother says. And I won't have it. I won't, do you hear?'

Kathleen interrupted. 'Now, Daniel, there's no need to go on so. Our Helen's a good lass, you know that. She'll never give in to owt.'

'She won't, that is certain. Because she'll not be tempted again, I'll see to that.'

'You're getting it all wrong, Dad. Alex is thinking of us being married one day.'

'That's as may be — and it doesn't affect my opinion. He's not right for you, Helen. You'd better school yourself to accept that. Whatever I thought of him afore, I can't take to a chap who's used his position to make a set at my daughter.'

'Alex hasn't a position to use, even if he would, Father. He doesn't own Stone's, it's Joseph who does. Alex and I are equals.'

'Whatever gave you that idea?' Daniel asked. 'Nay, lass, I thought you were brighter nor that. He's a man, isn't he? And the boss's son. There'll never be any sort of equality between you.'

'That's the only thing that worries us, love,' Kathleen said gently. 'But it's a big worry. He's bound to treat you differently from a young woman whose family had a similar standing.'

'You're worrying unnecessarily,' she told them. 'It's me that Alex wants.' Hadn't she been thrilled because that was so?

It was the wrong thing entirely. '*Wants?*' her father shouted, springing to his feet and simultaneously slamming both hands flat on the table. 'Aye, I reckon that just about sums it up — and that's why I'll have no more of this talk. His sort have allus thought they were entitled to take everything they wanted. Time somebody learned 'em different!'

'I'm sorry, love,' said Kathleen after they had both

watched him stomp to the foot of the stairs then listened while his boots creaked on every step and along the landing.

'Happen he'll come round. Maybe if you could have a word with him . . .' Helen began.

'I'm sorry,' her mother repeated. 'But your dad was really speaking for us both, even if I wouldn't have put it quite so strongly. Folk like the Stones don't settle down with people like us, love. Can't you just forget that couple of days you were away? We know Alex is nice-looking, but he's not the only one.'

Her parents' opposition to any relationship between herself and Alexander immediately focused all Helen's feelings towards him. After a restless night, she set out for work the following morning, more certain than ever that he was the man she wanted to marry.

Her mum and dad just didn't understand, she thought, watching raindrops running down the bus window. They ought to be able to see that because she and Alex had grown together during all these years there were no barriers of the kind they visualised. And hadn't he said, right from their first term in college, that he didn't think of her in the same way as the lasses he used to mess around with?

His behaviour as soon as she arrived at the office seemed to confirm his affection for her. The walk from the bus was across a bridge, then up the steepest slope she'd encountered anywhere. Pouring with rain, as it was today, there was no way of avoiding a drenching. Nobody, however young they were, could have hurried up that hill.

As soon as she opened the inner door of the office, Alex came to take her dripping raincoat.

'Eh, love!' he exclaimed. 'Haven't you got an umbrella?'

117

'I have an' all. I've just left it in the stand by the entrance. But it was blowing that hard across from t'other side of the valley nothing would have kept the rain off.'

'Well, come and sit down. I'll make you a cup of tea. Sally's not in yet, gone to the dentist.' Sally was the firm's secretary.

Before putting the kettle on, however, Alex drew Helen towards him.

'Steady on,' she said. 'Not here, love.'

He chuckled. 'Dad and Frank Barclay won't be in, they've got a meeting. Called all of a sudden, with the builders of the new factory.'

'Trouble?'

'Nothing that Stone's can't handle — something to do with the distance they are from the mains services. I gather the builders are creating because they hadn't allowed sufficient for laying everything on.'

'And is that our fault?'

Alex shook his head. 'Hardly. It was plain enough on the plans. But we shouldn't be worrying about that. This is the first time we've had the place to ourselves.'

'And what if Sally walks in?'

'Her appointment isn't till half-past nine, in Halifax.'

Before Helen could say any more his mouth was covering hers, and he was holding her to him, so close that his suit buttons were prodding at her breast.

'I've been thinking about what you were saying,' he told her as he eventually moved his head away. 'And getting married is the only way. My feelings for you are so strong, love. I just seem unable to think about anything else.' After once being with Helen, his freedom appeared a small sacrifice to be made in exchange for having her always.

'You'll have to convince my father first, I'm afraid.'

'All fathers are alike about their daughters, aren't they?' he said dismissively, and kissed her again. 'Nobody's good enough for them. Anyway, you're not that young that you require his permission.'

'I'd prefer not to marry against his wishes.'

'Of course, love. Naturally.' He leaned a little away from her to smile into her eyes. 'So long as I can convince *you*, that's what bothers me most. Especially at this moment.'

His arm still about her, he took her through with him into his father's inner office.

Helen frowned. 'I don't think we should, Alex. What if a client comes?'

'They never do, do they? Not without an appointment.' Those who had their own transport were obliged to take a circuitous route all along the hillside; those who came on foot had to suffer the climb which Helen daily endured. Neither was undertaken when there might well be a wasted journey.

Going behind the impressive desk, Alex seated himself in the no less imposing leather chair. 'Suits me, don't you think? But nothing like as much as you suit me . . .'

He drew her down on to his lap, one hand travelling to her breast while the other went to the back of her head, tilting it so that their lips met. His tongue parted her teeth, tracing them, sending her giddy with longing.

'Touch me,' he groaned. 'Hold me, Helen, hold me.'

'Nay, Alex, not in the office. We're here to work.'

'All right then. Just a few more kisses . . .'

His mouth returned greedily to hers, alerting all her senses again, compelling her to stir as he was stirring.

'I suppose you're right,' he admitted eventually. 'This only makes it more frustrating. I just can't live without you, Helen.'

She smiled, brushed her lips affectionately over his cheek, and was swept yet again into a fervour of urgent kisses. He had loosened the fastening of her blouse, and she felt his fingers insistently tracing first her breast and then her nipple. Deep within her the tremors of yearning increased, impelling her to kiss him back, to explore his teeth with the point of her tongue.

'We've got to stop,' he gasped. 'Or I'll have to take you in here, on the floor. Just promise you'll see me tonight, love, somewhere alone.'

'You're not going to come and speak to my parents then?' Helen needed to have everything sorted, couldn't make love with Alex repeatedly without knowing they would one day marry.

'Are you making that a condition?'

'No, love. Not really.'

'But you were brought up to marry first. I know. So was I.' He sighed, then turned it into a smile. 'I'll come and see them tonight. Get them to agree, somehow. But then I shall want you to arrange to come and stay at the house sometime soon. Very soon.'

Working that day was extremely difficult. The desire Alex aroused didn't simply go away because he returned to sitting at his drawing board while Helen worked at her own. And even when their secretary came in after her dental visit there was little to break the tense silence surrounding them. Sally had needed an extraction and was scarcely in a state for making conversation.

By the time they were leaving the office at five-thirty, Helen felt dazed by the force of her feelings.

'I'll run you home,' Alex suggested. 'Speak to them straight away.'

'If you don't mind, I'd rather you let me tackle them on my own first. That way they might be in a more receptive frame of mind when you arrive.'

Helen had been over-optimistic. When Alexander knocked on the door, she admitted him to a room that felt positively chilled by parental reluctance. Sure enough, Daniel Clegg only managed a bluff 'Evening' in answer to his greeting. But then Alex turned to Kathleen.

'I gather Helen has been telling you both how much I hope you'll agree to our marrying?'

'That's right, love,' she responded, automatically offering him a seat near the fire.

'I can understand your reservations,' he continued genially. 'You've not had the opportunity to get to know me yet, and you naturally wish to be assured that I'll make Helen a fitting husband. She has a warm and loving personality – much like your own, Mrs Clegg.'

Helen saw that her father was scrutinising Alex, trying to see beneath the charm and the flattery.

But Alex persisted in addressing her mother. 'In a way, you know, you're responsible for bringing all this about. On the first occasion I met you I was struck very forcibly by what a wonderful homemaker you are.'

Kathleen sat more upright in her chair, smiling as she smoothed the flowered pinafore she rarely discarded.

'Having grown up in a home deprived of a mother, I'm bound to notice such things. You made me long for a place to which I could always return and find a heart-warming welcome. And I needed to look no further than Helen to know that she's inherited all the skills which would provide just that.'

'There — did you hear, Daniel?' Kathleen enthused.

He wasn't in the least impressed. 'I heard all right. I was just wondering when I might get a word in.'

'My apologies, Mr Clegg. My unbounded love for Helen does tend to run away with . . .'

'And that's just it, isn't it?' her father observed. 'You young folk seem to think it's in order to let feelings run away with you.'

'I did say *love*,' Alex reminded him, his tone respectfully quiet.

'I'm not going to argue the toss over words. It's feelings I'm concerned about, and how they get the upper hand. Don't think I don't know.'

Glancing at him, Helen wondered if a man who could look as dour as her father was looking at present could ever have warmed enough to experience love.

'I have feelings an' all, you know. Feelings about the daughters I've raised. I've seen how our Marian has had to struggle while they were getting on their feet. Not that it seems to have harmed her. What concerns me about our Helen here is that her struggles might be of a very different nature.'

'She'll always be well provided for, you have my word.'

'Ah, yes. That's what I'm coming to. Believe it or not, I've been beholden to nobody all my life, and that's how my two lasses were brought up. And now you come along, with your nice manners and your expensive clothes, and this "love" you keep harping on about. But money'll never buy the kind of loyalty that ought to exist between husband and wife. And nor does it prove you'll allus put what's best for Helen afore owt else.' He paused, challenging Alex with darkening hazel eyes. 'That's about it. I'm not saying you shouldn't get wed. Just that you should wait — to make sure you're the man our Helen thinks you are.

122

It'll soon pass. I thought a couple of years, that's all.'

'Oh, Dad,' Helen sighed.

'Have you considered, Daniel, that by asking them to do this, you might force them to take matters into their own hands?' Kathleen asked her husband agitatedly.

'Helen has more sense nor that.'

'Might I say something further?' Alex began. In answer to a curt nod, he went on: 'There's the possibility of war to be considered also. Isn't this a time when we all need more security, not less? Something of substance to which we can hold on . . .'

'He's right, you know,' Kathleen said, and was stilled to silence by a frown from her husband. His eventual sigh sounded exasperated.

'You'll do as you like, I suppose, in the end,' he said finally. 'I'm not daft enough to put my foot down and have you both exclude us from your lives. Just don't expect me to be pleased if you decide to rush things.'

For Helen, her father's grudging acceptance that she would marry Alexander was a real dampener. But Alex himself was too elated to let her remain subdued for long. And he kept her to the promise that she would go out with him that evening. She certainly wasn't sorry to do that. Her father's attitude was hardly encouraging her to remain at home.

Alex had parked at the end of the street, and she was astonished to see Joseph Stone's Rolls-Royce in place of the Morris.

Alex grinned when he saw her expression. 'Well, I told Father what my mission was, and he endorsed my opinion that I needed to give my chances a boost by appearing in this.'

Helen had grown perturbed. 'Don't either of you understand at all the sort of folk we are? If your father had heard Dad tonight, he'd have been in no doubt

that this would finish everything before ever it began!'
And how could Alex set so much store by evidence of
wealth?

But he merely hugged her to him and laughed. 'Stop
worrying, love. Once we're married, everything will
sort itself out.' And he meant that to be far sooner
than any two years. 'Your dad will come round,' he
assured her. 'Give him a while to get used to the idea.'

And, meanwhile, he wouldn't permit her to
concentrate on anything beyond the two of them.
Without consulting her, he drove out of Halifax, down
past the Calder and Hebble and out towards West Vale
and Greetland. He didn't stop until they were far
beyond civilisation, where only birds roamed the skies
above the darkening moors.

'I don't think so, Alex,' she protested when he
suggested moving into the back of the car. She hadn't
forgotten all his tales about the girls he'd taken out in
this Rolls-Royce Phantom.

There was no possibility, though, that she would
hold back when his arm went around her and he began
kissing her – just as if nobody in the whole world but
Helen Clegg could ever have meant a thing to him.

'I love you so much,' he said, glad the words came
readily now, for he was indeed becoming increasingly
pleased with the prospect of their eventual marriage.
Helen was clever enough to be a wife who'd do him
credit, with her qualifications and latent homemaking
ability. And what could be finer than never being
denied her glorious sensuality?

He had pulled her close against him and was tracing
her ear with a thumb, while his other hand began its
descent from her breast. Her hair was cool against his
cheek, and sweet-scented. These days she wore it
longer, falling towards her shoulders in waves that
glinted with red-gold highlights. Now she was offering

124

kiss for kiss, no less eager than he to explore this wonderful new pleasure, inciting him to obey the hammering in his veins. He was wondering how he'd resist, how in the world he would hold out as he privately had vowed he must, when she shifted uncomfortably, trying to ease the cramp induced by being trapped against the car door.

'It really would be more comfortable in the back,' he reminded her. 'Only for a cuddle, if you like. Let's be practical — these cars aren't designed to give the driver all the luxury, are they?'

He settled her into one corner of the rear seat, then stretched out against her, smothering her face and neck with delicate kisses. Her arms soon came around him, drawing him closer still.

'What sort of an engagement ring will you choose?' he inquired into the soft hollow of her throat. 'I'll take you to buy one on Saturday.'

'I haven't thought yet,' Helen answered breathily, suddenly dazed by the pace and excitement of it all.

'We'll have fun looking. That's what I want for you, you know, love — *fun*. You've had to work so hard and so long.'

'And haven't you?'

'Getting to know you is my reward.'

His lips were devouring hers again, filling her with the ache to be his once more, to ease this need that seemed to swallow every thought but those about Alex. She could hardly think beyond his lips — his lips and his fingers which had found the secret places he had schooled to receive him.

'You said not here, and I won't insist,' he murmured huskily, while desire hardened him.

How could she be cruel to them both? thought Helen. How deny him?

He deserved some consideration for his refusal to let

her father prevent their getting wed. *And they were going to marry* . . .

The confines of the car and the luxurious scent of its upholstery seemed to heighten her sensuality. The proximity of this attractive man whom she'd grown to love as well as to like was compelling her to heed her impulses. She was only faintly surprised by her own eagerness when she began unfastening his buttons.

For several delicious minutes Alex held himself against her, and then there was no longer any possibility of their holding back. He loved her with careful skill, gently at first and then ever more urgently, matching his desire to hers until their joy soared with the skylark which rose from the nearby heather.

'We'll marry soon, my love,' he said, glad they hadn't received a bald 'no' from her parents. 'When we're in our own home there'll be nobody happier.'

Their home was the one thing that caused reservations in Helen, purely because the house was owned by Alexander's father. Liking Joseph Stone as she had from the first, and being delighted that he was pleased about their plans, still didn't prevent her wishing he had left them to find their own place. A small though detached property, it was built on the same parcel of land as Stone's offices. Alex himself was so thankful that a home had been found so readily that he was prepared to live with its Victorian styling. 'Aren't we lucky, love?' he exclaimed to her after they had been given the key for a preliminary inspection.

Unable to bring herself to mention to him that she didn't like the idea of his father providing their home, Helen had fallen back on admiring the generous proportions of its rooms and the high ceilings. If only it had been a house which they themselves had been able to purchase, she would have devoted herself wholeheartedly to living here. Even while it was still influenced by the previous inhabitant's taste for drab decor, she could visualise lighter walls and beautiful curtaining at those lovely big sash windows. But how she wished she didn't have this dreadful feeling that she was being *bought* by the Stone family.

In time, her practical nature made her accept that neither she nor Alex could have afforded even the deposit on a house, and as their wedding day approached she began looking forward to having her own home.

They had talked her father round to the idea of their marrying in July, which allowed little time for making her wedding dress, something that Helen decided was essential when she first began looking around at gowns in the more stylish shops. She was glad to be occupied, initially with designs and then with making up the gown on her mother's ancient treadle machine.

Kathleen was elated to be asked to help with fittings, and had to be chased out of her daughter's room for Helen really wanted the dress to be her own work. As she sewed she often found her mind racing, and not always forwards to the day when it would be worn. Although she felt sure that she loved Alex, this was a time for adjusting to reality as it was. And for surrendering past dreams.

Only just over a year ago she had been in Switzerland, and in that glorious abbey had met Christopher Maitland. Until quite recently she had succeeded in convincing herself that meeting Chris had been an experience touched with romance, though scarcely connected with the real world. She had come to believe that refusing to dream of how life might have been with him was all that was required. Now, however, imagination plagued her anew with fantasies while memory furnished mind pictures of his thick dark hair and the sherry brown eyes which had smiled into her own. Silly little things, like the concern shown in his buttoning her coat against the cold, arrived out of nowhere to lodge in her head, tantalising her with yearning.

Each night when Helen laid aside her sewing she put away her memories too, reminding herself that when the gown was completed she must relinquish thoughts of Christopher, for good. She was firm in her resolve about putting all she'd got into this marriage. She wouldn't contemplate going to Alex accompanied by any remnant of what she had felt for Chris.

They were marrying in St Paul's church and their reception was to be held in the nearby Queens Hall. Joseph had offered them The Stone House for the occasion, and Helen had found a tactful refusal difficult. Somehow, though, she had managed to remain on good terms with her future father-in-law whilst conveying her own father's determination that he would provide the reception.

A meeting between the two families had taken place, on Kathleen's insistence in the Cleggs' home, and Helen had been relieved as well as delighted when Joseph Stone had appeared at ease there. Her father had pleased her by offering sherry — not something which normally appeared there — and if his own abstention was noticed it certainly didn't depress the atmosphere.

'A most convivial evening,' was Joseph Stone's verdict as he and Alex rose to leave. 'I hope that it means we shall continue to meet like this after the young people's plans have come to fruition.'

Although doubting that was likely, Helen had been glad, especially when the get-together seemed to have tempered her father's disapproval of the marriage. She was compelled to admit that he was showing good grace now that there could be no turning back, and Alex appeared to have dismissed the earlier opposition he'd received from Daniel. Kathleen helped, of course. Her concern for the lad who'd grown up without a mother was revealed nearly every time that Alexander arrived in their home. If she wasn't offering him some titbit from her recent batch of baking, she would be spotting a button that hung by a thread and obliging with a hasty repair.

'I did tell your mum that we have a housekeeper, didn't I?' he asked Helen one evening. 'We're not exactly neglected over there, are we?'

Helen laughed. 'She loves fussing over you, don't spoil things for her. It saves you mentioning owt that needs doing when you're at home.'

He grinned. 'If your mother did but know it, Mrs Hartley has been complaining for years that neither Dad nor I have any system for bringing such jobs to her attention.'

'You'd better make the most of all this — once we're wed you'll find out how little I notice holey socks and missing buttons.'

Although said lightly enough, the phrase brought a frown to his pleasant features which perturbed Helen.

'What's up now?' she inquired. 'It was only a bit of a joke.'

'I know, love, I know.' He was smiling again.

Later when he was alone Alex returned to considering what his future bride had said. And he began to acknowledge that his idea of their life together mightn't entirely coincide with hers. He had visualised the sensual side, of course, and how good it would be to have a home where they were free to live as they chose, without any of the restraints he'd experienced in his father's household. What he hadn't acknowledged fully perhaps was Helen's obsession with her work — which he knew, in fact, to be stronger than his own. And suddenly he had foreseen that she could be less than enthusiastic about the domestic scene, and certainly would have little time for what he saw as housewifely tasks.

I wonder, he thought, am I tying myself to someone who'll put me second to her own ambition?

Chapter 7

Alexander had no such reservations on 15 July when Helen walked down the aisle of St Paul's church towards him. Her dress of brilliant white seemed to make her hair appear darker as it gleamed through the delicate net of her veil, and her face glowed with such radiance that she looked quite beautiful. Thank goodness he'd persuaded her to wear white, he thought, unable to contemplate her being dressed any differently. There had been an entire evening's discussion, though, the other week, while she experienced all that ridiculous guilt because she'd already given herself to him.

For the life of him, he hadn't been able to see how Helen could suppose she ought to advertise the fact that she was no longer a virgin. He definitely felt no remorse, but nor did he wish to have his father — much less *hers* — inquiring the reason why she hadn't dressed traditionally.

Gazing at her fondly as she drew near to his side, Alex experienced a feeling of relief for today's especial happiness. Only last week Helen had assured him that she'd received the monthly evidence that he'd been as careful as he'd hoped. Strangely, he realised now, it was as much for his future mother-in-law as for anyone that he was glad there'd be no awkwardness.

Helen herself, these days, possessed so much

assurance that he felt positive she wouldn't have quailed for long had the true details of their relationship emerged. Kathleen Clegg, however, was an altogether different woman: thoroughly good and well intentioned, but possessed by a naivety which he found touching.

Now that Helen was beside him Alex collected his thoughts, preparing to face the vicar who had instructed them in the service until he, at least, felt confident about the responses.

As the ceremony progressed Alex was surprised for Helen appeared not only assertive as she made her vows, but when she glanced his way he read in her vibrant grey eyes such intense joy that he dismissed every doubt about her attitude towards this marriage.

He felt quite overwhelmed by his good fortune, hardly a familiar emotion. Whatever they set out to achieve in the future, Helen would not only be a desirable partner but a confident one. He felt his father's gaze on them, and sensed across the yards separating them the total approval which Joseph had not always accorded him.

By the time they had returned from the vestry after signing the register, Helen felt like singing. Alex's dad had claimed a kiss, smiling down at her and remarking in a voice that was surprisingly unsteady with emotion that she looked very lovely. Her own father had been quiet since that morning when she'd appeared dressed like this in their tiny living room and, though she suspected he wouldn't say, she knew that he too had been astonished by the transformation in her.

Mum had given her a hug in the vestry, beaming at her from beneath tear-sparkled lashes. 'Your frock's fair lovely, bless you − and you are an' all. I'm that proud today.'

Even Marian had tended to be a bit emotional,

kissing her on both cheeks as she adjusted the veil for her before they processed back into the church. 'I'm that glad for you, Helen. It weren't right the way you had to sacrifice so much *life* until you qualified,' she said earnestly, before turning away to restrain Mark and Linda who were becoming over-excited about attending the bride.

Alex had invited Harold Tilsley to be his best man, which increased the entertainment factor of what, otherwise, might have become a somewhat serious reception. Even the solemn little speech that Daniel Clegg delivered with nervous sincerity was concluded by a comment from Harold which had them all laughing. And the bridegroom's words were interrupted so frequently that, despite her amusement, Helen began wondering if her new husband might lose patience. A dapper young man with suave dark hair, Harold relished having an audience. The only time that he became at all uneasy was when Joseph Stone insisted on adding a special finale.

'Dear friends,' Joseph began, 'for all my relatives, I'm glad to say, are also friends to me — dear friends, this is quite the happiest day I can remember, since poor Cynthia was taken from me. As most of you know, when Alexander and Helen were near to completing their training, I became aware that I wanted her in my firm. I couldn't have dreamed then that I might be so fortunate as to be welcoming her into my family in the way that I am today.

'Helen, I do welcome you, most warmly, as you become a Stone. You must always consider me an ally if that should be what you need — and certainly someone on whom you can lean. You will, I hope, believe that Alex will always keep you so happy you'll require nothing more of anyone. But please remember this — it is for you *both* that I am here. You have a good father, I know, also a wonderful mother. But here's a second father now – "in-law" and, I hope, for life.'

Helen left her place beside Alex to go and kiss his father and everyone applauded before taking their cue from her and beginning to move around and mingle. She was glad to see that Joseph Stone was taking her parents with him to meet members of the family. What a lovely man he was!

Alex came to her side, encircling her waist with one arm. 'You look marvellous, Mrs Stone,' he murmured into her ear. 'Come away with me now, this instant.'

She laughed. She was enjoying their day so much that it didn't seem very long before they were getting into the maroon Standard Flying Nine which was Joseph Stone's wedding gift.

Helen had already been hurried by car to her old home to change into the silver grey silk-textured dress and coat she'd chosen for going away. Kathleen had helped her get ready, and Helen had been feeling very emotional as the car took them back to the reception. 'You're a lovely mother, have I ever told you?' she'd said, her grey eyes glistening while she grasped Kathleen's hand.

Her mother had only smiled and squeezed her fingers, but neither of them could speak until, after swallowing hard, they'd regained their composure and opened the door of the room where their guests were assembled.

Alex was waiting near the door, only half his attention on his father who seemed to be having a solemn talk with him. Seeing Helen, he shook his father's hand and waited, his impatience thinly veiled, until Helen had hugged Joseph and her own parents.

'Can't wait to get you on my own,' he confessed as he started up the gleaming new Standard. 'It was a day to remember, but I found it a bit of a strain.'

'Not you!' Helen contradicted, smiling.

But Alex had spoken the truth. He had felt more at ease in church while he needed to concentrate on what was happening, but had been less happy afterwards while they seemed just to be on show. And having everybody telling him how lucky he was to have Helen for his bride had induced an unaccustomed inadequacy, making him wonder if he would measure up.

They were spending the first two nights in the Devonshire Arms at Bolton Abbey before travelling farther up Wharfedale. By the time they reached the hotel they both felt glad they had chosen somewhere fairly close to home.

'Getting married's an exhausting business,' Helen remarked, kicking off her grey kid shoes and removing her coat and the dashing little hat which she'd worn tilted provocatively over one eye.

'I know,' Alex agreed. He grinned engagingly. 'The bed looks tempting if you're in need of a rest.'

Although she smiled back, Helen was wishing that this was all new to them, that they'd never before slept in each other's arms. She'd have loved to have had the excitement today of discovering one another, which maybe would have roused her from this sudden tiredness.

They undressed and slipped into bed. Alex seemed eager to make love to her, and she wouldn't disappoint him, but the sleep which followed seemed to be what she herself most wanted.

The next day was better. They both wakened early to passionate kisses which quickly led to feverish consummation of their love. After lingering over breakfast they strolled beside the abbey, and then walked along the wooded banks of the Wharfe.

That night they dined in the hotel and sat over drinks until their need for each other eventually took them up to their room.

'I'm glad we came here,' said Alex the day they moved on. 'We'll never find a more beautiful spot to concentrate on being together.'

Their honeymoon had been a short spell of stepping back from everyday life. Returning a week later to their new home, they both realised that war was fast approaching. Listening to the wireless, they had thrust upon them the fact that while they had been away two thousand Nazi guards had been sent to Danzig.

By the end of July Britain was threatening to go to the assistance of the Polish people there if force should become necessary to support them against German infiltration. And it wasn't only here that concern was growing; an Anglo-French delegation had travelled to Moscow for discussion of a three-power defence pact.

In common with most men in business, Joseph Stone was extremely uneasy, sharp with everyone because of his preoccupation with every scrap of news from across the Channel. He'd known for well over a year that the peace was fragile but had willed himself to believe it could hold. Times should have been so good for Stone's, with his son now qualified and Helen adding her flair as well.

Alex was proving to have sound business sense, a complement to his reliability as a designer which boded well for the future. If only the firm was permitted to concentrate on work.

By 9 August, however, the King was inspecting an auxiliary fleet comprising over 130 ships. Less than a fortnight later Britain was reaffirming her promise to assist Poland amid constant stories of German activity on the border with Upper Silesia. Before the end of the month children were being evacuated from Paris and London. And treasures from principal museums, art galleries and Westminster Abbey were being removed to places of safety. On the last day of August reservists of both the army and RAF were being called up, while mobilisation of the Royal Navy was beginning.

'War's inevitable, isn't it?' Helen said with a sigh that evening, alarmed by the prospect of all building work ceasing, and men being compelled to enlist in the forces. How would she bear it if Alex was sent away while they were still adjusting to each other? Playing at living together. Although they seemed to get on, this life of theirs didn't yet seem real. There was so much more that she'd hoped to do towards establishing a sound marriage.

'Yes, there'll be no turning back now.'

She gave him a look. 'You don't sound all that sorry.'

'I'd miss you, of course, if I was forced to join up.'

'You'd miss our work as well, surely? Stone's . . .'

He shrugged. Today he was less than sure on that score. Already depressed by the curtailing of so many of their schemes, he had lunched alone with his father in order to discuss contingency arrangements pending the outbreak of hostilities. And Joseph Stone had said something which had slapped him in the eye.

'Helen's had the same training as yourself, remember, Alexander. If you're conscripted, we'll cope between us.'

Alex hadn't liked that. 'And, after all, there'll be precious little civilian building going on,' he'd observed quickly.

'Even if there were more,' his father had continued, 'I don't question her ability to cope. She has a natural instinct.'

'Are you saying I haven't?'

'Since you press the point, I reckon you'll always excel at making a good deal, keeping us afloat. Your comprehension of architecture is quite adequate, don't get me wrong . . .'

'Quite adequate' had stuck in Alex's throat. Despite his feelings for Helen he couldn't help wishing she was employed anywhere but in their family firm. It would take more than this constant physical need of her to make him regret the prospect of some breathing space.

Alex was still trying to decide which of the armed forces he would prefer when he received a confidential communication. As soon as war was declared men were being sought who possessed the knowledge that would help construct aircraft hangars, off-shore and coastal defences, command posts. He volunteered immediately, rather than risking call-up which might intervene to take him into something less congenial.

Helen felt torn when he told her. A part of her was thankful that he would be involved in an aspect of the war which carried less threat of real danger. On the other hand was his imminent departure, and that seemed well-nigh impossible to accept.

On his last night at home he took her fiercely as if compelling her with his body to acknowledge his strength, his superiority even.

Towards dawn, she turned to him again, seeking a gentler, loving reassurance. But Alex was sated still, and more than that, aware that permitting too much tenderness might sap his will to leave.

'It's only London I'm going to, initially, love. I'll be home for weekends, I dare say.'

Before he returned, though, there were nights to endure in the little house on the hill which hadn't yet lost its air of unfamiliarity. Her father-in-law had suggested at once that she might move into The Stone House. Helen had thanked him and declined. She couldn't say as much to him, but if she went anywhere it would be to her own parents, not that she intended resorting to that either.

Both Kathleen and Daniel regretted her making that decision, they'd have welcomed her company. They, too, were having their lives disrupted. Daniel's engineering skill had ensured that he was one of the first men locally to be sent to work on munitions. And Kathleen was faced with the prospect of taking more responsibility for Marian's children.

'Denis is volunteering for a special unit,' Marian had announced one Sunday. 'It's for keeping the troops entertained – ENSA. He's going to adore being involved in that.'

'And what about you, love?' her mother asked, some additional sense warning her already that young Mark and Linda would soon be seeing very little of either parent.

'I can drive, can't I? They'll need lots of drivers. I'm trying to get taken on for handling an ambulance.'

'Round here, do you mean?' Daniel asked, frowning.

'Probably, not sure yet. But you could cope, Mum, couldn't you, with the children.'

The arrangement seemed far from ideal, but Kathleen wasn't the sort to protest without giving it a try. Both Mark and Linda were used to her, after all. Linda had started school, would have lessons to occupy her. And besides, it was a lot worse for children down south who were being sent to strangers.

Helen's working life was totally changed. All civilian construction had ceased, to be followed by a period of visiting sites and checking that the builders concerned were ensuring they were left in such a state that they wouldn't deteriorate too drastically while work was halted. An abnormal stillness settled on the office. Frank Barclay had joined the navy. Joseph himself had been turned down as unfit for the First World War on account of some problem with his heart. He was pretty certain to remain where he was this time.

He was also much older than Helen had suspected. At fifty-five he was unlikely to have been conscripted had he been fit. And suddenly he seemed to age, whiling away time, keeping the firm ticking over, but with all purpose drained from him.

'Do you think they'll happen want you doing something similar to Alex?' Helen had asked one day, hating to see him so inactive.

Dismally, Joseph had shaken his head. 'Their reply wasn't encouraging when I offered my services. Maybe they think I'm past it.'

Alex arrived home one weekend, delighting Helen as well as bringing relief from her anxiety. He wasn't given to writing letters, and in all the weeks he'd been away had only managed an occasional short note to her. He had telephoned her in the office, but had told her so little that his calls had merely left her aching with the frustration of learning nothing about his new life.

'So tell me all about it,' she began now that he was home.

They had flung themselves into bed half an hour after his arrival, and now were glowing in the aftermath of their lovemaking. Helen felt she was relaxing for the first time since he'd gone away.

'Not much I can tell, I'm afraid, love. Top secret, most of it.'

'You can tell *me*, surely? What're you designing? where are you working — in London itself?'

Even that couldn't be revealed. She was dreadfully

disappointed, and strangely hurt, so hurt that she felt choked. It was over seven years since she had first had a part in Alexander's life. Now they were married and he was excluding her as he never had in the past.

Things seemed no better on the next occasion that he returned to the West Riding, and by this time her life at Stone's had grown so uninteresting that Helen felt she was being stifled.

'You don't really need me here, do you?' she said to her father-in-law on the day that Alex had gone off again.

Joseph smiled. 'You'll always have a place in Stone's, Helen my dear, you know that.'

'And nowt to do until the duration?'

'Terribly boring, isn't it?' he admitted. 'Bad enough for an old fellow like me. It's particularly hard for people like yourself who've only just become qualified.'

'What would you do if I found something more useful, just while the war was on, of course?'

'Stay here, much the same as I'm doing now. But I've got something else on — I'm becoming involved in the Local Defence Volunteers. Matter of fact, I'm making parts of The Stone House available to them.'

'That's good.'

'Gives me something to think about.'

'A bit of purpose, aye. Well then, happen you won't object to my idea. I had enough of factories when I worked evenings at that biscuit place, I want to avoid that if I can. What I thought was — well, they're crying out for women to help with growing food.'

'The Land Army, you mean? Good thinking, Helen.'

'With a bit of luck, I mightn't get sent too far away from home,' she began. She felt a certain responsibility towards quite a few people, including old Mr March, who must be visited as well as her family. 'I could keep an eye on my mum and dad — you know she's looking after our Marian's two? And I could still pop over to see you.'

Joseph was so obviously pleased that she was thinking of him that she was reminded all over again what a *genuine* man he was, and not a bit of side to him.

The farm where Helen began her introduction to the Women's Land Army certainly was nearer to home than she had dared to hope. Just the far side of Huddersfield, quite close to Holmfirth, it spread acre upon acre across bleak but beautiful hills. Because of the altitude, and exposure to the winds which drove in from all directions, it was a cold spot in that spring of 1940. She shuddered to think what it would be like in winter.

She was greeted on that first day by a broad, harassed-looking woman who came tramping out into the farmyard, shooing ahead of her a couple of hens which evidently had wandered indoors.

'Mrs Templer?' Helen inquired, and announced her own name. 'I'm one of your land-girls.'

'*Miss* Templer,' she was corrected fiercely. The hand which was offered was the size of a man's, and felt stronger. 'Thank goodness one on you's arrived. I'm on my own here, you know. Have been since my brother was taken.'

'Oh, dear,' said Helen sympathetically. 'Was his illness sudden like?'

Miss Templer laughed. 'Not dead, lass — taken to work in Sheffield. The war effort, of course. Ordnance factory.'

'Oh, I see.'

'It were his own fault. Farming's a reserved occupation, but no — he had to go and do summat different. Men! Any road, we'll show 'em, soon as I get more like you.'

'Are you expecting others soon?' Helen inquired as she was led through a hall reeking of cabbage towards some steep stairs.

'I were expecting somebody day afore yesterday, but no one turned up. There's no organisation, you know, all at sixes and sevens. I could do better myself.'

Helen was to discover that this last remark was applied to most tasks which affected any part of Miss Templer's life. For the present, she was allowed no time to consider what had been said. The third door along the landing was flung wide, revealing six camp beds with a mere foot of space between them, one drab brown wardrobe and a small chest of drawers.

'Nothing fancy, I'm afraid. I daresay you'll be too tired to notice, any road. Unless you're used to farm work?'

'Not really.'

'None of 'em will be. You'll learn. Dump your stuff for now, will you? I were just thinking of rounding up ready for milking.'

Her hostess had clomped along the landing and down to the foot of the stairs by the time Helen had emerged from the bedroom and closed the door behind her. When she eventually reached the outer door, a bellow greeted her from the far side of a drystone wall.

'Over here. Is that t'fastest you can move?'

The pasture was tussocky, very wet, and spattered with the inevitable cow dung. The first time Helen slithered in an evil-smelling patch brought the smile back to Miss Templer's face. 'You'll get plenty of that, lass.'

A high-pitched whistle summoned the farm dog, a black and white animal, part collie, part indeterminate, which bounded past Helen, lashing her with its dusty tail. The cattle were scattered over the field, munching contentedly but beginning to show interest as the dog went from one to the next, snuffling around their heels and emitting an occasional tiny bark.

'Ranger's better nor any cow-hand for bringing 'em in . . . just you watch.'

Helen was impressed. One by one the brown and white beasts turned towards the centre of the field and ambled on, the dog nudging them into line and onwards to the gate.

'You'll not have done any milking, I suppose?'

'Afraid not, Mrs — Miss Templer.'

'You'd better watch this time then. You can have a go tomorrow.'

It was the only thing over which Helen was allowed any lenience. After milking, the sheep had to be fed.

'The ground were frozen solid all winter, and now they've cropped it bare. Fodder's in the barn over yonder. And you can see where they're grazing, just under the brow of the hill. You'll need to look sharp or it'll be dark afore you've fed 'em. Oh — and keep your eyes open, will you? There's none due for lambing till next week, but if there's any dropping them now, you must think on to call me.'

Helen's arms had never ached so much in the whole of her life and her back felt as if it simply wouldn't straighten again. Who'd have thought that spreading feed for a few sheep would be such hard work! The slope of the hill hadn't helped, either. She was breathless by the time she'd finished, and scratched by the numerous beds of thistles.

'You're married, I see,' Miss Templer remarked, during supper, nodding towards Helen's left hand. 'Joined up, has he, your husband?'

'No — actually he's involved in designing war

144

defences, that kind of thing.'

'Oh, brainy, is he? Good job there's others like us, isn't it, lass? Not too proud to do a bit of hard graft. Pity about you being wed,' she added.

When the other Land Army girls arrived next morning, Helen noticed Miss Templer taking great interest in whether or not they were married. She began wondering if the woman's disapproval of men was extended to include anyone who had a male in her life.

One day shortly afterwards a telephone call from the ministry advised them that they were to be joined by three fellows who had proved unfit for factory work or the services.

'Never mind, we'll give them all the boring jobs and them that's furthest from t'farm,' Miss Templer assured the girls with relish.

When the men arrived, Helen soon found she was glad of the bit of spice which their presence brought. Mealtimes were very lively, with plenty of banter from the men, who all seemed to be around forty. Each of them was married, happy to pass around family photographs, and glad of any opportunity to dash off home to Sheffield. The heavy industry there made the city a target for enemy aircraft, and they needed regular reassurance that all was well.

One of the men, Kenneth Potter, rather reminded her of Alex. He had similar golden hair, and was of roughly the same build. Kenneth was asthmatic, and was quite badly affected by many of the grains they were obliged to handle, and by some of the local plants. He remained cheerful, nevertheless, and grateful when Helen and the other girls relieved him of some of the tasks among things that made him react badly.

'I'm determined to do my bit,' he told Helen one

day while she distributed fodder. 'And, much as it mightn't look that way, I'm a lot better here nor I were in yon factory.'

They teamed up as much as possible after that, as often as they could without Miss Templer becoming aware of it, exchanging jobs so that Kenneth tackled some of the digging and planting while Helen dealt with anything that hindered his breathing.

To her relief, Miss Templer seemed unaware that any changes were made to her allocation of work. 'She never appears particularly bothered what I'm doing so long as I never let up,' Helen confided to one of the other girls when they happened to be the only two in their cramped room one June evening.

Jessie, a pretty dark-haired lass who never looked strong enough for manual work, gave her a funny look. 'Well, she wouldn't, would she? Templer's only interested in girls who are single. The rest of us are just hands that get the work done somehow.'

'How do you mean?' asked Helen, bewildered.

Jessie's astonishingly loud laugh startled her. 'Nay, Helen — don't tell me you haven't spotted what's going on? You've been here longer than any of us.'

'Going on?'

'Where do you think Iris gets to when she slopes off while we're out in t'fields? And like t'other night when her bed wasn't slept in . . .'

'Wasn't she off with some chap? I thought happen she'd gone over to Kirkburton or Holmfirth or somewhere.'

'Not she! It's not fellows that her and Templer need. Surely you noticed how the old girl was eyeing up the talent when we all got here? She tried it on with Mavis, I believe, but she weren't having any. Mavis is keen on a chap in the navy, and certainly wouldn't look at another woman.'

'And you're saying that some lasses — that Iris . . .?' Helen was incredulous.

Again, Jessie's loud laughter echoed round the room. She glanced towards the door, checking it was closed. 'Do you mean to tell me this is t'first you've heard of owt like this? Didn't you mix with a lot of lasses in your job back home?'

'I studied architecture, that's the work I've been doing. With mainly males all around.'

'Lucky you! I see now why you've not met anybody with lesbian tendencies afore.'

'I'm beginning to think I should be thankful for that. What do they get out of it, though? I mean — whatever do they do?'

Jessie seemed to find this hilarious. 'That I can't tell you, love. But it seems to keep 'em happy. Just you watch. Even old Templer softens up when Iris is about. And Iris is always making up to her.'

For some weeks after learning this Helen was very observant whenever Miss Templer and Iris were both around at the same time. And although she still found the idea of two women having some sort of sexual relationship rather incredible, she couldn't deny that they did behave like a pair of lovers.

She felt terribly naive for having had no previous knowledge that such relationships could exist, and wondered for a few days if the other lasses might think she was a bit simple. If ever they laughed without her being aware of the cause she would ask herself if they could be making fun of her.

Suddenly, though, without warning, Alex returned to Yorkshire and gave her something more serious to think about. The first she knew of his visit was when he came striding along the lane that skirted the field where she was busy. She had been forking hay all day

147

and had paused to wipe sweat from her face, laughing up at Kenneth who was driving the cart. After the weeks of hard work toughening up her muscles, she enjoyed tossing hay, and Ken appreciated sitting where he was, far enough from the horse to protect his allergies, and at a relatively safe distance from the crop.

'Do you reckon I'm getting conditioned to this, any road?' he asked her.

'Could be, I suppose.'

'I certainly haven't had a bad wheezing do for a while.'

'That's good, love,' she replied, then turned from him to grin towards one of the other fellows who was propelling a massive bale in their direction.

'You'll have muscles like a prize fighter, shifting all that hay, Helen,' he called.

She laughed. 'Aye, won't that be champion?'

'And will it be champion having a face parched by the sun, and hands that're calloused?' asked a serious voice from the other side of the drystone wall.

'Alex!' Helen exclaimed. 'Eh — this is a lovely surprise!'

'Is it?' he inquired, the grey-green eyes unsmiling.

'Well, of course. Look, there's the gate over yonder. Come on through. Meet Kenneth and . . .'

'I'll stay where I am, thanks. Not dressed for trudging among that lot.' From his expression he was less suited for meeting the men working alongside her than for tramping through hay.

Helen went to join him in the lane, gave him a hug, and thrust down her disappointment when he didn't kiss her. Happen he found having the others looking on inhibiting.

'You'd like Kenneth,' she said, 'the other two an' all. They're all three of them about as used to farm work as the rest of us! But we all muck in . . .'

'Evidently.' Alex had taken one of her hands and was inspecting it closely, noting the blackened and splintered nails, the blisters and overall roughness. Sighing, he planted a kiss on her cracked knuckles, then grasped the hand between both of his. 'We must talk,' he said. 'Soon. Can you wangle a night off? It is our anniversary, after all.'

Helen swallowed. 'I'll try, love. I ought to be able to square it with Miss Templer. I haven't been taking time off, we've been that busy.' So busy that she hadn't given their anniversary a thought. How could she have overlooked it? No wonder Alex seemed so disgruntled.

When he refused to go up to the farm to wait for her, she explained that there was a little tea room half a mile away. 'They lay on a decent cuppa. Come back for me at half-past five, I'll have a word with old Templer before then.'

Having got the night off, and the following day as well, Helen should have been feeling elated when she joined Alex that evening. Somehow, though, their earlier encounter had induced a sense of foreboding.

'I needn't be back till last thing tomorrow night,' she announced, getting into the Standard while he held the door for her. 'Where are we going?'

'Home, naturally. You do recall that we have a home, I suppose?'

'Oh, Alex, don't be like that. There's no need.'

'No? When I arrive back there and find how neglected it feels?'

'You know I'm working over here.'

'It's not the other side of the earth. If I can make it from London, you could exert a bit of effort.'

'There was nothing wrong there, was there? Sally promised she'd keep an eye on the place for us.'

149

'Sally's not with the firm any longer − joined the ATS or something. She handed the key back to Father. You didn't believe he'd feel obliged to keep going to the house, lighting fires and so on? And Mrs Hartley's not getting any younger. She has enough on these days keeping house for Father, and no other help there now.'

'I didn't expect either of them to do owt. But somebody could have let me know. I'd have made time to pop over then.' She couldn't help wishing she was working further from home so that this would never have arisen. 'Let's not argue, eh, love? I'll do what I can while we're there.'

Alex seemed not to be listening. He started up the car and drew out into the lane before speaking. 'Father's not at all well.'

'Eh, I am sorry. We'll go and see him then. What's wrong? Is it his heart?'

'Nothing like that. Nothing you can define. He just − isn't himself. Half the time he doesn't even seem to listen to what you're saying. And he asked me when I arrived if I could tell him what his sister's name was. Said it had slipped his mind. Not at all like him, you must agree.'

'Well, this war is an upset to everybody. Happen if we go and cheer him up a bit . . .'

'We'll see,' said Alex glumly. He'd managed to obtain a decent bottle of wine, and had asked Mrs Hartley to buy them a couple of chops or something. All he wanted was Helen and himself in their own home, celebrating this special day of theirs which she gave every sign of ignoring.

All the way back towards Halifax and out in the direction of Luddenden Foot Helen was willing herself not to suggest they should go elsewhere. Strange though it was, she was dreading returning to their home, terribly scared by the thought that she'd be unable to tear herself away afterwards.

'Do you want to just pop along and see your father first?' she asked before they turned left off the main road.

'He'll be having dinner. Leave it till tomorrow.'

As soon as they unlocked the door and went inside, Helen realised that she'd been wrong to feel reluctant about coming here. This was where they belonged, where they must rediscover one another. And Alex had done his best to make their living room welcoming. There were flowers on the table, and he'd set it — however crookedly — with her best drawn-threadwork tablecloth and their one good set of china.

'Eh, love, you've made it look right grand!' she exclaimed, and hugged him.

His kisses were feverish over her lips, but he didn't part them, and nor did he press close in the way he had of urging her to equal his passion. Helen wondered whatever was going wrong.

Whoever Mrs Hartley had bribed to supply the chops, she'd done a good job. They tasted delicious, accompanied by vegetables which Helen had been pressed to accept by Miss Templer.

Pleasantly mellowed by the unaccustomed wine, Helen washed the dishes afterwards while Alex leaned into the doorframe, watching. She'd have appreciated a hand with the drying up, but reminded herself that Alex hadn't been brought up to understand that such chores existed, much less that he should assist with them. If she continued expecting too much of him, she was in for a lot of disappointments. And he had provided the basis of a lovely meal. She just wished she wasn't almost asleep on her feet . . .

They talked for a while afterwards, mostly about the war which had halted their careers even though, in this part of Yorkshire, folk had yet to face any real danger. Only a few days previously the Luftwaffe had attacked British convoys in the Channel, and Alex was afraid this indicated it wouldn't be long before there was fierce bombardment of the mainland.

'How safe are you, love?' Helen asked anxiously.

He reassured her quickly. 'Very safe — don't forget the government needs chaps like us to design features essential to their strategy.'

It sounded extremely important. If she didn't enjoy her own farmwork so much she would be envying him. But suddenly when he spoke again she felt agitation rise within her.

'I wish I could say I approved of what you are doing,' he began. 'I'm afraid I can't. I hated seeing you labouring in the fields, and look what it's doing to you. Your hair's all dried up.'

'That's the sun. Once the summer's over it'll get back to normal.'

'It's taken the colour out of it as well. And your hands are dreadful, Helen.'

She laughed. 'That's summat and nowt. I'll try and get some Glymiel jelly. That's supposed to make 'em smooth again.'

Alex didn't laugh with her. There was more than the effect upon his wife's appearance to trouble him, but he wouldn't mention the other factor that made him loathe what she was doing. Seeing her smiling up at the chap who was handling the hay cart, and grinning at the other fellow, had cut right through him. He couldn't blame the two of them for responding. Helen had a smashing figure, these days; no doubt the exercise had pared away every ounce of surplus fat. And this one thing that hadn't been ruined by that damned job was making her more attractive to men like those two. He felt like giving her what for, though, because she had seemed to be egging them on.

'Shall we get to bed?' Helen suggested, and felt relieved when Alex agreed. She missed him while he was away, she was certain about that, but when he was home they seemed to be on edge with each other.

How good it was to have fine cotton sheets, she thought, slipping into bed, and a proper mattress instead of that camp bed. It was utter bliss to escape from the chatter of the other five lasses, and to have no smokers in the room. She could smell honeysuckle and night-scented stocks wafting in through the open window. And it was so quiet here, with no crashing around from the attic above where other farm workers had to shift the stirrup-pump and precautionary buckets of sand in order to reach their beds.

Maybe if she had a good night's sleep while she was at home she'd feel better able to withstand Alexander's disapproval, which kept upsetting her so much that the lump in her throat seemed permanent.

Helen was nearly asleep when she felt Alex get in beside her. She tried to respond when he started kissing and caressing her, but she was too exhausted to hold out against her own weariness. She was hardly conscious when he began making love to her.

Chapter 8

Alexander seemed unforgiving at breakfast. Only afterwards when Helen insisted that they should go back upstairs did he begin to smile again. She couldn't blame him. Falling asleep like that when he'd come all this way was something no man would consider a compliment! But still he kept condemning her farm job.

'I know you were tired out, but this work's ruining everything, Helen. Surely there's some other way you could help the war effort?'

'I like what I'm doing. Though not the way it's annoying you. Come on, love — don't let's spoil our bit of time together arguing.'

This lovemaking more than made up for the previous night's. Alex's mood improved and he suggested later that they should call on her mother. 'I suppose your father'll be at work.'

'I expect so. Wait a minute, though — he could be in. I'm sure they're working shifts. Don't forget there's your dad, an' all. I want to see him.'

'That's only a few strides away, isn't it? He'll be in the office, won't he? It's a Tuesday, not the weekend.'

Joseph Stone greeted them both with his old enthusiasm, and hugged Helen so hard that her ribs felt bruised.

'You're looking well, love,' he told her, delighting

her so much that she had to curb the impulse to give Alex a triumphant glance.

'Must be the fresh air,' she said lightly. 'And I daresay all that exercise does no harm. But how are you?'

'Bored,' he admitted ruefully. 'There's precious little to occupy me here at work. I'm only content when I'm doing something for the LDVs – or Home Guard, as we're going to be called. It's no secret that's the new name that Winston Churchill is giving us. We've got some grand fellows there, you know. Just because some of them are getting on a bit or have a disability that keeps them out of the forces, doesn't mean that they can't fulfil a useful function.'

He began asking her about the Land Army and showed all the interest which had been lacking in his son's attitude. But then, thought Helen, he's not personally involved in the way that Alex is – he won't take it to heart because my hair's a mess, and my hands are rough.

Her own parents were both in the house, although Daniel was just pulling on his overalls ready for going on shift at two o'clock.

'I hate this shift work,' her mother told them after a round of hugs and kisses. 'We have to have our meals at peculiar times, and your dad can't seem to sleep the same, specially when he's on nights.'

'I don't suppose having Mark and Linda during the day will help when you're trying to get to sleep, eh, Dad?'

Her father stifled a sigh. 'I wouldn't say that. They're not naughty, either on 'em. And Linda's at school during t'day, of course.'

'Where's Mark today then, Mum?' asked Helen.

'Marian's got the day off. Worked a solid fortnight, she has, on them ambulances.'

'Round here? I didn't think there'd have been the need. There's not been owt much in the way of air-raids.'

'Eh, no. But she's over in Sheffield these days. They were crying out for ambulance drivers.'

'I see. So you've got the little ones most of the time then?'

'Aye. Not that I mind. They're getting to be right good company. And I'm glad of that, the hours your dad's working. But never mind us, we're all right really. What about you two?'

When Alexander said very little, Kathleen began prompting him. 'Are they looking after you proper down south? It is there that you've gone, isn't it? They're not like us, are they? Don't seem so thorough somehow. All top show, eh?'

'I've no complaints, Mother,' he responded swiftly.

Helen had never heard him address her mum like that before. Things could be so good, if he'd only stay so agreeable. He was talking right enough now, telling Kathleen the Tower of London moat had been dug up to make allotments. She just wished he'd stop going on about her Land Army work; knowing how strongly he disapproved would make her miserable when she returned to the farm.

In fact, Helen felt no more than the odd twinge of homesickness once she arrived back there. Naturally she'd been sorry to say goodbye to Alex when he set off for London, but she was relieved of the tension of wondering what he'd say next in condemnation of this place.

She couldn't deny that she'd been disappointed that he had been so critical, but she was determined it wasn't going to spoil what she was doing. Helping to feed the nation and to prevent merchant ships making so many trips across dangerous seas was bound to do nothing but good. And perhaps by the next time he came home she would have thought up a way to make him happier about it all.

She had more notice of his next visit to Yorkshire, had used one of her days off to go over and brighten up the house, and had reflected hard during the intervening weeks, coming up with a plan that ought to get them through the couple of days more cheerfully. They weren't going to dwell on the way things were now, nor on how it had been in the past when they weren't suffering the frustration of having their careers suspended. She wouldn't let this war ruin their marriage. They were going to discuss the future, imagine how grand it would be when they were in their own home permanently, and working to build up Stone's again. How they would design such splendid buildings!

They had enjoyed the pie she had made for dinner, even though the meagre amount of meat had been eked out with plenty of potatoes; and the baked custard she'd made using dried egg and household milk powder hadn't tasted bad at all. They'd had a treat afterwards — Miss Templer had given her a bottle of the plum port which she'd made out of damsons and some of their precious sugar. Alex had grimaced when he compared it with real port, but it had made a nice change, and seemed to give Helen a bit more spirit.

While she was feeling bright she began her attempt at encouraging him to look forward to the future. 'We'll really appreciate it, won't we, love, when we can get back to our own work again? It'll be such fun designing together.'

'Except that we don't agree on that any more than we do on most things, do we? Or are you prepared to acknowledge now that it is time that we architects came up to date in what we're offering?'

Why should I be the one to change? wondered Helen. Why is it *my* ideas that always are wrong? Suddenly deflated, she could arouse no enthusiasm for the future, and certainly none for the prospect of surrendering all her notions to her husband's. She told herself that the war was to blame for this inability to look forward together to the peace that was bound to come; the lives they were living now were so abnormal that they couldn't be expected to plan ahead.

Somehow, though, each time that she and Alex managed to be together, her doubts about their affinity were increased. Nothing she said seemed to be right. And he upset her deeply with his efforts to get her to try some other kind of war work.

As she learned more about farming, Helen was growing steadily more enthusiastic about what she was doing. Since she couldn't get on with her career, she'd put her heart into this job. She made friends among the other girls, and if some of them moved on to different areas, Jessie remained at Miss Templer's. The three men stayed there. During some of the coldest months Kenneth's asthma confined him to bed, and Miss Templer threatened to have him replaced by someone in better health, but that didn't come to anything. And eventually, in the autumn of 1942, when Italian prisoners of war were allocated to local farms, their team was increased by Vittore Fabri.

Vittore was a striking young man, with his black hair and eyes that were scarcely any lighter; although he wasn't quite as tall as Helen herself, he was extremely strong. It wasn't for any physical reason, however, that Helen first was drawn to him. Indeed, after their initial introduction, she hardly noticed Vittore until a day or two later.

It was Kenneth who called her across one morning while they were finishing off the milking. 'What do you think, Helen — this chap's an architect an' all.'

'You're not, are you?' she exclaimed. 'Well, I never!'

Vittore's usually solemn expression warmed into a massive smile. 'But yes, I am. And most surprised, I do assure you, to learn that architecture is your work also.'

Helen grinned as she glanced up from the pail she was lifting. 'Oh, aye? I hope your surprise isn't because I'm a female in your line of business?'

He shrugged ruefully. 'A little perhaps. But mostly, I must emphasise, because you are the first fellow architect whom I have met since I left my home in Florence to join our navy.'

'And you come from Florence — by, but that's a grand city!' Helen was so excited that she hardly noticed the milk splashing out of the pail she was handling carelessly.

'Steady on, lass,' said Ken, glancing down at the milk seeping into the ground.

Helen grimaced. 'Don't let on about that to Miss Templer, will you? But I'm that thrilled to know what you do, Vittore. You and me will have to have a long talk.'

They soon began the first of many lengthy, revealing conversations. Digging potatoes and other vegetables, tending stock on the windswept hillside or collecting eggs, they revelled in discussing the similarities and the differences in their backgrounds.

'Your training was much like my husband's,' Helen remarked on learning that Vittore's late father was an architect. 'I did it the hard way — although I was very lucky to be helped by a bursary.' She grew silent, remembering Fenny March, and wishing her twenty-five shillings weekly wages (though it was more than the minimum) allowed her to put back some of the money which had enabled her to study. And wishing as well that she could snatch more than the very occasional couple of hours for going to see Mr March.

'Perhaps, though, *you* appreciate more the training which has resulted in your ability to practise architecture?'

'Do you know, Vittore, I think you're right. There was a lot that Alex took for granted. So much so that I believe some aspects of our work bored him.'

'And you were never bored?'

'I didn't have much time to be. We'd hardly got started after all the years of training when the war came. What about you?'

'Through being in my father's firm, I had considerable practical experience. Also, I am older than you, I think. The day I was captured in the Mediterranean it was my thirtieth birthday.'

'How awful for you. What happened – do you want to talk about it? Or not to anybody on our side maybe?'

Vittore grinned. 'Since coming here I have not been made to feel conscious of there being "sides".'

'Or not until you get back to camp every night, eh? Well, then . . .'

'We were manning a cruiser which, along with two destroyers, was sunk by British forces. Initially, I was more thankful to be pulled out of the sea than perturbed to be taken prisoner.'

'I seem to remember hearing summat about the incident on the wireless. When did you say it was?'

'In June – the sixteenth.'

Helen nodded. 'I bet that was what we called the "Battle of the Convoys". They gave it out on the nine o'clock news.'

Trudging one day over the scrubby hillside as they brought the sheep down to a lower pasture, Helen remarked on Vittore's English. 'It's that good, I keep forgetting you're foreign!'

Laughing, he thanked her. 'You are the second person to say that. When I arrived over here I worked on making buildings safe after they had been bombed. Hadgraft — the boss — seemed quite impressed because we could converse. He wanted to know why my English was so correct.'

'And why is it? You must have studied a long time?'

'Certainly, I did. At university. And it began mainly because of architecture. I am a great fan of Edwin Lutyens, discovering more about his work was easier in English.'

'But surely reading foreign books is difficult, though?'

'A challenge at first, perhaps. After a time I became so fascinated that I persevered until I was even thinking in your language.'

When Vittore never mentioned either his wife or any family, Helen was eventually driven by curiosity to ask if he was single.

'No, I am married, but my wife . . . she did not live with me any longer, even before I went to sea. I do not talk about this. In Italy, you understand, is big disgrace. My family are Roman Catholic, very devout.'

'I see.'

'The Catholic faith has much to answer for, I think. Holding people together when they no longer love.'

And keeping them apart when they love too well and unsuitably, thought Helen fiercely. Suddenly, she was overwhelmed again by the emotions which Christopher Maitland had evoked. Beginning to think of him, she was seized by a need to know where Chris was, to be reassured that he wasn't endangered by this wretched war.

'What is wrong?' Vittore inquired gently. 'You are distressed.'

Helen sighed. 'It's something I thought I'd got over long since.' For no reason that she understood, she began telling him about the meeting with Chris, and how his vocation had prevented their relationship developing. 'I've never told anyone else about him,' she added.

Vittore was smiling wistfully. 'Then I thank you for confiding in me. You should not regret your meeting with this priest in training, you know — it cannot be easy for them to resign themselves to living without the warmth of close relationships. Who knows? Perhaps meeting you has given him a more comprehensive understanding of human feelings.'

'I wish I could believe that. All it's done for me is provide comparisons that I should never be making.'

His dark eyes were frowning suddenly. 'But your marriage, surely, is happy?'

'It will be,' Helen asserted fervently. 'When this lot's over and we can be together again, then it'll be a right good partnership.' She had got to believe that — had got to use all her determination to make her life with Alex work.

For the present, there was very little that she could do to hold their marriage together. She wrote frequently to Alex, but he replied only rarely, and his visits home had become rarer still. There were times when some little reminder brought her up sharp, making her wonder if they would ever be a proper family. A few days ago she had caught herself staring at one of the 'Lend to Defend' posters designed to encourage investment in National Savings Certificates. She had realised all of a sudden that *she* wanted a fair-

163

haired lad who might be gazing into the future like the one depicted with a Meccano set.

Even though there were fewer air-raids here in the north, wartime was biting. One of the other land-girls had got married the other week and Helen had felt deeply sorry for her. The best the confectioner could provide as a wedding cake was a rented one constructed of cardboard with 'icing' made out of chalk. Helen was glad she'd been able to help out by lending her own wedding outfit. The poor lass had been upset that day, as well. The news at breakfast time was of a bad raid on Canterbury which was her home town.

Instead of going to her new husband's parents for their one-night honeymoon, the youngsters had set off by train to find out how her own folk had stood up to the bombing in Canterbury. The only good thing had been seeing her family. She'd been disappointed earlier that her parents' work prevented their travelling to Yorkshire for the wedding.

'They were so glad to see me,' she told Helen afterwards, 'we sat up talking most of the night. My new hubby wasn't half cross!'

Overhearing, Vittore cast his expressive dark gaze towards the sky above their heads which was heavy with rain clouds. 'I can sympathise. I hope that you were very nice to him to compensate!'

From the shade of the young bride's cheeks, it seemed that she had been. Vittore laughed and turned to Helen. 'Now I know that it is true what they say — you English do not share our hot blood.'

'You reckon?' she asked, thinking of her own husband. 'I daresay it's more true that we're a bit of a mixture. Some of us have our moments . . .'

He grinned back at her and winked.

It was only then that she realised that her remark

could have been interpreted as flirtatious — something which she certainly hadn't intended. She was thankful that they were jolted out of the light-hearted discussion by sounds of great frivolity from the kitchen.

The first large drops of the gathering storm drove them to abandon the potatoes they were picking. They were due for a tea break and dashed in through the kitchen door.

The laughter they'd heard was Miss Templer and Iris, in fits over the latter's attempt at helping with the cooking. They were making a Somerset recipe, Rook Pie, and a fiddly job it was proving. After soaking overnight, the rooks had to be skinned.

Miss Templer was still wiping tears from her round face. 'I thought I were cack-handed in t'kitchen,' she exclaimed, 'but Iris, bless 'er, beats me.'

'But they're such titchy things to skin. And I didn't know you could only use meat off their breasts and legs.'

'Go on, you're doing champion,' Miss Templer encouraged her. 'You've picked out all them nasty bitter pieces of meat that you shouldn't ought to use. It'll be right enough now. And the topping you've made for it'll be fair scrumptious.'

'I hope so,' said Iris. 'It's just a pity you lot came in while it's at this stage.'

Miss Templer laughed again, but not unkindly. 'Don't take on, Iris love, it's same whatever we serve these days. You know what the Ministry of Food advise — don't tell folk what the dish is made from, until they've eaten it.'

The Rook Pie wasn't a tremendous success, but it did provide another substantial hot meal, essential this high on the bleak hills, and Miss Templer defended Iris from the others' ribbing.

Looking around the farmhouse table that evening, Helen realised all over again what a happy bunch they were, much like a big family of widely differing individuals. Somehow, though, it was always with Vittore that she felt the strongest affinity now. They'd spent so many hours talking about Florentine architecture while they tackled milking, harvesting and other strenuous tasks, that Helen felt it was only recently that she'd visited Italy.

She wouldn't have admitted anything of the kind to one of her companions, but privately she was growing aware that she looked for Vittore's arrival from the detention camp each morning. She also felt his absence when he returned there at nightfall. Even while summer was kinder to them, the farm was isolated.

They occasionally made their own amusement. Ken suggested that Miss Templer might be able to obtain permission for Vittore to stay later at the farm one evening. They had decided to hold a harvest supper. They weren't short of vegetables, and could hoard their meat rations for the occasion. Miss Templer had bottled masses of rhubarb, and custard made with powdered milk would combine well with it. Ken and the other two chaps had arranged for their wives to come over for the night, and the newly married girl was bringing her husband.

Vittore was so grateful to be allowed to attend that he had given a large chunk of his wages to provide beer which, despite its wartime wateriness, would be acceptable to all.

As an antidote to their sheer hard slog, gathering in the farm parlour which had been opened up especially soon proved to be a tonic. The three wives who'd arrived at teatime from Sheffield had all brought home-made cakes to add to the feast. Most of all, though, they had come with spirits high at the prospect of a night with their loved ones. Helen began wishing that Alex might have been present, then almost at once recognised that he wouldn't really have fitted in here. A lump rose in her throat as she wondered where she'd failed with him.

Strangely, Vittore mentioned her husband's absence. 'I suppose you would give anything if he could be with us tonight?'

'It'd be good to see him, aye. He's not been home for a while. I've got to admit, though, that I was just thinking he might not feel all that comfortable here.'

'And why is that? Surely, everyone is most agreeable.'

'They are an' all.' Even Miss Templer was mellowing as her relationship with Iris progressed.

When she didn't elaborate, Helen felt Vittore looking at her, concern shadowing his dark eyes. He knows there's summat not quite right between me and Alex, she thought, and was less perturbed than she'd anticipated to have him understand that difficulties existed.

The night wasn't meant for introspection, however, and as soon as all the food had been devoured Iris turned to Miss Templer.

'Why don't we have a bit of dancing? Just for fun. We can clear the table out of here, bring in the gramophone . . .'

They began with country dancing, Miss Templer showed she was particularly adept at demonstrating routines long-forgotten by most of them. They were followed by the Waltz Cotillion and The Lancers, both suggested by Ken's wife. Although frequently protesting that he couldn't follow any of these dances, Vittore was hauled on to the floor and pushed and pulled through the steps, partnered in the main by Helen.

Taking a breather at last, they walked towards a couple of chairs, laughing still with exhilaration. All at once, however, he grew serious, compelling her to look him in the eyes. She was astonished to see unshed tears below the dark irises.

'I am so happy tonight,' he told her quietly. 'Impossible though that may sound when I am a prisoner in England. And you are the one who makes my stay in your country a pleasure not a punishment.'

'Nay, get away with you. It's not just me,' she began.

Vittore continued nevertheless. 'Your attitude to me has always been so generous. You have never treated me like an enemy, simply as another human being whose life is disrupted by war.'

Helen was strangely moved by his admission, and anything but sorry when Jessie had found a record of dance music and Vittore drew her to her feet again. She was glad everybody else seemed to have got up for this one, she wouldn't have wished to make the pair of them conspicuous, but it did feel good to have his arms holding her close, to have his breath stirring tendrils of hair about her neck. That dance led to another, but just as Helen was admitting privately that she couldn't enjoy herself more the sirens began their dismal wailing.

'It would have to happen tonight!' somebody exclaimed, while one of the wives from Sheffield said they must have drawn the bombers away from the city. 'Can't we have one night off without this lot?'

Almost immediately the electricity was cut off, leaving them with only the light from the fire that was already dying to ashes in the grate.

'Come on, into t'kitchen, I'll find us some candles,' Miss Templer's voice commanded. 'Then we'd best see if we need to take cover in the cellar.' Only rarely here were they troubled with air-raids so serious that they need go underground for protection.

Vittore's grasp grew tighter over Helen's hand. 'One moment, please.'

They let the others go and remained as they were, standing where the dance had been interrupted. 'Helen?' he inquired, gazing steadily at her in the firelight.

Slowly, she nodded. Equally slowly, Vittore's head came closer until his mouth was brushing hers. Gentle as the touch of a moth's wing, his lips savoured her own. 'Helen,' he murmured gravely. 'You are so strong, you give me endurance to survive. And so warm that even the summer heat of my own country seems tepid . . .'

'Bit of a romantic, aren't you?' she said, smiling against his cheek.

His lips returned to her mouth and the arm about her drew her nearer. And now his kisses were more passionate, pressing urgently yet still without parting her lips.

'If we were free,' he said huskily. 'I free to live life as I wished, and you free to consider all the promises I would make to you . . .'

'Only we're not,' she responded, trying to lighten her tone, though she recognised deep in the private places of her soul that not being free induced heavy feelings of regret. 'And we're also a couple of sensible beings who won't go wishing for something they can't have.'

Although he nodded his agreement, Vittore continued to hold her and his mouth again claimed hers, though still he did not part her lips. There was no overt sensuality in his embrace, yet they were standing very close and Helen became fully aware of his arousal. Answering tremors of excitement developed

169

deep inside her, urging the release which she'd been denied for too long. Not clinging to him required every scrap of will-power that she could muster.

'We should join the others, I think,' Vittore murmured huskily, and took her hand as they went out and along the darkened passageway.

His fingers were stirring over her own, caressing in mute expression of emotions which must be submerged.

For days afterwards Helen remained acutely aware of Vittore, sensing his approach before she glimpsed him, coming alive to his nearness in the farm kitchen or wherever they worked together.

But she also grew aware that she knew very little of the real Vittore. She could only form a picture from what he had told her about his work, about his home life. *His* version of the way things were. Here in England, he might be a prisoner but he was free of responsibilities, able to concentrate on projecting his friendly disposition, on making himself liked. She was aware that she was seeing Vittore in a very particular and not entirely natural situation.

Alex eventually came home once more and they spent a cheerful couple of days, relishing being in their house together, and spreading their good humour among her family until, on their last afternoon, they visited Alexander's father.

In spite of his enthusiasm for the Home Guard, Joseph seemed to be ageing fast. When she'd seen him previously, Helen had felt reassured that he appeared far better than she had feared from Alex's description; today, he gave the impression of being exhausted and not quite orientated. The minute he asked what day it was, she felt Alex stiffening beside her in alarm, but his next question made them even more perturbed.

'There was a chap worked with me — he joined one

of the services, but I'll be hanged if I can remember which. I can't quite recall his name, Alex . . .'

'Frank Barclay,' was the terse answer.

After he'd replied Alex drew in a sighing breath. Helen wasn't surprised he was shaken. How could Joseph have failed to remember someone who'd worked with him so long, and so closely? 'I don't like leaving him on his own any more,' Alex admitted on their way back home. 'I think it might be an idea if you accepted his suggestion of living at The Stone House. For the duration at any rate.'

Helen was shattered. She had never known that Alex had been aware of that suggestion's being made, but what disturbed her most was his supposition that she could simply give up her war work just like that.

'I know it's upsetting,' she began, nearly in tears herself, 'I don't like seeing him that way any more than you do. But he does have Mrs Hartley. She's a very responsible sort, and devoted to him.'

'Family would be better.'

Helen resisted the impulse to suggest that *he* might spend more time there. And even continuing with this government job, Alex could write letters, give his father enough attention to ensure that he wasn't quite so cut off from the stimulation of familiar, caring company. Instead, she found herself promising to come over more frequently.

The offer wasn't sufficient for Alexander, but she ignored his baleful look and willed him not to persist in demanding that she give up her job completely. She doubted whether she'd have been permitted to stop working on the land anyway, but certainly resented his voicing that particular suggestion.

Later that night, on the last bus back to the farm, Helen felt crushed by her husband's picture of what her life ought to be. Had he no understanding at all, expecting her to resign herself to keeping an eye on his father and doing nothing else while millions of folk were slaving their guts out to bring this wretched war to an end? Did he think there was anything to do in the business, these days, when it couldn't even keep Joseph occupied?

Vittore could hardly miss her agitation next morning. They were milking, a task which normally was enlivened by discussions about architecture. Today, Helen hardly spoke at all to him.

'Have I said something to irritate you?' he inquired, passing her as he moved on to the next cow.

'Course not,' she assured him. 'Take no notice. It's only me getting on my high horse again over summat and nowt.'

'Do you wish to tell me?'

She sighed, leaned her head into the beast's side, and replied without glancing away from the warm milk beginning to stream into the pail. 'Aye, go on. But you'll only think I'm proper daft. Alexander's father isn't too well — we're not sure what's wrong, or even if anything really is . . . only he often seems a bit confused — distant, like, from the rest of us. Any road, Alex thinks I ought to give this up and go and look after the old chap. I wouldn't mind, but he's got a perfectly good housekeeper.'

'And your husband has been unwilling all along for you to work here.'

'He'd do under and over to try and stop me, if he thought it'd do the trick,' said Helen, wondering how much else Vittore understood about her and Alex.

'I do not suppose there is much chance that you would be allowed to leave the Land Army in those circumstances,' Vittore reassured her. 'I think perhaps you need not worry too greatly.'

Maybe not, thought Helen, but remained perturbed

that Alex could even expect it of her.

During his next visit to Yorkshire they were both greatly relieved to find Joseph in better spirits, with no sign of memory loss. He told them eagerly that he was working as an advisor, helping some of the builders recalled from the forces to reconstruct war-damaged property.

'Some of the chaps are good workers but don't possess sufficient knowledge on the theory of construction. That's where I come in.'

Vittore smiled when she explained this to him on her return to the farm. 'Is very good, I think,' he said, nodding. 'I feel sure there will be much rebuilding in my own country also when the war finally ceases.'

'I hope there aren't too many famous buildings ruined.'

Vittore seemed not to know. Although newspapers and broadcasts carried word of all the campaigns, such details didn't always emerge. And in any case, he seemed these days to have conditioned himself to not dwelling on the situation in Italy until the war ended.

On Christmas Eve in that grim December of 1942 Helen was reminded how truly he had involved himself in life over here. It was a Thursday and they were all preparing for having not only Christmas Day but the Saturday and Sunday in their homes. All, that is, except Vittore.

Helen's heart was wrung when she found him, depressed, sitting on an upturned pail in the cowshed. The rest of them were rushing through their chores before sitting down to the special meal Miss Templer was concocting as a start to the festivities.

'Eh, love,' Helen exclaimed, 'I bet you're wishing it were possible for you to get home for Christmas . . .'

Vittore shook his head, surprising her. 'On the contrary. I just wish, selfishly, that none of you was going away. This place has become home to me these past months.' He went on to explain that he had volunteered to work during the Christmas break. 'But with none of you others here, I shall feel sad.'

Helen suddenly longed to get permission to invite him home with her, but realised just as suddenly that such a gesture would be confronted by her husband's disapproval. Alex would understand her sympathy for the Italian even less than he understood her farm work.

'It'll soon pass,' she assured Vittore, which won a grin from him.

'You must think me like a small boy who needs to be coaxed through a difficulty,' he said ruefully.

She shook her head, but only afterwards did she fully comprehend that she thought of Vittore as anything but a small boy.

The meal had been enjoyable, with plenty of banter to lift their minds above the food which, although plentiful, was only a token of what a farm Christmas dinner should be. The men had each bought a small gift for one of the girls, and Helen wondered how much wangling had gone on when Vittore was the one chosen to give something to her.

He was the last to make a presentation, and did so as the party was breaking up and people were getting ready to depart for their homes.

'You need not open it yet,' he told her awkwardly, handing over the quite large package.

'Of course I've got to,' Helen insisted. 'I can't wait.'

The box she unwrapped had a hinged lid, carefully constructed so that she could look inside without disturbing the contents. As soon as she opened the lid, she gasped in sheer pleasure.

'Oh, it's a model − of the cathedral in Florence!'

'Only made with matchsticks. It was all I had available.'

'Well, it's a credit to you, Vittore, really lovely.'

She kissed him then, full on the lips, and felt his arms come around her.

'I would give you everything,' he said seriously, 'if only that were possible.'

Chapter 9

Helen felt quite furtive placing Vittore's gift in one of her cupboards as soon as she arrived home for Christmas, but there was no sense in antagonising Alex, which she knew she would if she explained who the donor was. They would have struggle enough to make this a happy time, with so many restrictions governing the food they were allowed, to say nothing of the penalties they invited if they dared to display festive lights. She wasn't going to risk anything that could destroy the season for her husband and herself.

Alex came in, exhausted, a couple of hours after Helen and just about managed to remain awake for the supper that she had made.

'I hope you're not wanting to get up early,' he remarked as they went up to bed.

'No, love. Eight or so will do nicely.'

'*Eight*? What on earth for?'

'I told you — my mum's expecting us all for dinner. Our Marian and the kids'll be there already. And now she's asked your father an' all, he's offered to pick us up on the way.'

'That's news to me.'

'Didn't you get my last letter, I posted it over a week since?'

Alex sighed. 'Maybe I did. It must have slipped my mind about Dad going there as well.'

177

Helen restrained the look which she felt like giving him. He was tired out, after all. But she'd been very pleasantly surprised that her mother was inviting Joseph Stone. She couldn't imagine anybody over-looking something as good as that.

'I don't suppose he'll mind hanging on a bit if we're not quite ready,' she said. 'I can show him some of the presents we've got.' It occurred to her then that the one thing he might enthuse over most was the only item she couldn't bring out here. *Was* it Alex who was difficult, she wondered, or would any man resent another chap giving his wife something at Christmas?

Just thinking about that delightful model of the cathedral made her long to look at it again. She was glad when Alex decided to have a bath, leaving her free to go to the cupboard. She couldn't help feeling touched. Vittore, bless him, had spent many an hour making this, and especially for her.

During Christmas Day Helen noticed how frequently she remembered the model, and with what delight. If she was honest with herself, she knew it had pleased her far more than the set of utility Celanese underwear for which Alex had sacrificed some of his clothing coupons. But being aware of this made her equally conscious of how readily Vittore impressed her. Far more than was good, she was sure. She would have to make a real effort not to think so much about him.

Despite shortages, or even partly because of them, that Christmas in Halifax was a lot of fun. Kathleen Clegg had them laughing over the few prunes, the five dates and the handful of sultanas which had been supplemented by finely chopped vegetables for the cake. And its topping tasted quite like marzipan, so long as you didn't know it was basically haricot beans with the addition of ground rice, almond essence, and a bit of precious sugar and margarine.

Marian's children seemed to love playing with their new toys, and didn't understand why anybody felt sorry for them. They had a renovated fort and dolls' house (both gleaned from jumble sales) and toys made out of cotton reels, matchboxes and other discarded objects. Neither Linda nor Mark was lacking in imagination. Extending it to convert makeshift items into whatever they fancied appeared only to increase the pleasure.

'We shall make it up to them, of course, once this lot's over,' Marian asserted several times, and hoped that Denis would make up to her for his long periods abroad.

Her husband's involvement with ENSA seemed to Marian to keep him away for even longer spells than if he'd been serving in one of the armed forces. He no sooner finished one tour than he was dispatched on another, and hardly ever given time for leave at home between them. She missed him quite fiercely. If it wasn't for her ambulance driving she would go crackers with yearning. Then there was the anxiety as well. She didn't half envy their Helen for having Alex still in England.

Denis was in North Africa now, from what she could gather, not that she was told very much. They were allowed to write more about the kind of shows they were putting on, and he was very happy about that. He was taking part in a lot of their sketches and doing a bit of singing which he enjoyed even more than the backstage work. And, naturally, as the sets they had for an entertainment out there were anything but complex, the stage management side wouldn't occupy him fully. Marian rather hoped he'd keep to appearing on stage after the war. She fancied having a husband who was an actor.

The children were playing nicely together today, first with Mark's things, then with Linda's. Marian was very thankful. They weren't always like this, not for her. They'd got that used to being with their grandmother that they usually played up when she herself was around. She would have hated that in front of Alex's father. Come to that, she'd not have been best pleased to have them letting her down with their Helen in the house.

She didn't know what it was about her sister — happen it was just this everlasting awareness that Helen had passed all those exams, had had so much education. Marian only knew that her sister made her keep wondering what she thought of them.

'You're looking a bit peaky, Marian,' Helen said now, smiling sympathetically. 'Have you been called out a lot at nights lately?'

Marian smiled back although she hadn't liked the implication that she was looking a wreck. 'Well, I've been on night duty this past week. But only so's I could get tonight off. I swapped turns with one of the other lasses. She wants New Year because her fiancé might be coming home.' She didn't go on to explain that she often took over nights from the other girls. It never seemed as bad being on her own in bed during the day.

Watching Alex sitting on the settee, an arm casually across Helen's shoulders, Marian felt her eyes filling. If only she could just see Denis, even for an hour, to know that he was all right.

Hurriedly, she stood up. 'Got to go down the steps,' she said and all but ran towards the outer door.

'I wanted to go to the lav,' Linda complained, surprised that her mother hadn't made the normal inquiry into her needs.

'Never mind, love,' Kathleen said, 'you can go out after.'

'Is Marian all right?' asked Helen. 'She looks quite poorly.'

'She misses him a lot, you know,' their father put in. Daniel Clegg didn't always say very much, but he was well aware of his family's emotions. 'They were married that young, you see. Marian never had much experience of standing on her own feet. And there's the responsibility,' he added softly, gazing fondly at Linda and Mark.

'Still, she's lucky to have such grand youngsters,' said Alex. 'It's what we all need. Somebody to plan for, to make you look to the future.'

Beyond her own instant panic, Helen noticed Alex's father raising an eyebrow at that, realised his astonishment was as great as her own. His gradual smile, though, revealed that he warmed to the prospect far more than she had herself.

Joseph nodded as his smile reached his eyes. 'Yes, well — there's one here who'll be delighted once there's a little Stone to continue our name. Maybe you'll think on that, you two!'

Helen tried to smile back at him, and didn't quite manage it. 'I hope you mean once the duration's here. I don't think somehow that it'd be such a good thing in wartime . . .'

Joseph inclined his head genially. '*Whenever*, my dear, whenever. I know these are difficult times — and I know also that you are as concerned as Alex here about keeping the family going.'

Alex wasn't saying anything. He's shot his bolt, thought Helen, and she was wary of being cornered into promising the old man a grandchild in the near future. She'd have to be careful, though, if Alex was thinking along those lines.

It wasn't that she never wanted children, she simply didn't want them yet. Especially while there were so many ways in which she felt she hardly knew Alex. Somehow, she would have to have a quiet word with their Marian. She knew how babies could be avoided.

There was an opportunity to talk privately while they were washing up. And, for once, Marian was entirely in agreement. 'You're right, love, not wanting to risk a bairn while the country's in this state.'

'So how do I go about it?'

'Well — t'easiest way is to get your Alex to wear summat.'

'Wear?' began Helen, not fully comprehending.

'You know, a rubber sheath.'

'I'm afraid he'd never do that.'

'It'll be up to you then. You want to go to the clinic. They'll fit you up with a sort of cap to go inside you, and there's a sponge an' all.'

Helen groaned. It sounded a terrible palaver, but maybe it would be worth it to ease her mind.

Marian grinned at her. 'It's not so nice going to the clinic the first time, but you get used to it, and to thinking on at home to get prepared.'

Confronted so suddenly with how real the risk of conceiving was, Helen hadn't considered that the nearest Marie Stopes clinic might not be open during her short Christmas break. When she finally screwed up her courage and went along then found the door locked, she glanced about hoping nobody she knew had seen her there, and walked away again. She couldn't pretend that she wasn't a bit relieved, although now she would worry each time that Alex made love to her.

Two days after returning to the farm Helen received evidence that she hadn't started a baby. For once, she endured feeling rough quite cheerfully. Since the moment that Alex had expressed his longing for a child, she had grown steadily more perturbed about beginning a family.

The war had been an unwelcome interruption, halting her career long before she'd begun to get her teeth into it. She and Alex had spent that long learning what it was about, but they'd been prevented from practising much real architecture. Even though she enjoyed her work on the farm, she looked on it as just a stop-gap, a means of doing something useful, but only until she could go back to her proper job. Did Alex honestly think she would be happy denying herself the opportunity to design all those buildings that seemed to be queuing up in her mind's eye, as impatiently as a lot of housewives outside a fish-monger's?

'You are looking very serious today, Helen, what is wrong?'

It was Vittore. He'd taken over from Ken behind the horse and plough laboriously working the frosted earth. Helen was in the next furrow, following on, taking out the larger stones they were turning up, a task that could only be done by hand. There were hundreds of stones as well — this was a field that hadn't been used for years, if ever. According to Miss Templer, it hadn't been considered worth cultivating for as long as she could remember.

Helen smiled back at Vittore. 'Nothing much, really, I were just thinking how grand it would be to get back to designing.'

'And for me also. During Christmas while you were all away, I sat in the camp working out what I would most like to plan.'

'You'll have to show me the designs, love.'

He merely shook his head. 'You have not understood — they are in my mind only. We are not permitted supplies of paper except when we write home.'

His words made her realise that by comparison her own difficulties were negligible. They also gave her an idea. Even during the winter they were often obliged to take packed lunches out into the fields. She ensured now that she also took a pencil and paper. It was awful stuff, like blotting paper — the result of salvaging — but Vittore valued it as greatly as the high grade paper produced pre-war.

'Are you sure you do not wish this yourself?' he asked on that first day.

'No, go on — so long as you let me watch. Do a bit of a sketch of the sort of buildings you'll design when you get back to Italy.'

Even well wrapped in coats and scarves, and sitting in the angle of a drystone wall to protect them from a keen wind which carried an occasional flurry of snow, they were chilled to the marrow. Somehow, though, they forgot all that while Vittore drew the outline of a splendid house which he dreamed of building on one of the hills surrounding Florence. There were echoes of the Palazzo Vecchio, though without being nearly so high, and with large ground-floor windows which acknowledged modern needs yet didn't detract from typical Florentine styling.

'I wish I could combine some of our older traditions with contemporary requirements,' Helen exclaimed. 'There seems to have been that much ultra-fashionable stuff that folk have dismissed anything built before about 1930 as not worth considering.'

Vittore grinned sideways at her, pausing as he completed a splendid doorway. 'It may be that you will — you could be the person who will eventually show other British architects that it does not have to be *either* old-fashioned or ultra-modern. That there is a place somewhere between the two. That way you create buildings that live happily alongside those from different eras.'

Helen was nodding. 'I'd like to think that was summat I could do. Happen it's a bit fanciful, though . . .'

Their designing sessions continued, however, and although ribbed by the others they both found not only enjoyment but fresh hope during the snatched minutes with pencil and paper. Beside him in a field, the sharp corners of the wall's uneven stones pressing into her back, Helen often gazed out across the range of snow-topped hills which seemed so high and open that they might have been the summit of the world. Despite the winter bleakness, she loved this part of Yorkshire for the sense of freedom it gave her, seeming to generate the belief that she might look forward to a better future.

Those interludes also brought Helen even closer to Vittore, widening their relationship, and yet at the same time narrowing her awareness of other lives beyond the farm. It was with a shock that she read in a rare letter from Alex that he would be with her for the last weekend in February. An even greater shock was her own private recognition that she would far rather remain here than go home to be with him.

Shattered by these emotions, she volunteered to take fodder to the sheep on the far slope of the hill. She needed to get away, especially from Vittore. She must school herself to remember that all the loyalty she had pledged was to Alex. But surrendering the stimulus of these past few weeks was more than she could face. Long after she had doled out the last of the kale and the water, Helen remained on the scrubby hillside, battling with the feelings which rebelled inside her.

It was all but dark. She started when a voice reached her above the sound of the wind sighing in nearby telephone wires.

'Helen . . .'

Vittore was on his way back to the prison camp. Thinking of him returning to that bleak place, and of herself steeling her will to set out the next day to meet Alex cheerfully, she gulped.

'Helen,' he repeated, running over the rough tussocky ground to reach her.

She had thought it was virtually dark. There was still just enough light to silhouette the crags against the sky. And to reveal to him the tears spilling from her eyes.

Wordlessly, Vittore raised a hand, touched the moisture on her cheek. 'Why, *cara?*'

Helen shook her head. 'Take no notice. It's just me being proper daft.'

He drew her against him. She felt the strength of arms which seemed to lock out the despair of their world.

'I hate this bloody war,' she said fiercely. 'What it's doing to you – and what it's doing to me, an' all, I suppose. Having everything disrupted. Never being able even to plan going back to our real work.' And, she added silently, for making me forget what I loved about my husband.

'You are to take a break, though, no? Tomorrow, is it – you will be in your own home?

'Aye. And happen that's what's wrong, because it doesn't feel like home. Nowhere does.' She paused. 'Where do I belong, Vittore?'

He yearned to say 'here', and convince her of his willingness to make *her* his home, his future. But he would say nothing of the kind. His own tattered marriage wasn't reason enough to draw her away from

186

her husband. It would have taken a tougher man than himself, though, to resist the appeal in these grey eyes gleaming with tears.

His kiss startled her but Helen didn't move one inch away. Her arms went around him and her lips returned to his mouth. There was no other way to express this immense longing.

Emotion surging through him, Vittore kissed her and went on kissing. His tongue parted her lips. God, but he had waited so long, aching to demonstrate the depth of his affection for her. And it was affection — something rarer by far than the desire which he had resigned himself to deny.

'Helen,' he gasped, and willed back anything further. Love was too vital a word for uttering and later dismissing. And dismiss it he must; she wasn't the sort of woman he would encourage into an illicit association. He fought to control his imagination before it presented him with pictures of the future they might have together.

'You're a good pal, Vittore,' she said lightly. 'I feel a lot better already.'

But there was nothing light about the way she returned his kiss. His hold on her tightened. Through the layers of thick winter clothing she felt bruised by his lean body. She heard the groan he stifled in his throat.

The prompting of their bodies could not be mistaken, any more than the depth and intensity of their kisses. About them on the hill keened the wind, stronger now, wailing in the telephone wires, rattling bare-branched trees, as wild as their attraction.

Iced by the elements, her cheeks and forehead felt exposed, the sharpest ever contrast with this heat raging within her.

Abruptly, Vittore released her, turned away and

ran, stumbling and staggering down the steepest part of the hillside. Helen listened for his footsteps on the gravel of the path, heard them out until they were swallowed by the wind.

Shakily, she started off towards the farm. Her legs weak, head woozy with longing, she hardly knew how to keep her feet. Thank heaven Vittore had stopped when he did. She'd been on the verge of losing awareness of where they were heading. And surrendering to this enormous need would have finished all that they meant to each other. Wanting him was such a small part of it all.

The sleet began driving across from the distant hills when she was still a quarter of a mile from the farm buildings. Wetter and far colder than rain, more gruelling than snow, Helen felt it was a just comment on her recklessness.

Travelling back towards Halifax in the bus next day, Helen began to recognise how seriously she had neglected to consider her marriage.

Even after she and Vittore had wrenched themselves apart, her only immediate thankfulness had been that they hadn't damaged the friendship between them. If she hadn't quite failed to remember that she was married, she had ceased to put her marriage first.

Alexander was at home before her, with a kettle boiling for tea to heat the chill out of her bones, and a warming invitation. 'Dad wants us there for lunch, Mrs Hartley is relishing doing something special.'

Helen smiled, picturing Mrs Hartley's thin form bustling round, her sparse white hair drawn back in its neat bun. 'Bless them both.'

Alex gave her an eager hug. 'I dropped in on Dad first thing. I got an overnight train.'

'What was the journey like, love?'

188

He grinned. 'Best forgotten. There were a lot of wounded on board, and other service chaps. I was forced to stay in the corridor, as per usual. There was too much stopping and starting, of course, because of raids. And that dim lighting gave me a thundering head.'

'Have you taken anything for it?'

'Didn't need to. I walked it off, from the station to The Stone House. Had an early breakfast with Father and his Home Guard cronies. What about you? You're looking done in.'

Helen made herself smile. The guilt she felt for her abandoned behaviour with Vittore was *her* problem. It mustn't be permitted to encroach on the happiness she should be creating for Alex.

Strangely, their time together did turn out to be happy; never once did they argue or voice misgivings about the future or anything else. And the news from Tripoli was good. Rommel was retreating as the Allies managed to turn around yet another offensive.

During that afternoon they visited Helen's mother and spent some time getting to know Marian's children all over again, noticing how they had grown up during those few weeks since Christmas.

'I know,' Kathleen agreed. 'I think it's summat to do with them being with your dad and me so much. It's many a year since we brought up you and our Marian, isn't it? I tend to forget and talk to this pair as if they were older than seven and eight.'

'That's not doing them any harm, any road, Mum,' said Alex, and gave her an affectionate squeeze.

Kathleen herself, though, was looking wan and exhausted. Helen insisted on helping make tea in the kitchen. 'Is it looking after the kiddies that's getting you down?' she asked.

'Nay, love, it's not them. They're not much trouble.'

Helen noticed then the extra plate waiting by the sink. 'Are you keeping an eye on old Mrs Tomlinson again?'

'Only a bit, and that's no hardship. She's nobbut next-door.'

'But she has family, surely?'

'They have their work to go to. They're tired out when they get home at night.'.

Tired? Wasn't her mother beyond tiredness? But she'd always been like this, helping whenever neighbours were in need. Popping in and out if somebody was too old or ill to manage on their own.

Alex was in the doorway, listening. 'It's grand of you to look after those who live around you, Mum. Just don't go overdoing things, mind.'

Alexander's loving concern for her mother made Helen even more aware of her thankfulness that she hadn't harmed her own relationship with him. Whatever happened from now on, she was conscious of the danger, must steel herself against all her feelings for Vittore.

He himself was the one who made this easier. Without saying one word about the way they had embraced out on the hill, he somehow conveyed that it would never be repeated. A subtle change in his manner allowed them to remain as friendly as in the past, yet left no doubt that the attraction they had both experienced would be disregarded.

They still continued to discuss architectural ideas, sitting over bits of paper while they ate lunch out in the fields or meadows or less frequently in the farmhouse kitchen. Both agreed that appalling though this war was, the destruction it wrought might afterwards generate a whole new wave of building.

190

Later that year several events abroad drew Vittore closer in spirit to everyone at the farm than ever he had felt towards the German cause which his country had supported. First of all, in July, came the US bombardment of Rome, when the Allied pilots concerned went in with strict warnings to avoid historic buildings and the Vatican.

'Do you hear that?' he asked as they all sat listening to the wireless while taking a break for tea. 'There is civilised behaviour, a fine example. When I learn something like that I wonder how ever my countrymen failed to see the difference between your Allies and the Nazis.'

He had even more cause later in the year to reiterate heartfelt thanks that it had been the British who had captured him. The announcement by General Eisenhower of Italy's surrender in that September of 1943 was followed by dreadful German atrocities.

'They have been looting in Rome,' Vittore announced horrified. 'Stealing valuable manuscripts, priceless works of art, old masters.'

That was only the beginning. A week or two afterwards, Vittore came to Helen as she was busy with the evening milking.

'You will never guess what is happening in Italy now,' he began, unable to check the tears spilling down his cheeks. 'Naples is suffering a reign of terror. The retreating German troops are taking revenge. The worst was that they planted land mines beneath a room into which they drove a hundred civilians. Then the mines were detonated.'

Hospitals were being ransacked and their food stocks ruined, water supplies were deliberately contaminated.

Italian soldiers were being herded into sealed trains and transported to Germany to be used as slave labour. The day this news reached Yorkshire, Vittore astonished Miss Templer by hugging her. 'I am just so glad to be here,' he kept repeating. 'I do not wish to leave all you good people, ever.'

By the end of October the Allied armies were 'like a bug on one leg', in Winston Churchill's words, as they tried to fight their way up the boot of Italy. By this time no one at the farm could bear to miss a news broadcast. They followed every detail of the troops' movements over marshy terrain towards Monte Casino, the monastery which the Nazis had rendered almost impregnable.

Although 1944 began with British and American forces landing at Anzio, making everyone share with Vittore the hope that the war in Italy soon could end, battle continued relentlessly on other fronts. The siege of Leningrad had been broken, but the launching of a massive assault on the Pacific came at the end of February, reminding them (if they had managed to forget) that more than one enemy was being confronted.

Wearied to death with years of anxiety, shortages on the home front and sheer hard work, they all seemed to grow progressively dispirited. More and more frequently Helen became depressed by the length of time that her career had been suspended. She began to take less interest in the designs that Vittore still enjoyed producing. She wouldn't dream of saying as much to him, but she very much feared that it might be many a year before anyone, anywhere, could start erecting buildings of the size and scope that thrilled them both.

There were highspots, like the day early in June when Rome was finally liberated by the Allies. Nobody at the farm was left out of the celebration that Vittore insisted on organising. And within days news of the D-Day landings had them rejoicing again. By the end of the month German forces were being driven out of Normandy, yet still Helen failed to remain optimistic for any length of time. All around on the Yorkshire hillsides harvesting and trees heavy with foliage proclaimed the heart-lifting spirit of summer, while she felt she had waited so long already that her own ambitions would never approach their zenith.

During July, when the Government announced that between three and four million houses would be constructed in the first decade after hostilities ceased, her emotions remained just as mixed as ever. Good though this planning for peacetime was, it appeared to leave little scope for the kind of work in which she yearned to be engaged.

She and Alex discussed these Government plans during his next visit to Yorkshire.

They were sitting up to the table, still surrounded by dirty dishes and the remains of the economy-style trifle which hadn't been anything like so tempting as the recipe had made it sound. She had never felt more exhausted, but admitting that to this husband of hers would only have invited another outburst against the work she was doing.

Alex himself was in fine fettle. He considered that much of the hardest work of *his* war had eased. He could afford time to look to a future when re-establishing Stone's as a lucrative practice would be their only worry.

'We'll cash in on everything that's happening, don't you fret,' he assured Helen now. 'So — building will initially be concentrated on supplying homes. We'll just have to prove our worth at that.'

'Aye, it'll be something, I know. Not very exciting, though — not when you think of all the things we dreamed of designing.'

'They'll be good houses, love, the best. They're determined on that, you know.'

'Who are — the Government?'

He nodded, smiling. 'Of course. They'll be the ones with the brass, and to issue restrictions. But they've promised new homes will be bigger — three-bed-roomed, and with larger windows. Once we've shown how up-to-date we can be with them, we shall be better positioned for proving ourselves on more complex assignments.'

Helen had restrained the look she might have given him when he was going on about being up-to-date. He was the same Alex. But she hadn't lost the hope that *she* might eventually be the one who would prove that it was possible to blend new buildings and modern facilities with the older styles existing in their vicinity. She loved her part of the West Riding, and couldn't bear the thought of it changing too drastically.

On one thing they were agreed: pulling Stone's back into shape as a going concern would be up to the pair of them. Sadly, the last few years of war had accelerated Joseph Stone's decline. Although he was quite often lucid enough when they were around, Mrs Hartley increasingly related evidence that his once-keen mind was, to say the least, unreliable.

'I doubt if Father will work again,' Alex confided now. 'Or only as a sleeping partner. We shan't be able to depend on him any longer.'

'Isn't old age sad?' said Helen. And was reminded by her husband that his father at sixty wasn't really all that old.

'I blame the war. So does his doctor. If Father had been permitted to carry on working as he had in the past, he'd never have lost touch with reality in the way that he's doing now.'

Helen could have wept. She'd grown to love Joseph

Stone as much as she'd always respected him. Whenever she'd managed to set aside difficulties wrought by the war and look beyond the duration to the future, she had pictured him there. She'd always wanted to show Joseph Stone that he'd been justified in having enough faith in her to take her into the firm. That she'd do him proud whatever she tackled.

When Alexander went back down south Helen, for the first time in longer than she cared to admit, began to panic that he might not return safely to her.

'It's proper daft,' she confessed to her mother who had asked whatever was wrong when Helen called in to say goodbye on her way back to the farm. 'He was there all through the blitz, and although, naturally, I was concerned, I didn't get all worked up about it.'

'You're worn out now, aren't you? We all are,' Kathleen said, and gave her a hug. 'They allus say the night's darkest afore the dawn — and we're hoping that this lot won't last much longer, aren't we?'

Her father, who had walked along the street with her as he came home from his shift at the factory, turned from washing his hands at the kitchen sink and gave her a tired grin. 'Your Alex is a survivor, you take my word for it — it'll take more nor Hitler to finish him! You're just a bit upset, like, seeing him off again. And we're all sick to death of war work, stands to reason everything gets us down.'

In the bus, though, Helen realised that it wasn't only weariness making her react like this to her husband's return to London with all its flying bombs. She was unnerved about everything, and especially by what he had said about his father's inability to cope with work in the future. Much as she reminded herself that she and Alex had grown up long since, and should possess the ability to restore Stone's to a thriving business, she couldn't stifle her misgivings. How would she get on if she was receiving no support from the old man whenever her ideas and Alexander's conflicted?

It wasn't for her sake alone, though, that she wanted Joseph Stone there: she longed to see him glad that the three of them had survived to breathe new life into the firm.

Chapter 10

Halifax looked damp and grey and miserable, as West Riding industrial towns excelled in looking during November when rain collected soot from the mill smoke, bespattering its townsfolk and muddying pavements. Helen's spirits felt hardly any better. Alex had asked her to go and see his father. He himself couldn't get away, and he didn't want the old man to be on his own today.

Yesterday, the Home Guard had been stood down. To lots of people its being disbanded was another sign that the war wouldn't last much longer. To a man like Joseph Stone, who had made it the interest that kept him going throughout the war, it was yet another sign that he was finished.

Helen had decided he mustn't be allowed to think that way. She was going to march into The Stone House and impress on her father-in-law that he was still needed in the business. She wasn't going to listen to any protests, nor to any suggestions that she and Alex would cope without him. When they re-opened after the duration, he would be there. Working.

Passing between the double row of shops as the bus was travelling through King Cross, Helen realised with something of a shock that they were only weeks away from Christmas. *I hope to goodness this is the last one of wartime austerity,* she thought, remembering how even these modest shops used to put on such a good display at this time of year. She had a lot of memories of saving up her spending money to buy presents or to treat herself when she was little. And of more recent years when the Co-op bazaar, its counters crammed with bargains, so often yielded just what you were seeking. Thinking further back, the things that she recalled were stranger — the shudder she always experienced when Mum took her into the tripe shop. Then there was the peculiar excitement induced (in the Co-op again) by the swish along overhead wires of those neat cylinders devised for conveying change from the cashier. She pictured the tiny Post Office which she could never recollect without tasting the tangy ironwork of its grille which must have been sampled in days long ago when her little tongue had to explore everything.

Her best memories of all, though, were of nearby Spring Edge and Savile Park — 'the moor' to local people. Had she even been there once in many a year? At one time she'd have been staggered that she could keep away from her favourite place. Yet trying to contact Fenny March was the last occasion that she remembered crossing the moor.

Helen was still thinking about Miss March when the bus approached Brearley. A part of her regretted being distracted from her intention of planning more of what she would say to Joseph but the other half felt curiously renewed by memories of her former art mistress. But for Fenny and the old man she'd never have trained, certainly wouldn't have met Alexander Stone or his father. She'd been fortunate. She would do all she could now to ensure Joseph's happiness.

Mrs Hartley opened the door and came close to hugging her as she ushered her into the chill of the hall.

'I'm that glad to see you!' she exclaimed, a wide

smile replacing an anxious frown. 'The master's been really down this morning. You're just the tonic he wants.'

As soon as she was taken through to the sitting room Helen saw how greatly in need of cheering Joseph was. Hunched into a chair, he was making no pretence of reading the book that was open on his knee. Even when Helen appeared before him, he took several seconds to recover his customary courtesy and rise.

He smiled then, however, and his eyes showed a glimmer of light. 'Helen, my dear — this is a nice surprise.'

She kissed his lined cheek, felt the prickle of unshaven whiskers. He wasn't himself.

But Joseph was brightening by the minute. He turned to Mrs Hartley. 'Have I had a cup of tea since breakfast?' Before she could reply he continued anyway. 'We'll have a pot now, any road.' He glanced towards Helen. 'Or do you prefer coffee? It might be only Camp, that chicory stuff?'

'Tea would be lovely, thanks.'

Discussion of his health lasted until the tray was brought in, and revealed nothing beyond his desire to conceal the way things really were. Maybe still caring what she thought was a good sign. Giving the tea in the pot a brisk stirring, Helen launched in on him.

'We're in a bit of a spot, Father — Alex and I. Fact is, we've decided it's high time we were looking to the future and getting the business operational again. The war's bound to end next year some time, and there's going to be a lot of folk crying out for builders — and that means architects besides.'

From beneath bushy white eyebrows, he was regarding her warily.

'Neither of us can get away for long enough to be any use,' Helen pressed on firmly. 'That's where you

199

come in. We don't even know what stocks we have of working materials, never mind how long it's going to take supplies to come through once they're being produced again.'

'You mean after . . .?' Joseph asked slowly.

'Once the war's over, aye. We want to be prepared, you see – need somebody who knows what they're about. Somebody who has the sense to see what we've run short of, and knows the suppliers who must be contacted.'

Her father-in-law was nodding. 'Firms who get their orders in now will stand more of a chance when production turns back to items required in peacetime.'

'We wondered if you could happen start sounding them out? Learn when we can expect supplies to begin trickling through. And then there's the jobs that were left unfinished when war broke out. There'll be sites to visit – we shall need to know what condition they're in now, especially if they've been used for other purposes. *And* what's happened to every company of builders that were working to our plans. Happen you worked with some on reconstructing?'

'That's going to take months . . .'

'Why do you think I've come to see you now, Father?' Helen said with a grin, handing a cup and saucer across. 'There's nobody else can set us ahead in this way. And I expect it'll be hectic once the Government begins rebuilding programmes. Every architect that's been forced to suspend work till the duration will be trying to muscle in on whatever's going. This way, Stone's won't be held up – we'll be there in front of all t'others.'

'By, but you're a grand lass, Helen!'

'These aren't just my ideas, you know. Alex wanted me to come and talk to you.'

'Oh, aye?'

He looked sceptical but not displeased. And Helen was aware as ever of how highly Joseph Stone esteemed her ability.

Suddenly, he startled her with a chuckle. 'I always thought that our Alexander was the one with more of a leaning towards the business side. I see now that you've as good a grasp of that as he has. And, as I've always said, you've that bit extra in your designing flair.'

She smiled back at him. 'It's to be hoped I still have — that I've lost nowt these past five years. You can't tell me that there isn't going to be a great deal of competition. No matter how many buildings have to be replaced up and down the country.'

'A lot of that will be down south, though,' he reminded her gravely. 'I've been thinking about that, and don't mind admitting I've been daunted by it. I'm past competing by dashing off to London.'

'Happen you are, and happen you're letting these years of being held up get on top of you. But it's here in Yorkshire we shall be needing somebody to anchor the whole business. You know as well as anybody, you can't run an efficient firm without sound management.'

'I could begin straight away — see what sort of shape the office is in. We might have to replace furniture and maybe some of the equipment when it's been shut up this long. I daresay after the war they'll be selling off a lot of army surplus . . .'

'What are your thoughts on staffing? Is Frank Barclay coming back into the business?'

'Afraid I don't know, my dear, rather lost touch. Suppose I could drop him a line tonight. He'd been given a shore job, last I heard — Portsmouth. He had a bad time of it on the Russian convoys.'

'Oh, aye — I think there was a bit about him in the

Halifax Courier. We shall need clerical staff an' all. What do you feel about having more than one secretary? If Alex or I have to go on long trips, we'll want somebody to cope with the paper work.'

'The girl we had afore — what was her name? I forget. She won't be coming back. Don't recall how I heard, but she had a couple of youngsters and one of them is disabled.'

'Poor lass, what a handful!'

'Her chap was lost as well, shot down over the Channel.'

They talked for a while longer, bringing up everything they could think of which might need sorting out before they could even begin running Stone's effectively again. By the time Helen left him her father-in-law was sufficiently alert for her to believe that her visit had been well worthwhile.

And Helen herself felt infinitely better. Just discussing the time when they would open up the practice again had made the end of the war seem nearer, and more inevitable. There were only two things that bothered her now: how would she ensure that she and Alex settled down happily together, and how endure saying goodbye to Vittore?

The break with the Italian architect came quite suddenly, during the following March and even before hostilities ended. The department responsible for prisoner-of-war camps had organised inspections with a view to winding them down, and the place where Vittore had spent the past few years was declared unfit for habitation.

He arrived for work one Monday, drawn-faced and dejected. Helen was the first to hear that he was being moved, and therefore would no longer be employed at the farm.

'I shall hate it, I know,' he stated grimly. 'I have become so attached to you.'

She tried to avoid considering that his words related to her personally. Vittore, however, soon left her in no doubt. 'You are a lovely woman, Helen, I only wish that we had met years ago.'

She had been about to remind him that he wouldn't have long to wait before being repatriated to Italy; somehow, the words seemed inappropriate now. When Vittore went on to speak less than enthusiastically about working there when he returned, she began to wonder if his home life was even worse than she'd suspected.

'Happen you'll feel better once you're back there again, and starting to get the firm on its feet. I know it's cheered me up since that day I saw Alex's father about our practice.'

Vittore only shook his head. 'Did I not tell you — since my father died, my partner is the brother of my wife. And you know how she and I live separate lives. Her brother wanted me out before the war; from the few letters I have received, it seems he is yet more antagonistic towards me.'

'What will you do then, join another firm?'

'Eventually, perhaps.'

Helen's sympathy for Vittore deepened during those last few days before the camp closed and he was moved from the area. Although he rallied and made an effort to conceal his misery, she couldn't help feeling depressed on his behalf even while the others laughed and joked throughout the tea party Miss Templer put on for him.

Vittore made a short speech, thanking Miss Templer and the rest of them for making him so welcome in and around the farm.

'You have given to me a home,' he told them, tears

glistening in his dark eyes. 'I shall never forget this place, nor any of you.'

He repeated the words about never forgetting to Helen when she walked alone with him towards the path that led to the camp. And now tears were tracing his cheeks, and the sigh he gave prevented him from continuing to talk.

'Nay, love,' said Helen gently. 'You mustn't take on like this. We knew all along, didn't we, that working here wouldn't last? We both have our careers to look to.'

'There will never be a time in mine when each design does not remind me of my sweet English lady architect.'

He drew her to him, lips salty from his tears. 'I pray we shall meet again,' he said huskily, kissing her fiercely.

'Maybe we will,' Helen answered carefully, but wondered already how that could ever come about while she was working over here, and with her husband.

Vittore's response was another kiss, more fevered, eloquent of passion.

After finally parting, Helen heard him running from her, resurrecting memories of that other occasion when they had clung so closely to each other. Walking slowly back to the farmhouse, she felt uneasy again, experiencing a strange premonition that she would meet Vittore at some time in the future, and that the encounter might not be entirely easy.

Once Vittore had left it began to seem that they were all, however unconsciously, winding down. Food rationing was intensifying, but with a lessening of the threat to vessels bringing supplies from overseas, there was hope that the situation would improve. Way back in the previous November when the last major German warship, the *Tirpitz*, had been sunk it had begun to look as though things would return eventually to normal. So long as nothing was wasted, work on the farm might be allowed gradually to diminish.

Helen was the next person to return home, shortly after street parties, bonfires and massive crowds gathering in front of Halifax Town Hall marked the end of the war in Europe. Having Joseph Stone back in the office had paid dividends, ensuring that their firm was, indeed, in the forefront of those architects who would work on designing homes for the millions of needy. No one could deny that she would fulfil as useful a role there as ever she had on the land.

Saying farewell, Helen wept over the other land-girls, especially Jessie who had remained at the farm throughout, and even over Miss Templer. Ken and the other chaps were each given a prolonged hugging. Ken was healthier by far than he had seemed on arriving there; his asthma attacks were less frequent and not half so alarming. Maybe the country air had helped.

Not greatly attracted by the prospect of living on her own until Alex was released from his war work, Helen had been toying with the idea of staying with her parents.

Her visit to them on the day she returned to Halifax quickly put that notion right out of her head. Young Mark and Linda were still being cared for by Kathleen Clegg; Marian's job driving ambulances was as necessary as ever, ferrying around the wounded arriving in the north for care in already overcrowded hospitals. Helen soon saw, though, how wearied her mother was looking after caring for the two youngsters.

Helen must not present her with another person to care for. She knew full well that she herself would be working long hours for Stone's and would have little time to spare for contributing much in the way of help at home.

I shall make the best of a bad job, she told herself firmly. I shan't like being alone in that house, but I shan't even think about the neighbourliness here. And it is on the doorstep of the office . . .

Working again with Joseph Stone was a joy which amply compensated for solitude elsewhere. There seemed to be no evidence now of the confusion which had plagued him during the war. Helen began to believe that getting him working again was all that had been required.

Because Halifax and its immediate surroundings had got off lightly, with only one direct hit from a bomb, a great deal of the permitted rebuilding was further afield. For a time Helen felt reluctant to use the car which Joseph had given them on their wedding day. She was unused to driving and really thought of the neat little Standard as belonging to Alex. Within a few weeks, however, she had seen the sense of using the petrol allowed for business, and was driving off to consult with builders and inspect construction sites.

One or two of these were in and around Sheffield, and she was glad to arrange meetings with her sister. On the first occasion that she saw Marian again, Helen was staggered.

With such a long interval since their last encounter, she had warned herself privately that there might be changes. Nothing on this earth could have prepared her for the overweight individual who had replaced the slender blonde whose beauty had always overshadowed hers.

Trying not to stare incredulously, Helen hugged her sister before following her inside the cinema cafe where they had arranged to have lunch together.

'Before you begin telling me, I know,' said Marian ruefully, grinning across the table, and pushing back a few strands of the fair hair which was wound around an old stocking in the 'Victory roll' style, encouraged to enable women to manage without hairpins. 'It's the sitting down that does it. In the ambulance, and when I get back home at night too tired to shift out of my chair.' She had a rented room in Sheffield to which she would not invite anyone. She believed living like a slob was her own business.

As soon as they ordered and began their meal, Helen saw also that Marian had lost all fastidiousness regarding food; she was wolfing down her bangers and mash, and made short work of one sausage which Helen left uneaten.

'I love potatoes, don't you?' she said, beaming. 'And they're easy to cook when you've been out all day. Must admit I fill up on them many a time. There's not been much else, has there? And I've got a sweet tooth these days. A lot of the lads we carry are Yanks. They're pretty free with their chocolate.'

Helen wondered what Denis would think of his vastly altered wife, and commanded herself not to ask. For once, Marian seemed quite interested in what her sister was doing. When she began asking about Stone's, Helen was glad to bring her up to date.

'And are you liking planning new houses for folk?' Marian inquired.

'It's all right for now, though a lot of it's council stuff. They reckon they want four local authority houses built for each private home. And all the private sector's regulated by licences. I just hope there'll be an opportunity later on for getting on with the kind of designing I really want to do.'

'I expect there will be. There's lots of public buildings have been destroyed, to say nothing of them

207

that would have been going up anyway, if the war had never happened.'

'Maybe so, but there's still these Government restrictions, you know – and will be for many a year, by the sound of things.'

'I see. And what does Alex think?'

'Oh, he's not home yet.'

'Really? But I thought – well, surely he was working on stuff for our defences. Hangars and coastal fortifications, wasn't he?'

'That sort of thing, aye. So far as I could tell. He wasn't supposed to talk about any of it. I imagine folk like him would be responsible for Bailey bridges an' all, and air-raid shelters.'

'Well, then – there's no call for them any longer, is there?'

'I know. But they seem to want to hang on to him for a while. Don't ask me why. He's got that used to not discussing his work, he doesn't tell me owt.'

'Never mind. You'll be all the more excited when he does come home for good.'

When Helen didn't respond, Marian gave her a searching look and reached across to grasp her arm. 'What's up, love? Everything is okay, isn't it, between you?'

Helen smiled. ''Course it is, so far as I know. It's just – well, we'd hardly got to know each other, had we, afore the war began? Since then, we're bound to have changed, both of us. And look how often our ideas collided head-on.'

'Happen he'll have mellowed a bit. Folk do, remember.'

Her sister snorted. 'Alex? Do you really think so? I reckon it's more likely he'll be even more fixed in his ideas. With all the years that have passed.' She couldn't help being thankful that Government stipulations would limit some of his concepts about architecture.

'It isn't only going to be up to Alex, though, is it? Your notions will be just as valid as his, surely?'

Helen caught herself gazing across the table at her sister, unable to speak, remembering an occasion all those years ago, in that other life which seemed now unrelated to her own, when a man training for the priesthood had reminded her of the value of her own thinking.

'And there's his dad, isn't there?' Marian continued. 'Isn't he the one who thinks you're the bee's knees?'

And *that* perhaps is more than half the trouble, Helen reflected, adding this to all the rest of her misgivings.

Within weeks of Alexander's final return to Yorkshire, some of Helen's doubts were proving justified. At home she felt awkward with him. It was so long since they'd been together there for more than the odd few nights that she might have been adapting to living with a stranger. And it didn't help when Alex so often appeared preoccupied that she began wondering if he'd ever again share his thoughts with her.

At work, sensing that her husband secretly resented her rejoining Stone's ahead of him, she kept trying to prove that this had given her no advantage. But his father's evident bias in her favour was undermining the relationship between them. Helen couldn't prevent Alex experiencing a certain resentment that she was bound to admit was only natural.

This surfaced in his criticism of her plans for half a dozen semi-detached houses. Very ordinary in appearance, their main asset the speed with which they might be constructed, there was scope for neither originality nor error. Alex, however, decided the elevations should be re-drawn.

'Any fool could have produced these,' he declared, dropping them on Helen's desk. 'Whoever's going to put up with places that are totally lacking in character?'

'Anybody that's been made homeless,' she answered swiftly.

'Oh, very smart. Pity your designs aren't equally sharp.'

'They're what's expected of us, love. You're as aware as I am of all the blessed instructions. They don't want owt fancy, they've got to build houses as fast as they can, haven't they?'

'Not necessarily by totally sacrificing taste. A kid like young Mark could have done a better drawing.'

Helen was relieved when Joseph came in before she could snap back at her husband. Because he had heard Alex's last sentence, though, he turned on him.

'That's uncalled for, Alexander. Helen's been doing a grand job ever since she came back here. Agreed, these designs are simplified — that's what everybody's after.'

His remarks didn't help. Alex swore under his breath, swallowed as if trying to contain his disgust, and faced his father. 'I don't care what the Government, Town and Country Planning, the local council or anyone else expects of us! We're the ones who will have to live with the crude buildings that are just being shoved up anyhow.'

'Folk need homes, it's that simple,' Joseph continued calmly, though Helen could see his patience was growing thin. 'I know round here we've been lucky and it isn't very obvious how severe the housing shortage is, but . . .'

'You don't need to talk to me about lack of housing. I spent most of the war amid all that bombing, didn't I?'

'Then you ought to understand we have to make this a priority. Once we tackle the problem of close on two million homes that have been either damaged or destroyed, we can look to all the niceties.'

'I still say we ought to do better than this,' Alex persisted, glowering at the plans which so offended him.

Helen couldn't pretend she wasn't put out. What was more she recognised that if she didn't make a stand now she'd have Alex criticising everything she ever did. She did, however, long to ease the antagonism that had flared between them.

That evening, when she was serving their meal, she smiled across at her husband who had hardly spoken since the disagreement.

'Happen we'd better make a pact not to fall out about work, love. It's not worth it, especially just now when our hands are tied by restrictions that govern every mortal thing we attempt.'

'Maybe you're right. I certainly didn't bargain with having this sort of conflict as soon as I got home.'

'And we won't let it happen again. After all, we know things are far from ideal. I'm just as eager as you, you know, to get my teeth into designing something big, something really original.'

'Yes.' Alex sighed. 'I daresay you are.' But he wouldn't have been half so perturbed if his own father didn't always side with Helen against him.

On the next occasion when this occurred, it was for rather different reasons. Amid all the replacement of housing that was being planned they were given the opportunity to design one really good scheme. A school in Manchester was to be rebuilt, and Joseph got wind of it before architect's drawings had been submitted.

'The school governors have specified that they want the new building to be in keeping with the present surroundings. I'm going over there tomorrow to have a look, but I gather that it's adjacent to a Victorian church which has survived intact. The nearby houses are Victorian and Edwardian and all. I want you, Helen, to come with me.'

She was torn. Delighted though she was finally to have this opportunity to work on the sort of thing for which she had first begun her training, she was only too aware that Alex felt slighted.

'It's not your style of building, I know,' she heard his father telling him. 'That's the only reason I've chosen Helen rather than you. You'll be far better getting on with something else, something more modern.'

Alex hadn't been appeased. Even the following weekend when he went with Helen to visit her parents, he was still disgruntled.

'Is something the matter, love?' Kathleen Clegg asked him while they were having tea. Her son-in-law wasn't normally so subdued.

'It's my fault, I'm afraid,' admitted Helen when Alex didn't answer. 'His dad's taken me to look at a site over Manchester way, and has given me the job of drawing up plans for a school.'

'By, but that's good, love,' her own father exclaimed quickly.

Helen wished that he hadn't. Alex was looking more downcast than ever. Her mother was glancing from one man to the other.

'How can you say that, Daniel?' she reproved her husband. 'Can't you tell that Alex is the one who ought to be given a job of that size?'

'It's only because of the style they're wanting,' Helen began explaining. 'They don't want anything too modern . . .'

'Do you have to make it sound as though I'm incapable of adapting to clients' wishes?' Alex demanded.

Helen pressed her lips together, determined to say no more. Whatever was said, the atmosphere only became steadily worse. Eh, love, she thought, gazing at her husband, can't you see it's because you've spent too long proving you're inflexible?

And even when some of the houses on which Alex was concentrating were allowing more scope for incorporating his ideas, he remained unhappy about the work Helen was doing. After her first visit to Manchester with his father, she returned there several times alone. On each occasion she was met with her husband's bad humour when she arrived home.

By the time her plans were drawn and approved, he was going around as though burdened by some massive problem. Nothing she did, either at home or in the office, seemed to make any difference. Things came to a head one Sunday evening as they got ready for bed.

Helen was planning an early start the following morning and had been checking the documents that she must take along. She had an on-site meeting with the construction company and the chairman of the school governors. The fact that Alex had a meeting also, to discuss details of a new development of council housing, cheered him not at all.

'Naturally, I'm disappointed,' he confessed. 'You would be as well if you were still waiting to begin on a decent job that would extend you a bit. Instead of all these footling little tasks that a trainee could manage with one hand tied behind him.'

'All right,' she said. 'And I do understand. Why don't we have a talk with your father before anything else worthwhile comes on the horizon?'

'If anybody talks to him, *I'll* be the one, thank you. I don't need somebody to speak up for me. And my patience is daily growing more exhausted. It seems as if all I ever do is wait — first it was wait for that God-damned war to end, now it's wait for this thing and then the other. There's nothing to look forward to any longer.'

Later that night, when they were in bed, Alex continued his catalogue of complaints. 'This is another thing I'm fed up of waiting for an' all. When folk were apart during the war, what was it they clung to most? Families. And where's ours, eh? You've put this off before, but I'm not going to hang on much longer, Helen. I want a child, preferably a son. And the sooner you accept that it's time you gave your mind to being a mother, the sooner we'll get back to a more agreeable way of life.'

It wasn't the most propitious, and certainly not the most romantic, way of coaxing her to make love. Helen wouldn't have denied him anything that night, but she couldn't obliterate certain feelings of resentment. Okay, so the war had kept them apart, had prevented their even really feeling married until now. But they were still young enough to be able to delay starting a family without either of them feeling deprived.

Alexander took her fiercely, making her recognise his determination to have her submit to his will. Helen caught herself hoping that they weren't conceiving a child in such disappointing circumstances. And immediately felt guilty. She shouldn't be hoping anything of the kind. Whatever was wrong between them these days? A few years ago they'd hardly been capable of resisting each other, and she'd been less worried then than she was now about bringing a bairn into the world.

It was this same problem again, she supposed. Having had to wait until now to really get cracking on her job. Even though she was better off than some folk. Architectural students who were returning from the forces were confronted with difficulties. There was a new requirement coming into force which could mean that they would have to spend an extra year acquiring work experience after the five-year course before they could even sit the Professional Practice and Practical Experience Examination.

Pondering the difficulties faced by present-day students, Helen was so preoccupied that she didn't realise that their lovemaking had ceased until Alexander's even breathing against her neck told her that he was asleep. She began feeling still more guilty, until it occurred to her that she was hardly to blame for his being totally absorbed in taking his pleasure without any regard for her own.

Whatever is happening to us? she wondered, appalled. During the rest of that wearisome night she lay thinking, summoning all her will-power until she eventually resolved that from tomorrow morning she would put more effort into making their marriage succeed. It was so often up to the wife to prevent a couple drifting apart.

She began by getting up early enough to prepare a decent breakfast, intending that they would eat it in comfort before she had to set off for Manchester. Alex, however, seemed to take forever washing and shaving and getting dressed. And then just as he finally sat down at the table, the telephone rang.

'I'll see who it is,' she said, rising from her chair.

'You get on with your breakfast, love.'

The caller was a woman. She sounded young and rather posh, Helen thought, and she was asking for Alexander.

'Just a minute, I'll get him for you. What's your name?'

'Candida. What's yours?' was the sharp reaction.

'Helen Stone, why?'

'I didn't know Alexander had a sister.'

'He hasn't — I'm his wife.'

Chapter 11

Helen missed her train for Manchester that morning, the first time ever that she'd set out late for an appointment. But she did catch the next train, even though she had only a vague grasp of what she was doing. It seemed to her that the already rocky state of her marriage to Alex was doomed to be reduced to tatters.

The cool manner with which he'd taken the receiver from her shaking hand had upset her as much as anything. He had made no pretence of being more than embarrassed by Candida's call, and nor had he troubled to disguise his end of the conversation that followed. By the time she heard the click as the receiver was replaced on its rest, Helen was in no doubt that his relationship with this Candida was, if nothing worse, very friendly.

'I had asked her never to call me here,' Alex began as he walked through from the hall.

Could he really believe wanting to keep her in the dark made it better? 'I'll bet you had!' Helen exclaimed. 'And how long has that been going on? All the time you were working away?'

'There isn't anything "going on" — we became friends, that was all, and only during the latter part of the war. Candida is a most efficient secretary. And, if you must know, enormous fun to be with.'

'While I'm just an old sober-sides?'

'Have I said that, have I? Be fair, Helen.' She read in his grey-green eyes the perpetual need to be liked.

'Fair? I like that! And is it fair — on either her or me — that you've concealed the fact that we are married? That I even exist!'

'You had friendships while you were away at the farm, you know you did. What about those chaps from Sheffield?'

Helen thought of Ken and the others. She thought of Vittoré Fabri, and of how hard she had found denying her emotions for him. Oh, yes, she had formed friendships. 'Yes, I agree,' she told him quietly. 'But every man I met was made well aware of the fact that I am married. I wish I thought for a minute that you have been equally straightforward.'

She had hurried out of the house at that. If she had remained, she'd have been compelled to keep on at him until she found out all there was to know about this Candida woman. And she'd have been in no state by then for setting out for a business meeting.

All the way over to Manchester in the train Helen was gathering her wits, summoning her self-possession so that she would be up to coping.

She mustn't think about it, that was all; by thrusting Alex and that wretched woman to the back of her mind, she would somehow be able to get through the next few hours.

The entire day felt nightmarish. Fortunately, her early work on the scheme had been very thorough, and the quantity surveyor had been efficient; this meant that the construction company's boss had a full understanding of what was required. Hour by hour, she witnessed agreement being reached between the builders and their client. When they both comp-limented her on doing a good job, she tried to smile.

All she could really feel though was dread, because now she had to go home and sort some kind of sense out of the mess between Alex and herself.

There was still a light in the office after Helen had climbed the hill at Luddenden Foot. When the house was empty she knew that she'd have to go along there. If Alexander was staying on late in order to avoid a confrontation with her, that wouldn't work. There was no way that she was going to leave this wretched business unsettled any longer than she was obliged to.

She was thankful to discover that Alex was alone there, and wasn't sorry that he had the grace to look shamefaced when she opened the door and went in.

'How did it go?' he asked, but she read in the shifting of his eyes how wary he was with her.

'Very well, thanks. Fortunately, I'd done most of my work, and didn't have to contribute too much today to ensure that it all went ahead smoothly.' If he says how sorry he is, she thought, and if he gives his word that nothing really wrong happened with that woman, I'll forgive him. It had begun in wartime, after all. Lots of folk were being flung together . . .

'It was only because of the war,' Alex said as if her thoughts had cued him. 'It didn't mean all that much. We were just . . .'

'. . . flung together?' she finished for him, falling back on the words already in her mind. But suddenly she *knew* that he had been unfaithful. And this woman had come back into his life, into their life. She felt her eyes narrowing. 'You had sex with her then, you don't deny that?'

'I'm not in love with her or anything. I've never even imagined I was.'

Helen straightened her shoulders, willed herself to be calm and firm. How could she go on living with him if whenever he was out of her sight she'd wonder who he was with and what he was doing? 'That's her hard lines, and yours. Because we're finished. You'd better beggar off to her now. If you couldn't keep our vows after that short time, there's not much hope for the future.'

'You don't know what you're saying, Helen. I've never cared for her, not like . . .'

'And while you're going, make sure you pack all your stuff. There's all your dirty underpants in the basket and four days' shirts.'

'Helen, you're not listening!'

'I heard enough this morning, enough to last a lifetime. You've as good as admitted you've been unfaithful, and *not* loving that woman makes it worse, not better.'

Too late, she heard the door behind her close. Alexander's face turned ashen as Joseph came in.

'What's all this?' he asked severely.

'Your son'll tell you. I'm going,' Helen began, swinging round ready to leave.

But her father-in-law caught her by the arm.

'Alexander?' he prompted.

'This is just between me and Helen,' said Alex hastily.

'I think not,' his father contradicted. 'Helen knows, and so do you, that I've always told her she can rely on me. Now there seems to be trouble between you. I want to see it sorted.'

His son said nothing. Helen again made as though to leave, and felt Joseph's fingers tighten, preventing her.

'So there's another woman — that it, Alexander?'

'I'm trying to explain, she doesn't mean a thing to me.'

'But you slept with her, I can't believe you didn't. And what do you suppose that means to Helen, here?

Why the hell didn't you give that a bit of thought before you lost your head? Nay, lad — I didn't bring you up to treat folk that badly!'

Helen could feel the old man shaking with rage. She was terrified he might have a seizure. He had problems with his heart, hadn't he — severe enough to keep him out of the forces?

'Let it go, Dad,' she said quietly. 'It's like Alex said, it's up to him and me to sort this.' Or not, she added to herself, certain that she was too shaken to continue living with this husband of hers.

'I'm damned if I'll let it go,' Joseph persisted.

'But it was only with being away from home,' Alex put in. 'You've got to understand . . .'

'Wrong,' his father contradicted. 'We don't *have* to understand anything, and Helen isn't even obliged to try to. You've done the most dreadful thing you could to her. No one would blame her for wanting you out of her life.'

Alex was growing increasingly alarmed. He saw himself being deprived of his work as well as his home, and all for one escapade! He'd have to grovel if that was the only way, promise anything so long as he wasn't kicked out of here as well as from the house. Thank God he literally didn't care enough about Candida to want to meet her again.

'I'll never see another woman as long as I live — and I'll make sure this one knows we shall never meet again. I'll be a model husband from now on.'

Happen so, thought Helen, but the fact remains that I shall never have an easy minute now. It seemed particularly ironic that after struggling for so long against her feelings for Vittore, she had been let down by Alex who hadn't hesitated to sleep with this Candida.

Nothing was resolved that day. She and Alexander

went off home together, but she could hardly bring herself to talk to him, her mind was in such turmoil. In a way, she could understand how easy it was to fall for somebody else, but succumbing to temptation was altogether different. And there was the way that Alex kept insisting that he *hadn't* fallen for this woman. She wondered if she'd ever really known him.

For weeks they remained in the same house and spent most of every working day in the same office, but the tension between them did not ease. They hadn't slept together since that first night. Helen had brought her pillow and spare bedclothes downstairs to sleep on the settee. She wanted to get as far away from him as she could, and certainly didn't want him to touch her.

'Don't be like this, Helen,' Alexander had pleaded.

'I can't help it. I know I shan't sleep with you near me.'

In the end he had taken the settee, and used it every night since.

On the next occasion when she visited her parents Helen intended going alone. She was desperate to talk to them. When she was getting ready, however, Alexander announced that he would accompany her.

'It's bad enough upsetting you. I don't want your mother finding out and thinking badly of me as well.'

Within five minutes of walking into the house, though, they learned that Kathleen and Daniel were aware of the situation.

'We've had a visitor,' Kathleen announced, while Helen was wondering why her parents looked as uncomfortable as she was feeling. 'Your father came here t'other night, Alexander. Told us there'd been a bit bother.'

'What on earth did he do that for?' Alex began.

His father-in-law answered him. 'He said as how he

didn't want owt going wrong between us families. And happen if we knew there'd be summat we could do.'

'*Is* there?' Kathleen asked, concernedly. 'We only want to help.'

'You'll help most by keeping out of something that just affects Helen and me,' said Alex. 'And I don't mean that unkindly – I appreciate your caring, only involving so many folk is making the whole business more important that it was.'

'More important?' Daniel demanded. 'What's more important than our daughter's happiness, that's what I want to know?'

Helen decided it was time she had her say. 'Dad – Mum, I know you mean all this for the best, but Alex is right about this. It is up to us to make up our minds whether we're going to stay together.'

'Eh, love – don't say it's come to that!' her mother exclaimed. 'You wouldn't separate?'

Helen didn't reply. The distress in Kathleen's grey eyes was bad enough now. She was determined not to make it worse.

'That's up to Helen,' said Alex eventually, with a sigh that seemed to emphasise his dread that their relationship was ending.

It wasn't until a further six weeks had passed that any conclusion was reached. And then it was for Joseph Stone's sake, rather than his son's, that Helen made a decision.

The old man had aged visibly during these weeks, and even in the office appeared to be quite disorientated. Helen had caught Alex watching him anxiously, but they never discussed anything but business these days.

One day, however, Alex was out meeting the local housing chief, and when their secretary had left for home Joseph detained Helen as she was tidying her desk.

'Have you a minute, love, for a bit of a chat?'

'Of course,' she said. 'What is it?'

'I wanted to talk to you about our Alex. All this trouble is playing havoc with me. I don't seem able to think straight. Somehow, folk's names keep going clean out of my head and . . .'

Helen smiled. 'That happens to all of us, at times.'

'Not every day, and for most of the day! And I keep forgetting what day it is, come to that — what month even. The other night, I wakened up in a right sweat. Couldn't remember for sure whether the war was over or not.'

'You know what, don't you? You want to put us two right out of your mind, forget what happened. It wasn't anything you could help, and if we can't sort it out . . .'

'It's you I'm concerned for most, Helen love,' her father-in-law interrupted. 'Alexander is the one who did wrong, he deserves what he gets. But I hate seeing you so miserable. There's the firm, as well, naturally. I'd always been that thankful that there was the pair of you to run it. I don't think I could bear it if it were to go downhill because of all this bother.'

'You want us to stay together, to patch things up?'

'Nothing would delight me more, love. I know it's more than Alex deserves, but he's not all bad.'

'I know that, Father. He's got a lot of you in him. I'd be sorry an' all to see Stone's go down. I can still recall how thrilled I was that first day you asked me to think about coming into the firm. And I suppose I can't have been all that sure I wanted us to split up when all this time has passed and I haven't done owt about it.'

She had a long talk with Alex that night. 'You've

made me feel terribly insecure in our marriage,' she
said finally. 'I don't know if I can put that behind me,
but I am prepared to have another try at making a go
of it.'

Alex rushed to hug her.

'You'll have to be patient with me,' she told him,
holding him a little away from her. 'It's going to take a
while to get over this. Things like sharing a bedroom
and that. I shan't be able to forget — well, you know.'

In the end, it was through Joseph Stone again that this
final barrier was overturned. She and Alex had been
called to The Stone House by Mrs Hartley. It was a
weekend and for days they had been concerned
because the old man was growing increasingly confused and unable to concentrate. Helen had caught
him out when he was supposedly studying a letter from
one of their clients. He had appeared to read every
word, turning over from one page to the next as
necessary. When they began discussing the details that
it contained, however, she quickly found that he
hadn't taken in anything. And now, a day or two later,
he had evidently lapsed again into an agitated state
where he could not be convinced that Britain wasn't
still at war.

'I can't get through to him, I'm afraid,' Mrs Hartley
said when she admitted them. 'And he won't let me
call the doctor.'

Joseph greeted them cheerfully enough, but his
ramblings did not cease, even when they had been
sitting talking with him for an hour or more. Alex
went to ring the doctor then sat with his father again
while Helen tried to learn all she could from Mrs
Hartley.

'He doesn't seem to take stuff in any more,' the
housekeeper confided, alarmed. 'He reckons he's

reading the paper, but I'll be hanged if he is. You talk to him five minutes later on, and he knows nowt about anything that's in it. He's the same about letters, an' all, I'm afraid. I found that out when somebody kept writing and then called to see us. Summat to do with that new-fangled washing machine that the master would insist on buying.'

When the doctor had given Joseph a thorough examination, he asked to speak with Alexander. After he had driven away, Helen went to find her husband. He was sitting near one of the large windows in that huge reception room which, except for a faint light from the moon beyond the glass, was in total darkness.

'He brought me up,' he said in a choking voice. 'There was just the pair of us for that long. I can't bear this, Helen, I can't.'

She crossed swiftly and put her arms round him. 'I know, love. I do know. I wish there was something I could do . . .'

Even while she was speaking she understood that there was. She wasn't certain it could help Joseph Stone now, but it would help this man of hers. 'He's resting now, isn't he? Let's see if Mrs Hartley has a room ready for us.'

'I had a feeling you might decide to stop the night,' the housekeeper told them. 'I've aired the bed in Mr Alexander's old room.'

After they had gone upstairs, however, Alex still needed to talk. Sitting at the desk which stood between two long windows, he faced the wall for a few seconds, thinking, then swivelled round to see what he could read in Helen's expression.

She was gazing at him, concern darkening the lovely grey eyes, while the distress of the past few weeks was evident in the shadows beneath them.

'I feel as if I'm losing everything,' he admitted. 'First you, now my father.'

'You haven't lost me, not entirely,' she reminded him calmly. 'We could still make this into a good marriage, but that's going to require commitment on both sides.'

'I can see that. You'll need convincing that you can trust me.'

'Aye,' Helen responded grimly, well aware that it would be a long time before she would be able to do that.

'I was weak, I'll confess,' he said miserably. 'Foolish. If you've not been tempted yourself, you'll doubtless find that hard to understand.'

'I've never said I haven't,' Helen began, and was checked by her husband's immediate surprise which soon changed to what seemed to be comprehension. 'That chap on the farm, I suppose? The one with chest trouble.'

Almost, Helen shook her head. Just in time she thought better of enlightening him. Ever since the war ended she had thought of Vittore, frequently and affectionately. When Alex was being difficult, she had yearned to get away from here to Italy. She could continue her career out there. But she'd kept her feelings to herself this far: now that Alex and his dad needed her, she'd ensure that they remained interred.

'As I see it,' she said firmly, 'we have got to leave the past where it is. Up to the other week, we haven't had any real reason to think we shan't make a go of it. Now there's your father's health to consider. And the business. I've always been very fond of your dad — you know that. I hate seeing him like this. And if our patching things up can help him to improve, that's what we'll do. It'll ease his mind a lot. As for the business — well, there's only us that's fit to build

Stone's up again. We'd best give our minds to that, and stop fratching.'

'Bless you, Helen – you're marvellous.'

'Time'll tell,' she responded enigmatically, far from convinced that she could carry out her own suggestions. She only knew that she felt compelled to put all she'd got into trying.

As she got into bed Helen noticed how exhausted she felt, like an old dishcloth. And Alex looked worse. She believed he genuinely was distressed by the rift between them, on top of that this anxiety about his father appeared to be more than he could take. Instinctively, she drew him against her.

'You've always been so good to me,' he murmured into her hair. 'Ever since that fire at Yeoman's Grange.'

Tired though they were, neither of them slept readily that night. Helen wasn't surprised when Alex began making love to her. And she wasn't sorry either. After keeping him off for so long, she'd been dreading a return to their normal relations. Like this, there was less awkwardness. And afterwards they managed to get off to sleep.

Joseph Stone rallied a little under his doctor's care, and seemed to regain more of a grasp on what was happening around him. He started taking an interest at the office again, and appeared to be able to follow what was going on there. And if Helen and Alex acknowledged in private that the old man no longer fulfilled a useful role, they agreed that he must be allowed to believe he was indispensable to them. Certainly, they both were far happier about his state of mind.

The news which was to really act as the tonic Joseph needed was their announcement that Helen was at last expecting a child. Alexander also was utterly delighted. And if she herself was less than thrilled about the timing, she was prepared to accept that this was an essential part of the pact to make their marriage work.

Having put Alex in such a good humour, she was compelled to admit that their life together took on a happier aspect. For once in his life, he became deeply concerned for someone other than himself, and within his limitations couldn't do enough for her. The limitations were as Helen might have expected. Reared with a housekeeper and other staff to tend every need, Alex simply wasn't aware of the innumerable tasks involved in keeping a home running. He failed to see that their carpets needed hoovering, or that the stack of dishes would remain beside the sink until somebody washed them.

When Helen's tiredness made him comment and she pointed out that she was trying to keep going both at home and in the office, it was at Stone's that Alex quickly suggested they should acquire some help.

His wife shook her head. 'No, that's not what I meant. I shall keep going there as long as I can. It's what I enjoy doing, isn't it? I had to wait all through the war for this, didn't I?'

Alexander didn't argue with her. He was learning that he shouldn't cross Helen too regularly. He would have to wait. With the old man still installed in the office, introducing another qualified architect might make for difficulties. And Helen was good at her job, and more reliable than somebody new might prove.

'I'll get someone to help with housework,' she announced one evening while they were sitting after finishing their evening meal. 'That way, I'll be able to carry on at Stone's, and happen just set somebody on there to cover for a month or two when I have the baby.'

'A month or two?' That didn't suit. 'That's not what I had in mind at all. I don't want my wife working when we have a family. It isn't as if you had to for the money.' The firm would do better once building licensing eased. And they didn't live extravagantly.

She managed a smile. 'Well, we'll have to see,' she said. But was conscious already that she would see to it that she continued to work after she became a mother.

Her sister told her she must be wrong in her head the first time that was mentioned in her hearing. Marian had asked her over to Leeds one Saturday to look at the cot which she had used for both children. Alex had taken his father to watch the local cricket club, and Helen was pleased to have the opportunity to go somewhere without him. She had included a visit to Harrogate as well, to see old Mr March who seemed to be taking on a new lease of life. His second daughter had been restored to him after the war had ended and the inmates of prison camps had been repatriated. Her husband hadn't survived, but she herself was gradually recovering from internment, and had settled in a pleasant flat not far from her father's nursing home.

In good spirits after being able to tell Mr March how the bursary was swelling now that she was earning good money again, Helen only laughed at Marian's astonishment. 'I'm beginning to think I'm not the maternal type, any road, though it's a bit late for deciding that. But it was to be an architect that I studied all those years. I'm not going to abandon that just when it's getting interesting again. There's going to be fewer building restrictions afore long, you know. That's what I've been waiting for.'

'But it'll be nowt but work still, Helen. Don't you want to have things a bit easier?'

'What for?' She could think of nothing more boring than just looking after the house and a bairn. Whatever would she do with all the designs and the schemes that still came surging into her head, just as they always had done?

'You could come over here more often, like this. We could go round the shops together. Lewis's is still there, you know, and Schofield's.'

'Look, love, I'm glad you enjoy that sort of thing, but it isn't for me, really it isn't.'

'Linda and Mark are looking forward to you having a baby, they'll love a little cousin. We could take them all into Roundhay Park, and further afield. We can both drive, can't we?'

It was mention of Linda and Mark that set Helen thinking. 'It's a pity you live so far away. I'd be asking you if you'd baby-sit for me, regular like. I'd be glad to pay you . . .'

When Marian beamed at her, Helen couldn't immediately understand why. But her sister soon enlightened her.

'You just might find we aren't living quite so far apart before very long. I wasn't going to say owt yet, but we mightn't be stopping in Leeds. You remember how Denis did a lot of acting with ENSA during the war?'

'Yes. Well?'

'Don't breathe a word to Mum and Dad yet, you know what a thing they have about being secure, but Denis is hankering to act again, says he's that sick of backstage work he'll take a cut in wages if he can get the job he wants. Anyhow, he's auditioning next week – in Halifax. The repertory company lost their male lead and are after somebody now. Wouldn't that be

231

great, getting taken on where he began as an A.S.M.!'

'Would it be a lot less money than he's getting as Stage Manager at Leeds Grand?'

'Don't know really, but he's afraid it would. It's not as important a theatre, is it? Wages in rep are notoriously low. But we're thinking of it as just a start. He could be fortunate and finish up in the West End. That's happened for more than one of the folk that he was with in ENSA.'

'And wouldn't you mind moving house again?'

Marian glanced around the lounge of the house which was comfortably, if not elaborately, furnished. 'Happen so — a bit. But this place hasn't felt quite the same since we came back when the war was over. I'd let it, you know, while I was in Sheffield and Denis away such a lot. The folk we had in kept it nice, but it hasn't felt like mine, if you know what I mean.'

Although determined not to set any great store by what her sister had told her, Helen couldn't help hoping that Denis would get the job which might ensure bringing them back to live near Halifax. The day that Marian telephoned with the news that this was what they were doing, it seemed almost as though their arrangements had co-ordinated to provide a means of securing her own way of continuing her career.

Before that could occur, however, the final months of her pregnancy must be endured. And without letting Alex see how greatly those summer months of 1946 were taxing her. Perhaps due to the proximity of the office to their home and consequent lack of exercise, or maybe simply her natural tendency, Helen had put on a great deal of weight. Even though she'd never considered West Riding summers particularly hot, in her condition this one felt extremely so, and endless. The baby was due in October and she was counting the weeks, not so much in anticipation as to have her burden eased.

To Alexander's relief, she had consented to work only part-time from July onwards and to cease coming into the office altogether four weeks before the birth was scheduled.

Helen hadn't breathed a word to anyone, but she and Marian had made a tentative arrangement that in the new year she would hand over care of the infant to her. She suspected that Alex would be appalled, but she would not let that deter her. Marian was good with kiddies, and liked not going out to work. Fortunately, on the occasions when they got together, Alex enjoyed the company of both Denis and Marian — he wouldn't have any reasons for objecting on the grounds of *who* would be caring for their child.

Towards the end of August Joseph Stone began declining again. Although he himself never admitted as much, both Helen and Alex concluded that he must realise that his active life was ending. Daily, he was driven as far as the office by the young woman who had been taken on to assist Mrs Hartley at The Stone House. And each day he tended to sit increasingly listlessly at his desk, making no pretence now of achieving any real work. Worst of all, he was becoming incontinent. Bad enough in the home, this created great difficulties in a professional office.

'We'll have to tell him to stay at home,' said Alex on the day when, for the second time, they'd had to summon the car to take his father back for dry clothing.

They were often obliged to find excuses for keeping clients out of the old man's office at times when he was in no state to meet anyone.

'Nay, love, we can't do that to him,' said Helen, her grey eyes filling. She had been recalling the fine man whom she had greatly admired and who had since commanded such a large slice of her affection.

Joseph had indeed recognised for himself that his working life had ceased. Although he might have appeared oblivious to the extent to which he was losing control of his bodily functions, he did experience quite lengthy lucid periods in which he was aware of the indignity such malfunction caused. He telephoned his son at home that evening.

'I shan't be coming in tomorrow,' he declared. 'Time I recognised that I'm getting to be nothing but a nuisance there. You and Helen will get on a lot better without me.'

On the next occasion when they visited the house, Joseph clearly was far more confused, rambling on about the war again, with no inkling that it had long since ceased. And Mrs Hartley was showing the effects of caring for him now. She herself was well on into her sixties and the additional washing, together with anxiety, was wearing her down.

Even the doctors admitted that there was little that they could do for the old man now. And he could linger on for years, thought Helen, while unable to bring herself to voice such a dread to her husband. But it was no sort of an existence for someone who had once been so fine a man. How would they all endure it if this continued indefinitely?

She and Alex were getting ready for bed one night in September. It was later than their usual time. Helen generally went up soon after nine-thirty these days, but tonight a fierce thunderstorm had torn its way back and forth along the valley since early evening. From the vantage point of their small house on the hill, they hadn't missed any of its alarming ferocity.

As she drew the bedroom curtains across lightning forked yet again and thunder rolled nearly overhead.

She didn't hear the telephone at first. Only as the rumbling faded did she become aware of its ringing. Alex was in the bathroom. Helen struggled back into her maternity smock, thankful that she hadn't taken off her skirt. Going downstairs, she glanced at her watch. It had gone eleven o'clock. This could only be an emergency.

Steeling herself, she lifted the receiver.

'It's Mr Stone, I'm afraid,' said Mrs Hartley agitatedly. 'I'm sorry to have to ring you, in your condition, but it's bad. I've called the doctor, he should be here any minute, but I thought you and Mr Alexander had better be told.'

'Of course, Mrs Hartley — how bad is it?'

'Well, I'm no expert, as you know, but I think he's had a sort of seizure.'

'We'll be there as soon as we can. You must stop worrying now, you've done everything you possibly could.'

Alex took the news badly when he came rushing down the stairs to join her. 'It's the end, I know it is!' he exclaimed, his face the shade of the mushrooms Helen had peeled for dinner that evening.

'We don't know that, love. We can only hope that it isn't, and just keep going to make sure we get there,' she added, wondering why words were so daft. You said what you felt you ought, yet all the while, deep inside, you were hoping the old man wouldn't drag on for ever like this. For his sake more than anybody's.

Rain drove at the windscreen all the way along the main road. 'Houses in Mytholmroyd'll be flooded if this doesn't ease up soon,' Helen remarked as lightning reflected back from water racing like rivers at the edge of the road.

'We don't have to go through there,' snapped Alex, and gave her a sideways glance that seemed to ask if she had lost her senses.

Helen didn't reply, but grew even more disturbed by recognising that he could spare no thought for anyone or anything that didn't affect his family.

The lane up to the house was awash as well, and smothered in the silt, sand and soil driven down the hillside by the force of the deluge. Despite their urgency, Alex was obliged to slow down as he negotiated every curve between the rough drystone walls.

The doctor's car was in the drive; Alex parked beside it rather than pausing to garage the Standard. Taking Helen's hand, he hastened through the downpour and began running up the steps.

Halfway to the door, Helen was obliged to free her hand and follow at her own pace. She had a stitch in her side already, and a pain was beginning to sear into her back.

The housekeeper had the door open and Alex was questioning her by the time Helen caught up.

'I'd just shown the doctor up there when you arrived, Mr Alexander. I daresay he'll be a while before he can tell us owt for certain.'

'And Dad — how did he seem? Is he conscious?'

Mrs Hartley was shaking her head. 'Eh, I wish I could tell you, I do that! But you know how he's been lately — never quite with you, in a manner of speaking. His eyes were open, though. Is that good?'

Before either of them could answer her, Helen felt something warm and wet cascading down her legs.

'Oh, no!' she exclaimed, shocked. 'I'm ever so sorry, it looks as if it's me now. I didn't even know I needed to go . . . I am sorry, Mrs Hartley, you've enough to do.'

But briefly the housekeeper's tired eyes lit up. 'Eh, love, don't take on. That's your waters, I'm sure!'

Chapter 12

Helen was still standing in the middle of the hall when
the doctor emerged from one of the bedrooms and
hurried down the beautiful curving staircase towards
them. Although somebody had taken her coat, and
someone else had produced a chair, she was too
uncomfortable about the pool on the floor to think of
sitting.

As Alex stepped forward to enquire after his father,
Mrs Hartley, for once in her life venturing to assert
herself, spoke first to the doctor.

'Is the master still holding on?' she asked swiftly,
and when satisfied with a nodded reply, continued:
'Then could you take a look at this lady please – Mr
Alexander's wife, you recall, Doctor? I think her
bairn's on its way.'

The doctor took charge at once, checking which
room was available and assisting Helen upstairs and
along the landing. Somewhere on the way he turned to
Alex who was following.

'You could go in and see your father. He doesn't
appear to be conscious of what's going on around him,
but there's still a good chance he might know you're
here.'

Alex ran towards his father's door.

'I wanted to see him again,' Helen protested, but
quite weakly. The pains had spread from her back

already, and felt to be dragging so much they could turn her inside out.

'And so you shall,' the doctor reassured her. 'He'll last beyond this night, if I'm any judge. You'll be showing him this fine infant that's in such a sudden hurry.'

If this is being in a hurry, thought Helen hours later as dawn paled the sky over the far hillside, I'd hate to have one that took its time! The doctor had summoned the midwife, a broad Scots woman, and after checking again that he could do nothing further for Joseph, had gone home to his interrupted sleep. Mrs Hartley had been persuaded by Jane, the young woman they employed, to go to her bed and rest. With Alex as well as the midwife popping in and out, Helen had no opportunity for feeling neglected. In fact, assured now that the birth would proceed quite normally, she wasn't sorry when the midwife left her on her own. The suddenness with which her labour had begun meant that she needed some time for settling her mind. Together with anxiety about her father-in-law, concern about this premature labour was whirling out of control.

Thunder still hung around, startling her every time that she supposed it had cleared right away. And lightning kept forking the early morning sky. Between the meteorological shocks and those inside her, moments for thinking were scarce. Helen felt no more at peace by the time the midwife returned to her room.

A large woman, who reminded Helen forcefully of Miss Templer at the farm, she conveyed efficiency with an underlying kindliness.

'Are the pains coming more frequently at all?' she inquired. She had been asked by Alexander Stone to remain at the house until the baby was safely delivered. No matter how long that took. She knew she would be well rewarded. The family were private patients. No one living at The Stone House would be on any doctor's panel.

'Sorry, I keep losing track,' said Helen. 'It's this storm interrupting.' Wanly, she smiled. 'Caught myself just now counting the gaps between the lightning and thunder instead.'

'Aye, it's been a cruel night, the worst we've had for ages. We'll time you for a while now, see what Doctor thinks.'

'He's still here then? I thought he'd gone. How's Mr Stone?'

'The doctor left not long after midnight, but turned up again not half an hour ago. And Mr Stone's still holding his own.'

'That was what Alex said.' He had visited often during the night before returning to doze in his father's room. 'Happen if I'm still like this in an hour or two I could go in and see my father-in-law? He's always been good to me.'

Another fierce pain interrupted. The midwife stood beside the bed, her attention divided between her watch and Helen's face. The next pain came sharply on the heels of its predecessor. Helen was too wearied to contain a little cry.

The midwife beamed, nodding to herself. 'Not long now, Mrs Stone. I'm just going to check downstairs that they have everything to hand. Shan't be a second.'

Alone again, Helen couldn't credit that her time was almost here. Maybe because of having so little real warning, she found picturing herself a mother before this day was out highly improbable. But then the pains recurred, stronger and more urgent. Thinking became impossible.

The midwife opened the door and ran towards the bed. 'Right, lassie — just try to do everything I say . . .'

Helen had wanted to remember the birth, to lodge in her mind each vital moment that was introducing this child of theirs to a separate life. But she was hurting too much to do more than reach through this agonising haze and grasp instructions from the large capable woman who was helping them. By the time she felt the final thrusting and the moist slithery being emerging between her legs, she could only pant, and pray a bit, and hope.

'Is it all right?' she gasped when the cord was cut. 'What is it?'

'A grand wee lad,' she was told, and that instant heard his first cry. 'Hear that now, Mrs Stone — hasn't he got fine lungs? And he's not over small for a bairn that's afore the time.'

Still blood-streaked, he was held up for Helen to see. 'I'll just clean the wee man up a mite, then you shall hold him.'

He felt heavier in her arms than she had feared, warm through the bit of blanket used as an improvised shawl. Helen pressed dry lips against his forehead.

'He is all right, isn't he?' she checked, unable to believe that the child was here and well.

The midwife chuckled. 'Aye — you may rest assured, there's no bits missing.'

'Has my husband been told? Can he come in now?'

'In a minute, lassie. When we've got you all clean and tidy again.'

Alex walked slowly across to the bed. He'd never felt so awed in the whole of his life. Helen looked different, pale with exhaustion and lack of sleep, but radiant, her beautiful grey eyes reflecting the early morning light. And the baby? He hardly dared to look. A part of him longed to stare and stare at his son, the product of their loving; yet the other half, the side unfamiliar with anything to do with this women's work, childbirth, might compel him to turn and run. He might so easily do or say something that was wrong.

He kissed Helen tentatively, aware of her sudden fragility, and risked one glance at the bundle that was his son.

Helen smiled after he had asked how she was. 'Bring up a chair, Alex. Then you can hold him.'

He didn't − wouldn't ever − know how.

'Nay, love − come on,' Helen chuckled, then grimaced when even a tiny laugh hurt. 'Just stick your arms out over the bed.'

He cradled the child against him, gazed down at the reddish, rather wizened face, wondered what colour his eyes were. When he asked, Helen said blue. She added that they always were, but might change later.

'How's your dad?' she asked. 'Any different?'

Alex shook his head, his eyes filling. 'It's been a long night.'

Helen grinned ruefully. 'You can say that again. But about your father − what did the doctor say this morning?'

'Won't commit himself, but he's coming back after surgery. It can't be so good.'

'The doctor's gone off again already, has he?'

'Not yet. Wants to take a look at you first.'

'I do wish your dad would come round − if only just so he'd know about his grandson. He used to be that keen to be assured the family would continue.'

Alex sighed, and blinked. Somehow, he couldn't keep the tears from reaching his lashes.

'Take the baby into his room, anyway, love. Please.'

'I − can't.'

He was saved by the door opening and the doctor

walking in. 'Let's have a look at the boy.'

He took the infant from his father, tested the weight, and smiled. 'I couldn't believe his birth weight, considering he's premature. That'll stand him in good stead, you know. There's no cause to be alarmed by his early arrival.' He glanced at Alex. 'If you'd just leave me with your wife for a minute or two . . .'

'Alex was just going to take the baby to his father.'

'Oh, no − I don't think so,' he protested.

'An excellent idea. Where's the problem?'

'Frankly, Doctor, when you came in I was just wondering how I could even manage to stand up while I was holding him!'

'Watch this − and you'd better catch on fast. There'll be some fetching and carrying while your wife's confined to bed.' Beaming to himself, the doctor beckoned with one hand and, still holding the baby carefully in one arm, conducted Alexander along to his father's room.

Alone with the old man and the infant, Alex glanced warily from the bundle in his arms to the frail features on the pillow. God, what a time! Even now that Helen was through her ordeal, he felt torn apart by anxiety. He couldn't have wanted this baby more − and a *son* − but the responsibility made him feel as though he were supporting the weight of this entire house on his shoulders. As, in another sense, he supposed he was.

Scarcely knowing how or why, he moved towards the bed, his steps faltering as he reluctantly drew closer to the presence of death. Almost unawares, he started speaking.

'He's here, Father, the grandson you wanted so much. I wish I knew what I ought to say, on his behalf *and* mine. I wish he'd come into our lives long before this, while you could appreciate him. He might have −

have helped. You'd have had a new interest, a bit of incentive to – well . . .' His voice dwindled on a sigh.

'Dad, listen, it's a boy. Helen's given me a boy. Given us . . .' He swallowed. Leaning forward, he laid his son close to the grandather who would have loved him. Feeling beneath the covers he located the hand, thin and wrinkled, almost bloodless but not quite cold. Gently, he pressed it beneath his own then held it gently against the baby's forehead.

'Dad, can't you feel? He's here now.'

Alex felt the fingers under his own stir slightly, as if caressing the still damp, fair down covering the front of his son's scalp. His glance jerking to his father's face, he saw the eyelids flicker, struggle to open with enormous effort.

Thinly, a voice emerged from cracked lips. 'A boy?'

'That's right, Dad. Your grandson. You're going to get well again, see him grow up . . .'

A strange sound rasped in his father's throat, his breath seemed to catch – and then was no more.

Alex stood there motionless while between his own hand and the infant, other fingers grew cold.

'At least it's meant that our son was born here, darling.'

Alex was with his wife and baby in a first-floor sitting room which hadn't been used for years. Helen had insisted on being up and about today, said she was feeling fine. And he couldn't have been more thankful for this one sign of their returning to a kind of normality.

The funeral was arranged for tomorrow. It had been a gruelling few days. As the only son, he had always known he would be obliged to see to everything alone. Somehow, perhaps because of Helen being confined to bed at the time, he had felt particularly isolated with his grief. Not that Helen's distress had been any less profound than his own. She had wept on several occasions and he'd noticed how her lovely grey eyes grew misty each time his father was mentioned. Including Joseph in the names they were giving their son was her suggestion — he would be Neil Joseph Stone.

'It'll be better once tomorrow's behind us,' she said now, smiling across at him.

Alex nodded. 'I expect so,' he said quietly, though in truth he could not imagine emerging from beneath this great burden.

It wasn't just the loss of the only parent he could remember clearly. That would have been bad enough but there was this place as well, and his total responsibility for the business. He wasn't acquainted in any detail with what the upkeep of The Stone House must be, but he had a good grasp of financial matters, could make an educated guess at the sum required. The house was too big to be run without staff. That Mrs Hartley would remain was not in question but Jane, the young woman whose primary task had been driving his father around, was already serving the notice which he'd been obliged to give her.

'It's getting you down, love, isn't it?'

That was Helen again, compassionate as ever, ready to share. Yet he'd not inflict on her the new anxieties induced by his father's death. He just wished he'd had more of an inkling that there might be so little available capital. Joseph Stone had been known for his wealth. Alex could hardly credit that, along with this place and Stone's, he'd inherited a budget which must be rigidly controlled.

'It'll take time, Helen, that's all,' he answered her, trying to lighten his tone. 'Just as it'll take a while to get used to living here.'

The way she paled so swiftly told him that she hadn't yet considered that they would be moving in. She didn't say, though, and he was compelled to admire the way her chin went up and a smile reappeared determinedly on her lips.

'I've always loved this house, you know that,' she assured him.

But would she love living here? The Stone House was so unlike the place where she felt she belonged. She yearned for life in a street where neighbours were friends. Maybe when Neil started to grow and was running about the house it might begin to be a bit like home. Until then she was afraid she'd feel as if she and Alex had been set down in a minor palace. Where she couldn't be herself. Still, once their Marian was looking after Neil so that she could get back to work, they wouldn't be spending all that much time here. And she'd always be busy at weekends. Ever since she'd got married, her hours at home had been crammed with more tasks than she would fit into them.

'I telephoned Harold Tilsley while I was in the office,' Alex announced. He didn't add that that had been days ago, and he'd sensed he was right to have reservations about telling her. 'There's a good chance that he'll come into Stone's.'

Helen frowned. 'But even if he is looking for a change, surely he'd not go for something temporary?'

'I can't manage on my own. I need somebody qualified in the office whenever the job takes me out of it.'

'I know that, don't I, love? But what I'm saying is – it'll only be a few months before I'm back there.'

'Will it?'

Helen swallowed down her immediate reply. She had seen his expression. And he'd had a lot of stress this week, tomorrow was his dad's funeral, this wasn't the time for asserting her views regarding her future at Stone's.

'We'll have to see, eh, Alex? See what we think when we've got used to coping with this young fellow here.' And living the different existence which this house will impose on us.

'I shall take Harold, if he's willing to come to us.'

Helen let him have the last word. For the present.

There was nothing funereal about the day, which was scorching for September. The sun had burned through the glass of the cars carrying them from the house to the church. Helen, who had insisted that she was well enough to attend, struggled with lightheadedness as she stood at the edge of the grave. She'd never seen such a big funeral, had felt overwhelmed by the throng congregating behind them in the church. As well as fellow architects and representatives of the many builders and contractors who were business contacts, present-day councillors and others who had served while Joseph Stone was mayor were present.

Thankfully, she saw that Alex seemed strengthened by the size of the gathering, or perhaps was helped by having to bear up in front of all these people. This morning he had cried desolately, trying to explain how he felt now he had no close kindred. But suddenly she understood that he would survive more than this ordeal.

Back at the house, she excused herself. It was Neil's feeding time, and she was glad to take him from her mother who had come for the day, giving help in whatever way she could. To Helen's pleased surprise, her dad had taken a day off work, as well, wanting to share their sorrow. He was with the others now, looking awkward among so many businessmen with

246

their expensive suits and wives darkly dressed but like fashion-plates. Helen had never loved him more.

'Did your dad have a private word with you both?' Kathleen asked now, kissing her grandson's drowsy face before handing him over.

'With me, yes. I'm afraid Alex was busy with somebody — it's been that sort of a day.'

'Aye, I suppose it has. Did everything go off all right?'

'So far as I could tell. Not being at my best, I was concentrating more on watching I stayed on my feet. It's that hot out!'

'But you are all right?'

''Course I am, thanks. Just a bit tired. I had to be there, Mum.'

'I know. And Alex'll allus remember that you were. Poor lad, he'll feel fair lost for a long while.'

'I've been thinking,' said Helen, unfastening her blouse and easing the baby into position. 'It's a right good thing this one here arrived when he did. Alex is that suited with him — when he has time to be — Neil will give him something else to think about.'

'Aye, love, he will that.'

'He believes his father knew, an' all. Did I tell you? Alex swears he understood. They were his last words: "A boy".'

'He'll know now for sure, any road. Joseph Stone won't neglect his grandson. He'll be watching him grow up. Him and Alexander's mother, they'll be together again now. Does your Alex ever say owt about his mother?'

Helen shook her head. 'Do you honestly believe all that, Mum — about when you die? About any of it, religion and that?'

'Of course. It's like your dad says, we're not alone, none of us. Not here, not when we pass on.'

247

'Must be a comfort.' All at once Helen recalled saying something of the kind years ago, to a man who long since would have become a priest. She wished she could talk to him now.

'I always look at it this way,' Kathleen persisted gently. 'I can only continue to trust, and there's lots of folk cleverer nor me who believe there's somebody there to put that trust in.'

Helen nodded pensively. Death and birth — they were times that set you thinking. And made you wish for powers greater than your own for coping with fresh responsibilities.

'If I don't get a word with your Alex afore we have to go,' said her mother, 'tell him that I shall expect you both to bring young Neil to us some Sunday before so long. Now think on — it's times like this when folk mustn't be allowed to forget that they aren't really on their own.'

During the ensuing weeks, Helen frequently wished that Alex could be persuaded to take up her mother's invitation. Although plainly besotted with their son, he appeared to have no time for anything outside Stone's. He was entirely caught up in so many matters that required serious thinking. Joseph Stone's will had been simple in content, leaving Alex the only benefic-iary, but had also named him the sole executor. And regarding the practice he was obliged to go through every file his father had handled, ascertaining which jobs remained unfinished. All too quickly, he had learned that his father's ability to work coherently had ceased far earlier than they had supposed.

Even Helen could not argue when he took Harold Tilsley into the firm. She could only plan for the future, and resolve that she also would have a place there as soon as Neil was big enough to be entrusted to her sister.

Moving all their possessions into the big house had created another upheaval, but one which Helen herself had enjoyed. Even if she still hadn't fully accepted the place as her home, she could make the best of things. No one would deny that it was a far more beautiful house than she'd ever aspired to, and at least she hadn't too many regrets about leaving the one on the hillside at Luddenden Foot.

Whilst busy clearing out their old home and packing, she had taken the opportunity to call into the office. It was hardly the best idea she'd ever had. Alex and Harold were evidently engaged in a man-to-man discussion on reallocating the work load. Alex made it plain that he didn't welcome the interruption, cutting her short while she was catching up on Harold's career to date, and suggesting she should have a cup of tea with their secretary if she felt like chatting.

There'll have to be changes, Helen thought determinedly, hurrying back to continue tidying out their old home. And straight after Christmas wouldn't be too soon. Admittedly, she'd had a lot on her hands, with the move and helping Mrs Hartley reorganise the household, to say nothing of the time devoted to Neil. But their Marian was settled into her new house in Halifax and was itching to help care for the baby. And in some ways his being born early had been a bonus. He'd be that much older and better able to adjust to seeing less of his mother.

Emptying the last of her cupboards that day, Helen had come across the box containing the model of Florence Cathedral which Vittore Fabri had constructed so carefully for her. Smiling at first, she had examined the beautifully crafted structure again. But suddenly tears had welled in her eyes. How could she deny her career, the impulse to create magnificent buildings, *how* − when she'd scarcely scratched at the surface of a job where she yearned to make an impression?

Christmas really seemed to creep up on them that year, and it wasn't until Kathleen Clegg reproached her younger daughter for not visiting earlier, and mentioned Christmas Day specifically, that Helen truly realised how near it was.

'We'd love to come to you for Christmas dinner, and no — I'm not going to check with Alex first. We're not stopping on our own in that big house, regretting that his father isn't still with us. We're coming to you. And if Neil's too little to know what it's about, *we're* going to enjoy our Christmas.'

To Helen's delight, Alex seemed thankful to have arrangements made on his behalf. 'I'll admit I was dreading Christmas Day, and feeling guilty about it as well. Knowing we've such a lot to be thankful for with Neil, yet knowing also that he's not old enough to appreciate a tree and Father Christmas and so on.'

'You'll enjoy seeing our Marian and Denis an' all. And the kids, they've really taken to little Neil. They're fair grand with him.'

On the day, however, it soon proved that Alex couldn't remain in agreement with his sister-in-law. It all began quite well, with Marian who was there already welcoming them in, and Kathleen appearing in the kitchen doorway to greet them while still continuing stirring the bread sauce she was making.

Denis was helping Helen's father who was trying to contain the excitement of Linda and Mark as they examined and re-examined some of the toys they had been given. Seeing their arrival, however, Denis straightened his back and strode across to hug Helen and kiss the sleeping baby before turning to Alex.

The two shook hands and Helen noticed how Denis brought his other hand up to grasp her husband's firmly. 'Glad to see you again, Alex. How are you now? We were both sorry about your father.'

Thanking him, Alex smiled. 'Yes – well, he's at peace now. Didn't have too much of that towards the end of his life. At least he lived to see his grandson.'

As Denis returned to the children, Daniel Clegg rose and came towards Helen. He put his arms round her as he kissed her, and surprised her then by holding them out again for the baby.

'Let's have a look at our Neil. I haven't seen him, have I, since we were over at the big house?'

Helen had visited her mother as well as Marian several times during the last few weeks, but always during the day while her father was at work. She was a firm believer in getting the baby home to bed early.

'You can make up for it today, Dad. I shan't mind if you take him over.'

'But I was going to look after Neil,' young Linda protested.

'You as well, of course,' said Helen, bending down to hug her niece.

'Are we really going to look after him soon like Mummy says?' Linda whispered.

'I hope so,' Helen whispered back, her entire body stiffening as she waited, wondering if Alex had heard.

If he had, he gave no sign and Mark was demanding attention now, rushing to his Uncle Alex with a clockwork car that Father Christmas had brought. Watching her husband with the lad, Helen recognised in his smile that he was savouring a sudden realisation of how it would feel when it was his own son who was sharing interests with him.

Lord, but I'm lucky, she thought. I might have ended up with a chap who didn't want a family. And, much as she looked forward to returning to her career, she'd grown to love Neil so deeply that she already wondered how ever she had been happy without him.

Just before family dinner Helen fed him, sitting in the bedroom which she once had shared with Marian. Gazing about her while Neil sucked away contentedly, she noticed how faded the walls were now, their distemper dulled from peach to a murky white where the sun had streamed in through the south-facing window. The curtains too had paled in streaks, so that the once-bright gold brocade now seemed tawdry. Marian had paid for the stuff for those curtains out of money saved from her first few wage packets, way back in the days when she was the only one of the sisters earning.

Helen was glad that she and Marian got on so well together these days. They had grown closer in outlook and in their interests over the years. And she could hardly believe how well Alex had taken to her brother-in-law. She'd expected somebody with his background would have found little in common with Denis who, despite the practical side which had made him a good stage manager, now appeared to be rather letting acting go to his head.

The two men were talking animatedly when Helen returned downstairs. She smiled to herself when she heard Alex holding forth.

'It's nationalisation that will turn this country around, isn't it? Give a bit of solidarity to some of the main industries.'

'True,' Denis agreed. 'As soon as we got Labour in control, I knew things would start looking up.'

Helen began wondering how her husband reconciled some of the views he held with his upbringing in a home the size of The Stone House, and waited on by servants. And what about owning a firm like theirs? She'd always known he was a bit of a Bolshie, hadn't she? All that stuff about not approving of the royal

252

family. But they had never discussed politics in all the years they'd been married. She could well believe he might not consider her opinion worth inviting.

Helen said nothing now, content to put Neil to sleep in his carrycot then join her mother and sister in the kitchen.

'Where's Dad gone?' she inquired, filling the bowl and starting on the washing up that had accumulated during the morning.

'He's taken our two for a walk,' Marian replied. 'Just as far as People's Park. Said he wanted to work up an appetite. I'm only glad it'll use up a bit of Linda and Mark's energy.'

'They love Christmas, don't they?' her mother put in. 'They were that excited when they got here.'

'Too excited,' said Marian, but with a smile. 'Still, this is the first Christmas since the war that there's been anything worthwhile in the shops.'

As soon as Marian's children returned with their grandfather they all gathered around the table. Daniel made a little speech, saying how pleased both he and Kathleen were to have all the family there together. 'I might not have appeared all that enthusiastic when either of you two young lasses wanted to get wed,' he admitted. 'But, by Jove, you're both making a good job of marriage.'

Alex found Helen's hand and squeezed and she saw Denis and Marian exchanging a loving glance. This Christmas is far better than ever I expected, she thought, sparing a moment's reflection for Joseph Stone while being thankful for her own folk. And most of all, of course, for Alex and baby Neil.

The discord began just as the meal was ending. Linda and Mark had already asked if they could leave the table, and the grown-ups were lingering over cups of tea.

253

'So how soon do you want me?' Marian asked Helen. 'I can manage all right, even before these two go back to school, if you like.'

Helen felt Alex stiffen beside her. She wished to goodness their Marian had spoken up while they were on their own. As it was, she would have to answer her. And before she'd even raised the subject again with Alex.

Grimly, she cleared her throat. 'We haven't got it all worked out yet, but probably the first week in the new year.'

'What's this?' Alex asked tersely.

'About me going back to work. I did mention it . . .'

'And I said I didn't approve.'

The raised voices disturbed Neil who began wailing. Please don't start, little love, thought Helen. Let me concentrate on this.

'There's no reason for you to come back into the firm, not now Harold Tilsley's joined us,' Alex asserted firmly.

Helen bit her lip. She wouldn't remind him of what she'd said about that, not in front of her family. She didn't want a full-scale quarrel.

Neil's cries had increased by several decibels. Marian, who was nearest to the cot, went to pick him up.

Helen hasn't even the decency to attend to him herself, thought Alex, inflamed by seeing another woman rushing to his son. And this was evidently the way Helen wished it to be. She wanted to surrender responsibility for their child to her sister.

Neil had stopped crying, and was attempting to grasp the beads Marian was wearing. Helen felt torn, a part of her thankful that her sister had quietened him so readily — she'd needed reassurance that he wouldn't suffer by this arrangement — but she was also disturbed. Did he ever respond so immediately when *she* picked him up?

'I'm not trying to neglect Neil. Anything but,' she told them quietly. 'But there are three of us to consider. Marian couldn't be better with him, just look at them now, and she is my only sister. It's not as if I'm trusting a stranger with him.'

Nobody spoke. Helen could feel her husband's antagonism, and the alarm of everyone else. But now this had been brought into the open she meant to make her point. Still quietly, she continued: 'If I have to resign myself to never working again, there'll be a whole area of my life where I'll feel unfulfilled. You all know what the war did to my career. I can't accept that all that hard work studying was just for that short while since 1945, and with so many restrictions preventing us getting to the sort of work we always dreamed of.'

If she had hoped that might get through to Alex, she soon understood that it had done no such thing. He still did not speak and nor did anyone else. It wasn't until her mother began collecting up the dirty dishes and they all moved away from the table that any kind of normal conversation recommenced. Fortunately, Linda and Mark were too young to remain inhibited by the atmosphere, but it was only due to their presence that the tension appeared gradually to ease.

Helen wasn't surprised when Alex suggested early in the evening that they ought to be getting Neil home to his cot. She was no longer even sorry that the gathering which had begun so promisingly was being cut short. Embarrassed as well as hurt by his opposition, she wanted to get him away from here in order to thrash out this problem.

'We'll see you tomorrow, any road, shan't we?' said

Marian, while they were putting on their coats. Earlier in the day, she and Denis had invited everyone to their new home for tea.

'I'm afraid not,' said Alex firmly before Helen could utter a word. 'We have something else arranged.'

In the car, Helen could wait no longer. She'd always been one for sorting out trouble before it could fester.

'You might have waited, instead of making me out to be a neglectful mother in front of everybody. You *know* I love Neil, that I'm potty about him. But that doesn't mean I want to spend my whole life stuck at home looking after him.'

'Evidently not. You make me wonder, Helen, if you even want to spend your life in The Stone House at all. You seem remarkably eager to get out of it as much as ever you can.'

'Since you've brought it up, I've never been all that keen on living there, but I decided after your dad died that so long as you were happy there, I'd give my mind to it.'

'Big of you!'

'Alex — don't let's be like this. All I want is an interest outside the home, the opportunity to continue as an architect. I'm not necessarily even suggesting that I work full time.'

Alex sighed. 'Why can't you be more like your own mother, eh? You saw today how content she is. She's a real homemaker, relishes cooking, caring for home and family . . .'

'And she's a different generation. They weren't brought up to have much in the way of expectations.'

'Why not try it my way, Helen? Give it a year or two, concentrating on Neil, and on making The Stone House into a real home. For too long now the place has been at the hands of a housekeeper, as well you

256

know. Mrs Hartley couldn't be better at that — but she's not the wife, not the person who should stamp her personality on the home.'

'Or we could try it my way, love?' Helen argued. 'Now, while Neil's too little to mind about having his auntie looking after him.'

Chapter 13

Alexander had eventually agreed to her going back to work, but he wasn't a good loser. Helen soon became aware that the next few weeks would be tough. And almost immediately after she had returned to Stone's he indicated very clearly that her insistence on taking her place was making life difficult.

She was working from ten in the morning until four, with an extended lunch hour in order to dash home to feed Neil. Unless she was to waste a lot of time waiting around for buses, this meant using the car. That didn't always fit in with her husband's arrangements, and became a nuisance when he needed to be out visiting sites or conferring with builders.

'I think I'm going to buy myself a little car,' she announced one evening while they were having dinner. 'I shall soon save enough. There's nothing else I need out of the money I earn, is there?'

Alex gave her a look, one she was learning to recognise as the prelude to objections.

'It's not only buying one, is it? There's running costs, insurance . . .'

'Can't they go down as the firm's expenses? Your car does.' And he'd recently invested in a new Rolls-Royce, having sold both his father's treasured Phantom and the little Standard.

'We're not making that much profit,' he told her

grimly. 'Think about it, Helen. There's Harold's salary coming out as well as what we're both taking from the firm.'

'Well, we'll wait a bit then. Now I'm back at work there are more designs being produced. That's bound to bring in more contracts.'

'You'd better resign yourself to a long wait, love. It'll be some time before profits increase substantially.'

Helen noticed during the following few weeks that Alex seemed to be quite obsessed with profitability. She wished he wasn't like that – it made her aware of the differences between them. That she wasn't always on about money; had been brought up in the belief that so long as she'd enough to survive on she could be content. But then, she thought, hadn't Alex always fancied showing off a bit? There'd been the way he always used to enjoy swanning around in his father's posh car. Wasn't the car he'd just bought equally impressive?

There are things about him that I've never really taken to, she reflected, although in many ways they were happy together now. Once she had started working again, she had insisted that they make a pact not to argue about her doing so. They were giving it a try, that was all. If Neil showed the least sign of being unhappy with this method of organising life, she would give it up.

Helen blessed their Marian for being so obliging. The only time she didn't turn up was during the worst of all the deep snow that fell early in 1947. And then, of course, Helen also was prevented from travelling to work. Normally, Marian arrived at The Stone House by nine-thirty every weekday, bringing Mark and Linda when they weren't at school. During lunch they all had a lovely time, chatting while they fed Neil and played with him.

Now that he was growing more interested in what was going on, he was charming Alex every evening with the little ways in which he was progressing. They had developed a routine which seemed to suit the three of them. Each day when Helen took over from Marian, she tidied the nursery and carried Neil with her down to the large kitchen where Mrs Hartley was preparing their meal. By the time Alex came in, she was ready to give Neil his bath, an occasion they savoured together, enjoying his antics before taking him to the night nursery.

This room was the one which Alex had used before him, and he began telling Helen snippets that he recalled from the days when his mother was alive. She smiled tenderly over his memories, aching for the lad who'd scarcely known a mother's caring, and remembering now his grief when Joseph Stone was lost to them.

Helen's deepest regret was that Marian's readiness to look after Neil seemed to have turned Alex against her. He denied that it was so, but Helen sensed that he blamed her sister for making it too easy for her to return to work. Instead of the outings with Marian and Denis and their kiddies which Helen had visualised, she was limited to the short encounters entailed in handing over responsibility for Neil.

As the year progressed and he developed, learning to stand and then to walk, Alex appeared engrossed in his son whenever he was at home, and Helen was no less enraptured by him. He was becoming a winning youngster, with her grey eyes but his father's glorious golden hair. His smile was the echo of his father's and employed as frequently as Alex's had been years ago.

He now smiled less readily, except with the boy. Helen noticed his new gravity, especially around their office. She couldn't understand the cause. Business would increase as soon as the emergency measures introduced that August were eased again and private housing permitted. Despite restrictions, schools were being planned for areas which had received heavy bombing. Stone's had submitted designs for more than one, and had been accepted. And there was the ever-present need for council houses and flats. These might not be the kind of jobs they would have chosen, but they did provide work for architects. When taxed with his gloomy appearance, Alex always hedged, seeming reluctant still to discuss any problems with her.

Anxious, Helen mentioned this one day to Harold Tilsley when Alex was out conferring with council officials.

'Do you want the truth, Helen?' he asked, seriously for him.

'Well, of course. When have I expected folk to mince words?'

'He's never really accepted you coming back to work again.'

'But Neil is fine — he truly is, Harold. He loves being with his Auntie Marian.'

'It's not only that. There's the contention here. Alex still doesn't agree with your ideas on design, does he? And he never will.'

'He doesn't say anything . . .'

'I suppose he knows it will do no good. Your ideas and his will never coincide. And he can't help resenting it when your designs are in favour.'

'But that's only part of the time. And, any road, it's not like him not to say . . .'

'It's not like the old Alex, agreed.'

Helen began observing then, seeing that her husband was indeed keeping to himself so much of what he was feeling. And not only in the office.

Ever since Neil's birth Alex had made love to her

less frequently. At first, she had accepted that her own health and the trauma of losing his father could be contributing to the waning of his passion. With each month, though, Helen began to fear that there might be some other cause, and dreaded learning that he was still hankering after that woman he'd known during the war.

Unable to bring herself to mention this, she was compelled nevertheless to tackle this matter which threatened to spoil their marriage. She chose a Monday evening when they both seemed relaxed after Neil's nightly routine, and neither of them was as tired as they became towards the end of every week.

'Is there something bothering you, love?' she asked while they were having dinner.

'Not especially, why?'

'Things aren't the same between us, are they, Alex? Is it — is it that you feel we ought to wait before risking another baby? If that's it, I think like you — and I could do something about that. There are clinics . . .'

'No,' he said firmly, gazing coldly across the table.

Helen wasn't sure whether he meant she mustn't try to prevent another child, or simply that the cause was different. 'Do you mean that you wouldn't want me doing that, because you'd like more children?'

'I would have liked more, yes. Not immediately, of course, Neil deserves some time as the sole focus of your attention.' He paused, sighing. 'But that's the whole crux of the matter, I'm afraid. It's you, Helen. You're just not the person I thought you were. Agreed, Neil doesn't appear neglected, but nor is he receiving the devotion I'd expected you to show.'

Helen swallowed and laid aside her knife and fork.

'I do love our baby, Alex, I keep telling you — far more deeply than I could have imagined. He has a good life the way things are. Marian couldn't be kinder or more fun for him. He dotes on her.'

'And doesn't that fact tell you anything?'

'That I should be disturbed because it isn't only us that he feels this way about? Once or twice, I admit, I've wished some little thing he's done, or a loving gesture, had been for me instead of my sister. But he knows well enough that we're his parents, Alex. And how much he matters to us.'

Her husband merely shrugged.

'In any case,' Helen continued, 'I don't think it's a bad idea for kiddies to be used to other folk from an early age. There's nothing worse than little 'uns that cling to their mummies. Especially lads.'

When Alex still said nothing, she took a deep breath. 'Any road, I didn't think we were talking about Neil so much as us — what's going wrong between us.'

'And you expect me to divide my general dissatisfaction from what happens in our bedroom, do you? Really, Helen, you can't seriously believe that's possible?'

'Dissatisfaction?' she uttered miserably. Her life seemed to be collapsing about her.

'You began this discussion, remember? I was prepared to wait, hope things might get better. Oh, Helen — why aren't you more like your mother?'

'You've said that before, and I wish you wouldn't. I couldn't live her sort of a life,' she told him earnestly, tears welling in her throat.

'Lots of women do, quite contentedly.'

'Used to, you mean. These days, they're beginning to want to be valued for themselves, for the things they're interested in . . .'

'You imply that your mother, and others like her, are boring.'

'No, I don't. Only that their lives would bore me.'

'Okay, leave it for now, eh?' Alex was sensing that if this conversation continued he'd not guarantee that he wouldn't say something irrevocable. And he didn't want that, he really didn't. It was early days still for their marriage, it should be given a chance.

'But how can I leave it? You're not happy, I can tell. And I . . .'

'You ought to be happy, Helen. Right from the start, you've done only what you wished. First insisting on that Land Army job . . .'

'But you weren't even here then,' she protested.

'Then wanting to delay starting a family. And now that Neil's here, you're just as determined to go your way and set him aside so you can satisfy your ambitions.'

If he was hoping she would give in and come out of the firm, it was more than Helen was willing to do. She couldn't sacrifice all the hopes and plans she had carried burning inside her for so many years. But how could she stick to her determination *and* make her marriage more contented again?

'Happen you're right, love – we ought to leave this for now. Maybe with a bit of time we'll sort something out. We do still love each other.'

Alex said nothing in reply, and from that day Helen began to believe that he no longer did love her.

For months there was no obvious alteration in their relationship. They still worked alongside each other and, together with Harold Tilsley, were improving the business as much as possible given continuing shortages and restrictions. They still relished the hours they spent with Neil. They still slept in the same bed, though that made no difference to the absence of love-making between them.

Helen began suspecting that Alex might have met someone else. His no longer needing sex was so totally unlike him. Certainly, for ages now, he hadn't said he loved her. And did she love him? Love, yes, she realised, though she was less sure that she was *in* love with him. She was beginning to wonder if she'd ever been in love with Alex.

Memories of that all-too-brief encounter with Christopher returned, and others of her friendship with Vittore Fabri. With each man she had known a soaring of the heart which she'd never experienced with her husband. But then, their relationship was very different, had developed so gradually over the years. It had none of the excitement of love at first sight, nor the rapture of the sudden discovery of the one person who might be the other half of one's self.

The quarrel developed one weekend during the following summer, after a day when they had taken Neil to the seaside at Scarborough. Helen was feeling happier than for some time when they had tucked up the tired youngster in his bed, and were going downstairs for dinner.

'By the way,' said Alex, holding the door for her as she preceded him into the dining room, 'I shan't be at home this coming week. I've got wind of a new development just outside London, and I'm determined to find out all I can.'

'Oh. You never said anything to me.'

'Didn't think you'd want to be involved. The developers have specified that they want something very up-to-date.'

'I see. I wish you'd told me, though. About not being at home. And there'll be things you'll want with you. I'll have to pack . . .'

He shook his head. 'No need – it's all taken care

of. Mrs Hartley knows I'll be away. And she has my packing in hand.'

'You've told her without mentioning it to me?' Helen felt hurt, and suddenly threatened.

'She is our housekeeper, after all. The reason we still employ her is because you don't care at all for the domestic scene.'

'Don't say that, it isn't true,' Helen interrupted.

'I wish to God it weren't! I'd give anything for a wife who wanted to concentrate on making this a home.'

'I have tried,' she insisted. 'But this is such a massive place, it'd take more than me to make it homely.'

'If you don't like it here, you could always move.'

Helen was shattered, could hardly believe what she had heard. For what felt like minutes neither of them spoke. Eventually, trying to level her voice, she said, 'Is it that you've met somebody else?'

'No. And while we stay together I'm not likely to, am I?'

'But that's what you want, that's what you're hoping for?'

'If it weren't for Neil, I'd have had the guts to say long since that you and I have made a terrible mistake.'

Despite everything that had been said, Helen was sorry to see Alex drive off next morning. Hugging Neil to her, she watched the Rolls until it went out of sight round a bend in the lane. Going back indoors, she continued to hug the boy, until his wriggling made her aware that the poor little fellow was being squeezed until it hurt.

'Come into the bedroom and watch me getting ready,' she suggested. Normally, he enjoyed playing with her jars of cream and powder. She had never used a lot of make-up, but it made her feel more confident when she was meeting clients. Today, she was desperate to disguise the effects of her sleepless night.

Neil seemed uninterested in her dressing-table, choosing instead to kneel on the windowseat, looking out for his Auntie Marian. Helen grew more depressed as she read the eagerness in his grey eyes and in his restlessly bobbing golden head. She hadn't needed this reminder that there was some truth in Alexander's assumptions about their son's allegiance to Marian.

By the time her sister arrived Helen wasn't far from tears, and they were too close for her distress to remain undetected.

'What's up, old love?' Marian asked, putting an arm round her.

'It's Alex. We're having trouble. And now he's gone off.'

'You don't mean he's left?'

'He wouldn't, would he? This place is his — the family home. No, actually it's a business trip. But he said some awful things last night. As good as told me I could clear out.'

'We all say stuff we don't mean, 'specially when we're het up. Take no notice, love, he wouldn't mean them.'

'Not so sure about that.'

'Haven't you been getting on at all lately?'

'Not really, not for ages. He's sort of — distant. And we've hardly made love ever since Neil was born.'

'Happen too much occurred all at once — losing his dad and becoming a father himself. Then there's the responsibility of the business.'

'Which he doesn't want me to share.'

'That as well, eh? Poor you. Still, I'm sure you'll sort it out between you. For Neil's sake, if nothing else. He adores that boy, doesn't he?'

Helen wasn't reassured. Quite the opposite. Because thinking of her husband's devotion to his son produced an appalling supposition. If Alex really meant that she must go, he might insist that he was given custody of young Neil.

The longcase clock in the hall was striking nine-forty-five. She would have to leave for work. And now she realised she could hardly bear to be separated from her son for even a few hours. Hugging him before she handed over to Marian, Helen felt as if she would never let go. A sigh rising all the way from her heart, she left the house and began running down the hill to catch a bus.

Waiting at the stop, she reflected that she'd never got the car that she had wanted, and now she'd not mention that again. In fact, during this week she must weigh very seriously whether all this contention was worth it. Wouldn't she do far better to accede to her husband's wishes? Surrender her career in the hope that the sacrifice might restore their marriage and their home life?

Harold could see how perturbed Helen was as soon as she walked into the office.

'What's wrong?' he inquired. 'Letting it get you down because your Alex has gone off for the week?'

'Something like that,' she responded quickly, her hurt increasing with the knowledge that Harold had been aware of his plans. Everybody but her.

He dispatched Wendy, their secretary, to make a pot of tea. 'Want to talk?' he asked. 'I know Alex of old, don't I? Look what a boor he was when we all went to Europe that time.'

Helen swallowed back a sigh. 'It's okay, thanks. I'll be fine once I get down to some work.'

'It's no bad thing to have one of us here keen on

more classical styles of architecture, you know. It's where proportion is based. And two like me and Alexander going for contemporary stuff is enough.'

Helen forced a smile to her lips. 'This time it's nothing to do with the way we always clash on that.'

The cup of tea helped to steady her for concentrating on plans and elevations. By eleven o'clock she was beginning to adopt the calm resignation that would get her through this week. And if at the end of it she would face a heart to heart with her husband, that wasn't for several days. Maybe the period without him would give her a chance to see a way out of this situation.

Hearing distantly a woman's voice and a child's in the outer office with Wendy, Helen was puzzled. Neither she nor Harold had appointments that day. They both intended catching up on desk work.

'There's somebody to see you, Mrs Stone,' Wendy announced awkwardly. 'Your sister.'

'Neil,' Helen gasped in horror. 'Something's happened to Neil?'

'No, love,' said Marian, entering. 'He's here, and he's all right. Just look at him.'

Seeing the distraught expression in her sister's eyes, Helen grasped her arm. 'Marian, what is it? Is summat up with one of your two?'

Grimly, Marian shook her head, began propelling Helen towards a chair. 'You'd better sit down, love. Your secretary's going to keep an eye on Neil for a minute.'

'Is it Mum, Dad?'

Again, her sister shook her head, swallowed. 'I don't know how to begin to tell you this, love. I'm afraid there's been an accident, on the way down south. It's your Alex . . .'

'Oh, God! How — how bad is he? Where've they taken him?'

'You'll have to be very brave, Helen,' Marian gulped, her blue eyes full of tears.

'You mean — you can't mean he's dead?'

'Instantaneous, the police say it was. He wouldn't know anything.'

Except that our marriage was a mess, a mistake, thought Helen dourly. Was that the reason he'd been driving less carefully?

'Some chap on the wrong side of the road,' said Marian. 'There wasn't a thing Alex could have done to avoid him.'

Helen called Neil into the office and pulled him against her, holding him to her heart and covering his face and head with kisses.

'I'll have to tell Harold,' she said presently. 'I can't stop here. There'll be things want seeing to. The police . . .'

'They went back to the station, but they'll come out to the house again.'

'Where did it happen?'

'Eh, I can't remember.'

'They'll tell me.' And will tell me more perhaps than I want to know. Because of when this happened, how bad things were between us. And now there'll never be a chance to put anything right.

In the taxi, driving up to The Stone House, Helen began weeping bitterly, as though the heart which had already felt brittle was finally disintegrating.

'I think you'd better go and lie down,' Marian suggested after settling with the taxi driver and helping her sister into the hall. Neil was running up and down, enjoying the sounds echoing from the floor yet darting puzzled looks towards his mother.

'If I lie down I might never get up again. No, we'll

271

give Neil his dinner, it must be about time. Then I'd better start sorting out what has to be done.'

'The police will tell you that, I daresay, help you find an undertaker.'

'There's the one we had for his father — there'll be details somewhere in Alexander's desk . . . Does Mrs Hartley know? Where is she?'

'Not yet, she's out shopping. I'd told her first thing that I could cope this dinnertime if she wanted to be out a bit longer.'

By the time the police returned Helen was nearly composed. She had made her mind up. All she had to do was get through this next few days without permitting herself to think. There'd be a lot to arrange, people to inform . . . Alexander had so many business contacts. Harold had said something about helping, being willing to do whatever he could. She wasn't going to let him. If she did everything herself, that might keep her mind busy. And it might begin to offset the harm she'd done to her marriage.

The Coroner's Officer came to the house. He had known Joseph Stone and couldn't do enough for his son's family now. The sergeant who was with him had more information about the accident, which had happened near Bakewell in Derbyshire. Helen remembered Marian driving through there on that visit to Stratford upon Avon all those years ago.

'The other driver was badly injured. As soon as he recovers consciousness, he'll be charged,' the sergeant added.

That seemed quite irrelevant to Helen. All she could wonder was what charge a Higher Authority would level at her — like sending her own husband to his death.

* * *

'You're pulling this on top of you, making yourself feel guilty, aren't you?'

That was Marian late that afternoon. She had been home, but only long enough to collect Linda and Mark from school and take them to her parents. During the evening, as soon as she'd made tea and cleared away, Kathleen was coming to stay at The Stone House.

'How dreadful!' she'd exclaimed on being told. 'I must get to our Helen as quick as I can. I know you're doing what you can, Marian love, but she is my daughter. I can't not go to her.'

In some ways, Helen was dreading her mother's arrival, was afraid she would sense the trouble there had been here. Kathleen Clegg had taken to Alexander from the start. She might have had reservations about their differences of class, but that had never stopped her trying to mother him. Marian's, though, was a soothing presence to have around. All day she had simply been here, neither fussing nor uttering all the trite things that people say, and which don't do a scrap of good when you're too upset to heed anything.

Marian had taken Neil out of the room when Helen needed quiet for telephoning or just for thinking. And she had brought him back in when even a few minutes' separation from the boy seemed intolerable. She had known better than to persist when Helen couldn't eat anything, and had had the sense to produce a stiff drink as an antidote for weeping.

'You'll have to get it out of your system,' she had said sympathetically. 'But you don't have to cry it all out in one day.'

Tomorrow the death would have to be registered and her father had insisted that he would take time off work to accompany her. He had telephoned Helen as soon as he arrived home and was told.

'We shall do everything we can from now on to help

273

you and the little lad, Helen, love. So just think on — there's to be none of the independence that you've allus shown.'

Although grateful, and relieved that she wouldn't have to set off on her own to see to things, Helen remained determined that she would be the one who did all the actual arranging that was necessary. Having her father there must not allow her to weaken and evade things.

Just seeing her mother brought another rush of tears, but familiar arms coming round her as well, and they began to help ease the pain.

'He'll be with his father at least,' said Kathleen, her own eyes awash. 'And with his mother an' all. You must try to think that, love. He won't be miserable.'

As he was with me, thought Helen, and wept more bitterly. Somehow, though, they got through the rest of the evening, and the night. Mrs Hartley had aired the room next to the master bedroom for Kathleen Clegg, before retiring early to her own bed, devastated by the accident killing the young man whom she had served so devotedly since he was a child.

The three women were dry-eyed the following morning, and although naturally sombre-faced seemed prepared to throw themselves into their tasks as an antidote to distress.

'Since I'm here I might as well look after Neil today,' Kathleen offered. 'I told our Marian that was what I'd do.' She had arranged to stay at The Stone House for two nights at least, and didn't intend sitting around idle.

Mrs Hartley was suggesting to Helen that some of the rooms should have a thorough turning out. 'There'll be folk coming for the funeral, won't there, Mrs Stone?'

Helen agreed. Everything felt so unreal that she

found it difficult to care what anybody else did. All she wanted was this week over and the funeral behind her. She had hardly slept last night for wondering how many people would detect that she was grieving for a marriage that had gone wrong as much as for the death of her husband?

Picking up her father at her old home, and watching him settle awkwardly into the taxi that she had hired, Helen recognised afresh how much effort he was putting into supporting her. He was even less accustomed to meeting the kind of officials they would see today than he was to riding round like this.

'Bless you, Dad,' she said, managing a smile. 'I'd have hated doing this on my own.'

She watched him swallow before he nodded. 'Where is it to be first then, Helen love?'

'The Registrar's, then the undertaker's.' The police had brought her the death certificate, and advised her on procedures.

A couple who were there to marry arrived at the register office just as Helen, with Daniel holding her elbow, approached the steps. The evident happiness of the pair seemed discordant, contrasting as it did with her own distress. She straightened her shoulders, though, hardening her resolve to get this matter attended to.

The registrar was younger than she had expected, and appeared nervous as he questioned her and completed documents. She caught herself wondering how such a fresh-faced man coped with confronting so much gloom, and hoped he got his share of wedding ceremonies to perform.

'You handled that right well,' her father said, grasping her arm as they emerged. 'I'm proud of you.'

Helen gave him a smile and hoped he wouldn't say

too much along those lines or she'd go all weepy on him.

The undertaker's was even worse than she'd been anticipating. When it came to choosing the coffin she realised how final and how real this was, and could contain her tears no longer. By the time they went out into the open air, her father was gazing at her in concern.

'Eh, lass – this is a bad do! I wish there was summat I could say that would make even a bit of difference.'

Helen nodded. 'I know, Dad, I know. But just being here for me is all I need.'

When all arrangements were made, however, and she left her father in Halifax and returned to The Stone House, Helen experienced no feeling of relief over what had been accomplished. I just wish there was something I could do, anything, she thought – anything that could change the state of mind in which Alexander had set out yesterday morning.

That night seemed even more intolerable than the one that had gone before. Helen grew so disturbed that she could no longer remain in the room that she and her husband had shared.

Neil was sleeping soundly in the nursery just across the landing, a small hand tucked beneath the cheek on which long pale lashes rested, his glorious hair already thick and golden, painfully like Alexander's. Quietly, she stood gazing down at his tiny bed, until she eventually calmed enough to find herself a chair. She sat there through the rest of the night, too full of emotion to even frame words in her head but silently promising him she would devote her life to compensating him for the loss of his father.

The funeral reminded Helen of Joseph's, only this

time the loss seemed a hundred times harder to bear. Even though they had appeared to get on so badly together during those last months of his life, Alexander had grown to be a part of her over such a long period. There had been the years before the war while their friendship was changing, developing; and then the war itself which had kept them apart such a lot; and afterwards the ups and downs between them. What was it all for? she wondered bleakly, and could only be thankful that their marriage had produced Neil.

They had advised her not to see Alexander. The Coroner's Officer had explained, very carefully, that many of his injuries had been to his face and head. She would not have recognised him, she was told, and the fact that identification had been made through his personal documents and dental records bore that out. All the same, this was one more thing that troubled her. If only she had seen his body she might have been able to accept that he was not going to walk into the office or through the front door of The Stone House again.

Marian and Denis were here this time and, of course, Helen's parents. Denis was being particularly kind, assuring her that neither he nor Marian had been put off by Alexander's cooling towards them.

'We know he only resented anybody making it easier for you to return to work. There's lots of men like that. It just looks as if, despite some of his modern ideas, he was a bit old-fashioned.'

If Helen hadn't witnessed the huge gathering for Joseph Stone's funeral, she would have been staggered by the numbers paying their final respects to his son. As it was, she could only feel heartened that so many people wished to attend, and be glad that they compelled her to keep going. In the church and at the graveside, she willed herself not to break down in front of such a crowd. Afterwards in the house she was thankful that she must give her attention to so many individuals.

At twilight, alone at last, Helen was standing near the windows of the large reception room where she'd first been welcomed to this house. Sounds carried on the still, summer evening. Distantly in the kitchen Mrs Hartley could be heard, giving the place a final tidying after the departure of the caterers. Across the valley the far hillside, darkening now, looked forbidding. Way below her on the road, cars and buses passed along the main thoroughfare between Halifax and Hebden Bridge, and made her ache to escape with them. Her parents had left an hour ago, on her insistence. Her pain wouldn't heal for many a month, if ever. Their remaining another night would only delay the need to confront the prospect of her life as it would be.

More than once today, Helen had been asked if she would keep on The Stone House. How she had yearned to explain that no, she had decided to move to somewhere smaller and more suitable. Instead, she had inclined her head, telling them that it was up to her now to ensure that this place stayed in the family.

Partly, the decision was for Neil. He deserved the home that would have been his had his father lived the expected life-span; and if her own unease here never altered, that was something she must endure. A sort of pledge towards her son's future. But it wasn't for Neil alone that she was so resolved. In this room especially, she felt them about her, Joseph and Alexander – not ghosts, but presences. When she could bear to let memories resurrect, the two would seem clearer still, their voices, faces, that glorious Stone family hair. She'd not abandon them to strangers.

How many years was it now since she had first entered this room – eleven, twelve? How many since Joseph asked her to work with him? And here it had been, not long ago, that she and Alexander had ended their initial estrangement. She wished to God that he could have lived to end their second.

Wearily, she turned from the room, crossed the echoing hall to thank Mrs Hartley and say goodnight. The day had passed as smoothly as anyone could expect.

When she eventually went upstairs Helen paused on the landing, glancing in both directions at the rows of closed doors. What a lot of empty rooms, and only herself, Neil and the housekeeper.

Neil's door was slightly ajar, the way she always left it at night so that the lightest cry would alert her. He wasn't crying but he was awake, his grey eyes large in the pallor of his face.

'Where's Daddy?' he asked. 'Why did you send him away?'

'Oh, Neil, love, I didn't. Daddy had to go away on business.'

'But he isn't coming back.' It wasn't a question. 'You were cross with him. I heard you shouting at him.'

Their son was not quite two years old, and they had been so proud of his early command of language.

Chapter 14

Returning to the office two days after the funeral was even harder than Helen had feared. Neil had clung to her, tearful and refusing to believe that she was coming home at lunchtime, until she had been obliged to hand him over forcibly to Marian.

'I'm sorry, Neil love, I truly am. But you loved being with Auntie Marian before, you'll have to get used to being with her again. I'm only going to work.'

He hadn't been appeased. And she herself was anything but calmed by opening up their offices. Alexander was all around her here as well, just as much as in the house. Steeling herself to endure, she entered the office he'd inherited from his father, now to be hers.

Once she'd rather envied him that partner's desk with its tooled leather top. Longer ago, in that other lifetime, he had held her close on this spot, had taken her with him on to that splendid chair. In those days they had wanted each other so much, their yearning so strong that it had coloured the whole of life, made it exciting.

It's no good, thought Helen firmly, I came here to work, and work I must. In no other way shall I survive, either to make Stone's succeed as it has in the past or to make any sense of my own life.

She would begin on tackling Alexander's desk.

Harold Tilsley had handed her the keys after the funeral. Evidently, Alexander had left them with him before setting out for London. She was too drained now by experiencing so many emotions to care that she hadn't been the recipient.

The windows faced west, making this office cool so early in the day. Even on a June morning the leather of the chair chilled her, making her shudder. Stilling a sigh, Helen fitted the key into the upper of the three drawers.

Wendy came into the outer office then appeared in the adjoining doorway, her attractive face revealing uncertainty as to whether a smile was appropriate. 'Good morning, Mrs Stone. It's − good to have you back.'

Helen smiled at her. 'Good morning, Wendy. Thank you. And thank you very much for being there at the funeral.' Bringing the word into the open ought to ease things and might help her to overcome her own feeling of unreality.

Wendy offered to make a cup of tea which Helen declined, smiling again.

'Not yet, thanks. Better get on.' And she mustn't shorten the day by too many interludes.

The papers in the first drawer appeared quite orderly. Helen began feeling thankful that her husband had possessed a flair for business, and had understood that efficiency meant economy. He had one specification partially completed on which she would need to consult Harold. The other documents were self-explanatory: items of correspondence clipped together and awaiting replies from council officers, builders or contractors. Each set bore the reference number of the relevant plans which would be on file.

The contents of the second drawer would require

more than this quick glance. Folders contained early sketches and notes of schemes proposed by clients. One out of the three related to a project on which she and Alexander had conferred. On the others she would again have to check with Harold.

Helen was unlocking the lowest drawer when he strode in. She heard his brief greeting tossed in Wendy's direction as he made his way through and then he was in the office with her, depositing on the stand the trilby hat he wore even in summer.

'Helen!'

He hadn't expected her, that was evident, as was his shock to find her in Alexander's place. He permitted himself no comment, but Helen read displeasure ill concealed in his eyes.

'How are you?' he inquired.

He might have been a client who had been told of her bereavement but wasn't sufficiently close to Stone's to attend the funeral. Nothing in his demeanour suggested he was an old friend of theirs, a fellow student, and now involved in their work.

'I'm all right, Harold, coping. There's plenty here to keep me occupied. I shall need to discuss some of these with you. Shall we say around ten?'

He had shared the third office with her, though half the time since her return to work he'd been closeted with her husband. She began to understand why he was feeling resentment, and compelled herself not to watch while he retrieved his hat and headed for the door. It was closed behind him but didn't seal off the sound of his footsteps as he went through and into the other office.

So that was it. Amid all the shock, grief and disorientation, it literally hadn't occurred to her that Harold might expect to become the senior partner. But he wasn't a Stone. *She* was, and equally well qualified.

Harold must not be allowed to forget that.

The rest of the morning was no worse, so long as she didn't let herself be swayed by this sudden awareness of Harold's expectations. He came in and sat at her side behind the desk, updating her on matters which Alexander had had in hand. Their conference over for the present, Helen thanked him warmly.

'I'll have to rely on you a lot.'

'Okay, then.' He rose swiftly and stalked out of her office. There had been no smile with the response. She would have to accept that Harold's smiles would now be rationed.

It was a relief to get out of the office and head for home at lunchtime. The insurers had supplied a vehicle on loan, replacing the one written-off in the crash. Helen was thankful this eased getting around, and more thankful still that since she'd requested a more modest car, it provided no gruelling memories.

Neil was much happier and appeared better adjusted. He came running from the doorway of his playroom, yelling for his aunt to follow.

'Mummy's here. Let's show her what we've been doing.'

They went out into the garden to the rear where the old man who came twice weekly grew vegetables to satisfy Mrs Hartley's demands for fresh produce.

'I've got my own little garden,' Neil declared, and demonstrated the couple of square yards marked out with string. 'I planted seeds.'

'That's lovely, darling. We'll enjoy watching them grow.'

'Auntie Marian showed me how.'

Helen turned to her sister. 'I hope she also chose something that'll spring up very quickly.'

Marian grinned. 'So do I! They were just a few ends of packets that your gardener had left over.'

Helen smoothed Neil's golden curls affectionately. 'We'll have to see this young man remembers to water them. I'll get him his own watering-can on Saturday.'

'*Now*, Mummy — today. I couldn't lift the other can.'

It was just like him to have tried. 'Saturday, I'm afraid. Unless Auntie Marian will take you to buy one.'

The interlude at home helped in two ways, reassuring her that Neil had settled again to being cared for by Marian, and giving her a break from the tension with Harold Tilsley. Helen was exhausted, nevertheless, by the end of the day, although she couldn't regret feeling so tired that eating her solitary meal became an effort. She would have an early night, and pray that being so weary might produce the first good sleep since losing Alexander.

During the ensuing few days Helen went out several times, visiting building sites or those where groundwork was in progress, consulting with builders and with clients. Away from the office, she felt more normal. Being compelled to concentrate was a boon and resulted in something resembling her old enthusiasm for her work. Her only regret was her awareness that she was seeking ways to stay out of the office.

It's just for a while, she told herself inwardly. Just until Harold has been given long enough to adjust to the new situation. And that shouldn't be too far into the future. He'd always seemed easy-going and adaptable. But would he be with her?

Neil's birthday was the next real hurdle, but Helen was up to planning carefully now, had schooled herself to shelve problems and anxieties in order to put him first. She had taken both parents as well as Marian and Denis into her confidence. Using two cars, they were organising a seaside picnic. St Anne's was their destination, chosen by Helen purely because it was the only resort within easy reach which they hadn't visited with Alexander.

The day began promisingly, with lots of laughter as Linda and Mark spilled out of the car where they had been crammed into the rear seats with their grandparents.

'These two lumps of trouble insist they want to travel with you and Neil,' said Denis, raising his eyes to the sky. 'Do you think you could bear it?'

'Sure, that's fine,' Helen replied swiftly. With three children in the back, she'd be permitted no time for brooding. Turning to her niece and nephew, she smiled. 'I need you both to look after Neil, you know. You must sit him between you.'

She was glad the car was only a two-door, and once in the rear they would effectively be imprisoned.

'Of course, Auntie Helen,' the pair chorused, for the present in accord.

'And try to restrain his jack-in-the-box tendencies, will you? I'm relying on you to cope.'

All the way along the road out through Hebden Bridge and Todmorden the children chatted behind her, leaving Helen free to concentrate on driving and keeping Denis's car in sight in her rear-view mirror. They skirted Burnley and stopped briefly in Padiham. When Marian checked that her two were behaving, Helen was able to reassure her.

'I've got them playing I-spy. Of course, Neil's hopeless, not knowing his alphabet, but he will keep trying to play. Linda and Mark think his efforts are hilarious.'

'So long as they're no worse than that,' said Denis. 'And if you stay in the lead you can always pull in to transfer them if they get too much for you.'

The children continued behaving remarkably well. It wasn't Linda's fault that she was so pedantic. The trouble began when Neil tired of playing games which he couldn't comprehend and resented losing the attention of the other two.

'My daddy's gone away,' he announced, conscious by now of the way in which this normally won some kind of warm assurance.

Swallowing, Helen listened for a reaction, not wishing to intervene if the youngsters could satisfy him.

'No,' said Linda carefully. 'That's not quite true.'

'He'll be coming home soon,' Neil continued, and Helen heard in his young voice the tiny tremor that invited confirmation. Lord, she thought, how many times have I had to contradict that particular statement already, and it doesn't penetrate? If only he were old enough to understand explanations about death. There is no way until then that he will even begin to accept what has happened.

'Neil love,' she began.

Linda spoke at the same moment, and had none of Helen's reservations about the blunt revelation of a fact. 'He won't, you know. Your daddy's dead, Neil. You're not stupid, you must know that.'

'What's dead?' he queried, awed.

'Not now, Linda,' Helen inserted hastily.

Mark, however, had concluded that such cautioning didn't apply to him.

'It's like our guinea pig was. It went all stiff and cold. Smelly, as well. We buried him under the tree.'

'And Sweetie the budgie,' Linda added. 'That was the year before the guinea pig.'

'My daddy's not smelly.'

'He will be now,' said Linda solemnly. 'Dead things are like that. That's why you put them in a box.'

287

Helen drew up at the side of the road, and turned in her seat.

'That's enough for now, Linda, Mark. Neil's too little to know all this. It's something I have to explain when he's more grown-up like you two.'

Denis had pulled in behind them, and Marian came round to the window beside Helen. 'Trouble?'

'They're not being naughty – don't whatever you do reprimand them. They just can't fathom that Neil's too young to know where Alexander is.'

'Right, you two – out. Into our car, sharp!'

'Can you get Mum or Dad to sit with Neil? He's a bit upset.'

'Sure, Helen love.'

The rest of the journey was all right, and the bracing wind at St Anne's seemed to drive away some of Helen's disturbance. Everyone gathered for a boisterous picnic, and it all seemed so homely and natural for them to be together that she felt quite guilty about not really missing Alexander.

During the homeward journey Neil slept, a smile on his face as he clutched a toy rabbit, one of the presents he'd been given.

That night, though, putting him to bed, Helen was appalled by another question.

'Did Daddy die because you didn't want him any more? If you're cross with me, will I die and be shut in a box?'

She hugged him close, weeping and cursing herself for having no real answer. What use was it to the child that she could only gasp out: 'No, my love, of course that wasn't the reason. And you won't die until you're very, very old. No matter how many times you're naughty.'

The declaration might have been a prediction. From that day he did seem to grow increasingly difficult.

Initially, however, the problems with him seemed to be overshadowed by the troubles at Stone's. One morning three months after Alexander had been killed, Helen found Harold Tilsley hovering in the outer office when she arrived. He was looking uncomfortable. She soon learned the reason when he asked for a private word.

'It's about my future here,' he began, even before they were seated. 'When I joined the firm Alex indicated that there was a good chance I would become a partner.'

'And?' Helen prompted when he paused.

'Well, unless that's still on offer . . .'

Nay, give me a chance, she thought. 'It may be, in time. As you should appreciate, I haven't yet sorted everything out after my husband's death.' The way she said 'my husband' sounded as though she was speaking to a stranger. And maybe that wasn't far out – Harold had been behaving as though that was what they were, and hurting her into the bargain.

'But you're not prepared, at this stage, to offer a partnership?'

'I'm afraid not, not just yet. Now that we're less hedged in with building restrictions business should pick up. Perhaps soon . . .'

'Forget it,' Harold interrupted. 'I've had a better offer, from another firm. I trust you'll agree to my leaving at the month end?'

There would have been no point in arguing had Helen wished to. As things were, she would only regret the loss of another pair of hands. She would look out for somebody younger, maybe a person returning to complete their architectural studies after war service. Meanwhile, for a time she would cope on her own. Wendy was a damned good secretary who hadn't been used to the full. And, if necessary, she herself could do some of the work at home. With Mrs Hartley in charge of organising the household, and Neil's bedtime so early in the evening, time hung very heavily in that great near-empty house. It wasn't as if she had any social life.

Even before Harold Tilsley left the firm, Helen began taking work home with her and found she rather enjoyed her evenings. As much as she enjoyed anything, these days. Having put Neil to bed, she was glad to have something to study while she ate in the dining room which felt so enormous and, because of the panelling, on dark days quite gloomy. Mrs Hartley had shaken her head at her in motherly fashion.

'Eh, dear, is that what you're forced to do now, Mrs Stone?'

Helen had smiled. 'Don't let it worry you, Mrs Hartley. I'm better when I'm busy.' And, she added silently, since you insist that I shouldn't just have a tray in front of the fire, this is one way of accepting circumstances.

There had been times since Alexander's death when Helen had felt like closing The Stone House and putting it on the market. Strangely, it was memories of Joseph Stone rather than his son which always prevented her. She was beginning to realise now that she would do her utmost to keep the house going. Although she knew already that it wouldn't necessarily prove easy.

One of the early shocks in sorting out Alexander's affairs had been learning that the business was doing little more than ticking over. And if she now understood that her husband's concern about its profitability had had a cause, this was outweighed by annoyance that he'd kept her in the dark.

I was his wife after all, she asserted frequently to

herself, he should have confided in me. For months Helen regulated the amount of thinking back she allowed herself; there was so much pain in gradually being compelled to recognise that in the office as well as in the home theirs had been anything but a true partnership.

She missed Alexander deeply, nevertheless, longing for the optimism which had graced their early friendship, most of all yearning for somebody to share her responsibilities.

Neil was missing him even more: there had been no reservations about his fondness for his father, just as there had been none in Alexander's behaviour towards his son. And since Helen had been the one always to correct or chastise, the boy's memories of his daddy were of an indulgent parent.

Even though Helen adhered strictly to keeping weekends free for him, Neil seemed to sense her preoccupation with Stone's and, not unnaturally, resented any attention it took away from him. Battles began when he learned that his father's former study had been taken over now for accommodating work which his mother brought home.

On the first occasion that she emerged from there for breakfast when Neil came downstairs, his little face glowered.

'That's Daddy's study,' he declared, accusingly.

'It was, I know,' she said gently. 'But I have to use it now.'

''Cos Daddy's dead.'

It was the first time since his birthday that Neil had referred to the fact. Helen had suspected she was being a coward in not explaining his father's death, but he was such a little boy still. And she had no one to advise her on *how* to explain and how soon he would be able to understand. 'There's time enough,' both her parents had said when she had confided her worry to them.

Gravely, she nodded, went down on one knee and drew Neil towards her. 'That's right, love. I'm afraid Daddy was hurt very badly and he couldn't be made better to come home to us.'

'Where did he go then?' he asked in a tiny voice that made him seem even younger than his two years.

'We think of the place as heaven. It's where good people go when they die, and we try to believe it's a happy place.'

Neil nodded seriously. He also appeared to understand when she explained that she was busier now because of doing his father's work.

How incomplete that assumption had been Helen learned on the following Friday. Tired out, she dumped all her papers in the study instead of taking some through to the dining room. As usual, she played with Neil for a while then got him ready for bed. He seemed fractious, though, refusing her offer of the customary bedtime story.

'Daddy knew better stories than you. He was more fun.'

That Helen could believe. There was no real fun in her life these days, not even any relaxation. The only time off that she could justify was time with Neil. And now it seemed what she did for him could never be good enough.

'Go to sleep then,' she said firmly. 'It's Saturday tomorrow, we'll go somewhere nice.'

'I'm not sleepy, not even a tiny bit.'

'Then you'll just have to do as you're told and lie there quietly.'

Because you're too busy to be with me, thought Neil, picturing her going downstairs to the room which had been special. His father's.

He waited, lying curled in bed. After a while, though, bored and wide awake, he decided to find his mother. Not having any story had been worse than not having his father's. And if he could see the work she was doing in that room downstairs and have Mummy explain it, he might feel nearer to Daddy again.

The door of the study was closed, but Neil had grown tall enough to reach the handle, and strong enough to turn it. When he entered the room he was smiling, ready to win his mother round and coax her to leave her work and amuse him. But she wasn't there.

Neil walked towards the desk, scrambled up on to the big chair, and began investigating.

The pile of documents was where Helen had left it, with two sets of plans uppermost. Seeing them, Neil frowned, puzzled. This wasn't work, this was drawing, like he did with Auntie Marian. And it was all in pencil. Mummy hadn't even done it properly, colouring between the lines like he did.

Neil glanced about on the top of the desk for crayons, and found only pens – they looked like the new Biro Daddy had given him. One was red, the other blue. If he coloured this for Mummy she wouldn't have to be so busy all the time.

Helen found him there when, her solitary meal over, she began crossing the hall and noticed the open study door.

'Neil, how could you!' she exclaimed, seeing all the scribbles covering the recently completed plans even before she glimpsed the smile dying on his face.

'I was doing colouring,' he said miserably. 'Helping . . .'

She swallowed down her anger, inwardly warning herself not to vent her distress on Neil. 'All right,' she said, more calmly. 'All right. But in future you're not to come in here when nobody's about. And you must never touch these papers.'

After she had returned Neil to his room, Helen came back to the study. Dejectedly, she sank on to the chair, gazed down at the ruined plans. Not satisfied with 'colouring' the top one, he had begun on the second. Both would have to be re-drawn and, tired or not, she must begin on that tonight.

It couldn't have been simply the copying of those two plans which threw her so far behind, but somehow after that evening Helen seemed to be coping less well. Often exhausted from working far into the night at home, she rarely felt well equipped for the day when she arrived in the office.

With no one else qualified to assist with routine, she was often obliged to rush meetings with prospective clients and with builders. She became aware that while the increasing availability of materials was making more business within the trade, less was coming to Stone's.

The day that her accountant issued the warning against further spending, Helen rushed home and ran to her room in tears. For weeks now she had been taking out only enough to cover food, Mrs Hartley's wages and the weekly sum which she paid Marian. She couldn't manage without someone to look after Neil. It seemed as though she would have to lose Mrs Hartley.

Helen couldn't sleep that night. There was no point in wondering where she had gone wrong. That was plain enough. In letting Harold Tilsley go she'd removed the back-up needed in the office, to say nothing of a second person's ideas which might have generated more business. But with nobody here to look after the house, how could she cope with the sheer physical work of caring for a place the size of this, to say nothing of providing meals for herself and

294

Neil? Then there would be washing, ironing . . .

Still wakeful at three in the morning, she left her room and walked slowly away along the landing. Pensively, step by step, she descended the exquisitely curved staircase. There, she turned towards the large reception room which seemed bigger still in the faint light from a distant half moon.

Joseph would never forgive me for selling this place, she thought, and then felt guiltier still for considering what he might have wished instead of his son. And thinking of Alexander reminded her of how *he* would have managed well enough without her. Indeed, had done so while she was absent from the firm after having Neil. But she wasn't stupid − wasn't even stupid enough to fail to acknowledge that trying to do everything on her own was what had resulted in loss of business.

There must be some way out, she thought, some way of economising even further, just to keep going.

We don't need this room, she recognised, nor that dining room in which I feel so ridiculously isolated. More than half of the upstairs rooms could be shut off. If that was done, she could manage somehow without a housekeeper. Lots of wives worked and still had no help in the home. It need only be for a short period, until she found a better way of coping at Stone's and started bringing in more business.

Her mind made up, Helen went to Mrs Hartley as soon as she heard her moving around in the kitchen that morning.

'Why, Mrs Stone, you do look poorly,' the housekeeper exclaimed. 'You'd better have a sit down, hadn't you?'

'I'm all right, thanks, Mrs Hartley. Fact is, I've got an unpleasant task and I'm wondering how best to tackle it.'

'Summat to do with me?'

'I'm afraid so. I'm dreadfully sorry, Mrs Hartley, but the business isn't picking up as it should be after the war. I really don't see how I can continue paying your wages.'

'Oh, is that all? Thank goodness it's nothing worse. You mustn't go moithering on about that, Mrs Stone. I know you'll pay me as soon as you can.'

'I don't think you quite understand,' said Helen, and forced down the lump developing in her throat. 'I can't see a way of keeping you on. I'm having to shut up part of the house. It's a case of that or selling it.'

'Eh, dear.' The housekeeper paused for a while, thinking. 'Well, happen this'll be just the opportunity I've been waiting for. I could take a holiday. That's summat I haven't done since afore the war. My cousin in Jersey keeps asking me to stay with her for a while.'

'Good idea,' said Helen, feeling relieved that Mrs Hartley wouldn't be entirely without a home.

'And then after I could maybe get in touch with you, see if things were any better. I've right taken to you, you know. I'd be ever so sorry if you couldn't manage to set me on again.'

Helen felt her eyes filling. 'Bless you, Mrs Hartley, you're being very understanding. I'll do my level best to get the firm on its feet again.'

'I hope you won't go overworking, mind. You look that peaky now, never mind when you'll be seeing to this place an' all.'

'I am exhausted,' Helen admitted, and suddenly tears were flowing again as she thought of how drastically things had changed since Joseph's death.

Before Mrs Hartley set out for Jersey she helped Helen decide which rooms must be closed, and went through them, covering furniture with dustsheets and ensuring that all items of any value were stored correctly. Once she had left, however, Helen immediately began wishing the housekeeper was back at The Stone House. The solitary evenings after Neil was put to bed seemed unbearable. Should I have sold up? she wondered. Living in a smaller house, perhaps nearer to her own family, would have been much more agreeable. In a street like theirs everybody was always so helpful.

'But I couldn't have let them down,' she said aloud one night, thinking yet again of Alexander and his father; and of her son who she'd always been determined would eventually inherit the house.

Until Mrs Hartley had gone Helen hadn't realised how fond of her Neil had become, although on reflection that was no great surprise. The housekeeper who had mothered Alexander would doubtless have gone on to make a fuss of the boy, especially while his mother was absent.

'She used to help me and Auntie Marian to cook cakes,' he said one Saturday morning. 'And I used to dry the dishes for her, ever so carefully.'

'And so you shall for me,' promised Helen. 'We could bake something today.'

The first problem was finding sufficient items for any of her favourite recipes. She was discovering that shopping, even just for the two of them, required more forethought than she seemed able to give it. Today, all she had in was the ingredients for making jam tarts.

'But I'm best at doing *cakes*,' Neil protested, sighing weightily.

'Never mind, you'll be learning something new if we tackle these.'

Rubbing fat into flour was more than a child not yet three years old could manage, but Helen allowed him to weigh everything into the bowl and eventually to pour in the water a few drops at a time until the dough was ready.

'I'll show you how to roll this out, then you can try,' she promised, demonstrating.

Neil took over eagerly, but his enthusiasm was far greater than his skill and the pastry soon was stretching and tearing beneath the rolling pin.

'Start again,' said Helen, gathering the dough into a ball and kneading it. 'And don't press quite so heavily this time.'

When at last the rolled-out pastry was fairly presentable, Helen began cutting it out.

'Me, me!' Neil insisted. 'I'll do that.'

'But the cutter's sharp.' Helen showed him the metal edge.

'Me, me!' he repeated, snatching the cutter from her.

There was a yell, followed by a sustained wailing. She grabbed the small hand and inspected the damage where the cutter had sliced into three of his fingers.

'Well, it was your own fault, Neil,' she reproved. 'It's rude to snatch. Happen you'll remember that now. Come on – we'll find dressings for those fingers. First, though, we must wash them.'

After patching him up and giving him a hug, Helen led the way back to the kitchen table.

'This time, you'll have to watch. Once we get them into the baking tins, though, you can spoon the jam into them.'

Again, however, Neil was not prepared to listen to advice. Because he loved jam he would insist on filling each tart to the rim.

'That'll all boil over and make a dreadful sticky mess when they get hot in the oven, love,' Helen told him. 'Don't put quite so much in them, please.'

'I like them this way,' he announced firmly, giving her a withering look.

Naturally, when the tarts were cooked all the divisions of the tin were covered with a hard mass of jam which was beginning to solidify, riveting the tarts into the tin, and welding them together. Helen concealed an exasperated smile.

'You get them out, Mummy,' said Neil urgently.

If he'd been a bit older she'd have told him to get on with that himself. As it was, she began trying with a knife to prise the tarts out. The first two crumbled, but the third emerged intact and she handed it to Neil.

'Careful, it's still warm,' she cautioned.

He inspected the tart, frowning at the grubby misshapen pastry, and its sticky covering. He sniffed at it, took a small bite which he spat out on to the floor. 'Ugh! That's nasty!' He hurled the rest of the tart across the kitchen.

'And so's your behaviour,' retorted Helen. Her patience, worn down by the laborious process of cooking at a child's pace, finally snapping. 'You're a rude, ungrateful boy. I'm ashamed of you.'

Neil began screaming.

Helen willed herself not to spank him, even though she wasn't at all certain that a smacked bottom was not what he needed.

'You're going to your room,' she said, and began marching him across the echoing hall.

The punishment appeared to be working. Neil quietened as they walked silently up the stairs and along to his bedroom.

'You needn't get undressed,' she told him, eager to get away from him for a break. 'Just take off those shoes and lie on top of the covers.'

On her way to the door, she looked back at him. 'I'll

tell you when you may get up again, so think on and stay there.'

'That's all right, Mummy,' responded Neil sweetly. 'I like bed.'

Returning downstairs, Helen was compelled to smile. Trust him to enjoy the punishment she devised. And she was the one who would now be obliged to do what she could with those wretched tarts and clean up the one that Neil had thrown.

Glancing at the clock, she decided that she would leave him where he was for a little while, giving her a chance to prepare lunch. They would go shopping this afternoon. Maybe that would enable her to keep him occupied whilst catching up on one job that needed doing.

Helen decided that the covered market in Halifax was one place where Neil might be interested in his surroundings. She, meanwhile, would have access to most of the items they required without dragging him in and out of a whole range of shops.

After the first ten minutes inside the market building, Helen was congratulating herself on choosing well. Neil seemed to love the brightly coloured stalls and the cheerful people who manned them. Remembering the ingredients that they had been lacking, Helen went around stocking up her store cupboard. She also selected enough fresh vegetables to see them through the next few days, and began looking for cakes as a treat for the boy.

He had been very good this afternoon, remaining close to her side while she was concentrating on choosing her purchases.

It was near at hand, just a little behind her, that the commotion began. First there was an alarming thud, followed by a sharp shriek, and then an agitated shouting.

'You little devil, you! Now look what you've done! How do you think I'm going to get up again?'

Turning, Helen was appalled to see an elderly lady on the ground, struggling to get to her feet, one of them encased in a surgical boot.

'Is he yours?' the woman snapped. 'Time you kept an eye on him. Pulled my stick away, that's what he did!'

'I'm most terribly sorry,' Helen began, bending to assist the old lady to her feet.

Faded brown eyes were regarding her keenly from behind thick-lensed spectacles. 'Well, I'll go to heck! It's Helen Clegg as was!'

'I'm afraid so,' she admitted wryly, recognising one of her mother's neighbours. 'Are you hurt?' she inquired in concern. 'Shall I get somebody to find you a chair?'

'Nay, lass, don't bother. I'm all right now I'm t'right way up again — it were nobbut my dignity as was hurt. As I reckon yours will be, many a time, afore this lad of yours is much older. I'm surprised at you, you know. Thought you'd have had more about you than letting him get away with daft tricks like that!'

'He hasn't got away with it, I can assure you,' said Helen, grasping Neil firmly by the arm. Unfortunately, though, she suspected that *she* was the one, rather than Neil, who would long remember the incident with mortifying regret.

Chapter 15

As Helen had feared, reprimanding Neil had been less than simple. Aware as she was by now that sending him to bed was no punishment, she resorted to a stern lecture, administered as soon as she had him in the car ready for going home.

'Why on earth did you do that to the poor lady?' she demanded.

'I wanted her to look at me,' he said plaintively.

Which she certainly did, thought Helen grimly. 'But why?' she persisted, determined to get to the bottom of her son's stupid action.

'She was looking at the ground, didn't even see I was there.'

'So — not everybody wants to make a fuss of you. And she probably needed to watch where she was putting her feet. That lady is lame, Neil, she has a poorly foot. And that's why she has to use a stick.'

'I didn't know, I only wanted her to smile at me.'

'If you keep on behaving like that, nobody'll ever smile at you again — and that includes me!'

He had studied her seriously for a minute after that. 'You don't smile much now, do you, Mummy?'

That, more than anything, had hurt, going deeper even than the mortification she had felt when being reproached for Neil's behaviour. And it convinced her that the time had come for reassessing her approach to the boy.

'What am I doing wrong, Marian?' she asked on the following Monday when she and her sister managed a private word before Neil came downstairs.

Marian was still stifling her amusement over the incident, but she attempted to be reassuring. 'You're happen trying to do too much, love, that's all. You're up to your eyes in problems, at Stone's and with the house, it's not surprising Neil gets you down.'

'But your two are so well brought up. How have you managed it?'

Her sister grinned. 'More luck than management, if you must know. And except for during the war they have had both of us around. Even then Mum and Dad gave them a lot of attention — I daresay more than they'd have got at home. Neil, now — well, he lost his dad and, in a way, lost a part of you at the same time, didn't he? Nowt's been the same since, has it? It's not your fault that you can't give him more attention, and it's not his either.'

'I think he was trying to get that poor woman to look at him. That's what he said, any road.'

'There you are then — happen he'll improve when he starts to feel more secure.'

But how will that come about, wondered Helen, now that Mrs Hartley has had to go out of our lives? And Neil is bound to sense how insecure I feel now that the business is doing so badly that we could even be forced into selling the house.

During the spring of 1949 Helen occasionally took Neil with her when she visited sites or even when she had brief meetings with clients. He seemed to respond to having this share in her working life and, if well supplied with books or crayons, could be left to amuse himself for short periods.

Helen wasn't certain the idea went down very well with clients whom she suspected might be seeing her as a part-time architect, more interested in her child. She could only hope the fact that she could leave him unsupervised for several minutes at a stretch indicated that she had trained him properly.

There came a day when she was obliged to leave Neil in the car. This seemed quite safe; from the temporary site office the car was in view, and she was only staying long enough to explain to the builder certain amendments in the plans she was delivering.

They couldn't have been talking more than a couple of minutes when the man interrupted their conversation.

'I say, Mrs Stone, isn't that your car?'

Looking up, Helen was horrified. The car was moving steadily downhill towards the centre of the site.

'Oh, God!' she exclaimed and ran outside.

'Didn't you set the handbrake?' he asked, running alongside her.

'Yes. I'm positive I did.' And then she saw that Neil had scrambled through from the back and on to the driver's seat. 'When it crashes he'll go through the windscreen,' she yelled.

Fortunately, a dumper truck had recently dropped a load of hardcore in a place right in line with the car's direction. In a welter of tiny stones and chippings the front of the car embedded itself in the heap.

Terrified, Neil began screaming.

'It's all right, my love,' Helen reassured him, opening the door and pulling him out to be hugged. 'You're quite safe now.'

'I only touched it a little bit, Mummy,' cried Neil, pointing to the handbrake.

'All right, all right,' she soothed, well aware that she had been at fault in leaving him alone in the car. This was something which would never be repeated.

Neil still wished to accompany her on some of her business outings and by taking Marian along Helen succeeded in finding a compromise, enabling her son to continue having more of a share in her world.

Having drained herself with the effort to increase Stone's business, Helen was pleased by that spring of 1949 to see more work coming her way. Much of the upturn was due to the enthusiasm of her secretary Wendy who had been offered the opportunity to extend her role. Instead of just attending to the routine of typing and keeping records she was learning more about architecture. This meant that she was capable of acting as Helen's personal assistant, coping with the office side of jobs and arranging meetings.

'I don't know what I'd do without you,' Helen often told her, deeply conscious that for the foreseeable future, until she could again take on another architect, she needed strong back-up.

Creating more business, however, had been achieved at considerable physical cost to Helen herself. She had thought in the past that she was tired. These days she was exhausted. And even now she wasn't really happy with the work in which she was engaged. The country as a whole hadn't recovered as everyone had hoped following the war. New building projects were often limited by shortages. Half the time Helen wondered why she still felt compelled to pour all this effort into Stone's.

Easter was approaching, and Marian had been pressing Helen to bring Neil away with them for a short break at Morecambe. It was one of those rare weeks when Denis hadn't a part in the current repertory production. They were going to give Linda

306

and Mark a treat, and tried to insist that Helen should join them.

Although grateful, she didn't really wish to do so. She was longing for a few days at home, simply letting go of everything and catching up on a few jobs. Working full-time ensured that household chores were repeatedly crowded out. She was also determined to make time to look at a prospective site for flats in the outskirts of Leeds. Initially the project hadn't sounded particularly interesting, but she had learned the developers were insisting they must be less like a fortress than the Quarry Hill flats completed before the war.

Helen thought she might go over there on Good Friday. Many West Riding firms took the Monday and Tuesday off instead, but she could manipulate any appointments to allow her to get away on that one day.

'Then why don't you let Neil come with us to Morecambe?' Marian suggested when Helen declined their offer. 'It's only for that few days. He's used to us, isn't he? And happen you'd manage a bit of a rest as well as getting on with jobs if you were on your own.'

Reluctantly, Helen agreed, and was glad when Neil seemed to be elated by the prospect of going away with his aunt, uncle and cousins. On the Friday morning he was awake early, demanding to know when he was going to Morecambe.

'Not till tomorrow night, love.' Denis had two shows on Saturdays, so they were setting off quite late. That was another excitement, although Helen hoped for everyone's sake that Neil would sleep during the journey.

Since Marian was busy with preparations, it had been agreed that Helen would leave Neil in their home on the Friday morning, rather than having Marian come out to The Stone House.

When she drew up outside, however, Helen was surprised to see Denis up and about already, and unlocking their car.

'Where are you off to?' she asked. 'It's not like you to be around at this time – you did have a performance last night?'

Her brother-in-law's grin was rueful. 'I did that! And I'm not going anywhere, and nor will any of us be, unless I get this thing fixed. It was playing up yesterday. Only just about got me home last night.'

'Oh, dear. Anything I can do?' she enquired.

'Not unless you can get me to the Ford dealer in Huddersfield. The local garage hasn't got the spares I need.'

'Oh.' Helen paused, thinking. If Denis didn't get the car put right today, they might all be stranded somewhere late at night tomorrow. 'Tell you what, you take mine for today. I can get a bus over to Leeds. You can't go carting spares around on buses.'

'I can't let you do that. Too much of a cheek.'

Helen grinned. 'When you've both offered to take Neil away for a few days? Don't talk daft, Denis. I'll still be in your debt after.'

'Well, then, if you're sure . . .'

'I'll just take him inside to Marian, and I'll be on my way.'

'Then you must at least let me run you to the bus stop.'

'Okay, fine.'

Helen didn't dislike the journey to Leeds. Sitting in the bus was in many ways more relaxing than driving. Especially when, these days, she found concentrating on anything quite an effort. Heading towards Leeds she discovered she was forgetting her purpose in coming here, lapsing into a sort of daydream that resurrected her student days. She had been so happy then and, despite the intensity of her studies, relatively carefree. Maybe if she had time after inspecting that prospective site, she would go into the city centre. It seemed years since she had been free to walk up and down the Headrow, to wander about, just looking.

The site was larger than she had anticipated from the details she had received. It wasn't difficult to believe that the flats to be constructed here might prove quite prestigious. Helen's resolve to submit designs to the developers grew stronger as she paced out the boundary and set her trained eye to making calculations.

The past few years had provided her with contacts among building contractors within a large area of this part of Yorkshire, and from them she had learned how the minds of most developers worked.

I could do it, she thought, already visualising the exterior of the flats. Suddenly, she smiled wryly to herself. This was just the kind of scheme Alexander would have favoured – modern design had been specified. Well, she too could cope with such requirements, if she had to.

When she had completed her examination of the site and made all the notes which might be of assistance later, Helen remembered her idea of taking a look around the city centre. She was tired now, but nevertheless jumped on a bus which would take her there.

Somehow, though, the prospect of going from store to store had palled. The absence of Neil, instead of leaving her free of anxiety as she had expected, was making her feel isolated. She stood for a while admiring the Town Hall, always her second favourite after the one in Bradford which had such an elegant tower and looked altogether more beautiful. I can't be like this, she silently asserted, I mustn't become possessive of Neil, just because I no longer trust myself alone with my thoughts. Ever since Alexander had died she had worked and worked, and worried about Neil, but wasn't that only in order to exclude facts even more difficult to face?

If Alexander had lived to come home from that trip to London, they might have been able to put their marriage to rights. But could she have contributed her share of tolerance and understanding towards making it work in the future? Had Alexander been all that far wrong in accusing her of never doing anything she didn't wish to?

Trying to obliterate her doubts, Helen headed towards Kirkgate covered market, but even its agreeable Edwardian styling didn't distract her. Weary beyond belief, she trudged along to queue for the bus. She would have to go and pick up the car, and Neil too of course. And now, from wishing he was with her, she had turned to dreading coping with him while she felt so exhausted. Before tomorrow evening she would also have to wash and iron all the clothes he would need with him in Morecambe.

Heavens, I'm becoming a proper Moaning Minnie, she thought, sinking on to the nearest seat as soon as the bus arrived. I'm never satisfied.

But what's it all for? she wondered dejectedly. Why do I have to work myself to a standstill? Every scrap of her earlier enthusiasm about producing plans for those flats had been eroded, all she felt now was the familiar dread of . . . yes, of *everything*.

Nothing makes sense, she thought miserably. Why does there seem no direction to my life? Where can I rediscover some purpose?

The bus was slowing in a line of cars. Presently it halted completely as the rest of the traffic turned left at an intersection. I'll never get home at this rate, she thought wretchedly, forgetting her previous reluctance to cope with the evening, and the next day.

Eventually the cause of their delay became evident, reminding her sharply of what today was.

A procession headed by a young man in cassock and surplice and carrying a simple wooden cross came into sight to the right of them. Flanked by a couple of boys of around twelve or so, he was walking gravely yet with a serenity that Helen envied. Behind him came a robed choir and following them a priest, looking rather austere in his long black cassock. Behind him came representatives of his congregation, but it was on the priest himself that Helen's gaze was riveted. *It was Christopher Maitland*. Regardless of the years that had intervened and despite the brief nature of their acquaintance, there could be no mistaking him.

All but hypnotised, she stared after him until he had passed out of sight along a road at right angles to the one where her bus was halted. As the congregation processed in front of her, Helen felt emotions surging through her, singing in her head. Not getting up and jumping off to catch up with Chris was requiring all her will-power.

When the bus slowly moved on again and began gathering speed, she experienced a curious conflict inside her. A part of her, reassured by seeing Chris again, was pleased that he had fulfilled his ambitions, and from the size of this procession of witness evidently had a good congregation. She was thankful as well to have this reminder that the values he upheld still carried some weight in these confusing times. For herself, though, she was saddened by the thought of how different her life might have been if she had been able to spend it with him.

All these years and the changes wrought by war and bereavement had left one thing unaltered. Those few seconds had proved that she would have gone to Chris today, if there'd been any hope that they might have a future together.

Approaching Halifax, Helen came out of her reverie with a feeling of shock. She was almost home. In another few minutes she'd be picking up Neil, and the car. She would have to pull herself together or their Marian would want to know whatever was wrong.

Her efforts mustn't have been nearly enough. As soon as her sister opened the door to her, she knew something was wrong.

'You look as if you've seen a ghost. Are you all right?'

'A bit tired, that's all. It's seemed a long day.'

'You shouldn't have let Denis have your car. He's ever so grateful, though, we both are.'

'Did he get your car fixed?'

'Yes, thanks.'

'Where's Neil?'

'In the garden, out the back. He's right enjoyed himself today. That's what I wanted to ask you — would it be all right if he stopped here tonight? Both Linda and Mark want him to, and he seems keen as well. It'd give you more time to yourself, and let him get used to being without you before we set off to a strange place.'

Helen hesitated, trying to focus the whole of her attention on to the question of Neil. 'Well, I suppose it'd be okay. But then, he hasn't got his pyjamas and things . . .'

'I can find him a pair that Mark's outgrown for tonight. And we can easily pick up his holiday things from you on our way tomorrow.'

'Thanks for the offer, love. We'll just see how he

reacts when he finds out I might be going home without him.'

Helen followed her sister through to the kitchen and while Marian was putting on the kettle she watched Neil through the window. He was sitting on the swing and Linda was pushing him with a degree of care that brought a lump to Helen's throat. Neil had some smashing cousins, bless them, and they seemed to compensate for the loneliness he must experience in his own home.

'I'll just go out and have a word,' she told her sister.

'Hello, Auntie Helen,' said Linda, steadying the swing to a gradual stop.

'Mummy!' Neil exclaimed, and sprang down to run to her.

While she was hugging him, however, Helen felt his small body tensing. 'You've come to take me home, haven't you?'

'Not if you'd rather stay here for tonight. Auntie Marian says you can . . .'

'Yes, please,' he said very swiftly.

Mark had caught the ball he was bouncing against the wall and ran towards them.

'Is Neil staying with us then? He's going to share my room.'

It will be very good for him, thought Helen as she got into the car and drove away. He'll experience living in somebody else's home as well as staying in that boarding house at Morecambe. And whilst the short holiday would be a real treat, tonight would provide a glimpse of ordinary family life.

Arriving back at The Stone House, Helen recognised that any reluctance to be parted from her son was diminishing. She wasn't even thinking about him. Seeing Christopher Maitland like that had generated such a mass of feelings. There was regret, of course, because of there being no opportunity to talk to him, just as there would always be this deeper regret that he wasn't free to share any aspect of his life with her. But there was much more besides.

Chris had been a part of all the wonder and the awe which she had experienced in the Abbey church at Einsiedeln. Seeing him again had brought her once more to the periphery of the beliefs on which his life was founded. During their first meeting she had quickly realised that he wasn't an unintelligent man, there must be some substance in his having faith in this God whom she could barely comprehend.

I wish I could understand, she thought, longing for stability and the strength to make her endure while her life seemed nothing but hard work and difficulties. If only she could recapture a fraction of the feeling induced by Einsiedeln, even just resurrect the once-vivid mind pictures that had faded with time. But she didn't remember taking even one photograph there.

After making and eating a meal, Helen admitted to herself that she had thought of nothing but the Abbey and Christopher since coming back home. She felt better, though, somehow strengthened, perhaps simply by taking a rest from dwelling on her problems.

I wish there was a church round here that could have that sort of effect on my attitude, she thought, yet knew in her heart that she wouldn't seek one out. Her father's non-conformist faith appeared to have seen him through, never wavering even during two world wars. Yet that had never seemed right for her, and she couldn't think she would find it any different now.

Throughout the evening Helen remained preoccupied. She washed their clothes and draped them over a clothes horse before the fire she had lit in the kitchen and on the overhead creel, but working automatically. She felt unable to think about anything else, even the ideas for those flats which had been so clear in her mind until beginning the journey home. Restless still, despite her resolve to have a much-needed early night, she began roaming through the silent house. The dust-covered furniture like so many strangely shaped ghosts seemed to inhabit the empty rooms, as if to warn her that she would be unwise to dwell on her isolation here.

Searching through Joseph Stone's library, Helen came upon the book; filed in the meticulous order on which he'd prided himself before ill health ravaged his intelligence. An illustrated volume on Swiss Architecture, it fell open on a group of photographs of Einsiedeln.

Memories came chasing back, of her father-in-law talking about the Abbey and, longer ago, of old Mr March, insisting that she must ensure she visited the place. How she yearned for the old days, most of all for her own original enthusiasm. Since the war, so much had altered, crushing her dreams and with them all her energy. There seemed so little inspiration, these days, with nothing but humdrum schemes for housing instead of the magnificent buildings she'd been longing for aeons to create. What could she do, what on earth could she do to renew the driving force that had urged her through all that training?

Still clutching that book as she went upstairs, the thought came to her. Whatever she did, be it mundane or exhilarating, contemporary or classical, she must display that same enthusiasm showed by good architects through the ages. The fact that a project was ordinary need not mean that her approach should be of a lower calibre.

Studying the pictures of Einsiedeln, reading some of the text, Helen fell asleep. In the night she wakened, smiling, recollecting that glimpse of the life Christopher had found for himself, beginning to wonder if her own life could somehow gain a measure of that same stability.

Helen always vowed that the changes in her attitude that day were responsible for her being contracted to design those flats in Leeds. Certainly the will and the energy to complete her initial designs appeared as if from nowhere, generating over that weekend ideas which previously might have taken weeks.

'I'm going to be busier than ever,' she announced to Wendy as she walked into the office on the Wednesday after Easter.

Her secretary smiled. 'You look better, any road. As if you've somehow shifted the load that was holding you back before.'

'Happen I have, Wendy, happen I have.' She went on to outline the information which they must gather. 'You'll enjoy helping, I hope. There'll be lots of regulations to be studied, things to be learned from the authorities in Leeds. I've begun making a list. I mean to have everything at my fingertips when I submit my first drawings.'

The speed with which Helen's early sketches brought a response from the developers provided just the boost that she needed.

'I don't care how hard I work now,' she confided to Wendy. 'It might not look like the kind of scheme I'd set my heart on, but this is the chance I've been waiting for.'

Without really knowing how, Helen completed further drawings, adding refinements, enlarging certain areas to show more detail, producing elevations. The good thing was that internally the flats were to be of only four basic designs. Fitting them together in an attractive arrangement within the overall dimensions taxed her skill, but proved fascinating.

When she took work home, she involved her son, although she knew well enough that he could understand only a fraction of what she was doing. But this seemed to suit Neil, he became more amenable, and so long as he was supplied with paper and pencils was relatively quiet.

The only serious problem was the eternal one of finance. Helen was ploughing back into Stone's amounts received in settlement for other smaller jobs, and taking hardly anything out beyond living expenses. For this large project, however, a model of the design was requested, something for which she lacked both the time and aptitude. Paying an outsider went against the grain, and reinforced her knowledge that to develop Stone's she needed more capital.

The day that the foundation stone was being laid, Helen permitted herself a rare site visit that wasn't for practical reasons. 'I'll be back in the office this afternoon,' she promised Wendy.

Unaccustomed as she was to social gatherings, even those connected with her work, Helen drove to Leeds feeling rather uneasy, wondering why she wasn't tackling something more worthwhile. Arriving at the site, however, she began to feel that the morning could be fun. And fun was rare in her life, these days. By this time she was well acquainted with their client, a developer who was beginning to make a name for himself throughout the West Riding. She could believe that in a few years' time, when restrictions eased further, and supplies permitted him to have his head, he would be showing the way to others.

One or two people concerned in Town and Country Planning she knew, and several local officials whom she had met on several occasions. And then there was a party of dignitaries and their friends: among them one woman, tall and dark-haired, appeared to be especially interested in Helen.

She came over and introduced herself after the brief stone-laying ceremony. 'I understand you're the architect, Mrs Stone. I'm Ophelia Hadgraft – and I'm delighted that a woman is responsible for such an ambitious project. The developers tell me that it's some time since you were involved in such a large scheme.'

'That's right. Not from choice, I assure you. If you're connected with the construction industry or the building trade, you'll know how bad things have been since the war. Still are, in fact.'

Ophelia Hadgraft was smiling. 'Actually, I'm not personally involved in either. I'm just interested in people who show a bit of enterprise.'

'I know what you mean. And I'm afraid this looks like being the last task of any size that I shall be tackling for a while. Again, that's not the way I want things. But I have to be realistic. A project this size takes a lot of time and considerable outlay. Unfortunately, being a one-woman outfit at present, I lack the resources to be choosy. Most of my work has to be bread-and-butter jobs.'

'Ah. Now that's what I was coming to. Mrs Stone, forgive my asking, but would you be interested in an injection of capital?'

'Would I!' Helen couldn't believe this was happening.

'Since my brother died and I sold the family business I've been looking for firms in which to invest. You seem to have all the qualities I visualise in someone who will be expected to make best use of my outlay.'

'Are you serious?' asked Helen, hardly daring to credit that her difficulties might shortly be solved.

'Try me. Show me your premises, outline your future plans, give me some indication of the number of shares you have available.'

Helen wished Alexander was still alive, that he was here to assess this woman's offer. He would have known if her suggestion was viable, and how to conduct all the arrangements. She could only use her common sense, and hope that by being cautious she wouldn't ruin all chance of receiving this assistance.

'I'm certainly willing to do all that. You would expect me, of course, to consult my accountant if you should wish to make this a firm offer.'

'Naturally, and your solicitor. You can't be too careful. And nor can I, although I feel that I already know enough about your capabilities. I've seen your plans, had them explained to me. When do you think would be convenient for my paying you a visit?'

'That's up to you. As soon as you like. With only myself and my secretary, there's not much to put in order at the office. We can't afford to be unmethodical.'

'But today would be too soon, I suppose?'

Helen smiled at the woman's eagerness. 'Not really, no. Having taken the morning off, I kept the afternoon free for catching up on paperwork. This sounds as though it could be more important.'

Important it was. Ophelia Hadgraft brought a certain dynamism along with her offer; Helen could feel herself being infected with new optimism. Having dismissed her chauffeur with instructions to call for her at Stone's offices at four that afternoon, Ophelia accepted the offer of a ride there with Helen.

'We need to talk, to get to know one another. This will start us off very nicely.'

Helen was wondering whatever she would find to say to the woman which might extend to fill the journey and beyond. Before they had driven for a couple of miles, however, she was beginning to believe that she had found a friend.

'I gather you are widowed,' Ophelia began, 'and that you have a son demanding your attention, as well as the practice?'

Helen smiled. 'Neil's a bit of a handful at times. He misses his father. And maybe he needs a firmer hand, though I don't think I'm soft with him.'

'And who cares for him now while you're working?'

'My sister, Marian. She's very good with children, has two of her own.' Helen paused, considering whether personal questions were in order, and decided that she could only follow the lead she'd been given. 'Did someone say that you're not married?'

'That's right. Lost my fiancé in the war. I was already older than most women who're seeking a husband. And there was my brother still at home. His wife was an invalid for years. When she died he came to live with me.'

She asked how old Helen's son was, and seemed surprised that he was only three. 'So it's not all that long since your husband died then?'

'Almost a year. Neil was nearly two.'

'Then you've done splendidly to get yourself together enough to take on a scheme like those flats.'

'Architecture's all I know, and next to Neil it's what I love best. I just wish there was more scope around here at present.'

'I can understand that. I know the south was more severely hit by the blitz, and therefore needs more development, but it seems sad to me that the West Riding isn't looking at these New Towns and the like.'

When Helen didn't immediately reply, her

companion gave her a sideways glance. 'Or aren't you enthusiastic about them?'

'I could be. I certainly applaud attempts at achieving some sort of cohesion in their planning. Just as I yearn to tackle projects that give rein to my imagination. I'm just a bit conservative about styling, prefer traditional to ultra-modern. Although, these days, I'll have a crack at anything that gets Stone's out of the rut.'

By the time they arrived at the office they had exchanged views on twentieth-century architecture and on a mass of other topics until Helen was feeling that she had known Ophelia Hadgraft for some time. This made her realise that she had been lacking a woman friend for many a year. In lots of ways, Marian had filled the gap, but there was also the need for a close association with somebody not influenced by family ties.

Wendy looked up in surprise on finding Helen with a companion, then after being introduced went to make tea for them.

'This is very good,' their visitor approved when she was led through to Helen's office. 'I'm glad you haven't skimped over providing somewhere to impress clients.'

'My father-in-law's doing, actually. Neither Alexander nor I had time to make substantial alterations.'

'And none were needed, if this is the way it's always looked. Did you manage to keep going through the war?'

Helen shook her head as she offered Ophelia a chair. 'Not really. For a time Alexander's father kept the office open, but there wasn't any business coming our way. I went into the Land Army – enjoyed it more than I expected. Then when the end of the war was nearing Father-in-law took away the mothballs, as it were.'

'And you've been fighting ever since to get back to normal? Well, here's hoping we may find a means of ensuring that is achieved even quicker.'

'Let's hope so, indeed,' said Helen, still wondering when she would waken up and find this was all a dream, too good to be true.

Chapter 16

The hopes generated on that day soon appeared to be coming to fruition. Before leaving in her chauffeur-driven car, Ophelia Hadgraft had indicated how much she was willing to invest in Stone's and it seemed to Helen a staggering amount of capital.

Mr Thorpe, her accountant, was equally impressed and suggested that, subject to his discreet inquiries proving satisfactory, Helen should agree to shares being made available.

When he came back with the information that Ophelia Hadgraft was entitled to be addressed as The Honourable, and the family money seemed to be well secured, he was as delighted as Helen that the deal should be completed.

'You will have more scope now, Mrs Stone, and I trust that will set your firm on the upward trend merited by all your hard work.'

Her solicitor also appeared well pleased that the arrangement held no hidden snags, and the transaction was arranged swiftly.

Although glad to be relieved of financial worries, Helen continued to be bound by the eternal regulations and shortages of materials which ensured that most of the work in which she was involved was no more exciting than local authority houses.

'I still need another really big project,' she confided

later during one of Ophelia's occasional visits to Stone's.

'Your opportunity will come,' she was assured. 'I'm certain of that. It's only a matter of waiting now for the right one.'

If only I could take on another architect, thought Helen. That would allow one of us to travel, to go down south and try our chances of getting involved in some of these plans for new towns. Despite the fact that Stone's was more secure, these days, she couldn't help being aware that Alexander would have been better able to generate the right kind of business.

I never expected to want a man to lean on as I practised architecture, Helen reflected, but she was compelled to admit how much she missed having one around. This wasn't only true of her working life. And nor was it true only of herself.

Neil was going through a phase of resenting female company. Even his beloved Auntie Marian was sometimes rejected by him with a cutting 'Don't be so soft!' It seemed that only when he was with Denis or Helen's own father did he blossom into the lovable lad who was too frequently concealed behind moody behaviour.

Unfortunately, Denis worked such long and erratic hours at the theatre that he was never a frequent visitor at The Stone House, and Daniel Clegg had aged so much since the war that he found his young grandson's antics rather wearing — welcome, but in small doses.

'You could always marry again, it's not impossible,' Marian remarked one day when Helen was expressing her anxiety about the absence of male influence in Neil's life.

'That is likely, I don't think!' she exclaimed with a wry grin. 'When do I ever go anywhere to meet a decent bloke?'

'Every day, or so I'd have thought,' Marian responded. 'Don't tell me you don't know anybody when you're always off meeting builders and council officials, and what about wealthy clients?'

Helen laughed. 'But they're different, just blokes I meet through my work.'

'What sort would you go for, if you did have another shot at marriage?' her sister persisted, certain that it was time Helen had an easier time, and someone special in her life.

'Eh, I don't know. I've no time to be bothered with such fanciful notions.'

'That's not like the old Helen. You were allus full of dreams. And there must have been somebody caught your eye once, as well as Alex.'

'Must there?' said Helen enigmatically. And refused to be drawn. Where was the sense in reviving memories, especially when they concerned longings that could never be satisfied? Ever since seeing Christopher Maitland earlier this year, she had willed herself not to wonder repeatedly how things might have been. She was thankful for the reminder that there might be some pattern to life, some higher scheme than any she herself could devise. Beyond that, she would not think – if she let her mind run on uncontrolled, she'd only make herself discontented. And, these days, things weren't all that bad. She had finally decided she could reopen some of the other rooms in the house; best of all, Mrs Hartley was coming back.

'What about them that you met in the war?' Marian persisted.

Although she smiled inwardly, recalling Vittore Fabri, Helen again revealed nothing. That night, though, long after Neil had gone to bed and as she herself was preparing for sleep, she thought about him once more. A smile on her lips, she got out of bed and went to the cupboard where the model of Florence Cathedral lay carefully packed in its box.

Dear Vittore, she thought affectionately, gazing at the tiny model of the cathedral, you were as good at dreaming as I was! Had his dreams materialised? she wondered, aching after all this time to know how he was. Had he patched things up with his wife? And how well had he set about restoring his firm? Were the Italians also restricted to designing mundane housing, or was he indulging his flair for the splendid places he had drawn whilst on a farm here in Yorkshire?

Although being reminded of Vittore like that made Helen think of him quite frequently, it certainly hadn't prepared her for seeing him again just a few months later in the autumn of 1949.

The first news of his arrival in England was a telephone call to the office. All Wendy told her was that a gentleman was ringing from London. Hearing his voice was an amazing shock. There was no mistaking his accent, even when all he said was, 'Helen?'

'Vittore! I can't believe it — are you really in London?'

'Why, yes, indeed. And hoping that we may arrange to meet.'

'We better had!' she exclaimed. 'I'll never forgive you if you go back to Italy without seeing me.'

'I certainly shall not do that. In fact, I am considering remaining over here, if that can be made possible.'

'Really? Whereabouts? In the south, I suppose. There's a lot more interesting work going on down there. Only wish I could get a share in it. And there's the Festival of Britain coming up . . .'

'But you're doing well, I hear? Something about a block of flats.'

'Fancy you hearing about that! Yes, I did enjoy that job, but it seems a long time ago already since my part in it was completed. Never mind, though, when can you come and see me?'

'Later this week, perhaps? Do you know a good hotel?'

'You don't have to stay in any hotel, don't be silly. Come to The Stone House.'

Vittore didn't hesitate. 'I would love that, if you are sure it would cause no inconvenience?'

'None at all, I insist. I've got my housekeeper back and she's itching to do a bit of entertaining. Stay as long as you like . . .'

Vittore arrived the following afternoon, coming to the office where he strode in looking so tanned and healthy that Helen only really recognised him by his voice. She was thankful she'd made time to rush to the shops and was feeling quite dashing in her bottle-green dress. Despite the sensible revers and long sleeves, it had the longer, flared skirt introduced by the New Look, and was very feminine.

Instinctively, they embraced, though his kiss was on her cheek — or both cheeks, which made her laugh. Briefly, he touched her glossy hair, which she wore to her shoulders and curled under.

Helen tried to contain the ripples of sheer excitement created by his touch. 'How fit you're looking now!' she exclaimed.

Vittore laughed back to her. 'All the Italian pasta, *cara*, and the glorious sunshine.'

'Yet you talk of maybe stopping over here. You can't mean that, surely?'

'If I could get the necessary permits, who knows?'

'Tell me all your news then — how well have you

done since going back there?'

His news was mixed. Business-wise, he appeared to have fared very well, accomplishing a lot more than Helen felt that she herself had. His home life, however, had deteriorated, even from what she had understood of his pre-war difficulties.

'My wife had taken a lover whilst I was interned. You will understand how this did not greatly surprise me. I told to you the way things had been. The lover was a Yank who insisted that she must marry him. Because of our Italian laws divorce had to be in the States. When that went through, my family as well as hers condemned me for letting her go. *Me*! I ask you, Helen, was that fair? And I the innocent person.'

'And you haven't married again?'

'Naturally, I have not. I told you, didn't I? I do not believe in divorce.'

'So you're on your own as well now?'

Nodding, his dark eyes solemn, he sighed. 'I was sorry to learn that you are alone, Helen.'

Briefly, she wondered who could have told him about Alexander. But there was so much to catch up on, and it was good to have an old friend here sympathising.

'Not entirely alone. I have my son, you know — Neil. He's old for his years, an' all. He'll soon be good company.'

'But not yet?'

'You'll see. Not very consistent, our Neil. One day he's very cooperative, interested in what's going on; the next he can be just as different. A thorough pest!'

'All little boys are naughty at times.'

She found herself telling Vittore of the episode when Neil had pulled away the woman's stick, and was surprised when he didn't laugh.

'You must have been horribly embarrassed.'

'You can say that again!' Helen smiled. 'Eh, Vittore, it is good to talk to you after all this time.'

They talked a great deal, in the office while she showed him some of her recent drawings and photographs of the present stage of construction on the flats in Leeds, and later at home, while Neil sat at the table entranced, as riveted by Vittore's gleaming dark eyes as he was thrilled to be allowed to sit up late for dinner.

Several hours afterwards, when Neil had finally gone to his room, Helen and Vittore were still talking. Reminiscing about the farm and the comradeship among the workers there, he instilled in her a strong desire to see the place again.

'Let's visit Miss Templer,' she suggested eagerly. 'This weekend, why not? We could take Neil, tell him what life was like there.' This was something Helen had never done. She realised now that not even mentioning the farm since she'd left had been because of Alexander's disapproval of her working there.

They were late setting out on that Saturday afternoon. Neil, who had grown possessive of their exciting visitor, had insisted that they inspect his tiny patch of garden. Somehow, out there a game had developed, kicking a ball around, and Helen hadn't had the heart to interrupt them. When the pair eventually came in for lunch, Neil was so grubby that a second bath had proved necessary.

Here they were now though, noting familiar landmarks as they drove out beyond Huddersfield. Neil, tired maybe after the morning's exertion, was quiet for once, staring out obligingly each time a once familiar spot was mentioned but clearly not comprehending. His lack of interest seemed to isolate the other two with the past, and with each other.

Briefly, Helen felt Vittore's hand on her arm, smiled as she gave him a sideways glance.

'I never thought I would come back,' he said seriously.

'Good thing you did, though,' she asserted. 'This has right taken me out of myself.'

'Mmm?'

He sounded puzzled. Helen smiled again, enlightened him. 'Sorry, what I mean is you've made me feel so different, much better, not nearly so entrenched in the humdrum life I lead.'

'That is good. Then I also am very pleased.'

They reached the farm and parked in the familiar yard, looking around them for some sign of Miss Templer. An oldish man was just visible beyond the drystone wall of the next field but one.

'I wonder if that's her brother?' said Helen as they got out of the car.

Knocking on the front door felt strange when they had both spent so many years wandering freely in and out of the farmhouse. And an answer was so long in coming that Helen was considering knocking again when the door opened.

'Well, I'll go to heck! It's Helen, isn't it?'

'That's right, Miss Templer, and this is my son, Neil. And you remember Vittore . . .'

'Well, I don't know! I wouldn't have owned you, you have bucked up,' she told Vittore. 'But I'm right glad to see you both, and the little lad − Neil, you say? Come in, come in.'

The big kitchen looked bare without farm workers on every available chair, but otherwise it seemed hardly to have changed.

'Did you really live here?' Neil asked, tugging on his mother's hand.

Helen grinned, turned to Vittore. 'Certainly brings

it all back, doesn't it, love?'

Miss Templer was standing, hands on hips, scrutinising them both. 'They were good days, weren't they?' she remarked, then seemed to recall the internment which had brought Vittore to Yorkshire.

But he smiled widely in response to her questioning grey eyebrow. 'For me also, yes – those times were very good.'

'And now?' Miss Templer enquired. 'Are you two, well . . .?'

Helen shook her head. 'It's just that we're still friends. Vittore's come back to England on a visit.'

'Not only a visit perhaps. If I can obtain the necessary permission,' he repeated, 'I would like to remain here. But tell us about yourself, Miss Templer, are you working as hard as ever?'

'When I'm able. I've got rheumatics, you see, 'specially in my knees. But we manage very well. My brother came back, shortly after t'end of the war.'

'We thought we saw somebody out there.'

'Some of t'others has been to call on me an' all, you know,' Miss Templer revealed, looking delighted. 'Kenneth, was it – the one with the bad chest? Him and one of the other fellows dropped in with their wives, must be two or three years ago now. And Iris comes to stay regular, of course.'

They chatted over tea while Neil played with the farm cat. And then they were given a tour of the fields, meeting Miss Templer's brother who appeared to be a man of few words.

'Miserable beggar!' their hostess muttered before they were quite out of earshot of him. 'I reckon he were far happier on munitions than ever he's been since. Pity they didn't keep him, I say!'

'Can we go home now?' Neil asked suddenly out of the blue.

Helen felt her colour rising. 'I'm sorry, Miss Templer, I'm afraid social graces were rationed when Neil was born. Although he does know better really than asking questions like that.'

'But I want to play football again, Vittore's super at it.'

'I'm afraid that'll have to wait till another day, my lad — by the time we get home it will be dark.'

'That's not fair,' the boy protested. 'It's boring here.'

'If you want summat to occupy you,' Miss Templer began, bending to speak to Neil, 'you can go and help my brother. He'll find you a job.'

That prospect didn't suit either. Neil stubbornly shook his head.

'I would like to walk,' Vittore suggested, then checked if that was all right with Miss Templer, and if she would join them.

'I'm afraid my old legs aren't up to it,' she told them. 'But you take a stroll round, enjoy yourselves. Not that there's much to see these days, except the view. We got rid of most of the sheep, and a lot of the fields where we grew crops have been turned over to cattle.'

The well-remembered vista of high, green hills spreading out towards the skyline was just as beautiful as ever. With the russet tones of autumn and the mauve of heather-capped moors it all seemed particularly lovely. Rain drops glistening on the leaves of an oak witnessed to an earlier shower which had bestowed its special clarity and brought the distant scene into sharper focus. At this altitude the expanse of hills seemed limitless and Helen relished the sense of freedom soaring through her. Today, she could believe that her future might be just as unrestricted.

They walked uphill to where the sheep used to graze,

and Neil began running about happily, exploring the entrances of rabbit burrows, and jumping off the low rocks that protruded from scrubby turf.

As they paused to gaze about them yet again, Helen heard the familiar sound of the wind in telegraph wires. All at once it returned her to the past, to the evening when Vittore had held her close, reassuring her.

Glancing his way, she caught him looking at her, some deep emotion turning his eyes almost to black and his smile to one of tender affection.

Neil had tired himself out. As soon as they said goodbye to Miss Templer and got into the car he yawned and started to drowse.

'It was good to go back to the farm,' said Vittore. 'I was reminded of so much that I experienced there.'

'A lot of hard work!' exclaimed Helen, though she had never considered the work alone out here.

Neil was asleep when they arrived at The Stone House. Before Helen could rouse him, Vittore caught her arm.

'Do not disturb him, there is no need. I will carry him upstairs for you.'

'He's not a tiny boy any longer.'

Vittore laughed. 'And I am not a tiny man.'

She hadn't needed any reminder of his presence which seemed so forceful that she ignored — as she always had — his height which was just about equal to her own. Now Vittore was here, Helen wondered how ever it was that he hadn't remained constantly in her thoughts since their very first meeting.

Following up the long curving staircase, she learned that he still had breath for speaking.

'Which room is Neil's, did you say?'

'Along to the left, here . . .'

She caught up with Vittore and opened the door. 'If

you don't mind putting him on the bed, I'll just slip his outdoor clothes off, and his shoes.'

Vittore was smiling again when he straightened up and faced her. 'Oh, to have the capacity of a child for sleeping well.'

'Don't you, then?' she asked, concerned.

He shrugged. 'Rarely. Especially since I went back to Italy.'

'Is it that bad?'

'Later, I will tell you. When you have attended to the boy.'

Mrs Hartley was waiting below in the hall, and showed Vittore into the large reception room which had just been reopened.

'If you'd like to wait in here, sir. Happen you'd like to help yourself to a drink while Mrs Stone is busy. She always expects her male guests to serve themselves.'

When Helen came downstairs after settling Neil she was surprised that Vittore asked if she did much entertaining.

'Because of the size of this room, you mean?' She shook her head. 'The house was built by my father-in-law. We took it over when he died. I hardly think I'd have gone for anything quite so big myself.'

'But it is indeed a beautiful house.'

'I agree with you. It's just a bit of a waste with only the two of us here now and Mrs Hartley.'

'You are young enough to marry again though, Helen.'

She laughed. 'You're as bad as our Marian! My sister. She was on at me not long since. As if I hadn't enough on my plate as it is.'

'But the right husband would share your responsibilities, would he not?'

'For the house, maybe. And for Neil an' all, I'd hope. But it's not only that, is it?'

'You mean the practice. Does that weigh heavily still?'

'Aye, I'm afraid so. Although a recent injection of capital has helped relieve the anxiety. I ought to be able to get away more, there's that little being built round here, and I don't have chance to go and look at what they're doing elsewhere. Alexander would have done all that.'

'You will miss him in so many ways.'

'Well, naturally. I'd known him so long, even before we were married, hadn't I?' Even to Vittore, she had no intention of revealing how drastically their relationship had deteriorated.

'And young Neil will miss him also.'

'He goes through phases, he's not so bad at present. Sometimes, he's really wilful and moody, and I can see he needs his daddy.'

After Mrs Hartley had announced that dinner was ready and they had gone through to the dining room they both became rather quiet. Helen was overcome by a sudden tiredness, and she suspected that Vittore was growing bored by her failure to provide more in the way of conversation.

The meal and the coffee which followed seemed to restore a little of her spirits, and she was content to return to sit near the fire.

'You were saying earlier, about the firm?' Vittore began carefully, glancing into the blaze rather than towards her. 'How the responsibility, to say nothing of the work, may be a little too much. Have you contemplated taking on another architect?'

'I have, but I've got to be realistic. I can only just survive paying Wendy, my secretary. If I had to fork out for anybody else, I'd be back to where I was before. Too hard up to run this place properly.'

'No, no – you have not understood. I mean as a

partner, someone who would invest in Stone's as well as working for — for you.'

'It'd have to be somebody who thought very much as I do about architecture. I had enough of opinions that clashed while Alexander was alive. So you see, Vittore, it'd have to be somebody pretty remarkable. He, or she, would have to have an eye for any up-to-date developments without wanting everything to be in ultra-modern style. It's a tall order. I'm reaching the conclusion that I'm damned difficult to please!'

'Not necessarily.' He was facing her now, the warmth in his fine dark eyes reminding her how good he was at beseeching with them. 'If I could be granted a permit to work over here, and I would even apply for naturalisation if that would help, I should like you to consider my joining you.'

'You? Eh, Vittore, if only you could. Didn't we used to get on well! I'm ever so glad we went to the farm today, aren't you?'

'But, yes, of course. We seem to have grown so close once more.'

And what good's that, thought Helen, when you still think of yourself as married? You haven't really come back to me. Where's the use in growing attached to you all over again, when it can lead nowhere? Except, possibly, with regard to work.

At around ten o'clock she rose and smiled across at him. 'Time I looked in on Neil to make sure he's sleeping all right. And then I'm going to bed. If you want to sit up, by all means do so. Make yourself at home. You know where the drinks are, and there's some of my father-in-law's books over there if you feel like a good read.'

Vittore chose instead to go up to his room. Tired but at ease, they hardly spoke as they walked side by side up the exquisite staircase.

At the door of her room, he took her wrist and drew her to him. His fingers were warm, powerful, and made her yearn to have him hold her and go on holding . . .

His kiss was firm on her lips. She felt his lips part.

'I need you so much, Helen,' he said huskily against her cheek. 'I've never stopped needing you.'

She made her voice light, rueful. 'And what I need is a good night's sleep, love.'

'There is one way of ensuring that,' Vittore persisted.

Helen shook her head at him. 'That's an old line — and I'm no bit of a lass that's going to fall for it. Sorry and all that, but you'll have to put that idea out of your head.'

'One more kiss then?'

One kiss, two, three — three hundred, she could no longer be sure. All she did know was the blood racing in her veins. Vittore was back, forcing her to acknowledge the acute awareness of him that was strong enough to cause her such fierce agony.

Vittore stayed for a further week in the house at Brearley, filling it with his good humour, often with his strong tenor voice. His fondness for opera seemed irrepressible, and clearly was encouraged when so many of the rooms proved to have good accoustics. Neil was entranced, and far better behaved than Helen remembered him. She herself delighted in having Vittore's companionship, and had to force into her subconscious the longing to have him share their life here permanently.

On the last Saturday of his stay he asked her to find somewhere for a special meal. Mrs Hartley was content to baby-sit for Neil. The restaurant was in Manchester, an elegant place which provided a small group of musicians to play for dancing.

'Remember the way we danced at the farm?' asked Vittore, holding her close as a foxtrot began.

Helen was willing herself not to. Her relationship with Alexander had been an almighty let-down. She wasn't going to be so vulnerable ever again. And besides, there was still everything that Vittore had said about his not being free. A proper fool she would be if she became involved with him now.

No amount of resolve could prevent her from enjoying this evening, however. Vittore's love of music made him an excellent partner. He couldn't know of her barely acknowledged yearning to be held by a loving man.

Helen could not protest when he repeatedly took her on to the floor, she could only revel in their well-matched steps and his mind-shattering nearness.

In the car going home he sat very close, his dark gaze going to her repeatedly so that driving required a serious effort of concentration. And when they went indoors he drew her to him at once, leaning with her into the massive oak door while his taut body spoke even more urgently than his kisses.

'Come to my room, Helen, please. Or allow me in yours. You are so completely desirable.'

'Not yet, Vittore, not so readily,' she said huskily, yet hating the good sense which compelled her to refuse. 'You've only just come back into my life. We've got to be reasonable about this. Sensible.'

'In here with me to the sofa then, just so I may hold you?'

Helen could no more deny herself than deny Vittore. But she would have to be extremely careful. She'd heard about Latin men and the heat of their passion. She mustn't forget how powerful desire could be.

Vittore drew her against him as they stood in the

light from the dying fire. His kisses became searching as they sank on to the sofa and held each other.

He was hard and he was stirring, driving Helen to acknowledge the rhythm of the blood which surged through her own veins. And she was moving with him. The hungry years had brought her to this day with every one of her senses sharpened. For how long they lay there, she could not reckon; only when forcing her own desire into submission grew almost impossible did she finally ease away from him.

'No more, Vittore, no more,' she stated firmly.

She liked him all the better for not attempting to argue. Instead, he assisted her to her feet and with one last kiss and a brief little hug, escorted her to the stairs.

'Sleep well, Helen.'

They were brisk and matter-of-fact with each other in the morning. Only their eyes, seeking and locking in long glances, revealed the yearning which had not diminished.

'May I return?' Vittore asked before they parted.

'There'll be trouble if you don't.'

The house felt emptier than ever in the past. Helen was thankful when work took her away to the office. And there, at least, thoughts of Vittore were permissible, taking on a different aspect. If he should find a way of working over here, nothing would stop her having him in the firm. Stone's would benefit from his expertise, to say nothing of his intended investment. And she would have a very good reason for welcoming him into this part of her life.

Neil began playing up during the week after Vittore's departure. Even Marian complained about his bad manners and spiteful little ways.

'It's not anything really wicked that he does,' she explained to Helen one evening. 'It's just that he really 'gets my goat by being downright awkward.'

Helen tried talking to her son, and got nowhere at all.

'It's no fun here any more,' he asserted, sounding nearer ten years old than three. 'Did you send Uncle Vittore away as well, like you sent Daddy?'

'I didn't send either of them away. And it's time you grew up a bit and got used to the idea that life can be disappointing. When Uncle Vittore came here it was only for a short stay. But he might come back again, especially if you try to become a likable person,' she added, and hated herself for attempting blackmail.

At the end of that week, Helen decided to confide in her mother. She wouldn't enjoy admitting how difficult Neil could be, but she was beginning to feel out of her depth with him again. And what were mothers for but to pass on advice down the generations?

Helen left Mrs Hartley keeping an eye on Neil while she drove over to Halifax during Saturday afternoon. Her father generally went off to the football match. She and her mother would be able to have a private heart-to-heart.

Kathleen seemed surprised that Helen was alone. She knew her daughter normally reserved weekends for Neil.

'Nothing's wrong, love, is it?' she asked from the kitchen doorway after putting on the kettle.

Helen sighed, staring across the street at the row of gaunt houses. 'Eh, I don't know, Mum. I've certainly come seeking your advice.'

Her mother grinned. 'Mine? Nay, I allus thought you were the clever one of this family.'

'I don't feel it. And definitely not where Neil's upbringing's concerned. I sometimes think I'm making a right hash of it.'

'Never! Not you. He's a grand little lad, a credit to you.'

'You only see him when he's on his best behaviour. He can be a proper little devil when things aren't to his liking.'

'I hope he wasn't naughty while you had that Italian chap staying? Our Marian told me you had a visitor.'

'Vittore, aye. No, Neil was very good, for him, while Vittore was there. It's since he's left that Neil's been playing up. He's so moody at times. Were we like that?'

'Not really, love. Marian was allus on the go, into everything, and you — well, you were quieter, of course, always reading or doing jigsaws if you weren't drawing. You were as good as gold.'

'I don't know if it's with me working and our Marian taking over from me, or what. He seems that changeable somehow. Just when I think he's learning to behave, he starts acting like a spoilt brat again.'

'I don't suppose it's with you going to work so much as him missing his dad. It's bound to have made him feel insecure, you know.'

'Aye, I daresay. He blames me for that an' all.'

'Nay, Helen, how can he? It were an accident killed Alexander.'

Helen swallowed, deciding the time had come for being honest about her great burden — the circumstances surrounding her husband's departure for London on that dreadful day.

'Aye, but we hadn't been getting on before he set off. Evidently, Neil had heard us arguing.'

'Lots of folk argue, love. You can't go punishing yourself for that.'

'We'd talked about splitting up.'

Kathleen's grey eyes narrowed. 'As bad as that, eh? Was — was there another woman again?'

'Not so far as I know. No, I'm pretty sure there wasn't. It was just me. Oh, Mum – he said I wasn't anything like the wife he wanted!'

'Did he now? And what did he expect? You gave him the son he was after, *and* worked in the family firm as well.'

'It was going back there after Neil was born that put Alexander's back up.'

'Yes, well, working wives do create a different home life, but that doesn't mean it has to be an unhappy one. And he had known you all the years you were studying – he couldn't seriously have expected you to give up your work.'

'Bless you, you're very understanding. But about Neil – what do you think I ought to do?'

'I don't rightly know, love. You'll have to be patient for a while maybe – till he grows up a bit. The best thing all round would be if you met somebody else, someone that'd be a father to him.'

Leaving her mother that afternoon, Helen felt a different kind of disturbance. Ever since Vittore had returned she had been fighting her own instincts. Perhaps that had been the wrong thing entirely?

Chapter 17

Helen was positive now that she was going to pull Stone's through — she would build up the business again until it regained the kind of reputation it had had while Joseph Stone was in charge. She began her campaign with visits to Sheffield, one of the places nearer to home that had suffered wartime bombardment.

There certainly was scope for redevelopment, and much of it where traditional styling would be more appropriate than anything modern. While she still had no one qualified in the office, she couldn't spend too long over each trip to Sheffield. She could find out what new building was required, though, and also widened her understanding of the area in long conversations with her sister.

Marian, despite the hazards from enemy bombing, had enjoyed her stay driving ambulances there. 'I'd love to see parts of it rebuilt by you, Helen,' she said, surprising her. 'You'd not choose stuff that would clash with what's there already.'

Helen smiled. She'd needed someone to understand her aims. 'Thanks. Eh, Marian — there's that much I long to get involved with. If I'd somebody experienced to leave in charge I'd be off all over the north, sniffing out where reconstruction should be done. Liverpool suffered very badly in the war, then there's Hull an' all.'

Since Ophelia Hadgraft had put money into Stone's Helen had been hoping she'd be justified in taking another architect into the firm, but here she was, still waiting and hoping, and being confronted by warnings from her accountant whenever she tried to expand further. Meanwhile, most of her work was confined to plans for housing. All she could do was remind herself how vital this was, and that when completed to her designs the homes produced were pleasing.

Autumn turned to winter, bringing biting winds that scoured hilltops and moors and tore through steep streets, until everyone felt that going out at all was a battle. Despite her resolve, Helen began to believe that a battle was the nearest description of the whole of her life. When she wasn't wearing herself out at work she was struggling to keep that massive house warm, and to survive Neil's moods.

It was mostly to try and make him feel happier that she became determined to provide a Christmas that was as good as possible. Last year, being the first after Alexander's death, she'd arranged hardly anything. Somehow, she would make up for that.

One Saturday early in December she and Neil arrived home from shopping feeling quite happy. He had been interested in plans for Christmas and in the items they were buying, and had behaved extremely well, reassuring Helen. Mrs Hartley greeted them in the hall with the news that there had been a telephone call.

'From that Italian – Mr Fabri,' she said. 'I told him you would be at home this evening, I hope that's all right?'

Helen spent the intervening hours trying to quell her excitement. Surely the fact that Vittore had phoned meant that he'd either remained in England or had

father had begun. Despite the large number of peop
present she was deeply conscious of a strange qu
that had nothing to do with silence. Indeed, the mu
was glorious, from the full-throated singing
Christmas hymns to the fervent intoning of the recto
all perfectly tuneful.

I wish I'd come to services here before, she though
aching to belong. I wonder why I've always felt I w
merely on the edge of worship, not quite participating

Glancing sideways at Vittore, she sensed th
although the doctrine was different from his own, l
was quite at home here.

When they went out into the crisp night air to wa
the short distance to the house he took her hand.

'Happy Christmas,' he said, and added, 'than
you.'

They drank hot coffee and ate mince pies left out fc
them by Mrs Hartley before going to their room
During this visit Vittore had avoided any hint that h
wished to make love to her. But Helen often read in hi
glance a longing which echoed her own. Sitting lik
this in her home, she could believe that the time woul
come when her restraint would give way.

She was awakened on Christmas morning by Nei
rushing into her room with some of his toys.

'Look, Mummy, look what Father Christmas ha
brought. And this one's special,' he declared, showing
er a magnificent model aeroplane. 'This is wha
Uncle Vittore asked him to bring.'

'He's very kind. You must be sure and thank him.'

'I said thank you already.'

Helen glanced at the clock. It was a quarter to seven.
ou didn't go into his room? Do you know that your
cle and I went to church last night — and didn't ge
me until after one o'clock!'

ittore, however, was showing no signs of lacking

returned here? He wouldn't be telephoning all the way
from Italy.

I might be proper daft, she thought, but I do want to
see him again. And I'd love more than anything to
have him working with me.

When the call came, Vittore made no such promises,
but he did say he had a lot to discuss with her. 'I was
wondering if it might be convenient for you if I visited
Yorkshire next weekend?'

Helen wouldn't have believed that a week could
drag so heavily even though she was so busy in the
office. Finally awakening on the Saturday morning,
she felt drained by days of enduring her own
impatience. She had never been like this before. But
then, of course, she'd never had to wait to see
somebody she'd grown found of.

Vittore arrived a few hours later, stepping from his
taxi and gazing up at The Stone House affectionately
and with an expert's approval in his dark eyes.
Watching from an upstairs window, Helen smiled to
herself. It might have been confirmation, had she
needed any, of how their tastes converged.

She only hoped his taste in fashion would appreciate
her New Look style. She was feeling self-conscious in a
dress that she'd originally bought for Christmas but
couldn't resist wearing today. In a soft wool that hung
in unpressed pleats from a nipped-in waistline, its
bodice fitted beautifully but seemed to emphasise her
breasts, a factor enhanced by the curving V neckline.
The long sleeves felt good, though, after years of
Utility skimpiness, as did the mid-calf skirt. And she
loved the material, a wedgwood shade that reflected a
tinge of blue into her grey eyes.

Running down the elegant staircase, she was in the
hall by the time Mrs Hartley had opened the door to
him. Neil, however, had beaten her to it. Hurling

himself at Vittore, he was lifted clear of the ground in an energetic hug.

Helen felt her throat tighten, and tears stung her eyes. But then Vittore was transferring the boy to one arm and extending the other for her. Holding her against him, he kissed her full on the lips, then kissed Neil also before setting him down.

'I feel as if I have returned home,' Vittore declared, beaming at the three of them as he turned slightly and greeted Mrs Hartley, 'Did I say hallo when you opened the door to me? You must forgive if my excitement took away my courtesy.'

Vittore appeared even fitter than on his previous visit, and was wearing a beautifully tailored suit in a creamy-coloured cloth that no one in the West Riding would have considered practical.

I can't stop myself wanting him here, thought Helen, regardless of all my resolutions. And I've only to look at Neil to know how much he likes his Uncle Vittore.

The rest of the day passed in a sort of daze. Helen was so elated that she'd lost all her customary steadiness. And Neil, bless him, was angelic, remaining surprisingly quiet while she and Vittore were talking, but cooperating with spirit when invited to show what he'd been doing during the past few weeks.

By Sunday evening Helen was growing accustomed to having Vittore around again, and was relishing his company. Early that morning they had walked uphill from the house and strolled along the ridge, glancing occasionally across the valley where frost had rimed bare branches and coated the dark stone walls like fine sugar.

'I love your Yorkshire,' he had told her, his breath frosting too in air that stung their faces.

That evening she wasn't surprised whe[n] announced his firm plans to settle here. 'I've man[aged] to secure permission,' he confided. 'Do not as[k me] how. I had to persuade someone to pull a few strin[gs. I] have also got most of my capital liquidised — [and] away from Italy. I am serious, Helen, about wishin[g to] join Stone's, if you would consider having me.'

She beamed at him. 'I think you know already t[hat] I'd love that. But you'll have to understand that I ca[n't] just leap into such an important decision instantly. [I'll] speak to my accountant, soon as I can, then you a[nd] me can talk again, sort out details.'

In the meantime, she asked him to extend his sta[y]. 'If you want to, you could stop with us till aft[er] Christmas. That would certainly suit Neil.'

'And you?' he asked quietly.

'And me an' all.'

'I should like to make up to you, Helen, for al[l the] loneliness you have endured since your husb[and's] accident.'

She could well believe that Vittore was capa[ble of] doing just that. He had been important to her f[or] a long time now. Having him back in her lif[e was as] good as recovering after an extended bout of s[ickness.]

On Christmas Eve Vittore startled her by s[uggesting] that they should attend mass at midnight.

'I wouldn't mind,' she said, 'but I'm no[t Catholic,] you know. I couldn't even tell you about the[nearest of] their church.'

'No matter. We would attend an Engli[sh one. I] should like that very much.'

The tiny church was almost full. The[y found seats] near the back and Helen felt the calm se[ttle over her.] Decorated for Christmas and full of s[uch a warm] atmosphere, she could hardly believe [this was the] place where the funerals of both A[lan and ...]

sleep. He was dressed in dark slacks and an elegant sweater, and talking with Mrs Hartley when Helen went down to the dining room. And maybe their rising early was for the best, she thought wryly. She had invited all her family over for Christmas dinner.

Asking them all to her was taking a chance. She couldn't be sure how they would get on with Vittore, and was also afraid that Marian, at least, would begin making five out of two and two.

Helen soon discovered, anyway, that her parents appreciated her sparing her mother the work of entertaining the whole family. And Denis, who had visited Italy with ENSA during the war, soon began talking animatedly with Vittore.

Having Mrs Hartley to attend to the actual meal was a great boon, freeing Helen to relax and chat with her guests.

Neil and his cousins were allowed to wrap up warm and romp in the garden just before dinner, an idea that paid dividends when they came in healthily hungry and with enough energy expended to give everyone a trouble-free meal.

During the late afternoon while the children were absorbed in a jigsaw puzzle, leaving the adults free to talk, Helen glanced towards Vittore.

Sitting on one of the sofas drawn up to the hearth in her large reception room, his smile was enhanced by the glow from the fire. His eyes, darker than ever in here, seemed to smile as much as his lips, and every line of his body looked perfectly at ease.

He appears to fit in so well here, Helen thought, smiling also to herself. There had been no awkwardness with any of her family — and his generosity to Neil was evidence of his affection for her son.

There had been a gift for Helen herself — one that

had taken her back to another Christmas. This time, the model he had given her was of St Peter's in Rome. She had been delighted to display them both on a side table in the dining room.

Marian had teased, as Helen had expected, while they were helping Mrs Hartley to clear the dirty dishes into the kitchen. But if she hadn't accepted Helen's explanation that Vittore was simply to become involved as a business partner, she had certainly ceased her questions about the relationship. Helen realised now that although she wouldn't wish to hurry through any part of this Christmas she would be glad to see her accountant afterwards and begin drawing up the deal to finalise their plans.

'You can't mean that!' Helen exclaimed, terribly disappointed. She had spent half the morning with Mr Thorpe, explaining how much Vittore was willing to invest in Stone's and how his expertise as an architect was just what she had been seeking. And here her accountant was, cautioning her against permitting another person to take a financial interest in the firm!

'I'm sorry, but I cannot think such a deal would be to your long-term advantage, Mrs Stone.'

'But whyever not?' Helen persisted. 'Haven't you been telling me for ages that we can't expand as things are? That we need more money behind us?'

'Ah, but there is a difference, you see,' Mr Thorpe persisted. 'I was thinking in terms of funds which were by way of being a ploughing back of your profits. If you let someone else in now you're leaving yourself wide open to difficulties in the future.'

'I don't see how.'

'Oh come, Mrs Stone, you're not that naive. You're already in a position where the Honourable Ophelia Hadgraft has a considerable say if it comes to boardroom wrangles. An additional shareholder would . . .'

'Oh, is that all?' said Helen thankfully, realising that he was visualising Vittore as a potential source of trouble. Nothing could be further from the truth. All Vittore wanted was to make things easier for her, to relieve her of some of the anxiety and increase the possibility of Stone's going after bigger and better projects.

'It's all right,' she went on to assure him. 'I've known Vittore Fabri for years. He's a lovely man who thinks as I do about architecture. About lots of things, if it comes to that. I'm grateful for your considering every aspect on my behalf, Mr Thorpe, but you really needn't have any qualms about this deal, none at all.'

When, a few days later, she saw Ophelia Hadgraft and told her that Vittore was coming into the firm, Helen was thankful that she didn't even express surprise.

'That will do wonders for Stone's, I'm sure. I'm delighted for you, Helen. His investment will indeed put the firm on a very sound footing, and his expertise will enable you to widen your scope.'

'I knew you'd be pleased. It just shows how right I was to trust my own instincts.'

Her instincts seemed to be working overtime since Christmas. Having seen how well integrated into her family Vittore was, she was beginning to lose all misgivings about his staying in her home. They frequently ended the day in each other's arms. And she was fully aware now that if he was to suggest their making love, she wouldn't refuse.

It was a total shock when Vittore himself decided he must move out of the house. On the day that he finally began working at Stone's he told her of his intention.

'Do not look so perturbed, Helen, there is nothing

wrong. You know how happy I am, how much I want to work alongside you. But you know also that I have experienced trouble in the past when involving business with my private life. And so the time has come to find myself accommodation. I have heard of a place that will be convenient for reaching the office, and I trust that you and I will continue to spend some of our leisure hours together, especially with young Neil.'

His decision was a blow, she couldn't find sufficient composure to pretend otherwise. It had come so suddenly, almost as though somebody had put the idea into his head. But if she was perturbed about their personal life she wouldn't let that spoil her happiness concerning their business relationship.

Within days Vittore seemed to have settled as readily into the office as she had once believed he'd been settled in her home. Seeing him each day compensated for missing him at The Stone House, and having Neil to herself again she noticed how he had blossomed under Vittore's influence. He had become a much more cheerful little boy, and much more cooperative.

During the second week that Vittore was in the office Helen realised that she was feeling infinitely better. Not only was she free to go out on business trips, she had regained the energy to enjoy doing so. Even this early in the new year she felt undaunted by the extreme cold and up to facing any falls of snow.

Hull was one of the first places Helen visited, and she learned of several schemes which she hoped might provide work for Stone's. Feeling some of the elation that she'd experienced when first qualified, she was driving back through Halifax when she recognised the car ahead of her as Ophelia Hadgraft's.

They arrived simultaneously at Stone's office and Ophelia, who evidently had recognised Helen's car in her rear-view mirror as they slowed to negotiate the bends of the approach road, waited for Helen by the steps.

'I thought you'd said you were going over to Hull today?' she said, and Helen noticed that although Ophelia was smiling her eyes hadn't warmed.

'That's it. I've had a right good day over there, there's plenty of scope for work. But I wanted to get back and make sure that Vittore was coping.'

As they entered the outer office Helen saw through the doorway of her own office that Vittore was sitting at her desk. He was speaking down the phone to someone and, seeing she had arrived, beckoned her.

'It is the construction company for those flats of yours nearing completion in Leeds.'

The query was minor and quickly answered, Helen's disturbance owed more to finding Vittore occupying her desk. It seemed all too reminiscent of Harold Tilsley. But I'm being paranoid, she reminded herself swiftly, and began introducing him to Ophelia Hadgraft.

Helen had wondered once or twice how the two would react to each other, and would have been horrified if they hadn't got on. It seemed, however, that she need not have worried.

Ophelia instantly extended a hand which Vittore grasped firmly and then raised to his lips. Amid effusive exclamations of 'How do you do?' 'I am so delighted to meet you' and 'I'm so glad that you have joined Stone's', the pair were beaming enthusiastically.

Privately, Helen smiled. It looked as if Ophelia was responding with an older woman's eagerness to flattery from a personable man. And Vittore, she supposed, had the typical Latin flair for impressing any female.

The three of them sat in Helen's office for an informal discussion of future plans. The other two seemed to think her visit to Hull had indeed provided lots of potential. And they readily applauded her idea of following this up with an exploratory trip to Liverpool.

When Ophelia glanced at her watch and announced that she had an engagement that evening and must be leaving, she added to Vittore: 'Can I offer you a lift perhaps? I shall be going through Halifax.'

He accepted readily, thanking her profusely, and tossing Helen a brief: 'Goodnight, see you in the morning.'

Driving home, Helen reflected that if Ophelia Hadgraft had been in less than her evident middle years, she herself might have been perturbed by the fuss Vittore was making of her. I seem to be in danger of becoming neurotic about his behaviour, she thought ruefully. Could this perhaps be a result of the mistrust which her own husband had once generated in her? Would she always doubt every man?

After playing with Neil and seeing him into bed that evening, Helen willed herself to concentrate on the notes that she had made over in Hull. But she seemed unable to forget her impression that there'd been more than the casual acceptance of a lift in the way the others had gone off together. She would just have to school herself to accept that whilst working so closely with anyone there were bound to be occasions when their behaviour appeared inexplicable.

Now that Vittore's presence made her feel easier about leaving the office, Helen found the next few months passing agreeably as well as swiftly. He didn't seem the sort of man who must have a hand in all the big schemes. He appeared happy enough to work on

Chapter 17

Helen was positive now that she was going to pull Stone's through — she would build up the business again until it regained the kind of reputation it had had while Joseph Stone was in charge. She began her campaign with visits to Sheffield, one of the places nearer to home that had suffered wartime bombardment.

There certainly was scope for redevelopment, and much of it where traditional styling would be more appropriate than anything modern. While she still had no one qualified in the office, she couldn't spend too long over each trip to Sheffield. She could find out what new building was required, though, and also widened her understanding of the area in long conversations with her sister.

Marian, despite the hazards from enemy bombing, had enjoyed her stay driving ambulances there. 'I'd love to see parts of it rebuilt by you, Helen,' she said, surprising her. 'You'd not choose stuff that would clash with what's there already.'

Helen smiled. She'd needed someone to understand her aims. 'Thanks. Eh, Marian — there's that much I long to get involved with. If I'd somebody experienced to leave in charge I'd be off all over the north, sniffing out where reconstruction should be done. Liverpool suffered very badly in the war, then there's Hull an' all.'

Since Ophelia Hadgraft had put money into Stone's Helen had been hoping she'd be justified in taking another architect into the firm, but here she was, still waiting and hoping, and being confronted by warnings from her accountant whenever she tried to expand further. Meanwhile, most of her work was confined to plans for housing. All she could do was remind herself how vital this was, and that when completed to her designs the homes produced were pleasing.

Autumn turned to winter, bringing biting winds that scoured hilltops and moors and tore through steep streets, until everyone felt that going out at all was a battle. Despite her resolve, Helen began to believe that a battle was the nearest description of the whole of her life. When she wasn't wearing herself out at work she was struggling to keep that massive house warm, and to survive Neil's moods.

It was mostly to try and make him feel happier that she became determined to provide a Christmas that was as good as possible. Last year, being the first after Alexander's death, she'd arranged hardly anything. Somehow, she would make up for that.

One Saturday early in December she and Neil arrived home from shopping feeling quite happy. He had been interested in plans for Christmas and in the items they were buying, and had behaved extremely well, reassuring Helen. Mrs Hartley greeted them in the hall with the news that there had been a telephone call.

'From that Italian – Mr Fabri,' she said. 'I told him you would be at home this evening, I hope that's all right?'

Helen spent the intervening hours trying to quell her excitement. Surely the fact that Vittore had phoned meant that he'd either remained in England or had returned here? He wouldn't be telephoning all the way from Italy.

I might be proper daft, she thought, but I do want to see him again. And I'd love more than anything to have him working with me.

When the call came, Vittore made no such promises, but he did say he had a lot to discuss with her. 'I was wondering if it might be convenient for you if I visited Yorkshire next weekend?'

Helen wouldn't have believed that a week could drag so heavily even though she was so busy in the office. Finally awakening on the Saturday morning, she felt drained by days of enduring her own impatience. She had never been like this before. But then, of course, she'd never had to wait to see somebody she'd grown found of.

Vittore arrived a few hours later, stepping from his taxi and gazing up at The Stone House affectionately and with an expert's approval in his dark eyes. Watching from an upstairs window, Helen smiled to herself. It might have been confirmation, had she needed any, of how their tastes converged.

She only hoped his taste in fashion would appreciate her New Look style. She was feeling self-conscious in a dress that she'd originally bought for Christmas but couldn't resist wearing today. In a soft wool that hung in unpressed pleats from a nipped-in waistline, its bodice fitted beautifully but seemed to emphasise her breasts, a factor enhanced by the curving V neckline. The long sleeves felt good, though, after years of Utility skimpiness, as did the mid-calf skirt. And she loved the material, a wedgwood shade that reflected a tinge of blue into her grey eyes.

Running down the elegant staircase, she was in the hall by the time Mrs Hartley had opened the door to him. Neil, however, had beaten her to it. Hurling himself at Vittore, he was lifted clear of the ground in an energetic hug.

Helen felt her throat tighten, and tears stung her eyes. But then Vittore was transferring the boy to one arm and extending the other for her. Holding her against him, he kissed her full on the lips, then kissed Neil also before setting him down.

'I feel as if I have returned home,' Vittore declared, beaming at the three of them as he turned slightly and greeted Mrs Hartley, 'Did I say hallo when you opened the door to me? You must forgive if my excitement took away my courtesy.'

Vittore appeared even fitter than on his previous visit, and was wearing a beautifully tailored suit in a creamy-coloured cloth that no one in the West Riding would have considered practical.

I can't stop myself wanting him here, thought Helen, regardless of all my resolutions. And I've only to look at Neil to know how much he likes his Uncle Vittore.

The rest of the day passed in a sort of daze. Helen was so elated that she'd lost all her customary steadiness. And Neil, bless him, was angelic, remaining surprisingly quiet while she and Vittore were talking, but cooperating with spirit when invited to show what he'd been doing during the past few weeks.

By Sunday evening Helen was growing accustomed to having Vittore around again, and was relishing his company. Early that morning they had walked uphill from the house and strolled along the ridge, glancing occasionally across the valley where frost had rimed bare branches and coated the dark stone walls like fine sugar.

'I love your Yorkshire,' he had told her, his breath frosting too in air that stung their faces.

That evening she wasn't surprised when he announced his firm plans to settle here. 'I've managed to secure permission,' he confided. 'Do not ask me how. I had to persuade someone to pull a few strings. I have also got most of my capital liquidised — and away from Italy. I am serious, Helen, about wishing to join Stone's, if you would consider having me.'

She beamed at him. 'I think you know already that I'd love that. But you'll have to understand that I can't just leap into such an important decision instantly. I'll speak to my accountant, soon as I can, then you and me can talk again, sort out details.'

In the meantime, she asked him to extend his stay. 'If you want to, you could stop with us till after Christmas. That would certainly suit Neil.'

'And you?' he asked quietly.

'And me an' all.'

'I should like to make up to you, Helen, for all the loneliness you have endured since your husband's accident.'

She could well believe that Vittore was capable of doing just that. He had been important to her for such a long time now. Having him back in her life felt as good as recovering after an extended bout of sickness.

On Christmas Eve Vittore startled her by suggesting that they should attend mass at midnight.

'I wouldn't mind,' she said, 'but I'm not Catholic, you know. I couldn't even tell you about the services in their church.'

'No matter. We would attend an English service. I should like that very much.'

The tiny church was almost full. They sat in a pew near the back and Helen felt the calm seeping into her. Decorated for Christmas and full of such a different atmosphere, she could hardly believe that it was the place where the funerals of both Alexander and his

347

father had begun. Despite the large number of people present she was deeply conscious of a strange quiet that had nothing to do with silence. Indeed, the music was glorious, from the full-throated singing of Christmas hymns to the fervent intoning of the rector, all perfectly tuneful.

I wish I'd come to services here before, she thought, aching to belong. I wonder why I've always felt I was merely on the edge of worship, not quite participating?

Glancing sideways at Vittore, she sensed that although the doctrine was different from his own, he was quite at home here.

When they went out into the crisp night air to walk the short distance to the house he took her hand.

'Happy Christmas,' he said, and added, 'thank you.'

They drank hot coffee and ate mince pies left out for them by Mrs Hartley before going to their rooms. During this visit Vittore had avoided any hint that he wished to make love to her. But Helen often read in his glance a longing which echoed her own. Sitting like this in her home, she could believe that the time would come when her restraint would give way.

She was awakened on Christmas morning by Neil rushing into her room with some of his toys.

'Look, Mummy, look what Father Christmas has brought. And this one's special,' he declared, showing her a magnificent model aeroplane. 'This is what Uncle Vittore asked him to bring.'

'He's very kind. You must be sure and thank him.'

'I said thank you already.'

Helen glanced at the clock. It was a quarter to seven. 'You didn't go into his room? Do you know that your uncle and I went to church last night — and didn't get home until after one o'clock!'

Vittore, however, was showing no signs of lacking

sleep. He was dressed in dark slacks and an elegant sweater, and talking with Mrs Hartley when Helen went down to the dining room. And maybe their rising early was for the best, she thought wryly. She had invited all her family over for Christmas dinner.

Asking them all to her was taking a chance. She couldn't be sure how they would get on with Vittore, and was also afraid that Marian, at least, would begin making five out of two and two.

Helen soon discovered, anyway, that her parents appreciated her sparing her mother the work of entertaining the whole family. And Denis, who had visited Italy with ENSA during the war, soon began talking animatedly with Vittore.

Having Mrs Hartley to attend to the actual meal was a great boon, freeing Helen to relax and chat with her guests.

Neil and his cousins were allowed to wrap up warm and romp in the garden just before dinner, an idea that paid dividends when they came in healthily hungry and with enough energy expended to give everyone a trouble-free meal.

During the late afternoon while the children were absorbed in a jigsaw puzzle, leaving the adults free to talk, Helen glanced towards Vittore.

Sitting on one of the sofas drawn up to the hearth in her large reception room, his smile was enhanced by the glow from the fire. His eyes, darker than ever in here, seemed to smile as much as his lips, and every line of his body looked perfectly at ease.

He appears to fit in so well here, Helen thought, smiling also to herself. There had been no awkwardness with any of her family – and his generosity to Neil was evidence of his affection for her son.

There had been a gift for Helen herself – one that

349

had taken her back to another Christmas. This time, the model he had given her was of St Peter's in Rome. She had been delighted to display them both on a side table in the dining room.

Marian had teased, as Helen had expected, while they were helping Mrs Hartley to clear the dirty dishes into the kitchen. But if she hadn't accepted Helen's explanation that Vittore was simply to become involved as a business partner, she had certainly ceased her questions about the relationship. Helen realised now that although she wouldn't wish to hurry through any part of this Christmas she would be glad to see her accountant afterwards and begin drawing up the deal to finalise their plans.

'You can't mean that!' Helen exclaimed, terribly disappointed. She had spent half the morning with Mr Thorpe, explaining how much Vittore was willing to invest in Stone's and how his expertise as an architect was just what she had been seeking. And here her accountant was, cautioning her against permitting another person to take a financial interest in the firm!

'I'm sorry, but I cannot think such a deal would be to your long-term advantage, Mrs Stone.'

'But whyever not?' Helen persisted. 'Haven't you been telling me for ages that we can't expand as things are? That we need more money behind us?'

'Ah, but there is a difference, you see,' Mr Thorpe persisted. 'I was thinking in terms of funds which were by way of being a ploughing back of your profits. If you let someone else in now you're leaving yourself wide open to difficulties in the future.'

'I don't see how.'

'Oh come, Mrs Stone, you're not that naive. You're already in a position where the Honourable Ophelia Hadgraft has a considerable say if it comes to

drawing plans, even for relatively mundane houses, while she set off farther afield, viewing potential development sites and eventually organising surveys for one or two projects which she succeeded in securing.

Vittore's evident rapport with Ophelia, which initially had caused Helen such surprise, was proving useful when the three of them met for formal business discussions. Helen was learning that Ophelia possessed a certain amount of understanding of what architecture involved, therefore they rarely wasted much time when discussing this side of running Stone's. For the first time since her father-in-law's death Helen began feeling happier about the way things were heading.

In her private life, too, she was reasonably content. She would have enjoyed seeing more of Vittore, but he did spend several weekends at The Stone House, and his relationship with Neil definitely seemed to be bringing out the best in the boy.

When the chilly West Riding spring developed into full summer and she could relish wearing lighter clothes and feeling the sun on her head while she was visiting sites, Helen believed that this, at last, might be the beginning of better times. She had struggled for so many years simply to do the work that she had wanted ever since she was a girl of fifteen. Now she was going to enjoy every minute of it.

She had been over to Sheffield on the day that she got home rather later than usual and found Marian sitting in the entrance hall, holding her throat and very clearly anxious to go home.

'Are you all right?' Helen asked straight away.

'I do feel a bit off colour,' her sister told her. 'I've had a sore throat for days. All of a sudden it's a lot worse and my neck's very stiff.'

'Eh, dear — I am sorry, love. And I'll bet Neil's led you a dance an' all. He generally does.' Even on a good day he possessed lots of surplus energy. Helen felt Marian's forehead which seemed to burn beneath her fingers.

'He's not been too bad. He's played out a lot. I've just left him having his tea now.'

'Good, thanks. Well, I hope you're soon feeling better, love. If you're not all right tomorrow you must stop at home. Mrs Hartley will keep an eye on Neil while I'm in the office. And I could always pop home at dinnertime.'

Although Helen was naturally concerned because Marian was unwell, she wasn't particularly alarmed. Yorkshire folk, however tough in constitution, were often plagued by the colds which flourished among the smoke of their chilly and frequently damp hills and valleys.

Hearing their mother's voice on the telephone the following morning, Helen immediately expected a message confirming that Marian was no better.

But Kathleen Clegg sounded as if she had been crying. 'It's our Marian, she's ever so poorly. Denis asked me to go and sit with her last night so he could get to the theatre.'

'She certainly wasn't so good when she left here,' said Helen. 'Is it 'flu she's got?'

'Eh, I wish to goodness that were all! I had to call the doctor to her late last night and whatever do you think? It's infantile paralysis . . .'

'Polio? No! Oh, heavens! I am sorry . . . How bad is she?'

'Well, the doctor was afraid for her breathing, evidently that can be affected. But he thought it was just her sore throat making that difficult. No, it's her legs — before I got her to bed she'd nearly lost the use

356

in them. Oh, Helen, I do hope she's not going to end up crippled!'

'So do I. But it's early days yet — we'll just have to hope the doctors can do summat for her. What about Linda and Mark, are they okay?'

'Up to now. The doctor's told us to keep them at home from school, of course, in case they might pass it on.'

God, thought Helen, that means Neil might have caught it already. But she mustn't think only of him just now. 'Are you there now, Mum, at Marian's?'

'Aye, I stopped here last night while Denis got home after the performance, then came straight round again this morning.'

'Are you coping all right? Do you want me to come over?'

'No, love, you mustn't bother. You have your work, and Neil to look after. I was wondering how you'd manage . . . if I ought to come on there?'

'No, Mum. I'll cope, thanks. You've enough on without that. Mrs Hartley will keep an eye on him. But shouldn't I . . .?'

'Marian's asleep now, the doctor gave her summat. And Denis is here an' all. You go to your work, love, we'll see you later on.'

Helen went straight to Neil's room where he was struggling to dress. He had his little underpants on back to front, and his vest was hanging outside them.

'Come here, love,' she said, and hugged him to her before even thinking of sorting out his clothes.

'You're squeezing too tight, Mummy, you're hurting!'

'Sorry, Neil, sorry . . .'

'What's happened, Mummy — don't cry.' He couldn't understand the distress in her eyes, nor the tears appearing in their corners. Mummies didn't cry, did they? That was babyish.

'It's your Auntie Marian, she's very poorly. She won't be able to look after you today.' And, she realised appalled, might never do so again.

When Helen had made the necessary arrangements with Mrs Hartley and finally set out for the office, she felt utterly shattered. On top of all the worry about her sister and anxiety in case Neil had picked up polio from her, was this deep concern about who would look after Neil in the future. For the time being, however, she would have to shelve that particular problem and work out how soon she could get over to see Marian.

The minute she walked into the office Wendy gave her a searching look. 'Whatever is wrong, Mrs Stone?'

'It's my sister, I'm afraid.'

'The one that looks after Neil?'

'Marian, aye. She's been taken ill. The doctor says it's polio.'

Wendy was commiserating with her when Vittore came out of his office. He too asked what was wrong, and crossed swiftly to put an arm about her shoulders. When he heard what the trouble was he sympathised at once.

'You must be wishing to be with her,' he added. 'Why do you not go there now? I can attend to everything here.'

'Thanks,' she said. 'But Denis is at home during the day, and my mother's there an' all. It'll be more use if I can go this evening while Denis is at the theatre.'

'Would it help if I sit with Neil then tonight?'

'Would you, Vittore? I'd be ever so grateful. Mrs Hartley will be tired out after having him all day.'

'I can arrange to stay the night, if you wish. That would mean you need not rush back from your sister's home.'

358

Marian was flushed still with her illness and didn't look as bad as Helen had expected. In fact, in her best lace-edged nightdress and negligee, she appeared delicate and rather beautiful. And because the doctor had prescribed something to ease her throat, she wasn't in as much discomfort as the previous day.

'Is Neil all right?' she asked almost as soon as Helen walked into the bedroom. 'I'll never forgive myself if he catches this as well.'

'He's fine so far, love, don't go worrying. And it's nothing you can help. It's not the sort of thing you go looking for.'

'You can say that again! It's a right bugger, Helen!' Marian's blue eyes were awash with tears. 'I can't move my left leg at all, you know. And the other one's not much better. I've tried not to show how upset I am in front of Mum, but I'm scared stiff I'll never be any different. Whatever am I going to do, Helen?'

She forced a smile on to her lips. 'You're going to stop worriting like this, that's what. They've only just started treating you, haven't they, love? And they can do a lot more these days than they could a few years ago,' she added, hoping with all her heart that this was true.

'Denis will go off me if I have to spend the rest of my life in a wheelchair, I know he will.'

'That's nonsense, Marian, and you know it is. You've got a champion husband who'll always cherish you, through thick and thin.'

'Cherish? Denis?'

'Isn't that what you've done for each other, all these years? You've made a right good home together and you've got two smashing kids.'

'That's another thing – I want to be with Linda and Mark while they're growing up. I couldn't bear to be stuck here in bed, or even only able to get about in the house.'

'You won't have to be like that. We'll see something's done. We're not going to let you end up in a bad way.'

Later, though, driving home, Helen was forced to admit that there didn't seem any kind of certainty that Marian would be cured. From what the doctor had told Kathleen Clegg, there was very little in the way of an acceptable treatment for poliomyelitis. And being told that the medical profession insisted that prevention was the answer did nothing to help them.

In her concern for Marian, Helen had virtually forgotten that Vittore was taking charge of things at The Stone House. Finding him walking towards her as she almost stumbled with exhaustion through the front door was a massive relief.

'Helen!' he exclaimed, rushing the last few paces to support her. 'Do not tell me you also are ill?'

She managed a weary grin as she shook her head. 'No, I'm just dead beat. Remember how we used to be after a hard day on the farm? But Neil — is he still all right?'

'If insisting on a game of Indians and Cowboys throughout your garden is "all right", that is what he is!'

'Thank goodness for that. Let's hope he stays that way. I meant to ask what the incubation period was, but I was so upset about our Marian, I didn't think.'

'Come and sit down. I sent Mrs Hartley off to her bed. The poor lady was quite exhausted.'

'I'm not surprised, coping with his lordship all day.'

'You certainly have one very active son.'

'Our Marian used to be the active one of us two,' Helen remarked sadly, and suddenly she was weeping. 'She was that *still* tonight. Propped up on the pillows, and hardly able to move except just her arms when she wanted something off the bedside table. I don't think I'll be able to bear it either if she doesn't get better.'

'Do not distress yourself, Helen, not yet. We can only hope and pray that she will improve in time.'

Pray? she thought, unable to believe that would do any good, unable to believe in anything.

'What's she ever done to deserve this, that's what I want to know?' she demanded fiercely, tears pouring down her cheeks. 'Look how she's helped with Neil. She'd do anything for me and him. This is so unfair.'

Vittore led her to the sofa and held her to him while she wept out a lot of the strain and distress. Eventually, he gave her brandy to drink then took her protectively by the arm and encouraged her to go upstairs to her room.

'I am here, do not forget,' he told her.

'Thank goodness you are, Vittore. I'd never have got through this day without you.'

'Sleep well, *cara*, try not to worry. You must give priority to your sister now. I shall take over more responsibility from you in the office.'

Chapter 18

As their days continued to be darkened by Marian's illness, Helen found she was thankful to be able to lean on Vittore for assistance. And he wasn't the only person concerned for her. When Ophelia Hadgraft next visited Stone's she was full of compassion.

'I didn't know she'd heard about Marian,' Helen remarked to Vittore afterwards.

'I suppose you must have mentioned it while you were so distressed. You probably don't remember,' he said.

Helen didn't reply. Although as disturbed as he'd supposed, she remained certain that she had said nothing about Marian to Ophelia. None of this really mattered, though it did increase an uneasy feeling that was developing at the back of her mind. Ridiculous though it seemed when Vittore couldn't have been more helpful, she often felt that there was some undercurrent which she ought to mistrust.

Life was too complex for delving into mere suspicions, however. Just getting through each week was requiring considerable planning. Between them, Kathleen Clegg and Mrs Hartley were minding Neil, enabling Helen to work. She herself wasn't happy about her mother taking on this additional responsibility while still assisting where she could in Marian's home, but for the present there seemed no alternative.

It was Marian who had insisted that Helen shouldn't make more permanent arrangements over caring for the boy, and none of them wanted to shatter her belief that she would eventually recover sufficiently to resume her original role.

Medical opinion was less specific about her future. The rest which had been prescribed appeared to have eased some of her debility, but only to a degree where she was able, with the aid of crutches, to get to and from the bathroom. The leg most gravely affected seemed to have regained only a fraction of its previous mobility.

The only good thing was that Marian herself got over her depression.

Nevertheless Helen could hardly face her frequent visits to her sister. Seeing Marian like that brought back so many memories of how energetic she'd always been. And Denis had confessed to his father-in-law that he was hard put to avoid breaking down in front of her sometimes. He wasn't sorry that an actor was trained to analyse emotions instead of giving in to them.

'I know, I know,' Daniel Clegg had said while he and Denis sat downstairs, leaving Helen and her mother with Marian. 'I feel the same.'

'I feel quite guilty being glad when it's time to set off to the theatre. Don't get me wrong — I love her just as much as ever . . .'

'I can see that, Denis, we all can. Nobody could be more devoted.'

'It hurts for her sake, you see — noticing all that she's missing with the children. And it isn't enough, just being thankful that my hours mean I can do more for Linda and Mark than if I had a nine-to-five job.'

'Aye, it's a bad do,' said Daniel, shaking his head. 'They've been good though, those two, haven't they? I gather they've started being very helpful.' The fact remained, however, that the whole family was hurt by seeing Marian stricken by such a serious illness.

There were times when Helen felt like letting everything slide simply to spend more time with her sister. The days Marian had passed at The Stone House looking after Neil had drawn them closer than ever in their lives before. Now Helen wanted to give a bit back, yet felt torn in three directions, especially with Neil needing her more because most of his time was spent with a couple of elderly women. And how could she neglect the architectural practice?

Vittore seemed to expect that she would do so. Helen had lost count of the number of occasions that he had urged her to take more time off. She wondered if the Italian devotion to family was responsible for his supposition that she would relinquish some of her duties at Stone's. Certainly, he seemed unable to understand that no matter how torn – or how tired – it wasn't in her nature to slacken her grasp on the reins.

Now that they were into the latter half of 1950 it looked to Helen as if they were at last on the verge of having more scope for exercising imaginative architecture. Indeed, had they been fortunate enough to be sited in the south of England, they could already have been engaged in designing part of one of the new towns. Stevenage had been followed by Harlow and Crawley, and others were on the way. Even though the modernity of some of these schemes wasn't to Helen's taste, she'd have been glad of the opportunity to participate in something so exciting. Secretly, she liked to think that she might have been able to influence the developers with more classical styling.

As it was, she contented herself with designs for reconstruction of buildings in those northern cities which had suffered bomb damage. And the days spent on site there were really as much as she wished to spend out of the office. It was *her* architectural practice, after all, and fond though she was of Vittore she wasn't going to leave him in charge there for extended periods.

She had been perturbed recently when Wendy told her that Vittore always took over her desk whenever she was out for the day.

'Have you told him to occupy your office when you're not in, Mrs Stone? I know it's not really owt to do with me, but I thought you ought to know what's going on.'

Helen had smiled, making light of the issue. If there was a certain amount of antagonism between Wendy and Vittore she didn't want to fuel it. 'I've nothing to hide there, Wendy, so I don't think you need to worry. And he does have all my papers to hand if he gets any queries.'

The day that Helen herself began to wonder if Vittore did cherish unvoiced ambitions she had been over to Liverpool.

She was already feeling rather dejected as she drove back again; the meeting with a potential client had been so unpromising that she was afraid that Stone's wouldn't be invited to submit drawings. He had been a blunt man who didn't trouble to disguise his assumption that a female architect would be below par.

She had also promised to go over and see Marian that evening, a visit which she'd postponed from the weekend when she was suffering from a heavy cold. Risking passing on any infection to Marian must be avoided. And now she was watching the time. Her call in at the office would have to be brief if she was to see much of Neil before a hasty meal and the journey to Halifax.

Helen was astonished when she found Ophelia Hadgraft's car parked outside Stone's. Some additional sense made her enter quietly. When she saw that the door of her own office was closed and then heard the murmur of conversation from beyond its panels, she greeted Wendy with a smile and a nod before crossing swiftly to open the door.

'Don't worry, she doesn't need to know,' Vittore was saying to Ophelia. 'If the worst happens, I can handle it. I'll see she agrees . . .'

The pair of them started simultaneously, and swung round to face the door.

'Hallo,' said Helen evenly, and added that she hadn't expected to see Ophelia.

The older woman's face coloured, an unusual reaction in someone of her sophistication.

'Ophelia was passing and called in, that is all,' Vittore announced, a shade too quickly.

Helen knew he was lying and, whilst she couldn't even guess why he should have cause to do so, that fact together with what she'd overheard made her decide to force the issue.

'It's time the three of us arranged another meeting, anyway,' she announced, pleased that she at least sounded calm. She watched each of the other two control the urge to exchange a glance. 'We're beginning to make a healthier profit,' she continued steadily. 'We've got to ensure that we build on that by not letting opportunities evade us.'

'Naturally,' said Ophelia, forcing a smile. 'And I'm sure that Vittore here is the man to give you all the back-up you require.'

Helen smiled back at her. 'You don't need to tell me that. Don't forget how long I've known him.'

Even if I'm starting to wonder if I don't know him thoroughly enough, she thought, and felt an enormous ache of foreboding and disappointment filling her heart.

The meeting they arranged for a week later passed off very smoothly, yet Helen was left with the feeling that it had all been a shade *too* smooth. Could it be that both Ophelia and Vittore were exerting every effort to maintain a false equilibrium at Stone's for some purpose of their own? It almost felt to her as though they were holding their breath in anticipation of . . . of what, she really could not imagine. And nor could she, for the life of her, see what they might hope to gain by anything covert.

Away from work, Vittore seemed as friendly as ever, when she and Neil saw him — which, these days, was rather less frequently. He appeared to enjoy keeping his personal life to himself; for instance, he'd never told her where exactly he was living, and certainly hadn't invited her there. It seemed odd when she reflected on how he had stayed in her home.

Helen began seriously to doubt his loyalty on the day when she was remaining in the office while he was travelling to Todmorden to survey the site of a house for an influential local businessman.

'Take my car, if you like,' she told him on the previous day. 'You needn't set out before I arrive at the office, and you'll be back before I'm ready for home.'

Vittore declined with a smile. 'I am afraid I cannot do that. I have no licence to drive in England. I thought of ordering a taxi.'

'That'll cost a packet. There's a very good bus service which stops close to the site. There's a timetable somewhere about the office, and I'll give you directions.'

Helen could see that didn't please, but was determined not to relent. Before having her own car, she had found public transport quite adequate. Stone's might be better off financially, these days, but was not yet in a position to throw money around.

Am I being hard? she wondered during the following day while Vittore was out, and then something Wendy said made her steel herself against softening.

'Mrs Stone,' she began while she was taking dictation in Helen's office, 'I hope you don't think I'm turning into a spy, but I can't help noticing that Mr Fabri is spending a lot of time talking on the phone to the Honourable Ophelia Hadgraft. I — well, just thought you ought to know, that's all. Happen there's nothing in it. Did they know each other before?'

'No, of course they didn't,' said Helen hastily. 'I introduced them.' Suddenly, though, her mind resurrected the scene of that introduction, and the prolonged greeting between Ophelia and Vittore which hadn't appeared very natural. 'I'm sure there is some perfectly ordinary explanation of these phone calls,' she added, and reflected that she herself was dissembling now.

Helen was too busy catching up on a backlog of deskwork to pay much heed to Wendy's information. When, during the afternoon, an agitated phone call from Mrs Hartley brought the news that Neil had fallen from a wall in the garden, hitting his head, everything else was driven from her mind.

Telling Wendy that she was popping home to check if Neil needed a visit from the doctor, she dashed out of the office to her car.

Neil seemed chirpy enough now he was over the shock of his fall, but Helen played safe and called the doctor in. After checking the boy thoroughly and reporting he was ninety-nine per cent certain there was no real damage, the doctor suggested a few hours' rest for him.

'You look as if a rest wouldn't come amiss for yourself either, Mrs Stone.'

She laughed. 'I'm fine, Doctor, honestly. I do have to keep going, but that's the way I like my life.'

'Not too many gaps that way, since you were widowed, eh?'

Helen agreed. 'And even before then I was never one for sitting around doing nothing.'

That surely still applied today, and once Neil was settled in his room with Mrs Hartley hovering, her ears alert, Helen decided to return to the office.

Waiting for a gap in the traffic enabling her to drive out on to the main road Helen was staggered to see Ophelia's car again, and even more staggered to recognise Vittore Fabri in the passenger seat.

This can't be coincidence, she thought. It just isn't likely that she would turn up over there by chance and give him a lift.

This time, she resolved, I shall get to the bottom of what's going on. All the way back to the office she was steeling herself to demand an answer to the questions mounting inside her.

Other cars had come along after Ophelia's, preventing Helen following immediately behind them, but they were still in sight when she approached Ludden-den Foot. The surprise came when she watched Ophelia continue along the main road rather than turning right for Stone's office.

So he's not even putting in a full day's work! she thought angrily. And grew angrier still as she realised this meant postponing her own questions.

By the next morning she couldn't wait a moment longer, and tackled Vittore as soon as he walked into the office.

'You didn't think it necessary to report back here yesterday after your visit to Todmorden then?'

'It was too late, I'm afraid. Trouble with the buses.'

'It was approximately three-thirty when you were passing through Brearley. And if that was a bus, it was a very splendid affair – and with Ophelia Hadgraft at the wheel.'

Vittore paled before a flush crept upwards from his immaculate shirt collar. 'But I did not see . . . where were you?'

'Just leaving the house. Neil had had a nasty fall.'

'Neil? Oh, I am sorry. How serious?' he began, but his eyes were veiled and the enquiry sounded automatic rather than concerned.

'Not very, fortunately. But I'd been home to call the doctor in to see him. That is why I wasn't where you expected,' she added sharply.

'There is nothing to cause you annoyance. Ophelia merely happened to be returning in the same direction.'

'Very convenient. Or it would be if I believed you. It's time you came clean, Vittore.'

'Came clean?' he enquired, feigning bewilderment.

'Told me the whole story,' she snapped. 'Like what's going on between you and Ophelia Hadgraft.'

Vittore stiffened, alarmed. How much did Helen know of what had happened months ago, while his wish to avoid Alexander Stone was preventing him from contacting her? Had she discovered that he had written from Italy to the man who had been so impressed by his command of English during the war? Colin Hadgraft.

Hoping that Hadgraft might provide useful introductions, he had been shaken at first to learn of his death. But the man's sister had written back in such genial terms that he had asked her for advice on the situation over here, including any information as to how Stone's was progressing. With Ophelia's second reply, Vittore had begun to believe his luck was turning.

The news was that Helen, now alone in the firm, was making a name for herself, to such an extent that Ophelia's investigations had prompted her to invest capital in Stone's. With Ophelia as an ally, and his own influence over Helen already established, he had believed there would be no boundaries to his future here.

He could not relinquish all that; he must bluster this out or risk being finished.

'What do you mean? You cannot be objecting to my being acquainted with her — she is a shareholder in Stone's. You yourself chose her.'

'And you seem to have become very friendly with her in a short space of time. Unless — *did* you know her before you joined the firm, Vittore?'

He was staring at her now, the dark eyes glittering with ill-contained fury. Helen guessed this was because of her having spotted some connivance, but his response gave her no more than a clue that she was correct.

'What right have you to question my friendships?' His voice was rising. 'If I knew Ophelia already, that is my concern, not yours.'

'And you did, didn't you?' Helen said, wondering what else he had been keeping from her since returning to England, and for what motive.

'We were already acquainted yes,' Vittore admitted at last.

'Did she tell you about Stone's?'

'Do not be stupid, Helen. You were the one who told me, years ago at the farm.'

'I don't mean that. Did she inform you that I was on

my own here, badly in need of capital?'

'I wanted to work with you, and I brought in money that you needed, isn't that sufficient?'

'Not when you're concealing things from me. Even though I don't understand your purpose in doing so. I can't work like that, Vittore,' she told him earnestly. 'What made you come back to Yorkshire? What made you choose Stone's?'

'I have told you, yours is the sort of practice where I wish to work. *Mama mia*, I have put capital into the firm, not taken money out! I cannot understand why you are creating such a scene.'

His mentioning the money for a second time in as many minutes distressed her, and made her more determined still to have the truth. 'Can't you? I should have thought that was obvious. You're making me wonder what is happening within my own practice.'

'How like a woman! This is business, Helen, you cannot logically expect to know all the details of everything.'

'When it affects the way that business is run, I can. And you had better believe me.'

'Have I been neglectful of my work? Have I ever? I tell you what is wrong, you are jealous of my private relationships. Have I no right to any life away from you?'

'This has no connection with your private life at all,' Helen stated icily. But she was already beginning to fear that the personal relationship once existing between them, and now displaced, was quite a factor in her distress.

The argument simmered to an uneasy halt, but only so that they might achieve some work that day. Much later, on her way home that evening, Helen began to understand how deeply she was wounded by Vittore's apparent deception of her. And to whom could she turn? She had scorned her accountant's advice when taking Vittore into Stone's, he would hardly sympathise now that she was perturbed.

The only good thing that day was the fact that Neil was his usual self, no worse for the fall, and full of all the things he'd been doing. He often seemed by now to be well able to amuse himself, although Helen was counting the weeks until he would be old enough for school. He would benefit from the stimulation of other children's company as well as the teachers'.

The necessity to put in a full day's work got them through the rest of the week at the office, and by the following Monday the atmosphere appeared to have returned to normal. Nothing in Vittore's attitude conveyed to Helen either resentment or the possibility that he might not be wholly loyal to her. And, these days, they seemed at last to be getting enough of the kind of work which was satisfying as well as made them a profit. Helen was thankful for a sort of truce between herself and Vittore; she couldn't afford to divide her attention when it still ought to be focused entirely on restoring Stone's to its pre-war success.

There was the Fenella March bursary also. For too many years Helen had been obliged to ignore her promise to put back the amount of money which had enabled her to study. Old Mr March was frail, but still hanging on to life. Although his other daughter had survived Nazi internment and had returned to live in Harrogate, he was always glad to see Helen who visited him whenever her commitments allowed. Her dearest wish now was to restore that bursary to its full amount while Mr March was alive to meet the next recipient.

By Christmas 1950 Marian had recovered sufficiently

to be able to get about her own home and, with the aid of a stick, to reach her local shops. Helen had invited her and Denis and the children to The Stone House where her parents would be joining them for Christmas Day. Kathleen Stone had declined the offer of a longer stay there.

'We need a bit of quiet on our own, these days,' she had explained. 'We're not getting any younger.'

Helen had nodded. She had been saddened to notice how the worry concerning Marian, to say nothing of the additional work, had aged their mother. And Daniel Clegg, never an ebullient man, often gave the impression of being weary.

'We love to see the kiddies full of energy, you know,' Kathleen had added. 'But we can only take all that noise and bounding around in small doses.'

When the time came, Helen wondered where her mother had gained the impression that any of the children would be exuberant. Both Linda and Mark had grown up a lot during their mother's illness and still were touchingly attentive to her.

'They really are a couple of loves, aren't they?' Marian exclaimed to her sister when Mark had offered her his arm as they came up the front steps of The Stone House, and Linda insisted on finding for her mother the most comfortable chair in the large reception room. They continued considerate throughout the stay, offering to fetch and carry, and playing quietly with the puzzles and games which they'd been given as presents.

For a four-year-old Neil was quiet also, but was disturbing Helen by reverting to his old uncongenial mood. He had demanded to be told why his Uncle Vittore wasn't there, not a question which she relished answering.

She hadn't expected that her terse reply that Vittore

hadn't been invited would satisfy, and it certainly didn't.

Neil's lip puckered as if he was going to cry, but what emerged was a massive wail of protest. 'You've told *him* now that we don't want him here, haven't you?' he accused her, his expression as well as his tone so reminiscent of his father that Helen itched to slap him.

'I haven't, Neil,' she replied through clenched teeth, the hands at her side equally tense. 'But you will have to accept that he has other friends, and isn't going to spend all his spare time with us.'

'But he likes me, I know he does,' her son insisted. 'It's only you that's nasty to him.'

Helen turned away. She hadn't needed any reminder of Vittore's absence, nor of the reason behind it. Ever since she had first begun to examine his behaviour regarding Stone's she had been compelled to question his motives in everything that had occurred since his return to Yorkshire. What of his apparent affection for her, his kisses, the warm embraces? Had they all been contrived towards the one end — that of having her accept him readily, not only as an architect with her firm but also a shareholder? Had even his attitude towards Neil been calculated as a way of ingratiating himself with her?

At any other time, she'd have found such possibilities cruel. At Christmas, with every corner of her home resurrecting memories of his being here a year ago, they felt unbearable.

For Marian's sake, however, Helen willed herself to set aside this ache that seemed to eat right through her. Her sister, Denis and the family were only just emerging from their own great anxiety. It was up to her now to ensure that they enjoyed the festivities.

Marian wasn't blind, though, and soon saw that Helen was far from happy.

'You've given us a lovely time, bless you,' she said on Boxing Day, 'but I'll be hanged if you look to be enjoying yourself. Is it because of Vittore? He's conspicuous by his absence.'

'Aye, it's him,' Helen admitted now that she was alone with her sister. 'Though not just because he isn't here. I don't mind you knowing that I think he's up to something to do with the firm.'

'To do with Stone's? Nay, he'd never! He's got money tied up in it now, hasn't he?'

'He has that, and I'm almost beginning to wish he hadn't.' She told her sister she felt sure that Vittore wasn't being straight with her. 'There's nowt much that I can put my finger on, a lot of it daft stuff like catching him and Ophelia Hadgraft with their heads together, but I'm sure he's up to something.'

'But what could he do — what would he want to do other than ensure that you continue to do bigger and better business?'

'Eh, I don't know, Marian, I really don't. Happen it's me that's wrong. It is mostly just this uneasy feeling.'

As soon as they were into the new year Helen's suspicions only grew stronger, yet still there was nothing concrete on which to base any further complaint against Vittore. She began arranging more frequent meetings in which the two of them and Ophelia discussed present and future projects. Her idea was that this might tighten their ship, permit fewer loopholes by which either he or Ophelia could manipulate things to her disadvantage.

If these meetings achieved this end Helen couldn't be sure, but what they did reveal was the affinity between the other two. Sometimes in an odd word or so which crept in, more frequently in glances which she intercepted, the evidence of a strong association between the pair grew steadily stronger.

As well as hurt, Helen felt rather foolish. No one enjoyed having advantage taken of them, and she felt positive this was what had been intended all along. She was also once again becoming reluctant to spend too much time out of the office. Wendy still reported anxiously that Vittore often telephoned Ophelia Hadgraft when Helen's back was turned.

She soon learned that although Vittore had lost his direct influence over her, he now had found another tack.

They were discussing the Festival of Britain. Although the style involved in much of the scheme wasn't really to her taste, Helen had once been keen to be one of the vast number of architects involved. The Dome of Discovery might not be to her liking, but from its plans it would seem to be the largest unsupported dome in the world. That, and other constructions on the site, would engage a lot of interest. Neither Vittore nor Ophelia had agreed to Stone's participating. They had given no real reason, and Helen could never see any sense in their refusal to contribute to something which would bring not only work but a considerable amount of prestige.

And then one day Wendy came to Helen with an item of correspondence. 'As you can see, it's on our headed paper, but I swear I didn't type it, Mrs Stone.'

The letter was in Vittore's name and concerned Stone's intention of becoming involved in a construction connected with the Festival of Britain.

'No wonder he didn't want me to look into the possibility of our doing this!' Helen exclaimed. *He* had already done so ages ago, and without so much as consulting her.

The meeting which Helen then called became exceedingly unpleasant. When challenged, Vittore met criticism with attack.

'I was only doing what you should have attempted years ago,' he told Helen, while Ophelia smiled across the table. 'You shouldn't be condemning me for showing enterprise.'

'I wouldn't be, if you'd consulted with me first. That would have been common courtesy as well as diplomacy. The fact that you didn't do so only reinforces my unease about your attitude here.'

'Oh, surely, Helen,' Ophelia interrupted, 'you needn't be put out? Granted, it must be galling for you that Vittore has been so much more perceptive regarding the direction Stone's should be taking, but I do think you should concede that he has our best interests at heart. After all, men are more accustomed to these matters . . .'

Ophelia got no further in this uncharacteristic observation. Springing to her feet, Helen slammed both hands down on the table. She might have been gratified by the way the other two started if she hadn't been too furious to register their reactions.

'That is just the bigoted view that I've been fighting since 1932. I'm surprised at you, Ophelia – even if I'm learning now not to be surprised when you two connive against me. But I'll have you understand, both of you, that this most certainly isn't an attitude that I permit to inhibit me.'

'But, Helen,' Vittore began quite quietly, 'there is no need for you to become angry simply because I have had a good idea. What we must do now is develop it in the best interests of Stone's.'

'Never! I don't care how much we lose by it, this scheme is not going ahead.'

'You *should* care how much we might lose. You

could at least examine it in detail,' Ophelia pointed out. 'Vittore has put in a lot of work . . .'

It was Helen's turn to interrupt again. 'And Vittore knows that he should not have done so in the first place without a word of it to me.' She faced him now. 'You could at the very least have put me in the picture when *I* was talking about the Festival.'

'What are you going to do then?' he demanded, leaning back in his chair and regarding her with all the calm of generations of Italian men who had dictated to their womenfolk. Although his voice was steady, the look in his dark eyes was anything but.

Lord, but I wish I could just sack you, thought Helen. As things stood, she could only offer to buy him out – buy the pair of them out, that's what she wanted to do. And there wasn't a hope in hell of raising the cash to do so.

She breathed in slowly to steady herself. 'All we can do is put our minds, jointly, to keeping Stone's running.' But she was going to need a lot of convincing that she could trust either Vittore or Ophelia again.

Helen couldn't let her mistrust of her fellow shareholders shackle her to the office, preventing her going out to prospective sites. There was one in particular which seemed to hold out possibilities of becoming just her kind of job. A large parish in Leeds had obtained the necessary consent for construction of a new church hall. The original building had been commandeered by the military during the war and had suffered considerable internal damage. Since then a fire had rendered the hall so unsafe that it had been demolished. It had been specified that the external appearance of the new building must harmonise with the adjacent Victorian church.

She might have been dispirited by the behaviour of

Vittore and Ophelia, but she wasn't too demoralised to know that this promised to be a scheme after her own heart. She was going all out to get it.

The site on that Monday morning looked much as Helen had imagined: at the top of a hill but surrounded by densely positioned, mostly terraced, houses. The church was medium-sized with a spire, and built of stone now darkened by a century of smoke. The newly cleared area for the church hall was to its left, at a minor junction along one of the popular routes running eastwards out of the city centre.

Helen spent several minutes standing on the opposite corner, just looking. The proportions of the church itself weren't spectacularly good, but not unpleasing either; she reckoned she'd be able to echo enough of its lines to help coordinate the new structure to be built alongside it. The Gothic windows might be echoed as well, but in a simplified form and on a larger scale. She wanted the hall to have plenty of light.

After crossing to the site itself, she began examining available space, checking with an expert eye the dimensions that had been supplied. Water, electricity, and mains drainage had, of course, been present for the original hall and this lessened the matters needing consideration. She was soon leaning against the church wall while she roughed in her first few sketches.

Ideas were coming swiftly, a sure sign that her heart was in the project. As soon as she'd completed drawings of front and side elevations, Helen turned happily to conceiving the interior. She had been given instructions that there should be one very large room to accommodate a stage and provide space for social functions. Leading off from this should be rooms of varying sizes, suitable for the different grades of Sunday School classes and for meetings of organisations such as Brownies, Guides, Scouts and so on.

The flexibility she was allowed in planning these meant that she could enjoy playing around with her ideas. Before she had spent very long on site, she was beginning to realise that the possible combinations were endless.

I wonder if I ought to ask if they have more detailed requirements? she thought, and turned to hurry towards the church in order to try and find someone. Beside its west door, she saw the noticeboard on which the vicar's name had been painted out. It was then that she remembered being told that the parish was going through an interregnum, something about the new incumbent being unwilling to leave his present curacy until his vicar there recovered after a long convalescence. It seemed there was going to be no quick answer but rather a long wait while she learned if amendments to her proposed design were to be requested by the parish council.

Helen continued forward into the church, however, wishing to get the feel of the place as well as to ascertain whether or not there might be something in its internal styling which again could be echoed in the hall.

The first thing she noticed was incense, still so heavy in the air from the previous day's services that she almost could see its mistiness about the altar. Instantly, Helen recalled Einsiedeln's Abbey church and briefly shut her eyes. Much as she was enjoying today's task, she yearned to return to the spirit of looking forward which had been so much a part of her life in those days. Now she seemed to spend most of her time fighting — if not to survive the eternal struggle at Stone's, then to preserve the house and, perhaps most of all, to rear Neil as a son of whom she could be proud.

'I don't want anything so extraordinary,' she said

aloud into the empty church. 'I only want to do a satisfying job, and find a way of being the right kind of mother to my boy.'

Grimacing ruefully and giving her head a little shake, Helen hauled herself together and began looking about. The church appeared quite spartan, severely furnished, until she neared the altar. There, a reredos carved with saints and painted mainly in red and gold provided the backdrop for a splendid gold crucifix. The altar table was dressed ceremonially in richly embroidered fabric where gold and jewel colours enhanced the thick material of a pale cream shade. The colour combination seemed to be another reminder of that very different church in Einsiedeln.

What would it be like, Helen wondered, to worship here? To spend long enough in this place to at least stand the chance of absorbing . . . *something*.

But work was beckoning again. She'd gathered little in here that would influence her decisions on details of her scheme for the hall next door. Once she arrived home, however, she would begin the serious planning. And then she could find that the very absence of firm guidelines allowed her freedom to let ideas flow. As for this church and the feelings it had aroused here, there would be other times, other visits.

Chapter 19

By the time Helen reached The Stone House that evening, she was itching to begin drawing the initial elevations for the church hall. Even calling in at the office, she had been too impatient to linger over catching up on the day's events. After signing the letters Wendy had prepared and having a brief chat with Vittore about the drawings on which he was engaged, she had been glad to run out to the car.

Neil was going through a more cooperative phase and they often shared supper while he told her about his day. Marian was coming to The Stone House again but, because of her leg, only on alternate days. This had been one of them and Neil was full of all the things they had done together.

After their meal he demanded to be shown the 'pictures' that Helen had brought home with her, so before putting him to bed she took him into the study.

'This is a large building which I am designing,' she told him. 'If the people buy my plans, you can go over to Leeds with me while it is being built. You'll be able to see it growing then.'

Sitting at the desk which Alexander and his father before him had used, Helen glanced sideways at her son. Neil's golden head was bowed in concentration, and his young face wore a half-smile of interest. She was reminded suddenly of an advertisement she had seen long ago of a lad with — was it a Meccano set? She had wished at that time for such a boy, for the opportunity to help shape his future. Would Neil follow his parents' inclinations? she wondered. She'd be happy to think of him continuing the Stone tradition.

The firm, however, seemed to have little prominence in her mind while she began on these church hall plans. Consulting the initial briefing again, she became absorbed in the requirements of that parish in Leeds, and grew so content in her work that she thought not at all of the publicity securing the commission might win for Stone's.

One aspect of the hall's use particularly interested her, and could have helped facilitate the granting of a licence to build. The parish as a whole and, evidently, the prospective new incumbent, were keen to incorporate a youth centre. From what she'd heard, they would cater for people not only of school age but those beyond who were either unemployed or for other reasons had too much time on their hands. In a city the size of Leeds, Helen could believe that would prevent many youngsters falling under bad influences.

All this, together with the ideas forming earlier that day, was running through her head while she completed elevations and began early drawing up of plans. As she continued to spend every spare moment on the project, Helen grew increasingly conscious that this, more than anything attempted in the past, was the work for which she had paid with all those long years of studying. This was *her* scheme above any other, yet she hadn't felt ready even to mention it in the office. And the night they were finished she was so eager to send off her early drawings that she used her private notepaper for the accompanying letter instead of waiting to pick up a few sheets of the firm's.

Vittore was working steadily on plans for council-built homes, and seemed remarkably quiet about his acceptance of this job which gave so little scope for his talents and ideas. Helen couldn't rid herself of the feeling that he was biding his time. The fact that she couldn't for the life of her think what he might be awaiting failed to quash this impression, even if it did leave her feeling she might be guilty now of misjudging him.

The day it all blew up began badly at home. Neil had developed a heavy cold which made him miserable and whiny. Dragging herself away from him was difficult, and certainly not helped by its not being a day for Marian to visit.

Only on the way to the office did Helen recall that she had arranged a meeting with Vittore and Ophelia for ten-thirty. Ever since their first disagreement she had dreaded each meeting as it approached. The number which had passed without altercation had done nothing to reassure her, reinforcing instead her own fear that she was becoming obsessive in her supposition that they would come to an ultimate confrontation.

Today, however, Vittore seemed his old genial self, and when she mentioned that Neil was unwell his sympathy appeared genuine. I'm being silly always looking for trouble, she thought, and was encouraged again when Ophelia came in chatting animatedly about her drive over and the late hour at which she'd left some function the previous evening.

It was that function which turned from a casual topic of conversation to the source of Helen's disquiet. It soon became evident that Vittore had attended with Ophelia, and that it had been hosted by a major local construction company. Helen could feel her eyebrows soaring. Because architects were forbidden to

387

advertise, making themselves known around was a matter of seizing every possible opportunity to publicise their work. If, as it seemed, these two had been representing Stone's, she wanted to know why – and why Vittore had evidently taken it upon himself to do so without her agreement.

'Did the invitation come to you personally?' Helen asked him, deliberately keeping her voice even.

'I know that you don't like to leave Neil of an evening,' he began steadily enough, though his dark eyes were evasive.

'Don't prevaricate with me. I believe in straight answers.'

When he didn't respond Helen rose from her seat, excused herself and went to find Wendy.

'I gather there was some kind of reception last night which Mr Fabri attended. Did the invitation come to this address?'

'Oh, yes, Mrs Stone. But Mr Fabri told me he would be attending, that it was all right because you'd said you didn't want to.'

That was enough. Helen strode through to join the others. 'A pity you chose to air where you'd been, Ophelia. If I'd been kept in the dark altogether, no one would have been any worse off. As it is, I'll remind you what I've said in the past.'

'But I was there for Stone's, we both were,' Vittore protested. 'Keeping our name before that particular construction company, seeing that we remain in line with our competitors.'

'You seem to forget that we're a team, that we should work together and not have one member excluded from *any part* of the life of the firm. Whatever do I have to say to convince you that I am determined to be consulted!'

'But this is such a small matter, Helen,' Ophelia put

in. 'Hardly worth your notice. We know you reserve evenings for family. All we did was go to a bit of a party.'

Helen, who had just seen from the invitation that the function was large enough for a civic hall, grew more furious still. She decided, however, to shelve the matter in favour of something more productive. There was nothing she could do here and now to rid herself of this contention. She needed time to think, and maybe to seek advice.

Over the next few weeks Vittore tested Helen's reaction on a series of occasions by leaving her out of consultations and decisions. After keeping silent for a time while he, and to a lesser degree Ophelia, made plain their desire to oust her, Helen concluded that she must make radical changes. She wasn't going to work like this.

She was bitterly hurt by having her trust in Vittore shattered. It seemed as if ambition had altered him completely, turning him so ruthless that he would go to any lengths to take the firm over. He wasn't a bit like the man who'd returned to England, and didn't resemble the one who had meant such a lot to her during the war.

If she could have, she would have raised sufficient capital to buy out the pair of them. But that would only have been possible by mortgaging The Stone House and that — to Helen — was Neil's heritage, sacrosanct.

The alternative, and one which she doubted would be approved by anyone, much less her solicitor or Mr Thorpe her accountant, was to sell her shares and get out.

Recent months had taught Helen to conceal her intentions. She began speaking in the office of wishing to spend more time with Neil during these formative years. She must, after all, act as father as well as mother to him. There was the difficulty also, since Marian's illness, of often having to leave him with either her mother or Mrs Hartley. Now that they were ageing, this was taxing for them and wasn't especially good for the boy. Helen surprised herself with the extent to which she could emphasise her reluctance to commit her time so completely to Stone's.

Pretending to care less about the firm was one of the hardest things she had ever attempted. Each time that she walked into the office, she steeled herself to give nothing away. Within her own family, she was aware of arousing curiosity by this attitude she seemed to be assuming towards her work. Here, she must exert even greater effort to assure Vittore of these new intentions. To put him off guard.

Meanwhile, working from home and among her many business contacts, she was strengthening her personal prestige. She was determined that as soon as she relinquished the reins here she would have everything ready for the next step in her career.

The day that she offered her shareholding to the other two, they were astonished, but they recovered within the week. And, presumably after putting their heads together, they made a joint bid for Helen's stake in the firm.

By the time they had been persuaded to raise the offer to a sum which she was prepared to accept, Helen was beginning to come round to believing that a life away from Stone's was possible.

But when the transaction had gone through and the day came for her finally to leave the office, she felt devastated and sick. Vittore had let her down so fearfully, changing from the man who had seemed to share so many of her interests and priorities into a schemer who wanted only to take over her business. It seemed a long time now since she had been fond of him, but memories of that affection too were plaguing her as she cleared her desk.

She was taking with her that desk, which had once been Joseph Stone's, and the draftsman's desks that she and Alexander had used.

'I can't leave them here,' she'd told the other two. 'They belong to our family.'

Saying goodbye to Wendy was as hard as anything. She had been an efficient, helpful secretary. Helen just wished she could take her with her.

Wendy was in tears when the parting came. 'I can't see me stopping here much longer, not when you've gone.'

Helen was surprised. There still wasn't full employment after the difficult years that had followed the ending of the war.

'Let me know if you do decide to leave, I might be able to help.'

Wendy gave her a curious look. 'But — do you mean looking after your little boy? I'm afraid I don't know so much about kids . . .'

Helen smiled, gave her a hug. 'Let's just see, eh?'

Passing the small house where she and Alexander had begun their married life, Helen realised even more deeply how a whole era was ending. She had fought a lot, struggled, but had also learned a great deal. And perhaps mostly about herself, and this ability she was acquiring to ensure that she mastered future opposition.

For a month, Helen seemed to devote herself entirely to her family, spending more time than she had for years with her parents. She relished playing with her son, teaching him new skills, and all during hours when normally she would have been at work. She spent more time with Marian, Denis and their children, and availed herself of theatre tickets which he offered. Sitting in the Grand Theatre, she compared her memories of that splendid new theatre in Stratford, where her ambitions had been nurtured, with this out-moded but still popular centre of repertory in Halifax. And somehow the company here seemed more deserving of credit for surmounting obstacles created by inadequate funding.

Underneath all this outward relaxation and time with the family, however, she was putting in the groundwork for her future. Mostly in her head, but also through contact with builders and others within the construction industry, she was asserting that Helen Stone wasn't finished.

And Helen Stone was the name under which all her new designs would be produced. Architects might not advertise, but she was delighted to discover that her name had already begun to mean something. Her greatest satisfaction came on the day she heard that the first project which would prove to everyone she was still very much in business would be the church hall for which she was being contracted.

I might win yet, she thought happily, for once submerging the very real dread that not enough business would come her way. Relying entirely on herself was at once reassuring and something of a weight. She now had behind her the capital raised by selling her shareholding in Stone's, though she had learned during these past few years how a house the size of theirs swallowed up money.

The Stone House, however, was now to play its part in the future she was mapping out for herself and Neil. She already had the study and was turning the sombre dining room into an office. Helen Stone's architectural practice would function from here. She felt certain Joseph would have been glad to see clients meeting her in rooms that he'd designed. She nodded approvingly when she'd installed desks and drawing boards, and placed filing cabinets against the panelled walls.

Working with Neil so close at hand was the proverbial bane as well as blessing. On days when Marian was unable to come out to them, Helen was glad to be there, lessening the responsibility which fell upon either her mother or Mrs Hartley. But both she herself and the boy had to exercise considerable discipline to ensure that some work was accomplished.

The day that building work on the church hall in Leeds began, Helen came home really elated. For the first time in months she felt on top of the world, and the enquiries which she had received since setting up again on her own seemed to indicate that this scheme would soon be followed by others. In the meantime, she had been asked to design a private house just beyond Mytholmroyd, one of the few for which a licence had been granted. Providing that she satisfied the potential owners, her fee would mean that she could face the next six months without dipping into her capital.

'We're going to be all right, love,' she told Neil that night. 'Even though there's only you and me now, we shan't have to do without anything.'

Neil, of course, was too young really to understand, but he did recognise that his mother was happier and therefore the whole atmosphere of the house was improving.

Helen kept her promise to take Neil along with her occasionally when she visited the church hall site. He seemed to enjoy getting thoroughly dirty there, and loved winning the attention of some of the building workers. He had learned some discipline by this time, and knew to obey when told he must keep out of the way.

'I want to make houses,' he confided one evening while they were driving back to The Stone House. 'I want to stick the stones on top of each other like the men do.'

Helen smiled sideways at him. 'You mean you'd rather do that than design the way they must be built, love?'

'Yes, 'cos you have more fun building.'

'Well, we'll have to see, shan't we? You'll soon be starting school, then there'll be all sorts of different things to interest you. You might end up wanting to do something else altogether.'

'No, I won't, Mummy. I'm going to make all the houses that you draw.'

Although she knew this was all just a childish fancy, Helen was nevertheless pleased. She couldn't have done all that badly as a mother if the lad would look forward to working with her.

For the present she was so happy with the way the church hall was taking shape that she could hardly keep away from the site. She had to force herself to ensure that she spent time making certain that new business continued to come in.

The evening that Wendy telephoned her, Helen was quite surprised. She had thought − and indeed had hoped for the girl's sake − that she would settle back into the routine at Stone's once she became accustomed to the new set-up. It soon was plain that this wasn't so.

'I've given in my notice, Mrs Stone. I couldn't stand another week there. That Ophelia Hadgraft is never out of the place now, and it isn't as if she does anything . . .'

'Except help to pay your wages,' Helen reminded her, trying to be fair.

'Oh, that. Any road, it's the way them two carry on that makes me sick. And I'll bet she's nearly old enough to be his mother. Did you know that it was through her that he got to know about you being left on your own an' all that?'

'Well, I can't say I'm surprised. They might have kept quiet about it for a while, but it had become evident that they were well acquainted before Vittore started work there.' Helen paused. 'Have you found another job then, Wendy?'

'Not yet. Haven't really started looking, though. All I wanted was to get out. I finish there on Friday.'

'Well, I can use some help here, although I have to say that I can't employ you full-time as yet.'

'That doesn't matter. I'd love to work with you again, you know that. You're working from home now, aren't you?'

'And loving it. I'd be very happy if you could join me.'

'I certainly will. I'll start on Monday if you like.'

Having Wendy there was good, leaving Helen free to concentrate while telephone calls were answered and letters written. And when she went out on business Helen was glad to know somebody was there, in control. Mrs Hartley was too nervous about business matters to be relied on to take more than the simplest of messages without becoming worried, and was growing too old to be schooled into adapting. Most of all, though, Helen appreciated Wendy's supportive manner.

The long years of training followed by others of being compelled to concentrate on her work had left Helen without any real women friends. Normally, this didn't trouble her unduly, especially since she and Marian had grown close, but she found that having another woman around was very enjoyable.

'I feel years younger suddenly,' she confessed one day when they were sharing a laugh over the strange phrasing of a letter that had come in that morning's post.

Helen could afford to feel light-hearted; the church hall was completed, and the local publicity it was earning her had already produced several enquiries regarding designs for similar buildings.

'I might even go to that,' Helen told Wendy a few days later when an invitation arrived for the opening of the hall.

'Well, of course you must,' Wendy insisted.

'I'll have to see. You know what I'm like — not used to socialising these days.'

'Were you ever?' asked Wendy wryly.

Helen grinned. 'You know me too well!' she admitted, wondering how or why she had accepted having so little social life.

She resolved there and then that she would attend that ceremonial opening.

Driving to Leeds on that afternoon in May, Helen felt strangely excited. And if an element of trepidation was present it seemed to be tempered with anticipation of seeing the hall furnished and joy to have it finally in use.

Entering, Helen paused just inside the front doorway, looking about her. Wide steps led up to the double doors of the main hall, while others to either side of them led down towards the cloakrooms. Before going through into that large main room, she glanced to each side of her, noting the doors that gave on to two of the smaller rooms.

The big hall was what most interested her, however, and she stood just inside the doors, gazing upwards to the windows and then all about her until she glanced towards the stage.

She was beginning to smile. It seemed almost perfect, she was compelled to acknowledge that the design was good, and it had been constructed exactly as she had visualised it. Now she saw it with people filing in to fill the rows of seats she experienced a curious sort of humility, as if she were scarcely able to believe that she was responsible for its planning.

Agreeing to attend, Helen had declined the invitation to sit with the dignitaries who would occupy the seats arranged on the platform. She felt quite conspicuous enough when shown to the place reserved in the front row for her, and she wanted to be free to experience this day without fear that all her emotions would be on show. Creating this hall, especially whilst struggling to overcome all the trouble within Stone's, had been quite a triumph. If she lived to be ninety and worked all the while, she'd never feel that any other place was quite so important.

The group of young musicians filed in first, playing guitars and recorders, violins and brass instruments. As soon as they had mounted the short flight of stairs leading up to the stage, they were joined by a further band of young people, many of them of Caribbean, Indian or Pakistani origin. All were unified by their unqualified joy. Their song, delivered with all the verve they could muster, filled Helen with a pang of sheer pleasure. Somewhere behind her a voice whispered these were the children belonging to the Sunday School. She felt glad to participate in their evident satisfaction that they belonged here.

When the last chords of their song died to silence, a middle-aged man stepped forward.

'As many of you know,' he began, 'I've been in charge of this group of young folk for years while I've been the superintendent of their classes. I've watched their predecessors grow up, and have seen some of them with children of their own. Never before have we had such a fine home for our Sunday classes, and we've certainly never had so splendid a place for concerts and the like. Today being special, we want to thank a lot of people who've made this possible. We also wish to welcome our Lord Bishop who is performing the act of dedication for us. And we are particularly pleased that our new vicar, Christopher Maitland, has at last torn himself away from his old parish!'

It must be a coincidence, thought Helen, so shaken by hearing his name that she couldn't pay any heed to the man who was continuing his speech with a welcome to the Lord Mayor. Christopher was a Catholic, a priest, not an Anglican vicar . . .

And now the city's Mace Bearer was leading in the procession. A fraction after everyone else, Helen rose to her feet. But she couldn't look, couldn't bear the depth of disappointment that she would feel learning he wasn't the Christopher she knew. Fixing her gaze on the hands clasped in front of her, she kept it lowered until she had heard out the movement of feet and the last scrape of a chair as they were all seated on the platform.

Only then did she permit herself to look.

It was Chris. Older, much older than she had expected, bespectacled, but unmistakably the Chris who had seemed to be a part of her life ever since that first short meeting. Her heart gave a distinct jolt. She glanced furtively to those on either side of her, wondering if they could have noticed.

The mayor was speaking. Helen couldn't take in more than the odd phrase. When he mentioned the high standard of the building's design she would have missed his words if it hadn't been for recognising her own name. And then, before she'd begun to recover her ragged composure, it was Christopher's turn to address them.

His voice was almost exactly as she recalled, so familiar that she ached to turn back the years and establish some sort of understanding. The only difference seemed to be that, these days, she could discern more forcefulness in it.

'How fortunate I am,' he began, 'to be commencing my ministry in this parish with such a marvellous crowd of people and in such a grand setting. As some of you are aware, I am particularly concerned for young folk – it's heartening to hear how well they perform together. Indeed, when they combine so well to make such music, I wonder if I'm going to be superfluous!' As laughter died, he continued: 'Seriously, though, I am extremely happy to be here at last. I know that these youngsters performing for us today consider this their "thank you" for these splendid premises. I know how hard they too have worked towards this end, helping to raise funds, warming everyone with their enthusiasm, and challenging others to work to produce just that bit more than anyone thought possible. And so now we have this magnificent hall. I trust that I, along with all of you, will continue their example and good work as we get on with the life of our parish.'

Briefly, Helen closed her eyes. She had designed this for him without knowing it; she had created this building, in which even her astute eyes could detect no fault, for Christopher. It seemed to her that she had worked through every one of the intervening years since they'd met for precisely this purpose.

She opened her eyes as the next speaker began addressing them. Chris was looking straight at her. She would never forget the delight shining in those sherry brown eyes, and bringing a smile to his rather austere face.

He came straight towards her after the bishop's blessing. For what felt like a full minute or more he stood before her, tall and lean, gazing hard into her eyes. And then he took both her hands in his strong yet slender fingers. 'Helen.'

She tried to answer, and couldn't. She simply looked at him, all the emotion contained for so many years gleaming in her grey eyes. Life might have aged them both a bit, nothing else had altered.

'We must talk,' he asserted firmly. 'After all this time, we've got to. And especially because you're responsible for this splendid place. Do you have to rush away? I'm afraid I'm expected to work, help keep things going . . .'

Smiling, Helen nodded. 'I'm sure. And I won't just disappear. There's no rush. My sister's looking after Neil — he's my son.'

Momentarily, the brown eyes clouded. Chris recovered swiftly. 'I'll extricate myself quickly from the others.'

He settled her at a table with the mayor and two or three councillors and their wives before walking away. Helen watched him.

All the time she was struggling to make conversation with the local dignitaries, her glance followed Christopher about the room. Every few paces, he paused to talk with someone. It might be a fur-coated lady who obviously was well connected, or maybe a shabbily dressed woman trailing a bunch of kiddies, but always he had the same ready smile, the same genuine interest in them. He would be the ideal vicar.

When he stopped to speak with the youngsters who had led the singing, she felt emotion choking her. Eagerly, they surrounded him, clearly warming already to the new incumbent to a degree where they weren't in the least awed by his clerical collar. She saw him bend down towards a little girl and give a mischievous pull at her braided hair. And she heard the immediate laughter as the girl and a couple of her friends retaliated by tugging at the short cape of his cassock.

'Ready?' Christopher said to her at last. They made a circuit of the room so that, beginning with the mayor, she could say goodbye to every important visitor.

'I'll see you to your car,' Chris offered then, taking her elbow as they left the room. In the entrance hall he grinned. 'Must preserve some show of decorum. Though actually I'm so thrilled I could toss away all caution and hug you.'

'I wish you could,' she admitted straightforwardly. 'Oh, Chris . . .' And suddenly she blurted: 'You're not Catholic, are you?'

He grinned. 'Catholic, yes — Roman, no. High Anglican's the word. I'll explain if you like?'

'Not just now. I . . . Oh, none of this is making much sense! Aren't you staggered? I mean, with our meeting again like this?'

He spoke as they began descending the steps to street level. 'I have to admit that my surprise isn't quite total. As prospective incumbent here, I was shown all the plans for the church hall. In giving my wholehearted approval, I was happy to know that I was agreeing to a scheme which you'd originated.'

'So you knew it was me?'

'There'd been a photograph in the *Yorkshire Post* at the time you designed that block of flats.'

'You knew then that I'd become Helen Stone?'

He nodded, rather gravely. 'Look — do you have to be home by a certain time?'

'Not so long as I'm not alarmingly late. My sister's not all that brilliant these days. She had polio.'

'I'm sorry.'

'She's come out of it — well, not too badly, but is easily tired.'

Christopher nodded. He was willing his attention away from the rings on her left hand. They ought not to matter to him. He shouldn't have been alerted quite so forcefully to the fact that she hadn't said one word about her husband.

He cleared his throat. 'If you can spare a few minutes, we'll go across to the vicarage. It's just round the corner.'

The house was Victorian, a larger edition of the one which had been her first home with Alexander. Although it was rather drab in itself, Chris had chosen furniture that brightened the high rooms, and pictures which seemed to shout his love of beauty and light.

He took her coat carefully, making her feel that his concern was being expressed in the simple action, and reminding her as well of the moment, aeons ago, when he'd buttoned the collar of that other coat for her. Helen told herself sternly to remember how he'd have shown similar attention to any and everyone back at the hall.

'Your son is how old then?' Chris inquired, his face impassive as he indicated a comfortable chair.

'Neil's four now. A bit of a handful, I'm afraid. Not his fault really,' she added. She was going to explain about losing his father, but Christopher was speaking again, almost as though he did not wish to hear.

'Most youngsters are, or so I believe. I often wonder how I would have coped with my own . . .' And now, suddenly, how it might have been to bring up a family with you, he thought. He forced a grin. 'Just as well I never married!'

'But I thought — I always thought you weren't permitted,' Helen began, before remembering that he wasn't a Roman Catholic priest.

'Yes, that. Bit of a facer really at the time, being told it wasn't likely to work for me. When I was preparing for ordination our Superior cautioned me against vows of celibacy. Strangely, as it turns out, I might just as well have been bound by them. There you go.' He shrugged. 'Enough about me. What's all this about your being on your own as an architect these days? I was sure the firm mentioned at the time of those flats going up was Stone's.'

'It was. I let myself in for a right packet there, and no mistake. You wouldn't believe how gullible I've been.'

'I might believe you'd take people at face value.'

Helen smiled. 'Thanks. First of all it was some woman who wished to invest in the firm, and I certainly needed capital if I was to get Stone's re-established after the war and the difficult years that followed. Then I took on another architect — someone I'd known during the war. He's Italian. He put money into Stone's as well. What I should have guessed was that the pair of them were associates — I didn't grasp that for long enough. By which time they were making life so awkward that the only solution for me was to extricate myself. I can only thank heaven that this job came along at the same time . . .'

'So can I,' Chris interrupted fervently. 'And now we've met up again — what next? Will you meet me some other time, Helen? On a day when you're not heading home and when I'm not tied up with all those people in that hall back there?'

Chapter 20

Helen left without giving a reply. She needed to think. She felt today as if she would need almost as long to get used to seeing him again as it had taken for him to reappear in her life. All the way back to Brearley she passed through smoky towns and stone-built villages without really seeing any of them, only coming to herself as she drove through Luddenden Foot.

Marian met her at the front door. 'By, but you look as though going out has done you the world of good! You've got colour in them pinched cheeks again.'

Helen knew she'd have to tell her, she couldn't keep this to herself. 'Where's Neil? Is he all right if we leave him for a minute? I've got that much to tell you . . .'

'He's fine. Mrs Hartley's giving him his supper. She's keeping yours hot for you.'

'I'm late, aren't I? And you ought to be getting home.'

'Stop fussing, love. Linda and Mark will be okay. I told Denis to get the lady next door to sit with them if I wasn't back when it was time for the theatre. It's only for once, isn't it? And, by the look of you, it's been a once in a lifetime occasion. Were they suited with the hall now it's finished?'

Just for a second, Helen stared at her sister, barely comprehending. 'Oh, yes – yes, thanks. Everybody seemed thrilled with it.'

'But there's more to tell, isn't there.' It wasn't a question.

'Aye, there is. Come and sit down.'

They went through to the sitting room. Marian eased herself down into an armchair, but Helen was so excited and agitated that she couldn't stand still, let alone sit.

'You'll never guess who the new vicar is at that place,' she began, and then checked herself, smiling ruefully. 'Well, of course you won't – nobody would. I've never told any of the family, ever. It was years ago, before the war, when I went on that trip to see Italy and Switzerland. There's an abbey in the Swiss Alps – Einsiedeln . . . I met him there and it was like – well, just like you read about, only believe it doesn't happen in real life. We couldn't stop talking right from the minute we bumped into each other. We thought the same way about so many things.'

'Only?'

Helen swallowed, met Marian's curious gaze. She couldn't imagine what she must sound like, didn't believe she would be making very much sense. 'Only he was training to be a priest. I thought he meant Roman Catholic – calling it "priest" and all that. I didn't understand – not with us being brought up non-conformist – it wasn't till today that I really found out that the Church of England calls them priests an' all. Anyway, it was Chris who said then that we couldn't go on meeting over here. At that time, he did intend taking vows. Only in the end he didn't – take them, I mean. But he hasn't been married, not ever.'

'And you're on your own now.'

'Marian, I mustn't even think that way. I really mustn't. He's got his life, and I've got mine. And there's Neil . . .'

'Needing a father.'

'Don't, love, don't say it. I've no right.'

'No right to happiness? That's the top and bottom of what you're thinking, isn't it? Why, love, why for heaven's sake?'

'I don't know. It's just the way I am. Happen it's still to do with Alexander, the way things were when he set off that day.'

'Whether any of that was your fault or not, and *I* don't think it was, you've paid since. Every day of your life since he died. Are you going to go on paying for the rest of your days?'

'I don't know, Marian, I wish I did. I wish I felt really sure about something. Anything.'

'When are you seeing him again?'

'I don't know that I am.'

'Did he let you come away without suggesting it?'

'No, as a matter of fact, he did want to see me.'

'In another twelve or thirteen years again maybe? Is that what you're saying?'

'Don't talk daft.'

'It's you that's proper daft! Nay, Helen, what do I always keep telling you? We're not practising for summat. This is it — the life we've had given us. You're what — thirty-three? How much longer are you going to wait before you settle for being happy?' When Helen made as though to speak Marian continued forcefully: 'And don't tell me how happy you were while Alex was here — I know he never really understood you. You've earned a bit of pleasure by now if anybody has, and it sounds as if it wouldn't do yon chap any harm.'

Despite her sister's advice Helen remained undecided about seeing Christopher again. Undecided, yet yearning with her entire being to be with him. Knowing every cranny of that church hall and enough about the church to visualise it quite freely, she couldn't avoid picturing him there. Each and every one of her days was coloured with him, filled with the enormous ache to learn more about what the years had done to him.

So many of her questions had not been asked, such a large portion of the time keeping them apart remained a blank to her. Wondering ate into her concentration, making her work suffer, and this time no amount of will-power seemed to overcome this obstacle that rose so consistently between herself and the tasks which she should accomplish.

The letter came one morning while Helen was attempting yet again to put a bit of life into the elevation of a house she was planning. Chris had written at some length, asking her understanding when he explained that he couldn't bring himself to accept that their brief meeting must remain just a tantalising glimpse of each other's lives. Somehow, she could not imagine how, he had unearthed the fact that she was now widowed. His taking the trouble to find this out was enough to convince her of how earnest he was. He was suggesting a meeting on neutral ground, 'where neither of us need pay any heed to anyone's reactions but our own'.

Helen telephoned him that day. She had intended writing back agreeing to see him, but had been overwhelmed by the need to hear his voice. And his voice alone assured her that, no matter how great her own need, it was matched by Christopher's. When he confirmed how urgently he wished to see her, Helen felt emotion rising in her throat.

'Can you make it one evening this week?' he asked her. 'I've got a Confirmation class on Wednesday but the rest are free. I thought we might meet somewhere halfway, but I don't know where to suggest. I'm afraid I'm more familiar with the North Riding after spending so long there.'

'I don't mind where, Chris, so long as it's not too out of the way. I shall be working until after five.'

'Then we'll make it somewhere in your direction. I can get away earlier than you. I'll pick you up if you wish.'

Driving his pre-war Ford through Halifax, Christopher glanced about him as much as traffic conditions permitted. Wasn't this where she'd grown up, the place which had shaped the young Helen? Seeing the drab streets of terraced houses radiating from the main road, and the huge textile mills that towered over almost every street corner, he marvelled that she hadn't become tougher.

Though I suppose I'm just very thankful that she seems as vulnerable as ever, he thought.

That story the other day of how Helen had been conned by the folk who'd infiltrated her architectural firm had resurrected the old yearning to protect her. God knew that he'd be glad to provide some sort of anchor for her.

Leaving Halifax behind as he headed towards the Calder Valley, Chris was glad to see green hills. Some wooded, others with fields and meadows bisected by staunch drystone walls, they were visible between the mills which, even out here, pronounced this industrial Yorkshire. His heart soared with the steep hillsides, reminding him of the ever-present hope which never quite became trampled beneath work or burdens or distress. Enduring was so often the only thing required of anyone. And now he might at last begin to believe that he was being granted the opportunity for which he had longed.

It had seemed such a long wait, while he'd felt bound to remain in his old parish until his colleague was fully recovered. And all the time he'd been tantalised by the sight of Helen's plans for the church hall, by news of her visits to check how building work was progressing. Looking back now, it seemed almost that those months had been longer than the whole of the previous twelve or so years put together.

So preoccupied that he had ceased noticing road signs, Chris was nearly past the turning that Helen had described to him. Changing down with a merciless grating of gears, he drove the little car up the winding lane. Smiling now, he spared a moment to take in the lushness of the fields to either side, and the view over the valley to another slope equally pastoral. This was an appropriately beautiful spot for their reunion.

He rounded the next bend between the rough stone walls, and open wrought-iron gates revealed a curving drive with beyond that The Stone House. If it hadn't been so solitary in this site dominating the hill, he might have thought he was mistaken in believing this her home. He would have been much happier to think he was mistaken.

He had been an utter fool considering these fantasies of his might hold some substance. Helen had it all, hadn't she? The skill and the acumen to succeed in her own architectural practice, the son on whom she centred all her devotion and future hopes, and this. Material evidence that she enjoyed circumstances utterly different from the abstemious life which was his. He'd never before considered the meagre financial rewards of his vocation any great hardship. Suddenly they were overburdening.

If he hadn't felt so exposed to all those massive windows which seemed to scan his every weakness, he would have turned in the narrow lane and fled.

Helen was ready when she saw Christopher's rather battered car nosing up the drive. After dressing carefully in a mauve skirt and new softly draped white blouse, chosen because it was so different from her usual tailored style, she had made certain he wouldn't have to come into the house and wait. She wasn't reluctant to invite him in, but had decided it was too soon for a confrontation between Chris and her son. Neil could be difficult, and this evening mattered too much to run that risk.

She noticed as she ran out to greet him that Chris seemed pensive. She began telling him about her day, and the enquiries coming in now from other folk who wanted buildings that were in accord with older properties surrounding them.

They drove up Cragg Vale where they ate at an unpretentious inn, relishing the good country cooking and the quiet and anonymity in which to talk. Chris held forth for a while, unable to remain subdued for long now that they were together. He enthused about how well he was settling into his new parish, and emphasised how her splendid hall was reawakening a sense of community there.

'I could spend every evening there, if I wanted. So many organisations have resurrected now they've somewhere so perfect for gathering. But, as you might have noticed, it's the youngsters who take priority in my interest.'

'They seem an enthusiastic bunch,' Helen observed, happy just to be there watching how his brown eyes lit, and wondering why no one else she'd ever met seemed to glow with his particular fervour.

'They're that, all right, and when you consider that up to now they've spent too much time on the streets, that's some achievement. Most of the kids have mothers who work, and haven't had sufficient time given to them.'

'I'll bet you're glad to rectify that.'

He grinned. 'Well, I do admit to a firm belief that all most of them need is somebody to show enough concern and interest in them. But I'm sure you don't need me to explain that, especially since you've been trying to be father as well as mother to your son.' When she said nothing Chris continued: 'Why didn't you tell me you were on your own now? Your husband died, didn't he?'

Helen nodded. 'In a car accident over two years ago, yes. And the only reason I didn't mention it the other day was lack of time. It was all a bit of a rush, wasn't it?'

Christopher couldn't argue with that. It had mostly been rather in the public eye as well. The trouble was that since setting out today, knowing that they were finally going to meet away from everyone, he'd grown less able to picture himself expressing his emotions. Seeing that house had made him more inhibited still, acutely aware of how little use he might be to her.

'It was dreadful when Alexander died,' Helen began. 'I know fatal accidents always produce shock, but this was particularly bad. We'd parted on such rotten terms. I'm afraid I didn't love him enough — not to sacrifice my career, which was what Alexander wanted. I've thought since how he couldn't have been unaware of how little I did care for him. It's no wonder he'd cooled towards me.'

'Was it really that bad? Are you certain you aren't remembering only the black side?'

'I'm certain.'

'But you did your best. It wouldn't be you if you'd been guilty of neglect.'

Wanly, she smiled. 'Thanks. I just wish I could put it all behind me. But there's too much that keeps bringing it all back into focus.'

'Your son, you mean?'

'Neil, yes, though he's the one aspect I don't regret. But there's the house as well. You saw what it's like. It's not the kind of place that makes forgetting easy. Joseph Stone — he was Alexander's father — designed the place, and it's got both of them stamped all over every room. I wish sometimes that Neil was grown up, then it'd be his.'

'You can't wish your life away like that, Helen.'

Startled, she gazed at him. What was the alternative? she wondered. Living on this treadmill of designing, raising Neil, everlastingly trying to bring more business her way? Alone.

Gently, Christopher smiled. He was beginning to see where her greatest need lay. He was better at this than at expressing his own longings. 'Come on, let's walk.'

Leaving the car where it was, they strode uphill, side by side, while the head wind buffeted them and drove away anxieties.

At the brow of the hill they paused, gazing beyond the heather and scrubland towards the horizon, hazed now with heat remaining from the summer day.

'It's grand out here,' said Chris. 'Should free you of a few cares, at least.'

'It is doing, or is that your company?'

'I'd like to think . . .' He stopped, sighed, then faced her. 'Helen, I'm no good at this. But it is what I want more than anything — to have some part in making you feel better. Even if it mostly has to be only at the other end of the telephone, being there for you, sharing.'

'You always have.' She sensed how startled he was, and then she was telling him. It all spilled out, in ragged half-sentences: every time when she had remembered, and felt him near. And that Good Friday when she had seen him yet been denied a meeting. 'It did help,' she added fervently. 'I'd reached the end of my tether, but somehow that reminder of the beliefs that anchor you made me keep going.'

'I remember that day. It wasn't my own parish. I'd gone over rather reluctantly to deputise for someone who'd fractured a leg. I'd have preferred to spend Easter in my neck of the woods. But I can see now how it maybe wasn't just chance.'

Helen felt slightly alarmed, perplexed by his steady acceptance of merely being what seemed to her like a pawn in some almighty scheme.

Only Chris had been speaking more directly of how events had conspired to help *her*. And once again all his reservations were overwhelmed by the inner certainty that he must hold on to this contact newly restored between them. No matter about their very different circumstances.

'We can't let life continually keep us apart, can we, Helen? Even if it's to be only as friends?'

'I'd certainly hate to go for years without seeing you again. And though I often feel my life is too full of things that need my attention, I know there's plenty of room for improvement.'

Christopher was nodding. 'Something beyond the everyday, more than all the thousand and one tasks that crowd in on us.' He turned to her. 'Let's make a pact to give each other some time — because it's what we both want.'

They left it at that, agreeing as they walked back to the car that they would keep in touch. Approaching The Stone House, Chris again felt it dominating him, filling him with awareness of an unfamiliar inability to cope.

In a sort of desperation, he suggested that they should next meet on a Saturday. 'I'll let you know when I have one free of weddings. I'd love to meet your son. We'll give him a day out somewhere.'

* * *

Much as she ached to talk about Christopher, Helen kept to herself the spiralling emotions generated by their evening and the prospect of another outing. It all felt so new and insubstantial that she was afraid revealing too much might place a jinx upon their relationship. She had sensed that Chris was holding back which, despite all he'd said, made her determined not to depend too much on having him around in the future.

Regardless of her reservations, though, he had changed her life. I can hope again now, she realised. The wonder of having circumstances bring him back in touch was giving her a whole new outlook. Work flowed more easily, and designs that had been causing her trouble seemed now to cohere. Most of all, though, it was her will that had been restored, simply because future possibilities appeared limitless.

Her father noticed on the Saturday afternoon when she called to see him after Marian had told her that he was unwell.

'It's only a cold, the doctor says,' Daniel assured her quickly. 'There's nowt for you to be worriting about. Although I'm bound to admit it has pulled me down.'

Helen grinned. 'It must have if it's kept you from watching cricket today!'

'Aye, well – there's a keen wind, isn't there, in spite of that nice bit of sunshine. I've got to get myself better for work by Monday, you know. I've had two or three days off as it is.'

It was then that he remarked on how much brighter she was looking. 'You've had me worried, love, many a time. I don't say so much, I know, but that doesn't mean I'm not concerned. You've looked that drawn for many a year, and naturally it's got worse since you lost your Alex.'

Helen smiled reassuringly, and was thankful that she was able to tell him truthfully that she was feeling better now. 'I did have a lot on my plate, especially when the firm was causing so many headaches. I'm finding I'm better working on my own. Happen I'm not so good at getting on with other folk!'

Daniel frowned, taking her remark very seriously. 'Nay, Helen, I won't have that. You've made such a success of your job, and I'm sure you wouldn't have if you couldn't manage to get on with folk. Any road, you do seem to be making a go of it without anybody else, from what I hear.'

'I've certainly as much work as I can handle, Dad. I sometimes think I ought to be widening my scope, but that'd mean going further afield. I can't do so much of that till Neil's a lot older.'

Hearing his name, Neil peered around the door of the kitchen where he was helping his grandmother who was baking.

'I'm a lot older now,' he asserted, his grey eyes sparkling.

Helen and her father exchanged glances and laughed. Neil was joined at the kitchen door by Kathleen Clegg who grasped him firmly by the shoulder.

'But are you old enough to concentrate on what you're supposed to be doing?' she inquired, looking down into his grinning face. 'I'm not wearing myself out beating this cake mixture while you're standing there talking and doing nowt!'

Giggling up at her, Neil slipped a floury hand into her wrinkled palm as they turned away.

'He's a grand little lad, bless him,' Daniel told his daughter.

Helen made a face. 'At times! I just wish I could rely on him to be like this always.'

'Eh, he's all right. You don't want to make a cissy out of him.'

'Have I said I do? No, Dad — it's only that I want him to behave properly, to grow up boyish without turning downright rude like he is sometimes.' And, she added silently, I wish to goodness there was some kind of guarantee that he would respond well to Christopher's suggestion of taking them both out.

The more she thought about that day the more she wished that he hadn't been so eager to meet Neil just yet. She would have liked more time alone with Chris first, time in which to set everything else aside while they became thoroughly reacquainted with each other.

Christopher's feelings were just the opposite to hers. He suspected that Neil could be the bridge which would cross the abyss of what he thought of as his own shortcomings, and bring him closer to Helen. He had seen how complete her world appeared, but believed he could provide something that her son was lacking. And he liked kids, always had done, even while wondering how he'd have coped with any of his own.

Smiling wryly to himself as he sat in his study supposedly working on next Sunday's sermon, Christopher seemed to hear his own parents. Seeing them only very rarely since they had emigrated to farm in Australia, he remembered most of what they had said during his only trip out there.

Concerned by his evident need of a life partner, his mother had asked if he never longed for a family. 'You're not getting any younger, Chris, and with us so far away you're on your own too much already. What's it going to be like later on, when you're not able to get about so readily?'

'I have a very big family wherever I'm working,' he'd assured her. 'Dozens of young folk around me in the parish. I'll never want for company while one generation succeeds another. I feel privileged, do you realise that? They share with me their interests and their dreams. They relish all the activities we arrange for them, but I bet I relish them more — for all the warm-heartedness and fun they generate.'

'That's as may be,' his father had said. 'But it's not a man's world, is it? You'll be missing a lot if you continue denying yourself a man's decisions, the role he plays in taking responsibility for the folk under his roof. All this talk of relating to youngsters is fine and good, as far as it goes. But you're never with them long enough to tackle anything head-on.'

Chris might have disputed that, but had chosen not to. And he could believe there was a lot of truth in his father's observations. He admitted to himself that he hadn't lived the kind of existence that broadened someone's concept of family life. From a boys-only grammar school he had entered university and theological college, and the latter certainly hadn't provided any taste of a mixed-sex adult community. His war service as an army chaplain had seemed male-orientated again, very tough, especially in the desert. Having parents who'd lived abroad after he'd reached his late teens, it was many a year since he'd experienced life as a family member.

It was indeed to a rapport with Helen's young son that he was looking. He forgot himself when he was with children.

On the day that he set out to pick up Helen and Neil at Brearley, Chris was feeling elated. He had in the car an old football abandoned weeks ago by choirboys in the vicarage garden. And there was a kite which he'd purchased yesterday especially for Neil. In reserve, in case the lad grew tired, was a slate, still with its special pencil. Its source long-forgotten, it had survived since before the war and often provided amusement for youngsters who'd never seen anything of the kind. Helen might be thankful if he could coax Neil to be quiet while he and the boy concentrated on drawing or beginning to write.

Even his first sight of The Stone House today appeared less daunting now he was prepared for his meeting with her son.

When Chris drew up outside, Helen was in the hall trying to persuade Neil into fetching a sweater from upstairs rather than ordering him. She hurried to open the front door, burning with the knowledge that Neil was regarding her reproachfully from the sitting-room doorway.

'Come in, Chris,' she said, beaming. 'Lovely to see you again.' Over her shoulder she called to her son, 'Neil — come on now, here's somebody I want you to meet.'

Scowling, the boy remained where he was, half-hidden by the door. She silently blessed Christopher for crossing to him unhesitatingly, his hand outstretched.

'Neil,' she said, 'this is a friend of mine. I think you'd better call him Uncle Chris.'

'But he's not my uncle.'

Helen's hopes plummeted.

'I know I'm not,' Chris was saying, down on one knee to meet Neil at his own level. 'But I was hoping you'd sort of adopt me.'

Stonily, Neil stared back at him. 'I've got two uncles — there's Uncle Denis and Uncle Vittore.' And his clamped lips and stern expression conveyed his reluctance to entertain any idea of acquiring any more.

'Uncle Vittore, eh?' Chris snatched at a possible lead to conversation. 'It doesn't sound as if he's English . . .'

'He used to live here with Mummy.'

Helen held back an appalled gasp. And explaining the ins and outs of Vittore's visits would only make matters worse.

This introduction was failing miserably.

Christopher had succeeded in taking Neil's right hand, but it lay motionless in his large one, as if witnessing that the boy had no desire to cooperate even as far as a greeting.

Helen was itching to scold her son, even to shake some sense into him. These days, he wasn't normally this unsociable.

'This is *our* house,' Neil stated abruptly, grey eyes icy with disdain. 'My daddy won't let you stay.'

Shaken, Christopher turned instinctively to Helen.

'He has been told,' she said. It was some months ago now that she had finally brought herself to try again to explain to the child that what his cousins had said was true, and his daddy couldn't come back here because he had been hurt too badly to go on living. He had seemed to accept the facts at last, to put behind him all need to cling to whatever remained of Alexander in his young memory.

'Uncle Chris is taking us out for the day in his car, and we're all going to have lots of fun together,' Helen reminded him firmly.

'I don't want to go.'

'I've brought a football, and there's a kite for you.'

'Not for Neil, I think, Chris,' said Helen sharply, sickened by her son's behaviour. 'Not if you've any sense. He doesn't deserve them.'

'We'll see.' He smiled encouragingly at the boy.

One small foot darted out but before it contacted his shin Christopher had seized it. 'Now what?' he challenged.

Biting his lip, Neil clung to the door for support.

With his other hand, Chris detained Helen as she

approached, intent on punishing Neil. But she had had enough.

'Get upstairs this minute, Neil. Fetch your sweater off the bed, and then we are going out right away.'

To her relief Neil trudged away, albeit unwillingly.

'We may as well sit down,' she said, leading the way into the large reception room. 'I'm afraid he won't exactly hurry.'

Chris went to a sofa opposite the chair where she was sitting.

Helen noticed his worried look and sighed before speaking. 'It's ages since he reacted this way about his father, pretending he's still alive. I don't know what . . .'

'Don't you? He's being presented with another trauma – in human shape.'

'Good heavens, don't blame yourself.'

'I'd lay money on being proved right. I'm the threat to the status quo, the person who's intruding on his relationship with you.'

'Then he'd better learn to adapt,' said Helen. 'I'll be hanged if I'm going to spend the rest of my life being dictated to by my own son. He'll just have to wait till – well, I suppose till time or something else shows him that I'm not going to disappear.'

Chris smiled slightly, but without meeting her eyes. Not for worlds would he spoil things between mother and son. But it was good to know that the mother, at least, seemed prepared to accept a few changes.

When Neil eventually came stomping back down the stairs, Helen was glad to see Chris stepping forward to help him wriggle into the sweater. And the child actually accepted his assistance.

Going out to the car, though, Neil rather spoiled all that. 'What a funny old car,' he said scornfully. 'My daddy's is newer than that. And very big.'

'Well, I'm not rich,' Chris told him briskly. 'So this is the car that I have. Would you like to sit in the front?'

'No.'

'No, what?' Helen reproved him.

'No, I don't. I don't want to go in his rotten car at all. But you'll make me.'

Wordlessly, Chris folded forward the front passenger seat and indicated that Neil should get into the back. Although he complied, there was a wail of protest when his mother settled into the front.

'Mummy, Mummy, in here! In here with me.'

'No. You're behaving just like a baby. I don't want to sit with somebody like that.'

After several minutes of very audible sniffing while they drove along, Neil quietened and began looking out of the window. The hated car wasn't all bad — being smaller than many it was nearer to the ground and gave him quite a good view of the places and people they were passing. He began pulling faces. Unfortunately, no one seemed to notice.

'I hope you're not going to be terribly sorry that you wished a certain small person on yourself today,' said Helen quietly.

Chris grinned. 'I'll survive. He's bound to resent anyone who claims any of your precious time.' I wonder who that 'Uncle' Vittore was, he thought, and why he didn't last? Assuming that he wasn't still in the picture somewhere. He couldn't be jealous of someone who seemed to have had a relationship with Helen in the days before he himself had come back into her life, but he'd have liked to have known more. If only how far it had gone. Hadn't Neil said this Vittore had lived with her? Strange that. He wouldn't have thought she was the sort.

'Mummy, I've got to wee!'

Again, Helen sighed. 'Chris, I'm sorry – could you stop somewhere along here, please? I'm afraid with all the fuss back there I never checked that he . . .'

Christopher laughed. 'That's all right. I can draw in just here. There's a field with a gate. And at least he warned us.'

After that the day improved. Neil began replying when spoken to and by the time Chris parked at a spot high on the moors, was showing much more interest.

'Did you say you've got a football?'

Chris kicked the ball around with him untiringly while Helen sat among the heather, relishing the fresh air and the hills ranged for miles all about them, but most of all the sight of the two males whom she loved enjoying a game together.

They picnicked from a handy rock and Neil delighted in passing around plates and mugs, and behaving with all the charm of the well-mannered child that Helen had been hoping he might become.

Afterwards Chris demonstrated patiently with the kite and then helped Neil to handle it until shrieks of pure joy rose with the song of neighbouring skylarks.

Leaning back into the slope of the moors, Helen closed eyes that suddenly were pricking with happy tears. Never in her life had she felt more contented. Seeing Neil responding at last to Christopher's interest was such a relief. And as for Chris himself, she could hardly believe the good fortune which had ensured their paths should cross again.

I couldn't let him go, not now, she realised. I couldn't bear never to see him again.

Opening her eyes, she was just in time to see Chris hauling in the kite, and grasping her son's hand as they ran back to join her.

'We're going to rest now,' he announced, plonking

Neil down beside her before hurrying to the car to fetch the slate and pencil.

'What's that for?' asked the boy, frowning at the battered frame of the slate and turning it over to find that the other side was no different.

'It's a slate, to draw on,' Helen told him, and smiled at Chris. 'I used to have one of these, Neil, and your Cousin Linda did a lot of drawing on one. I don't know where Uncle Chris found this, but it's a long time since I saw any.'

'How about showing me how clever you are?' Chris suggested, lowering himself on to the ground beside them. 'Are you going to draw, or can you write your name now you're growing so fast?'

Neil, scowling again, examined the slate pencil then tested it by drawing a long line down one side of the slate.

The half-forgotten screech made both Helen and Chris laugh, but Neil's reaction was anything but amusement.

'That's horrible,' he shouted. 'I hate it!' He flung away both slate and pencil as hard as he could.

The pencil disappeared through low-growing bilberries. The slate struck rock and fell apart, the frame broken and the slate itself split in two.

Helen sprang to her feet. 'You hateful boy! That was very rude and ungrateful. That slate didn't belong to you, it wasn't yours to break. I won't have such awful behaviour.'

But Chris checked her by grasping her hand as she made to hasten past him. Still smiling, although concernedly, he shook his head at her.

'Leave it,' he murmured.

His steady brown gaze seemed to lock on to hers, while his expression told her that they shared too much for it to be destroyed by one small boy's aggression.

God, but I do love you, she thought. And yet she still seemed to feel apprehension gathering about her just as electricity might charge the air, presaging the storm that would ravage these tranquil moors.

Chapter 21

Exhausted by the conflicting emotions of the day, Helen decided on an early night. When Christopher left after having tea with them at the house, she took Neil straight upstairs.

'You were naughty today, and it's only thanks to your Uncle Chris that you didn't get the smacked bottom I was itching to give you,' she told him seriously. 'Now he might be patient with you, but I'm not going to be. You've been taught how to behave and I won't have you showing me up, especially when people are being kind to you.'

'Sorry, Mummy,' he murmured huskily, the eyelashes so like his father's suddenly fringed with tears.

Helen still felt disturbed by the time she went to her own bed, though there was more now to keep her awake. During the day, while they had been with Chris, she had been aware of him throughout the whole of her body. With each accelerating pulse and every tremor deep within her she had been conscious of the growing attraction between them.

Alone in her room, she longed to show him a bit of affection; to have him near, to trace the firm line of his jaw, to feel that crisp dark hair beneath her fingers, to have his arms round her. She longed to kiss those barely remembered lips, to cling as they had just that once in the past, and to have him touch her.

For hours she lay needing sleep, yet torn between surrendering to its calm and remaining with this awareness of being alive again, reawakened by him.

Towards morning she became troubled by misgivings. Wasn't she rushing headlong again, letting emotions overrule good sense? Had she learned nothing from the trauma caused by her poor judgement of Vittore? With him, there had been that long period of working together on the farm — yet she'd still had to discover the hard way how little she had really known him.

There was her disappointing marriage as well, the early years of working alongside Alexander had failed to reveal how ill matched they were. Now Chris had come back into her life after all this time without any contact between them. And here she was like a bit of a girl, preparing to stake all her happiness on their having a future together. She must slow down and *think* before setting the scene for a third disaster.

'I've always loved you though,' she whispered into the darkness where only trees stirring in the breeze interrupted utter silence. More than Vittore who once seemed to matter to me, she reflected, and more by far than I ever loved my husband.

Alongside this needing and this love there was also this great renewal of hope — again, because of Christopher. I'd never ask for another thing, she resolved, if we could make this relationship work.

Screams from Neil's room wakened Helen almost as soon as she began dozing. Struggling out of bed, she stumbled towards the door and, almost staggering with weariness, ran to him.

His eyes were dry, but they seemed the only dry thing about him. The bed and his pyjamas were saturated. She didn't need to ask why he was distressed.

'I'm wet, Mummy,' he announced unnecessarily, sounding indignant.

'And whose fault's that?' she demanded, before reminding herself that reprimanding him would solve nothing. 'Okay, let's have you out of there. Find some clean pyjamas while I change this bed.'

For night after night Neil continued wetting, and although Mrs Hartley calmly accepted all the extra washing, Helen could not concur with her opinion that it didn't really matter. She knew that it did, if only as a symptom of her son's disturbance. Neil had been an easy boy to train. She'd always been proud of how soon he was dry at night as well as during the day. And now this regression. She could only blame her renewed friendship with Chris and the changes it was producing.

Helen tried being particularly loving with Neil, spoiling him far more than she'd ever thought wise. He responded by becoming more demanding, pestering for new toys and trying emotional blackmail as a means of gaining more of her time. And he still wet the bed with distressing regularity.

Chris was keeping in touch with her by telephone, and suggested that she and Neil should come to him for a weekend. 'You've never heard me preach and it's our patronal festival on Sunday. I've got the whole of Saturday free. We could take a trip out, maybe up into the Dales.'

Helen wouldn't stay the night in Leeds, and made the excuse that she had work to do on the Sunday. She wouldn't explain about Neil's bed-wetting, not so much because it reflected on her but rather for her own certainty that it was on Christopher's account that her son had reverted to babyish traits. Chris himself was just as likely to reach that same assumption.

Having agreed just to go over on the Saturday,

Helen soon became convinced that she had made the right decision, if for different reasons. The minute that she'd told him their plans Neil retorted that he was not going to go and see Uncle Christopher.

'He's not my uncle, and I don't want to go anywhere in his rotten car.'

'For heaven's sake, Neil, stop being so silly. You're downright ungrateful. Your Uncle Chris wants to make both of us happy, and if you'd only be agreeable for once you'd begin enjoying yourself.'

On the day itself Neil was silent and withdrawn, making Helen long to shake him. After they had set out from the vicarage – in her car because he had muttered about not liking Christopher's – he lapsed into misery from which no attempts at conversation roused him.

'I'm terribly sorry, Chris,' Helen said fervently, tears filling her grey eyes, when they stopped for a picnic lunch and nothing that Chris had insisted on preparing for them suited the lad. 'I wish I'd left him with our Marian or my mother.'

But leaving Neil with anyone else would be no lasting solution. She couldn't go on for ever like this, being wrenched apart by her love for her son and for Christopher.

They were sitting beside the river at Grassington after driving out via Fewston where they'd stopped to admire the picturesque reservoir. Helen had been thinking that she'd never enjoyed so much lovely scenery, until Neil's sullenness intruded yet again.

During the journey back to Leeds as surrounding limestone rocks gave way to the darker sandstone, Chris said the one thing which Helen had longed for years to hear. Neil was asleep on the back seat. They were running downhill through a sunlit dale, with a river meandering between meadows dotted with grazing cattle and sheep. Woods clothed the steeply sloping hills, with purple moors beyond and craggs on the horizon.

'I love you, Helen, I want you to marry me,' Chris said quietly. 'Lord knows, I've waited long enough. There's only ever been you, and I can't bear the thought that even now we might not end up together.'

'Oh, Chris, I'd love us to marry. If only . . .'

'Neil?' he murmured. 'I do understand, love, that you have to put him first. But I'm not giving up hope that he'll come round. I do know how he must feel — that he can't bear to have me monopolising the bit of free time that you do have. And I think we can win him round, if we put it to him in the right manner.'

They tried that evening after tea at the vicarage, during which Neil had been persuaded into talking to Chris, if only about some of his toys. There had been one difficult moment when he had mentioned the aeroplane that Uncle Vittore had given him. Helen could have done without that particular reminder at this time, but no one else appeared perturbed by it. One day she would explain to Chris that Vittore was the person who'd joined her at Stone's, and how he'd shattered her by trying to take over.

'Would you like to see the room where I think you'd enjoy playing with all your toys?' Chris had suggested as tea was ending.

'I have a playroom, thank you,' Neil responded, rigidly, icily polite.

'Yes, but you see — your mother and I are hoping that some day you might both come to live here.'

'No, never. I want to live in my house, always and always.'

Helen had taken Neil firmly by the hand and after reminding him to say thank you for his tea, led him

431

along in the wake of Chris as he headed towards the rather dark staircase.

The room was large, but had dingy wallpaper and despite a window that overlooked the back of the church seemed drab. Glancing about, Helen noticed that someone had hastily covered the centre of the floor with an ageing carpet. It wasn't quite parallel with the walls, and to one end the polished boards were revealed through a layer of dust in squares and rectangles where boxes had been stored. Picturing Chris trying to put the room to rights for her son, Helen felt her eyes blurring.

Her response this afternoon to his proposal had been instinctive. She would love to marry him. But she mustn't risk making another terrible mistake. While putting Neil forward as the obstacle, she'd known in her heart that she was really protecting them all from the possibility of future disappointment. This room, more than anything, convinced her of the depth of Christopher's feelings for them both. This was reality, down-to-earth evidence of his eagerness to make a place for them with him.

But, although she would never hurt Chris by expressing any fears that he, too, might eventually let her down, she still had to be reassured that none of them would suffer by trying to make a life together. The time needed for persuading Neil would provide a breathing space. Opportunity for them all to become more sure about one another.

'It's lovely and big,' she exclaimed, smiling appreciatively.

'This would be just for you,' Chris told Neil, bending down so that his eyes were level with the boy's defiant grey ones. 'You could do exactly as you liked in here. Nobody would make a fuss about any mess or anything . . .'

432

'No, thank you,' Neil interrupted coldly. 'I don't like it here. I don't, I don't!'

'But, Neil,' Helen persisted. 'Just think, Uncle Chris wants to look after us both, and especially to look after you. He wants to teach you games, just the way your daddy would have taught you.'

'No. I want to live in my house.'

'But why?' Christopher asked gently. 'You would be surrounded by all your own books and toys, everything that belongs to you. This would be your home. Let me show you the room where we'd put your own little bed.'

Solemnly, Neil continued shaking his head. Helen and Chris exchanged a despairing glance.

'I know,' said Neil after a moment's thought. 'Mummy can live with you, I'll live at Auntie Marian's house. With her and Uncle Denis and Mark and Linda. I like it there.'

Utterly shaken, so wretched that she was on the verge of weeping, Helen gulped. She turned swiftly to stare out of the window.

Chris was trying to catch her attention, but she was in no state for even listening to what he intended as reassurance.

'There's time,' he said calmly. 'I daresay this is too soon.'

It isn't for me, she thought. It feels as if I've waited a lifetime already. And on every occasion that we meet it seems that our ever belonging to each other grows increasingly unlikely.

When she controlled her emotions sufficiently, she faced Neil and spoke sternly. 'There's no chance that you'll ever go and live with your Auntie Marian. You can put that idea right out of your head.'

Helen did decide, though, that if Chris still wanted to see her again she would leave Neil with Marian, perhaps even overnight. Chris was entitled to some private life, if she herself was finding arranging any virtually impossible.

All the way home that evening, Helen grew more and more sickened by what Neil had said. Did she mean so little to him that he could so readily contemplate living with her sister? This reminder brought hurtling back every opinion of Alexander's about Marian caring for Neil. She was thankful that there was no sound from the back seat where her son had fallen asleep again. She hadn't the heart to chatter away as they normally did during car journeys.

For days Helen remained so distressed by Neil's suggestion that she had to force herself to do any work at her drawing board or desk. But if the boy was succeeding in ruining everything else for her, she certainly wasn't going to let him affect her job. While discussing meals or other household matters, Mrs Hartley would frown and ask whatever was wrong. Helen didn't like dismissing the kindly enquiry with a hasty 'nothing', but she had no intention of admitting Neil's hurtful assertion to anyone.

The words had cut so deeply. How could a four-year-old boy be willing to live apart from his mother, especially when he'd already lost his father? Reflecting on how he'd reacted ever since Alexander's death, Helen began believing that Neil must think a lot more of him than ever he had of her. Yet it was over two years now since the accident. She was surprised that Neil had any clear memories of his father. Where was she going wrong?

It was then that she recalled how Alexander had accused her of only ever doing what she wanted. Was that the reason behind this trouble? But that couldn't be true, could it, not of her behaviour towards Neil? Apart from her work, which was after all for both their sakes, she'd spent the whole of the last two years putting Neil before herself. *Until renewing acquaintance with Christopher.*

Helen was compelled to admit that it must seem to the boy that his position as sole claimant on her love and attention was being displaced. Grimly, she began to wonder if the only way of restoring Neil's contentment was by sacrificing her own.

There was still her work. And a great deal that was of interest was going on in architecture now. The contest for designing the new cathedral at Coventry had produced some fascinating ideas. For the first time ever, she herself had fallen for a modern scheme. Perhaps because of its planned use of uncoursed pink sandstone for the exterior or maybe for his decision to incorporate the adjacent ruins of the original, she was very much in favour of the controversial winning design by Basil Spence.

And being delighted by such an up-to-date concept, Helen had felt her own ambitions widening. If only I was free to get around and visit more potential development sites, she thought longingly, I might extend myself. Perhaps in doing so I would discover satisfaction.

It was she herself, after all, who had mapped out her life, selecting this career and working always to achieve her aims. Maybe having some degree of success in that was all she deserved. Wasn't she expecting too much by aching for personal happiness? For love?

The church was empty and, except for birdsong and the thrum of traffic, strangely silent. Chris was accustomed by now to the sound of the congregation behind him; even at early weekday Communion, to the presence of one or two parishioners. Today, though, he had sought this solitude, urged by his own disquiet to pause in his busy life and examine this, his failure.

How long, he wondered, how long have I been deluding myself about my ability to relate to youngsters? This belief in his own affinity with children and teenagers had developed throughout his first curacy and increased ever since. He had thought he understood the way their minds worked, from the blessed simplicity of the very young, right the way through the difficulties of adolescence to the ambitions of late teenage.

Well, if he'd been arrogant in assuming he had some such spark, this certainly was his comeuppance! And the circumstances couldn't have been more distressing. The irony of having Helen restored to him in such a miraculous fashion, only to have their hopes thwarted by her son's attitude, was unbearable. Had he been so very wrong to believe that he might have a real home at last, with the one woman who had awakened him to this yearning for a deeper expression of loving? Why, *how*, had he failed in his determined effort to bring more love into the life of her small son?

God help him, but he was drained now, wrung dry by trying to please the lad, to give him the kind of fun a child should be enjoying, and this additional love. Always love — love which normally is healing.

Heaven knew if there existed any way now in which he might get through to Neil. He literally would do anything, if it were any use, would wear himself out over any means which could reconcile the lad to him. As things stood, it looked as though he would eventually have to resign himself to spending the rest of his life apart from Helen. He had seen the tears in her eyes the other day, couldn't put her through much more of the distress of being torn in two directions.

Proposing to her had been an impulse which he

couldn't have withheld for much longer. She couldn't know how many years ago it was, nor how far away that lifetime now seemed, when he had become convinced that he would marry no other woman.

Thinking back now, the heat of the desert oppressed him, its sand scratched beneath his lowered eyelids. The stink of death filled his nostrils. His hands felt heavy with the spade that too often had been employed to inter his comrades. All too frequently, it had been a solitary business. Forces at war couldn't always spare time from fighting to bury the men dying beside them.

There'll be better times, he had assured himself, just as he had assured his men. He liked to think that some of them, if not all, had believed him. Even when they had been shot to pieces, to lie in the heat, trying to come to terms with severed limbs, nerves completely shattered, or eyes that would remain sightless.

With them and through them, he had suffered his own hell. Had hurt because they were hurting, and he could bring them no real relief. For there were no answers, only the hope which he had tried to hold before them.

His own endurance of that North African campaign had been through moments of escape: when his soul, troubled past bearing by the carnage all around, had sought the only sources of tranquillity which he'd ever discovered. Still fresh in his memory at that time, he'd pictured so often the glorious day of his ordination, and the weeks which had preceded that most solemn occasion.

Being accepted as he was had been the greatest joy of all. In that final term he had laid before their College Superior every one of his doubts about himself. And had found they were understood. That, more than anything, had convinced him that he stood a chance of making a fair job of being a clergyman. Eventually.

Compelled by his innate straightforwardness to lay bare every private misgiving, he'd brought out all the emotions that had troubled him since that day in 1938. He could see now that drab, worn study, and the elderly priest who so often looked no less worn. And he experienced afresh the enormous relief which had followed the old man's opinion.

'Do not try yourself too hard, my son, this isn't an easy life you've selected. Don't make it unnecessarily harder.'

Unnecessarily? But he'd always thought, had believed, that by committing himself to a celibate life he would be making a better offering. Would have become a better priest. More use even . . .

His Superior had smiled, knowingly, knowing him. 'Give all you can — the Lord understands. He won't fail to smile on you, should you feel the need of an earthly partner. Come now, Chris, you're forgetting where your feelings originated.'

War had followed only weeks after that Trinity Ordination in 1939. There had been little time for thinking, scarcely any for private prayer after becoming an army chaplain. And then he had found himself in the desert. The place where he'd confronted the reality that is war, and had been driven by the lives deprived of a future to reconsider his own life.

All those years ago, he'd been bothered still by the readiness with which he'd been relieved of the obligation to commit himself to living a sexless existence. It had seemed to him then to have one purpose only. Freedom to marry had granted him freedom to remember her, his ideal woman.

The impact of that short encounter with Helen had remained as clear in his mind as the Swiss mountain air. Every intonation of her voice had resurrected for him, along with that smile and those exquisite grey eyes. Surrounded by battle, he had turned the eye of his mind inward to find her, and silently to make another vow.

During the intervening years in his first two parishes he'd met no serious challenge to his resolution. There had been attractive young women, of course, the proverbial bevy of them had constituted a part of the congregation. Most had flirted with him, two or three had been intelligent enough to engage more than his male vanity, but there wasn't one among them who'd made him wish to reconsider.

His search for Helen had begun after the war, once he returned to Yorkshire. It had lasted all of an hour. He had remembered she was training to be an architect and, although he had at first been unable to find her under her maiden name in the directory of Architects he'd tracked down, he'd remembered her mentioning Alexander Stone and his architect father. And there he'd found her. Under Helen Stone, her married name.

And now here he was, again brought to his knees, and this time despite their reunion. They had come so near. How could he give up now? He could only set his mind to making more of an effort.

'I want to see you,' he said over the phone, after working his way through extended preliminaries about the weather and other matters of no consequence. 'I'm hoping there might be some way of getting Neil to adjust to the prospect of the three of us having some kind of future together. I thought if perhaps you and I could have a talk, alone . . .'

Even while she was agreeing, Helen felt no more optimistic than she had when they'd last said goodbye. But she was utterly depressed by not seeing Chris and would do almost anything so long as they could meet.

'I've left him with our Marian,' she said as soon as Chris opened the door to her. 'If I'm not back this evening she'll put him to bed, and I've told her I'll pick him up by tomorrow afternoon at the latest. At least Neil's happy about that arrangement.'

'But you're not.' He ached for her. She looked so ill, thinner than ever he'd seen her. Her silky-looking skirt and blouse were navy blue, exquisitely cut, but for the woman she once had been — certainly two sizes larger. All the lustre was gone from the grey eyes which seemed to stare distractedly from her haggard face.

Helen shrugged. 'Would you be happy if your only son had turned round and told you he'd rather live permanently with your sister?'

'It's all my fault.'

'No, Chris, it isn't. You mustn't think that, love, not ever. It's me — something I lack that prevents me providing Neil with the kind of mother he needs.' Her eyes were awash with tears now, bringing a lump to his own throat.

'That's nonsense, Helen.'

'No, it's the truth. Alexander saw it. He was always telling me I ought to be a better mother, that I ought to give all my time to Neil.'

'And make the lad unduly self-centred in the process?'

His words checked her. 'But, Chris, it wouldn't have that effect surely? It's the way I am that's made him so wretchedly insecure he needs all my attention.'

'Rubbish! That's due to losing his father so young.'

It was the sort of thing other people had said. She wished with all her heart that she might begin to believe it. 'But that wouldn't make him want to live at our Marian's.'

'No — and I think that's another, simpler issue. Because being with her family is fun, exciting. Lots of children go through phases of preferring to stay with cousins or friends.'

'Well, it doesn't seem like that to me.'

'Of course not. You're extremely vulnerable to every breath of criticism. And with a son like Neil, I'm afraid there's plenty of that around.'

'There wouldn't be if I always handled him properly.'

'Oh, Helen!' Smiling ruefully, he took her hands and pulled her to him. Locking his arms about her, he kissed her fervently on the mouth. 'I'd do anything, anything — to stop you being hurt.'

She swallowed, looked up at him. 'I wish I knew where to turn. This is all so bloody.'

'I know. That's why I wanted to talk — see if we can sort something.'

'There is no solution. I'm sorry, Chris, but that is the way things stand. Neil won't budge, and I can't see that any of us will be happy while he can't accept the prospect of our being together.' She was weeping now, tears trickling down her cheeks and dripping off her chin.

Chris continued hugging her. 'Leave it for now then, eh? I'll take you out somewhere instead, where we can have a quiet meal, concentrate on each other.'

They drove to Otley where, following their meal, they walked in the evening sunlight beside the River Wharfe. On the water couples rowed tiny boats peacefully back and forth while elderly folk strolled along the path or paused to rest on green-painted seats adjacent to fragrant rosebeds. Near the opposite bank houses, terraced and of stone, stood comfortably with each other and with the tranquil scene. Helen envied quite fiercely all the folk here, visible and unseen, for the absence from their lives of her own massive burden.

'I love you, that's why I want us to marry,' Chris reminded her, taking her hand, smoothing it with his fingers. 'Let me take your anxieties, about Neil, about everything.'

She shook her head. Her smile was sad. 'I wish you could, I wish I could let you. Though you probably carry more than enough weight as it is, through your work.'

'That's different. I'm not so deeply and personally involved.'

'But it can't be easy.'

His short laugh was rueful. 'Nothing is, ever. Remember what you once said, all those years ago? About the "comfort" in believing. I ought to feel that it's there. Somehow I can never even bring myself to preach that it is. What comfort is there among the losses that come in everyone's life, or in wars, in disagreements that arise often simply from expressing one's beliefs, or in circumstances which enforce grave disappointment? Faith doesn't bring an automatic palliative.'

'What then?' Helen asked, more interested now in his thoughts than her own difficulties.

Christopher shrugged. 'Endurance, I suppose. To ensure that one survives long enough to accept whatever's dealt out.'

On the way back to Leeds they both fell quiet, each preoccupied with matters already aired, and to no satisfactory end.

The scenery through which they drove was still lovely, but Helen could hardly bear to look. For most of her life she had been moved by beautiful countryside, perhaps even more so than by the exquisite man-made buildings that had inspired her.

Viewing these splendid hills of her native Yorkshire, she'd often experienced intense yearning simply to share it all with somebody who mattered. And now here they were, so close that their arms were touching in the car, and all she knew was dread that Neil would keep them apart. For ever.

'It's strange, you know,' said Chris, leading the way indoors, 'I could have sworn that it was right for us to end up together, that it was meant.' He ached to tell her of his thoughts during the war. And knew that he couldn't without forcing her hand.

'Me too.' She sounded forlorn. 'I love you so much, Chris. I've realised recently that I've wanted you for so long that nobody else ever stood a chance of measuring up.'

He drew her to him again, kissing her repeatedly, on her hair, her eyelids, and then her lips. 'God, but I don't want to live without you.'

Starved of each other, they clung, bodies feverish with need.

'Lord, but I need you,' Christopher sighed, his yearning somehow increased by reflecting on his miserable failure to win Neil's approval. 'Hold me, Helen, hold me.'

Her arms slid round him, making him groan with delight. Her breasts felt hard against his chest. The force straining from deep within him was moving beyond his will, developing its own impetus.

His hand went between them, caressing her breast, then passing over her flat stomach. A tiny moan of sheer pleasure escaped her lips.

'Yes, Chris, yes . . .'

He drew her down with him on to his old sofa, too eager now even to ensure her comfort. Pushing the material of her skirt aside, he traced her inner thigh, hesitated.

'Don't stop now,' she cried, her lips seeking his mouth.

He felt slender fingers on him, urging him to love her, while her tongue tested his own, willing him to seal their union. His every pulse was awake, beating in echo of this massive lifetime's need. He'd never imagined an impulse so strong, could not think how he had existed without making her belong to him.

And then he thought of Neil, and how the boy would fight to the end to keep them apart. He couldn't do this to Helen. Neil was the centre of her world. Even her work was in aid of the future she would create for him. A future that would be full and interesting without Chris Maitland, the man who only aroused her son's antagonism.

'I'm sorry,' he said quietly. 'I shouldn't have gone this far. The situation's intolerable, isn't it? I'd not forgive myself for letting the worst happen when we know there's precious little hope of marriage.'

'It wouldn't be the worst, Chris. I want to love you.'

Too weak with longing to ignore her words, he closed his eyes, savouring the touch of her hands, surrendering to kisses no less passionate than his own. For this he had waited throughout the whole of his life. Through study, training, the war, and afterwards. To come to this time, this place, to her.

'Let's go up to bed, Chris.'

Her words alerted him to how close they had come, to the hair's breadth that stood between them and . . .

'I'll show you to your room,' he stated carefully, rising as he spoke and willing his light-headedness to disperse. There seemed no chance that the rest of his enormous discomfort would ever be relieved.

He returned downstairs swiftly the moment that he'd seen her to her room. Grimly, recognising that he literally was removing himself from temptation, he went towards his study and closed the door.

It was two in the morning when Chris finally went upstairs, after wrestling for hours to master himself and concentrate on the sermon he must finish.

The door of her room was ajar. Lit by the bedside lamp, her hair gleamed with lights, gilding its brown strands. Her face was as pale as her cream silk nightgown, and looked stricken. A lump rose in his throat to choke him.

'Helen? Are you all right?'

'We neither of us are, are we? I can't bear this.'

He hurried to the bed, sat on its edge and pulled her into his arms. What use was love when he was denied using it for the one person who meant the world to him? For the two people . . .

Chris couldn't avoid kissing her any more than he could curtail this need to hold her. When she leaned back into the pillows he moved with her, pressed his face into the hollow of her throat. Her perfume was delicate, hardly more than a hint, but it filled his nostrils, while her taste beneath his lips seemed sweet, utterly delicious.

He could only draw nearer, sliding one arm beneath her as he edged his body over hers. Helen's sigh was blissful. She raised a hand to his head, then met his mouth with her lips.

Beneath the covers keeping them apart, she began stirring, her hips urging him to move with her. His need tremendous again, Chris could not resist, but only surrender his will. His own hardness alarmed him, renewing awareness of where its force might lead. Not yet, though, he murmured within his head to the cautious half of his nature, while desire drove him to intensify their kisses and to continue this relentless stirring.

There was no solution. They parted after a while,

445

their glances rueful, admitting that regardless of their needs, they must be realistic, that there were too many obstacles. And remembering that he was a priest.

'But I am also a man,' Christopher added gravely. 'You know how much I want you. Continued self-denial simply isn't practical.'

Helen heard the telephone ringing at five-thirty in the morning, and Chris running downstairs to answer it. I suppose vicars are much like doctors for being called out at all hours, she thought.

Five minutes later he appeared in the doorway of her room. He was tying the cord of the dressing gown he'd grabbed. She'd never seen him looking as anxious.

'I'm terribly sorry, love, that was for you. Your sister. I'm afraid . . .'

'Oh, God – Neil!' Helen interrupted. 'Whatever's happened, is he ill?'

'No, love. There's probably a simple explanation, but – well, he seems to have disappeared.'

'He can't have! He's only little. Children his age don't just go wandering away.' She began scrambling out of bed. 'Is Marian still on the line?'

'No, she rang off.' Marian had said she was phoning the police, but he didn't believe knowing that would help Helen. 'She'd told me all she could. Evidently he seemed to settle all right last night, and she took him to the bathroom around three o'clock. But when her son wakened a couple of hours later Neil wasn't in his bed.'

Helen turned icily cold and was shuddering with dread. 'Have they searched the garden? It's nothing like as big as at The Stone House, but happen he's hiding. I'll have to get there, straight away.'

They took her car, it was speedier and more reliable, but Chris drove. Helen was so shattered that all she could do was sit huddled into her seat, worrying. Even when they began driving into Halifax she could hardly compose herself enough to direct him to her sister's.

Marian was at the door of the terraced house before Helen had hurtled up the short path.

'Denis has gone looking for him with them,' she said. 'Eh, love, I'm that sorry! But I only said it for the best, because I was sure it was what you'd want me to say . . .'

'Said? Want you to say? Whatever's been going on?'

'Come and sit down a minute, both of you.'

'Nay, I'll not,' Helen contradicted. 'I'm off searching as soon as I find out what you've been up to.'

'Well, it was last night, just before he went up to bed. They'd all been having a right good time playing out. And Neil said summat about wanting to come and live here. Well, what could I say? I couldn't let him go on thinking that was likely, could I? So I told him that he belonged with you, that he'd live with you till he grew up and had a home of his own.'

Helen heard Christopher's deep sigh, and then a voice which appeared to be her own saying, 'You were quite right, Marian, love, you mustn't blame yourself.'

Leaving Marian by the telephone, they set out on foot. A thin drizzle was falling, making the terraced houses look greyer than ever, sending Helen's panic racing out of control.

'He'll be wet through in this. He'll get his death of cold, pneumonia even . . . That's if we ever find him.'

'Somebody'll come across him before so long,' Chris began assuring her. 'Now the police are out.'

'Police? *Police*? That means they think he's been kidnapped, doesn't it, or worse?'

'It means nothing of the kind, love. Simply that they're doing their utmost to find him.'

They turned a corner and saw two uniformed officers going from door to door, knocking people up where necessary, and looking into yards and gardens. It all made Neil's disappearance more real and alarming.

'Maybe we can be more use if we investigate some of his haunts. Or has he made any little friends round here?' said Chris.

'Not that I know of. He was usually quite content to play with Mark and Linda. Mostly in their garden. I think sometimes Denis or Marian took them to the park.'

'Is it far?'

'Just across Warley Road — that's the one over there across the top of Hopwood Lane.'

'And the park's not locked at night?'

'I don't know.'

'I don't suppose it's had any gates since they were all taken for salvage. We'll make that our first call, shall we?'

'If you think that's best,' Helen replied, unable to think rationally any longer.

What will I do if something's happened to him? she thought, panicking again. Whatever will I do? I'll never forgive myself.

Chapter 22

The curtains at the lodge were still closed. There wasn't another person visible as far as they could see across the park.

'Do you think we ought to try and find the park keeper?' Helen asked.

Chris shook his head. 'Not for the minute, love. Might as well take a look for ourselves. If he hasn't come on duty yet, he'll not have seen anything either.'

Hurriedly, they followed the curving path, defying the rain driving into their faces as they glanced sideways towards flowerbeds, herbaceous borders, and shrubs.

'We'll investigate those more thoroughly if we don't find him soon,' Chris stated.

'He could be anywhere,' Helen said. 'Even if he is in the park, anywhere at all.'

'Well, we'll have to see.' Chris was thankful there was no evidence of people sleeping rough here.

They came to a terrace balustraded in stone, and stood for a few seconds looking to left and right, and then down to where the ground fell away sharply below them.

In the distance ahead, where the view over the valley should have been, everything was whited out by rain as opaque as cloud.

'Come on,' Chris urged her, taking her elbow and heading towards steps. 'Looks like there's more than one path, we'll have to be systematic. Where does all this lead?'

'Eventually, down to Burnley Road. That's the one that goes out our way.'

'Do you think somebody might have told Neil that, have shown him the direction of The Stone House perhaps?' But surely a lad that age wouldn't have set out to walk there?

'I've no idea.'

They took the first path on the left, began following it downhill. Helen slithered on the surface treacherous with rain and Chris caught her against him. She closed her eyes, yearning just to be held there, to be able to cease thinking.

'What's that?' he exclaimed, suddenly, making her jump.

'Oh, God, let him be all right!' she exclaimed, freeing herself and starting to run across grass that soaked her feet.

In a slight hollow, shielded on one side by a large rock and on another by a collection of shrubs, was a hunched figure. His bright gold hair darkened by the rain, and bare legs tucked beneath him, he was clutching his coat round him. The buttons were fastened wrongly, leaving a gap at the neck and one bottom corner dangling.

'Neil! Oh, my darling!'

'Mummy, Mummy!'

He tried to stand and couldn't. His legs had been cramped too long while he waited there, miserably lost.

'I wanted to go home,' he said. And didn't protest when Chris scooped him up and prepared to carry him back to Marian's. 'Don't forget my things,' he said though, and pointed to a now muddy bundle beside the rock.

Even distressed as she had been, Helen was compelled to smile. The bundle was knotted clumsily to a stick that she recognised from Mark's drumkit.

'I couldn't find a spotted hanky,' Neil explained, quite cheerfully now. 'I took a cover off Linda's doll's pram. It was only big enough for my pyjama bottoms. And some marshmallows — I ate those when the rain started.'

They met Denis with the police after crossing Warley Road again, and were whisked by police car back to the terraced house where Marian hugged first Helen and then young Neil. The next hour was a jumble of thanking the police and relating where the boy had been discovered, while Marian and Denis rushed around in the kitchen cooking breakfast.

Neil was plonked in a hot bath, and emerged to enjoy all the attention, demonstrating to his cousins how he had carried his pack on his shoulder just like the boy in his story book.

Eventually, Chris looked at his watch. 'I'm sorry, but I'll have to be on my way.'

Denis volunteered to drive him back to Leeds as soon as Helen had assured everyone that she was up to taking Neil home.

'I'm all right now, really,' she insisted. But even while she was thanking Chris for everything that he had done she was thinking that this crisis had proved that she couldn't put their life before Neil's wishes. No matter how much heartache she was creating for herself, she couldn't continue upsetting her son.

Helen rushed to answer the telephone. Despite her determination, she couldn't school herself not to hope that Chris might be on the line. He had rung the day after Neil's escapade and had mentioned a concert his church youngsters were giving. Although she'd tried to explain about not seeing him, she'd felt a bald 'no' was unwarranted. This time, anyway, the caller was her father.

'I don't like bothering you on a Saturday, love, not when you've been busy all week. But it's your mum. I'm afraid she's not a bit well.'

'Whatever's wrong, Dad?'

'Eh, I don't know. I'd been at work, you see, this morning. When I came round t'corner of the street, there was quite a crowd gathering in front of our house. I ran t'rest of the way and there she were — your mother. Somebody had fetched a chair out, and she were sat there, her hair all anyhow — you know how she keeps it tidy — and her face the colour of a floorcloth.'

'What had happened then?' asked Helen agitatedly, wishing he didn't take so long to get to the point.

'Seemingly, she'd passed clean out, just as she were coming out of their gate. You know how she will persist in looking after her next-door . . . Any road, as luck would have it, that young woman opposite happened to see. She were t'first to help her up.'

'And Mum — how is she now?'

'She says she's all right, but she never says owt else, does she? Won't have the doctor, of course. I keep telling her that's what this 'ere National Health is for.'

'I'll come on and see what I think, Dad. All right?'

Helen was arranging for Mrs Hartley to keep an eye on Neil for the afternoon when the telephone rang again. Her heart pounding as she imagined her mother having taken a turn for the worse, Helen tore across to lift the receiver.

This time it was Christopher. 'I'm on my way to see you, Helen. I'm going to have another shot at getting Neil on to my side. I love the boy, love both of you. I can't just give up.'

'Eh, Chris — I wish you'd let me know sooner. I've got to go out. My dad's just rung to tell me my mother's had some kind of a blackout. She's refusing to see a doctor, and I'm on my way there to try and sort something out.'

'That's in Halifax, isn't it?'

'Yes, but . . .' Helen jerked around to face the clock. She'd have to get moving.

'Give me the address. I'll meet you there.'

'But, Chris . . .'

'For God's sake — won't you even let me do one thing to help you?'

There wasn't time to argue. Helen sighed and told him the street and house number.

His old Ford was in the familiar street when Helen drew up there. She remembered then that he'd already been on his way over from Leeds. Getting out of her own car and locking it, Helen hurried up the short path to the door.

Chris opened it to her, making her wonder where her father was. Surely nothing had happened to him as well? 'Hallo,' she said. 'Where's Dad?'

'He's only down the steps,' called her mother. 'He won't be a minute.'

'Hallo, Mum,' said Helen, crossing swiftly to the armchair where she was sitting. 'Are you any better now?'

'Aye — I'm as right as rain again, bless you. I were just starting to tell Mr Maitland . . .' Surprising Helen, she laughed. 'I couldn't help seeing the funny side of it all. I said — didn't I, Mr Maitland, when you came through the door? — I thought, "Well, I'll go to heck. Somebody must think I'm not long for this world — they've fetched t'parson." '

Chris gave Helen a rueful smile. 'I'm hoping to convince her that all my work isn't funereal.'

'Aye, well, it looks as though it mightn't be today. We're ever so grateful,' Helen said, trying not to think how good it was to have him around when there was a crisis. 'Have you introduced yourself?' she asked Chris, and he beamed at her.

'As an old friend of yours. And as such I feel I ought to advise calling in the doctor, if only as a precaution.'

'I was going to, anyway. I'll just run to the 'phone box.'

Kathleen Clegg didn't argue against her decision. Hurrying along the street, Helen realised her mother must have been worried. She herself was badly shaken. Learning her parents weren't indestructible had brought her up sharp.

Some while later, Helen and Chris had retreated to the kitchen so that Kathleen, who refused to go up to a bedroom, could be examined by the doctor.

'I'm glad I'm here,' he told her quietly, leaning against the sink.

Helen gave him a look. 'You enjoy picking up the pieces when my family are in trouble, do you?' she asked dryly, sitting on the small table crammed in between the cupboard on one wall and her mother's Baby Belling oven which had stood against the other since replacing the fire range before the war.

'It's what life's about. And I've seen far worse. Blood, severed limbs, mangled corpses — in the desert.'

'So that's where the war took you?' She gazed at him, her grey eyes widening, remembering how she'd wondered at the farm where he might be, had been concerned for his safety. 'You've never told me.'

'One day I will.'

She didn't like there being a part of his life about which she knew nothing. 'Where else did you serve?'

'Various places, though the desert was where I was confronted by any actual fighting. That's how I got involved with wounded men. There's often only chaplains around who aren't combatant.'

Talking of the war brought back all her feelings about its failure to restore them to a really satisfactory peace. Suddenly, she needed to hear his answers. As she did to discuss so many things with him.

'What was it all for, Chris? All the bloodshed, I mean. We're not that much better off, are we? Here we are in the fifties, and we're nowhere near over the legacy of shortages, restrictions, and general dissatisfaction. *What was it for?*'

'Neither you nor I can say that for sure, Helen. Maybe simply to show us that war mustn't occur again. That it needn't.'

'A bit of a costly lesson.'

'Aren't they all?'

'You sound too cynical for somebody wearing their collar that way round!'

Christopher smiled. 'Not cynical, A realist maybe. I hope that I am. There's not much to recommend religion if it's not relevant to real life, is there?'

'Don't ask me — not my subject. Never has been. I'm just as confused as I was in Switzerland.'

'Oh, I don't think so. You're a survivor, Helen, a fighter. They don't struggle on unless they've found some hope.'

Hope, though, was something she found rather elusive during the next few weeks, although her mother had been pronounced by the doctor to be reasonably fit for her age and had felt well enough to discount his advice to take things easier. The blackout was attributed to nothing more alarming than doing too much when she hadn't eaten for hours. After the scare, Helen had realised that her father was nearing retirement age, even though he swore he'd never stop working. And her mother was four years his senior.

This sudden threat made her think. They've had a grand life together, she considered; ordinary, but grand. In their quiet way they had lived out the selflessness in which they believed, and would continue to the end to make this inconspicuous witness.

And what have I done, she often wondered in the night, except go out of my way to prove I could be an architect? No matter what the cost to other people.

There was precious little satisfaction now, even in the way her work was increasing. She had sent Chris away, albeit with her thanks, after that strange interlude in Halifax. Seeing him in her old home, eager to help her folk, had produced emotions in her far stronger than she could ignore. She'd wanted him then, in so many ways, and far more intensely than with mere desire.

If he couldn't continue being a part of her life, then she didn't know how she was going to exist. But there was Neil to consider as well — and he had to come first. He'd always blamed her, hadn't he, for causing his father's loss? She couldn't compel him to live with Chris when he so evidently hated the whole idea. And nor could she continue seeing Christopher, not when they knew that there must be no physical contact between them. She couldn't steel herself for that. Even in front of her mum and dad, she'd hardly known how not to hug him, just for being there. And she knew herself. She couldn't stop at a hug, nor at a kiss, and once she began . . . She'd only ever felt like this with Chris, driven by love as well as all her other senses. She couldn't keep on resisting.

On the day, Helen was wishing with all her heart that she'd been firmer about not going over for the

Sunday School concert. Since that parting on her mother's doorstep she had tussled with the conflict deep inside her.

This had got to stop. After today, it must. She would have to find a way of putting Chris right out of her mind; out of her life. She needed him too much. This had grown obsessive, beyond all proportion. And she needed Neil as well. More importantly, he needed her, would do so for many years to come. And he really would never resign himself to accepting Chris — he'd proved that, hadn't he, by running away? She had felt torn at times in the past, between her work and her son. The pain of that was nothing compared with this massive hurt.

That day over at her mother's had only convinced her more deeply how right she and Chris might have been together. Having come so close to being a part of his world, she couldn't unmake the dreams imagination had fashioned. The only way was to cease everything that brought them back to life.

Schooling herself now to accepting that this would be their final meeting, Helen resolved that she would be stern — with Chris, in permitting no persuasion, but most of all with herself against surrendering to this force compelling her to love him. She would be matter-of-fact, friendly but cool, and firm in her farewell.

The telephone sliced into her thoughts and, relieved to have an interruption, she ran to lift the receiver.

'It's me — Marian. I'm ever so sorry, love, but I can't make it today. I've dropped the frying pan — and before you say owt, no, it wasn't full or anything, it wasn't hot either. But it caught my bad leg, right on the shin bone. Denis would have the doctor, and he's forbidden me to put any weight on it for a day or two.'

After checking that the doctor considered no lasting damage had been done, Helen sympathised, assured Marian that she would cope and promised to ring the following day. Replacing the receiver, she felt further relief wash right through her. She didn't have to go over to Leeds now. She would let Chris know immediately. Not seeing him would enable her to be as firm as she ought to have been already about the future.

'Sorry about your sister,' he said swiftly. 'But what about your housekeeper — Mrs Hartley?'

'She's having a week off, bit of a holiday.'

'Bring Neil with you then.'

'You must be joking!' said Helen. 'Hasn't he been disruptive enough already? And it isn't as if . . .' She stopped speaking, swallowed. She had been going to say '. . . as if it mattered now.' And maybe she should have said it. However far from the real truth it was. She ought to have made him believe that none of this did matter. How otherwise would she — *they* — learn to accept the facts?

'Helen, it's not like you to let me down.'

There had been more, much of it scarcely sounding like Chris, for the words were harsh, almost unforgiving. And she couldn't let it end this way — with sourness between them. She would have to risk going there with Neil.

Chris was backstage when they arrived, but came through from one of the dressing rooms as soon as he learned they were there. Neil was his usual unforthcoming self, barely speaking when Chris said hallo, but he did comply uncomplainingly for once when they were taken through to see the young people preparing for the concert.

'Better not show you in there,' Chris said with a grin, passing the dressing rooms. 'Some are getting changed now. We'll go through to watch folk being made-up. I was sort of supervising. The woman in charge has rather a heavy hand with the Leichner — don't want them looking over-painted, especially the lads.'

'There you are, Father,' said one of the older boys. 'Is this okay? Feels cissy, but I know because of the lights . . .'

'You look great,' said Chris, nodding approvingly. 'And I like the outfit — how's the guitar today?'

'Much better, I think.'

Chris turned to Helen. 'His guitar is second-hand. Unfortunately strings kept snapping, but we believe we've fixed it now.'

'Father,' someone called from across the room, 'Harry's been sick again.'

'Is someone with him?' Chris enquired.

'Aye — Miss Gilbert. And he's all right again now, any road.'

Smiling ruefully, Chris turned to Helen. 'I'm told this happens every time they do anything out of the ordinary. He's rather highly strung, and exceptionally intelligent. Matter of fact, he has ambitions to try something in your line. Sadly, his home circumstances are going to make that virtually impossible.'

'Happen he could try for a scholarship. That was the only way I . . .' Suddenly, she stopped speaking, thought for a minute and smiled. 'Of course — that's it! The Fenella March Bursary. I've finished paying back all that I had from old Mr March, and a bit more besides. Money doesn't go as far, these days. Does this Harry seriously want to study architecture?'

'I'll arrange for you to have a chat with him after the concert, but from what I've heard since coming to the parish, he talks of little else.'

'How old is he?'

'Sixteen or so, I suppose. He's in a bit of a dead-end job at present, that I do know.'

Neil was remarkably well behaved throughout the performance. On the whole the youngsters were very good instrumentalists as well as singers. They had chosen the programme themselves which perhaps accounted for its appealing to Neil. During the interval Helen only saw Chris briefly, from a distance, when he emerged to have a word with the ladies organising refreshments.

She wasn't sorry to have nothing more to distract her than keeping an eye on Neil and watching the concert herself. She needed to think. Her own ready offer regarding the bursary might mean that she wouldn't be making such a clean break with Christopher as she'd intended. She'd pictured herself keeping right away from him, from the folk in his parish. And just seeing him today was resurrecting all the emotions compounded over the years, and especially during these past few months. Her need for him didn't lessen, and she sensed that it never would. How could she live with that if she didn't make the effort she'd decided on, and put him completely out of her life?

Neil was clapping enthusiastically as the concert drew to a close with every young person from five years old to eighteen coming forward to bow to the audience.

'Can we come here again, Mummy?' he asked excitedly, bouncing on his chair.

Why on earth couldn't he have formed some attachment to the place when that was vital? thought Helen. Does everything in my life always have to come too late?

Chris came to them as members of the audience were heading for the exit.

'If you're sure about having a word with Harry Winter,' he said, 'he'd be delighted if you'd come backstage now. Naturally, I've made no promises on your behalf. I simply said you were interested to hear about his ambitions.'

'Okay then, fine,' she said, but glanced down at Neil.

'He'll come with me, won't you, old chap? I'll bet you'd like to have a go at my guitar . . .'

Neil gazed up at him. 'Have you got one, have you really?'

'Yes, indeed. I lent it to Sharon for the concert. Has anyone ever shown you how the guitar is played?'

Harry Winter was waiting in a corner of the room where the other youngsters were having make-up removed. A worried-looking young fellow, whom Helen remembered having played the drums with a gusto which belied his solemn appearance, he invited her to sit as soon as Chris had introduced them.

'I'm afraid it's bedlam in here, Mrs Stone, sorry. But I think all the other rooms are in use.'

'That's all right, Harry. So long as we can hear each other, that's all that matters.'

'Father Christopher says you're the person who designed this building. I think that's super — you must have been so excited when it was opened.'

Helen would rather have avoided thinking about that particular occasion. Subsequent events were proving such a let-down after the soaring hopes awakened by meeting Chris again. With an effort, she smiled.

'It's always great when you see something that has been completed to your designs. I hope, though, that you're not just being carried away by the glamour of that side of things? This job's much more a matter of sheer hard slog.'

'I do realise that,' he said earnestly. 'It's more that I think it must be a very interesting career – planning, and all that. My mum got me to go with her to see about our house when they were being built. Council, of course. I'm the eldest, you see, of five. Since my dad were killed in t'war I've tried to give her a bit of help. Any road, they let us see the plans. I think that were what started me off. Folk were that thankful to be getting somewhere decent to live. I reckoned I'd love to do summat worthwhile like that.'

'And are you any good at art? There's so much drawing involved you'll need to be better than average. And there's figure work an' all – if you can't do calculations, you'll never make an architect.'

When Chris left them to talk, he took Neil's hand and led him up the steps behind the stage. In the wings the electrician was dismantling part of the lighting system, helped by a youth of about fifteen.

'Hallo, Father Christopher,' the lad called, beaming. 'Did all right, didn't we? We never missed one cue, and Mr Jarvis let me work some of the switches.'

Neil was watching and listening, wondering at this strange world and wishing he could join in something that seemed to make everybody all happy and excited. He'd never seen so many children together in one place. It would be even more fun than playing with Linda and Mark. He gazed longingly towards some of the instruments being packed carefully away. He wished he could have a go on them.

'Oh, there you are, Father Christopher,' a teenaged girl exclaimed, smiling as she looked around one end of a section of scenery. 'Here's the guitar – thank you ever so much for lending it to me. I hope you agreed that it sounded infinitely better than that old thing of mine!'

'You certainly made good use of it, Sharon. Well done!'

Pausing while Chris chatted to first one youngster and then another, Neil followed him across to one of the dressing rooms that now was empty.

'Let's see if I can make this sound almost as good as Sharon did, eh?'

For a while, Neil watched, fascinated, while Chris conjured music from the guitar. 'Can I try?' he asked. 'Please . . .'

'You might be disappointed. Your hands are still small for coping with this, but you can certainly have a go,' Christopher offered, drawing Neil towards him and positioning the boy's thumb and fingers near the strings.

Managing a few notes, however tunelessly, delighted Neil and sent him off into high-pitched giggles. 'What else can you play?' he asked, and listened rather wistfully to one of the melodies that he'd heard during the concert.

'I want to do that,' he announced.

'Perhaps when you're a bit bigger. For now, you might find the recorder more your size.'

'Show me,' Neil demanded, grinning.

'I'm afraid I can't play one,' Chris confessed.

A girl who was passing the open doorway smiled cheekily towards them. 'Don't tell me there's something you can't do, Father Christopher!' she exclaimed, then ran off, her plaited hair bouncing.

'Is she your little girl as well?' asked Neil, the forehead beneath his golden curls wrinkling in bewilderment. 'Are all these children yours?'

Chris smiled. 'Not in the way that you mean, Neil. They belong to my church, and because I've come here to help look after them they have become mine. But they don't all live in my house. There'd never be room, would there?'

Thinking of the rather old-fashioned vicarage, Neil shook his head fiercely and continued listening.

'And they're not mine in the same way that you belong to your mummy, or even to your grandma and grandad — they aren't related to me. But I do often think they are like a big family gathered all around me.'

Neil was silent, staring down at the scuffed toes of his shoes. 'But they call you "Father Christopher"?'

'Yes, and I think that's rather nice, don't you?'

Again, Neil nodded. 'Father's like a daddy, isn't it?'

'That's right.'

'My daddy won't come back, Mummy says. He died, and it wasn't because she was cross with him.'

'No, and it wasn't because he didn't wish to come home either. It was simply something very sad which happened. And sometimes when things like that occur, nobody can explain them.'

'Not even you?' The child's eyes looked enormous, their blue-tinged whites emphasising the beautiful grey irises.

'Not even me! We may not see a reason, because it isn't always what someone wants to do — it can be what God plans for them.'

'Who's God? And why did He make my daddy go away?'

Chris was thrown, but did his best to answer in a way that Neil might understand.

'Those are hard questions. And I can't really tell you why He decided to take your daddy. But perhaps if I try to explain what I believe about God you will understand a bit better.'

464

Neil was nodding, which seemed encouraging.

'Well, love, I think God is like a father, but belonging to everyone, and especially to those who want Him to be their special person. And the best thing about God is that, although we can't see Him, He is there and knows what we are doing.'

'But why did he make my daddy dead?'

Chris swallowed. 'We can't be sure, but we can only think that dying was perhaps the only way to stop your daddy hurting. You know that he was in the car, and there was an accident . . .'

Neil nodded, 'Mummy told me.'

'Well, sometimes when people are hurt so badly, God has to decide that it would be cruel to let them live if they would always be in pain.'

' 'Cos they wouldn't be happy,' Neil asserted.

'That's right, my boy. Now, shall we go and find your mummy?'

'In a minute.'

'You want to hear some more music, do you? See if we can find more instruments?'

Neil shook his head. He seemed to be struggling as if to surface from clinging, tangled reeds. 'No, not today. Another day. I was just − thinking. Why aren't you *my* Father Christopher?'

'I can be, straight away. Because it's what you want.'

From the look Neil was giving him, Chris realised that this was a longing which had been developing during the entire evening.

Walking along backstage in search of her son and Chris, Helen was feeling overwhelmed with emotion again. Young Harry Winter had been full of all the eagerness to design which she so clearly remembered from her own early days. She felt sure she'd be right to recommend that Mr March should offer him the bursary.

It was this place, though — the church hall — which was getting to her. Sounds of sheer enjoyment from the youngsters busy packing up after their concert were filling its rooms, and making her look at the place again. Whatever happened in the future, this would always remain to her the most important of her designs. She had watched it come alive and that, surely, was the real test of any building? Regret because this was the last time she would come here now choked her.

Glimpsing Neil through the open dressing-room door, she saw his interested expression and experienced a moment's relief. At least he wasn't being fractious today.

'Ah, there you are,' she said, trying to quell all her emotions and smile as if she meant it. 'Time we were off, Neil.'

'How did it go?' Chris asked as he looked up and saw her. 'I hope young Harry was duly grateful.'

'Grateful? He was over the moon. As I explained to him, it's really up to Mr March to choose the next recipient for the bursary, but he's old and very frail now, and I don't think I'm being big-headed when I say I'm sure he'll be guided by me. I'm going to have a preliminary word with the old man, then get in touch with Harry if he does agree to see him.'

'That's splendid! Thanks so much, Helen, for thinking of it. Now there's something I've got to discuss with you . . .'

'Sorry, Chris,' she said sharply. 'It's high time we were getting home. Neil should have been in bed long before this.'

'Helen, *please*,' he persisted. 'It's to do with Neil, what he's been saying. We've had a good chat, and now I've got to talk to you.'

'But there's too many folk around here, and you're still busy.'

'I don't have to be. I need only check that the Sunday School Superintendent or somebody will lock up. Come with me to the vicarage, we can talk privately there.'

'Five minutes then. After that we shall have to be on our way.'

'Me as well, Father Christopher, I'm coming with you.' Tugging at Christopher's cassock, Neil was smiling beseechingly up at him.

Helen's gaze had jerked down to scrutinise her son. 'Is that what you meant?' she asked Chris in a shaken whisper.

He nodded. 'I told you we had a bit of a chat,' he explained as they set out. 'About his daddy, and about why everybody here calls me Father Christopher. Neil seems to have taken to the term.'

This made a difference, a vast one, but Helen had grown so used to facing the worst that she couldn't believe it would change things completely.

Once inside his living room, Chris offered to make a pot of tea.

'No, it's all right, thanks,' she said. 'We really do have to be on our way shortly.'

'Can I have a glass of milk please, Father Christopher?'

'Certainly, Neil. Come and help me get it.'

When they returned from the kitchen Helen was still standing. Chris gave her a look. Lord, but she was determined about not hanging on to hear him out.

'You could sit, you know,' he said, anxiety making him sound brusque. 'I shan't chain you to the chair.'

Neil was making himself at home on the sofa. After a couple of sips of milk his fair head began nodding.

'Just look at him,' Helen murmured. 'He's tired out.'

We could find him a bed upstairs, thought Chris, but wouldn't suggest it. If Helen was that determined to get away he wasn't going to interfere. But he would make certain that she didn't go before he'd made her fully aware of her son's apparent change of heart. He couldn't let her decide without a proper understanding of the situation.

Neil dozed, then his head jerked upwards and he regarded Chris through half-closed eyelids. 'Didn't you say that I could have my bed here?'

'I did, and you may. But until then would you like to have a sleep on one of my beds?'

'Can I? Ooh, please.'

Helen couldn't argue. Together they all went upstairs, and after settling Neil on one of the spare beds she and Chris stood looking down at him from the doorway. Eyes closing already, Neil was relaxed, with all dread of the unknown removed.

She was reminded of the times years ago when she and Alexander had gazed at their sleeping son. So like, yet unlike, this occasion that it brought a complex mixture of emotions rushing through her. But it no longer seemed wrong to have Christopher's arm about her shoulders as they went downstairs. She was right to trust him with their future. But she must ensure that Chris understood what marriage to her would be like.

'Before I say another thing,' he said suddenly, 'how is your mother now? I'm sorry. I clean forgot to ask.' He had been so agitated about their meeting and trying to make everything right between them.

Helen grinned as she went to the armchair that he moved towards the fire for her. 'Back to normal, thanks. She says she's not felt the slightest bit dizzy since that day. Nobody'll alter her, though. Dad neither. I daresay they'll both die on the go, just as busy as ever.'

'There are worse ways.'

She gave him a look as he took the chair across the hearth from her own. 'Aye, I suppose so.'

Chris was smiling. 'You've no room to talk. You're their daughter, all right! When did you last let up?'

'Well — you know how it is.'

'Helen, I meant what I said. I do love you, profoundly. I want to make your life easier. Now that Neil's coming round . . .'

'If only that could last!'

'I don't doubt that there'll be times still when he hates my guts — if only for trying to take too much of a share of your time. But it's the load I want you to share with me most of all, Helen, some of the responsibility.'

When she swallowed but said nothing, he continued all the more earnestly: 'It won't be easy, I'm not pretending it will. We've got to face this squarely or not at all. There's the way you'd be uprooting yourself for a start. You must be extremely fond of that beautiful house.'

Helen gave a tiny snort. 'That's one thing you wouldn't have to worry about. I've never wanted to live there. Oh, I thought The Stone House was gorgeous the first time I saw it, when Joseph Stone was living. And I like it now as the place where I do my job — it seems particularly suitable for discussions with clients, and as somewhere to work. I'm glad, an' all, to think of Neil living there one day, when he's grown-up. But I'm much more at home in somewhere less pretentious. Happen you're right, and I am very like my mother.'

'You could have a free hand here, that goes without saying. As you can tell, I've done no more than move in with my possessions. Just about every room needs decorating, but with your ideas and my wholehearted cooperation we could make the place rather nice.'

'Don't rush me, Chris. You're making this sound so tempting.'

'Rush you? How many years is it since we met? If this is rushing, I've never understood the meaning of the word!'

'But you haven't thought this through, love, not properly. You can't have, or you'd never have proposed. I made a real hash of marriage once.'

'Marriage takes two people — to ruin it, just as much as to make it succeed. And I can't see a thing wrong with your decision to stick to your career.'

'Ah, but would you say the same in a year or two — when I can't be content without dashing off up and down the country? Because I know that's what I want. I've missed a lot, being tied to the north while Neil was little. I don't think there's much chance now of my becoming involved in any aspect of the Festival of Britain or anything it's spawning, but I'm determined I'm not going to miss out on anything more. They've had that contest for designing the new cathedral for Coventry. There'll be others, and more new towns.'

'I was coming to that,' he said. 'It's what I've thought all along. Because of my work there's many a time when I could be at home during the week, for Neil.'

I'd be happy to leave him in your care, thought Helen, and realised how much had altered in a few hours. 'It'd be good for him an' all,' she said pensively. 'It's time he had somebody different keeping an eye on him. Me and our Marian indulge him too much, and Mum and Mrs Hartley are worse still. They spoil him something shocking!'

'I hope you're not casting me in the role of

disciplinarian?' Chris said with a grin.

'Only as strict as any father would be.'

'There's nothing I'd rather be — unless it's your husband. That goes without saying. I was badly shaken, you know, when Neil didn't respond to me at all.'

'I am sorry,' said Helen, rising and going to him. 'I wouldn't have brought you trouble for worlds.'

'I know. Stop worrying.'

He was standing as well, gazing into her eyes with such complete affection that she felt the breath catch her throat.

'You're not going home tonight, are you?' he asked, and his dark eyes lit with a brilliant smile when she shook her head.

Strangely, though, Helen sensed that they wouldn't be sleeping together tonight. The attraction had in no way lessened, but had become a promise of happiness in the future — a future that was drawing so close that waiting a little while longer wouldn't hurt.

'Do you want me to go up and see if Neil has settled?' he asked.

'No, I will, thanks.'

She wanted to see her son asleep in Christopher's home, needed assurance that what she believed to be happening was fact.

The boy had hardly stirred, breathing slowly and steadily, quite content on the strange bed and totally oblivious to being almost fully dressed still. Helen hadn't the heart to disturb him by insisting on taking off his clothes. She picked up his scuff-toed shoes and placed them together neatly. They would both have to learn new ways, not to obtrude too forcibly perhaps on Christopher's bachelor existence.

Gazing out of the window, Helen wondered what changes there would be, in her outlook and her way of life. All of them she would face with a smile, sensing already that the hardest going had been tackled. From now on she could look forward to things getting better.

Beyond the vicarage garden was the church. Beside that the hall which had brought her back into Christopher's life. All around were the clustered streets so typical of Yorkshire urban life. They wouldn't seem unfamiliar much longer. Settling here would be like coming home.

Turning from the window, she found Neil's grey eyes wide open.

'Guess what, Mummy? Father Christopher's going to teach me to play his guitar when I'm a bit bigger.'

'You're very lucky,' said Helen. And, she realised, I might at long last be very lucky too.

HARRY BOWLING

The new Cockney saga from the bestselling author of GASLIGHT IN PAGE STREET

The Girl from Cotton Lane

Cotton Lane in dockland Bermondsey is one of the many small cobbled streets which serve the wharves. And on the corner is Bradley's Dining Rooms, the favourite eating place of the rivermen, trade union officials and horse and motor drivers. Since her marriage to Fred Bradley, Carrie has been building up the business, and trade has picked up considerably since the end of the Great War. Yet everything is not well between Carrie and Fred. And though they have a little daughter they both adore, neither of them is truly happy.

Carrie's parents, Nellie and William Tanner, live in Bacon Buildings, the tenement they were forced to move into when George Galloway sacked William after thirty-seven years. But their hearts lie in Page Street, their old home, and with their friends there: redoubtable Florrie 'Hairpin' Axford and her gossiping companions; scruffy old Broomhead Smith; the fighting Sullivans, and young Billy, who, unable to box after a wound sustained in the trenches, is determined to set up a gymnasium to help the local youngsters keep off the streets; and new arrivals, Joe Maitland, who's doing well with his warehouse in Dockhead, though his dealings are not always strictly above board, and Red Ellie, the stalwart Communist who brings the street together to fight their slum landlord, George Galloway.

Don't miss Harry Bowling's previous Cockney sagas, GASLIGHT IN PAGE STREET, PARAGON PLACE, IRONMONGER'S DAUGHTER, TUPPENCE TO TOOLEY STREET and CONNER STREET'S WAR, also available from Headline.

FICTION/GENERAL   0 7472 3869 3

A selection of bestsellers from Headline

THE LADYKILLER	Martina Cole	£5.99 ☐
JESSICA'S GIRL	Josephine Cox	£5.99 ☐
NICE GIRLS	Claudia Crawford	£4.99 ☐
HER HUNGRY HEART	Roberta Latow	£5.99 ☐
FLOOD WATER	Peter Ling	£4.99 ☐
THE OTHER MOTHER	Seth Margolis	£4.99 ☐
ACT OF PASSION	Rosalind Miles	£4.99 ☐
A NEST OF SINGING BIRDS	Elizabeth Murphy	£5.99 ☐
THE COCKNEY GIRL	Gilda O'Neill	£4.99 ☐
FORBIDDEN FEELINGS	Una-Mary Parker	£5.99 ☐
OUR STREET	Victor Pemberton	£5.99 ☐
GREEN GROW THE RUSHES	Harriet Smart	£5.99 ☐
BLUE DRESS GIRL	E V Thompson	£5.99 ☐
DAYDREAMS	Elizabeth Walker	£5.99 ☐

All Headline books are available at your local bookshop or newsagent, or can be ordered direct from the publisher. Just tick the titles you want and fill in the form below. Prices and availability subject to change without notice.

Headline Book Publishing PLC, Cash Sales Department, Bookpoint, 39 Milton Park, Abingdon, OXON, OX14 4TD, UK. If you have a credit card you may order by telephone – 0235 831700.

Please enclose a cheque or postal order made payable to Bookpoint Ltd to the value of the cover price and allow the following for postage and packing:
UK & BFPO: £1.00 for the first book, 50p for the second book and 30p for each additional book ordered up to a maximum charge of £3.00.
OVERSEAS & EIRE: £2.00 for the first book, £1.00 for the second book and 50p for each additional book.

Name ....

Address ....

....

....

If you would prefer to pay by credit card, please complete:
Please debit my Visa/Access/Diner's Card/American Express (delete as applicable) card no:

Signature .... Expiry Date ....